# THE BEST
# GHOST
# STORIES
## EVER TOLD

# THE BEST
# GHOST
# STORIES
## EVER TOLD

### EDITED AND INTRODUCED BY
# STEPHEN BRENNAN

Skyhorse Publishing

Skyhorse Publishing books may be purchased in bulk at special discounts for sales promotion, corporate gifts, fund-raising, or educational purposes. Special editions can also be created to specifications. For details, contact the Special Sales Department, Skyhorse Publishing, 307 West 36th Street, 11th Floor, New York, NY 10018 or info@skyhorsepublishing.com.

Skyhorse® and Skyhorse Publishing® are registered trademarks of Skyhorse Publishing, Inc.®, a Delaware corporation.

www.skyhorsepublishing.com

10 9 8 7 6 5 4 3 2 1

Library of Congress Cataloging-in-Publication Data

The best ghost stories ever told / edited and introduced by Stephen Brennan.
    p. cm.
 ISBN 978-1-61608-364-9 (alk. paper)
 1. Ghost stories. I. Brennan, Stephen Vincent.
 PN6071.G45B47 2011
 808.83'8733--dc23
                2011016980

Printed in the United States of America

# CONTENTS

# INTRODUCTION

*And so, it is said, you are haunted!*
*My friend, we are haunted all;*

—Isabella Banks

Boo! Did I scare you? Did you jump? Well, surprise is only part of it. There is also memory, regret, fear, romance, humor—yes, humor too, else how would you deal with the horror—and a dozen other elemental human constructs and emotions.

Do you believe in ghosts? I'm sure I do. Samuel Johnson said somewhere or other that while reason is against it, everyone believes in ghosts. That is, when asked, you deny your belief in any such thing, and yet deep in your secret heart, you *do* believe. And so, I think, it is with most of us. Nevertheless, the very fact that this question continues to be among the most asked, by all peoples, in all places, of all time (do you know of any person who has not asked it, either of themselves or of another?) attests to the fearsome grip this idea of an encounter with the spirit world has now—has darn near always had—upon us. It would seem that spooks have always been with us. They come—some bidden, some unbidden. Frequently they are the ghosts of our past, prompted by anything from guilty memory to dyspeptic digestion. Remember too, it is not required that a ghost be seen to be believed. A specter may just as well be heard, or smelled, or otherwise sensed. And though it is true that the extent of our sensitivity has much to do with our vulnerability and attraction to this same *spirit world,* even the most levelheaded rationalist cannot deny the sudden start that makes the heart go *thump,* the tingle of fear down the spine, the hair on end at the nape of the neck, the barest scent on a breath of air that instantly transports you to another place and time, or the lost lover's name you're sure you can hear in the center of a howling wind.

I best like to hear a ghost story told by camp or bonfire light. There's something about an outdoor blaze, late at night, with the darkness all around, that suits a tale of visitation from beyond. I like the incense of wood-smoke, the pop and crack of burning log, the thousand sparks riding skyward on the rising heat— sacerdotal token of a million propitiations to fearful gods, the blaze in Plato's cave, the burning bush that is not consumed—all the long history of man's (or woman's) grappling with her mysterious present, his half-remembered past, their unknown future. (Scrooge was visited by these very three ghosts.) And I like the huddled camaraderie of the auditors of the story, snuggled together against, and in appreciation of, the terror out there.

Because within the fire-lit circle there is safety, whereas in the darkness beyond . . . ? This is primal stuff. The teller, standing in for all of us, conjures an impossible, fearful story, and by his very uttering or outing of the tale makes us all safe from it, by rendering the spooky story into something, if not commonplace, then at least manageable, and perhaps laughed at as well. And if the teller is any good at all, we are entertained, beguiled, and chilled, when at last we go from the fire, without fear, to our beds.

The ghost story has a long and honorable provenance in the lore and literature of our tribe. Aboriginal and First Peoples regarded it much as I've described above. The holy men and women mediated between the living and their dead ancestors, and then worked it all out around the flicker and glow of the communal campfire. This is the ghost story as sacred rite also, and some of this mingling persists in the writings that were to become the Bible.

It may be heresy, but it can be no sacrilege to merely note that Jesus' several appearances after dying on the cross are in effect ghost stories—to say nothing of the raising of Lazarus, or of the living Christ's confabs in the desert with the Devil. The ancient Greek and Romans organized their understanding of visitations from the spirit world by giving the shades an actual place to dwell— Hades, and if you would visit with them, you must go to hell to do it. (The exceptions of course were the unburied dead who roamed the earth frightening the dogs and making a general nuisance of themselves.) With the Renaissance and Enlightenment we see a definite split between the telling of ghost stories and the literatures and practices of faith. Much as when the actors are kicked out of the churches, the ghost stories are no longer regarded as sacred, but now secular. Shakespeare's ghosts: old King Hamlet, Banquo and Caesar's ghost, are cultural figures rather than religious. With the nineteenth century, the "ghost story" comes into its own as a discrete and separate genre of short story. With the advent of mechanized printing, there was a great demand for ghostly tales, and all the best writers turned their hands to writing them. It is of some interest to note the comparatively large number of women writers who succeeded in getting their ghost stories into print. One can almost imagine their publishers and their editors, as they bought into the stereotypical cant about the female author with words something like: "Ah yes, we need an author who is good with character and with romance, with fear and with hysteria. Let's have a woman write it." Hmmm . . .

Be pleased to find here, between these covers, forty-odd examples of the very best ghost stories ever written. Just take a peek at the table of contents— Impressive, what? Even the briefest glimpse at this dream team of authors leaves no doubt as to the significance and popularity of ghost stories in our literature and in our lives. Personally, I'm with Bertie Wooster in holding that there are few pleasures equal to curling up with a good goose-flesher.

Now, you may regard yourself as a wholly rational being, or in twentieth century parlance, *a clear-eyed realist*. Or materialism may be your thing, nineteenth century or otherwise. Or you may reckon you have boxed the psycho-metaphysical compass with your understanding of the social and anthropomorphic origins of spooky tales. You may even figure that with your learning, your sophistication, and your sangfroid you are proof against the pleasurable terror of the best ghost stories. If that be the case, then I adjure you, attend this book.

As the man said—*Boo!*

Stephen Brennan
West Cornwall, Connecticut, 2011

# THE MONKEY'S PAW
## W. W. JACOBS

Without, the night was cold and wet, but in the small parlour of Laburnam Villa the blinds were drawn and the fire burned brightly. Father and son were at chess, the former, who possessed ideas about the game involving radical changes, putting his kings into such sharp and unnecessary perils that it even provoked comment from the white-haired old lady knitting placidly by the fire.

"Hark at the wind," said Mr. White, who, having seen a fatal mistake after it was too late, was amiably desirous of preventing his son from seeing it.

"I'm listening," said the latter, grimly surveying the board as he stretched out his hand. "Check."

"I should hardly think that he'd come tonight," said his father, with his hand poised over the board.

"Mate," replied the son.

"That's the worst of living so far out," bawled Mr. White, with sudden and unlooked-for violence; "of all the beastly, slushy, out-of-the-way places to live in, this is the worst. Pathway's a bog, and the road's a torrent. I don't know what people are thinking about. I suppose because only two houses in the road are let, they think it doesn't matter."

"Never mind, dear," said his wife, soothingly; "perhaps you'll win the next one."

Mr. White looked up sharply, just in time to intercept a knowing glance between mother and son. The words died away on his lips, and he hid a guilty grin in his thin grey beard.

"There he is," said Herbert White, as the gate banged to loudly and heavy footsteps came towards the door.

The old man rose with hospitable haste, and opening the door, was heard condoling with the new arrival. The new arrival also condoled with himself, so that Mrs. White said, "Tut, tut!" and coughed gently as her husband entered the room, followed by a tall, burly man, beady of eye and rubicund of visage.

"Sergeant-Major Morris," he said, introducing him.

The sergeant-major shook hands, and taking the proffered seat by the fire, watched contentedly while his host got out whisky and tumblers and stood a small copper kettle on the fire.

At the third glass his eyes got brighter, and he began to talk, the little family circle regarding with eager interest this visitor from distant parts, as he squared his broad shoulders in the chair and spoke of wild scenes and doughty deeds; of wars and plagues and strange peoples.

"Twenty-one years of it," said Mr. White, nodding at his wife and son. "When he went away he was a slip of a youth in the warehouse. Now look at him."

"He don't look to have taken much harm," said Mrs. White, politely.

"I'd like to go to India myself," said the old man, "just to look round a bit, you know."

"Better where you are," said the sergeant-major, shaking his head. He put down the empty glass, and sighing softly, shook it again.

"I should like to see those old temples and fakirs and jugglers," said the old man. "What was that you started telling me the other day about a monkey's paw or something, Morris?"

"Nothing," said the soldier hastily. "Leastways nothing worth hearing."

"Monkey's paw?" said Mrs. White, curiously.

"Well, it's just a bit of what you might call magic, perhaps," said the sergeant-major off-handedly.

His three listeners leaned forward eagerly. The visitor absent-mindedly put his empty glass to his lips and then set it down again. His host filled it for him.

"To look at," said the sergeant-major, fumbling in his pocket, "it's just an ordinary little paw, dried to a mummy."

He took something out of his pocket and proffered it. Mrs. White drew back with a grimace, but her son, taking it, examined it curiously.

"And what is there special about it?" inquired Mr. White as he took it from his son, and having examined it, placed it upon the table.

"It had a spell put on it by an old fakir," said the sergeant-major, "a very holy man. He wanted to show that fate ruled people's lives, and that those who interfered with it did so to their sorrow. He put a spell on it so that three separate men could each have three wishes from it."

His manner was so impressive that his hearers were conscious that their light laughter jarred somewhat.

"Well, why don't you have three, sir?" said Herbert White cleverly.

The soldier regarded him in the way that middle age is wont to regard presumptuous youth. "I have," he said quietly, and his blotchy face whitened.

"And did you really have the three wishes granted?" asked Mrs. White.

"I did," said the sergeant-major, and his glass tapped against his strong teeth.

"And has anybody else wished?" persisted the old lady.

"The first man had his three wishes. Yes," was the reply; "I don't know what the first two were, but the third was for death. That's how I got the paw."

His tones were so grave that a hush fell upon the group.

"If you've had your three wishes, it's no good to you now, then, Morris," said the old man at last. "What do you keep it for?"

The soldier shook his head. "Fancy, I suppose," he said slowly. "I did have some idea of selling it, but I don't think I will. It has caused enough mischief already. Besides, people won't buy. They think it's a fairy tale; some of them, and those who do think anything of it want to try it first and pay me afterwards."

"If you could have another three wishes," said the old man, eyeing him keenly, "would you have them?"

"I don't know," said the other. "I don't know."

He took the paw, and dangling it between his forefinger and thumb, suddenly threw it upon the fire. White, with a slight cry, stooped down and snatched it off.

"Better let it burn," said the soldier solemnly.

"If you don't want it, Morris," said the other, "give it to me."

"I won't," said his friend doggedly. "I threw it on the fire. If you keep it, don't blame me for what happens. Pitch it on the fire again like a sensible man."

The other shook his head and examined his new possession closely. "How do you do it?" he inquired.

"Hold it up in your right hand and wish aloud," said the sergeant-major, "but I warn you of the consequences."

"Sounds like the *Arabian Nights,*" said Mrs. White as she rose and began to set the supper. "Don't you think you might wish for four pairs of hands for me?"

Her husband drew the talisman from his pocket, and then all three burst into laughter as the sergeant-major, with a look of alarm on his face, caught him by the arm.

"If you must wish," he said gruffly, "wish for something sensible."

Mr. White dropped it back in his pocket, and placing chairs, motioned his friend to the table. In the business of supper the talisman was partly forgotten, and afterwards the three sat listening in an enthralled fashion to a second instalment of the soldier's adventures in India.

"If the tale about the monkey's paw is not more truthful than those he has been telling us," said Herbert, as the door closed behind their guest, just in time for him to catch the last train, "we shan't make much out of it."

"Did you give him anything for it, father?" inquired Mrs. White, regarding her husband closely.

"A trifle," said he, colouring slightly. "He didn't want it, but I made him take it. And he pressed me again to throw it away."

"Likely," said Herbert, with pretended horror. "Why, we're going to be rich, and famous and happy. Wish to be an emperor, father, to begin with; then you can't be henpecked."

He darted round the table, pursued by the maligned Mrs. White armed with an antimacassar.

Mr. White took the paw from his pocket and eyed it dubiously. "I don't know what to wish for, and that's a fact," he said slowly. "It seems to me I've got all I want."

"If you only cleared the house, you'd be quite happy wouldn't you?" said Herbert, with his hand on his shoulder. "Well, wish for two hundred pounds, then; that'll just do it."

His father, smiling shamefacedly at his own credulity, held up the talisman, as his son, with a solemn face, somewhat marred by a wink at his mother, sat down at the piano and struck a few impressive chords.

"I wish for two hundred pounds," said the old man distinctly.

A fine crash from the piano greeted the words, interrupted by a shuddering cry from the old man. His wife and son ran towards him.

"It moved," he cried, with a glance of disgust at the object as it lay on the floor. "As I wished, it twisted in my hand like a snake."

"Well, I don't see the money," said his son as he picked it up and placed it on the table, "and I bet I never shall."

"It must have been your fancy, father," said his wife, regarding him anxiously.

He shook his head. "Never mind, though; there's no harm done, but it gave me a shock all the same."

They sat down by the fire again while the two men finished their pipes. Outside, the wind was higher than ever, and the old man started nervously at the sound of a door banging upstairs. A silence unusual and depressing settled upon all three, which lasted until the old couple rose to retire for the night.

"I expect you'll find the cash tied up in a big bag in the middle of your bed," said Herbert, as he bade them good night, "and something horrible squatting up on top of the wardrobe watching you as you pocket your ill-gotten gains."

He sat alone in the darkness, gazing at the dying fire, and seeing faces in it. The last face was so horrible and so simian that he gazed at it in amazement. It got so vivid that, with a little uneasy laugh, he felt on the table for a glass containing a little water to throw over it. His hand grasped the monkey's paw, and with a little shiver he wiped his hand on his coat and went up to bed.

\* \* \* \* \*

In the brightness of the wintry sun next morning as it streamed over the breakfast table he laughed at his fears. There was an air of prosaic wholesomeness about the room which it had lacked on the previous night, and the dirty, shrivelled little paw was pitched on the sideboard with a carelessness which betokened no great belief in its virtues.

"I suppose all old soldiers are the same," said Mrs. White. "The idea of our listening to such nonsense! How could wishes be granted in these days? And if they could, how could two hundred pounds hurt you, father?"

"Might drop on his head from the sky," said the frivolous Herbert.

"Morris said the things happened so naturally," said his father, "that you might if you so wished attribute it to coincidence."

"Well, don't break into the money before I come back," said Herbert as he rose from the table. "I'm afraid it'll turn you into a mean, avaricious man, and we shall have to disown you."

His mother laughed, and following him to the door, watched him down the road; and returning to the breakfast table, was very happy at the expense of her husband's credulity. All of which did not prevent her from scurrying to the door at the postman's knock, nor prevent her from referring somewhat shortly to retired sergeant-majors of bibulous habits when she found that the post brought a tailor's bill.

"Herbert will have some more of his funny remarks, I expect, when he comes home," she said, as they sat at dinner.

"I dare say," said Mr. White, pouring himself out some beer; "but for all that, the thing moved in my hand; that I'll swear to."

"You thought it did," said the old lady soothingly.

"I say it did," replied the other. "There was no thought about it; I had just— What's the matter?"

His wife made no reply. She was watching the mysterious movements of a man outside, who, peering in an undecided fashion at the house, appeared to be trying to make up his mind to enter. In mental connection with the two hundred pounds, she noticed that the stranger was well dressed, and wore a silk hat of glossy newness. Three times he paused at the gate, and then walked on again. The fourth time he stood with his hand upon it, and then with sudden resolution flung it open and walked up the path. Mrs. White at the same moment placed her hands behind her, and hurriedly unfastening the strings of her apron, put that useful article of apparel beneath the cushion of her chair.

She brought the stranger, who seemed ill at ease, into the room. He gazed at her furtively, and listened in a preoccupied fashion as the old lady apologised for the appearance of the room, and her husband's coat, a garment which he usually reserved for the garden. She then waited as patiently as her sex would permit, for him to broach his business, but he was at first strangely silent.

"I—was asked to call," he said at last, and stooped and picked a piece of cotton from his trousers. "I come from 'Maw and Meggins'."

The old lady started. "Is anything the matter?" she asked breathlessly. "Has anything happened to Herbert? What is it? What is it?"

Her husband interposed. "There, there, mother," he said hastily. "Sit down, and don't jump to conclusions. You've not brought bad news, I'm sure, sir"; and he eyed the other wistfully.

"I'm sorry—" began the visitor.

"Is he hurt?" demanded the mother wildly.

The visitor bowed in assent. "Badly hurt," he said quietly, "but he is not in any pain."

"Oh, thank God!" said the old woman, clasping her hands. "Thank God for that! Thank—"

She broke off suddenly as the sinister meaning of the assurance dawned upon her and she saw the awful confirmation of her fears in the other's averted face. She caught her breath, and turning to her slower-witted husband, laid her trembling old hand upon his. There was a long silence.

"He was caught in the machinery," said the visitor at length in a low voice.

"Caught in the machinery," repeated Mr. White, in a dazed fashion, "yes."

He sat staring blankly out at the window, and taking his wife's hand between his own, pressed it as he had been wont to do in their old courting-days nearly forty years before.

"He was the only one left to us," he said, turning gently to the visitor. "It is hard."

The other coughed, and rising, walked slowly to the window. "The firm wished me to convey their sincere sympathy with you in your great loss," he said, without looking round. "I beg that you will understand I am only their servant and merely obeying orders."

There was no reply; the old woman's face was white, her eyes staring, and her breath inaudible; on the husband's face was a look such as his friend the sergeant-major might have carried into his first action.

"I was to say that Maw and Meggins disclaim all responsibility," continued the other. "They admit no liability at all, but in consideration of your son's services, they wish to present you with a certain sum as compensation."

Mr. White dropped his wife's hand, and rising to his feet, gazed with a look of horror at his visitor. His dry lips shaped the words, "How much?"

"Two hundred pounds," was the answer.

Unconscious of his wife's shriek, the old man smiled faintly, put out his hands like a sightless man, and dropped, a senseless heap, to the floor.

\* \* \* \* \*

In the huge new cemetery, some two miles distant, the old people buried their dead, and came back to a house steeped in shadow and silence. It was all over so quickly that at first they could hardly realise it, and remained in a state of expectation as though of something else to happen —something else which was to lighten this load, too heavy for old hearts to bear.

But the days passed, and expectation gave place to resignation—the hopeless resignation of the old, sometimes mis-called, apathy. Sometimes they hardly exchanged a word, for now they had nothing to talk about, and their days were long to weariness.

It was about a week after that the old man, waking suddenly in the night, stretched out his hand and found himself alone. The room was in darkness, and the sound of subdued weeping came from the window. He raised himself in bed and listened.

"Come back," he said tenderly. "You will be cold."

"It is colder for my son," said the old woman, and wept afresh.

The sound of her sobs died away on his ears. The bed was warm, and his eyes heavy with sleep. He dozed fitfully, and then slept until a sudden wild cry from his wife awoke him with a start.

*"The paw!"* she cried wildly. "The monkey's paw!"

He started up in alarm. "Where? Where is it? What's the matter?"

She came stumbling across the room towards him. "I want it," she said quietly. "You've not destroyed it?"

"It's in the parlour, on the bracket," he replied, marvelling. "Why?"

She cried and laughed together, and bending over, kissed his cheek.

"I only just thought of it," she said hysterically. "Why didn't I think of it before? Why didn't *you* think of it?" "Think of what?" he questioned.

"The other two wishes," she replied rapidly. "We've only had one."

"Was not that enough?" he demanded fiercely.

"No," she cried triumphantly; "we'll have one more. Go down and get it quickly, and wish our boy alive again."

The man sat up in bed and flung the bedclothes from his quaking limbs. "Good God, you are mad!" he cried, aghast.

"Get it," she panted; "get it quickly, and wish— Oh, my boy, my boy!"

Her husband struck a match and lit the candle. "Get back to bed," he said unsteadily. "You don't know what you are saying."

"We had the first wish granted," said the old woman feverishly; "why not the second?"

"A coincidence," stammered the old man.

"Go and get it and wish," cried his wife, quivering with excitement.

The old man turned and regarded her, and his voice shook. "He has been dead ten days, and besides he—I would not tell you else, but—I could only recognise him by his clothing. If he was too terrible for you to see then, how now?"

"Bring him back," cried the old woman, and dragged him towards the door. "Do you think I fear the child I have nursed?"

He went down in the darkness, and felt his way to the parlour, and then to the mantelpiece. The talisman was in its place, and a horrible fear that the unspoken wish might bring his mutilated son before him ere he could escape from the room seized upon him, and he caught his breath as he found that he had lost the direction of the door. His brow cold with sweat, he felt his way round the table, and groped along the wall until he found himself in the small passage with the unwholesome thing in his hand.

Even, his wife's face seemed changed as he entered the room. It was white and expectant, and to his fears seemed to have an unnatural look upon it. He was afraid of her.

"*Wish!*" she cried, in a strong voice.

"It is foolish and wicked," he faltered.

"*Wish!*" repeated his wife.

He raised his hand. "I wish my son alive again."

The talisman fell to the floor, and he regarded it fearfully. Then he sank trembling into a chair as the old woman, with burning eyes, walked to the window and raised the blind.

He sat until he was chilled with the cold, glancing occasionally at the figure of the old woman peering through the window. The candle-end, which had burned below the rim of the china candlestick, was throwing pulsating shadows on the ceiling and walls, until, with a flicker larger than the rest, it expired. The old man, with an unspeakable sense of relief at the failure of the talisman, crept back to his bed, and a minute or two afterwards the old woman came silently and apathetically beside him.

Neither spoke, but lay silently listening to the ticking of the clock. A stair creaked, and a squeaky mouse scurried noisily through the wall. The darkness was oppressive, and after lying for some time screwing up his courage, he took the box of matches, and striking one, went downstairs for a candle.

At the foot of the stairs the match went out, and he paused to strike another; and at the same moment a knock, so quiet and stealthy as to be scarcely audible, sounded on the front door.

The matches fell from his hand and spilled in the passage. He stood motionless, his breath suspended until the knock was repeated. Then he turned and fled swiftly back to his room, and closed the door behind him. A third knock sounded through the house.

*"What's that?"* cried the old woman, starting up.

"A rat," said the old man in shaking tones—"a rat. It passed me on the stairs."

His wife sat up in bed listening. A loud knock resounded through the house.

"It's Herbert!" she screamed. "It's Herbert!"

She ran to the door, but her husband was before her, and catching her by the arm, held her tightly.

"What are you going to do?" he whispered hoarsely.

"It's my boy; it's Herbert!" she cried, struggling mechanically. "I forgot it was two miles away. What are you holding me for? Let go. I must open the door."

"For God's sake don't let it in," cried the old man, trembling.

"You're afraid of your own son," she cried, struggling. "Let me go. I'm coming, Herbert; I'm coming."

There was another knock, and another. The old woman with a sudden wrench broke free and ran from the room. Her husband followed to the landing, and called after her appealingly as she hurried downstairs. He heard the chain rattle back and the bottom bolt drawn slowly and stiffly from the socket. Then the old woman's voice, strained and panting.

"The bolt," she cried loudly. "Come down. I can't reach it."

But her husband was on his hands and knees groping wildly on the floor in search of the paw. If he could only find it before the thing outside got in. A perfect fusillade of knocks reverberated through the house, and he heard the scraping of a chair as his wife put it down in the passage against the door. He heard the creaking of the bolt as it came slowly back, and at the same moment he found the monkey's paw, and frantically breathed his third and last wish.

The knocking ceased suddenly, although the echoes of it were still in the house. He heard the chair drawn back, and the door opened. A cold wind rushed up the staircase, and a long loud wail of disappointment and misery from his wife gave him courage to run down to her side, and then to the gate beyond. The street lamp flickering opposite shone on a quiet and deserted road.

# GREEN TEA
## JOSEPH SHERIDAN LE FANU

### PROLOGUE

*Martin Hesselius, the German Physician*

Though carefully educated in medicine and surgery, I have never practised either. The study of each continues, nevertheless, to interest me profoundly. Neither idleness nor caprice caused my secession from the honourable calling which I had just entered. The cause was a very trifling scratch inflicted by a dissecting knife. This trifle cost me the loss of two fingers, amputated promptly, and the more painful loss of my health, for I have never been quite well since, and have seldom been twelve months together in the same place.

In my wanderings I became acquainted with Dr. Martin Hesselius, a wanderer like myself, like me a physician, and like me an enthusiast in his profession. Unlike me in this, that his wanderings were voluntary, and he a man, if not of fortune, as we estimate fortune in England, at least in what our forefathers used to term "easy circumstances." He was an old man when I first saw him; nearly five-and-thirty years my senior.

In Dr. Martin Hesselius, I found my master. His knowledge was immense, his grasp of a case was an intuition. He was the very man to inspire a young enthusiast, like me, with awe and delight. My admiration has stood the test of time and survived the separation of death. I am sure it was well-founded.

For nearly twenty years I acted as his medical secretary. His immense collection of papers he has left in my care, to be arranged, indexed and bound. His treatment of some of these cases is curious. He writes in two distinct characters. He describes what he saw and heard as an intelligent layman might, and when in this style of narrative he had seen the patient either through his own hall-door, to the light of day, or through the gates of darkness to the caverns of the dead, he returns upon the narrative, and in the terms of his art and with all the force and originality of genius, proceeds to the work of analysis, diagnosis and illustration.

Here and there a case strikes me as of a kind to amuse or horrify a lay reader with an interest quite different from the peculiar one which it may possess for an expert. With slight modifications, chiefly of language, and of course a change of names, I copy the following. The narrator is Dr. Martin Hesselius. I find it among the voluminous notes of cases which he made during a tour in England about sixty-four years ago.

It is related in series of letters to his friend Professor Van Loo of Leyden. The professor was not a physician, but a chemist, and a man who read history and metaphysics and medicine, and had, in his day, written a play.

The narrative is therefore, if somewhat less valuable as a medical record, necessarily written in a manner more likely to interest an unlearned reader.

These letters, from a memorandum attached, appear to have been returned on the death of the professor, in 1819, to Dr. Hesselius. They are written, some in English, some in French, but the greater part in German. I am a faithful, though I am conscious, by no means a graceful translator, and although here and there I omit some passages, and shorten others, and disguise names, I have interpolated nothing.

# CHAPTER I

## *Dr. Hesselius Relates How He Met the Rev. Mr. Jennings*

The Rev. Mr. Jennings is tall and thin. He is middle-aged, and dresses with a natty, old-fashioned, high-church precision. He is naturally a little stately, but not at all stiff. His features, without being handsome, are well formed, and their expression extremely kind, but also shy.

I met him one evening at Lady Mary Heyduke's. The modesty and benevolence of his countenance are extremely prepossessing.

We were but a small party, and he joined agreeably enough in the conversation, He seems to enjoy listening very much more than contributing to the talk; but what he says is always to the purpose and well said. He is a great favourite of Lady Mary's, who it seems, consults him upon many things, and thinks him the most happy and blessed person on earth. Little knows she about him.

The Rev. Mr. Jennings is a bachelor, and has, they say, sixty thousand pounds in the funds. He is a charitable man. He is most anxious to be actively employed in his sacred profession, and yet though always tolerably well elsewhere, when he goes down to his vicarage in Warwickshire, to engage in the actual duties of his sacred calling, his health soon fails him, and in a very strange way. So says Lady Mary.

There is no doubt that Mr. Jennings' health does break down in, generally, a sudden and mysterious way, sometimes in the very act of officiating in his old and pretty church at Kenlis. It may be his heart, it may be his brain. But so it has happened three or four times, or oftener, that after proceeding a certain way in the service, he has of a sudden stopped short, and after a silence, apparently quite unable to resume, he has fallen into solitary, inaudible prayer, his hands and his eyes uplifted, and then pale as death, and in the agitation of a strange shame and horror, descended trembling, and got into the vestry-room, leaving his congregation, without explanation, to themselves. This occurred when his curate was absent. When he goes down to Kenlis now, he always takes care to provide a clergyman to share his duty, and to supply his place on the instant should he become thus suddenly incapacitated.

When Mr. Jennings breaks down quite, and beats a retreat from the vicarage, and returns to London, where, in a dark street off Piccadilly, he inhabits a very narrow house, Lady Mary says that he is always perfectly well. I have my own opinion about that. There are degrees of course. We shall see.

Mr. Jennings is a perfectly gentlemanlike man. People, however, remark something odd. There is an impression a little ambiguous. One thing which certainly contributes to it, people I think don't remember; or, perhaps, distinctly remark. But I did, almost immediately. Mr. Jennings has a way of looking sidelong upon the carpet, as if his eye followed the movements of something there. This, of course, is not always. It occurs now and then. But often enough to give a certain oddity, as I have said, to his manner, and in this glance travelling along the floor there is something both shy and anxious.

A medical philosopher, as you are good enough to call me, elaborating theories by the aid of cases sought out by himself, and by him watched and scrutinised with more time at command, and consequently infinitely more minuteness than the ordinary practitioner can afford, falls insensibly into habits of observation, which accompany him everywhere, and are exercised, as some people would say, impertinently, upon every subject that presents itself with the least likelihood of rewarding inquiry.

There was a promise of this kind in the slight, timid, kindly, but reserved gentleman, whom I met for the first time at this agreeable little evening gathering. I observed, of course, more than I here set down; but I reserve all that borders on the technical for a strictly scientific paper.

I may remark, that when I here speak of medical science, I do so, as I hope some day to see it more generally understood, in a much more comprehensive sense than its generally material treatment would warrant. I believe the entire natural world is but the ultimate expression of that spiritual world from which, and in which alone, it has its life. I believe that the essential man is a spirit, that the spirit is an organised substance, but as different in point of material from what we ordinarily understand by matter, as light or electricity is; that the material body is, in the most literal sense, a vesture, and death consequently no interruption of the living man's existence, but simply his extrication from the natural body—a process which commences at the moment of what we term death, and the completion of which, at furthest a few days later, is the resurrection "in power."

The person who weighs the consequences of these positions will probably see their practical bearing upon medical science. This is, however, by no means the proper place for displaying the proofs and discussing the consequences of this too generally unrecognized state of facts.

In pursuance of my habit, I was covertly observing Mr. Jennings, with all my caution—I think he perceived it—and I saw plainly that he was as cautiously observing me. Lady Mary happening to address me by my name, as Dr. Hesselius, I saw that he glanced at me more sharply, and then became thoughtful for a few minutes.

After this, as I conversed with a gentleman at the other end of the room, I saw him look at me more steadily, and with an interest which I thought I understood. I then saw him take an opportunity of chatting with Lady Mary, and was, as one always is, perfectly aware of being the subject of a distant inquiry and answer.

This tall clergyman approached me by-and-by; and in a little time we had got into conversation. When two people, who like reading, and know books and places, having travelled, wish to discourse, it is very strange if they can't find topics. It was not accident that brought him near me, and led him into conversation. He knew German and had read my *Essays on Metaphysical Medicine* which suggest more than they actually say.

This courteous man, gentle, shy, plainly a man of thought and reading, who moving and talking among us, was not altogether of us, and whom I already suspected of leading a life whose transactions and alarms were carefully concealed, with an impenetrable reserve from, not only the world, but his best beloved friends—was cautiously weighing in his own mind the idea of taking a certain step with regard to me.

I penetrated his thoughts without his being aware of it, and was careful to say nothing which could betray to his sensitive vigilance my suspicions respecting his position, or my surmises about his plans respecting myself.

We chatted upon indifferent subjects for a time but at last he said:

"I was very much interested by some papers of yours, Dr. Hesselius, upon what you term Metaphysical Medicine—I read them in German, ten or twelve years ago—have they been translated?"

"No, I'm sure they have not—I should have heard. They would have asked my leave, I think."

"I asked the publishers here, a few months ago, to get the book for me in the original German; but they tell me it is out of print."

"So it is, and has been for some years; but it flatters me as an author to find that you have not forgotten my little book, although," I added, laughing, "ten or twelve years is a considerable time to have managed without it; but I suppose you have been turning the subject over again in your mind, or something has happened lately to revive your interest in it."

At this remark, accompanied by a glance of inquiry, a sudden embarrassment disturbed Mr. Jennings, analogous to that which makes a young lady blush and look foolish. He dropped his eyes, and folded his hands together uneasily, and looked oddly, and you would have said, guiltily, for a moment.

I helped him out of his awkwardness in the best way, by appearing not to observe it, and going straight on, I said: "Those revivals of interest in a subject happen to me often; one book suggests another, and often sends me back a wild-goose chase over an interval of twenty years. But if you still care to possess a copy, I shall be only too happy to provide you; I have still got two or three by me—and if you allow me to present one I shall be very much honoured."

"You are very good indeed," he said, quite at his ease again, in a moment: "I almost despaired—I don't know how to thank you."

"Pray don't say a word; the thing is really so little worth that I am only ashamed of having offered it, and if you thank me any more I shall throw it into the fire in a fit of modesty."

Mr. Jennings laughed. He inquired where I was staying in London, and after a little more conversation on a variety of subjects, he took his departure.

## CHAPTER II

*The Doctor Questions Lady Mary and She Answers*

"I like your vicar so much, Lady Mary," said I, as soon as he was gone. "He has read, travelled, and thought, and having also suffered, he ought to be an accomplished companion."

"So he is, and, better still, he is a really good man," said she. "His advice is invaluable about my schools, and all my little undertakings at Dawlbridge, and he's so painstaking, he takes so much trouble—you have no idea—wherever he thinks he can be of use: he's so good-natured and so sensible."

"It is pleasant to hear so good an account of his neighbourly virtues. I can only testify to his being an agreeable and gentle companion, and in addition to what you have told me, I think I can tell you two or three things about him," said I.

"Really!"

"Yes, to begin with, he's unmarried." "Yes, that's right—go on."

"He has been writing, that is he *was,* but for two or three years perhaps, he has not gone on with his work, and the book was upon some rather abstract subject—perhaps theology."

"Well, he was writing a book, as you say; I'm not quite sure what it was about, but only that it was nothing that I cared for; very likely you are right, and he certainly did stop—yes."

"And although he only drank a little coffee here to-night, he likes tea, at least, did like it extravagantly."

"Yes, that's *quite* true."

"He drank green tea, a good deal, didn't he?" I pursued. "Well, that's very odd! Green tea was a subject on which we used almost to quarrel."

"But he has quite given that up," said I. "So he has."

"And, now, one more fact. His mother or his father, did you know them?"

"Yes, both; his father is only ten years dead, and their place is near Dawl-bridge. We knew them very well," she answered.

"Well, either his mother or his father—I should rather think his father, saw a ghost," said I.

"Well, you really are a conjurer, Dr. Hesselius."

"Conjurer or no, haven't I said right?" I answered merrily.

"You certainly have, and it *was* his father: he was a silent, whimsical man, and he used to bore my father about his dreams, and at last he told him a story about a ghost he had seen and talked with, and a very odd story it was. I remember it particularly, because I was so afraid of him. This story was long before he died—when I was quite a child—and his ways were so silent and moping, and he used to drop in sometimes, in the dusk, when I was alone in the drawing-room, and I used to fancy there were ghosts about him."

I smiled and nodded.

"And now, having established my character as a conjurer, I think I must say good-night," said I. "But how *did* you find it out?"

"By the planets, of course, as the gipsies do," I answered, and so, gaily we said good-night.

Next morning I sent the little book he had been inquiring after, and a note to Mr. Jennings, and on returning late that evening, I found that he had called at my lodgings, and left his card. He asked whether I was at home, and asked at what hour he would be most likely to find me.

Does he intend opening his case, and consulting me "professionally," as they say? I hope so. I have already conceived a theory about him. It is supported by Lady Mary's answers to my parting questions. I should like much to ascertain from his own lips. But what can I do consistently with good breeding to invite a confession? Nothing. I rather think he meditates one. At all events, my dear Van L., I shan't make myself difficult of access; I mean to return his visit tomorrow. It will be only civil in return for his politeness, to ask to see him. Perhaps something may come of it. Whether much, little, or nothing, my dear Van L., you shall hear.

## CHAPTER III

*Dr. Hesselius Picks Up Something in Latin Books*

Well, I have called at Blank Street.

On inquiring at the door, the servant told me that Mr. Jennings was engaged very particularly with a gentleman, a clergyman from Kenlis, his parish in the country. Intending to reserve my privilege, and to call again, I merely intimated that I should try another time, and had turned to go, when the servant begged my pardon, and asked me, looking at me a little more attentively than well-bred persons of his order usually do, whether I was Dr. Hesselius; and, on learning that I was, he said, "Perhaps then, sir, you would allow me to mention it to Mr. Jennings, for I am sure he wishes to see you."

The servant returned in a moment, with a message from Mr. Jennings, asking me to go into his study, which was in effect his back drawing-room, promising to be with me in a very few minutes.

This was really a study—almost a library. The room was lofty, with two tall slender windows, and rich dark curtains. It was much larger than I had expected, and stored with books on every side, from the floor to the ceiling. The upper carpet—for to my tread it felt that there were two or three—was a Turkey carpet. My steps fell noiselessly. The bookcases standing out, placed the windows, particularly narrow ones, in deep recesses. The effect of the room was, although extremely comfortable, and even luxurious, decidedly gloomy, and aided by the silence, almost oppressive. Perhaps, however, I ought to have allowed something for association. My mind had connected peculiar ideas with Mr. Jennings. I stepped into this perfectly silent room, of a very silent house, with a peculiar foreboding; and its darkness, and solemn clothing of books, for except where two narrow looking-glasses were set in the wall, they were everywhere, helped this somber feeling.

While awaiting Mr. Jennings' arrival, I amused myself by looking into some of the books with which his shelves were laden. Not among these, but immediately under them, with their backs upward, on the floor, I lighted upon a complete set of Swedenborg's "Arcana Caelestia," in the original Latin, a very fine folio set, bound in the natty livery which theology affects, pure vellum, namely, gold letters, and carmine edges. There were paper markers in several of these volumes, I raised and placed them, one after the other, upon the table, and opening where these papers were placed, I read in the solemn Latin phraseology, a series of sentences indicated by a pencilled line at the margin. Of these I copy here a few, translating them into English.

"When man's interior sight is opened, which is that of his spirit, then there appear the things of another life, which cannot possibly be made visible to the bodily sight..."

"By the internal sight it has been granted me to see the things that are in the other life, more clearly than I see those that are in the world. From these considerations, it is evident that external vision exists from interior vision, and this from a vision still more interior, and so on..."

"There are with every man at least two evil spirits..."

"With wicked genii there is also a fluent speech, but harsh and grating. There is also among them a speech which is not fluent, wherein the dissent of the thoughts is perceived as something secretly creeping along within it."

"The evil spirits associated with man are, indeed from the hells, but when with man they are not then in hell, but are taken out thence. The place where they then are, is in the midst between heaven and hell, and is called the world of spirits—when the evil spirits who are with man, are in that world, they are not in any infernal torment, but in every thought and affection of man, and so, in all that the man himself enjoys. But when they are remitted into their hell, they return to their former state..."

"If evil spirits could perceive that they were associated with man, and yet that they were spirits separate from him, and if they could flow in into the things of his body, they would attempt by a thousand means to destroy him; for they hate man with a deadly hatred..."

"Knowing, therefore, that I was a man in the body, they were continually striving to destroy me, not as to the body only, but especially as to the soul; for to destroy any man or spirit is the very delight of the life of all who are in hell; but I have been continually protected by the Lord. Hence it appears how dangerous it is for man to be in a living consort with spirits, unless he be in the good of faith..."

"Nothing is more carefully guarded from the knowledge of associate spirits than their being thus conjoint with a man, for if they knew it they would speak to him, with the intention to destroy him..."

"The delight of hell is to do evil to man, and to hasten his eternal ruin."

A long note, written with a very sharp and fine pencil, in Mr. Jennings' neat hand, at the foot of the page, caught my eye. Expecting his criticism upon the text, I read a word or two, and stopped, for it was something quite different, and began with these words, *Deus misereatur mei*—"May God compassionate me." Thus warned of its private nature, I averted my eyes, and shut the book, replacing all the volumes as I had found them, except one which interested me, and in which, as men studious and solitary in their habits will do, I grew so absorbed as to take no cognisance of the outer world, nor to remember where I was.

I was reading some pages which refer to "representatives" and "correspondents," in the technical language of Swedenborg, and had arrived at a passage, the substance of which is, that evil spirits, when seen by other eyes than those of their infernal associates, present themselves, by "correspondence," in the shape of the beast *(fera)* which represents their particular lust and life, in aspect direful and atrocious. This is a long passage, and particularises a number of those bestial forms.

## CHAPTER IV

### *Four Eyes Were Reading the Passage*

I was running the head of my pencil-case along the line as I read it, and something caused me to raise my eyes.

Directly before me was one of the mirrors I have mentioned, in which I saw reflected the tall shape of my friend, Mr. Jennings, leaning over my shoulder, and reading the page at which I was busy, and with a face so dark and wild that I should hardly have known him.

I turned and rose. He stood erect also, and with an effort laughed a little, saying:

"I came in and asked you how you did, but without succeeding in awaking you from your book; so I could not restrain my curiosity, and very impertinently, I'm afraid, peeped over your shoulder. This is not your first time of looking into those pages. You have looked into Swedenborg, no doubt, long ago?"

"Oh dear, yes! I owe Swedenborg a great deal; you will discover traces of him in the little book on Metaphysical Medicine, which you were so good as to remember."

Although my friend affected a gaiety of manner, there was a slight flush in his face, and I could perceive that he was inwardly much perturbed.

"I'm scarcely yet qualified, I know so little of Swedenborg. I've only had them a fortnight," he answered, "and I think they are rather likely to make a solitary man nervous—that is, judging from the very little I have read—I don't say that they have made me so," he laughed; "and I'm so very much obliged for the book. I hope you got my note?"

I made all proper acknowledgments and modest disclaimers.

"I never read a book that I go with, so entirely, as that of yours," he continued. "I saw at once there is more in it than is quite unfolded. Do you know Dr. Harley?" he asked, rather abruptly.

In passing, the editor remarks that the physician here named was one of the most eminent who had ever practised in England.

I did, having had letters to him, and had experienced from him great courtesy and considerable assistance during my visit to England.

"I think that man one of the very greatest fools I ever met in my life," said Mr. Jennings.

This was the first time I had ever heard him say a sharp thing of anybody, and such a term applied to so high a name a little startled me.

"Really! and in what way?" I asked.

"In his profession," he answered.

I smiled.

"I mean this," he said: "he seems to me, one half, blind—I mean one half of all he looks at is dark—preternaturally bright and vivid all the rest; and the worst of it is, it seems *willful*. I can't get him—I mean he won't—I've had some experience of him as a physician, but I look on him as, in that sense, no better than a paralytic mind, an intellect half dead. I'll tell you—I know I shall some time—all about it," he said, with a little agitation. "You stay some months longer in England. If I should be out of town during your stay for a little time, would you allow me to trouble you with a letter?"

"I should be only too happy," I assured him.

"Very good of you. I am so utterly dissatisfied with Harley."

"A little leaning to the materialistic school," I said.

"A *mere* materialist," he corrected me; "you can't think how that sort of thing worries one who knows better. You won't tell any one—any of my friends you know—that I am hippish; now, for instance, no one knows—not even Lady Mary—that I have seen Dr. Harley, or any other doctor. So pray don't mention it; and, if I should have any threatening of an attack, you'll kindly let me write, or, should I be in town, have a little talk with you."

I was full of conjecture, and unconsciously I found I had fixed my eyes gravely on him, for he lowered his for a moment, and he said:

"I see you think I might as well tell you now, or else you are forming a conjecture; but you may as well give it up. If you were guessing all the rest of your life, you will never hit on it."

He shook his head smiling, and over that wintry sunshine a black cloud suddenly came down, and he drew his breath in, through his teeth as men do in pain.

"Sorry, of course, to learn that you apprehend occasion to consult any of us; but, command me when and how you like, and I need not assure you that your confidence is sacred."

He then talked of quite other things, and in a comparatively cheerful way and after a little time, I took my leave.

## CHAPTER V

### *Dr. Hesselius is Summoned to Richmond*

We parted cheerfully, but he was not cheerful, nor was I. There are certain expressions of that powerful organ of spirit—the human face—which, although I have seen them often, and possess a doctor's nerve, yet disturb me profoundly. One look of Mr. Jennings haunted me. It had seized my imagination with so dismal a power that I changed my plans for the evening, and went to the opera, feeling that I wanted a change of ideas.

I heard nothing of or from him for two or three days, when a note in his hand reached me. It was cheerful, and full of hope. He said that he had been for some little time so much better—quite well, in fact—that he was going to make a little experiment, and run down for a month or so to his parish, to try whether a little work might not quite set him up. There was in it a fervent religious expression of gratitude for his restoration, as he now almost hoped he might call it.

A day or two later I saw Lady Mary, who repeated what his note had announced, and told me that he was actually in Warwickshire, having resumed his clerical duties at Kenlis; and she added, "I begin to think that he is really perfectly well, and that there never was anything the matter, more than nerves and fancy; we are all nervous, but I fancy there is nothing like a little hard work for that kind of weakness, and he has made up his mind to try it. I should not be surprised if he did not come back for a year."

Notwithstanding all this confidence, only two days later I had this note, dated from his house off Piccadilly:

"Dear Sir,—I have returned disappointed. If I should feel at all able to see you, I shall write to ask you kindly to call. At present, I am too low, and, in fact, simply unable to say all I wish to say. Pray don't mention my name to my friends. I can see no one. By-and-by, please God, you shall hear from me. I mean to take a run into Shropshire, where some of my people are. God bless you! May we, on my return, meet more happily than I can now write."

About a week after this I saw Lady Mary at her own house, the last person, she said, left in town, and just on the wing for Brighton, for the London season was quite over. She told me that she had heard from Mr. Jennings' niece,

Martha, in Shropshire. There was nothing to be gathered from her letter, more than that he was low and nervous. In those words, of which healthy people think so lightly, what a world of suffering is sometimes hidden!

Nearly five weeks had passed without any further news of Mr. Jennings. At the end of that time I received a note from him. He wrote:

"I have been in the country, and have had change of air, change of scene, change of faces, change of everything—and in everything—but *myself.* I have made up my mind, so far as the most irresolute creature on earth can do it, to tell my case fully to you. If your engagements will permit, pray come to me to-day, to-morrow, or the next day; but, pray defer as little as possible. You know not how much I need help. I have a quiet house at Richmond, where I now am. Perhaps you can manage to come to dinner, or to luncheon, or even to tea. You shall have no trouble in finding me out. The servant at Blank Street, who takes this note, will have a carriage at your door at any hour you please; and I am always to be found. You will say that I ought not to be alone. I have tried everything. Come and see."

I called up the servant, and decided on going out the same evening, which accordingly I did.

He would have been much better in a lodging-house, or hotel, I thought, as I drove up through a short double row of sombre elms to a very old-fashioned brick house, darkened by the foliage of these trees, which overtopped, and nearly surrounded it. It was a perverse choice, for nothing could be imagined more triste and silent. The house, I found, belonged to him. He had stayed for a day or two in town, and, finding it for some cause insupportable, had come out here, probably because being furnished and his own, he was relieved of the thought and delay of selection, by coming here.

The sun had already set, and the red reflected light of the western sky illuminated the scene with the peculiar effect with which we are all familiar. The hall seemed very dark, but, getting to the back drawing-room, whose windows command the west, I was again in the same dusky light.

I sat down, looking out upon the richly-wooded landscape that glowed in the grand and melancholy light which was every moment fading. The corners of the room were already dark; all was growing dim, and the gloom was insensibly toning my mind, already prepared for what was sinister. I was waiting alone for his arrival, which soon took place. The door communicating with the front room opened, and the tall figure of Mr. Jennings, faintly seen in the ruddy twilight, came, with quiet stealthy steps, into the room.

We shook hands, and, taking a chair to the window, where there was still light enough to enable us to see each other's faces, he sat down beside me, and, placing his hand upon my arm, with scarcely a word of preface began his narrative.

# CHAPTER VI

## *How Mr. Jennings Met His Companion*

The faint glow of the west, the pomp of the then lonely woods of Richmond, were before us, behind and about us the darkening room, and on the stony face of the sufferer—for the character of his face, though still gentle and sweet, was changed—rested that dim, odd glow which seems to descend and produce, where it touches, lights, sudden though faint, which are lost, almost without gradation, in darkness. The silence, too, was utter: not a distant wheel, or bark, or whistle from without; and within the depressing stillness of an invalid bachelor's house.

I guessed well the nature, though not even vaguely the particulars of the revelations I was about to receive, from that fixed face of suffering that so oddly flushed stood out, like a portrait of Schalken's, before its background of darkness.

"It began," he said, "on the 15th of October, three years and eleven weeks ago, and two days—I keep very accurate count, for every day is torment. If I leave anywhere a chasm in my narrative tell me.

"About four years ago I began a work, which had cost me very much thought and reading. It was upon the religious metaphysics of the ancients."

"I know," said I, "the actual religion of educated and thinking paganism, quite apart from symbolic worship? A wide and very interesting field."

"Yes, but not good for the mind—the Christian mind, I mean. Paganism is all bound together in essential unity, and, with evil sympathy, their religion involves their art, and both their manners, and the subject is a degrading fascination and the Nemesis sure. God forgive me!

"I wrote a great deal; I wrote late at night. I was always thinking on the subject, walking about, wherever I was, everywhere. It thoroughly infected me. You are to remember that all the material ideas connected with it were more or less of the beautiful, the subject itself delightfully interesting, and I, then, without a care."

He sighed heavily.

"I believe, that every one who sets about writing in earnest does his work, as a friend of mine phrased it, *on* something—tea, or coffee, or tobacco. I suppose there is a material waste that must be hourly supplied in such occupations, or that we should grow too abstracted, and the mind, as it were, pass out of the body, unless it were reminded often enough of the connection by actual sensation. At all events, I felt the want, and I supplied it. Tea was my companion—at first the ordinary black tea, made in the usual way, not too strong: but I drank a good deal, and increased its strength as I went on. I never experienced an uncomfortable symptom from it. I began to take a little green tea. I found the effect pleasanter, it cleared and intensified the power of thought so, I had come to take it frequently, but not stronger than one might take it for pleasure. I wrote a great deal out here, it was so quiet, and in this room. I used to sit up very late, and it became a habit with me to sip my tea—green tea—every now and then as my work proceeded. I had a little kettle on my table, that swung over a lamp, and made tea two or three times between eleven o'clock and two or three in the morning, my hours of going to bed. I used to go into town every day. I was not a monk, and, although I spent an hour or two in a library, hunting up authorities and looking out lights upon my theme, I was in no morbid state as far as I can judge. I met my friends pretty much as usual and enjoyed their society, and, on the whole, existence had never been, I think, so pleasant before.

"I had met with a man who had some odd old books, German editions in mediaeval Latin, and I was only too happy to be permitted access to them. This obliging person's books were in the City, a very out-of-the-way part of it. I had rather out-stayed my intended hour, and, on coming out, seeing no cab near, I was tempted to get into the omnibus which used to drive past this house. It was darker than this by the time the 'bus had reached an old house, you may have remarked, with four poplars at each side of the door, and there the last passenger but myself got out. We drove along rather faster. It was twilight now. I leaned back in my corner next the door ruminating pleasantly.

"The interior of the omnibus was nearly dark. I had observed in the corner opposite to me at the other side, and at the end next the horses, two small circular reflections, as it seemed to me of a reddish light. They were about two inches apart, and about the size of those small brass buttons that yachting men used to put upon their jackets. I began to speculate, as listless men will, upon this trifle, as it seemed. From what centre did that faint but deep red light come, and from what—glass beads, buttons, toy decorations—was it reflected? We were lumbering along gently, having nearly a mile still to go. I had not solved the puzzle, and it became in another minute more odd, for these two luminous points, with a sudden jerk, descended nearer and nearer the floor, keeping still their relative distance and horizontal position, and then, as suddenly, they rose to the level of the seat on which I was sitting and I saw them no more.

"My curiosity was now really excited, and, before I had time to think, I saw again these two dull lamps, again together near the floor; again they disappeared, and again in their old corner I saw them.

"So, keeping my eyes upon them, I edged quietly up my own side, towards the end at which I still saw these tiny discs of red.

"There was very little light in the 'bus. It was nearly dark. I leaned forward to aid my endeavour to discover what these little circles really were. They shifted position a little as I did so. I began now to perceive an outline of something black, and I soon saw, with tolerable distinctness, the outline of a small black monkey, pushing its face forward in mimicry to meet mine; those were its eyes, and I now dimly saw its teeth grinning at me.

"I drew back, not knowing whether it might not meditate a spring. I fancied that one of the passengers had forgot this ugly pet, and wishing to ascertain something of its temper, though not caring to trust my fingers to it, I poked my umbrella softly towards it. It remained immovable—up to it—*through* it. For through it, and back and forward it passed, without the slightest resistance.

"I can't, in the least, convey to you the kind of horror that I felt. When I had ascertained that the thing was an illusion, as I then supposed, there came a misgiving about myself and a terror that fascinated me in impotence to remove my gaze from the eyes of the brute for some moments. As I looked, it made a little skip back, quite into the corner, and I, in a panic, found myself at the door, having put my head out, drawing deep breaths of the outer air, and staring at the lights and trees we were passing, too glad to reassure myself of reality.

"I stopped the bus and got out. I perceived the man look oddly at me as I paid him. I dare say there was something unusual in my looks and manner, for I had never felt so strangely before."

## CHAPTER VII

### *The Journey: First Stage*

"When the omnibus drove on, and I was alone upon the road, I looked carefully round to ascertain whether the monkey had followed me. To my indescribable relief I saw it nowhere. I can't describe easily what a shock I had received, and my sense of genuine gratitude on finding myself, as I supposed, quite rid of it.

"I had got out a little before we reached this house, two or three hundred steps. A brick wall runs along the footpath, and inside the wall is a hedge of yew, or some dark evergreen of that kind, and within that again the row of fine trees which you may have remarked as you came.

"This brick wall is about as high as my shoulder, and happening to raise my eyes I saw the monkey, with that stooping gait, on all fours, walking or creeping, close beside me, on top of the wall. I stopped, looking at it with a feeling of loathing and horror. As I stopped so did it. It sat up on the wall with its long hands on its knees looking at me. There was not light enough to see it much more than in outline, nor was it dark enough to bring the peculiar light of its eyes into strong relief. I still saw, however, that red foggy light plainly enough. It did not show its teeth, nor exhibit any sign of irritation, but seemed jaded and sulky, and was observing me steadily.

"I drew back into the middle of the road. It was an unconscious recoil, and there I stood, still looking at it. It did not move.

"With an instinctive determination to try something—anything, I turned about and walked briskly towards town with askance look, all the time, watching the movements of the beast. It crept swiftly along the wall, at exactly my pace.

"Where the wall ends, near the turn of the road, it came down, and with a wiry spring or two brought itself close to my feet, and continued to keep up with me, as I quickened my pace. It was at my left side, so close to my leg that I felt every moment as if I should tread upon it.

"The road was quite deserted and silent, and it was darker every moment. I stopped dismayed and bewildered, turning as I did so, the other way—I mean, towards this house, away from which I had been walking. When I stood still, the monkey drew back to a distance of, I suppose, about five or six yards, and remained stationary, watching me.

"I had been more agitated than I have said. I had read, of course, as everyone has, something about 'spectral illusions,' as you physicians term the phenomena of such cases. I considered my situation, and looked my misfortune in the face.

"These affections, I had read, are sometimes transitory and sometimes obstinate. I had read of cases in which the appearance, at first harmless, had, step by step, degenerated into something direful and insupportable, and ended by wearing its victim out. Still as I stood there, but for my bestial companion, quite alone, I tried to comfort myself by repeating again and again the assurance, 'the thing is purely disease, a well-known physical affection, as distinctly as small-pox or neuralgia. Doctors are all agreed on that, philosophy demonstrates it. I must not be a fool. I've been sitting up too late, and I daresay my digestion is quite wrong, and, with God's help, I shall be all right, and this is but a symptom of nervous dyspepsia.' Did I believe all this? Not one word of it, no more than any other miserable being ever did who is once seized and riveted in this satanic captivity. Against my convictions, I might say my knowledge, I was simply bullying myself into a false courage.

"I now walked homeward. I had only a few hundred yards to go. I had forced myself into a sort of resignation, but I had not got over the sickening shock and the flurry of the first certainty of my misfortune.

"I made up my mind to pass the night at home. The brute moved close beside me, and I fancied there was the sort of anxious drawing toward the house, which one sees in tired horses or dogs, sometimes as they come toward home.

"I was afraid to go into town, I was afraid of any one's seeing and recognizing me. I was conscious of an irrepressible agitation in my manner. Also, I was afraid of any violent change in my habits, such as going to a place of amusement, or walking from home in order to fatigue myself. At the hall door it waited till I mounted the steps, and when the door was opened entered with me.

"I drank no tea that night. I got cigars and some brandy and water. My idea was that I should act upon my material system, and by living for a while in sensation apart from thought, send myself forcibly, as it were, into a new groove. I came up here to this drawing-room. I sat just here. The monkey then got upon a small table that then stood *there*. It looked dazed and languid. An irrepressible uneasiness as to its movements kept my eyes always upon it. Its eyes were half closed, but I could see them glow. It was looking steadily at me. In all situations, at all hours, it is awake and looking at me. That never changes.

"I shall not continue in detail my narrative of this particular night. I shall describe, rather, the phenomena of the first year, which never varied, essentially. I shall describe the monkey as it appeared in daylight. In the dark, as you shall presently hear, there are peculiarities. It is a small monkey, perfectly black. It had only one peculiarity—a character of malignity—unfathomable malignity. During the first year it looked sullen and sick. But this character of intense malice and vigilance was always underlying that surly languor. During all that time it acted as if on a plan of giving me as little trouble as was consistent with watching me. Its eyes were never off me. I have never lost sight of it, except in my sleep, light or dark, day or night, since it came here, excepting when it withdraws for some weeks at a time, unaccountably.

"In total dark it is visible as in daylight. I do not mean merely its eyes. It is *all* visible distinctly in a halo that resembles a glow of red embers, and which accompanies it in all its movements.

"When it leaves me for a time, it is always at night, in the dark, and in the same way. It grows at first uneasy, and then furious, and then advances towards me, grinning and shaking, its paws clenched, and, at the same time, there comes the appearance of fire in the grate. I never have any fire. I can't sleep in the room where there is any, and it draws nearer and nearer to the chimney, quivering, it seems, with rage, and when its fury rises to the highest pitch, it springs into the grate, and up the chimney, and I see it no more.

"When first this happened, I thought I was released. I was now a new man. A day passed—a night—and no return, and a blessed week—a week—another week. I was always on my knees, Dr. Hesselius, always, thanking God and praying. A whole month passed of liberty, but on a sudden, it was with me again."

## CHAPTER VIII

### *The Second Stage*

"It was with me, and the malice which before was torpid under a sullen exterior, was now active. It was perfectly unchanged in every other respect. This new energy was apparent in its activity and its looks, and soon in other ways.

"For a time, you will understand, the change was shown only in an increased vivacity, and an air of menace, as if it were always brooding over some atrocious plan. Its eyes, as before, were never off me."

"Is it here now?" I asked.

"No," he replied, "it has been absent exactly a fortnight and a day—fifteen days. It has sometimes been away so long as nearly two months, once for three. Its absence always exceeds a fortnight, although it may be but by a single day. Fifteen days having past since I saw it last, it may return now at any moment."

"Is its return," I asked, "accompanied by any peculiar manifestation?"

"Nothing—no," he said. "It is simply with me again. On lifting my eyes from a book, or turning my head, I see it, as usual, looking at me, and then it remains, as before, for its appointed time. I have never told so much and so minutely before to any one."

I perceived that he was agitated, and looking like death, and he repeatedly applied his handkerchief to his forehead; I suggested that he might be tired, and told him that I would call, with pleasure, in the morning, but he said:

"No, if you don't mind hearing it all now. I have got so far, and I should prefer making one effort of it. When I spoke to Dr. Harley, I had nothing like so much to tell. You are a philosophic physician. You give spirit its proper rank. If this thing is real—" He paused looking at me with agitated inquiry. "We can discuss it by-and-by, and very fully. I will give you all I think," I answered, after an interval.

"Well—very well. If it is anything real, I say, it is prevailing, little by little, and drawing me more interiorly into hell. Optic nerves, he talked of. Ah! well—there are other nerves of communication. May God Almighty help me! You shall hear.

"Its power of action, I tell you, had increased. Its malice became, in a way, aggressive. About two years ago, some questions that were pending between me and the bishop having been settled, I went down to my parish in Warwickshire, anxious to find occupation in my profession. I was not prepared for what happened, although I have since thought I might have apprehended something like it. The reason of my saying so is this—"

He was beginning to speak with a great deal more effort and reluctance, and sighed often, and seemed at times nearly overcome. But at this time his manner was not agitated. It was more like that of a sinking patient, who has given himself up.

"Yes, but I will first tell you about Kenlis, my parish. It was with me when I left this place for Dawlbridge. It was my silent travelling companion, and it remained with me at the vicarage. When I entered on the discharge of my duties, another change took place. The thing exhibited an atrocious determination to thwart me. It was with me in the church—in the reading-desk, in the pulpit, within the communion rails. At last, it reached this extremity, that while I was reading to the congregation, it would spring upon the book and squat there, so that I was unable to see the page. This happened more than once.

"I left Dawlbridge for a time. I placed myself in Dr. Harley's hands. I did everything he told me. He gave my case a great deal of thought. It interested him, I think. He seemed successful. For nearly three months I was perfectly free from a return. I began to think I was safe. With his full assent I returned to Dawlbridge.

"I travelled in a chaise. I was in good spirits. I was more—I was happy and grateful. I was returning, as I thought, delivered from a dreadful hallucination, to the scene of duties which I longed to enter upon. It was a beautiful sunny evening, everything looked serene and cheerful, and I was delighted. I remember looking out of the window to see the spire of my church at Kenlis among the trees, at the point where one has the earliest view of it. It is exactly where the little stream that bounds the parish passes under the road by a culvert, and where it emerges at the road-side, a stone with an old inscription is placed. As we passed this point, I drew my head in and sat down, and in the corner of the chaise was the monkey.

"For a moment I felt faint, and then quite wild with despair and horror. I called to the driver, and got out, and sat down at the road-side, and prayed to God silently for mercy. A despairing resignation supervened. My companion was with me as I reentered the vicarage. The same persecution followed. After a short struggle I submitted, and soon I left the place.

"I told you," he said, "that the beast has before this become in certain ways aggressive. I will explain a little. It seemed to be actuated by intense and increasing fury, whenever I said my prayers, or even meditated prayer. It amounted at last to a dreadful interruption. You will ask, how could a silent immaterial phantom effect that? It was thus, whenever I meditated praying; It was always before me, and nearer and nearer.

"It used to spring on a table, on the back of a chair, on the chimney-piece, and slowly to swing itself from side to side, looking at me all the time. There is in its motion an indefinable power to dissipate thought, and to contract one's attention to that monotony, till the ideas shrink, as it were, to a point, and at last to nothing—and unless I had started up, and shook off the catalepsy I have felt as if my mind were on the point of losing itself. There are other ways," he sighed heavily; "thus, for instance, while I pray with my eyes closed, it comes closer and closer, and I see it. I know it is not to be accounted for physically, but I do actually see it, though my lids are closed, and so it rocks my mind, as it were, and overpowers me, and I am obliged to rise from my knees. If you had ever yourself known this, you would be acquainted with desperation."

## CHAPTER IX

### *The Third Stage*

"I see, Dr. Hesselius, that you don't lose one word of my statement. I need not ask you to listen specially to what I am now going to tell you. They talk of the optic nerves, and of spectral illusions, as if the organ of sight was the only point assailable by the influences that have fastened upon me—I know better.

For two years in my direful case that limitation prevailed. But as food is taken in softly at the lips, and then brought under the teeth, as the tip of the little finger caught in a mill crank will draw in the hand, and the arm, and the whole body, so the miserable mortal who has been once caught firmly by the end of the finest fibre of his nerve, is drawn in and in, by the enormous machinery of hell, until he is as I am. Yes, Doctor, as I am, for a while I talk to you, and implore relief, I feel that my prayer is for the impossible, and my pleading with the inexorable."

I endeavoured to calm his visibly increasing agitation, and told him that he must not despair.

While we talked the night had overtaken us. The filmy moonlight was wide over the scene which the window commanded, and I said:

"Perhaps you would prefer having candles. This light, you know, is odd. I should wish you, as much as possible, under your usual conditions while I make my diagnosis, shall I call it—otherwise I don't care."

"All lights are the same to me," he said; "except when I read or write, I care not if night were perpetual. I am going to tell you what happened about a year ago. The thing began to speak to me."

"Speak! How do you mean—speak as a man does, do you mean?

"Yes; speak in words and consecutive sentences, with perfect coherence and articulation; but there is a peculiarity. It is not like the tone of a human voice. It is not by my ears it reaches me—it comes like a singing through my head.

"This faculty, the power of speaking to me, will be my undoing. It won't let me pray, it interrupts me with dreadful blasphemies. I dare not go on, I could not. Oh! Doctor, can the skill, and thought, and prayers of man avail me nothing!"

"You must promise me, my dear sir, not to trouble yourself with unnecessarily exciting thoughts; confine yourself strictly to the narrative of facts; and recollect, above all, that even if the thing that infests you be, you seem to suppose a reality with an actual independent life and will, yet it can have no power to hurt you, unless it be given from above: its access to your senses depends mainly upon your physical condition—this is, under God, your comfort and reliance: we are all alike environed.

It is only that in your case, the *'paries'* the veil of the flesh, the screen, is a little out of repair, and sights and sounds are transmitted. We must enter on a new course, sir,—be encouraged. I'll give to-night to the careful consideration of the whole case.

"You are very good, sir; you think it worth trying, you don't give me quite up; but, sir, you don't know, it is gaining such an influence over me: it orders me about, it is such a tyrant, and I'm growing so helpless. May God deliver me!"

"It orders you about—of course you mean by speech?"

"Yes, yes; it is always urging me to crimes, to injure others, or myself. You see, Doctor, the situation is urgent, it is indeed. When I was in Shropshire, a few weeks ago" (Mr. Jennings was speaking rapidly and trembling now, holding my arm with one hand, and looking in my face), "I went out one day with a party of friends for a walk: my persecutor, I tell you, was with me at the time. I lagged behind the rest: the country near the Dee, you know, is beautiful. Our path happened to lie near a coal mine, and at the verge of the wood is a perpendicular shaft, they say, a hundred and fifty feet deep. My niece had remained behind with me—she knows, of course nothing of the nature of my sufferings. She knew, however, that I had been ill, and was low, and she remained to prevent my being quite alone. As we loitered slowly on together, the brute that accompanied me was urging me to throw myself down the shaft. I tell you now—oh, sir, think of it!—the one consideration that saved me from that hideous death was the fear lest the shock of witnessing the occurrence should be too much for the poor girl. I asked her to go on and walk with her friends, saying that I could go no further. She made excuses, and the more I urged her the firmer she became. She looked doubtful and frightened. I suppose there was something in my looks or manner that alarmed her; but she would not go, and that literally saved me. You had no idea, sir, that a living man could be made so abject a slave of Satan," he said, with a ghastly groan and a shudder.

There was a pause here, and I said, "You *were* preserved nevertheless. It was the act of God. You are in His hands and in the power of no other being: be therefore confident for the future."

## CHAPTER X

*Home*

I made him have candles lighted, and saw the room looking cheery and inhabited before I left him. I told him that he must regard his illness strictly as one dependent on physical, though *subtle* physical causes. I told him that he had evidence of God's care and love in the deliverance which he had just described, and that I had perceived with pain that he seemed to regard its peculiar features as indicating that he had been delivered over to spiritual reprobation. Than such a conclusion nothing could be, I insisted, less warranted; and not only so, but more contrary to facts, as disclosed in his mysterious deliverance from that murderous influence during his Shropshire excursion. First, his niece had been retained by his side without his intending to keep her near him; and, secondly, there had been infused into his mind an irresistible repugnance to execute the dreadful suggestion in her presence.

As I reasoned this point with him, Mr. Jennings wept. He seemed comforted. One promise I exacted, which was that should the monkey at any time return, I should be sent for immediately; and, repeating my assurance that I would give neither time nor thought to any other subject until I had thoroughly investigated his case, and that to-morrow he should hear the result, I took my leave.

Before getting into the carriage I told the servant that his master was far from well, and that he should make a point of frequently looking into his room. My own arrangements I made with a view to being quite secure from interruption.

I merely called at my lodgings, and with a travelling-desk and carpet-bag, set off in a hackney carriage for an inn about two miles out of town, called "The Horns," a very quiet and comfortable house, with good thick walls. And there I resolved, without the possibility of intrusion or distraction, to devote some hours of the night, in my comfortable sitting-room, to Mr. Jennings' case, and so much of the morning as it might require.

(There occurs here a careful note of Dr. Hesselius' opinion upon the case, and of the habits, dietary, and medicines which he prescribed. It is curious—some persons would say mystical. But, on the whole, I doubt whether it would sufficiently interest a reader of the kind I am likely to meet with, to warrant its being here reprinted. The whole letter was plainly written at the inn where he had hid himself for the occasion. The next letter is dated from his town lodgings.)

I left town for the inn where I slept last night at half-past nine, and did not arrive at my room in town until one o'clock this afternoon. I found a letter in Mr. Jennings' hand upon my table. It had not come by post, and, on inquiry, I learned that Mr. Jennings' servant had brought it, and on learning that I was not to return until to-day, and that no one could tell him my address, he seemed very uncomfortable, and said his orders from his master were that that he was not to return without an answer. I opened the letter and read:

"Dear Dr. Hesselius.—It is here. You had not been an hour gone when it returned. It is speaking. It knows all that has happened. It knows everything—it knows you, and is frantic and atrocious. It reviles. I send you this. It knows every word I have written—I write. This I promised, and I therefore write, but I fear very confused, very incoherently. I am so interrupted, disturbed.

Ever yours, sincerely yours, Robert Lynder Jennings."

"When did this come?" I asked.

"About eleven last night: the man was here again, and has been here three times to-day. The last time is about an hour since."

Thus answered, and with the notes I had made upon his case in my pocket, I was in a few minutes driving towards Richmond, to see Mr. Jennings.

I by no means, as you perceive, despaired of Mr. Jennings' case. He had himself remembered and applied, though quite in a mistaken way, the principle which I lay down in my Metaphysical Medicine, and which governs all such cases. I was about to apply it in earnest. I was profoundly interested, and very anxious to see and examine him while the "enemy" was actually present.

I drove up to the sombre house, and ran up the steps, and knocked. The door, in a little time, was opened by a tall woman in black silk. She looked ill, and as if she had been crying. She curtseyed, and heard my question, but she did not answer. She turned her face away, extending her hand towards two men who were coming down-stairs; and thus having, as it were, tacitly made me over to them, she passed through a side-door hastily and shut it.

The man who was nearest the hall, I at once accosted, but being now close to him, I was shocked to see that both his hands were covered with blood.

I drew back a little, and the man, passing downstairs, merely said in a low tone, "Here's the servant, sir."

The servant had stopped on the stairs, confounded and dumb at seeing me. He was rubbing his hands in a handkerchief, and it was steeped in blood.

"Jones, what is it? what has happened?" I asked, while a sickening suspicion overpowered me.

The man asked me to come up to the lobby. I was beside him in a moment, and, frowning and pallid, with contracted eyes, he told me the horror which I already half guessed.

His master had made away with himself.

I went upstairs with him to the room—what I saw there I won't tell you. He had cut his throat with his razor. It was a frightful gash. The two men had laid him on the bed, and composed his limbs. It had happened, as the immense pool of blood on the floor declared, at some distance between the bed and the window. There was carpet round his bed, and a carpet under his dressing-table, but none on the rest of the floor, for the man said he did not like a carpet on his bedroom. In this sombre and now terrible room, one of the great elms that darkened the house was slowly moving the shadow of one of its great boughs upon this dreadful floor.

I beckoned to the servant, and we went downstairs together. I turned off the hall into an old-fashioned panelled room, and there standing, I heard all the servant had to tell. It was not a great deal.

"I concluded, sir, from your words, and looks, sir, as you left last night, that you thought my master was seriously ill. I thought it might be that you were afraid of a fit, or something. So I attended very close to your directions. He sat up late, till past three o'clock. He was not writing or reading. He was talking a great deal to himself, but that was nothing unusual. At about that hour I assisted him to undress, and left him in his slippers and dressing-gown. I went back softly in about half-an-hour. He was in his bed, quite undressed, and a pair of candles lighted on the table beside his bed. He was leaning on his elbow, and looking out at the other side of the bed when I came in, I asked him if he wanted anything, and he said No."

"I don't know whether it was what you said to me, sir, or something a little unusual about him, but I was uneasy, uncommon uneasy about him last night.

"In another half hour, or it might be a little more, I went up again. I did not hear him talking as before. I opened the door a little. The candles were both out, which was not usual. I had a bedroom candle, and I let the light in, a little bit, looking softly round. I saw him sitting in that chair beside the dressing-table with his clothes on again. He turned round and looked at me. I thought it strange he should get up and dress, and put out the candles to sit in the dark, that way. But I only asked him again if I could do anything for him. He said, No, rather sharp, I thought. I asked him if I might light the candles, and he said, 'Do as you like, Jones.' So I lighted them, and I lingered about the room, and he said, 'Tell me truth, Jones; why did you come again—you did not hear anyone cursing?' 'No, sir,' I said, wondering what he could mean.

"'No,' said he, after me, 'of course, no;' and I said to him, 'Wouldn't it be well, sir, you went to bed? It's just five o'clock;' and he said nothing, but, 'Very likely; good-night, Jones.' So I went, sir, but in less than an hour I came again. The door was fast, and he heard me, and called as I thought from the bed to know what I wanted, and he desired me not to disturb him again. I lay down and slept for a little. It must have been between six and seven when I went up again. The door was still fast, and he made no answer, so I did not like to disturb him, and thinking he was asleep, I left him till nine. It was his custom to ring when he wished me to come, and I had no particular hour for calling him. I tapped very gently, and getting no answer, I stayed away a good while, supposing he was getting some rest then. It was not till eleven o'clock I grew really uncomfortable about him—for at the latest he was never, that I could remember, later than half-past ten. I got no answer. I knocked and called, and still no answer. So not being able to force the door, I called Thomas from the stables, and together we forced it, and found him in the shocking way you saw."

Jones had no more to tell. Poor Mr. Jennings was very gentle, and very kind. All his people were fond of him. I could see that the servant was very much moved.

So, dejected and agitated, I passed from that terrible house, and its dark canopy of elms, and I hope I shall never see it more. While I write to you I feel like a man who has but half waked from a frightful and monotonous dream. My memory rejects the picture with incredulity and horror. Yet I know it is true. It is the story of the process of a poison, a poison which excites the reciprocal action of spirit and nerve, and paralyses the tissue that separates those cognate functions of the senses, the external and the interior. Thus we find strange bed-fellows, and the mortal and immortal prematurely make acquaintance.

## CONCLUSION

### *A Word for Those Who Suffer*

My dear Van L—, you have suffered from an affection similar to that which I have just described. You twice complained of a return of it.

Who, under God, cured you? Your humble servant, Martin Hesselius. Let me rather adopt the more emphasised piety of a certain good old French surgeon of three hundred years ago: "I treated, and God cured you."

Come, my friend, you are not to be hippish. Let me tell you a fact.

I have met with, and treated, as my book shows, fifty-seven cases of this kind of vision, which I term indifferently "sublimated," "precocious," and "interior."

There is another class of affections which are truly termed—though commonly confounded with those which I describe—spectral illusions. These latter I look upon as being no less simply curable than a cold in the head or a trifling dyspepsia.

It is those which rank in the first category that test our promptitude of thought. Fifty-seven such cases have I encountered, neither more nor less. And in how many of these have I failed? In no one single instance.

There is no one affliction of mortality more easily and certainly reducible, with a little patience, and a rational confidence in the physician. With these simple conditions, I look upon the cure as absolutely certain.

You are to remember that I had not even commenced to treat Mr. Jennings' case. I have not any doubt that I should have cured him perfectly in eighteen months, or possibly it might have extended to two years. Some cases are very rapidly curable, others extremely tedious. Every intelligent physician who will give thought and diligence to the task, will effect a cure.

You know my tract on "The Cardinal Functions of the Brain." I there, by the evidence of innumerable facts, prove, as I think, the high probability of a circulation arterial and venous in its mechanism, through the nerves. Of this system, thus considered, the brain is the heart. The fluid, which is propagated hence through one class of nerves, returns in an altered state through another, and the nature of that fluid is spiritual, though not immaterial, anymore than, as I before remarked, light or electricity are so.

By various abuses, among which the habitual use of such agents as green tea is one, this fluid may be affected as to its quality, but it is more frequently disturbed as to equilibrium. This fluid being that which we have in common with spirits, a congestion found upon the masses of brain or nerve, connected with the interior sense, forms a surface unduly exposed, on which disembodied spirits may operate: communication is thus more or less effectually established. Between this brain circulation and the heart circulation there is an intimate sympathy. The seat, or rather the instrument of exterior vision, is the eye. The seat of interior vision is the nervous tissue and brain, immediately about and above the eyebrow. You remember how effectually I dissipated your pictures by the simple application of iced eau-de-cologne. Few cases, however, can be treated exactly alike with anything like rapid success. Cold acts powerfully as a repellant of the nervous fluid. Long enough continued it will even produce that permanent insensibility which we call numbness, and a little longer, muscular as well as sensational paralysis.

I have not, I repeat, the slightest doubt that I should have first dimmed and ultimately sealed that inner eye which Mr. Jennings had inadvertently opened. The same senses are opened in delirium tremens, and entirely shut up again when the overaction of the cerebral heart, and the prodigious nervous congestions that attend it, are terminated by a decided change in the state of the body. It is by acting steadily upon the body, by a simple process, that this result is produced—and inevitably produced—I have never yet failed.

Poor Mr. Jennings made away with himself. But that catastrophe was the result of a totally different malady, which, as it were, projected itself upon the disease which was established. His case was in the distinctive manner a complication, and the complaint under which he really succumbed, was hereditary suicidal mania. Poor Mr. Jennings I cannot call a patient of mine, for I had not even begun to treat his case, and he had not yet given me, I am convinced, his full and unreserved confidence. If the patient do not array himself on the side of the disease, his cure is certain.

# THE STRANGE RIDE OF MORROWBIE JUKES

## RUDYARD KIPLING

*Alive or dead—there is no other way*

Native Proverb

There is, as the conjurers say, no deception about this tale. Jukes by accident stumbled upon a village that is well known to exist, though he is the only Englishman who has been there. A somewhat similar institution used to flourish on the outskirts of Calcutta, and there is a story that if you go into the heart of Bikanir, which is in the heart of the Great Indian Desert, you shall come across not a village but a town where the Dead who did not die but may not live have established their headquarters. And, since it is perfectly true that in the same Desert is a wonderful city where all the rich money lenders retreat after they have made their fortunes (fortunes so vast that the owners cannot trust even the strong hand of the Government to protect them, but take refuge in the waterless sands), and drive sumptuous C-spring barouches, and buy beautiful girls and decorate their palaces with gold and ivory and Minton tiles and mother-'n'-pearl, I do not see why Jukes's tale should not be true. He is a Civil Engineer, with a head for plans and distances and things of that kind, and he certainly would not take the trouble to invent imaginary traps. He could earn more by doing his legitimate work. He never varies the tale in the telling, and grows very hot and indignant when he thinks of the disrespectful treatment he received. He wrote this quite straightforwardly at first, but he has since touched it up in places and introduced Moral Reflections, thus:

In the beginning it all arose from a slight attack of fever. My work necessitated my being in camp for some months between Pakpattan and Muharakpur—a desolate sandy stretch of country as every one who has had the misfortune to go there may know. My coolies were neither more nor less exasperating than other gangs, and my work demanded sufficient attention to keep me from moping, had I been inclined to so unmanly a weakness.

On the 23d December, 1884, I felt a little feverish. There was a full moon at the time, and, in consequence, every dog near my tent was baying it. The brutes assembled in twos and threes and drove me frantic. A few days previously I had shot one loud-mouthed singer and suspended his carcass *in terrorem* about fifty yards from my tent-door. But his friends fell upon, fought for, and ultimately devoured the body; and, as it seemed to me, sang their hymns of thanksgiving afterward with renewed energy.

The light-heartedness which accompanies fever acts differently on different men. My irritation gave way, after a short time, to a fixed determination to slaughter one huge black and white beast who had been foremost in song and first in flight throughout the evening. Thanks to a shaking hand and a giddy head I had already missed him twice with both barrels of my shot-gun, when it struck me that my best plan would be to ride him down in the open and finish him off with a hog-spear. This, of course, was merely the semi-delirious notion of a fever patient; but I remember that it struck me at the time as being eminently practical and feasible.

I therefore ordered my groom to saddle Pornic and bring him round quietly to the rear of my tent. When the pony was ready, I stood at his head prepared to mount and dash out as soon as the dog should again lift up his voice. Pornic, by the way, had not been out of his pickets for a couple of days; the night air was crisp and chilly; and I was armed with a specially long and sharp pair of persuaders with which I had been rousing a sluggish cob that afternoon. You will easily believe, then, that when he was let go he went quickly. In one moment, for the brute bolted as straight as a die, the tent was left far behind, and we were flying over the smooth sandy soil at racing speed.

In another we had passed the wretched dog, and I had almost forgotten why it was that I had taken the horse and hogspear.

The delirium of fever and the excitement of rapid motion through the air must have taken away the remnants of my senses. I have a faint recollection of standing upright in my stirrups, and of brandishing my hog-spear at the great white Moon that looked down so calmly on my mad gallop; and of shout-log challenges to the camel-thorn bushes as they whizzed past. Once or twice I believe, I swayed forward on Pornic's neck, and literally hung on by my spurs— as the marks next morning showed.

The wretched beast went forward like a thing possessed, over what seemed to be a limitless expanse of moonlit sand. Next, I remember, the ground rose suddenly in front of us, and as we topped the ascent I saw the waters of the Sutlej shining like a silver bar below. Then Pornic blundered heavily on his nose, and we rolled together down some unseen slope.

I must have lost consciousness, for when I recovered I was lying on my stomach in a heap of soft white sand, and the dawn was beginning to break dimly over the edge of the slope down which I had fallen. As the light grew stronger I saw that I was at the bottom of a horseshoe-shaped crater of sand, opening on one side directly on to the shoals of the Sutlej. My fever had altogether left me, and, with the exception of a slight dizziness in the head, I felt no bad effects from the fall over night.

Pornic, who was standing a few yards away, was naturally a good deal exhausted, but had not hurt himself in the least. His saddle, a favorite polo one, was much knocked about and had been twisted under his belly. It took me some time to put him to rights, and in the meantime I had ample opportunities of observing the spot into which I had so foolishly dropped.

At the risk of being considered tedious, I must describe it at length: inasmuch as an accurate mental picture of its peculiarities will be of material assistance in enabling the reader to understand what follows.

Imagine then, as I have said before, a horseshoe-shaped crater of sand with steeply graded sand walls about thirty-five feet high. (The slope, I fancy, must have been about 65 degrees.) This crater enclosed a level piece of ground about fifty yards long by thirty at its broadest part, with a crude well in the centre. Round the bottom of the crater, about three feet from the level of the ground proper, ran a series of eighty-three semi-circular ovoid, square, and multilateral holes, all about three feet at the mouth. Each hole on inspection showed that it was carefully shored internally with drift-wood and bamboos, and over the mouth a wooden drip-board projected, like the peak of a jockey's cap, for two feet. No sign of life was visible in these tunnels, but a most sickening stench pervaded the entire amphitheatre—a stench fouler than any which my wanderings in Indian villages have introduced me to.

Having remounted Pornic, who was as anxious as I to get back to camp, I rode round the base of the horseshoe to find some place whence an exit would be practicable. The inhabitants, whoever they might be, had not thought fit to put in an appearance, so I was left to my own devices. My first attempt to "rush" Pornic up the steep sand-banks showed me that I had fallen into a trap exactly on the same model as that which the ant-lion sets for its prey. At each step the shifting sand poured down from above in tons, and rattled on the drip-boards of the holes like small shot. A couple of ineffectual charges sent us both rolling down to the bottom, half choked with the torrents of sand; and I was constrained to turn my attention to the river-bank.

Here everything seemed easy enough. The sand hills ran down to the river edge, it is true, but there were plenty of shoals and shallows across which I could gallop Pornic, and find my way back to *terra firma* by turning sharply to the right or left. As I led Pornic over the sands I was startled by the faint pop of a rifle across the river; and at the same moment a bullet dropped with a sharp *"whit"* close to Pornic's head.

There was no mistaking the nature of the missile—a regulation Martini-Henry "picket." About five hundred yards away a country-boat was anchored in midstream; and a jet of smoke drifting away from its bows in the still morning air showed me whence the delicate attention had come. Was ever a respectable gentleman in such an *impasse?* The treacherous sand slope allowed no escape from a spot which I had visited most involuntarily, and a promenade on the river frontage was the signal for a bombardment from some insane native in a boat. I'm afraid that I lost my temper very much indeed.

Another bullet reminded me that I had better save my breath to cool my porridge; and I retreated hastily up the sands and back to the horseshoe, where I saw that the noise of the rifle had drawn sixty-five human beings from the badger-holes which I had up till that point supposed to be untenanted. I found myself in the midst of a crowd of spectators—about forty men, twenty women, and one child who could not have been more than five years old. They were all scantily clothed in that salmon-colored cloth which one associates with Hindu mendicants, and, at first sight, gave me the impression of a band of loathsome *fakirs*. The filth and repulsiveness of the assembly were beyond all description, and I shuddered to think what their life in the badger-holes must be.

Even in these days, when local self-government has destroyed the greater part of a native's respect for a Sahib, I have been accustomed to a certain amount of civility from my inferiors, and on approaching the crowd naturally expected that there would be some recognition of my presence. As a matter of fact there was; but it was by no means what I had looked for.

The ragged crew actually laughed at me—such laughter I hope I may never hear again. They cackled, yelled, whistled, and howled as I walked into their midst; some of them literally throwing themselves down on the ground in convulsions of unholy mirth. In a moment I had let go Pornic's head, and, irritated beyond expression at the morning's adventure, commenced cuffing those nearest to me with all the force I could. The wretches dropped under my blows like nine-pins, and the laughter gave place to wails for mercy; while those yet untouched clasped me round the knees, imploring me in all sorts of uncouth tongues to spare them.

In the tumult, and just when I was feeling very much ashamed of myself for having thus easily given way to my temper, a thin, high voice murmured in English from behind my shoulder: "Sahib! Sahib! Do you not know me? Sahib, it is Gunga Dass, the telegraph-master."

I spun round quickly and faced the speaker. Gunga Dass, (I have, of course, no hesitation in mentioning the man's real name) I had known four years before as a Deccanee Brahmin loaned by the Punjab Government to one of the Khalsia States. He was in charge of a branch telegraph-office there, and when I had last met him was a jovial, full-stomached, portly Government servant with a marvelous capacity for making bad puns in English—a peculiarity which made me remember him long after I had forgotten his services to me in his official capacity. It is seldom that a Hindu makes English puns.

Now, however, the man was changed beyond all recognition. Caste-mark, stomach, slate-colored continuations, and unctuous speech were all gone. I looked at a withered skeleton, turban-less and almost naked, with long matted hair and deep-set codfish-eyes. But for a crescent-shaped scar on the left cheek—the result of an accident for which I was responsible—I should never have known him. But it was indubitably Gunga Dass, and—for this I was thankful—an English-speaking native who might at least tell me the meaning of all that I had gone through that day.

The crowd retreated to some distance as I turned toward the miserable figure, and ordered him to show me some method of escaping from the crater. He held a freshly plucked crow in his hand, and in reply to my question climbed slowly on a platform of sand which ran in front of the holes, and commenced lighting a fire there in silence. Dried bents, sand-poppies, and driftwood burn quickly; and I derived much consolation from the fact that he lit them with an ordinary sulphur-match. When they were in a bright glow, and the crow was nearly spitted in front thereof, Gunga Dass began without a word of preamble:

"There are only two kinds of men, Sar. The alive and the dead. When you are dead, you are dead, but when you are alive, you live." (Here the crow demanded his attention for an instant as it twirled before the fire in danger of being burned to a cinder.) "If you die at home and do not die when you come to the ghat to be burned you come here."

The nature of the reeking village was made plain now, and all that I had known or read of the grotesque and the horrible paled before the fact just communicated by the ex-Brahmin. Sixteen years ago, when I first landed in Bombay, I had been told by a wandering Armenian of the existence, somewhere in India, of a place to which such Hindus as had the misfortune to recover from trance or catalepsy were conveyed and kept, and I recollect laughing heartily at what I was then pleased to consider a traveler's tale.

Sitting at the bottom of the sand-trap, the memory of Watson's Hotel, with its swinging punkahs, white-robed attendants, and the sallow-faced Armenian, rose up in my mind as vividly as a photograph, and I burst into a loud fit of laughter. The contrast was too absurd!

Gunga Dass, as he bent over the unclean bird, watched me curiously. Hindus seldom laugh, and his surroundings were not such as to move Gunga Dass to any undue excess of hilarity. He removed the crow solemnly from the wooden spit and as solemnly devoured it. Then he continued his story, which I give in his own words:

"In epidemics of the cholera you are carried to be burned almost before you are dead. When you come to the riverside the cold air, perhaps, makes you alive, and then, if you are only little alive, mud is put on your nose and mouth and you die conclusively. If you are rather more alive, more mud is put; but if you are too lively they let you go and take you away. I was too lively, and made protestation with anger against the indignities that they endeavored to press upon me. In those days I was Brahmin and proud man. Now I am dead man and eat"—here he eyed the well-gnawed breast bone with the first sign of emotion that I had seen in him since we met— "crows, and other things. They took me from my sheets when they saw that I was too lively and gave me medicines for one week, and I survived successfully. Then they sent me by rail from my place to Okara Station, with a man to take care of me; and at Okara Station we met two other men, and they conducted we three on camels, in the night, from Okara Station to this place, and they propelled me from the top to the bottom, and the other two succeeded, and I have been here ever since two and a half years. Once I was Brahmin and proud man, and now I eat crows."

"There is no way of getting out?"

"None of what kind at all. When I first came I made experiments frequently and all the others also, but we have always succumbed to the sand which is precipitated upon our heads."

"But surely," I broke in at this point, "the river-front is open, and it is worth while dodging the bullets; while at night"—I had already matured a rough plan of escape which a natural instinct of selfishness forbade me sharing with Gunga Dass. He, however, divined my unspoken thought almost as soon as it was formed; and, to my intense astonishment, gave vent to a long low chuckle of derision—the laughter, be it understood, of a superior or at least of an equal.

"You will not"—he had dropped the Sir completely after his opening sentence—"make any escape that way. But you can try. I have tried. Once only."

The sensation of nameless terror and abject fear which I had in vain attempted to strive against overmastered me completely. My long fast—it was now close upon ten o'clock, and I had eaten nothing since tiffin on the previous day—combined with the violent and unnatural agitation of the ride had exhausted me, and I verily believe that, for a few minutes, I acted as one mad. I hurled myself against the pitiless sand-slope, I ran round the base of the crater, blaspheming and praying by turns. I crawled out among the sedges of the river-front, only to be driven back each time in an agony of nervous dread by the rifle-bullets which cut up the sand round me—for I dared not face the death of a mad dog among that hideous crowd—and finally fell, spent and raving, at the curb of the well. No one had taken the slightest notion of an exhibition which makes me blush hotly even when I think of it now.

Two or three men trod on my panting body as they drew water, but they were evidently used to this sort of thing, and had no time to waste upon me. The situation was humiliating. Gunga Dass, indeed, when he had banked the embers of his fire with sand, was at some pains to throw half a cupful of fetid water over my head, an attention for which I could have fallen on my knees and thanked him, but he was laughing all the while in the same mirthless, wheezy key that greeted me on my first attempt to force the shoals. And so, in a semi-comatose condition, I lay till noon. Then, being only a man after all, I felt hungry, and intimated as much to Gunga Dass, whom I had begun to regard as my natural protector. Following the impulse of the outer world when dealing with natives, I put my hand into my pocket and drew out four annas. The absurdity of the gift struck me at once, and I was about to replace the money.

Gunga Dass, however, was of a different opinion. "Give me the money," said he; "all you have, or I will get help, and we will kill you!" All this as if it were the most natural thing in the world!

A Briton's first impulse, I believe, is to guard the contents of his pockets; but a moment's reflection convinced me of the futility of differing with the one man who had it in his power to make me comfortable; and with whose help it was possible that I might eventually escape from the crater. I gave him all the money in my possession, Rs. 9-8-5—nine rupees eight annas and five pie—for I always keep small change as bakshish when I am in camp. Gunga Dass clutched the coins, and hid them at once in his ragged loin cloth, his expression changing to something diabolical as he looked round to assure himself that no one had observed us.

"*Now* I will give you something to eat," said he. What pleasure the possession of my money could have afforded him I am unable to say; but inasmuch as it did give him evident delight, I was not sorry that I had parted with it so readily, for I had no doubt that he would have had me killed if I had refused. One does not protest against the vagaries of a den of wild beasts; and my companions were lower than any beasts. While I devoured what Gunga Dass had provided, a coarse *chapatti* and a cupful of the foul well-water, the people showed not the faintest sign of curiosity—that curiosity which is so rampant, as a rule, in an Indian village.

I could even fancy that they despised me. At all events they treated me with the most chilling indifference, and Gunga Dass was nearly as bad. I plied him with questions about the terrible village, and received extremely unsatisfactory answers. So far as I could gather, it had been in existence from time immemorial— whence I concluded that it was at least a century old—and during that time no one had ever been known to escape from it. (I had to control myself here with both hands, lest the blind terror should lay hold of me a second time and drive me raving round the crater.) Gunga Dass took a malicious pleasure in emphasizing this point and in watching me wince. Nothing that I could do would induce him to tell me who the mysterious "They" were.

"It is so ordered," he would reply, "and I do not yet know any one who has disobeyed the orders."

"Only wait till my servants find that I am missing," I retorted, "and I promise you that this place shall be cleared off the face of the earth, and I'll give you a lesson in civility, too, my friend."

"Your servants would be torn in pieces before they came near this place; and, besides, you are dead, my dear friend. It is not your fault, of course, but none the less you are dead and buried."

At irregular intervals supplies of food, I was told, were dropped down from the land side into the amphitheatre, and the inhabitants fought for them like wild beasts. When a man felt his death coming on he retreated to his lair and died there. The body was sometimes dragged out of the hole and thrown on to the sand, or allowed to rot where it lay.

The phrase "thrown on to the sand" caught my attention, and I asked Gunga Dass whether this sort of thing was not likely to breed a pestilence.

"That," said he with another of his wheezy chuckles, "you may see for yourself subsequently. You will have much time to make observations."

Whereat, to his great delight, I winced once more and hastily continued the conversation: "And how do you live here from day to day? What do you do?" The question elicited exactly the same answer as before—coupled with the information that "this place is like your European heaven; there is neither marrying nor giving in marriage."

Gunga Dass had been educated at a Mission School, and, as he himself admitted, had he only changed his religion "like a wise man," might have avoided the living grave which was now his portion. But as long as I was with him I fancy he was happy.

Here was a Sahib, a representative of the dominant race, helpless as a child and completely at the mercy of his native neighbors. In a deliberate lazy way he set himself to torture me as a schoolboy would devote a rapturous half-hour to watching the agonies of an impaled beetle, or as a ferret in a blind burrow might glue himself comfortably to the neck of a rabbit. The burden of his conversation was that there was no escape "of no kind whatever," and that I should stay here till I died and was "thrown on to the sand." If it were possible to forejudge the conversation of the Damned on the advent of a new soul in their abode, I should say that they would speak as Gunga Dass did to me throughout that long afternoon. I was powerless to protest or answer; all my energies being devoted to a struggle against the inexplicable terror that threatened to overwhelm me again and again. I can compare the feeling to nothing except the struggles of a man against the overpowering nausea of the Channel passage—only my agony was of the spirit and infinitely more terrible.

As the day wore on, the inhabitants began to appear in full strength to catch the rays of the afternoon sun, which were now sloping in at the mouth of the crater. They assembled in little knots, and talked among themselves without even throwing a glance in my direction. About four o'clock, as far as I could judge Gunga Dass rose and dived into his lair for a moment, emerging with a live crow in his hands. The wretched bird was in a most draggled and deplorable condition, but seemed to be in no way afraid of its master. Advancing cautiously to the river front, Gunga Dass stepped from tussock to tussock until he had reached a smooth patch of sand directly in the line of the boat's fire. The occupants of the boat took no notice. Here he stopped, and, with a couple of dexterous turns of the wrist, pegged the bird on its back with outstretched wings. As was only natural, the crow began to shriek at once and beat the air with its claws. In a few seconds the clamor had attracted the attention of a bevy of wild crows on a shoal a few hundred yards away, where they were discussing something that looked like a corpse. Half a dozen crows flew over at once to see what was going on, and also, as it proved, to attack the pinioned bird. Gunga Dass, who had lain down on a tussock, motioned to me to be quiet, though I fancy this was a needless precaution. In a moment, and before I could see how it happened, a wild crow, who had grappled with the shrieking and helpless bird, was entangled in the latter's claws, swiftly disengaged by Gunga Dass, and pegged down beside its companion in adversity. Curiosity, it seemed, overpowered the rest of the flock, and almost before Gunga Dass and I had time to withdraw to the tussock, two more captives were struggling in the upturned claws of the decoys. So the chase—if I can give it so dignified a name—continued until Gunga Dass had captured seven crows. Five of them he throttled at once, reserving two for further operations another day. I was a good deal impressed by this, to me, novel method of securing food, and complimented Gunga Dass on his skill.

"It is nothing to do," said he. "Tomorrow you must do it for me. You are stronger than I am."

This calm assumption of superiority upset me not a little, and I answered peremptorily: "Indeed, you old ruffian! What do you think I have given you money for?"

"Very well," was the unmoved reply "Perhaps not to-morrow, nor the day after, nor subsequently; but in the end, and for many years, you will catch crows and eat crows, and you will thank your European God that you have crows to catch and eat."

I could have cheerfully strangled him for this; but judged it best under the circumstances to smother my resentment. An hour later I was eating one of the crows; and, as Gunga Dass had said, thanking my God that I had a crow to eat. Never as long as I live shall I forget that evening meal. The whole population were squatting on the hard sand platform opposite their dens, huddled over tiny fires of refuse and dried rushes. Death, having once laid his hand upon these men and forborne to strike, seemed to stand aloof from them now; for most of our company were old men, bent and worn and twisted with years, and women aged to all appearance as the Fates themselves. They sat together in knots and talked—God only knows what they found to discuss—in low equable tones, curiously in contrast to the strident babble with which natives are accustomed to make day hideous. Now and then an access of that sudden fury which had possessed me in the morning would lay hold on a man or woman; and with yells and imprecations the sufferer would attack the steep slope until, baffled and bleeding, he fell back on the platform incapable of moving a limb. The others would never even raise their eyes when this happened, as men too well aware of the futility of their fellows' attempts and wearied with their useless repetition. I saw four such outbursts in the course of the evening.

Gunga Dass took an eminently business-like view of my situation, and while we were dining—I can afford to laugh at the recollection now, but it was painful enough at the time— propounded the terms on which he would consent to "do" for me. My nine rupees eight annas, he argued, ar the rate of three annas a day, would provide me with food for fifty-one days, or about seven weeks; that is to say, he would be willing to cater for me for that length of time. At the end of it I was to look after myself. For a further consideration—*videlicet* my boots—he would be willing to allow me to occupy the den next to his own, and would supply me with as much dried grass for bedding as he could spare.

"Very well, Gunga Dass," I replied; "to the first terms I cheerfully agree, but, as there is nothing on earth to prevent my killing you as you sit here and taking everything that you have" (I thought of the two invaluable crows at the time), "I flatly refuse to give you my boots and shall take whichever den I please."

The stroke was a bold one, and I was glad when I saw that it had succeeded. Gunga Dass changed his tone immediately, and disavowed all intention of asking for my boots. At the time it did not strike me as at all strange that I, a civil engineer, a man of thirteen years' standing in the Service, and, I trust, an average Englishman, should thus calmly threaten murder and violence against the man who had, for a consideration it is true, taken me under his wing. I had left the world, it seemed, for centuries. I was as certain then as I am now of my own existence, that in the accursed settlement there was no law save that of the strongest; that the living dead men had thrown behind them every canon of the world which had cast them out; and that I had to depend for my own life on my strength and vigilance alone. The crew of the ill-fated *Mignonette* are the only men who would understand my frame of mind. "At present," I argued to myself, "I am strong and a match for six of these wretches. It is imperatively necessary that I should, for my own sake, keep both health and strength until the hour of my release comes—if it ever does."

Fortified with these resolutions, I ate and drank as much as I could, and made Gunga Dass understand that I intended to be his master, and that the least sign of insubordination on his part would be visited with the only punishment I had it in my power to inflict—sudden and violent death. Shortly after this I went to bed. That is to say, Gunga Dass gave me a double armful of dried bents which I thrust down the mouth of the lair to the right of his, and followed myself, feet foremost; the hole running about nine feet into the sand with a slight downward inclination, and being neatly shored with timbers. From my den, which faced the river-front, I was able to watch the waters of the Sutlej flowing past under the light of a young moon and compose myself to sleep as best I might.

The horrors of that night I shall never forget. My den was nearly as narrow as a coffin, and the sides had been worn smooth and greasy by the contact of innumerable naked bodies, added to which it smelled abominably. Sleep was altogether out of question to one in my excited frame of mind. As the night wore on, it seemed that the entire amphitheatre was filled with legions of unclean devils that, trooping up from the shoals below, mocked the unfortunates in their lairs.

Personally I am not of an imaginative temperament,—very few engineers are,—but on that occasion I was as completely prostrated with nervous terror as any woman. After half an hour or so, however, I was able once more to calmly review my chances of escape. Any exit by the steep sand walls was, of course, impracticable. I had been thoroughly convinced of this some time before. It was possible, just possible, that I might, in the uncertain moonlight, safely run the gauntlet of the rifle shots. The place was so full of terror for me that I was prepared to undergo any risk in leaving it. Imagine my delight, then, when after creeping stealthily to the river-front I found that the infernal boat was not there. My freedom lay before me in the next few steps!

By walking out to the first shallow pool that lay at the foot of the projecting left horn of the horseshoe, I could wade across, turn the flank of the crater, and make my way inland. Without a moment's hesitation I marched briskly past the tussocks where Gunga Dass had snared the crows, and out in the direction of the smooth white sand beyond. My first step from the tufts of dried grass showed me how utterly futile was any hope of escape; for, as I put my foot down, I felt an indescribable drawing, sucking motion of the sand below. Another moment and my leg was swallowed up nearly to the knee. In the moonlight the whole surface of the sand seemed to be shaken with devilish delight at my disappointment. I struggled clear, sweating with terror and exertion, back to the tussocks behind me and fell on my face.

My only means of escape from the semicircle was protected with a quicksand!

How long I lay I have not the faintest idea; but I was roused at last by the malevolent chuckle of Gunga Dass at my ear "I would advise you, Protector of the Poor" (the ruffian was speaking English) "to return to your house. It is unhealthy to lie down here. Moreover, when the boat returns, you will most certainly be rifled at." He stood over me in the dim light of the dawn, chuckling and laughing to himself. Suppressing my first impulse to catch the man by the neck and throw him on to the quicksand, I rose sullenly and followed him to the platform below the burrows.

Suddenly, and futilely as I thought while I spoke, I asked: "Gunga Dass, what is the good of the boat if I can't get out *anyhow?*"

I recollect that even in my deepest trouble I had been speculating vaguely on the waste of ammunition in guarding an already well protected foreshore.

Gunga Dass laughed again and made answer: "They have the boat only in daytime. It is for the reason that *there is a way.* I hope we shall have the pleasure of your company for much longer time. It is a pleasant spot when you have been here some years and eaten roast crow long enough."

I staggered, numbed and helpless, toward the fetid burrow allotted to me, and fell asleep. An hour or so later I was awakened by a piercing scream—the shrill, high-pitched scream of a horse in pain. Those who have once heard that will never forget the sound. I found some little difficulty in scrambling out of the burrow. When I was in the open, I saw Pornic, my poor old Pornic, lying dead on the sandy soil. How they had killed him I cannot guess. Gunga Dass explained that horse was better than crow, and "greatest good of greatest number is political maxim. We are now Republic, Mister Jukes, and you are entitled to a fair share of the beast. If you like, we will pass a vote of thanks. Shall I propose?"

Yes, we were a Republic indeed! A Republic of wild beasts penned at the bottom of a pit, to eat and fight and sleep till we died. I attempted no protest of any kind, but sat down and stared at the hideous sight in front of me. In less time almost than it takes me to write this, Pornic's body was divided, in some unclear way or other; the men and women had dragged the fragments on to the platform and were preparing their normal meal. Gunga Dass cooked mine. The almost irresistible impulse to fly at the sand walls until I was wearied laid hold of me afresh, and I had to struggle against it with all my might. Gunga Dass was offensively jocular till I told him that if he addressed another remark of any kind whatever to me I should strangle him where he sat. This silenced him till silence became insupportable, and I bade him say something.

"You will live here till you die like the other Feringhi," he said, coolly, watching me over the fragment of gristle that he was gnawing.

"What other Sahib, you swine? Speak at once, and don't stop to tell me a lie."

"He is over there," answered Gunga Dass, pointing to a burrow-mouth about four doors to the left of my own. "You can see for yourself. He died in the burrow as you will die, and I will die, and as all these men and women and the one child will also die."

"For pity's sake tell me all you know about him. Who was he? When did he come, and when did he die?"

This appeal was a weak step on my part. Gunga Dass only leered and replied: "I will not—unless you give me something first."

Then I recollected where I was, and struck the man between the eyes, partially stunning him. He stepped down from the platform at once, and, cringing and fawning and weeping and attempting to embrace my feet, led me round to the burrow which he had indicated.

"I know nothing whatever about the gentleman. Your God be my witness that I do not. He was as anxious to escape as you were, and he was shot from the boat, though we all did all things to prevent him from attempting. He was shot here." Gunga Dass laid his hand on his lean stomach and bowed to the earth.

"Well, and what then? Go on!"

"And then—and then, Your Honor, we carried him in to his house and gave him water, and put wet cloths on the wound, and he laid down in his house and gave up the ghost."

"In how long? In how long?"

"About half an hour, after he received his wound. I call Vishnu to witness," yelled the wretched man, "that I did everything for him. Everything which was possible, that I did!"

He threw himself down on the ground and clasped my ankles. But I had my doubts about Gunga Dass's benevolence, and kicked him off as he lay protesting.

"I believe you robbed him of everything he had. But I can find out in a minute or two. How long was the Sahib here?"

"Nearly a year and a half. I think he must have gone mad. But hear me swear Protector of the Poor! Won't Your Honor hear me swear that I never touched an article that belonged to him? What is Your Worship going to do?"

I had taken Gunga Dass by the waist and had hauled him on to the platform opposite the deserted burrow. As I did so I thought of my wretched fellow-prisoner's unspeakable misery among all these horrors for eighteen months, and the final agony of dying like a rat in a hole, with a bullet-wound in the stomach. Gunga Dass fancied I was going to kill him and howled pitifully. The rest of the population, in the plethora that follows a full flesh meal, watched us without stirring.

"Go inside, Gunga Dass," said I, "and fetch it out."

I was feeling sick and faint with horror now. Gunga Dass nearly rolled off the platform and howled aloud.

"But I am Brahmin, Sahib—a high-caste Brahmin. By your soul, by your father's soul, do not make me do this thing!"

"Brahmin or no Brahmin, by my soul and my father's soul, in you go!" I said, and, seizing him by the shoulders, I crammed his head into the mouth of the burrow, kicked the rest of him in, and, sitting down, covered my face with my hands.

At the end of a few minutes I heard a rustle and a creak; then Gunga Dass in a sobbing, choking whisper speaking to himself; then a soft thud—and I uncovered my eyes.

The dry sand had turned the corpse entrusted to its keeping into a yellow-brown mummy. I told Gunga Dass to stand off while I examined it. The body—clad in an olive-green hunting-suit much stained and worn, with leather pads on the shoulders—was that of a man between thirty and forty, above middle height, with light, sandy hair, long mustache, and a rough unkempt beard. The left canine of the upper jaw was missing, and a portion of the lobe of the right ear was gone. On the second finger of the left hand was a ring—a shield-shaped bloodstone serin gold, with a monogram that might have been either "B.K." or "B.L." On the third finger of the right hand was a silver ring in the shape of a coiled cobra, much worn and tarnished. Gunga Dass deposited a handful of trifles he had picked out of the burrow at my feet, and, covering the face of the body with my handkerchief, I turned to examine these. I give the full list in the hope that it may lead to the identification of the unfortunate man:

1. Bowl of a briarwood pipe, serrated at the edge; much worn and blackened; bound with string at the crew.
2. Two patent-lever keys; wards of both broken.
3. Tortoise-shell-handled penknife, silver or nickel, name-plate, marked with monogram "B.K."
4. Envelope, postmark undecipherable, bearing a Victorian stamp, addressed to "Miss Mon—" (rest illegible)—"ham"—"nt."
5. Imitation crocodile-skin notebook with pencil. First forty-five pages blank; four and a half illegible; fifteen others filled with private memoranda relating chiefly to three persons—a Mrs. L. Singleton, abbreviated several times to "Lot Single," "Mrs. S. May," and "Garmison," referred to in places as "Jerry" or "Jack."
6. Handle of small-sized hunting-knife. Blade snapped short. Buck's horn, diamond cut, with swivel and ring on the butt; fragment of cotton cord attached.

It must not be supposed that I inventoried all these things on the spot as fully as I have here written them down. The notebook first attracted my attention, and I put it in my pocket with a view of studying it later on.

The rest of the articles I conveyed to my burrow for safety's sake, and there being a methodical man, I inventoried them. I then returned to the corpse and ordered Gunga Dass to help me to carry it out to the river-front. While we were engaged in this, the exploded shell of an old brown cartridge dropped out of one of the pockets and rolled at my feet. Gunga Dass had not seen it; and I fell to thinking that a man does not carry exploded cartridge-cases, especially "browns," which will not bear loading twice, about with him when shooting. In other words, that cartridge-case had been fired inside the crater. Consequently there must be a gun somewhere. I was on the verge of asking Gunga Dass, but checked myself, knowing that he would lie. We laid the body down on the edge of the quicksand by the tussocks. It was my intention to push it out and let it be swallowed up—the only possible mode of burial that I could think of. I ordered Gunga Dass to go away.

Then I gingerly put the corpse out on the quicksand. In doing so, it was lying face downward, I tore the frail and rotten khaki shooting-coat open, disclosing a hideous cavity in the back. I have already told you that the dry sand had, as it were, mummified the body. A moment's glance showed that the gaping hole had been caused by a gun-shot wound; the gun must have been fired with the muzzle almost touching the back. The shooting-coat, being intact, had been drawn over the body after death, which must have been instantaneous. The secret of the poor wretch's death was plain to me in a flash. Some one of the crater, presumably Gunga Dass, must have shot him with his own gun—the gun that fitted the brown cartridges. He had never attempted to escape in the face of the rifle-fire from the boat.

I pushed the corpse out hastily, and saw it sink from sight literally in a few seconds. I shuddered as I watched. In a dazed, half-conscious way I turned to peruse the notebook. A stained and discolored slip of paper had been inserted between the binding and the back, and dropped out as I opened the pages. This is what it contained: *"Four out from crow-clump: three left; nine out; two right; three back; two left; fourteen out; two left; seven out; one left; nine back; two right; six back; four right; seven back."* The paper had been burned and charred at the edges. What it meant I could not understand. I sat down on the dried bents turning it over and over between my fingers, until I was aware of Gunga Dass standing immediately behind me with glowing eyes and outstretched hands.

"Have you got it?" he panted. "Will you not let me look at it also? I swear that I will return it." "Got what? Return what?" asked.

"That which you have in your hands. It will help us both." He stretched out his long, bird-like talons, trembling with eagerness.

"I could never find it," he continued. "He had secreted it about his person. Therefore I shot him, but nevertheless I was unable to obtain it."

Gunga Dass had quite forgotten his little fiction about the rifle-bullet. I received the information perfectly calmly. Morality is blunted by consorting with the Dead who are alive.

"What on earth are you raving about? What is it you want me to give you?"

"The piece of paper in the notebook. It will help us both. Oh, you fool! You fool! Can you not see what it will do for us? We shall escape!"

His voice rose almost to a scream, and he danced with excitement before me. I own I was moved at the chance of my getting away.

"Don't skip! Explain yourself. Do you mean to say that this slip of paper will help us? What does it mean?"

"Read it aloud! Read it aloud! I beg and I pray you to read it aloud."

I did so. Gunga Dass listened delightedly, and drew an irregular line in the sand with his fingers.

"See now! It was the length of his gun-barrels without the stock. I have those barrels. Four gun-barrels out from the place where I caught crows. Straight out; do you follow me? Then three left. Ah! How well I remember when that man worked it out night after night. Then nine out, and so on. Out is always straight before you across the quicksand. He told me so before I killed him."

"But if you knew all this why didn't you get out before?"

"I did *not* know it. He told me that he was working it out a year and a half ago, and how he was working it out night after night when the boat had gone away, and he could get out near the quicksand safely. Then he said that we would get away together. But I was afraid that he would leave me behind one night when he had worked it all out, and so I shot him. Besides, it is not advisable that the men who once get in here should escape. Only I, and I am a Brahmin."

The prospect of escape had brought Gunga Dass's caste back to him. He stood up, walked about and gesticulated violently. Eventually I managed to make him talk soberly, and he told me how this Englishman had spent six months night after night in exploring, inch by inch, the passage across the quicksand; how he had declared it to be simplicity itself up to within about twenty yards of the river bank after turning the flank of the left horn of the horseshoe. This much he had evidently not completed when Gunga Dass shot him with his own gun.

In my frenzy of delight at the possibilities of escape, I recollect shaking hands effusively with Gunga Dass, after we had decided that we were to make an attempt to get away that very night. It was weary work waiting throughout the afternoon.

About ten o'clock, as far as I could judge, when the Moon had just risen above the lip of the crater, Gunga Dass made a move for his burrow to bring out the gun-barrels whereby to measure our path. All the other wretched inhabitants had retired to their lairs long ago. The guardian boat had drifted downstream some hours before, and we were utterly alone by the crow-clump. Gunga Dass, while carrying the gun-barrels, let slip the piece of paper which was to be our guide. I stooped down hastily to recover it, and, as I did so, I was aware that the diabolical Brahmin was aiming a violent blow at the back of my head with the gun-barrels. It was too late to turn round. I must have received the blow somewhere on the nape of my neck. A hundred thousand fiery stars danced before my eyes, and I fell forwards senseless at the edge of the quicksand.

When I recovered consciousness, the Moon was going down, and I was sensible of intolerable pain in the back of my head. Gunga Dass had disappeared and my mouth was full of blood. I lay down again and prayed that I might die without more ado. Then the unreasoning fury which I had before mentioned, laid hold upon me, and I staggered inland toward the walls of the crater. It seemed that some one was calling to me in a whisper— "Sahib! Sahib! Sahib!" exactly as my bearer used to call me in the morning. I fancied that I was delirious until a handful of sand fell at my feet. Then I looked up and saw a head peering down into the amphitheatre—the head of Dunnoo, my dog-boy, who attended to my collies. As soon as he had attracted my attention, he held up his hand and showed a rope. I motioned, staggering to and fro for the while, that he should throw it down. It was a couple of leather punkah-ropes knotted together, with a loop at one end. I slipped the loop over my head and under my arms; heard Dunnoo urge something forward; was conscious that I was being dragged, face downward, up the steep sand slope, and the next instant found myself choked and half fainting on the sand hills overlooking the crater. Dunnoo, with his face ashy grey in the moonlight, implored me not to stay but to get back to my tent at once.

It seems that he had tracked Pornic's footprints fourteen miles across the sands to the crater; had returned and told my servants, who flatly refused to meddle with any one, white or black, once fallen into the hideous Village of the Dead; whereupon Dunnoo had taken one of my ponies and a couple of punkah-ropes, returned to the crater, and hauled me out as I have described.

To cut a long story short, Dunnoo is now my personal servant on a gold mohur a month—a sum which I still think far too little for the services he has rendered. Nothing on earth will induce me to go near that devilish spot again, or to reveal its whereabouts more clearly than I have done. Of Gunga Dass I have never found a trace, nor do I wish to do. My sole motive in giving this to be published is the hope that some one may possibly identify, from the details and the inventory which I have given above, the corpse of the man in the olive-green hunting-suit.

# THE MYSTERY OF BARNEY O'ROURKE

## JOHN KENDRICK BANGS

Avery irritating thing has happened. My hired man, a certain Barney O'Rourke, an American citizen of much political influence, a good gardener, and, according to his lights, a gentleman, has got very much the best of me, and all because of certain effusions which from time to time have emanated from my pen. It is not often that one's literary chickens come home to roost in such a vengeful fashion as some of mine have recently done, and I have no doubt that as this story progresses he who reads will find much sympathy for me rising up in his breast. As the matter stands, I am torn with conflicting emotions. I am very fond of Barney, and I have always found him truthful hitherto, but exactly what to believe now I hardly know. The main thing to bring my present trouble upon me, I am forced to believe, is the fact that my house has been in the past, and may possibly still be, haunted. Why my house should be haunted at all I do not know, for it has never been the scene of any tragedy that I am aware of. I built it myself, and it is paid for. So far as I am aware, nothing awful of a material nature has ever happened within its walls, and yet it appears to be, for the present at any rate, a sort of club-house for inconsiderate if not strictly horrid things, which is a most unfair dispensation of the fates, for I have not deserved it. If I were in any sense a Bluebeard, and spent my days cutting ladies' throats as a pastime; if I had a pleasing habit of inviting friends up from town over Sunday, and dropping them into oubliettes connecting my library with dark, dank, and snaky subterranean dungeons; if guests who dine at my house came with a feeling that the chances were, they would never return to their families alive—it might be different. I shouldn't and couldn't blame a house for being haunted if it were the dwelling-place of a bloodthirsty ruffian such as I have indicated, but that is just what it is not. It is not the home of a lover of fearful crimes. I would not walk ten feet for the pleasure of killing any man, no matter who he is. On the contrary, I would walk twenty feet to avoid doing it, if the emergency should ever arise, aye, even if it were that fiend who sits next me at the opera and hums the opera through from beginning to end. There have been times, I must confess, when I have wished I might have had the oubliettes to which I have referred constructed beneath my library and leading to the coal-bins or to some long-forgotten well, but that was two or three years ago, when I was in politics for a brief period, and delegations of willing and thirsty voters were daily and nightly swarming in through every one of the sixteen doors on the ground-floor of my house, which my architect, in a riotous moment, smuggled into the plans in the guise of "French windows." I shouldn't have minded then if the earth had opened up and swallowed my whole party, so long as I did not have to go with them, but under such provocation as I had I do not feel that my residence is justified in being haunted after its present fashion because such a notion entered my mind. We cannot help our thoughts, much less our notions, and punishment for that which we cannot help is not in strict accord with latter-day ideas of justice. It may occur to some hypercritical person to suggest that the English language has frequently been murdered in my den, and that it is its horrid corpse which is playing havoc at my home, crying out to heaven and flaunting its bloody wounds in the face of my conscience, but I can pass such an aspersion as that by with contemptuous silence, for even if it were true it could not be set down as wilful assassination on my part, since no sane person who needs a language as much as I do would ever in cold blood kill any one of the many that lie about us. Furthermore, the English language is not dead. It may not be met with often in these days, but it is still encountered with sufficient frequency in the works of Henry James and Miss Libby to prove that it still lives; and I am told that one or two members of our consular service abroad can speak it-though as for this I cannot write with certainty, for I have never encountered one of these exceptions to the general rule.

The episode with which this narrative has to deal is interesting in some ways, though I doubt not some readers will prove sceptical as to its realism. There are suspicious minds in the world, and with these every man who writes of truth must reckon. To such I have only to say that it is my desire and intention to tell the truth as simply as it can be told by James, and as truthfully as Sylvanus Cobb ever wrote!

Now, then, the facts of my story are these:

In the latter part of last July, expecting a meeting of friends at my house in connection with a question of the good government of the city in which I honestly try to pay my taxes, I ordered one hundred cigars to be delivered at my residence. I ordered several other things at the same time, but they have nothing whatever to do with this story, because they were all—every single bottle of them—consumed at the meeting; but of the cigars, about which the strange facts of my story cluster, at the close of the meeting a goodly two dozen remained. This is surprising, considering that there were quite six of us present, but it is true. Twenty-four by actual count remained when the last guest left me. The next morning, I and my family took our departure for a month's rest in the mountains. In the hurry of leaving home, and the worry of looking after three children and four times as many trunks, I neglected to include the cigars in my impedimenta, leaving them in the opened box upon my library table. It was careless of me, no doubt, but it was an important incident, as the sequel shows. The incidents of the stay in the hills were commonplace, but during my absence from home strange things were going on there, as I learned upon my return.

The place had been left in charge of Barney O'Rourke, who, upon my arrival, assured me that everything was all right, and I thanked and paid him.

"Wait a minute, Barney," I said, as he turned to leave me; "I've got a cigar for you." I may mention incidentally that in the past I had kept Barney on very good terms with his work by treating him in a friendly, sociable way, but, to my great surprise, upon this occasion he declined advances.

His face flushed very red as he observed that he had given up smoking.

"Well, wait a minute, anyhow," said I. "There are one or two things I want to speak to you about." And I went to the table to get a cigar for myself.

Instantly the suspicion which has doubtless flashed through the mind of the reader flashed through my own—Barney had been tempted, and had fallen.

I recalled his blush, and on the moment realized that in all my vast experience with hired men in the past I had never seen one blush before. The case was clear. My cigars had gone to help Barney through the hot summer.

"Well, I declare!" I cried, turning suddenly upon him. "I left a lot of cigars here when I went away, Barney."

"I know ye did, sorr," said Barney, who had now grown white and rigid. "I saw them meself, sorr. There was twenty-foor of 'em."

"You counted them, eh?" I asked, with an elevation of my eyebrows which to those who know me conveys the idea of suspicion.

"I did, sorr. In your absence I was responsible for everyt'ing here, and the mornin' ye wint awaa I took a quick invintery, sorr, of the removables," he answered, fingering his cap nervously. "That's how it was, sorr, and thim twenty-foor segyars was lyin' there in the box forninst me eyes."

"And how do you account for the removal of these removables, as you call them, Barney?" I asked, looking coldly at him. He saw he was under suspicion, and he winced, but pulled himself together in an instant.

"I expected the question, sorr," he said, calmly, "and I have me answer ready. Thim segyars was shmoked, sorr."

"Doubtless," said I, with an ill-suppressed sneer. "And by whom? Cats?" I added, with a contemptuous shrug of my shoulders. His answer overpowered me, it was so simple, direct, and unexpected.

"Shpooks," he replied, laconically.

I gasped in astonishment, and sat down. My knees simply collapsed under me, and I could no more have continued to stand up than fly.

"What?" I cried, as soon as I had recovered sufficiently to gasp out the word.

"Shpooks," replied Barney. "Ut came about like this, sorr. It was the Froiday two wakes afther you left, I became un'asy loike along about nine o'clock in the avenin', and I fought I'd come around here and see if everything was sthraight. Me wife sez ut's foolish of me, sorr, and I sez maybe so, but I can't get ut out o' me head thot somet'ing's wrong.

"'Ye locked everything up safe whin ye left?' sez she.

"'I always does,' sez I.

"'Thin ut's a phwhim,' sez she.

"'No,' sez I. 'Ut's a sinsation. If ut was a phwim, ut'd be youse as would hov' it'; that's what I sez, severely loike, sorr, and out I shtarts. It was tin o'clock whin

I got here. The noight was dark and blow-in' loike March, rainin' and t'underin' till ye couldn't hear yourself fink.

"I walked down the walk, sorr, an' barrin' the t'under everyt'ing was quiet. I troid the dures. All toight as a politician. Shtill, finks I, I'll go inoside. Quiet as a lamb ut was, sorr; but on a suddent, as I was about to go back home again, I shmelt shmoke!"

"Fire?" I cried, excitedly.

"I said shmoke, sorr," said Barney, whose calmness was now beautiful to look upon, he was so serenely confident of his position. "Doesn't smoke involve a fire?" I demanded. "Sometimes," said Barney. "I fought ye meant a conflagrashun, sorr. The shmoke I shmelt was segyars."

"Ah," I observed. "I am glad you are coming to the point. Go on. There *is* a difference."

"There is thot," said Barney, pleasantly, he was getting along so swimmingly. "This shmoke, as I say, was segyar shmoke, so I gropes me way cautious loike up the back sthairs and listens by the library dure. All quiet as a lamb. Thin, bold loike, I shteps into the room, and nearly drops wid the shcare I have on me in a minute. The room was dark as a b'aver hat, sorr, but in different shpots ranged round in the chairs was six little red balls of foire!"

"Barney!" I cried.

"Thrue, sorr," said he. "And tobacky shmoke rollin' out till you'd 'a' fought there was a foire in a segyar-store! Ut queered me, sorr, for a minute, and me impulse is to run; but I gets me courage up, springs across the room, touches the electric button, an' bzt! every gas-jet on the flu re loights up!"

"That was rash, Barney," I put in, sarcastically.

"It was in your intherest, sorr," said he, impressively.

"And you saw what?" I queried, growing very impatient

"What I hope niver to see again, sorr," said Barney, compressing his lips solemnly. *"Six impty chairs,* sorr, wid six segyars as hoigh up from the flure as a man's mout', puffin' and a-blowin' out shmoke loike a chimbley! An' ivery oncet in a whoile the segyars would go down kind of an' be tapped loike as if wid a finger of a shmoker, and the ashes would fall off onto the flure!"

"Well?" said I. "Go on. What next?"

"I wanted to run awaa, sorr, but I shtood rutted to the shpot wid th' surproise I had on me, until foinally ivery segyar was burnt to a shtub and trun into the foireplace, where I found 'em the nixt mornin' when I came to clane up, provin' ut wasn't ony dhrame I'd been havin'."

I arose from my chair and paced the room for two or three minutes, wondering what I could say. Of course the man was lying, I thought. Then I pulled myself together.

"Barney," I said, severely, "what's the use? Do you expect me to believe any such cock-and-bull story as that?"

"No, sorr," said he. "But thim's the facts."

"Do you mean to say that this house of mine is haunted?" I cried.

"I don't know," said Barney, quietly. "I didn't t'ink so before."

"Before? Before what? When?" I asked.

"Whin you was writin' shtories about ut, sorr," said Barney, respectfully. "You've had a black horse-hair sofy turn white in a single noight, sorr, for the soight of horror ut's witnessed. You've had the hair of your own head shtand on ind loike tin penny nails at what you've seen here in this very room, yourself, sorr. You've had ghosts doin' all sorts of tings in the shtories you've been writin' for years, and *you've always swore they was thrue, sorr.* I didn't believe 'em when I read 'em, but whin I see thim segyars bein' shmoked up before me eyes by invisible tings, I sez to meself, sez I, the boss ain't such a dommed loiar afther all. I've follyd your writin', sorr, very careful and close loike; an I don't see how, afther the tales you've told about your own experiences right here, you can say consishtently that this wan o' mine ain't so!"

"But why, Barney," I asked, to confuse him, "when a thing like this happened, didn't you write and tell me?"

Barney chuckled as only one of his species can chuckle.

"Wroite an' tell ye?" he cried. "Be gorry, sorr, if I could wroite at all at all, ut's not you oi'd be wroitin' that tale to, but to the edithor of the paper that you wroite for. A tale loike that is wort' tin dollars to any man, eshpecially if ut's thrue. But I niver learned the art!"

And with that Barney left me overwhelmed. Subsequently I gave him the ten dollars which I think his story is worth, but I must confess that I am in a dilemma. After what I have said about my supernatural guests, I cannot discharge Barney for lying, but I'll be blest if I can quite believe that his story is accurate in every respect. If there should happen to be among the readers of this tale any who have made a sufficiently close study of the habits of hired men and ghosts to be able to shed any light upon the situation, nothing would please me more than to hear from them.

I may add, in closing, that Barney has resumed smoking.

# THE RED-HAIRED GIRL
## SABINE BARING-GOULD

### A WIFE'S STORY

In 1876 we took a house in one of the best streets and parts of B—. I do not
give the name of the street or the number of the house, because the circumstances that occurred in that place were such as to make people nervous, and
shy—unreasonably so—of taking those lodgings, after reading our experiences
therein.

We were a small family—my husband, a grown-up daughter, and myself;
and we had two maids—a cook, and the other was house and parlourmaid in
one. We had not been a fortnight in the house before my daughter said to me
one morning. "Mamma, I do not like Jane"—that was our house-parlourmaid.

"Why so?" I asked. "She seems respectable, and she does her work system-
atically. I have no fault to find with her, none whatever."

"She may do her work," said Bessie, my daughter, "but I dislike
inquisitiveness."

"Inquisitiveness!" I exclaimed. "What do you mean? Has she been looking into your drawers?"

"No, mamma, but she watches me. It is hot weather now, and when I am in my room, occasionally, I leave my door open whilst writing a letter, or doing any little bit of needlework, and then I am almost certain to hear her outside. If I turn sharply round, I see her slipping out of sight. It is most annoying. I really was unaware that I was such an interesting personage as to make it worth anyone's while to spy out my proceedings."

"Nonsense, my dear. You are sure it is Jane?"

"Well—I suppose so." There was a slight hesitation in her voice. "If not Jane, who can it be?"

"Are you sure it is not cook?"

"Oh, no, it is not cook; she is busy in the kitchen. I have heard her there, when I have gone outside my room upon the landing, after having caught that girl watching me."

"If you have caught her," said I, "I suppose you spoke to her about the impropriety of her conduct."

"Well, caught is the wrong word. I have not actually *caught* her at it. Only to-day I distinctly heard her at my door, and I saw her back as she turned to run away, when I went towards her."

"But you followed her, of course?"

"Yes, but I did not find her on the landing when I got outside."

"Where was she, then?" "I don't know."

"But did you not go and see?"

"She slipped away with astonishing celerity," said Bessie. "I can take no steps in the matter. If she does it again, speak to her and remonstrate."

"But I never have a chance. She is gone in a moment."

"She cannot get away so quickly as all that."

"Somehow she does."

"And you are sure it is Jane?" again I asked; and again she replied:

"If not Jane, who else can it be? There is no one else in the house."

So this unpleasant matter ended, for the time. The next intimation of something of the sort proceeded from another quarter—in fact, from Jane herself. She came to me some days later and said, with some embarrassment in her tone—"If you please, ma'am, if I do not give satisfaction, I would rather leave the situation."

"Leave!" I exclaimed. "Why, I have not given you the slightest cause. I have not found fault with you for anything as yet, have I, Jane? On the contrary,

I have been much pleased with the thoroughness of your work. And you are always tidy and obliging."

"It isn't that, ma'am; but I don't like being watched whatever I do."

"Watched!" I repeated. "What do you mean? You surely do not suppose that I am running after you when you are engaged on your occupations. I assure you I have other and more important things to do."

"No, ma'am, I don't suppose you do."

"Then who watches you?"

"I think it must be Miss Bessie."

"Miss Bessie!"

I could say no more, I was so astounded.

"Yes, ma'am. When I am sweeping out a room, and my back is turned, I hear her at the door; and when I turn myself about, I just catch a glimpse of her running away. I see her skirts—"

"Miss Bessie is above doing anything of the sort."

"If it is not Miss Bessie, who is it, ma'am?"

There was a tone of indecision in her voice.

"My good Jane," said I, "set your mind at rest. Miss Bessie could not act as you suppose. Have you seen her on these occasions and assured yourself that it is she?"

"No, ma'am, I've not, so to speak, seen her face; but I know it ain't cook, and I'm sure it ain't you, ma'am; so who else can it be?" I considered for some moments, and the maid stood before me in dubious mood.

"You say you saw her skirts. Did you recognise the gown? What did she wear?"

"It was a light cotton print—more like a maid's morning dress."

"Well, set your mind at ease; Miss Bessie has not got such a frock as you describe."

"I don't think she has," said Jane; "but there was someone at the door, watching me, who ran away when I turned myself about."

"Did she run upstairs or down?"

"I don't know. I did go out on the landing, but there was no one there. I'm sure it wasn't cook, for I heard her clattering the dishes down in the kitchen at the time."

"Well, Jane, there is some mystery in this. I will not accept your notice; we will let matters stand over till we can look into this complaint of yours and discover the rights of it."

"Thank you, ma'am. I'm very comfortable, here, but it is unpleasant to suppose that one is not trusted, and is spied on wherever one goes and whatever one is about."

A week later, after dinner one evening, when Bessie and I had quitted the table and left my husband to his smoke, Bessie said to me, when we were in the drawing-room together: "Mamma, it is not Jane."

"What is not Jane?" I asked.

"It is not Jane who watches me."

"Who can it be, then?"

"I don't know."

"And how is it that you are confident that you are not being observed by Jane?"

"Because I have seen her—that is to say, her head." "When? Where?"

"Whilst dressing for dinner, I was before the glass doing my hair, when I saw in the mirror someone behind me. I had only the two candles lighted on the table, and the room was otherwise dark. I thought I heard someone stirring—just the sort of stealthy step I have come to recognise as having troubled me so often. I did not turn, but looked steadily before me into the glass, and I could see reflected therein someone—a woman with red hair. Then I moved from my place quickly. I heard steps of some person hurrying away, but I saw no one then."

"The door was open?"

"No, it was shut."

"But where did she go?"

"I do not know, mamma. I looked everywhere in the room and could find no one. I have been quite upset. I cannot tell what to think of this. I feel utterly unhinged."

"I noticed at table that you did not appear well, but I said nothing about it. Your father gets so alarmed, and fidgets and fusses, if he thinks that there is anything the matter with you. But this is a most extraordinary story."

"It is an extraordinary fact," said Bessie.

"You have searched your room thoroughly?"

"I have looked into every corner."

"And there is no one there?"

"No one. Would you mind, mamma, sleeping with me to-night? I am so frightened. Do you think it can be a ghost?" "Ghost? Fiddlesticks!"

I made some excuse to my husband and spent the night in Bessie's room. There was no disturbance that night of any sort, and although my daughter was excited and unable to sleep till long after midnight, she did fall into refreshing slumber at last, and in the morning said to me: "Mamma, I think I must have fancied that I saw something in the glass. I dare say my nerves were overwrought."

I was greatly relieved to hear this, and I arrived at much the same conclusion as did Bessie, but was again bewildered, and my mind unsettled by Jane, who came to me just before lunch, when I was alone, and said—

"Please, ma'am, it's only fair to say, but it's not Miss Bessie."

"What is not Miss Bessie? I mean, who is not Miss Bessie?"

"Her as is spying on me."

"I told you it could not be she. Who is it?"

"Please, ma'am, I don't know. It's a red-haired girl."

"But, Jane, be serious. There is no red-haired girl in the house."

"I know there ain't, ma'am. But for all that, she spies on me."

"Be reasonable, Jane," I said, disguising the shock her words produced on me. "If there be no red-haired girl in the house, how can you have one watching you?"

"I don't know; but one does."

"How do you know that she is red-haired?"

"Because I have seen her."

"When?"

"This morning."

"Indeed?"

"Yes, ma'am. I was going upstairs, when I heard steps coming softly after me—the backstairs, ma'am; they're rather dark and steep, and there's no carpet on them, as on the front stairs, and I was sure I heard someone following me; so I twisted about, thinking it might be cook, but it wasn't. I saw a young woman in a print dress, and the light as came from the window at the side fell on her head, and it was carrots—reg'lar carrots."

"Did you see her face?"

"No, ma'am; she put her arm up and turned and ran downstairs, and I went after her, but I never found her."

"You followed her—how far?"

"To the kitchen. Cook was there. And I said to cook, says I: 'Did you see a girl come this way?' And she said, short-like: 'No.'"

"And cook saw nothing at all?"

"Nothing. She didn't seem best pleased at my axing. I suppose I frightened her, as I'd been telling her about how I was followed and spied on."

I mused a moment only, and then said solemnly—

"Jane, what you want is a *pill*. You are suffering from hallucinations. I know a case very much like yours; and take my word for it that, in your condition of liver or digestion, a pill is a sovereign remedy. Set your mind at rest; this is a mere delusion, caused by pressure on the optic nerve. I will give you a pill tonight when you go to bed, another to-morrow, a third on the day after, and that will settle the red-haired girl. You will see no more of her."

"You think so, ma'am?"

"I am sure of it."

On consideration, I thought it as well to mention the matter to the cook, a strange, reserved woman, not given to talking, who did her work admirably, but whom, for some inexplicable reason, I did not like. If I had considered a little further as to how to broach the subject, I should perhaps have proved more successful; but by not doing so I rushed the question and obtained no satisfaction. I had gone down to the kitchen to order dinner, and the difficult question had arisen how to dispose of the scraps from yesterday's joint.

"Rissoles, ma'am?"

"No," said I, "not rissoles. Your master objects to them."

"Then perhaps croquettes?"

"They are only rissoles in disguise."

"Perhaps cottage pie?"

"No; that is inorganic rissole, a sort of protoplasm out of which rissoles are developed."

"Then, ma'am, I might make a hash."

"Not an ordinary, barefaced, rudimentary hash?"

"No, ma'am, with French mushrooms, or truffles, or tomatoes."

"Well—yes—perhaps. By the way, talking of tomatoes, who is that red-haired girl who has been about the house?"

"Can't say, ma'am."

I noticed at once that the eyes of the cook contracted, her lips tightened, and her face assumed a half-defiant, half-terrified look. "You have not many friends in this place, have you, cook?"

"No, ma'am, none."

"Then who can she be?"

"Can't say, ma'am."

"You can throw no light on the matter? It is very unsatisfactory having a person about the house—and she has been seen upstairs—of whom one knows nothing."

"No doubt, ma'am."

"And you cannot enlighten me?"

"She is no friend of mine."

"Nor is she of Jane's. Jane spoke to me about her. Has she remarked concerning this girl to you?"

"Can't say, ma'am, as I notice all Jane says. She talks a good deal."

"You see, there must be someone who is a stranger and who has access to this house. It is most awkward."

"Very so, ma'am."

I could get nothing more from the cook. I might as well have talked to a log; and, indeed, her face assumed a wooden look as I continued to speak to her on the matter. So I sighed, and said—

"Very well, hash with tomato," and went upstairs. A few days later the house-parlourmaid said to me, "Please, ma'am, may I have another pill?" "Pill!" I exclaimed. "Why?"

"Because I have seen her again. She was behind the curtains, and I caught her putting out her red head to look at me." "Did you see her face?"

"No; she up with her arm over it and scuttled away."

"This is strange. I do not think I have more than two podophyllin pills left in the box, but to those you are welcome. Only I should recommend a different treatment. Instead of taking them yourself, the moment you see, or fancy that you see, the red-haired girl, go at her with the box and threaten to administer the pills to her. That will rout her, if anything will."

"But she will not stop for the pills."

"The threat of having them forced on her every time she shows herself will disconcert her. Conceive, I am supposing, that on each occasion Miss Bessie, or I, were to meet you on the stairs, in a room, on the landing, in the ball, we were to rush on you and force, let us say, castor-oil globules between your lips. You would give notice at once."

"Yes; so I should, ma'am."

"Well, try this upon the red-haired girl. It will prove infallible."

"Thank you, ma'am; what you say seems reasonable."

Whether Bessie saw more of the puzzling apparition, I cannot say. She spoke no further on the matter to me; but that may have been so as to cause me no further uneasiness. I was unable to resolve the question to my own satisfaction—whether what had been seen was a real person, who obtained access to the house in some unaccountable manner, or whether it was, what I have called an apparition.

As far as I could ascertain, nothing had been taken away. The movements of the red-haired girl were not those of one who sought to pilfer. They seemed to me rather those of one not in her right mind; and on this supposition I made inquiries in the neighbourhood as to the existence in our street, in any of the adjoining houses, of a person wanting in her wits, who was suffered to run about at will. But I could obtain no information that at all threw light on a point to me so perplexing.

Hitherto I had not mentioned the topic to my husband. I knew so well that I should obtain no help from him, that I made no effort to seek it. He would "Pish!" and "Pshaw!" and make some slighting reference to women's intellects, and not further trouble himself about the matter. But one day, to my great astonishment, he referred to it himself.

"Julia," said he, "do you observe how I have cut myself in shaving?"

"Yes, dear," I replied. "You have cotton-wool sticking to your jaw, as if you were growing a white whisker on one side."

"It bled a great deal," said he.

"I am sorry to hear it."

"And I mopped up the blood with the new toilet-cover."

"Never!" I exclaimed. "You haven't been so foolish as to do that?"

"Yes. And that is just like you. You are much more concerned about your toilet-cover being stained than about my poor cheek which is gashed."

"You were very clumsy to do it," was all I could say. Married people are not always careful to preserve the amenities in private life. It is a pity, but it is so.

"It was due to no clumsiness on my part," said he; "though I do allow my nerves have been so shaken, broken, by married life, that I cannot always command my hand, as was the case when I was a bachelor. But this time it was due to that new, stupid, red-haired servant you have introduced into the house without consulting me or my pocket."

"Red-haired servant!" I echoed.

"Yes, that red-haired girl I have seen about. She thrusts herself into my study in a most offensive and objectionable way. But the climax of all was this morning, when I was shaving. I stood in my shirt before the glass, and had lathered my face, and was engaged on my right jaw, when that red-haired girl rushed between me and the mirror with both her elbows up, screening her face with her arms, and her head bowed. I started back, and in so doing cut myself."

"Where did she come from?"

"How can I tell? I did not expect to see anyone."

"Then where did she go?"

"I do not know; I was too concerned about my bleeding jaw to look about me. That girl must be dismissed."

"I wish she could be dismissed," I said.

"What do you mean?"

I did not answer my husband, for I really did not know what answer to make. I was now the only person in the house who had not seen the red-haired girl, except possibly the cook, from whom I could gather nothing, but whom I suspected of knowing more concerning this mysterious apparition than she chose to admit. That what had been seen by Bessie and Jane was a supernatural visitant, I now felt convinced, seeing that it had appeared to that least imaginative and most commonplace of all individuals, my husband. By no mental process could he have been got to imagine anything. He certainly did see this red-haired girl, and that no living, corporeal maid had been in his dressing-room at the time I was perfectly certain.

I was soon, however, myself to be included in the number of those before whose eyes she appeared. It was in this wise.

Cook had gone out to do some marketing. I was in the breakfast-room, when, wanting a funnel to fill a little phial of brandy I always keep on the washstand in case of emergencies, I went to the head of the kitchen stairs, to descend and fetch what I required. Then I was aware of a great clattering of the fire-irons below, and a banging about of the boiler and grate. I went down the steps very hastily and entered the kitchen.

There I saw a figure of a short, set girl in a shabby cotton gown, not over clean, and slipshod, stooping before the stove, and striking the fender with the iron poker. She had fiery red hair, very untidy.

I uttered an exclamation.

Instantly she dropped the poker, and covering her face with her arms, uttering a strange, low cry, she dashed round the kitchen table, making nearly the complete circuit, and then swept past me, and I heard her clattering up the kitchen stairs.

I was too much taken aback to follow. I stood as one petrified. I felt dazed and unable to trust either my eyes or my ears.

Something like a minute must have elapsed before I had sufficiently recovered to turn and leave the kitchen. Then I ascended slowly and, I confess, nervously. I was fearful lest I should find the red-haired girl cowering against the wall, and that I should have to pass her.

But nothing was to be seen. I reached the hall, and saw that no door was open from it except that of the breakfast-room. I entered and thoroughly examined every recess, corner, and conceivable hiding-place, but could find no one there. Then I ascended the staircase, with my hand on the balustrade, and searched all the rooms on the first floor, without the least success. Above were the servants' apartments, and I now resolved on mounting to them. Here the staircase was uncarpeted. As I was ascending, I heard Jane at work in her room. I then heard her come out hastily upon the landing. At the same moment, with a rush past me, uttering the same moan, went the red-haired girl. I am sure I felt her skirts sweep my dress. I did not notice her till she was close upon me, but I did distinctly see her as she passed. I turned, and saw no more.

I at once mounted to the landing where was Jane. "What is it?" I asked.

"Please, ma'am, I've seen the red-haired girl again, and I did as you recommended. I went at her rattling the pill-box, and she turned and ran downstairs. Did you see her, ma'am, as you came up?"

"How inexplicable!" I said. I would not admit to Jane that I had seen the apparition.

The situation remained unaltered for a week. The mystery was unsolved. No fresh light had been thrown on it. I did not again see or hear anything out of the way; nor did my husband, I presume, for he made no further remarks relative to the extra servant who had caused him so much annoyance. I presume he supposed that I had summarily dismissed her. This I conjectured from a smugness assumed by his face, such as it always acquired when he had carried a point against me—which was not often.

However, one evening, abruptly, we had a new sensation. My husband, Bessie, and I were at dinner, and we were partaking of the soup, Jane standing by, waiting to change our plates and to remove the tureen, when we dropped our spoons, alarmed by fearful screams issuing from the kitchen. By the way, characteristically, my husband finished his soup before he laid down the spoon and said—

"Good gracious! What is that?"

Bessie, Jane, and I were by this time at the door, and we rushed together to the kitchen stairs, and one after the other ran down them. I was the first to enter, and I saw cook wrapped in flames, and a paraffin lamp on the floor broken, and the blazing oil flowing over it.

I had sufficient presence of mind to catch up the cocoa-nut matting which was not impregnated with the oil, and to throw it round cook, wrap her tightly in it, and force her down on the floor where not overflowed by the oil. I held her thus, and Bessie succoured me. Jane was too frightened to do other than scream. The cries of the burnt woman were terrible. Presently my husband appeared.

"Dear me! Bless me! Good gracious!" he said.

"You go away and fetch a doctor," I called to him; "you can be of no possible service here—you only get in our way."

"But the dinner?"

"Bother the dinner! Run for a surgeon."

In a little while we had removed the poor woman to her room, she shrieking the whole way upstairs; and, when there, we laid her on the bed, and kept her folded in the cocoa-nut matting till a medical man arrived, in spite of her struggles to be free. My husband, on this occasion, acted with commendable promptness; but whether because he was impatient for the completion of his meal, or whether his sluggish nature was for once touched with human sympathy, it is not for me to say.

All I know is that, so soon as the surgeon was there, I dismissed Jane with, "There, go and get your master the rest of his dinner, and leave us with cook."

The poor creature was frightfully burnt. She was attended to devotedly by Bessie and myself, till a nurse was obtained from the hospital. For hours she was as one mad with terror as much as with pain.

Next day she was quieter and sent for me. I hastened to her, and she begged the nurse to leave the room. I took a chair and seated myself by her bedside, and expressed my profound commiseration, and told her that I should like to know how the accident had taken place.

"Ma'am, it was the red-haired girl did it."

"The red-haired girl!"

"Yes, ma'am. I took a lamp to look how the fish was getting on, and all at once I saw her rush straight at me, and I-—I backed, thinking she would knock me down, and the lamp fell over and smashed, and my clothes caught, and—"

"Oh, cook! You should not have taken the lamp."

"It's done. And she would never leave me alone till she had burnt or scalded me. You needn't be afraid—she don't haunt the house. It is *me* she has haunted, because of what I did to her."

"Then you know her?"

"She was in service with me, as kitchen maid, at my last place, near Cambridge. I took a sort of hate against her, she was such a slattern and so inquisitive. She peeped into my letters, and turned out my box and drawers, she was ever prying; and when I spoke to her, she was that saucy! I reg'lar hated her. And one day she was kneeling by the stove, and I was there, too, and I suppose the devil possessed me, for I upset the boiler as was on the hot-plate right upon her, just as she looked up, and it poured over her face and bosom, and arms, and scalded her that dreadful, she died. And since then she has haunted me. But she'll do so no more. She won't trouble you further. She has done for me, as she has always minded to do, since I scalded her to death."

The unhappy woman did not recover.

"Dear me! No hope?" said my husband, when informed that the surgeon despaired of her. "And good cooks are so scarce. By the way, that red-haired girl?"

"Gone—gone for ever," I said.

# THE MAN AND THE SNAKE
## AMBROSE BIERCE

Stretched at ease upon a sofa, in gown and slippers, Harker Brayton smiled as he read the foregoing sentence in old Morryster's "Marvells of Science." "The only marvel in the matter," he said to himself, "is that the wise and learned in Morryster's day should have believed such nonsense as is rejected by most of even the ignorant in ours."

A train of reflection followed—for Brayton was a man of thought—and he unconsciously lowered his book without altering the direction of his eyes. As soon as the volume had gone below the line of sight, something in an obscure corner of the room recalled his attention to his surroundings. What he saw, in the shadow under his bed, were two small points of light, apparently about an inch apart. They might have been reflections of the gas jet above him, in metal nail heads; he gave them but little thought and resumed his reading. A moment later something—some impulse which it did not occur to him to anal-yse—impelled him to lower the book again and seek for what he saw before. The points of light were still there. They seemed to have become brighter than before, shining with a greenish lustre which he had not at first observed. He thought, too, that they might have moved a trifle—were somewhat nearer. They were still too much in the shadow, however, to reveal their nature and origin to an indolent attention, and he resumed his reading. Suddenly something in the text suggested a thought which made him start and drop the book for the third time to the side of the sofa, whence, escaping from his hand, it fell sprawling to the floor, back upward. Brayton, half-risen, was staring intently into the obscurity beneath the bed, where the points of light shone with, it seemed to him, an added fire. His attention was now fully aroused, his gaze eager and imperative. It disclosed, almost directly beneath the foot-rail of the bed, the coils of a large serpent—the points of light were its eyes! Its horrible head, thrust flatly forth from the innermost coil and resting upon the outermost, was directed straight towards him, the definition of the wide, brutal jaw and the idiotlike forehead serving to show the direction of its malevolent gaze. The eyes were no longer merely luminous points; they looked into his own with a meaning, a malign significance.

A snake in a bedroom of a modern city dwelling of the better sort is, happily, not so common a phenomenon as to make explanation altogether needless. Harker Brayton, a bachelor of thirty-five, a scholar, idler, and something of an athlete, rich, popular, and of sound health, had returned to San Francisco from all manner of remote and unfamiliar countries. His tastes, always a trifle luxurious, had taken on an added exuberance from long privation; and the resources of even the Castle Hotel being inadequate for their perfect gratification, he had gladly accepted the hospitality of his friend, Dr. Druring, the distinguished scientist. Dr. Druring's house, a large, old-fashioned one in what was now an obscure quarter of the city, had an outer and visible aspect of reserve. It plainly would not associate with the contiguous elements of its altered environment, and appeared to have developed some of the eccentricities which come of isolation. One of these was a "wing," conspicuously irrelevant in point of architecture, and no less rebellious in the matter of purpose; for it was a combination of laboratory, menagerie, and museum. It was here that the doctor indulged the scientific side of his nature in the study of such forms of animal life as engaged his interest and comforted his taste—which, it must be confessed, ran rather to the lower forms. For one of the higher types nimbly and sweetly to recommend itself into his gentle senses, it had at least to retain certain rudimentary characteristics allying it to such "dragons of the prime" as toads and snakes. His scientific sympathies were distinctly reptilian; he loved nature's vulgarians and described himself as the Zola of zoology. His wife and daughters, not having the advantage to share his enlightened curiosity regarding the works and ways of our ill-starred fellow-creatures, were, with needless austerity, excluded from what he called the Snakery, and doomed to companionship with their own kind; though to soften the rigours of their lot, he had permitted them, out of his great wealth, to outdo the reptiles in the gorgeousness of their surroundings and to shine with a superior splendour.

Architecturally, and in point of "furnishing," the Snakery had a severe simplicity befitting the humble circumstances of its occupants, many of whom, indeed, could not safely have been entrusted with the liberty which is necessary to the full enjoyment of luxury, for they had the troublesome peculiarity of being alive. In their own apartments, however, they were under as little personal restraint as was compatible with their protection from the baneful habit of swallowing one another; and, as Brayton had thoughtfully been apprised, it was more than a tradition that some of them had at divers times been found in parts of the premises where it would have embarrassed them to explain their presence. Despite the Snakery and its uncanny associations—to which, indeed, he gave little attention—Brayton found life at the Druring mansion very much to his mind.

Beyond a smart shock of surprise and a shudder of mere loathing, Mr. Brayton was not greatly affected. His first thought was to ring the call bell and bring a servant, but, although the bell cord dangled within easy reach, he made no movement towards it; it had occurred to his mind that the act might subject him to the suspicion of fear, which he certainly did not feel. He was more keenly conscious of the incongruous nature of the situation than affected by its perils; it was revolting, but absurd.

The reptile was of a species with which Brayton was unfamiliar. Its length he could only conjecture; the body at the largest visible part seemed about as thick as his forearm. In what way was it dangerous, if in any way? Was it venomous? Was it a constrictor? His knowledge of nature's danger signals did not enable him to say; he had never deciphered the code.

If not dangerous, the creature was at least offensive. It was *de trop*—"matter out of place"—an impertinence. The gem was unworthy of the setting. Even the barbarous taste of our time and country, which had loaded the walls of the room with pictures, the floor with furniture, and the furniture with *bric-a-brac*, had not quite fitted the place for this bit of the savage life of the jungle. Besides—

insupportable thought!—the exhalations of its breath mingled with the atmosphere which he himself was breathing!

These thoughts shaped themselves with greater or less definition in Brayton's mind, and begot action. The process is what we call consideration and decision. It is thus that we are wise and unwise. It is thus that the withered leaf in an autumn breeze shows greater or less intelligence than its fellows, falling upon the land or upon the lake. The secret of human action is an open one—something contracts our muscles. Does it matter if we give to the preparatory molecular changes the name of will?

Brayton rose to his feet and prepared to back softly away from the snake, without disturbing it, if possible, and through the door. People retire so from the presence of the great, for greatness is power, and power is a menace. He knew that he could walk backward without obstruction, and find the door without error. Should the monster follow, the taste which had plastered the walls with paintings had consistently supplied a rack of murderous Oriental weapons from which he could snatch one to suit the occasion. In the meantime the snake's eyes burned with a more pitiless malevolence than ever.

Brayton lifted his right foot free of the floor to step backward. That moment he felt a strong aversion to doing so.

"I am accounted brave," he murmured; "is bravery, then, no more than pride? Because there are none to witness the shame shall I retreat?"

He was steadying himself with his right hand upon the back of a chair, his foot suspended.

"Nonsense!" he said aloud; "I am not so great a coward as to fear to seem to myself afraid."

He lifted the foot a little higher by slightly bending the knee, and thrust it sharply to the floor—an inch in front of the other! He could not think how that occurred. A trial with the left foot had the same result; it was again in advance of the right. The hand upon the chair back was grasping it; the arm was straight, reaching somewhat backward. One might have seen that he was reluctant to lose his hold. The snake's malignant head was still thrust forth from the inner coil as before, the neck level. It had not moved, but its eyes were now electric sparks, radiating an infinity of luminous needles.

The man had an ashy pallor. Again he took a step forward, and another, partly dragging the chair, which, when finally released, fell upon the floor with a crash. The man groaned; the snake made neither sound nor motion, but its eyes were two dazzling suns. The reptile itself was wholly concealed by them.

They gave off enlarging rings of rich and vivid colours, which at their greatest expansion successively vanished like soap bubbles; they seemed to approach his very face, and anon were an immeasurable distance away. He heard, somewhere, the continual throbbing of a great drum, with desultory bursts of far music, inconceivably sweet, like the tones of an aeolian harp. He knew it for the sunrise melody of Memnon's statue, and thought he stood in the Nileside reeds, hearing, with exalted sense, that immortal anthem through the silence of the centuries.

The music ceased; rather, it became by insensible degrees the distant roll of a retreating thunderstorm. A landscape, glittering with sun and rain, stretched before him, arched with a vivid rainbow, framing in its giant curve a hundred visible cities. In the middle distance a vast serpent, wearing a crown, reared its head out of its voluminous convolutions and looked at him with his dead mother's eyes. Suddenly this enchanting landscape seemed to rise swiftly upwards, like the drop scene at a theatre, and vanished in a blank. Something struck him a hard blow upon the face and breast. He had fallen to the floor; the blood ran from his broken nose and his bruised lips. For a moment he was dazed and stunned, and lay with closed eyes, his face against the door. In a few moments he had recovered, and then realised that his fall, by withdrawing his eyes, had broken the spell which held him. He felt that now, by keeping his gaze averted, he would be able to retreat. But the thought of the serpent within a few feet of his head, yet unseen—perhaps in the very act of springing upon him and throwing its coils about his throat—was too horrible. He lifted his head, stared again into those baleful eyes, and was again in bondage.

The snake had not moved, and appeared somewhat to have lost its power upon the imagination; the gorgeous illusions of a few moments before were not repeated.

Beneath that flat and brainless brow its black, beady eyes simply glittered, as at first, with an expression unspeakably malignant. It was as if the creature, knowing its triumph assured, had determined to practice no more alluring wiles.

Now ensued a fearful scene. The man, prone upon the floor, within a yard of his enemy, raised the upper part of his body upon his elbows, his head thrown back, his legs extended to their full length. His face was white between its gouts of blood; his eyes were strained open to their uttermost expansion. There was froth upon his lips; it dropped off in flakes. Strong convulsions ran through his body, making almost serpentine undulations. He bent himself at the waist, shifting his legs from side to side. And every moment left him a little nearer to the snake. He thrust his hands forward to brace himself back, yet constantly advanced upon his elbows.

Dr. Druring and his wife sat in the library. The scientist was in rare good humour.

"I have just obtained, by exchange with another collector," he said, "a splendid specimen of the *Ophiophagus*."

"And what may that be?" the lady inquired with a somewhat languid interest.

"Why, bless my soul, what profound ignorance! My dear, a man who ascertains after marriage that his wife does not know Greek is entitled to a divorce. The *Ophiophagus* is a snake which eats other snakes."

"I hope it will eat all yours," she said, absently shifting the lamp. "But how does it get the other snakes? By charming them, I suppose."

"That is just like you, dear," said the doctor, with an affectation of petulance. "You know how irritating to me is any allusion to that vulgar superstition about the snake's power of fascination."

The conversation was interrupted by a mighty cry which ran through the silent house like the voice of a demon shouting in a tomb. Again and yet again it sounded, with terrible distinctness. They sprang to their feet, the man confused, the lady pale and speechless with fright. Almost before the echoes of the last cry had died away the doctor was out of the room, springing up the staircase two steps at a time. In the corridor, in front of Brayton's chamber, he met some servants who had come from the upper floor. Together they rushed at the door without knocking. It was unfastened, and gave way. Brayton lay upon his stomach on the floor, dead. His head and arms were partly concealed under the foot-rail of the bed. They pulled the body away, turning it upon the back. The face was daubed with blood and froth, the eyes were wide open, staring—a dreadful sight!

"Died in a fit," said the scientist, bending his knee and placing his hand upon the heart. While in that position he happened to glance under the bed. "Good God!" he added, "how did this thing get in here?"

He reached under the bed, pulled out the snake, and flung it, still coiled, to the centre of the room, whence, with a harsh, shuffling sound, it slid across the polished floor till stopped by the wall, where it lay without motion. It was a stuffed snake; its eyes were two shoe buttons.

# THE OPEN WINDOW
## SAKI (H. H. MUNRO)

"My aunt will be down presently, Mr. Nuttel," said a very self possessed young lady of fifteen; "in the meantime you must *try* and put up with me."

Framton Nuttel endeavored to say the correct something which should duly flatter the niece of the moment without unduly discounting the aunt that was to come. Privately he doubted more than ever whether these formal visits on a succession total strangers would do much towards helping the nerve cure which he was supposed to be undergoing.

"I know how it will be," his sister had said when he was preparing to migrate to this rural retreat; "you will bury yourself down there and not speak to a living soul, and your nerves will be worse than ever from moping. I shall just give you letter of introduction to all the people I know there. Some of them, far as I can remember, were quite nice."

Framton wondered whether Mrs. Sappleton, the lady to whom he was presenting one of the letters of introduction, came in the nice division.

"Do you know many of the people round here?" asked the niece, when she judged that they had had sufficient silent communion.

"Hardly a soul," said Framton. "My sister was staying at the rectory, you know, some four years ago, and she gave me letters of introduction to some of the people here."

He made the last statement in a tone of distinct regret.

"Then you know practically nothing about my aunt?" pursued the self-possessed young lady.

"Only her name and address," admitted the caller. He was wondering whether Mrs. Sappleton was in the married or widowed state. An indefinable something about the room seemed suggest masculine habitation.

"Her great tragedy happened just three years ago," said the child; 'that would be since your sister's time."

"Her tragedy?" asked Framton; somehow in this restful country spot tragedies seemed out of place.

"You may wonder why we keep that window wide open on October afternoon," said the niece, indicating a large French window that opened on to a lawn.

"It is quite warm for the time of the year," said Framton; "but has that window got anything to do with the tragedy?"

"Out through that window, three years ago to a day, her husband and her two young brothers went off for their day's shooting. They never came back. In crossing the moor to their favourite snipe-shooting ground, they were all three engulfed in a treacherous piece of bog. It had been that dreadful wet summer, you know, and places that were safe in other years gave way suddenly without warning. Their bodies were never recovered. That was the dreadful part of it. Here the child's voice lost its self-possessed note and became falteringly human. "Poor aunt always thinks that they will come back some day, they and the little brown spaniel that was lost with them, and walk in at that window just as they used to do. That is why the window is kept open every evening till it is quite dusk. Poor dear aunt, she has often told me how they went out, her husband with his white waterproof coat over his arm, and Ronnie, her youngest brother, singing 'Bertie, why do you bound?' as he always did to tease her, because she said it got on her nerves. Do you know, sometimes on still, quiet evenings like this, I almost get a creepy feeling that they will all walk in through that window—"

She broke off with a little shudder. It was a relief to Framton when the aunt bustled into the room with a whirl of apologies for being late in making her appearance.

"I hope Vera has been amusing you?" she said.

"She has been very interesting," said Framton.

"I hope you don't mind the open window," said Mrs. Sappleton briskly; "my husband and brothers will be home directly from shooting, and they always come in this way. They've been out for snipe in the marshes to-day, so they'll make a fine mess over my poor carpets. So like you men-folks, isn't it?"

She rattled on cheerfully about the shooting and the scarcity of birds, and the prospects for duck in the winter. To Framton it was all purely horrible. He made a desperate but only partially successful effort to turn the talk on to a less ghastly topic; he was conscious that his hostess was giving him only a fragment of her attention, and her eyes were constantly straying past him to the open window and the lawn beyond. It was certainly an unfortunate coincidence that he should have paid his visit on this tragic anniversary.

"The doctors agree in ordering me complete rest, an absence of mental excitement, and avoidance of anything in the nature of violent physical exercise," announced Framton, who laboured under the tolerably widespread delusion that total strangers and chance acquaintances are hungry for the least detail of one's ailments and infirmities, their cause and cure. "On the matter of diet they are not so much in agreement," he continued.

"No?" said Mrs. Sappleton, in a voice which only replaced a yawn at the last moment. Then she suddenly brightened into alert attention—but not to what Framton was saying.

"Here they are at last!" she cried. "Just in time for tea, and don't they look as if they were muddy up to the eyes!"

Framton shivered slightly and turned toward the niece with a look intended to convey sympathetic comprehension. The child was staring out through the open window with dazed horror in her eyes. In a chill shock of nameless fear, Framton swung round in his seat and looked in the same direction.

In the deepening twilight three figures were walking across the lawn towards the window; they all carried guns under their arms, and one of them was additionally burdened with a white coat hung over his shoulders. A tired brown spaniel kept close at their heels. Noiselessly they neared the house, and then a hoarse young voice chanted out of the dusk: "I said, Bertie, why do you bound?"

Framton grabbed wildly at his stick and hat; the hall door, the gravel drive, and the front gate were dimly noted stages in his headlong retreat. A cyclist coming along the road had to run into the hedge to avoid imminent collision.

"Here we are, my dear," said the bearer of the white mackintosh, coming in through the window; "fairly muddy, but most of it's dry. Who was that who bolted out as we came up?"

"A most extraordinary man, a Mr. Nuttel," said Mrs. Sappleton; "could only talk about his illness, and dashed off without a word of good-bye or apology when you arrived. One would think he had seen a ghost."

"I expect it was the spaniel," said the niece calmly; "he told me he had a horror of dogs. He was once hunted into a cemetery somewhere on the banks of the Ganges by a pack of pariah dogs, and had to spend the night in a newly dug grave with the creatures snarling and grinning and foaming just above him. Enough to make anyone lose their nerve."

Romance at short notice was her specialty.

# THE STORY OF SALOME
## AMELIA B. EDWARDS

A few years ago, no matter how many, I, Harcourt Blunt, was travelling with my friend Coventry Tumour and it was on the steps of our hotel that I received from him the announcement - he sent one to me - that he was again in love.

'I tell you, Blunt,' said my fellow-traveller, 'she's the loveliest creature I ever beheld in my life.'

I laughed outright.

'My dear fellow,' I replied, 'you've so often seen the loveliest creature you ever beheld in your life.'

'Ay, but I am in earnest now for the first time.'

'And you have so often been in earnest for the first time! Remember the innkeeper's daughter at Cologne.' 'A pretty housemaid, whom no training could have made presentable.' Then there was the beautiful American at Interlachen.'

'Yes; but—'

'And the Bella Marchesa at Prince Torlonia's ball.'

'Not one of them worthy to be named in the same breath with my imperial Venetian. Come with me to the Merceria and be convinced. By taking a gondola to St Mark's Place we shall be there in a quarter of an hour.'

I went, and he raved of his new flame all the way. She was a Jewess - he would convert her. Her father kept a shop in the Merceria - what of that? He dealt only in costliest Oriental merchandise, and was as rich as a Rothschild. As for any probable injury to his own prospects, why need he hesitate on that account? What were 'prospects' when weighed against the happiness of one's whole life? Besides, he was not ambitious. He didn't care to go into Parliament. If his uncle Sir Geoffrey cut him off with a shilling, what then? He had a moderate independence of which no one living could deprive him, and what more could any reasonable man desire?

I listened, smiled, and was silent. I knew Coventry Tumour too well to attach the smallest degree of importance to anything that he might say or do in a matter of this kind. To be distractedly in love was his normal condition. We had been friends from boyhood; and since the time when he used to cherish a hopeless attachment to the young lady behind the counter of the tart-shop at Harrow, I had never known him 'fancy-free' for more than a few weeks at a time. He had gone through every phase of no less than three grandes passions during the five months that we had now been travelling together; and having left Rome about eleven weeks before with every hope laid waste, and a heart so broken that it could never by any possibility be put together again, he was now, according to the natural course of events, just ready to fall in love again.

We landed at the traghetto San Marco. It was a cloudless morning towards the middle of April, just ten years ago. The ducal palace glowed in the hot sunshine; the boatmen were clustered, gossiping, about the Molo; the orange-vendors were busy under the arches of the piazzetta; the flaneurs were already eating ices and smoking cigarettes outside the cafes. There was an Austrian military band, strapped, buckled, moustachioed, and white-coated, playing just in front of St Mark's; and the shadow of the great bell-tower slept all across the square.

Passing under the low round archway leading to the Merceria, we plunged at once into that cool labyrinth of narrow, intricate, and picturesque streets, where the sun never penetrates - where no wheels are heard, and no beast of burden is seen - where every house is a shop, and every shop-front is open to the ground, as in an Oriental bazaar - where the upper balconies seem almost to meet overhead, and are separated by only a strip of burning sky - and where more than three people cannot march abreast in any part. Pushing our way as best we might through the motley crowd that here chatters, cheapens, buys, sells, and perpetually bustles to and fro, we came presently to a shop for the sale of Eastern goods. A few glass jars filled with spices, and some pieces of stuff, untidily strewed the counter next the street; but within, dark and narrow though it seemed, the place was crammed with costliest merchandise. Cases of gorgeous Oriental jewellery, embroideries and fringes of massive gold and silver bullion, precious drugs and spices, exquisite toys in filigree, miracles of carving in ivory, sandal-wood, and amber, jewelled yataghans, scimitars of state rich with 'barbaric pearl and gold', bales of Cashmere shawls, China silks, India muslins, gauzes, and the like, filled every inch of available space from floor to ceiling, leaving only a narrow lane from the door to the counter, and a still narrower passage to the rooms beyond the shop.

We went in. A young woman, who was sitting reading on a low seat behind the counter, laid aside her book, and rose slowly. She was dressed wholly in black. I cannot describe the fashion of her garments. I only know that they fell about her in long, soft, trailing folds, leaving a narrow band of fine cambric visible at the throat and wrists; and that, however graceful and unusual this dress may have been, I scarcely observed it, so entirely was I taken up with admiration of her beauty.

For she was indeed very beautiful - beautiful in a way that I had not anticipated. Coventry Tumour, with all his enthusiasm, had failed to do her justice. He had raved of her eyes - her large, lustrous, melancholy eyes - of the transparent paleness of her complexion, of the faultless delicacy of her features; but he had not prepared me for the unconscious dignity, the perfect nobleness and refinement, that informed her every look and gesture. My friend requested to see a bracelet at which he had been looking the day before. Proud, stately, silent, she unlocked the case in which it was kept, and laid it before him on the counter. He asked permission to take it over to the light. She bent her head, but answered not a word. It was like being waited upon by a young empress.

Tumour took the bracelet to the door and affected to examine it. It consisted of a double row of gold coins linked together at intervals by a bean-shaped ornament, studded with pink coral and diamonds. Coming back into the shop he asked me if I thought it would please his sister, to whom he had promised a remembrance of Venice.

'It is a pretty trifle,' I replied; 'but surely a remembrance of Venice should be of Venetian manufacture. This, I suppose, is Turkish.'

The beautiful Jewess looked up. We spoke in English; but she understood and replied:

'E Greco, signore,' she said coldly.

At this moment an old man came suddenly forward from some dark counting-house at the back - a grizzled, bearded, eager-eyed Shylock, with a peri behind his ear.

'Go in, Salome - go in, my daughter,' he said hurriedly. 'I will serve these gentlemen.'

She lifted her eyes to his for one moment - then moved silently away, and vanished in the gloom of the room beyond.

We saw her no more. We lingered awhile, looking over the contents of the jewel-cases; but in vain. Then Tumour bought his bracelet, and we went out again into the narrow streets, and back to the open daylight of the Gran' Piazza.

'Well,' he said breathlessly, 'what do you think of her?'

'She is very lovely.'

'Lovelier than you expected?'

'Much lovelier. But—'

'But what?'

'The sooner you succeed in forgetting her, the better.'

He vowed, of course, that he never would and never could forget her. He would hear of no incompatibilities, listen to no objections, believe in no obstacles. That the beautiful Salome was herself not only unconscious of his passion and indifferent to his person, but ignorant of his very name and station, were facts not even to be admitted on the list of difficulties. Finding him thus deaf to reason, I said no more.

It was all over, however, before the week was out.

'Look here, Blunt,' he said, coming up to me one morning in the coffee-room of our hotel just as I was sitting down to answer a pile of home-letters; 'would you like to go on to Trieste tomorrow? There, don't look at me like that - you can guess how it is with me. I was a fool ever to suppose she would care for me - a stranger, a foreigner, a Christian. Well, I'm horribly out of sorts anyhow - and - and I wish I was a thousand miles off at this moment!'

We travelled on together to Athens, and there parted, Tumour being bound for England, and I for the East. My own tour lasted many months longer. I went first to Egypt and the Holy Land; then joined an exploring party on the Euphrates; and at length, after just twelve months of Oriental life, found myself back again at Trieste about the middle of April in the year following that during which occurred the events I have just narrated. There I found that batch of letters and papers to which I had been looking forward for many weeks past; and amongst the former, one from Coventry Tumour. This time he was not only irrecoverably in love, but on the eve of matrimony. The letter was rapturous and extravagant enough. The writer was the happiest of men; his destined bride the loveliest and most amiable of her sex; the future a paradise; the past a melancholy series of mistakes. As for love, he had never, of course, known what it was till now. And what of the beautiful Salome?

Not one word of her from beginning to end. He had forgotten her as utterly as if she had never existed. And yet how desperately in love and how desperately in despair he was 'one little year ago'! Ah, yes; but then it was 'one little year ago'; and who that had ever known Coventry Tumour would expect him to remember la plus grande des grandes passions for even half that time?

I slept that night at Trieste, and went on next day to Venice. Somehow, I could not get Tumour and his love affairs out of my head. I remembered our visit to the Merceria. I was haunted by the image of the beautiful Jewess. Was she still so lovely? Did she still sit reading in her wonted seat by the open counter, with the gloomy shop reaching away behind, and the cases of rich robes and jewels all around?

An irresistible impulse prompted me to go to the Merceria and see her once again. I went. It had been a busy morning with me, and I did not get there till between three and four o'clock in the afternoon. The place was crowded. I passed up the well-remembered street, looking out on both sides for the gloomy little shop with its unattractive counter; but in vain. When I had gone so far that I thought I must have passed it, I turned back. House by house I retraced my steps to the very entrance, and still could not find it. Then, concluding that I had not gone far enough at first, I turned back again till I reached a spot where several streets diverged. Here I came to a standstill, for beyond this point I knew I had not passed before.

It was now only too evident that the Jew no longer occupied his former shop in the Merceria, and that my chance of discovering his whereabouts was exceedingly slender. I could not inquire of his successor, because I could not identify the house. I found it impossible even to remember what trades were carried on by his neighbours on either side. I was ignorant of his very name. Convinced, therefore, of the inutility of making any further effort, I gave up the search, and comforted myself by reflecting that my own heart was not made of adamant, and that it was, perhaps, better for my peace not to see the beautiful

Salome again. I was destined to see her again, however, and that ere many days had passed over my head.

A year of more than ordinarily fatiguing Eastern travel had left me in need of rest, and I had resolved to allow myself a month's sketching in Venice and its neighbourhood before turning my face homewards. As, therefore, it is manifestly the first object of a sketcher to select his points of view, and as no more luxurious machine than a Venetian gondola was ever invented for the use of man, I proceeded to employ the first days of my stay in endless boatings to and fro: now exploring all manner of canals and canaletti; rowing out in the direction of Murano; now making for the islands beyond San Pietro Castello, and in the course of these pilgrimages noting down an infinite number of picturesque sites, and smoking art infinite number of cigarettes. It was, I think, about the fourth or fifth day of this pleasant work, when my gondolier proposed to take me as far as the Lido. It wanted about two hours to sunset, and the great sandbank lay not more than three or four miles away; so I gave the word, and in another moment we had changed our route and were gliding farther and farther from Venice at each dip of the oar. Then the long dull distant ridge that had all day bounded the shallow horizon rose gradually above the placid level of the Lagune, assumed a more broken outline, resolved itself into hillocks and hollows of tawny sand, showed here and there a patch of parched grass and tangled brake, and looked like the coasts of some inhospitable desert beyond which no traveller might penetrate. My boatman made straight for a spot where some stakes at the water's edge gave token of a landing-place; and here, though with some difficulty, for the tide was low, ran the gondola aground. I landed. My first step was among graves.

'E'l cimeterio giudaico, signore,' said my gondolier, with a touch of his cap.

The Jewish cemetery! The ghetto of the dead! I remembered now to have read or heard long since how the Venetian Jews, cut off in death as in life from the neighbourhood of their Christian rulers, had been buried from immemorial time upon this desolate waste. I stooped to examine the headstone at my feet. It was but a shattered fragment, crusted over with yellow lichens, and eaten away by the salt sea air. I passed on to the next, and the next. Some were completely matted over with weeds and brambles; some were half-buried in the drifting sand; of some, only a corner remained above the surface. Here and there a name, a date, a fragment of heraldic carving, or part of a Hebrew inscription, was yet legible; but all were more or less broken and effaced.

Wandering on thus among graves and hillocks, ascending at every step, and passing some three or four glassy pools overgrown with gaunt-looking reeds, I presently found that I had reached the central and most elevated part of the Lido, and that I commanded an uninterrupted view on every side. On the one hand lay the broad, silent Lagune bounded by Venice and the Euganean hills—on the other, stealing up in long, lazy folds, and breaking noiselessly against the endless shore, the blue Adriatic. An old man gathering shells on the seaward side, a distant gondola on the Lagune, were the only signs of life for miles around.

Standing on the upper ridge of this narrow barrier, looking upon both waters, and watching the gradual approach of what promised to be a gorgeous sunset, I fell into one of those wandering trains of thought in which the real and unreal succeed each other as capriciously as in a dream. I remembered how Goethe here conceived his vertebral theory of the skull - how Byron, too lame to walk, kept his horse on the Lido, and here rode daily to and fro - how Shelley loved the wild solitude of the place, wrote of it in Julian and Maddalo, listened, perhaps from this very spot, to the mad-house bell on the island of San Giorgio. Then I wondered if Titian had ever come hither from his gloomy house on the other side of Venice, to study the gold and purple of these western skies - if Othello had walked here with Desdemona - if Shylock was buried yonder, and Leah whom he loved 'when he was a bachelor.'

And then in the midst of my reverie, I came suddenly upon another Jewish cemetery.

Was it indeed another, or but an outlying portion of the first? It was evidently another, and a more modem one. The ground was better kept. The monuments were newer. Such dates as I had succeeded in deciphering on the broken sepulchres lower down were all of the fourteenth and fifteenth centuries; but the inscriptions upon these bore reference to quite recent interments.

I went on a few steps farther. I stopped to copy a quaint Italian couplet on one tomb - to gather a wild forget-me-not from the foot of another - to put aside a bramble that trailed across a third - and then I became aware for the first time of a lady sitting beside a grave not a dozen yards from the spot on which I stood.

I had believed myself so utterly alone, and was so taken by surprise, that for the first moment I could almost have persuaded myself that she also was of the stuff that dreams are made of. She was dressed from head to foot in the deepest mourning; her face turned from me, looking towards the sunset; her cheek resting in the palm of her hand. The grave by which she sat was obviously recent. The scant herbage round about had been lately disturbed, and the marble headstone looked as if it had not yet undergone a week's exposure to wind and weather.

Persuaded that she had not observed me, I lingered for an instant looking at her. Something in the grace and sorrow of her attitude, something in the turn of her head and the flow of her sable draperies, arrested my attention. Was she young? I fancied so. Did she mourn a husband? A lover? A parent? I glanced towards the headstone. It was covered with Hebrew characters; so that, had I even been nearer, it could have told me nothing.

But I felt that I had no right to stand there, a spectator of her sorrow, an intruder on her privacy. I proceeded to move noiselessly away. At that moment she turned and looked at me.

It was Salome.

Salome, pale and worn as from some deep and wasting grief, but more beautiful, if that could be, than ever. Beautiful, with a still more spiritual beauty than of old; with cheeks so wan and eyes so unutterably bright and solemn, that my very heart seemed to stand still as I looked upon them. For one second I paused, half fancying, half hoping that there was recognition in her glance; then, not daring to look or linger longer, turned away. When I had gone far enough to do so without discourtesy, I stopped and gazed back. She had resumed her former attitude, and was looking over towards Venice and the setting sun. The stone by which she watched was not more motionless.

The sun went down in glory. The last flush faded from the domes and bell-towers of Venice; the western peaks changed from rose to purple, from gold to grey; a scarcely perceptible film of mist became all at once visible upon the surface of the Lagune; and overhead, the first star trembled into light. I waited and watched till the shadows had so deepened that I could no longer distinguish one distant object from another. Was that the spot? Was she still there? Was she moving? Was she gone? I could not tell. The more I looked, the more uncertain I became. Then, fearing to miss my way in the fast-gathering twilight, I shuck down towards the water's edge, and made for the point at which I had landed.

I found my gondolier fast asleep, with his head on a cushion, and his bit of gondola-carpet thrown over him for a counterpane. I asked if he had seen any other boat put off from the Lido since I left. He rubbed his eyes, started up, and was awake in a moment.

'Per Bacco, signore, I have been asleep,' he said apologetically: 'I have seen nothing.'

'Did you observe any other boat moored hereabouts when we landed?'
'None, signore.'

'And you have seen nothing of a lady in black?' He laughed and shook his
head.

'Consolatevi, signore,' he said archly. 'She will come tomorrow.'

Then, finding that I looked grave, he touched his cap, and with a gentle,
'Scusate, signore,' took his place at the stem, and there waited. I bade him row
to my hotel; and then, leaning dreamily back in my little dark cabin, I folded my
arms, closed my eyes, and thought of Salome.

How lovely she was! How infinitely more lovely than even my first remembrance of her! How was it that I had not admired her more that day in the Merceria? Was I blind, or had she become indeed more beautiful? It was a sad and
strange place in which to meet her again. By whose grave was she watching? By
her father's? Yes, surely by her father's. He was an old man when I saw him, and
in the course of nature had not long to live. He was dead: hence my unavailing
search in the Merceria. He was dead. His shop was let to another occupant. His
stock-in-trade was sold and dispersed. And Salome - was she left alone? Had
she no mother? No brother? No lover? Would her eyes have had that look of
speechless woe in them if she had any very near or dear tie left on earth? Then I
thought of Coventry Tumour, and his approaching marriage. Did he ever really
love her? I doubted it. 'True love,' saith an old song, 'can ne'er forget'; but he
had forgotten, as though the past had been a dream. And yet he was in earnest
while it lasted - would have risked all for her sake, if she would have listened to
him. Ah, if she had listened to him! And then I remembered that he had never
told me the particulars of that affair. Did she herself reject him, or did he lay
his suit before her father? And was he rejected only because he was a Christian?
I had never cared to ask these things while we were together; but now I would
have given the best hunter in my stables to know every minute detail connected
with the matter.

Pondering thus, travelling over the same ground again and again, wondering whether she remembered me, whether she was poor, whether she was indeed
alone in the world, how long the old man had been dead, and a hundred other
things of the same kind I scarcely noticed how the watery miles glided past,
or how the night closed in. One question, however, recurred oftener than any
other: How was I to see her again?

I arrived at my hotel; I dined at the table d'hote. I strolled out, after dinner,
to my favourite cafe in the piazza; I dropped in for half an hour at the Fenice,

and heard one act of an extremely poor opera. I came home restless, uneasy, wakeful; and sitting for hours before my bedroom fire, asked myself the same perpetual question: how was I to see her again?

Fairly tired out at last, I fell asleep in my chair, and when I awoke the sun was shining upon my window.

I started to my feet. I had it now. It flashed upon me, as if it came with the sunlight. I had but to go again to the cemetery, copy the inscription upon the old man's tomb, ask my learned friend Professor Nicolai, of Padua, to translate it for me, and then, once in possession of names and dates, the rest would be easy. In less than an hour, I was once more on my way to the Lido.

I took a rubbing of the stone. It was the quickest way, and the surest; for I knew that in Hebrew everything depended on the pointing of the characters, and I feared to trust my own untutored skill. This done, I hastened back, wrote my letter to the professor, and dispatched both letter and rubbingby the midday train.

The professor was not a prompt man. On the contrary he was a pre-eminently slow man; dreamy, indolent, buried in Oriental lore. From any other correspondent one might have looked for a reply in the course of the morrow; but from Nicolai of Padua it would have been folly to expect one under two or three days. And in the meanwhile? Well, in the meanwhile there were churches and palaces to be seen, sketches to be made, letters of introduction to be delivered. It was, at all events, of no use to be impatient.

And yet I was impatient - so impatient that I could neither sketch, nor read, nor sit still for ten minutes together. Possessed by an uncontrollable restlessness, I wandered from gallery to gallery, from palace to palace, from church to church. The imprisonment of even a gondola was irksome to me. I was, as it were, impelled to be moving and doing; and even so, the day seemed endless.

The next was even worse. There was just the possibility of a reply from Padua, and the knowledge of that possibility unsettled me for the day. Having watched and waited for every post from eight to four, I went down to the traghetto of St Mark's, and was there hailed by my accustomed gondolier.

He touched his cap and waited for orders.

'Where to, signore?' he asked, finding that I remained silent.

'To the Lido.'

It was an irresistible temptation, and I yielded to it; but I yielded in opposition to my judgment. I knew that I ought not to haunt the place. I had resolved that I would not. And yet I went.

Going along, I told myself that I had only come to reconnoitre. It was not unlikely that she might be going to the same spot about the same hour as before; and in that case I might overtake her gondola by the way, or find it moored somewhere along the shore. At all events, I was determined not to land. But we met no gondola beyond San Pietro Castello; saw no sign of one along the shore. The afternoon was far advanced; the sun was near going down; we had the Lagune and the Lido to ourselves.

My boatman made for the same landing-place, and moored his gondola to the same stake as before. He took it for granted that I meant to land; and I landed. After all, however, it was evident that Salome could riot be there, in which case I was guilty of no intrusion. I might stroll in the direction of the cemetery, taking care to avoid her, if she were anywhere about, and keeping well away from that part where I had last seen her. So I broke another resolve, and went up towards the top of the Lido. Again I came to the salt pools and the reeds; again stood with the sea upon my left hand and the Lagune upon my right, and the endless sandbank reaching on for miles between the two. Yonder lay the new cemetery. Standing thus I overlooked every foot of the ground. I could even distinguish the headstone of which I had taken the rubbing the morning before. There was no living thing in sight. I was, to all appearance, as utterly alone as Enoch Arden on his desert island.

Then I strolled on, a little nearer, and a little nearer still; and then, contrary to all my determinations, I found myself standing upon the very spot, beside the very grave, which I had made my mind on no account to approach.

The sun was now just going down - had gone down, indeed, behind a bank of golden-edged cumuli - and was flooding earth, sea, and sky with crimson. It was at this hour that I saw her. It was upon this spot that she was sitting. A few scant blades of grass had sprung up here and there upon the grave. Her dress must have touched them as she sat there - her dress; perhaps her hand. I gathered one, and laid it carefully between the leaves of my note-book.

At last I turned to go, and, turning, met her face to face!

She was distant about six yards, and advancing slowly towards the spot on which I was standing. Her head drooped slightly forward; her hands were clasped together; her eyes were fixed upon the ground. It was the attitude of a nun. Startled, confused, scarcely knowing what I did, I took off my hat, and drew aside to let her pass.

She looked up - hesitated - stood still - gazed at me with a strange, steadfast, mournful expression - then dropped her eyes again, passed me without another glance, and resumed her former place and attitude beside her father's grave.

I turned away. I would have given worlds to speak to her; but I had not dared, and the opportunity was gone. Yet I might have spoken! She looked at me - looked at me with so strange and piteous an expression in her eyes - continued looking at me as long as one might have counted five . . . I might have spoken. I surely might have spoken! And now - ah! now it was impossible. She had fallen into the old thoughtful attitude with her cheek resting on her hand. Her thoughts were far away. She had forgotten my very presence.

I went back to the shore, more disturbed and uneasy than ever. I spent all the remaining daylight in rowing up and down the margin of the Lido, looking for her gondola - hoping, at all events, to see her put off - to follow her, perhaps, across the waste of waters. But the dusk came quickly on, and then darkness, and I left at last without having seen any further sign or token of her presence.

Lying awake that night, tossing uneasily upon my bed, and thinking over the incidents of the last few days, I found myself perpetually recurring to that long, steady, sorrowful gaze which she fixed upon me in the cemetery. The more I thought of it, the more I seemed to feel that there was in it some deeper meaning than I, in my confusion, had observed at the time. It was such a strange look - a look almost of entreaty, of asking for help or sympathy; like the dumb appeal in the eyes of a sick animal. Could this really be? What, after all, more possible than that, left alone in the world - with, perhaps, not a single male relation to advise her - she found herself in some position of present difficulty, and knew not where to turn for help? All this might well be. She had even, perhaps, some instinctive feeling that she might trust me. Ah! if she would indeed trust me ...

I had hoped to receive my Paduan letter by the morning delivery; but morning and afternoon went by as before, and still no letter came. As the day began to decline, I was again on my way to the Lido; this time for the purpose, and with the intention, of speaking to her. I landed, and went direct to the cemetery. It had been a dull day. Lagune and sky were both one leaden uniform grey, and a mist hung over Venice.

I saw her from the moment I reached the upper ridge. She was walking slowly to and fro among the graves, like a stately shadow. I had felt confident, somehow, that she would be there; and now, for some reason that I could not have defined for my life, I felt equally confident that she expected me.

Trembling and eager, yet half dreading the moment when she should discover my presence, I hastened on, printing the loose sand at every noiseless step.

A few moments more, and I should overtake her, speak to her, hear the music of her voice - that music which I remembered so well, though a year had gone by since I last heard it. But how should I address her? What had I to say? I knew not. I had no time to think. I could only hurry on till within some ten feet of her trailing garments; stand still when she turned, and uncover before her as if she were a queen.

She paused and looked at me, just as she had paused and looked at me the evening before. With the same sorrowful meaning in her eyes; with even more than the same entreating expression. But she waited for me to speak.

I did speak. I cannot recall what I said; I only know that I faltered something of an apology - mentioned that I had had the honour of meeting her before, many months ago; and, trying to say more - trying to express how thankfully and proudly I would devote myself to any service, however humble, however laborious, I failed both in voice and words, and broke down utterly.

Having come to a stop, I looked up, and found her eyes Still fixed upon me.

'You are a Christian,' she said.

A trembling came upon me at the first sound of her voice. It was the same voice; distinct, melodious, scarce louder than a whisper - and yet it was not quite the same. There was a melancholy in the music, and, if I may use a word which, after all, fails to express my meaning, a remoteness, that fell upon my ear like the plaintive cadence in an autumnal wind.

I bent my head, and answered that I was.

She pointed to the headstone of which I had taken a rubbing a day or two before.

'A Christian soul lies there,' she said, 'laid in earth without one Christian prayer - with Hebrew rites - in a Hebrew sanctuary. Will you, stranger, perform an act of piety towards the dead?'

'The Signora has but to speak,' I said. 'All that she wishes shall be done.'

'Read one prayer over this grave; trace a cross upon this stone.'

'I will.'

She thanked me with a gesture, slightly bowed her head, drew her outer garment more closely round her, and moved away to a rising ground at some little distance. I was dismissed. I had no excuse for lingering - no right to prolong the interview - no business to remain there one moment longer. So I left her there, nor once looked back till I reached the last point from which I knew I should be able to see her. But when I turned for that last look, she was no longer in sight.

I had resolved to speak to her, and this was the result. A stranger interview never, surely, fell to the lot of man! I had said nothing that I meant to say - had learnt nothing that I sought to know. With regard to her circumstances, her place of residence, her very name, I was no wiser than before. And yet I had, perhaps, no reason to be dissatisfied. She had honoured me with her confidence, and entrusted to me a task of some difficulty and importance. It now only remained for me to execute that task as thoroughly and as quickly as possible. That done, I might fairly hope to win some place in her remembrance - by and by, perhaps, in her esteem.

Meanwhile, the old question rose again - whose grave could it be? I had settled this matter so conclusively in my own mind from the first, that I could scarcely believe even now that it was not her father's. Yet that he should have died a secret convert to Christianity was incredible. Whose grave could it be? A lover's? A Christian lover's? Alas! it might be. Or a sister's? In either of these cases it was more than probable that Salome was herself a convert. But I had no time to waste in conjecture. I must act, and act promptly.

I hastened back to Venice as fast as my gondolier could row me; and as we went along I promised myself that all her wishes should be carried out before she visited the spot again. To at once secure the services of a clergyman who would go with me to the Lido at early dawn, and there read some portion, at least, of the burial-service! and at the same time to engage a stonemason to cut the cross - to have all done before she, or anyone, should have approached the place next day, was my especial object. And that object I was resolved to carry out, though I had to search Venice through before I laid my head upon the pillow.

I found my clergyman without difficulty. He was a young man occupying rooms in the same hotel, and on the same floor as myself. I had met him each day at the table d'hote, and conversed with him once or twice in the reading-room. He was a North countryman, had not long since taken orders, and was both gentlemanly and obliging. He promised in the readiest manner to do all that I required, and to breakfast with me at six the next morning, in order that we might reach the cemetery by eight.

To find my stonemason, however, was not so easy; and yet I went to work methodically enough. I began with the Venetian Directory; then copied a list of stonemasons' names and addresses; then took a gondola a due rame, and started upon my voyage of discovery.

But a night's voyage of discovery among the intricate back canaletti of Venice is no very easy and no very safe enterprise. Narrow, tortuous, densely populated, often blocked by huge hay, wood, and provision barges, almost wholly unlighted, and so perplexingly alike that no mere novice in Venetian topography need ever hope to distinguish one from another, they baffle the very gondoliers, arid are a terra incognita to all but the dwellers therein.

I succeeded, however, in finding three of the places entered on my list. At the first I was told that the workman of whom I was in quest was working by the week somewhere over by Murano, and would not be back again till Saturday night. At the second and third, I found the men at home, supping with their wives and children at the end of the day's work; but neither would consent to undertake my commission. One, after a whispered consultation with his son, declined reluctantly. The other told me plainly that he dared not do it, and that he did not believe I should find a stonemason in Venice who would be bolder than himself.

The Jews, he said, were rich and powerful; no longer an oppressed people; no longer to be insulted even in Venice with impunity. To cut a Christian cross upon a Jewish headstone in the Jewish cemetery, would be 'a sort of sacrilege,' and punishable, no doubt, by the law. This sounded like truth; so finding that my rowers were by no means confident of their way, and that the canaletti were dark as the catacombs, I prevailed upon the stonemason to sell me a small mallet and a couple of chisels, and made up my mind to commit the sacrilege myself.

With this single exception, all was done next morning as I had planned to do. My new acquaintance breakfasted with me, accompanied me to the Lido, read such portions of the burial-service as seemed proper to him, and then, having business in Venice, left me to my task. It was by no means an easy one. To a skilled hand it would have been, perhaps, the work of half an hour; but it was my first effort, and rude as the thing was - a mere grooved attempt at a Latin cross, about two inches and a half in length, cut close at the bottom of the stone, where it could be easily concealed by a little piling of the sand - it took me nearly four hours to complete. While I was at work, the dull grey morning grew duller and greyer; a thick sea fog drove up from the Adriatic, and a low moaning wind came and went like the echo of a distant requiem. More than once I started, believing that she had surprised me there - fancying I saw the passing of a shadow - heard the rustling of a garment - the breathing of a sigh. But no. The mists and the moaning wind deceived me. I was alone.

When at length I got back to my hotel, it was just two o'clock. The hall-porter put a letter into my hand as I passed through. One glance at that crabbed superscription was enough. It was from Padua. I hastened to my room, tore open the envelope, and read these words:

'CARO SIGNORE,

The rubbing you send is neither ancient nor curious, as I fear you suppose it to be. Aftro; it is of yesterday. It merely records that one Salome, the only and beloved child of a certain Isaac da Costa, died last autumn on the eighteenth of October, aged twenty-one years, and that by the said Isaac da Costa this monument is erected to the memory of her virtues and his grief.

I pray you *cam signore,* to receive the assurance of my sincere esteem.

NICOLO NICOLAI

Padua, April 27th, 1857.'

The letter dropped from my hand. I seemed to have read without understanding it. I picked it up; went through it again, word by word; sat down; rose up; took a turn across the room; felt confused, bewildered, incredulous.

Could there, then, be two Salomes? Or was there some radical and extraordinary mistake?

I hesitated; I knew not what to do. Should I go down to the Merceria, and see whether the name of da Costa was known in the quartier? Or find out the registrar of births and deaths for the Jewish district? Or call upon the principal rabbi, and learn from him who this second Salome had been, and in what degree of relationship she stood towards the Salome whom I knew? I decided upon the last course. The chief rabbi's address was easily obtained. He lived in an ancient house on the Giudecca, and there I found him - a grave, stately old man, with a grizzled beard reaching nearly to his waist.

I introduced myself, and stated my business. I came to ask if he could give me any information respecting the late Salome da Costa, who died on the 18th of October last, and was buried on the Lido.

The rabbi replied that he had no doubt he could give me any information I desired, as he had known the lady personally, and was the intimate friend of her father.

'Can you tell me,' I asked, 'whether she had any dear friend or female relative of the same name - Salome?' the rabbi shook his head.

'I think not,' he said. 'I remember no other maiden of that name.'

'Pardon me, but I know there was another,' I replied. 'There was a very beautiful Salome living in the Merceria when I was last in Venice, just this time last year.'

'Salome da Costa was very fair,' said the rabbi; 'and she dwelt with her father in the Merceria. Since her death, he hath removed to the neighbourhood of the Rialto.'

'This Salome's father was a dealer in Oriental goods,' I said, hastily.

'Isaac da Costa is a dealer in Oriental goods,' replied the old man very gently. 'We are speaking, my son, of the same persons.'

'Impossible!'

He shook his head again.

'But she lives!' I exclaimed, becoming greatly agitated. 'She lives. I have seen her. I have spoken to her. I saw her only last evening.'

'Nay,' he said compassionately, 'this is some dream. She of whom you speak is indeed no more.'

'I saw her only last evening,' I repeated.

"Where did you suppose you beheld her?'

'On the Lido.'

'On the Lido?'

'And she spoke to me. I heard her voice - heard it as distinctly as I hear my own at this moment.'

The rabbi stroked his beard thoughtfully, and looked at me. 'You think you heard her voice!' he ejaculated. 'That is strange. What said she?'

I was about to answer. I checked myself - a sudden thought flashed upon me, and I trembled from head to foot.

'Have you - have you any reason for supposing that she died a Christian?' I faltered.

The old man started, and changed colour.

'I -I - that is a strange question,' he stammered. 'Why do you ask it?'

'Yes or no?' I cried wildly. 'Yes or no?'

He frowned, looked down, hesitated. 'I admit,' he said, after a moment or two - 'I admit that I may have heard something tending that way. It may be that the maiden cherished some secret doubt. Yet she was no professed Christian.'

*Laid in earth without one Christian prayer; with Hebrew rites; in a Hebrew sanctuary!* I repeated to myself.

'But I marvel how you come to have heard of this,' continued the rabbi. 'It was known only to her father and myself.'

'Sir,' I said solemnly, 'I know now that Salome da Costa is dead; I have seen her spirit thrice, haunting the spot where—'

My voice broke. I could not utter the words.

'Last evening, at sunset,' I resumed, 'was the third time. Never doubting that - that I indeed beheld her in the flesh, I spoke to her. She answered me. She - she told me this.'

The rabbi covered his face with his hands, and so remained for some time, lost in meditation. 'Young man,' he said at length, 'your story is strange, and you bring strange evidence to bear upon it. It may be as you say; it may be that you are the dupe of some waking dream - I know not.'

He knew not; but I - ah! I knew, only too well. I knew now why she had appeared to me clothed with such unearthly beauty. I understood now that look of dumb entreaty in her eyes - that tone of strange remoteness in her voice. The sweet soul could not rest amid the dust of its kinsfolk, 'unhoused, unanointed, unaneal'd', lacking even 'one Christian prayer' above its grave. And now - was it all over? Should I never see her more?

Never - ah! Never. How I haunted the Lido at sunset for many a month, till spring had blossomed into autumn, and autumn had ripened into summer; how I wandered back to Venice year after year, at the same season, while yet any vestige of that wild hope remained alive; how my heart has never throbbed, my pulse never leaped, for love of mortal woman since that time - are details into which I need not enter here. Enough that I watched and waited but that her gracious spirit appeared to me no more. I wait still, but I watch no longer. I know now that our place of meeting will not be here.

# THE BLACK CAT

## EDGAR ALLAN POE

For the most wild yet most homely narrative which I am about to pen, I neither expect nor solicit belief. Mad indeed would I be to expect it, in a case where my very senses reject their own evidence. Yet, mad am I not—and very surely do I not dream. But tomorrow I die, and today I would unburden my soul. My immediate purpose is to place before the world, plainly, succinctly, and without comment, a series of mere household events. In their consequences, these events have terrified—have tortured—have destroyed me. Yet I will not attempt to expound them. To me, they have presented little but horror—to many they will seem less terrible than *baroques*. Hereafter, perhaps, some intellect may be found which will reduce my phantasm to the commonplace—some intellect more calm, more logical, and far less excitable than my own, which will perceive, in the circumstances I detail with awe, nothing more than an ordinary succession of very natural causes and effects.

From my infancy I was noted for the docility and humanity of my disposition. My tenderness of heart was even so conspicuous as to make me the jest of my companions. I was especially fond of animals, and was indulged by my parents with a great variety of pets. With these I spent most of my time, and never was so happy as when feeding and caressing them. This peculiarity of character grew with my growth, and, in my manhood, I derived from it one of my principal sources of pleasure. To those who have cherished an affection for a faithful and sagacious dog, I need hardly be at the trouble of explaining the. nature or the intensity of the gratification thus derivable. There is something in the unselfish and self-sacrificing love of a brute, which goes directly to the heart of him who has had frequent occasion to test the paltry friendship and gossamer fidelity of mere *man*.

I married early, and was happy to find in my wife a disposition not uncongenial with my own. Observing my partiality for domestic pets, she lost no opportunity of procuring those of the most agreeable kind. We had birds, goldfish, a fine dog, rabbits, a small monkey, and a *cat*.

This latter was a remarkably large and beautiful animal, entirely black, and sagacious to an astonishing degree. In speaking of his intelligence, my wife, who at heart was not a little tinctured with superstition, made frequent allusion to the ancient popular notion, which regarded all black cats as witches in disguise. Not that she was ever *serious* upon this point—and I mention the matter at all for no better reason that that it happens, just now, to be remembered.

Pluto—this was the cat's name—was my favorite pet and playmate. I alone fed him, and he attended me wherever I went about the house. It was even with difficulty that I could prevent him from following me through the streets.

Our friendship lasted, in this manner, for several years, during which my general temperament and character—through the instrumentality of the Fiend Intemperance had (I blush to confess it) experienced a radical alteration for the worse. I grew, day by day, more moody, more irritable, more regardless of the feelings of others. I suffered myself to use intemperate language to my wife. At length, I even offered her personal violence. My pets, of course, were made to feel the change in my disposition. I not only neglected, but ill-used them. For Pluto, however, I still retained sufficient regard to restrain me from maltreating him, as I made no scruple of maltreating the rabbits, the monkey, or even the dog, when, by accident, or through affection, they came in my way. But my disease grew upon me—for what disease is like alcohol—and at length even Pluto, who was now becoming old, and consequently somewhat peevish—even Pluto began to experience the effects of my ill temper.

One night, returning home, much intoxicated, from one of my haunts about town, I fancied that the cat avoided my presence. I seized him; when, in his fright at my violence, he inflicted a slight wound upon my hand with his teeth. The fury of a demon instantly possessed me. I knew myself no longer. My original soul seemed, at once, to take its flight from my body; and a more than fiendish malevolence, gin-nurtured, thrilled every fibre of my frame. I took from my waistcoat-pocket a penknife, opened it, grasped the poor beast by the throat, and deliberately cut one of its eyes from the socket! I blush, I burn, I shudder, while I pen the damnable atrocity.

When reason returned with the morning—when I had slept off the fumes of the night's debauch—I experienced a sentiment half of horror, half of remorse, for the crime of which I had been guilty; but it was, at best, a feeble and equivocal feeling, and the soul remained untouched. I again plunged into excess, and soon drowned in wine all memory of the deed.

In the meantime the cat slowly recovered. The socket of the lost eye presented, it is true, a frightful appearance, but he no longer appeared to suffer any pain. He went about the house as usual, but, as might be expected, fled in extreme terror at my approach. I had so much of my old heart left, as to be at first grieved by this evident dislike on the part of a creature which had once so loved me. But this feeling soon gave place to irritation. And then came, as if to my final and irrevocable overthrow, the spirit of *Perverseness*. Of this spirit philosophy takes no account. Yet I am not more sure that my soul lives, than I am that perverseness is one of the primitive impulses of the human heart—one of the indivisible primary faculties, or sentiments, which give direction to the character of Man. Who has not, a hundred times, found himself committing a vile or a stupid action, for no other reason than because he knows he should *not*? Have we not a perpetual inclination, in the teeth of our best judgment, to violate that which is *Law,* merely because we understand it to be such? This spirit of perverseness, I say, came to my final overthrow. It was this unfathomable longing of the soul to *vex itself*—to offer violence to its own nature—to do wrong for the wrong's sake only—that urged me to continue and finally to consummate the injury I had inflicted upon the unoffending brute. One morning, in cold blood, I slipped a noose about its neck and hung it to the limb of a tree;—hung it with the tears streaming from my eyes, and with the bitterest remorse at my heart;—hung it *because* I knew that it had loved me, and *because* I felt it had given me no reason of offence;—hung it *because* I knew that in so doing I was committing a sin—a deadly sin that would so jeopardize my immortal soul as to place it—if such a thing were possible—even beyond the reach of the infinite mercy of the Most Merciful and Most Terrible God.

On the night of the day on which this most cruel deed was done, I was aroused from sleep by the cry of fire. The curtains of my bed were in flames. The whole house was blazing. It was with great difficulty that my wife, a servant, and myself, made our escape from the conflagration. The destruction was complete. My entire worldly wealth was swallowed up, and I resigned myself thenceforward to despair.

I am above the weakness of seeking to establish a sequence of cause and effect, between the disaster and the atrocity. But I am detailing a chain of facts—and wish not to leave even a possible link imperfect. On the day succeeding the fire, I visited the ruins. The walls, with one exception, had fallen in. This exception was found in a compartment wall, not very thick, which stood about the middle of the house, and against which had rested the head of my bed. The plastering had here, in great measure, resisted the action of the fire—a fact which I attributed to its having been recently spread. About this wall a dense crowd were collected, and many persons seemed to be examining a particular portion of it with very minute and eager attention. The words "strange!" "singular!" and other similar expressions, excited my curiosity. I approached and saw, as if graven in *bas-relief* upon the white surface, the figure of a gigantic *cat*. The impression was given with an accuracy truly marvellous. There was a rope about the animal's neck.

When I first beheld this apparition—for I could scarcely regard it as less—my wonder and my terror were extreme. But at length reflection came to my aid. The cat, I remembered, had been hung in a garden adjacent to the house. Upon the alarm of fire, this garden had been immediately filled by the crowd—by some one of whom the animal must have been cut from the tree and thrown, through an open window, into my chamber. This had probably been done with the view of arousing me from sleep. The falling of other walls had compressed the victim of my cruelty into the substance of the freshly-spread plaster; the lime of which, with the flames, and the *ammonia* from the carcass, had then accomplished the portraiture as I saw it.

Although I thus readily accounted to my reason, if not altogether to my conscience, for the startling fact just detailed, it did not the less fail to make a deep impression upon my fancy. For months I could not rid myself of the phantasm of the cat; and, during this period, there came back into my spirit a half-sentiment that seemed, but was not, remorse. I went so far as to regret the loss of the animal, and to look about me, among the vile haunts which I now habitually frequented, for another pet of the same species, and of somewhat similar appearance, with which to supply its place.

One night as I sat, half stupefied, in a den of more than infamy, my attention was suddenly drawn to some black object, reposing upon the head of one of the immense hogsheads of gin, or of rum, which constituted the chief furniture of the apartment. I had been looking steadily at the top of this hogshead for some minutes, and what now caused me surprise was the fact that I had not sooner perceived the object thereupon. I approached it, and touched it with my hand. It was a black cat—a very large one—fully as large as Pluto, and closely resembling him in every respect but one. Pluto had not a white hair upon any portion of his body; but this cat had a large, although indefinite splotch of white, covering nearly the whole region of the breast.

Upon my touching him, he immediately arose, purred loudly, rubbed against my hand, and appeared delighted with my notice.

This, then, was the very creature of which I was in search. I at once offered to purchase it of the landlord; but this person made no claim to it—knew nothing of it—had never seen it before.

I continued my caresses, and when I prepared to go home, the animal evinced a disposition to accompany me. I permitted it to do so; occasionally stooping and patting it as I proceeded. When it reached the house it domesticated itself at once, and became immediately a great favorite with my wife.

For my own part, I soon found a dislike to it arising within me. This was just the reverse of what I had anticipated; but—I know not how or why it was—its evident fondness for myself rather disgusted and annoyed me. By slow degrees these feelings of disgust and annoyance rose into the bitterness of hatred. I avoided the creature; a certain sense of shame, and the remembrance of my former deed of cruelty, preventing me from physically abusing it. I did not, for some weeks, strike, or otherwise violently ill use it; but gradually—very gradually—I came to look upon it with unutterable loathing, and to flee silently from its odious presence, as from the breath of a pestilence.

What added, no doubt, to my hatred of the beast, was the discovery, on the morning after I brought it home, that, like Pluto, it also had been deprived of one of its eyes. This circumstance, however, only endeared it to my wife, who, as I have already said, possessed, in a high degree, that humanity of feeling which had once been my distinguishing trait, and the source of many of my simplest and purest pleasures.

With my aversion to this cat, however, its partiality for myself seemed to increase. It followed my footsteps with a pertinacity which it would be difficult to make the reader comprehend. Whenever I sat, it would crouch beneath my chair, or spring upon my knees, covering me with its loathsome caresses. If I arose to walk it would get between my feet and thus nearly throw me down, or, fastening its long and sharp claws in my dress, clamber, in this manner, to my breast. At such times, although I longed to destroy it with a blow, I was yet withheld from so doing, partly by a memory of my former crime, but chiefly—let me confess it at once—by absolute *dread* of the beast.

This dread was not exactly a dread of physical evil—and yet I should be at a loss how otherwise to define it. I am almost ashamed to own-yes, even in this felon's cell, I am almost ashamed to own—that the terror and horror with which the animal inspired me, had been heightened by one of the merest chimeras it would be possible to conceive. My wife had called my attention, more than once, to the character of the mark of white hair, of which I have spoken, and which constituted the sole visible difference between the strange beast and the one I had destroyed. The reader will remember that this mark, although large, had been originally very indefinite; but, by slow degrees—degrees nearly imperceptible, and which for a long time my reason struggled to reject as fanciful-it had, at length, assumed a rigorous distinctness of outline. It was now the representation of an object that I shudder to name-and for this, above all, I loathed, and dreaded, and would have rid myself of the monster *had I dared* —it was now, I say, the image of a hideous—of a ghastly thing— of the *Gallows!*—oh, mournful and terrible engine of Horror and of Crime—of Agony and of Death!

And now was I indeed wretched beyond the wretchedness of mere Humanity. And *a brute beast*—whose fellow I had contemptuously destroyed—a *brute beast* to work out for me—for me, a man fashioned in the image of the High God—so much of insufferable woe! Alas! Neither by day nor by night knew I the blessing of rest any more! During the former the creature left me no moment alone, and in the latter I started hourly from dreams of unutterable fear to find the hot breath of *the thing* upon my face, and its vast weight—an incarnate nightmare that I had no power to shake off—incumbent eternally upon my *heart!*

Beneath the pressure of torments such as these the feeble remnant of the good within me succumbed. Evil thoughts became my sole intimates-the darkest and most evil of thoughts. The moodiness of my usual temper increased to hatred of all things and of all mankind; while from the sudden, frequent, and ungovernable outbursts of a fury to which I now blindly abandoned myself, my uncomplaining wife, alas, was the most usual and the most patient of sufferers.

One day she accompanied me, upon some household errand, into the cellar of the old building which our poverty compelled us to inhabit. The cat followed me down the steep stairs, and, nearly throwing me headlong, exasperated me to madness. Uplifting an axe, and forgetting in my wrath the childish dread which had hitherto stayed my hand, I aimed a blew at the animal, which, of course, would have proved instantly fatal had it descended as I wished. But this blow was arrested by the hand of my wife. Goaded by the interference into a rage more than demoniacal, I withdrew my arm from her grasp and buried the axe in her brain. She fell dead upon the spot without a groan.

This hideous murder accomplished, I set myself forthwith, and with entire deliberation, to the task of concealing the body. I knew that I could not remove it from the house, either by day or by night, without the risk of being observed by the neighbors. Many projects entered my mind. At one period I thought of cutting the corpse into minute fragments, and destroying them by fire. At another, I resolved to dig a grave for it in the floor of the cellar. Again, I deliberated about casting it in the well in the yard—about packing it in a box, as if merchandise, with the usual arrangements, and so getting a porter to take it from the house. Finally I hit upon what I considered a far better expedient than either of these. I determined to wall it up in the cellar, as the monks of the Middle Ages are recorded to have walled up their victims.

For a purpose such as this the cellar was well adapted. Its walls were loosely constructed, and had lately been plastered throughout with a rough plaster, which the dampness of the atmosphere had prevented from hardening. Moreover, in one of the walls was a projection, caused by a false chimney, or fireplace, that had been filled up and made to resemble the rest of the cellar. I made no doubt that I could readily displace the bricks at this point, insert the corpse, and wall the whole up as before, so that no eye could detect anything suspicious.

And in this calculation I was not deceived. By means of a crowbar I easily dislodged the bricks, and, having carefully deposited the body against the inner wall, I propped it in that position, while with little trouble I relaid the whole structure as it originally stood. Having procured mortar, sand, and hair, with every possible precaution, I prepared a plaster which could not be distinguished from the old, and with this I very carefully went over the new brick-work. When I had finished, I felt satisfied that all was right. The wall did not present the slightest appearance of having been disturbed. The rubbish on the floor was picked up with the minutest care. I looked around triumphantly, and said to myself: "Here at least, then, my labor has not been in vain."

My next step was to look for the beast which had been the cause of so much wretchedness; for I had, at length, firmly resolved to put it to death. Had I been able to meet with it at the moment, there could have been no doubt of its fate; but it appeared that the crafty animal had been alarmed at the violence of my previous anger, and forbore to present itself in my present mood. It is impossible to describe or to imagine the deep, the blissful sense of relief which the absence of the detested creature occasioned in my bosom. It did not make its appearance during the night; and thus for one night, at least, since its introduction into the house, I soundly and tranquilly slept; aye, *slept* even with the burden of murder upon my soul.

The second and the third day passed, and still my tormentor came not. Once again I breathed as a freeman. The monster, in terror, had fled the premises for ever! I should behold it no more! My happiness was supreme! The guilt of my dark deed disturbed me but little. Some few inquiries had been made, but these had been readily answered. Even a search had been instituted—but of course nothing was to be discovered. I looked upon my future felicity as secured.

Upon the fourth day of the assassination, a party of the police came, very unexpectedly, into the house, and proceeded again to make rigorous investigation of the premises. Secure, however, in the inscrutability of my place of concealment, I felt no embarrassment whatever. The officers bade me accompany them in their search. They left no nook or corner unexplored. At length, for the third or fourth time, they descended into the cellar. I quivered not in a muscle. My heart beat calmly as that of one who slumbers in innocence. I walked the cellar from end to end. I folded my arms upon my bosom, and roamed easily to and fro. The police were thoroughly satisfied and prepared to depart. The glee at my heart was too strong to be restrained. I burned to say if but one word, by way of triumph, and to render doubly sure their assurance of my guiltlessness.

"Gentlemen," I said at last, as the party ascended the steps, "I delight to have allayed your suspicions. I wish you all health and a little more courtesy. By the bye, gentlemen, this—this is a very well-constructed house," (in the rabid desire to say something easily, I scarcely knew what I uttered at all),—"I may say an *excellently* well-constructed house. These walls—are you going, gentlemen?—these walls are solidly put together"; and here, through the mere frenzy of bravado, I rapped heavily with a cane which I held in my hand, upon that very portion of the brick-work behind which stood the corpse of the wife of my bosom.

But may God shield and deliver me from the fangs of the Arch-Fiend! No sooner had the reverberation of my blows sunk into silence, than I was answered by a voice from within the tomb!— by a cry, at first muffled and broken, like the sobbing of a child, and then quickly swelling into one long, loud, and continuous scream, utterly anomalous and inhuman—a howl—a wailing shriek, half of horror and half of triumph, such as might have arisen only out of hell, conjointly from the throats of the damned in their agony and of the demons that exult in the damnation.

Of my own thoughts it is folly to speak. Swooning, I staggered to the opposite wall. For one instant the party on the stairs remained motionless, through extremity of terror and awe. In the next a dozen stout arms were toiling at the wall. It fell bodily. The corpse, already greatly decayed and clotted with gore, stood erect before the eyes of the spectators. Upon its head, with red extended mouth and solitary eye of fire, sat the hideous beast whose craft had seduced me into murder, and whose informing voice had consigned me to the hangman. I had walled the monster up within the tomb.

# JOHN CHARRINGTON'S WEDDING

## E. NESBIT

No one ever thought that May Forster would marry John Charrington; but he thought differently, and things which John Charrington intended had a queer way of coming to pass. He asked her to marry him before he went up to Oxford. She laughed and refused him. He asked her again next time he came home. Again she laughed, tossed her dainty blonde head, and again refused. A third time he asked her; she said it was becoming a confirmed bad habit, and laughed at him more than ever.

John was not the only man who wanted to marry her: she was the belle of our village *coterie,* and we were all in love with her more or less; it was a sort of fashion, like heliotrope ties or Inverness capes. Therefore we were as much annoyed as surprised when John Gharrington walked into our little local Club—we held it in a loft over the saddler's, I remember—and invited us all to his wedding.

"Your wedding?"

"You don't mean it?"

"Who's the happy fair? When's it to be?"

John Gharrington filled his pipe and lighted it before he replied. Then he said:

"I'm sorry to deprive you fellows of your only joke—but Miss Forster and I are to be married in September."

"You don't mean it?"

"He's got the mitten again, and it's turned his head."

"No," I said, rising, "I see it's true. Lend me a pistol someone or a first class fare to the other end of Nowhere. Gharrington has bewitched the only pretty girl in pur twenty-mile radius. Was it mesmerism, or a love-potion, Jack?"

"Neither, sir, but a gift you'll never have—perseverance —and the best luck a man ever had in this world."

There was something in his voice that silenced me, and all chaff of the other fellows failed to draw him further.

The queer thing about it was that when we congratulated Miss Forster, she blushed and smiled and dimpled, for all the world as though she were in love with him, and had been in love with him all the time. Upon my word, I think she had. Women are strange creatures.

We were all asked to the wedding. In Brixham everyone who was anybody knew everybody else who was anyone. My sisters were, I truly believe, more interested in the *trousseau* than the bride herself, and I was to be best man. The coming marriage was much canvassed at afternoon tea-tables, and at our little Club over the saddler's, and the question was always asked: "Does she care for him?"

I used to ask that question myself in the early days of their engagement, but after a certain evening in August I never asked it again. I was coming home from the Club through the churchyard. Our church is on a thyme-grown hill, and the turf about it is so thick and soft that one's footsteps are noiseless.

I made no sound as I vaulted the low lichened wall, and threaded my way between the tombstones. It was at the same instant that I heard John Charrington's voice, and saw her. May was sitting on a low flat gravestone, her face turned towards the full splendour of the western sun. Its expression ended, at once and forever, any question of love for him; it was transfigured to a beauty I should not have believed possible, even to that beautiful little face.

John lay at her feet, and it was his voice that broke the stillness of the golden August evening.

"My dear, my dear, I believe I should come back from the dead if you wanted me!"

I coughed at once to indicate my presence, and passed on into the shadow fully enlightened.

The wedding was to be early in September. Two days before I had to run up to town on business. The train was late, of course, for we are on the South-Eastern, and as I stood grumbling with my watch in my hand, whom should I see but John Gharrington and May Forster. They were walking up and down the unfrequented end of the platform, arm in arm, looking into each other's eyes, careless of the sympathetic interest of the porters.

Of course I knew better than to hesitate a moment before burying myself in the booking-office, and it was not till the train drew up at the platform, that I obtrusively passed the pair with my Gladstone, and took the corner in a first-class smoking-carriage. I did this with as good an air of not seeing them as I could assume. I pride myself on my discretion, but if John were travelling alone I wanted his company. I had it.

"Hullo, old man," came his cheery voice as he swung his bag into my carriage; "here's luck; I was expecting a dull journey!"

"Where are you off to?" I asked, discretion still bidding me turn my eyes away, though I saw, without looking, that hers were red-rimmed.

"To old Branbridge's," he answered, shutting the door and leaning out for a last word with his sweetheart.

"Oh, I wish you wouldn't go, John," she was saying in a low, earnest voice. "I feel certain something will happen."

"Do you think I should let anything happen to keep me, and the day after tomorrow our wedding-day?"

"Don't go," she answered, with a pleading intensity which would have sent my Gladstone onto the platform and me after it. But she wasn't speaking to me. John Gharrington was made differently; he rarely changed his opinions, never his resolutions.

He only stroked the little ungloved hands that lay on the carriage door.

"I must, May. The old boy's been awfully good to me, and now he's dying I must go and see him, but I shall come home in time for—" the rest of the parting was lost in a whisper and in the rattling lurch of the starting train.

"You're sure to come?" she spoke as the train moved.

"Nothing shall keep me," he answered; and we steamed out. After he had seen the last of the little figure on the platform he leaned back in his corner and kept silence for a minute.

When he spoke it was to explain to me that his godfather, whose heir he was, lay dying at Peasmarsh Place, some fifty miles away, and had sent for John, and John had felt bound to go.

"I shall be surely back tomorrow," he said, "or, if not, the day after, in heaps of time. Thank Heaven, one hasn't to get up in the middle of the night to get married nowadays!"

"And suppose Mr. Branbridge dies?"

"Alive or dead I mean to be married on Thursday!" John answered, lighting a cigar and unfolding *The Times.*

At Peasmarsh station we said "good-bye," and he got out, and I saw him ride off; I went on to London, where I stayed the night.

When I got home the next afternoon, a very wet one, by the way, my sister greeted me with:

"Where's Mr. Charrington?"

"Goodness knows," I answered testily. Every man, since Cain, has resented that kind of question.

"I thought you might have heard from him," she went on, "as you're to give him away tomorrow."

"Isn't he back?" I asked, for I had confidently expected to find him at home.

"No, Geoffrey,"—my sister Fanny always had a way of jumping to conclusions, especially such conclusions as were least favourable to her fellow-creatures—"he has not returned, and, what is more, you may depend upon it he won't. You mark my words, there'll be no wedding tomorrow."

My sister Fanny has a power of annoying me which no other human being possesses.

"You mark my words," I retorted with asperity, "you had better give up making such a thundering idiot of yourself. There'll be more wedding tomorrow than ever you'll take the first part in." A prophecy which, by the way, came true.

But though I could snarl confidently to my sister, I did not feel so comfortable when late that night, I, standing on the doorstep of John's house, heard that he had not returned. I went home gloomily through the rain. Next morning brought a brilliant blue sky, gold sun, and all such softness of air and beauty of cloud as go to make up a perfect day. I woke with a vague feeling of having gone to bed anxious, and of being rather averse to facing that anxiety in the light of full wakefulness.

But with my shaving-water came a note from John which relieved my mind and sent me up to the Forster's with a light heart.

May was in the garden. I saw her blue gown through the hollyhocks as the lodge gates swung to behind me. So I did not go up to the house, but turned aside down the turfed path.

"He's written to you too," she said, without preliminary greeting, when I reached her side.

"Yes, I'm to meet him at the station at three, and come straight on to the church."

Her face looked pale, but there was a brightness in her eyes, and a tender quiver about the mouth that spoke of renewed happiness.

"Mr. Branbridge begged him so to stay another night that he had not the heart to refuse," she went on. "He is so kind, but I wish he hadn't stayed."

I was at the station at half-past two. I felt rather annoyed with John. It seemed a sort of slight to the beautiful girl who loved him, that he should come as it were out of breath, and with the dust of travel upon him, to take her hand, which some of us would have given the best years of our lives to take.

But when the three o'clock train glided in, and glided out again having brought no passengers to our little station, I was more than annoyed. There was no other train for thirty-five minutes; I calculated that, with much hurry, we might just get to the church in time for the ceremony; but, oh, what a fool to miss that first train! What other man could have done it?

That thirty-five minutes seemed a year, as I wandered round the station reading the advertisements and the timetables, and the company's bye-laws, and getting more and more angry with John Charrington. This confidence in his own power of getting everything he wanted the minute he wanted it was leading him too far. I hate waiting. Everyone does, but I believe I hate it more than anyone else. The three thirty-five was late, of course.

I ground my pipe between my teeth and stamped with impatience as I watched the signals. Click. The signal went down. Five minutes later I flung myself into the carriage that I had brought for John.

"Drive to the church!" I said, as someone shut the door. "Mr. Charrington hasn't come by this train."

Anxiety now replaced anger. What had become of the man? Could he have been taken suddenly ill? I had never known him have a day's illness in his life. And even so he might have telegraphed. Some awful accident must have happened to him. The thought that he had played her false never—no, not for a moment—entered my head. Yes, something terrible had happened to him, and on me lay the task of telling his bride. I almost wished the carriage would upset and break my head so that someone else might tell her, not I, who—but that's nothing to do with this story.

It was five minutes to four as we drew up at the churchyard gate. A double row of eager onlookers lined the path from lychgate to porch. I sprang from the carriage and passed up between them. Our gardener had a good front place near the door. I stopped.

"Are they waiting still, Byles?" I asked, simply to gain time, for of course I knew they were by the waiting crowd's attentive attitude.

"Waiting, sir? No, no, sir; why, it must be over by now."

"Over! Then Mr. Gharrington's come?"

"To the minute, sir; must have missed you somehow, and I say, sir," lowering his voice, "I never see Mr. John the least bit so afore, but my opinion is he's been drinking pretty free. His clothes was all dusty and his face like a sheet. I tell you I didn't like the looks of him at all, and the folks inside are saying all sorts of things. You'll see, something's gone very wrong with Mr. John, and he's tried liquor. He looked like a ghost, and in he went with his eyes straight before him, with never a look or a word for none of us: him that was always such a gentleman!"

I had never heard Byles make so long a speech. The crowd in the churchyard were talking in whispers and getting ready rice and slippers to throw at the bride and bridegroom. The ringers were ready with their hands on the ropes to ring out the merry peal as the bride and bridegroom should come out.

A murmur from the church announced them; out they came. Byles was right. John Gharrington did not look himself. There was dust on his coat, his hair was disarranged.

He seemed to have been in some row, for there was a black mark above his eyebrow. He was deathly pale. But his pallor was not greater than that of the bride, who might have been carved in ivory—dress, veil, orange blossoms, face and all.

As they passed out the ringers stooped—there were six of them—and then, on the ears expecting the gay wedding peal, came the slow tolling of the passing bell.

A thrill of horror at so foolish a jest from the ringers passed through us all. But the ringers themselves dropped the ropes and fled like rabbits out into the sunlight. The bride shuddered, and grey shadows came about her mouth, but the bridegroom led her on down the path where the people stood with the handfuls of rice; but the handfuls were never thrown, and the wedding-bells never rang. In vain the ringers were urged to remedy their mistake: they protested with many whispered expletives that they would see themselves further first.

In a hush like the hush in the chamber of death the bridal pair passed into their carriage and its door slammed behind them.

Then the tongues were loosed. A babel of anger, wonder, conjecture from the guests and the spectators.

"If I'd seen his condition, sir," said old Forster to me as we drove off, "I would have stretched him on the floor of the church, sir, by Heaven I would, before I'd have let him marry my daughter!"

Then he put his head out of the window.

"Drive like hell," he cried to the coachman; "don't spare the horses."

He was obeyed. We passed the bride's carriage. I forbore to look at it, and old Forster turned his head away and swore. We reached home before it.

We stood in the hall doorway, in the blazing afternoon sun, and in about half a minute we heard wheels crunching the gravel. When the carriage stopped in front of the steps old Forster and I ran down.

"Great Heaven, the carriage is empty! And yet—"

I had the door open in a minute, and this is what I saw—

No sign of John Charrington; and of May, his wife, only a huddled heap of white satin lying half on the floor of the carriage and half on the seat.

"I drove straight here, sir," said the coachman, as the bride's father lifted her out; "and I'll swear no-one got out of the carriage."

We carried her into the house in her bridal dress and drew back her veil. I saw her face. Shall I ever forget it? White, white and drawn with agony and horror, bearing such a look of terror as I have never seen since except in dreams. And her hair, her radiant blonde hair, I tell you it was white like snow.

As we stood, her father and I, half mad with the horror and mystery of it, a boy came up the avenue—a telegraph boy. They brought the orange envelope to me. I tore it open.

*Mr. Charrington was thrown from the dogcart on his way to the station at half-past one. Killed on the spot!*

And he was married to May Forster in our parish church at *half-past three*, in presence of half the parish.

*"I shall be married, dead or alive!"*

What had passed in that carriage on the homeward drive? No one knows—no one will ever know. Oh, May! Oh, my dear!

Before a week was over they laid her beside her husband in our little churchyard on the thyme-covered hill—the churchyard where they had kept their love-trysts.

Thus was accomplished John Charrington's wedding.

# THE OLD NURSE'S STORY
## ELIZABETH GASKELL

You know, my dears, that your mother was an orphan, and an only child; and I dare say you have heard that your grandfather was a clergyman up in Westmoreland, where I come from. I was just a girl in the village school, when, one day, your grandmother came in to ask the mistress if there was any scholar there who would do for a nurse-maid; and mighty proud I was, I can tell ye, when the mistress called me up, and spoke to my being a good girl at my needle, and a steady honest girl, and one whose parents were very respectable, though they might be poor. I thought I should like nothing better than to serve the pretty young lady, who was blushing as deep as I was, as she spoke of the coming baby, and what I should have to do with it. However, I see you don't care so much for this part of my story, as for what you think is to come, so I'll tell you at once. I was engaged and settled at the parsonage before Miss Rosamond (that was the baby, who is now your mother) was born. To be sure, I had little enough to do with her when she came, for she was never out of her mother's arms, and slept by her all night long; and proud enough was I sometimes when missis trusted her to me. There never was such a baby before or since, though you've all of you been fine enough in your turns; but for sweet, winning ways, you've none of you come up to your mother. She took after her mother, who was a real lady born; a Miss Furnivall, a granddaughter of Lord Furriivall's, in Northumberland. I believe she had neither brother nor sister, and had been brought up in my lord's family till she had married your grandfather, who was just a curate, son to a shopkeeper in Carlisle—but a clever, fine gentleman as ever was—and one who was a right-down hard worker in his parish, which was very wide, and scattered all abroad over the Westmoreland Fells. When your mother, little Miss Rosamond, was about four or five years old, both her parents died in a fortnight one after the other. Ah! That was a sad time. My pretty young mistress and me was looking for another baby, when my master came home from one of his long rides, wet, and tired, and took the fever he died of; and then she never held up her head again, but just lived to see her dead baby, and have it laid on her breast before she sighed away her life. My mistress had asked me, on her death-bed, never to leave Miss Rosamond; but if she had never spoken a word, I would have gone with the little child to the end of the world.

The next thing, and before we had well stilled our sobs, the executors and guardians came to settle the affairs. They were my poor young mistress's own cousin, Lord Furnivall, and Mr. Esthwaite, my master's brother, a shopkeeper in Manchester; not so well-to-do then as he was afterwards, and with a large family rising about him. Well! I don't know if it were their settling, or because of a letter my mistress wrote on her death-bed to her cousin, my lord; but somehow it was settled that Miss Rosamond and me were to go to Furnivall Manor House, in Northumberland, and my lord spoke as if it had been her mother's wish that she should live with his family, and as if he had no objections, for that one or two more or less could make no difference in so grand a household. So though that was not the way in which I should have wished the coming of my bright and pretty pet to have been looked at—who was like a sunbeam in any family, be it never so grand I was well pleased that all the folks in the Dale should stare and admire, when they heard I was going to be the young lady's maid at my Lord Furnivall's at Furnivall Manor.

But I made a mistake in thinking we were to go and live where my lord did. It turned out that the family had left Furnivall Manor House fifty years or more. I could not hear that my poor young mistress had ever been there, though she had been brought up in the family; and I was sorry for that, for I should have liked Miss Rosamond's youth to have passed where her mother's had been.

My lord's gentleman, from whom I asked so many questions as I durst, said that the Manor House was at the foot of the Cumberland Fells, and a very grand place; that an old Miss Furnivall, a great-aunt of my lord's, lived there, with only a few servants; but that it was a very healthy place, and my lord had thought that it would suit Miss Rosamond very well for a few years, and that her being there might perhaps amuse his old aunt.

I was bidden by my lord to have Miss Rosamond's things ready by a certain day. He was a stern proud man, as they say all the Lords Furnivall were; and he never spoke a word more than was necessary. Folk did say he had loved my young mistress; but that, because she knew that his father would object, she would never listen to him, and married Mr. Esthwaite; but I don't know. He never married, at any rate. But he never took much notice of Miss Rosamond; which I thought he might have done if he had cared for her dead mother. He sent his gentleman with us to the Manor House, telling him to join him at Newcastle that same evening; so there was no great length of time for him to make us known to all the strangers before he, too, shook us off; and we were left, two lonely young things (I was not eighteen), in the great old Manor House. It seems like yesterday that we drove there. We had left our own dear parsonage very early, and we had both cried as if our hearts would break, though we were travelling in my lord's carriage, which I thought so much of once. And now it was long past noon on a September day, and we stopped to change horses for the last time at a little smoky town, all full of colliers and miners. Miss Rosamond had fallen asleep, but Mr. Henry told me to waken her, that she might see the park and the Manor House as we drove up. I thought it rather a pity; but I did what he bade me, for fear he should complain of me to my lord. We had left all signs of a town, or even a village, and were then inside the gates of a large wild park—not like the parks here in the north, but with rocks, and the noise of running water, and gnarled thorn-trees, and old oaks, all white and peeled with age.

The road went up abdut two miles, and then we saw a great and stately house, with many trees close around it, so close that in some places their branches dragged against the walls when the wind blew; and some hung broken down; for no one seemed to take much charge of the place; to lop the wood, or to keep the moss-covered carriageway in order. Only in front of the house all was clear. The great oval drive was without a weed; and neither tree nor creeper was allowed to grow over the long, many-windowed front; at both sides of which a wing projected, which were each the ends of other side fronts; for the house, although it was so desolate, was even grander than I expected. Behind it rose the Fells, which seemed unenclosed and bare enough; and on the left hand of the house, as you stood facing it, was a little, old-fashioned flower-garden, as I found out afterwards. A door opened out upon it from the west front; it had been scooped out of the thick dark wood for some old Lady Furnivall; but the branches of the great forest trees had grown and overshadowed it again, and there were very few flowers that would live there at that time.

When we drove up to the great front entrance, and went into the hall, I thought we should be lost—it was so large, and vast, and grand. There was a chandelier all of bronze, hung down from the middle of the ceiling; and I had never seen one before, and looked at it all in amaze. Then, at one end of the hall, was a great fireplace, as large as the sides of the houses in my country, with massy andirons and dogs to hold the wood; and by it were heavy old-fashioned sofas. At the opposite end of the hall, to the left as you went in on the western side, was an organ built into the wall, and so large that it filled up the best part of that end.

Beyond it, on the same side, was a door; and opposite, on each side of the fireplace, were also doors leading to the east front; but those I never went through as long as I stayed in the house; so I can't tell you what lay beyond.

The afternoon was closing in, and the hall, which had no fire lighted in it, looked dark and gloomy, but we did not stay there a moment. The old servant, who had opened the door for us, bowed to Mr. Henry, and took us in through the door at the further side of the great organ, and led us through several smaller halls and passages into the west drawing-room, where he said that Miss Furnivall was sitting. Poor little Miss Rosamond held very tight to me, as if she were scared and lost in that great place, and as for myself, I was not much better. The west drawing-room was very cheerful-looking, with a warm fire in it, and plenty of good, comfortable furniture about. Miss Furnivall was an old lady not far from eighty, I should think, but I do not know. She was thin and tall, and had a face as full of fine wrinkles as if they had been drawn all over it with a needle's point. Her eyes were very watchful, to make up, I suppose, for her being so deaf as to be obliged to use a trumpet. Sitting with her, working at the same great piece of tapestry, was Mrs. Stark, her maid and companion, and almost as old as she was. She had lived with Miss Furnivall ever since they were both young, and now she seemed more like a friend than a servant; she looked so cold and grey, and stony as if she had never loved or cared for any one; and I don't suppose she did care for any one, except her mistress; and, owing to the great deafness of the latter, Mrs. Stark treated her very much as if she were a child. Mr. Henry gave some message from my lord, and then he bowed good-bye to us all, - taking no notice of my sweet little Miss Rosamond's outstretched hand - and left us standing there, being looked at by the two old ladies through their spectacles.

I was right glad when they rung for the old footman who had shown us in at first, and told him to take us to our rooms. So we went out of that great drawing-room, and into another sitting-room, and out of that, and then up a great flight of stain, and along a broad gallery—which was something like a library, having books all down one side, and windows and writing-tables all down the other—till we came to our rooms, which I was not sorry to hear were just over the kitchens; for I began to think I should be lost in that wilderness of a house. There was an old nursery that had been used for all the little lords and ladies long ago, with a pleasant fire burning in the grate, and the kettle boiling on the hob, and tea-things spread out on the table; and out of that room was the night-nursery, with a little crib for Miss Rosamond close to my bed. And old James called up Dorothy, his wife, to bid us welcome; and both he and she were so hospitable and kind, that by and by Miss Rosamond and me felt quite at home; and by the time tea was over, she was sitting on Dorothy's knee, and chattering away as fast as her little tongue could go. I soon found out that Dorothy was from Westmoreland, and that bound her and me together, as it were; and I would never wish to meet with kinder people than were old James and his wife. James had lived pretty nearly all his life in my lord's family, and thought there was no one so grand as they. He even looked down a little on his wife; because, till he had married her, she had never lived in any but a farmer's household. But he was very fond of her, as well he might be. They had one servant under them, to do all the rough work. Agnes they called her; and she and me, and James and Dorothy, with Miss Furnivall and Mrs. Stark, made up the family; always remembering my sweet little Miss Rosamond! I used to wonder what they had done before she came, they thought so much of her now. Kitchen and drawing-room, it was all the same. The hard, sad Miss Furnivall, and the cold Mrs. Stark, looked pleased when she came fluttering in like a bird, playing and pranking hither and thither, with a continual murmur, and pretty prattle of gladness. I am sure, they were sorry many a time when she flitted away into the kitchen, though they were too proud to ask her to stay with them, and were a little surprised at her taste; though to be sure, as Mrs. Stark said it was not to be wondered at, remembering what stock her father had come of. The great, old rambling house was a famous place for little Miss Rosamond. She made expeditions all over it, with me at her heels; all, except the east wing, which was never opened, and whither we never thought of going. But in the western and northern part was many a pleasant room; full of things that were curiosities to us, though they might not have been to people who had seen more. The windows were darkened by the sweeping boughs of the trees, and the ivy which had overgrown them: but, in the green gloom, we could manage to see old China jars and carved ivory boxes, and great heavy boob, and, above all, the old pictures!

Once, I remember, my darling would have Dorothy go with us to tell us who they all were; for they were all portraits of some of my lord's family, though Dorothy could not tell us the names of every one. We had gone through most of the rooms, when we came to the old state drawing-room over the hall, and there was a picture of Miss Furnivall; or, as she was called in those days, Miss Grace, for she was the younger sister. Such a beauty she must have been! but with such a set, proud look, and such scorn looking out of her handsome eyes, with her eyebrows just a little raised, as if she were wondering how any one could have the impertinence to look at her; and her lip curled at us, as we stood there gazing. She had a dress on, the like of which I had never seen before, but it was all the fashion when she was young: a hat of some soft white stuff like beaver, pulled a little over her brows, and a beautiful plume of feathers sweeping round it on one side; and her gown of blue satin was open in front to a quilted white stomacher.

"Well, to be sure!" said I, when I had gazed my fill. "Flesh is grass, they do say; but who would have thought that Miss Furnivall had been such an out-and-out beauty, to see her now?"

"Yes," said Dorothy. "Folks change sadly. But if what my master's father used to say was true, Miss Furnivall, the elder sister, was handsomer than Miss Grace. Her picture is here somewhere; but, if I show it you, you must never let on, even to James, that you have seen it. Can the little lady hold her tongue, think you?" asked she.

I was not so sure, for she was such a little sweet, bold, open-spoken child, so I set her to hide herself; and then I helped Dorothy to turn a great picture, that leaned with its face towards the wall, and was not hung up as the others were. To be sure, it beat Miss Grace for beauty; and, I think, for scornful pride, too, though in that matter it might be hard to choose. I could have looked at it an hour, but Dorothy seemed half frightened at having shown it to me, and hurried it back again, and bade me run and find Miss Rosamond, for that there were some ugly places about the house, where she should like ill for the child to go. I was a brave, high-spirited girl, and thought little of what the old woman said, for I liked hide-and-seek as well as any child in the parish; so off I ran to find my little one.

As winter drew on, and the days grew shorter, I was sometimes almost certain that I heard a noise as if some one was playing on the great organ in the hall. I did not hear it every evening; but, certainly, I did very often; usually when I was sitting with Miss Rosamond, after I had put her to bed, and keeping quite still and silent in the bedroom. Then I used to hear it booming and swelling away in the distance. The first night, when I went down to my supper, I asked Dorothy who had been playing music, and James said very shortly that I was a gowk to take the wind soughing among the trees for music: but I saw Dorothy look at him very fearfully, and Bessy, the kitchen-maid, said something beneath her breath, and went quite white. I saw they did not like my question, so I held my peace till I was with Dorothy alone, when I knew I could get a good deal out of her. So, the next day, I watched my time, and I coaxed and asked her who it was that played the organ; for I knew that it was the organ and not the wind well enough, for all I had kept silence before James. But Dorothy had had her lesson, I'll warrant, and never a word could I get from her. So then I tried Bessy, though I had always held my head rather above her, as I was evened to James and Dorothy, and she was little better than their servant. So she said I must never, never tell; and if I ever told, I was never to say *she* had told me; but it was a very strange noise, and she had heard it many a time, but most of all pn winter nights, and before storms; and folks did say, it was the old lord playing on the great organ in the hall, just as he used to when he was alive; but who the old lord was, or why he played, and why he played on stormy winter evenings in particular, she either could not or would not tell me. Well! I told you I had a brave heart; and I thought it was rather pleasant to have that grand music rolling about the house, let who would be the player; for now it rose above the great gusts of wind, and wailed and triumphed just like a living creature, and then it fell to a softness most complete; only it was always music and tunes, so it was nonsense to call it the wind. I thought at first that it might be Miss Furnivall who played, unknown to Bessy; but one day when I was in the hall by myself, I opened the organ and peeped all about it and around it, as I had done to the organ in Crosthwaite Church once before, and I saw it was all broken and destroyed inside, though it looked so brave and fine; and then, though it was noonday, my flesh began to creep a little, and I shut it, and run away pretty quickly to my own bright nursery; and I did not like hearing the music for some time after that, any more than James and Dorothy did. All this time Miss

Rosamond was making herself more and more beloved. The old ladies liked her to dine with them at their early dinner; James stood behind Miss Furnivall's chair, and I behind Miss Rosamond's all in state; and, after dinner, she would play about in a corner of the great drawing-room, as still as any mouse, while Miss Furnivall slept, and I had my dinner in the kitchen. But she was glad enough to come to me in the nursery afterwards; for, as she said, Miss Furnivall was so sad, and Mrs. Stark so dull; but she and I were merry enough; and, by-and-by, I got not to care for that weird rolling music, which did one no harm, if we did not know where it came from.

That winter was very cold. In the middle of October the frosts began, and lasted many, many weeks. I remember, one day at dinner, Miss Furnivall lifted up her sad, heavy eyes, and said to Mrs. Stark, "I am afraid we shall have a terrible winter," in a strange kind of meaning way. But Mrs. Stark pretended not to hear, and talked very loud of something else. My little lady and I did not care for the frost; not we! As long as it was dry we climbed up the steep brows, behind the house, and went up on the Fells, which were bleak, and bare enough, and there we ran races in the fresh, sharp air; and once we came down by a new; path that took us past the two old gnarled holly-trees, which grew about half-way down by the east side of the house. But the days grew shorter and shorter; and the old lord, if it was he, played more and more stormily and sadly on the great organ. One Sunday afternoon—it must have been towards the end of November—I asked Dorothy to take charge of little Missey when she came out of the drawing-room, after Miss Furnivall had had her nap; for it was too cold to take her with me to church, and yet I wanted to go. And Dorothy was glad enough to promise, and was so fond of the child that all seemed well; Bessy and I set off very briskly, though the sky hung heavy and black over the white earth, as if the night had never fully gone away; and the air, though still, was very biting and keen.

"We shall have a fall of snow," said Bessy to me. And sure enough, even while we were in church, it came down thick, in great large flakes, so thick it almost darkened the windows. It had stopped snowing before we came out, but it lay soft, thick and deep beneath our feet, as we tramped home. Before we got to the hall the moon rose, and I think it was lighter then—what with the moon, and what with the white dazzling snow—than it had been when we went to church, between two and three o'clock. I have not told you that Miss Furnivall and Mrs. Stark never went to church: they used to read the prayers together, in their quiet gloomy way; they seemed to feel the Sunday very long without their tapestry-work to be busy at. So when I went to Dorothy in the kitchen, to fetch Miss Rosamond and take her upstairs with me, I did not much wonder when the old woman told me that the ladies had kept the child with them, and that she had never come to the kitchen, as I had bidden her, when she was tired of behaving pretty in the drawing-room. So I took off my things and went to find her, and bring her to her supper in the nursery. But when I went into the best drawing-room there sat the two old ladies, very still and quiet, dropping out a word now and then but looking as if nothing so bright and merry as Miss Rosamond had ever been near them. Still I thought she might be hiding from me; it was one of her pretty ways; and that she had persuaded them to look as if they knew nothing about her; so I went softly peeping under this sofa, and behind that chair, making believe I was sadly frightened at not finding her.

"What's the matter, Hester?" said Mrs. Stark, sharply. I don't know if Miss Furnivall had seen me, for, as I told you, she was very deaf, and she sat quite still, idly staring into the fire, with her hopeless face.

"I'm only looking for my little Rosy-Posy," replied I, still thinking that the child was there, and near me, though I could not see her.

"Miss Rosamond is not here," said Mrs. Stark. "She went away more than an hour ago to find Dorothy." And she too turned and went on looking into the fire.

My heart sank at this, and I began to wish I had never left my darling. I went back to Dorothy and told her. James was gone out for the day, but she and me and Bessy took lights and went up into the nursery first, and then we roamed over the great large house, callingyand entreating Miss Rosamond to come out of her hiding-place, and riot frighten us to death in that way. But there was no answer; no sound.

"Oh!" said I at last, "Can she have got into the east wing and hidden there?"

But Dorothy said it was not possible, for that she herself had never been there; that the doors were always locked, and my lord's steward had the keys, she believed; at any rate, neither she nor James had ever seen them: so I said I would go back, and see if, after all, she was not hidden in the drawing-room, unknown to the old ladies; and if I found her there, I said, I would whip her well for the fright she had given me; but I never meant to do it. Well, I went back to the west drawing-room, and I told Mrs. Stark we could not find her anywhere, and asked for leave to look all about the furniture there, for I thought now, that she might have fallen asleep in some warm hidden corner; but no! We looked, Miss Furnivall got up and looked, trembling all over, and she was nowhere there; then we set off again, every one in the house, and looked in all the places we had searched before, but we could not find her. Miss Furnivall shivered and shook so much that Mrs. Stark took her back into the warm drawing-room; but not before they had made me promise to bring her to them when she was found. Well, what a day! I began to think she never would be found, when I bethought me to look out into the great front court, all covered with snow. I was upstairs when I looked out; but it was such clear moonlight, I could see, quite plain, two little footprints, which might be traced from the hall door, and round the corner of the east wing. I don't know how I got down, but I tugged open the great, stiff hall door; and, throwing the skirt of my gown over my head for a cloak, I ran out. I turned the east corner, and there a black shadow fell on the snow; but when I came again into the moonlight, there were the little footmarks going up—up to the Fells. It was bitter cold; so cold that the air almost took the skin off my face as I ran, but I ran on, crying to think how my poor little darling must be perished, and frightened. I was within sight of the holly-trees when I saw a shepherd coming down the hill, bearing something in his arms wrapped in his maud. He shouted to me, and asked me if I had lost a bairn; and, when I could not speak for crying, he bore towards me, and I saw my wee bairnie lying still, and white, and stiff, in his arms, as if she had been dead. He told me he had been up the Fells to gather in his sheep, before the deep cold of night came on, and that under the holly-trees (black marks on the hillside, where no other bush was for miles around) he had found my little lady—my lamb—my queen—my darling—stiff and cold, in the terrible sleep which is frost-begotten. Oh! The joy, and the tears of having her in my arms once again! For I would not let him carry her; but took her, maud and all, into my own arms, and held her near my own warm neck and heart, and felt the life stealing slowly back again into her little gentle limbs. But she was still insensible when we reached the hall, and I had no breath for speech. We went in by the kitchen door.

"Bring the warming-pan," said I; and I carried her upstairs and began undressing her by the nursery fire, which Bessy had kept up. I called my little lammie all the sweet and playful names I could think of—even while my eyes were blinded by my tears; and at last, oh! At length she opened her large blue eyes. Then I put her into her warm bed, and sent Dorothy down to tell Miss Furnivall that all was well; and I made up my mind to sit by my darling's bedside the live-long night. She fell away into a soft sleep as soon as her pretty head had touched the pillow, and I watched her until morning light; when she wakened up bright and clear, or so I thought at first, and, my dears, so I think now.

She said that she had fancied that she should like to go to Dorothy, for that both the old ladies were asleep, and it was very dull in the drawing-room; and that, as she was going through the west lobby, she saw the snow through the high window falling, falling soft and steady; but she wanted to see it lying pretty and white on the ground; so she made her way into the great hall; and then, going to the window, she saw it bright and soft upon the drive; but while she stood there, she saw a little girl, not so old as she was, "but so pretty," said my darling, "and this little girl beckoned to me to come out; and oh, she was so pretty and so sweet, I could not choose but to go." And then this other little girl had taken her by the hand, and side by side the two had gone round the east corner.

"Now you are a naughty little girl, and telling stories," said I. "What would your good mamma, that is in heaven, and never told a story in her life, say to her little Rosamond, if she heard her—and I dare say she does—telling stories!"

"Indeed, Hester," sobbed out my child, "I'm telling you true. Indeed I am."

"Don't tell me!" said I, very stern. "I tracked you by your footmarks through the snow; there were only yours to be seen: and if you had had a little girl to go hand-in-hand with you up the hill, don't you think the footprints would have gone along with yours?"

"I can't help it, dear, dear Hester," said she, crying, "if they did not; I never looked at her feet, but she held my hand fast and tight in her little one, and it was very, very cold. She took me up the Fell-path, up to the holly-trees; and there I saw a lady weeping and crying; but when she saw me, she hushed her weeping, and smiled very proud and grand, and took me on her knee, and began to lull me to sleep; and that's all, Hester—but that is true; and my dear mamma knows it is," said she, crying. So I thought the child was in a fever, and pretended to believe her, as she went over her story—over and over again, and always the same. At last Dorothy knocked at the door with Miss Rosamond's breakfast; and she told me the old ladies were down in the eating parlour, and that they wanted to speak to me. They had both been into the night-nursery the evening before, but it was after Miss Rosamond was asleep; so they had only looked at her—not asked me any questions.

"I shall catch it," thought I to myself, as I went along the north gallery. "And yet," I thought, taking courage, "it was in their charge I left her; and it's they that's to blame for letting her steal away unknown and unwatched." So I went in boldly, and told my story. I told it all to Miss Furnivall, shouting close to her ear; but when I came to the mention of the other little girl out in the snow, coaxing and tempting her out, and willing her up to the grand and beautiful lady by the holly-tree, she threw her arms up—her old and withered arms—and cried aloud, "Oh! Heaven, forgive! Have mercy!"

Mrs. Stark took hold of her; roughly enough, I thought; but she was past Mrs. Stark's management, and spoke to me, in a kind of wild warning and authority.

"Hester! Keep her from that child! It will lure her to her death! That evil child! Tell her it is a wicked, naughty child." Then Mrs. Stark hurried me out of the room; where, indeed, I was glad enough to go; but Miss Furnivall kept shrieking out, "Oh! have mercy! Wilt Thou never forgive! It is many a long year ago—"

I was very uneasy in my mind after that. I would never leave Miss Rosamond, night or day, for fear lest she might slip off again, after some fancy or other; and all the more because I thought I could make out that Miss Furnivall was crazy, from their odd ways about her; and I was afraid lest something of the same kind (which might be in the family, you know) hung over my darling. And the great frost never ceased all this time; and whenever it was a more stormy night than usual, between the gusts, and through the wind, we heard the old lord playing on the great organ. But, old lord, or not, wherever Miss Rosamond went, there I followed; for my love for her, pretty helpless orphan, was stronger than my fear for the grand and terrible sound. Besides, it rested with me to keep her cheerful and merry, as beseemed her age. So we played together, and wandered together, here and there, and everywhere; for I never dared to lose sight of her again in that large and rambling house. And so it happened, that one afternoon, not long before Christmas Day, we were playing together on the billiard-table in the great hall (not that we knew the way of playing, but she liked to roll the smooth ivory balls with her pretty hands, and I liked to do whatever she did); and, by-and-by, without our noticing it, it grew dusk indoors, though it was still light in the open air, and I was thinking of taking her back into the nursery, when, all of a sudden, she cried out:

"Look, Hester! Look! There is my poor little girl out in the snow!" I turned towards the long narrow windows, and there, sure enough, I saw a little girl, less than my Miss Rosamond—dressed all unfit to be out-of-doors such a bitter night—crying, and beating against the window-panes, as if she wanted to be let in. She seemed to sob and wail, till Miss Rosamond could bear it no longer, and was flying to the door to open it, when, all of a sudden, and close up upon us, the great organ pealed out so loud and thundering, it fairly made me tremble; and all the more when I remembered me that, even in the stillness of that dead-cold weather, I had heard no sound of little battering hands upon the window-glass, although the Phantom Child had seemed to put forth all its force; and, although I had seen it wail and cry, no faintest touch of sound had fallen upon my ears. Whether I remembered all this at the very moment, I do not know; the great organ sound had so stunned me into terror; but this I know, I caught up Miss Rosamond before she got the hall door opened, and clutched her, and carried her away, kicking and screaming, into the large bright kitchen, where Dorothy and Agnes were busy with their mince-pies.

"What is the matter with my sweet one?" cried Dorothy, as I bore in Miss Rosamond, who was sobbing as if her heart would break.

"She won't let me open the door for my little girl to come in; and she'll die if she is out on the Fells all night. Cruel, naughty Hester," she said, slapping me; but she might have struck harder, for I had seen a look of ghastly terror on Dorothy's face, which made my very blood run cold.

"Shut the back-kitchen door fast, and bolt it well," said she to Agnes. She said no more; she gave me raisins and almonds to quiet Miss Rosamond: but she sobbed about the little girl in the snow, and would not touch any of the good things. I was thankful when she cried herself to sleep in bed. Then I stole down to the kitchen, and told Dorothy I had made up my mind. I would carry my darling back to my father's house in Applethwaite; where, if we lived humbly, we lived at peace. I said I had been frightened enough with the old lord's organ-playing; but now, that I had seen for myself this little moaning child, all decked out as no child in the neighbourhood could be, beating and battering to get in, yet always without any sound or noise - with the dark wound on its right shoulder; and that Miss Rosamond had known it again for the phantom that had nearly lured her to her death (which Dorothy knew was true); I would stand it no longer.

I saw Dorothy change colour once or twice. When I had done, she told me she did not think I could take Miss Rosamond with me, for that she was my lord's ward, and I had no right over her; and she asked me, would I leave the child that I was so fond of, just for sounds and sights that could do me no harm; and that they had all had to get used to in their turns? I was all in a hot, trembling passion; and I said it was very well for her to talk, that knew what these sights and noises betokened, and that had, perhaps, had something to do with the Spectre-Child while it was alive. And I taunted her so, that she told me all she knew, at last; and then I wished I had never been told, for it only made me afraid more than ever.

She said she had heard the tale from old neighbours, that were alive when she was first married; when folks used to come to the hall sometimes, before it had got such a bad name on the countryside: it might not be true, or it might, what she had been told.

The old lord was Miss Furnivall's father—Miss Grace as Dorothy called her, for Miss Maude was the elder, and Miss Furnivall by rights. The old lord was eaten up with pride. Such a proud man was never seen or heard of; and his daughters were like funis No one was good enough to wed them, although they had choice enough; for they were the great beauties of their day, as I had seen by their portraits, where they hung in the state drawing-room. But, as the old saying is, 'Pride will have a fall'; and these two haughty beauties fell in love with the same man, and he no better than a foreign musician, whom their father had down from London to play music with him at the Manor House. For, above all things, next to his pride, the old lord loved music. He could play on nearly every instrument that ever was heard of: and it was a strange thing it did not soften him; but he was a fierce dour old man, and had broken his poor wife's heart with his cruelty, they said. He was mad after music, and would pay any money for it. So he got this foreigner to come; who made such beautiful music, that they said the very birds on the trees stopped their singing to listen. And, by degrees, this foreign gentleman got such a hold over the old lord, that nothing would serve him but that he must come every year; and it was he that had the great organ brought from Holland, and built up in the hall,, where it stood now. He taught the old lord to play on it; but many and many a time, when Lord Furnivall was thinking of nothing but his fine organ, and his finer music, the dark for-eigner was walking abroad in the woods with one of the young ladies; now Miss Maude, and then Miss Grace.

Miss Maude won the day and carried off the prize, such as it was; and he and she were married, all unknown to any one; and before he made his next yearly visit, she had been confined of a little girl at a farm-house on the Moors, while her father and Miss Grace thought she was away at Doncaster Races. But though she was a wife and a mother, she was not a bit softened, but as haughty and as passionate as ever; and perhaps more so, for she was jealous of Miss Grace, to whom her foreign husband paid a deal of court—by way of blinding her—as he told his wife. But Miss Grace triumphed over Miss Maude, and Miss Maude grew fiercer and fiercer, both with her husband and with her sister; and the former—who could easily shake off what was disagreeable, and hide himself in foreign countries—went away a month before his usual time that summer, and half-threatened that he would never come back again. Meanwhile the little girl was left at the farm-house, and her mother used to have her horse saddled and gallop wildly over the hills to see her once every week, at the very least—for where she loved, she loved; and where she hated, she hated. And the old lord went on playing—playing on his organ; and the servants thought the sweet music he made had soothed down his awful temper, of which (Dorothy said) some terrible tales could be told. He grew infirm too, and had to walk with a crutch; and his son—that was the present Lord Furnivall's father—was with the army in America, and the other son at sea; so Miss Maude had it pretty much her own way, and she and Miss Grace grew colder and bitterer to each other every day; till at last they hardly ever spoke, except when the old lord was by. The foreign musician came again the next summer, but it was for the last time; for they led him such a life with their jealousy and their passions, that he grew weary, and went away, and never was heard of again. And Miss Maude, who had always meant to have her marriage acknowledged when her father should be dead, was left now a deserted wife—whom nobody knew to have been married—with a child that she dared not own, although she loved it to distraction; living with a father whom she feared, and a sister whom she hated. When the next summer passed over and the dark foreigner never came, both Miss Maude and Miss Grace grew gloomy and sad; they had a haggard look about them, though they looked handsome as ever. But by-and-by Miss Maude brightened; for her father grew more and more infirm, and more than ever carried away by his music; and she and Miss Grace lived almost entirely apart, having separate rooms, the one on the west side, Miss Maude on the east—those very rooms which were now shut up. So she thought she might have her little girl with her, and no one need ever know except those who dared not speak about it, and were bound to believe that it was, as she said, a cottager's child she had taken a fancy to. All this, Dorothy said, was pretty well known; but what came afterwards no one knew, except Miss Grace, and Mrs. Stark, who was even then her maid, and much more of a friend to her than ever her sister had been. But the servants supposed, from words that were dropped, that Miss Maude had triumphed over Miss Grace, and told her that all the time the dark foreigner had been mocking her with pretended love—he was her own husband; the colour left Miss Grace's cheek and lips that very day for, ever, and she was heard to say many a time that sooner or later she would have her revenge; and Mrs. Stark was for ever spying about the east rooms.

One fearful night, just after the New Year had come in, when the snow was lying thick and deep, and the flakes were still falling, fast enough to blind any one who might be out and abroad, there was a great and violent noise heard, and the old lord's voice above all, cursing and swearing awfully—and the cries of a little child—and the proud defiance of a fierce woman—and the sound of a blow—and a dead stillness—and moans and waitings dying away on the hill-side! Then the old lord summoned all his servants, and told them, with terrible oaths, and words more terrible, that his daughter had disgraced herself, and that he had turned her out of doors—her, and her child—and that if ever they gave her help or food or shelter, he prayed that they might never enter Heaven. And, all the while, Miss Grace stood by him, white and still as any stone; and when he had ended she heaved a great sigh, as much as to say her work was done, and her end was accomplished. But the old lord never touched his organ again, and died within the year; and no wonder! For, on the morrow of that wild and fearful night, the shepherds, coming down the Fell side, found Miss Maude sitting, all crazy and smiling, under the holly-trees, nursing a dead child with a terrible mark on its right shoulder. "But that was not what killed it," said Dorothy; "it was the frost and the cold;—every wild creature was in its hole, and every beast in its fold, while the child and its mother were turned out to wander on the Fells! And now you know all! And I wonder if you are less frightened now?"

I was more frightened than ever; but I said I was not. I wished Miss Rosamond and myself well out of that dreadful house for ever; but I would not leave her, and I dared not take her away. But oh! How I watched her, and guarded her! We bolted the doors and shut the window-shutters fast, an hour or more before dark, rather than leave them open five minutes too late. But my little lady still heard the weird child crying and mourning; and not all we could do or say could keep her from wanting to go to her, and let her in from the cruel wind and the snow. All this time, I kept away from Miss Furnivall and Mrs. Stark, as much as ever I could; for I feared them, I knew no good could be about them, with their grey hard faces, and their dreamy eyes, looking back into the ghastly years that were gone. But, even in my fear, I had a kind of pity for Miss Furnivall, at least. Those gone down to the pit can hardly have a more hopeless look than that which was ever on her face. At last I even got so sorry for her—who never said a word but what was quite forced from her—that I prayed for her; and I taught Miss Rosamond to pray for one who had done a deadly sin; but often when she came to those words, she would listen, and start up from her knees, and say, 'I hear my little girl complaining and crying very sad—"Oh! Let her in, or she will die!'

One night, just after New Year's Day had come at last, and the long winter had taken a turn, as I hoped I heard the west drawing-room bell ring three times, which was a signal for me. I would not leave Miss Rosamond alone, for all she was asleep—for the old lord had been playing wilder than ever—and I feared lest my darling should waken to hear the Spectre-Child; see her I knew she could not. I had fastened the windows too well for that. So I took her out of her bed and wrapped her up in such outer clothes as were most handy, and carried her down to the drawing-room, where the old ladies sat at their tapestry-work as usual. They looked up when I came in, and Mrs. Stark asked, quite astounded, "Why did I bring Miss Rosamond there, out of her warm bed?"

I had begun to whisper, "Because I was afraid of her being tempted out while I was away, by the wild child in the snow," when she stopped me short (with a glance at Miss Furnivall), and said Miss Furnivall wanted me to undo some work she had done wrong, and which neither of them could see to unpick. So I laid my pretty dear on the sofa, and sat down on a stool by them, and hardened my heart against them, as I heard the wind rising and howling.

Miss Rosamond slept on sound, for all the wind blew so; and Miss Furnivall said never a word, nor looked round when the gusts shook the windows. All at once she started up to her full height, and put up one hand, as if to bid us listen.

"I hear voices!" said she, "I hear terrible screams—I hear my father's voice!"

Just at that moment, my darling wakened with a sudden start: "My little girl is crying, oh, how she is crying!" And she tried to get up and go to her, but she got her feet entangled in the blanket, and I caught her up; for my flesh had begun to creep at these noises, which they heard while we could catch no sound. In a minute or two the noises came, and gathered fast, and filled our ears; we, too, heard voices and screams and no longer heard the winter's wind that raged abroad. Mrs. Stark looked at me, and I at her, but we dared not speak. Suddenly Miss Furnivall went towards the door, out into the ante-room, through the west lobby, and opened the door into the great hall. Mrs. Stark followed, and I durst not be left, though my heart almost stopped beating for fear. I wrapped my darling tight in my arms, and went out with them. In the hall the screams were louder than ever; they sounded to come from the east wing—nearer and nearer—close on the other side of the locked-up doors—close behind them. Then I noticed that the great bronze chandelier seemed all alight, though the hall was dim, and that a fire was blazing in the vast hearth-place, though it gave no heat; and I shuddered up with terror, and folded my darling closer to me. But as I did so the east door shook, and she, suddenly struggling to get free from me, cried, "Hester, I must go! My little girl is there; I hear her; she is coming! Hester, I must go!"

I held her tight with all my strength; with a set will, I held her. If I had died, my hands would have grasped her still, I was so resolved in my mind. Miss Furnivall stood listening, and paid no regard to my darling, who had got down to the ground, and whom I, upon my knees now, was holding with both my arms clasped round her neck; she still striving and crying to get free.

All at once the east door gave way with a thundering crash, as if torn open in a violent passion, and there came into that broad and mysterious light, the figure of a tall old man, with grey hair and gleaming eyes. He drove before him, with many a relentless gesture of abhorrence, a stern and beautiful woman, with a little child clinging to her dress.

"O Hester! Hester!" cried Miss Rosamond. "It's the lady! The lady below the holly-trees; and my little girl is with her. Hester! Hester! Let me go to her; they are drawing me to them. I feel them—I feel them. I must go!"

Again she was almost convulsed by her efforts to get away; but I held her tighter and tighter, till I feared I should do her a hurt; but rather that than let her go towards those terrible phantoms. They passed along towards the great hall-door, where the winds howled and ravened for their prey; but before they reached that, the lady turned; and I could see that she defied the old man with a fierce and proud defiance; but then she quailed, and then she threw up her arms wildly and piteously to save her child—her little child—from a blow from his uplifted crutch.

And Miss Rosamond was torn as if by a power stronger than mine, and writhed in my arms and sobbed (for by this time the poor darling was growing faint).

"They want me to go with them on to the Fells—they are drawing me to them. Oh, my little girl! I would come, but cruel, wicked Hester holds me very tight." But when she saw the uplifted crutch, she swooned away, and I thanked God for it. Just at this moment—when the tall old man, his hair streaming as in the blast of a furnace, was going to strike the little shrinking child—Miss Furnivall, the old woman by my side, cried out, "Oh, father! Father! Spare the little innocent child!" But just then I saw—we all saw—another phantom shape itself and grow clear out of the blue and misty light that filled the hall; we had not seen her till now, for it was another lady who stood by the old man, with a look of relentless hate and triumphant scorn. That figure was very beautiful to look upon, with a soft white hat drawn down over the proud brows and a red and curling lip. It was dressed in an open robe of blue satin. I had seen that figure before. It was the likeness of Miss Furnivall in her youth; and the terrible phantoms moved on, regardless of old Miss Furnivall's wild entreaty, and the uplifted crutch fell on the right shoulder of the little child, and the younger sister looked on, stony and deadly serene. But at that moment the dim lights, and the fire that gave no heat, went out of themselves, and Miss Furnivall lay at our feet stricken down by the palsy—death-stricken.

Yes! She was carried to her bed that night never to rise again. She lay with her face to the wall muttering low but muttering always: "Alas! Alas! What is done in youth can never be undone in age! What is done in youth can never be undone in age!"

# THE BUSINESS OF
# MADAME JAHN
## VINCENT O'SULLIVAN

H ow we all stared, how frightened we all were, how we passed opinions, on
that morning when Gustave Herbout was found swinging by the neck
from the ceiling of his bedroom! The whole *Faubourg*, even the ancient folk who
had not felt a street under them for years, turned out and stood gaping at the
house with amazement and loud conjecture. For why should Gustave Herbout,
of all men, take to the rope? Only last week he had inherited all the money of
his aunt, Madame Jahn, together with her house and the shop with the five
assistants, and life looked fair enough for him. No; clearly it was not wise of
Gustave to hang himself!

Besides, his aunt's death had happened at a time when Gustave was in
sore straits for money. To be sure, he had his salary from the bank in which
he worked; but what is a mere salary to one who (like Gustave) threw off the
clerkly habit when working hours were over to assume the dress and lounge
of the accustomed *boulevardier*: while he would relate to obsequious friends

vague but satisfactory stories of a Russian Prince who was his uncle, and of an extremely rich English lady to whose death he looked forward with hope. Alas! With a clerk's salary one cannot make much of a figure in Paris. It took all of that, and more, to maintain the renown he had gained among his acquaintance of having to his own a certain little lady with yellow hair who danced divinely. So he was forced to depend on the presents which Madame Jahn gave him from time to time; and for those presents he had to pay his aunt a most sedulous and irksome attention. At times, when he was almost sick from his craving for the *boulevard*, the *cafe*, the theatre, he would have to repair as the day grew to an end, to our *Faubourg*, and the house behind the shop, where he would sit down to an old-fashioned supper with his aunt, and listen with a sort of dull impatience while she asked him when he had last been at Confession, and told him long dreary stories of his dead father and mother. Punctually at nine o'clock the deaf servant, who was the only person besides Madame Jahn that lived in the house, would let in the fat old priest, who came for his game of dominoes, and betake herself to bed. Then the dominoes would begin, and with them the old man's prattle which Gustave knew so well: about his daily work, about the uselessness of all things here on earth, and the happiness and glory of the Kingdom of Heaven; and, of course, our *boulevard-ier* noticed, with the usual cheap sneer of the modern, that whilst the priest talked of the Kingdom of Heaven he yet showed the greatest anxiety if he had symptoms of a cold, or any other petty malady. However, Gustave would sit there with a hyprocrite's grin and inwardly raging, till the clock chimed eleven. At that hour Madame Jahn would rise, and, if she was pleased with her nephew, would go over to her writing-desk and give him, with, a rather pretty air of concealment from the priest, perhaps fifty or a hundred francs. Whereupon Gustave would bid her a manifestly affectionate good night! and depart in the company of the priest. As soon as he could get rid of the priest, he would hasten to his favourite *cafes*, to discover that all the people worth seeing had long since grown tired of waiting and had departed on their own affairs. The money, indeed, was a kind of consolation; but then there were nights when he did not get a *sou*. Ah! They amuse themselves in Paris, but not in this way—this is not amusing.

One cannot live a proper life upon a salary and an occasional gift of fifty or a hundred francs. And it is not entertaining to tell men that your uncle, the Prince at Moscow, is in a sorry case, and even now lies a-dying, or that the rich English lady is in the grip of a vile consumption and is momently expected to succumb, if these men only shove up their shoulders, wink at one another, and continue to present their bills. Further, the little Mademoiselle with yellow hair had lately shown signs of a very pretty temper, because her usual flowers and *bon-bons* were not apparent. So, since things were come to this dismal pass, Gustave fell to attending the race-meetings at Chan-tilly. During the first week Gustave won largely, for that is sometimes the way with ignorant men: during that week, too, the little Mademoiselle was charming, for she had her *bouquets* and boxes of *bon-bons*. But the next week Gustave lost heavily, for that is also very often the way with ignorant men: and he was thrown into the blackest despair, when one night at a place where he used to sup, Mademoiselle took the arm of a great fellow whom he much suspected to be a German, and tossed him a scornful nod as she went off.

On the evening after this happened, he was standing between five and six o'clock, in the *Place de la Madeleine,* blowing on his fingers and trying to plan his next move, when he heard his name called by a familiar voice, and turned to face his aunt's adviser, the priest.

"Ah, Gustave, my friend, I have just been to see a colleague of mine here!" cried the old man, pointing to the great church. "And are you going to your good aunt tonight?" he added, with a look at Gustave's neat dress.

Gustave was in a flame that the priest should have detected him in his gay clothes, for he always made a point of appearing at Madame Jahn's clad staidly in black; but he answered pleasantly enough:

"No, my Father, I'm afraid I can't tonight. You see I'm a little behind with my office work, and I have to stay at home and catch up."

"Well, well!" said the priest, with half a sigh, "I suppose young men will always be the same. I myself can only be with her till nine o'clock to-night because I must see a sick parishioner. But let me give you one bit of advice, my friend," he went on, taking hold of a button on Gustave's coat: "Don't neglect your aunt; for, mark my words, one day everything of Madame Jahn's will be yours!" And the omnibus he was waiting for happening to swing by at that moment, he departed without another word.

Gustave strolled along the *Boulevard des Capucines* in a study. Yes; it was certain that the house, and the shop with the five assistants, would one day be his; for the priest knew all his aunt's affairs. But how soon would they be his? Madame Jahn was now hardly sixty; her mother had lived to be ninety; when she was ninety he would be—And meanwhile, what about the numerous bills; what (above all!) about the little lady with yellow hair? He paused and struck his heel on the pavement with such force, that two men passing nudged one another and smiled. Then he made certain purchases, and set about wasting his time till nine o'clock.

It is curious to consider, that although when he started out at nine o'clock, Gustave was perfectly clear as to what he meant to do, yet he was chiefly troubled by the fear that the priest had told his aunt about his fine clothes. But when he had passed through the deserted *Faubourg,* and had come to the house behind the shop, he found his aunt only very pleased to see him, and a little surprised. So he sat with her, and listened to her gentle, homely stories, and told lies about himself and his manner of life, till the clock struck eleven. Then he rose, and Madame Jahn rose too and went to her writing-desk and opened a small drawer.

"You have been very kind to a lonely old woman tonight, my Gustave," said Madame Jahn, smiling.

"How sweet of you to say that, dearest aunt!" replied Gustave. He went over and passed his arm caressingly across her shoulders, and stabbed her in the heart.

For a full five minutes after the murder he stood still; as men often do in a great crisis when they know that any movement means decisive action. Then he started, laid hold of his hat, and made for the door. But there the stinging knowledge of his crime came to him for the first time; and he turned back into the room. Madame Jahn's bedroom candle was on a table: he lit it, and passed through a door which led from the house into the shop. Crouching below the counters covered with white sheets, lest a streak of light on the windows might attract the observation of some passenger, he proceeded to a side entrance to the shop, unbarred and unlocked the door and put the key in his pocket. Then, in the same crouching way, he returned to the room, and started to ransack the small drawer. The notes he scattered about the floor; but two small bags of coin went into his coat. Then he took the candle and dropped some wax on the face and hands and dress of the corpse; he spilt wax, too, over the carpet, and then he broke the candle and ground it under his foot. He even tore with long nervous fingers at the dead woman's bodice until her breasts lay exposed; and plucked out a handful of her hair and threw it on the floor to stick to the wax. When all these things had been accomplished he went to the house door and listened. The *Faubourg* is always very quiet about twelve o'clock, and a single footstep falls on the night with a great sound. He could not hear the least noise; so he darted out and ran lightly until he came to a turning. There he fell into a sauntering walk, lit a cigarette, and, hailing a passing *fiacre,* directed the man to drive to the *Pont Saint-Michel*. At the bridge he alighted, and noting that he was not eyed, he threw the key of the shop into the river. Then assuming the swagger and assurance of a half-drunken man, he marched up the *Boulevard* and entered the *Cafe d'Harcourt*.

The place was filled with the usual crowd of men and women of the *Quartier Latin*. Gustave looked round, and observing a young student with a flushed face who was talking eagerly about the rights of man, he sat down by him. It was his part to act quickly: so before the student had quite finished a sentence for his ear, the murderer gave him the lie. The student, however, was not so ready for a fight as Gustave had supposed; and when he began to argue again, Gustave seized a glass full of brandy and water and threw the stuff in his face. Then indeed there was a row, till the *gendarmes* interfered, and haled Gustave to the station. At the police station he bitterly lamented his misdeed, which he attributed to an extra glass of absinthe, and he begged the authorities to carry word of his plight to his good aunt, Madame Jahn, in our *Faubourg*. So to the house behind the shop they went, and there they found her—sitting with her breasts hanging out, her poor head clotted with blood, and a knife in her heart.

The next morning, Gustave was set free. A man and a woman, two of the five assistants in the shop, had been charged with the murder. The woman had been severely reprimanded by Madame Jahn on the day before, and the man was known to be the girl's paramour. It was the duty of the man to close at night all the entrances into the shop, save the main entrance, which was closed by Madame Jahn and her deaf servant; and the police had formed a theory (worked out with the amazing zeal and skill which cause the Paris police so often to overreach themselves!) that the man had failed to bolt one of the side doors, and had, by his subtlety, got possession of the key whereby he and his accomplice re-entered the place about midnight. Working on this theory, the police had woven a web round the two unfortunates with threads of steel; and there was little doubt that both of them would stretch their necks under the guillotine, with full consent of Press and public. At least, this was Gustave's opinion; and Gustave's opinion now went for a great deal in the *Faubourg*. Of course there were a few who murmured that it was a good thing poor Madame Jahn had not lived to see her nephew arrested for a drunken brawler; but with full remembrance of who owned the house and shop we were most of us inclined to say, after the priest: That if the brave Gustave had been with his aunt, the shocking affair could never have occurred. And, indeed, what had we more inspiring than the inconsolable grief he showed? Why! On the day of the funeral, when he heard the earth clatter down on the coffin-lid in *Pere Lachaise,* he even swooned to the ground, and had to be carried out in the midst of the mourners. "Oh, yes," (quoth the gossips), "Gustave Herbout loved his aunt passing well!"

On the night after the funeral, Gustave was sitting alone before the fire in Madame Jahn's room, smoking and making his plans. He thought, that when all this wretched mock grief and pretence of decorum was over, he would again visit the *cafes* which he greatly savoured, and the little Mademoiselle with yellow hair would once more smile on him delicious smiles with a gleaming regard. Thus he was thinking when the clock on the mantelpiece tinkled eleven; and at that moment a very singular thing happened The door was suddenly opened: a girl came in, and walked straight over to the writing-desk, pulled out the small drawer, and then sat staring at the man by the fire. She was distinctly beautiful; although there was a certain old-fashionedness in her peculiar silken dress, and the manner of wearing her hair. Not once did it occur to Gustave, as he gazed in terror, that he was gazing on a mortal woman: the doors were too well bolted to allow anyone from outside to enter, and besides, there was a strange baffling familiarity in the face and mien of the intruder. It might have been an hour as he sat there; and then, the silence becoming too horrible, by a supreme effort of his wonderful courage he rushed out of the room and upstairs to get his hat. There in his murdered aunt's bedroom—there, smiling at him from the wall—was a vivid presentment of the dread vision that sat below: a portrait of Madame Jahn as a girl. He fled into the street, and walked, perhaps two miles, before he thought at all. But when he did think, he found that he was drawn against his will back to the house to see if *It* was still there: just as the police here believe a murderer is drawn to the *Morgue* to view the body of his victim. Yes; the girl was there still, with her great reproachless eyes; and throughout that solemn night Gustave, haggard and mute, sat glaring at her. Towards dawn he fell into an uneasy doze; and when he awoke with a scream, he found that the girl was gone.

At noon the next day Gustave, heartened by several glasses of brandy, and cheered by the sunshine in the *Champs-Elysees,* endeavoured to make light of the affair. He would gladly have arranged not to go back to the house: but then people would talk so much, and he could not afford to lose any custom out of the shop. Moreover, the whole matter was only an hallucination—the effect of jaded nerves. He dined well, and went to see a musical comedy; and so contrived, that he did not return to the house until after two o'clock. There was someone waiting for him, sitting at the desk with the small drawer open; not the girl of last night, but a somewhat older woman— and the same reproachless eyes. So great was the fascination of those eyes, that, although he left the house at once with an iron resolution not to go back, he found himself drawn under them again, and he sat through the night as he had sat through the night before, sobbing and stupidly glaring. And all day long he crouched by the fire shuddering; and all the night till eleven o'clock; and then a figure of his aunt came to him again, but always a little older and more withered. And this went on for five days; the figure that sat with him becoming older and older as the days ran, till on the sixth night he gazed through the hours at his aunt as she was on the night he killed her. On these nights he was used sometimes to start up and make for the street, swearing never to return; but always he would be dragged back to the eyes. The policemen came to know him from these night walks, and people began to notice his bad looks: these could not spring from grief, folks said, and so they thought he was leading a wild life.

On the seventh night there was a delay of about five minutes after the clock had rung eleven, before the door opened. And then—then, merciful God! The body of a woman in grave-clothes came into the room, as if borne by unseen men, and lay in the air across the writing-desk, while the small drawer flew open of its own accord. Yes—there was the shroud and the brown scapular, the prim white cap, the hands folded on the shrunken breast. Grey from slimy horror, Gustave raised himself up, and went over to look for the eyes. When he saw them pressed down with pennies, he reeled back and vomited into the grate. And blind, and sick, and loathing, he stumbled upstairs.

But as he passed by Madame Jahn's bedroom the corpse came out to meet him, with the eyes closed and the pennies pressing them down. Then, at last, reeking and dabbled with sweat, with his tongue lolling out, and the spittle running down his beard, Gustave breathed:

"Are you alive?"

"No, no!" wailed the *thing*, with a burst of awful weeping; "I have been dead many days."

# THE CANTERVILLE GHOST
## OSCAR WILDE

### 1

When Mr. Hiram B. Otis, the American Minister, bought Canterville Chase, every one told him he was doing a very foolish thing, as there was no doubt at all that the place was haunted. Indeed, Lord Canterville himself, who was a man of the most punctilious honour, had felt it his duty to mention the fact to Mr. Otis when they came to discuss terms.

"We have not cared to live in the place ourselves," said Lord Canterville, "since my grandaunt, the Dowager Duchess of Bolton, was frightened into a fit, from which she never really recovered, by two skeleton hands being placed on her shoulders as she was dressing for dinner, and I feel bound to tell you, Mr. Otis, that the ghost has been seen by several living members of my family, as well as by the rector of the parish, the Rev. Augustus Dampier, who is a Fellow of King's College, Cambridge. After the unfortunate accident to the Duchess, none of our younger servants would stay with us, and Lady Canterville often got very little sleep at night, in consequence of the mysterious noises that came from the corridor and the library."

"My Lord," answered the Minister, "I will take the furniture and the ghost at a valuation. I have come from a modern country, where we have everything that money can buy; and with all our spry young fellows painting the Old World red, and carrying off your best actors and prima-donnas, I reckon that if there were such a thing as a ghost in Europe, we'd have it at home in a very short time in one of our public museums, or on the road as a show."

"I fear that the ghost exists," said Lord Canterville, smiling, "though it may have resisted the overtures of your enterprising impresarios. It has been well known for three centuries, since 1584 in fact, and always makes its appearance before the death of any member of our family."

"Well, so does the family doctor for that matter, Lord Canterville. But there is no such thing, sir, as a ghost, and I guess the laws of Nature are not going to be suspended for the British aristocracy."

"You are certainly very natural in America," answered Lord Canterville, who did not quite understand Mr. Otis's last observation, "and if you don't mind a ghost in the house, it is all right. Only you must remember I warned you."

A few weeks after this, the purchase was concluded, and at the close of the season the Minister and his family went down to Canterville Chase. Mrs. Otis, who, as Miss Lucretia R. Tappan, of West 53d Street, had been a celebrated New York belle, was now a very handsome, middle-aged woman, with fine eyes, and a superb profile. Many American ladies on leaving their native land adopt an appearance of chronic ill-health, under the impression that it is a form of European refinement, but Mrs. Otis had never fallen into this error. She had a magnificent constitution, and a really wonderful amount of animal spirits. Indeed, in many respects, she was quite English, and was an excellent example of the fact that we have really everything in common with America nowadays, except, of course, language. Her eldest son, christened Washington by his parents in a moment of patriotism, which he never ceased to regret, was a fair-haired, rather good-looking young man, who had qualified himself for American diplomacy by leading the German at the Newport Casino for three successive seasons, and even in London was well known as an excellent dancer. Gardenias and the peerage were his only weaknesses. Otherwise he was extremely sensible. Miss Virginia E. Otis was a little girl of fifteen, lithe and lovely as a fawn, and with a fine freedom in her large blue eyes. She was a wonderful Amazon, and had once raced old Lord Bilton on her pony twice round the park, winning by a length and a half, just in front of the Achilles statue, to the huge delight of the young Duke of Cheshire, who proposed for her on the spot, and was sent back to Eton that very night by his guardians, in floods of tears. After Virginia came the twins, who were usually called "The Star and Stripes," as they were always getting swished. They were delightful boys, and, with the exception of the worthy Minister, the only true republicans of the family.

As Canterville Chase is seven miles from Ascot, the nearest railway station, Mr. Otis had telegraphed for a waggonette to meet them, and they started on their drive in high spirits. It was a lovely July evening, and the air was delicate with the scent of the pinewoods. Now and then they heard a wood-pigeon brooding over its own sweet voice, or saw, deep in the rustling fern, the burnished breast of the pheasant. Little squirrels peered at them from the beech-trees as they went by, and the rabbits scudded away through the brushwood and over the mossy knolls, with their white tails in the air. As they entered the avenue of Canterville Chase, however, the sky became suddenly overcast with clouds, a curious stillness seemed to hold the atmosphere, a great flight of rooks passed silently over their heads, and, before they reached the house, some big drops of rain had fallen.

Standing on the steps to receive them was an old woman, neatly dressed in black silk, with a white cap and apron. This was Mrs. Umney, the housekeeper, whom Mrs. Otis, at Lady Canterville's earnest request, had consented to keep in her former position. She made them each a low curtsey as they alighted, and said in a quaint, old-fashioned manner, "I bid you welcome to Canterville Chase."

Following her, they passed through the fine Tudor hall into the library, a long, low room, panelled in black oak, at the end of which was a large stained glass window. Here they found tea laid out for them, and, after taking off their wraps, they sat down and began to look round, while Mrs. Umney waited on them. Suddenly Mrs. Otis caught sight of a dull red stain on the floor just by the fireplace, and, quite unconscious of what it really signified, said to Mrs. Umney, "I am afraid something has been spilt there."

"Yes, madam," replied the old housekeeper in a low voice, "blood has been spilt on that spot."

"How horrid!" cried Mrs. Otis; "I don't at all care for blood-stains in a sitting-room. It must be removed at once."

The old woman smiled, and answered in the same low, mysterious voice, "It is the blood of Lady Eleanore de Canterville, who was murdered on that very spot by her own husband, Sir Simon de Canterville, in 1575. Sir Simon survived her nine years, and disappeared suddenly under very mysterious circumstances. His body has never been discovered, but his guilty spirit still haunts the Chase. The blood-stain has been much admired by tourists and others, and cannot be removed."

"That is all nonsense," cried Washington Otis; "Pinkerton's Champion Stain Remover and Paragon Detergent will clean it up in no time," and before the terrified housekeeper could interfere, he had fallen upon his knees, and was rapidly scouring the floor with a small stick of what looked like a black cosmetic. In a few moments no trace of the blood-stain could be seen.

"I knew Pinkerton would do it," he exclaimed, triumphantly, as he looked round at his admiring family; but no sooner had he said these words than a terrible flash of lightning lit up the sombre room, a fearful peal of thunder made them all start to their feet, and Mrs. Umney fainted.

"What a monstrous climate!" said the American Minister, calmly, as he lit a long cheroot. "I guess the old country is so overpopulated that they have not enough decent weather for everybody. I have always been of opinion that emigration is the only thing for England."

"My dear Hiram," cried Mrs. Otis, "what can we do with a woman who faints?"

"Charge it to her like breakages," answered the Minister; "she won't faint after that;" and in a few moments Mrs. Umney certainly came to. There was no doubt, however, that she was extremely upset, and she sternly warned Mr. Otis to beware of some trouble coming to the house.

"I have seen things with my own eyes, sir," she said, "that would make any Christian's hair stand on end, and many and many a night I have not closed my eyes in sleep for the awful things that are done here." Mr. Otis, however, and his wife warmly assured the honest soul that they were not afraid of ghosts, and, after invoking the blessings of Providence on her new master and mistress, and making arrangements for an increase of salary, the old housekeeper tottered off to her own room.

## II

The storm raged fiercely all that night, but nothing of particular note occurred. The next morning, however, when they came down to breakfast, they found the terrible stain of blood once again on the floor. "I don't think it can be the fault of the Paragon Detergent," said Washington, "for I have tried it with everything. It must be the ghost." He accordingly rubbed out the stain a second time, but the second morning it appeared again. The third morning also it was there, though the library had been locked up at night by Mr. Otis himself, and the key carried up-stairs. The whole family were now quite interested; Mr. Otis began to suspect that he had been too dogmatic in his denial of the existence of ghosts, Mrs. Otis expressed her intention of joining the Psychical Society, and Washington prepared a long letter to Messrs. Myers and Podmore on the subject of the Permanence of Sanguineous Stains when connected with Crime. That night all doubts about the objective existence of phantasmata were removed for ever.

The day had been warm and sunny; and, in the cool of the evening, the whole family went out to drive. They did not return home till nine o'clock, when they had a light supper. The conversation in no way turned upon ghosts, so there were not even those primary conditions of receptive expectations which so often precede the presentation of psychical phenomena. The subjects discussed, as I have since learned from Mr. Otis, were merely such as form the ordinary conversation of cultured Americans of the better class, such as the immense superiority of Miss Fanny Devonport over Sarah Bernhardt as an actress; the difficulty of obtaining green corn, buckwheat cakes, and hominy, even in the best English houses; the importance of Boston in the development of the world-soul; the advantages of the baggage-check system in railway travelling; and the sweetness of the New York accent as compared to the London drawl. No mention at all was made of the supernatural, nor was Sir Simon de Canterville alluded to in any way. At eleven o'clock the family retired, and by half-past all the lights were out. Some time after, Mr. Otis was awakened by a curious noise in the corridor, outside his room. It sounded like the clank of metal, and seemed to be coming nearer every moment. He got up at once, struck a match, and looked at the time. It was exactly one o'clock. He was quite calm, and felt his pulse, which was not at all feverish. The strange noise still continued, and with it he heard distinctly the sound of footsteps. He put on his slippers, took a small oblong phial out of his dressing-case, and opened the door. Right in front of him he saw, in the wan moonlight, an old man of terrible aspect. His eyes were as red burning coals; long grey hair fell over his shoulders in matted coils; his garments, which were of antique cut, were soiled and ragged, and from his wrists and ankles hung heavy manacles and rusty gyves.

"My dear sir," said Mr. Otis, "I really must insist on your oiling those chains, and have brought you for that purpose a small bottle of the Tammany Rising Sun Lubricator. It is said to be completely efficacious upon one application, and there are several testimonials to that effect on the wrapper from some of our most eminent native divines. I shall leave it here for you by the bedroom candles, and will be happy to supply you with more, should you require it." With these words the United States Minister laid the bottle down on a marble table, and, closing his door, retired to rest.

For a moment the Canterville ghost stood quite motionless in natural indignation; then, dashing the bottle violently upon the polished floor, he fled down the corridor, uttering hollow groans, and emitting a ghastly green light. Just, however, as he reached the top of the great oak staircase, a door was flung open, two little white-robed figures appeared, and a large pillow whizzed past his head! There was evidently no time to be lost, so, hastily adopting the Fourth dimension of Space as a means of escape, he vanished through the wainscoting, and the house became quite quiet. On reaching a small secret chamber in the left wing, he leaned up against a moonbeam to recover his breath, and began to try and realize his position. Never, in a brilliant and uninterrupted career of three hundred years, had he been so grossly insulted. He thought of the Dowager Duchess, whom he had frightened into a fit as she stood before the glass in her lace and diamonds; of the four housemaids, who had gone into hysterics when he merely grinned at them through the curtains on one of the spare bedrooms; of the rector of the parish, whose candle he had blown out as he was coming late one night from the library, and who had been under the care of Sir William Gull ever since, a perfect martyr to nervous disorders; and of old Madame de Tremouillac, who, having wakened up one morning early and seen a skeleton seated in an armchair by the fire reading her diary, had been confined to her bed for six weeks with an attack of brain fever, and, on her recovery, had become reconciled to the Church, and broken off her connection with that notorious sceptic, Monsieur de Voltaire. He remembered the terrible night when the wicked Lord Canterville was found choking in his dressing-room, with the knave of diamonds half-way down his throat, and confessed, just before he died, that he had cheated Charles James Fox out of £50,000 at Crockford's by means of that very card, and swore that the ghost had made him swallow it. All his great achievements came back to him again, from the butler who had shot himself in the pantry because he had seen a green hand tapping at the window-pane, to the beautiful Lady Stutfield, who was always obliged to wear a black velvet band round her throat to hide the mark of five fingers burnt upon her white skin, and who drowned herself at last in the carp-pond at the end of the King's Walk. With the enthusiastic egotism of the true artist, he went over his most celebrated performances, and smiled bitterly to himself as he recalled to mind his last appearance as "Red Reuben, or the Strangled Babe," his *debut* as "Guant Gibeon, the Blood-sucker of Bexley Moor," and the *furore* he had excited one lovely June evening by merely playing ninepins with his own bones upon the lawn-tennis ground. And after all this some wretched modern Americans were to come and offer him the Rising Sun Lubricator, and throw pillows at his head! It was quite unbearable. Besides, no ghost in history had ever been treated in this manner. Accordingly, he determined to have vengeance, and remained till daylight in an attitude of deep thought.

## III

The next morning, when the Otis family met at breakfast, they discussed the ghost at some length. The American Minister was naturally a little annoyed to find that his present had not been accepted. "I have no wish," he said, "to do the ghost any personal injury, and I must say that, considering the length of time he has been in the house, I don't think it is at all polite to throw pillows at him,"-a very just remark, at which, I am sorry to say, the twins burst into shouts of laughter. "Upon the other hand," he continued, "if he really declines to use the Rising Sun Lubricator, we shall have to take his chains from him. It would be quite impossible to sleep, with such a noise going on outside the bedrooms."

For the rest of the week, however, they were undisturbed, the only thing that excited any attention being the continual renewal of the blood-stain on the library floor. This certainly was very strange, as the door was always locked at night by Mr. Otis, and the windows kept closely barred. The chameleon-like colour, also, of the stain excited a good deal of comment. Some mornings it was a dull (almost Indian) red, then it would be vermilion, then a rich purple, and once when they came down for family prayers, according to the simple rites of the Free American Reformed Episcopalian Church, they found it a bright emerald-green. These kaleidoscopic changes naturally amused the party very much, and bets on the subject were freely made every evening. The only person who did not enter into the joke was little Virginia, who, for some unexplained reason, was always a good deal distressed at the sight of the blood-stain, and very nearly cried the morning it was emerald-green.

The second appearance of the ghost was on Sunday night. Shortly after they had gone to bed they were suddenly alarmed by a fearful crash in the hall. Rushing down-stairs, they found that a large suit of old armour had become detached from its stand, and had fallen on the stone floor, while seated in a high-backed chair was the Canterville ghost, rubbing his knees with an expression of acute agony on his face. The twins, having brought their pea-shooters with them, at once discharged two pellets on him, with that accuracy of aim which can only be attained by long and careful practice on a writing-master, while the American Minister covered him with his revolver, and called upon him, in accordance with Californian etiquette, to hold up his hands! The ghost started up with a wild shriek of rage, and swept through them like a mist, extinguishing

Washington Otis's candle as he passed, and so leaving them all in total darkness. On reaching the top of the staircase he recovered himself, and determined to give his celebrated peal of demoniac laughter. This he had on more than one occasion found extremely useful. It was said to have turned Lord Rakers wig grey in a single night, and had certainly made three of Lady Canterville's French governesses give warning before their month was up. He accordingly laughed his most horrible laugh, till the old vaulted roof rang and rang again, but hardly had the fearful echo died away when a door opened, and Mrs. Otis came out in a light blue dressing-gown. "I am afraid you are far from well," she said, "and have brought you a bottle of Doctor Dobell's tincture. If it is indigestion, you will find it a most excellent remedy." The ghost glared at her in fury, and began at once to make preparations for turning himself into a large black dog, an accomplishment for which he was justly renowned, and to which the family doctor always attributed the permanent idiocy of Lord Canterville's uncle, the Hon. Thomas Horton. The sound of approaching footsteps, however, made him hesitate in his fell purpose, so he contented himself with becoming faintly phosphorescent, and vanished with a deep churchyard groan, just as the twins had come up to him.

On reaching his room he entirely broke down, and became a prey to the most violent agitation. The vulgarity of the twins, and the gross materialism of Mrs. Otis, were naturally extremely annoying, but what really distressed him most was that he had been unable to wear the suit of mail. He had hoped that even modern Americans would be thrilled by the sight of a Spectre in armour, if for no more sensible reason, at least out of respect for their natural poet Longfellow, over whose graceful and attractive poetry he himself had whiled away many a weary hour when the Cantervilles were up in town. Besides it was his own suit. He had worn it with great success at the Kenilworth tournament, and had been highly complimented on it by no less a person than the Virgin Queen herself. Yet when he had put it on, he had been completely overpowered by the weight of the huge breastplate and steel casque, and had fallen heavily on the stone pavement, barking both his knees severely, and bruising the knuckles of his right hand.

For some days after this he was extremely ill, and hardly stirred out of his room at all, except to keep the blood-stain in proper repair. However, by taking great care of himself, he recovered, and resolved to make a third attempt to frighten the American Minister and his family. He selected Friday, August 17th, for his appearance, and spent most of that day in looking over his wardrobe, ultimately deciding in favour of a large slouched hat with a red feather, a winding-sheet frilled at the wrists and neck, and a rusty dagger. Towards evening a violent storm of rain came on, and the wind was so high that all the windows and doors in the old house shook and rattled. In fact, it was just such weather as he loved. His plan of action was this. He was to make his way quietly to Washington Otis's room, gibber at him from the foot of the bed, and stab himself three times in the throat to the sound of low music. He bore Washington a special grudge, being quite aware that it was he who was in the habit of removing the famous Canterville blood-stain by means of Pinkerton's Paragon Detergent. Having reduced the reckless and foolhardy youth to a condition of abject terror, he was then to proceed to the room occupied by the American Minister and his wife, and there to place a clammy hand on Mrs. Otis's forehead, while he hissed into her trembling husband's ear the awful secrets of the charnel-house. With regard to little Virginia, he had not quite made up his mind. She had never insulted him in any way, and was pretty and gentle. A few hollow groans from the wardrobe, he thought, would be more than sufficient, or, if that failed to wake her, he might grabble at the counterpane with palsy-twitching fingers. As for the twins, he was quite determined to teach them a lesson. The first thing to be done was, of course, to sit upon their chests, so as to produce the stifling sensation of nightmare. Then, as their beds were quite close to each other, to stand between them in the form of a green, icy-cold corpse, till they became paralyzed with fear, and finally, to throw off the winding-sheet, and crawl round the room, with white, bleached bones and one rolling eyeball, in the character of "Dumb Daniel, or the Suicide's Skeleton," a *role* in which he had on more than one occasion produced a great effect, and which he considered quite equal to his famous part of "Martin the Maniac, or the Masked Mystery."

At half-past ten he heard the family going to bed. For some time he was disturbed by wild shrieks of laughter from the twins, who, with the light-hearted gaiety of schoolboys, were evidently amusing themselves before they retired to rest, but at a quarter-past eleven all was still, and, as midnight sounded, he sallied forth. The owl beat against the window-panes, the raven croaked from the old yew-tree, and the wind wandered moaning round the house like a lost soul; but the Otis family slept unconscious of their doom, and high above the rain and storm he could hear the steady snoring of the Minister for the United States. He stepped stealthily out of the wainscoting, with an evil smile on his cruel, wrinkled mouth, and the moon hid her face in a cloud as he stole past the great oriel window, where his own arms and those of his murdered wife were blazoned in azure and gold. On and on he glided, like an evil shadow, the very darkness seeming to loathe him as he passed. Once he thought he heard something call, and stopped; but it was only the baying of a dog from the Red Farm, and he went on, muttering strange sixteenth-century curses, and ever and anon brandishing the rusty dagger in the midnight air. Finally he reached the corner of the passage that led to luckless Washington's room. For a moment he paused there, the wind blowing his long grey locks about his head, and twisting into grotesque and fantastic folds the nameless horror of the dead man's shroud. Then the clock struck the quarter, and he felt the time was come. He chuckled to himself, and turned the corner; but no sooner had he done so than, with a piteous wail of terror, he fell back, and hid his blanched face in his long, bony hands. Right in front of him was standing a horrible spectre, motionless as a carven image, and monstrous as a madman's dream! Its head was bald and burnished; its face round, and fat, and white; and hideous laughter seemed to have writhed its features into an eternal grin. From the eyes streamed rays of scarlet light, the mouth was a wide well of fire, and a hideous garment, like to his own, swathed with its silent snows the Titan form. On its breast was a placard with strange writing in antique characters, some scroll of shame it seemed, some record of wild sins, some awful calendar of crime, and, with its right hand, it bore aloft a falchion of gleaming steel.

Never having seen a ghost before, he naturally was terribly frightened, and, after a second hasty glance at the awful phantom, he fled back to his room, tripping up in his long winding-sheet as he sped down the corridor, and finally dropping the rusty dagger into the Minister's jack-boots, where it was found in the morning by the butler. Once in the privacy of his own apartment, he flung himself down on a small pallet-bed, and hid his face under the clothes. After a time, however, the brave old Canterville spirit asserted itself, and he determined to go and speak to the other ghost as soon as it was daylight. Accordingly, just as the dawn was touching the hills with silver, he returned towards the spot where he had first laid eyes on the grisly phantom, feeling that, after all, two ghosts were better than one, and that, by the aid of his new friend, he might safely grapple with the twins. On reaching the spot, however, a terrible sight met his gaze. Something had evidently happened to the spectre, for the light had entirely faded from its hollow eyes, the gleaming falchion had fallen from its hand, and it was leaning up against the wall in a strained and uncomfortable attitude. He rushed forward and seized it in his arms, when, to his horror, the head slipped off and rolled on the floor, the body assumed a recumbent posture, and he found himself clasping a white dimity bed-curtain, with a sweeping-brush, a kitchen cleaver, and a hollow turnip lying at his feet! Unable to understand this curious transformation, he clutched the placard with feverish haste, and there, in the grey morning light, he read these fearful words:-

Ye On lie True and Originale Spook,
Beware of Ye Imitationes.
All others are counterfeite.

The whole thing flashed across him. He had been tricked, foiled, and out-witted! The old Canterville look came into his eyes; he ground his toothless gums together; and, raising his withered hands high above his head, swore according to the picturesque phraseology of the antique school, that, when Chanticleer had sounded twice his merry horn, deeds of blood would be wrought, and murder walk abroad with silent feet.

Hardly had he finished this awful oath when, from the red-tiled roof of a distant homestead, a cock crew. He laughed a long, low, bitter laugh, and waited. Hour after hour he waited, but the cock, for some strange reason, did not crow again. Finally, at half-past seven, the arrival of the housemaids made him give up his fearful vigil, and he stalked back to his room, thinking of his vain oath and baffled purpose. There he consulted several books of ancient chivalry, of which he was exceedingly fond, and found that, on every occasion on which this oath had been used, Chanticleer had always crowed a second time. "Perdition seize the naughty fowl," he muttered, "I have seen the day when, with my stout spear, I would have run him through the gorge, and made him crow for me an 'twere in death!" He then retired to a comfortable lead coffin, and stayed there till evening.

## IV

The next day the ghost was very weak and tired. The terrible excitement of the last four weeks was beginning to have its effect. His nerves were completely shattered, and he started at the slightest noise. For five days he kept his room, and at last made up his mind to give up the point of the blood-stain on the library floor. If the Otis family did not want it, they clearly did not deserve it. They were evidently people on a low, material plane of existence, and quite incapable of appreciating the symbolic value of sensuous phenomena. The question of phantasmic apparitions, and the development of astral bodies, was of course quite a different matter, and really not under his control. It was his solemn duty to appear in the corridor once a week, and to gibber from the large oriel window on the first and third Wednesdays in every month, and he did not see how he could honourably escape from his obligations. It is quite true that his life had been very evil, but, upon the other hand, he was most conscientious in all things connected with the supernatural. For the next three Saturdays, accordingly, he traversed the corridor as usual between midnight and three o'clock, taking every possible precaution against being either heard or seen. He removed his boots, trod as lightly as possible on the old worm-eaten boards, wore a large black velvet cloak, and was careful to use the Rising Sun Lubricator for oiling his chains. I am bound to acknowledge that it was with a good deal of difficulty that he brought himself to adopt this last mode of protection. However, one night, while the family were at dinner, he slipped into Mr. Otis's bedroom and carried off the bottle. He felt a little humiliated at first, but afterwards was sensible enough to see that there was a great deal to be said for the invention, and, to a certain degree, it served his purpose. Still in spite of everything he was not left unmolested. Strings were continually being stretched across the corridor, over which he tripped in the dark, and on one occasion, while dressed for the part of "Black Isaac, or the Huntsman of Hogley Woods," he met with a severe fall, through treading on a butter-slide, which the twins had constructed from the entrance of the Tapestry Chamber to the top of the oak staircase. This last insult so enraged him, that he resolved to make one final effort to assert his dignity and social position, and determined to visit the insolent young Etonians the next night in his celebrated character of "Reckless Rupert, or the Headless Earl."

He had not appeared in this disguise for more than seventy years; in fact, not since he had so frightened pretty Lady Barbara Modish by means of it, that she suddenly broke off her engagement with the present Lord Canterville's grandfather, and ran away to Gretna Green with handsome Jack Castletown, declaring that nothing in the world would induce her to marry into a family that allowed such a horrible phantom to walk up and down the terrace at twilight. Poor Jack was afterwards shot in a duel by Lord Canterville on Wandsworth Common, and Lady Barbara died of a broken heart at Tunbridge Wells before the year was out, so, in every way, it had been a great success. It was, however an extremely difficult "makeup," if I may use such a theatrical expression in connection with one of the greatest mysteries of the supernatural, or, to employ a more scientific term, the higher-natural world, and it took him fully three hours to make his preparations. At last everything was ready, and he was very pleased with his appearance. The big leather riding-boots that went with the dress were just a little too large for him, and he could only find one of the two horse-pistols, but, on the whole, he was quite satisfied, and at a quarter-past one he glided out of the wainscoting and crept down the corridor. On reaching the room occupied by the twins, which I should mention was called the Blue Bed Chamber, on account of the colour of its hangings, he found the door just ajar. Wishing to make an effective entrance, he flung it wide open, when a heavy jug of water fell right down on him, wetting him to the skin, and just missing his left shoulder by a couple of inches. At the same moment he heard stifled shrieks of laughter proceeding from the four-post bed. The shock to his nervous system was so great that he fled back to his room as hard as he could go, and the next day he was laid up with a severe cold. The only thing that at all consoled him in the whole affair was the fact that he had not brought his head with him, for, had he done so, the consequences might have been very serious.

He now gave up all hope of ever frightening this rude American family, and contented himself, as a rule, with creeping about the passages in list slippers, with a thick red muffler round his throat for fear of draughts, and a small arquebuse, in case he should be attacked by the twins. The final blow he received occurred on the 19th of September. He had gone down-stairs to the great entrance-hall, feeling sure that there, at any rate, he would be quite unmolested, and was amusing himself by making satirical remarks on the large Saroni photographs of the American Minister and his wife which had now taken the place of the Canterville family pictures. He was simply but neatly clad in a long shroud, spotted with churchyard mould, had tied up his jaw with a strip of yellow linen, and carried a small lantern and a sexton's spade. In fact, he was dressed for the character of "Jonas the Graveless, or the Corpse-Snatcher of Chertsey Barn," one of his most remarkable impersonations, and one which the Cantervilles had every reason to remember, as it was the real origin of their quarrel with their neighbour, Lord Rufford. It was about a quarter-past two o'clock in the morning, and, as far as he could ascertain, no one was stirring. As he was strolling towards the library, however, to see if there were any traces left of the blood-stain, suddenly there leaped out on him from a dark corner two figures, who waved their arms wildly above their heads, and shrieked out "BOO!" in his ear.

Seized with a panic, which, under the circumstances, was only natural, he rushed for the staircase, but found Washington Otis waiting for him there with the big garden-syringe, and being thus hemmed in by his enemies on every side, and driven almost to bay, he vanished into the great iron stove, which, fortunately for him, was not lit, and had to make his way home through the flues and chimneys, arriving at his own room in a terrible state of dirt, disorder, and despair.

After this he was not seen again on any nocturnal expedition. The twins lay in wait for him on several occasions, and strewed the passages with nutshells every night to the great annoyance of their parents and the servants, but it was of no avail. It was quite evident that his feelings were so wounded that he would not appear. Mr. Otis consequently resumed his great work on the history of the Democratic Party, on which he had been engaged for some years; Mrs. Otis organized a wonderful clam-bake, which amazed the whole county; the boys took to lacrosse, euchre, poker, and other American national games, and Virginia rode about the lanes on her pony, accompanied by the young Duke of Cheshire, who had come to spend the last week of his holidays at Canterville Chase. It was generally assumed that the ghost had gone away, and, in fact, Mr. Otis wrote a letter to that effect to Lord Canterville, who, in reply, expressed his great pleasure at the news, and sent his best congratulations to the Minister's worthy wife.

The Otises, however, were deceived, for the ghost was still in the house, and though now almost an invalid, was by no means ready to let matters rest, particularly as he heard that among the guests was the young Duke of Cheshire, whose grand-uncle, Lord Francis Stilton, had once bet a hundred guineas with Colonel Carbury that he would play dice with the Canterville ghost, and was found the next morning lying on the floor of the card-room in such a helpless paralytic state that, though he lived on to a great age, he was never able to say anything again but "Double Sixes." The story was well known at the time, though, of course, out of respect to the feelings of the two noble families, every attempt was made to hush it up, and a full account of all the circumstances connected with it will be found in the third volume of Lord Tattle's *Recollections of the Prince Regent and his Friends.* The ghost, then, was naturally very anxious to show that he had not lost his influence over the Stiltons, with whom, indeed, he was distantly connected, his own first cousin having been married *en secondes noces* to the Sieur de Bulkeley, from whom, as every one knows, the Dukes of Cheshire are lineally descended. Accordingly, he made arrangements for appearing to Virginia's little lover in his celebrated impersonation of "The Vampire Monk, or the Bloodless Benedictine," a performance so horrible that when old Lady Startup saw it, which she did on one fatal New Year's Eve, in the year 1764, she went off into the most piercing shrieks, which culminated in violent apoplexy, and died in three days, after disinheriting the Cantervilles, who were her nearest relations, and leaving all her money to her London apothecary. At the last moment, however, his terror of the twins prevented his leaving his room, and the little Duke slept in peace under the great feathered canopy in the Royal Bedchamber, and dreamed of Virginia.

## V

A few days after this, Virginia and her curly-haired cavalier went out riding on Brockley meadows, where she tore her habit so badly in getting through a hedge that, on their return home, she made up her mind to go up by the back staircase so as not to be seen. As she was running past the Tapestry Chamber, the door of which happened to be open, she fancied she saw some one inside, and thinking it was her mother's maid, who sometimes used to bring her work there, looked in to ask her to mend her habit. To her immense surprise, however, it was the Canterville Ghost himself! He was sitting by the window, watching the ruined gold of the yellowing trees fly through the air, and the red leaves dancing madly down the long avenue. His head was leaning on his hand, and his whole attitude was one of extreme depression. Indeed, so forlorn, and so much out of repair did he look, that little Virginia, whose first idea had been to run away and lock herself in her room, was filled with pity, and determined to try and comfort him. So light was her footfall, and so deep his melancholy, that he was not aware of her presence till she spoke to him.

"I am so sorry for you," she said, "but my brothers are going back to Eton to-morrow, and then, if you behave yourself, no one will annoy you."

"It is absurd asking me to behave myself," he answered, looking round in astonishment at the pretty little girl who had ventured to address him, "quite absurd. I must rattle my chains, and groan through keyholes, and walk about at night, if that is what you mean. It is my only reason for existing."

"It is no reason at all for existing, and you know you have been very wicked. Mrs. Umney told us, the first day we arrived here, that you had killed your wife."

"Well, I quite admit it," said the Ghost, petulantly, "but it was a purely family matter, and concerned no one else."

"It is very wrong to kill any one," said Virginia, who at times had a sweet puritan gravity, caught from some old New England ancestor.

"Oh, I hate the cheap severity of abstract ethics! My wife was very plain, never had my ruffs properly starched, and knew nothing about cookery. Why, there was a buck I had shot in Hogley Woods, a magnificent pricket, and do you know how she had it sent to table? However, it is no matter now, for it is all over, and I don't think it was very nice of her brothers to starve me to death, though I did kill her."

"Starve you to death? Oh, Mr. Ghost-I mean Sir Simon, are you hungry? I have a sandwich in my case. Would you like it?"

"No, thank you, I never eat anything now; but it is very kind of you, all the same, and you are much nicer than the rest of your horrid, rude, vulgar, dishonest family."

"Stop!" cried Virginia, stamping her foot, "it is you who are rude, and horrid, and vulgar, and as for dishonesty, you know you stole the paints out of my box to try and furbish up that ridiculous blood-stain in the library. First you took all my reds, including the vermilion, and I couldn't do any more sunsets, then you took the emerald-green and the chrome-yellow, and finally I had nothing left but indigo and Chinese white, and could only do moonlight scenes, which are always depressing to look at, and not at all easy to paint. I never told on you, though I was very much annoyed, and it was most ridiculous, the whole thing; for who ever heard of emerald-green blood?"

"Well, really," said the Ghost, rather meekly, "what was I to do? It is a very difficult thing to get real blood nowadays, and, as your brother began it all with his Paragon Detergent, I certainly saw no reason why I should not have your paints. As for colour, that is always a matter of taste: the Cantervilles have blue blood, for instance, the very bluest in England; but I know you Americans don't care for things of this kind."

"You know nothing about it, and the best thing you can do is to emigrate and improve your mind. My father will be only too happy to give you a free passage, and though there is a heavy duty on spirits of every kind, there will be no difficulty about the Custom House, as the officers are all Democrats. Once in New York, you are sure to be a great success. I know lots of people there who would give a hundred thousand dollars to have a grandfather, and much more than that to have a family ghost."

"I don't think I should like America."

"I suppose because we have no ruins and no curiosities," said Virginia, satirically.

"No ruins! No curiosities!" answered the Ghost; "You have your navy and your manners."

"Good evening; I will go and ask Papa to get the twins an extra week's holiday."

"Please don't go, Miss Virginia," he cried; "I am so lonely and so unhappy, and I really don't know what to do. I want to go to sleep and I cannot."

"That's quite absurd! You have merely to go to bed and blow out the candle. It is very difficult sometimes to keep awake, especially at church, but there is no difficulty at all about sleeping. Why, even babies know how to do that, and they are not very clever."

"I have not slept for three hundred years," he said sadly, and Virginia's beautiful blue eyes opened in wonder; "for three hundred years I have not slept, and I am so tired." Virginia grew quite grave, and her little lips trembled like rose-leaves. She came towards him, and kneeling down at his side, looked up into his old withered face.

"Poor, poor Ghost," she murmured; "have you no place where you can sleep?"

"Far away beyond the pine-woods," he answered, in a low, dreamy voice, "there is a little garden. There the grass grows long and deep, there are the great white stars of the hemlock flower, there the nightingale sings all night long. All night long he sings, and the cold crystal moon looks down, and the yew-tree spreads out its giant arms over the sleepers."

Virginia's eyes grew dim with tears, and she hid her face in her hands.

"You mean the Garden of Death," she whispered.

"Yes, death. Death must be so beautiful. To lie in the soft brown earth, with the grasses waving above one's head, and listen to silence. To have no yesterday, and no to-morrow. To forget time, to forget life, to be at peace. You can help me. You can open for me the portals of death's house, for love is always with you, and love is stronger than death is."

Virginia trembled, a cold shudder ran through her, and for a few moments there was silence. She felt as if she was in a terrible dream.

Then the ghost spoke again, and his voice sounded like the sighing of the wind.

"Have you ever read the old prophecy on the library window?"

"Oh, often," cried the little girl, looking up; "I know it quite well. It is painted in curious black letters, and is difficult to read. There are only six lines:

'When a golden girl can win
Prayer from out the lips of sin,
When the barren almond bears,
And a little child gives away its tears,
Then shall all the house be still
And peace come to Canterville.'

But I don't know what they mean."

"They mean," he said, sadly, "that you must weep with me for my sins, because I have no tears, and pray with me for my soul, because I have no faith, and then, if you have always been sweet, and good, and gentle, the angel of death will have mercy on me. You will see fearful shapes in darkness, and wicked voices will whisper in your ear, but they will not harm you, for against the purity of a little child the powers of Hell cannot prevail."

Virginia made no answer, and the ghost wrung his hands in wild despair as he looked down at her bowed golden head. Suddenly she stood up, very pale, and with a strange light in her eyes. "I am not afraid," she said firmly, "and I will ask the angel to have mercy on you."

He rose from his seat with a faint cry of joy, and taking her hand bent over it with old-fashioned grace and kissed it. His fingers were as cold as ice, and his lips burned like fire, but Virginia did not falter, as he led her across the dusky room. On the faded green tapestry were broidered little huntsmen. They blew their tasselled horns and with their tiny hands waved to her to go back. "Go back! Little Virginia," they cried, "go back!" but the ghost clutched her hand more tightly, and she shut her eyes against them. Horrible animals with lizard tails and goggle eyes blinked at her from the carven chimneypiece, and murmured, "Beware! Little Virginia, beware! We may never see you again," but the Ghost glided on more swiftly, and Virginia did not listen. When they reached the end of the room he stopped, and muttered some words she could not understand. She opened her eyes, and saw the wall slowly fading away like a mist, and a great black cavern in front of her. A bitter cold wind swept round them, and she felt something pulling at her dress. "Quick, quick," cried the Ghost, "or it will be too late," and in a moment the wainscoting had closed behind them, and the Tapestry Chamber was empty.

## VI

About ten minutes later, the bell rang for tea, and, as Virginia did not come down, Mrs. Otis sent up one of the footmen to tell her. After a little time he returned and said that he could not find Miss Virginia anywhere. As she was in the habit of going out to the garden every evening to get flowers for the dinner-table, Mrs. Otis was not at all alarmed at first, but when six o'clock struck, and Virginia did not appear, she became really agitated, and sent the boys out to look for her, while she herself and Mr. Otis searched every room in the house. At half-past six the boys came back and said that they could find no trace of their sister anywhere. They were all now in the greatest state of excitement, and did not know what to do, when Mr. Otis suddenly remembered that, some few days before, he had given a band of gipsies permission to camp in the park. He accordingly at once set off for Blackfell Hollow, where he knew they were, accompanied by his eldest son and two of the farm-servants. The little Duke of Cheshire, who was perfectly frantic with anxiety, begged hard to be allowed to go too, but Mr. Otis would not allow him, as he was afraid there might be a scuffle. On arriving at the spot, however, he found that the gipsies had gone, and it was evident that their departure had been rather sudden, as the fire was still burning, and some plates were lying on the grass.

Having sent off Washington and the two men to scour the district, he ran home, and despatched telegrams to all the police inspectors in the county, telling them to look out for a little girl who had been kidnapped by tramps or gipsies. He then ordered his horse to be brought round, and, after insisting on his wife and the three boys sitting down to dinner, rode off down the Ascot road with a groom. He had hardly, however, gone a couple of miles, when he heard somebody galloping after him, and, looking round, saw the little Duke coming up on his pony, with his face very flushed, and no hat. "I'm awfully sorry, Mr. Otis," gasped out the boy, "but I can't eat any dinner as long as Virginia is lost. Please don't be angry with me; if you had let us be engaged last year, there would never have been all this trouble. You won't send me back, will you? I can't go! I won't go!"

The Minister could not help smiling at the handsome young scapegrace, and was a good deal touched at his devotion to Virginia, so leaning down from his horse, he patted him kindly on the shoulders, and said, "Well, Cecil, if you won't go back, I suppose you must come with me, but I must get you a hat at Ascot."

"Oh, bother my hat! I want Virginia!" cried the little Duke, laughing, and they galloped on to the railway station. There Mr. Otis inquired of the station-master if any one answering to the description of Virginia had been seen on the platform, but could get no news of her. The station-master, however, wired up and down the line, and assured him that a strict watch would be kept for her, and, after having bought a hat for the little Duke from a linen-draper, who was just putting up his shutters, Mr. Otis rode off to Bexley, a village about four miles away, which he was told was a well-known haunt of the gipsies, as there was a large common next to it. Here they roused up the rural policeman, but could get no information from him, and, after riding all over the common, they turned their horses' heads homewards, and reached the Chase about eleven o'clock, dead-tired and almost heart-broken. They found Washington and the twins waiting for them at the gate-house with lanterns, as the avenue was very dark. Not the slightest trace of Virginia had been discovered. The gipsies had been caught on Brockley meadows, but she was not with them, and they had explained their sudden departure by saying that they had mistaken the date of Chorton Fair, and had gone off in a hurry for fear they should be late. Indeed, they had been quite distressed at hearing of Virginia's disappearance, as they were very grateful to Mr. Otis for having allowed them to camp in his park, and four of their number had stayed behind to help in the search. The carp-pond had been dragged, and the whole Chase thoroughly gone over, but without any result. It was evident that, for that night at any rate, Virginia was lost to them; and it was in a state of the deepest depression that Mr. Otis and the boys walked up to the house, the groom following behind with the two horses and the pony. In the hall they found a group of frightened servants, and lying on a sofa in the library was poor Mrs. Otis, almost out of her mind with terror and anxiety, and having her forehead bathed with eau de cologne by the old housekeeper. Mr. Otis at once insisted on her having something to eat, and ordered up supper for the whole party. It was a melancholy meal, as hardly any one spoke, and even the twins were awestruck and subdued, as they were very fond of their sister. When they had finished, Mr. Otis, in spite of the entreaties of the little Duke, ordered them all to bed, saying that nothing more could be done that night, and that he would telegraph in the morning to Scotland Yard for some detectives to be sent down immediately. Just as they were passing out of the dining-room, midnight began to boom from the clock tower, and when the last stroke sounded they heard a crash and a sudden shrill cry; a dreadful peal of thunder shook the house, a strain of unearthly music floated through the air, a panel at the top of the staircase flew back with a loud noise, and out on the landing, looking very pale and white, with a little casket in her hand, stepped Virginia. In a moment they had all rushed up to her. Mrs. Otis clasped her passionately in her arms, the Duke smothered her with violent kisses, and the twins executed a wild war-dance round the group.

"Good heavens! Child, where have you been?" said Mr. Otis, rather angrily, thinking that she had been playing some foolish trick on them. "Cecil and I have been riding all over the country looking for you, and your mother has been frightened to death. You must never play these practical jokes any more."

"Except on the Ghost! Except on the Ghost!" shrieked the twins, as they capered about.

"My own darling, thank God you are found; you must never leave my side again," murmured Mrs. Otis, as she kissed the trembling child, and smoothed the tangled gold of her hair.

"Papa," said Virginia, quietly, "I have been with the Ghost. He is dead, and you must come and see him. He had been very wicked, but he was really sorry for all that he had done, and he gave me this box of beautiful jewels before he died."

The whole family gazed at her in mute amazement, but she was quite grave and serious; and, turning round, she led them through the opening in the wain-scoting down a narrow secret corridor, Washington following with a lighted candle, which he had caught up from the table. Finally, they came to a great oak door, studded with rusty nails. When Virginia touched it, it swung back on its heavy hinges, and they found themselves in a little low room, with a vaulted ceiling, and one tiny grated window. Embedded in the wall was a huge iron ring, and chained to it was a gaunt skeleton, that was stretched out at full length on the stone floor, and seemed to be trying to grasp with its long fleshless fingers an old-fashioned trencher and ewer, that were placed just out of its reach. The jug had evidently been once filled with water, as it was covered inside with green mould. There was nothing on the trencher but a pile of dust. Virginia knelt down beside the skeleton, and, folding her little hands together, began to pray silently, while the rest of the party looked on in wonder at the terrible tragedy whose secret was now disclosed to them.

"Hallo!" suddenly exclaimed one of the twins, who had been looking out of the window to try and discover in what wing of the house the room was situated. "Hallo! The old withered almond-tree has blossomed. I can see the flowers quite plainly in the moonlight."

"God has forgiven him," said Virginia, gravely, as she rose to her feet, and a beautiful light seemed to illumine her face. "What an angel you are!" cried the young Duke, and he put his arm round her neck, and kissed her.

## VII

Four days after these curious incidents, a funeral started from Canterville Chase at about eleven o'clock at night. The hearse was drawn by eight black horses, each of which carried on its head a great tuft of nodding ostrich-plumes, and the leaden coffin was covered by a rich purple pall, on which was embroidered in gold the Canterville coat-of-arms. By the side of the hearse and the coaches walked the servants with lighted torches, and the whole procession was wonderfully impressive. Lord Canterville was the chief mourner, having come up specially from Wales to attend the funeral, and sat in the first carriage along with little Virginia. Then came the United States Minister and his wife, then Washington and the three boys, and in the last carriage was Mrs. Umney. It was generally felt that, as she had been frightened by the ghost for more than fifty years of her life, she had a right to see the last of him. A deep grave had been dug in the corner of the churchyard, just under the old yew-tree, and the service was read in the most impressive manner by the Rev. Augustus Dampier. When the ceremony was over, the servants, according to an old custom observed in the Canterville family, extinguished their torches, and, as the coffin was being lowered into the grave, Virginia stepped forward, and laid on it a large cross made of white and pink almond-blossoms. As she did so, the moon came out from behind a cloud, and flooded with its silent silver the little churchyard, and from a distant copse a nightingale began to sing. She thought of the ghost's description of the Garden of Death, her eyes became dim with tears, and she hardly spoke a word during the drive home.

The next morning, before Lord Canterville went up to town, Mr. Otis had an interview with him on the subject of the jewels the ghost had given to Virginia. They were perfectly magnificent, especially a certain ruby necklace with old Venetian setting, which was really a superb specimen of sixteenth-century work, and their value was so great that Mr. Otis felt considerable scruples about allowing his daughter to accept them.

"My lord," he said, "I know that in this country mortmain is held to apply to trinkets as well as to land, and it is quite clear to me that these jewels are, or should be, heirlooms in your family. I must beg you, accordingly, to take them to London with you, and to regard them simply as a portion of your property which has been restored to you under certain strange conditions. As for my daughter, she is merely a child, and has as yet, I am glad to say, but little interest in such appurtenances of idle luxury. I am also informed by Mrs. Otis, who, I may say, is no mean authority upon Art,-having had the privilege of spending several winters in Boston when she was a girl,-that these gems are of great monetary worth, and if offered for sale would fetch a tall price. Under these circumstances, Lord Canterville, I feel sure that you will recognize how impossible it would be for me to allow them to remain in the possession of any member of my family; and, indeed, all such vain gauds and toys, however suitable or necessary to the dignity of the British aristocracy, would be completely out of place among those who have been brought up on the severe, and I believe immortal, principles of Republican simplicity. Perhaps I should mention that Virginia is very anxious that you should allow her to retain the box, as a memento of your unfortunate but misguided ancestor. As it is extremely old, and consequently a good deal out of repair, you may perhaps think fit to comply with her request. For my own part, I confess I am a good deal surprised to find a child of mine expressing sympathy with mediaevalism in any form, and can only account for it by the fact that Virginia was born in one of your London suburbs shortly after Mrs. Otis had returned from a trip to Athens."

Lord Canterville listened very gravely to the worthy Minister's speech, pulling his grey moustache now and then to hide an involuntary smile, and when Mr. Otis had ended, he shook him cordially by the hand, and said: "My dear sir, your charming little daughter rendered my unlucky ancestor, Sir Simon, a very important service, and I and my family are much indebted to her for her marvellous courage and pluck. The jewels are clearly hers, and, egad, I believe that if I were heartless enough to take them from her, the wicked old fellow would be out of his grave in a fortnight, leading me the devil of a life. As for their being heirlooms, nothing is an heirloom that is not so mentioned in a will or legal document, and the existence of these jewels has been quite unknown. I assure you I have no more claim on them than your butler, and when Miss Virginia grows up, I dare say she will be pleased to have pretty things to wear. Besides, you forget, Mr. Otis, that you took the furniture and the ghost at a valuation, and anything that belonged to the ghost passed at once into your possession, as, whatever activity Sir Simon may have shown in the corridor at night, in point of law he was really dead, and you acquired his property by purchase."

Mr. Otis was a good deal distressed at Lord Canterville's refusal, and begged him to reconsider his decision, but the good-natured peer was quite firm, and finally induced the Minister to allow his daughter to retain the present the ghost had given her, and when, in the spring of 1890, the young Duchess of Cheshire was presented at the Queen's first drawing-room on the occasion of her marriage, her jewels were the universal theme of admiration. For Virginia received the coronet, which is the reward of all good little American girls, and was married to her boy-lover as soon as he came of age. They were both so charming, and they loved each other so much, that every one was delighted at the match, except the old Marchioness of Dumbleton, who had tried to catch the Duke for one of her seven unmarried daughters, and had given no less than three expensive dinner-parties for that purpose, and, strange to say, Mr. Otis himself. Mr. Otis was extremely fond of the young Duke personally, but, theoretically, he objected to titles, and, to use his own words, "was not without apprehension lest, amid the enervating influences of a pleasure-loving aristocracy, the true principles of Republican simplicity should be forgotten." His objections, however, were completely overruled, and I believe that when he walked up the aisle of St. George's, Hanover Square, with his daughter leaning on his arm, there was not a prouder man in the whole length and breadth of England.

The Duke and Duchess, after the honeymoon was over, went down to Canterville Chase, and on the day after their arrival they walked over in the afternoon to the lonely churchyard by the pine-woods. There had been a great deal of difficulty at first about the inscription on Sir Simon's tombstone, but finally it had been decided to engrave on it simply the initials of the old gentleman's name, and the verse from the library window. The Duchess had brought with her some lovely roses, which she strewed upon the grave, and after they had stood by it for some time they strolled into the ruined chancel of the old abbey. There the Duchess sat down on a fallen pillar, while her husband lay at her feet smoking a cigarette and looking up at her beautiful eyes. Suddenly he threw his cigarette away, took hold of her hand, and said to her, "Virginia, a wife should have no secrets from her husband."

"Dear Cecil! I have no secrets from you."

"Yes, you have," he answered, smiling, "you have never told me what happened to you when you were locked up with the ghost."

"I have never told any one, Cecil," said Virginia, gravely.

"I know that, but you might tell me."

"Please don't ask me, Cecil, I cannot tell you. Poor Sir Simon! I owe him a great deal. Yes, don't laugh, Cecil, I really do. He made me see what Life is, and what Death signifies, and why Love is stronger than both."

The Duke rose and kissed his wife lovingly.

"You can have your secret as long as I have your heart," he murmured.

"You have always had that, Cecil."

"And you will tell our children some day, won't you?"

Virginia blushed.

# A HAUNTED ISLAND
## ALGERNON BLACKWOOD

The following events occurred on a small island of isolated position in a large Canadian lake, to whose cool waters the inhabitants of Montreal and Toronto flee for rest and recreation in the hot months. It is only to be regretted that events of such peculiar interest to the genuine student of the psychical should be entirely uncorroborated. Such unfortunately, however, is the case.

Our own party of nearly twenty had returned to Montreal that very day, and I was left in solitary possession for a week or two longer, in order to accomplish some important 'reading' for the law which I had foolishly neglected during the summer.

It was late in September, and the big trout and maskinonge were stirring themselves in the depths of the lake, and beginning slowly to move up to the surface waters as the north winds and early frosts lowered their temperature. Already the maples were crimson and gold, and the wild laughter of the loons echoed in sheltered bays that never knew their strange cry in the summer.

With a whole island to oneself, a two-storey cottage, a canoe, and only the chipmunks, and the farmer's weekly visit with eggs and bread, to disturb one, the opportunities for hard reading might be very great. It all depends!

The rest of the party had gone off with many warnings to beware of Indians, and not to stay late enough to be the victim of a frost that thinks nothing of forty below zero. After they had gone, the loneliness of the situation made itself unpleasantly felt. There were no other islands within six or seven miles, and though the mainland forests lay a couple of miles behind me, they stretched for a very great distance unbroken by any signs of human habitation. But, though the island was completely deserted and silent, the rocks and trees that had echoed human laughter and voices almost every hour of the day for two months could not fail to retain some memories of it all; and I was not surprised to fancy I heard a shout or a cry as I passed from rock to rock, and more than once to imagine that I heard my own name called aloud.

In the cottage there were six tiny little bedrooms divided from one another by plain unvarnished partitions of pine. A wooden bedstead, a mattress, and a chair, stood in each room, but I only found two mirrors, and one of these was broken.

The boards creaked a good deal as I moved about, and the signs of occupation were so recent that I could hardly believe I was alone. I half expected to find someone left behind, still trying to crowd into a box more than it would hold. The door of One room was stiff, and refused for a moment to open, and it required very little persuasion to imagine someone was holding the handle on the inside, and that when it opened I should meet a pair of human eyes.

A thorough search of the floor led me to select as my own sleeping quarters a little room with a diminutive balcony over the verandah roof. The room was very small, but the bed was large, and had the best mattress of them all. It was situated directly over the sitting-room where I should live and do my 'reading', and the miniature window looked out to the rising sun. With the exception of a narrow path which led from the front door and verandah through the trees to the boat-landing, the island was densely covered with maples, hemlocks, and cedars. The trees gathered in round the cottage so closely that the slightest wind made the branches scrape the roof and tap the wooden walls. A few moments after sunset the darkness became impenetrable, and ten yards beyond the glare of the lamps that shone through the sitting-room windows—of which there were four—you could not see an inch before your nose, nor move a step without running up against a tree.

The rest of that day I spent moving my belongings from my tent to the sitting-room, taking stock of the contents of the larder, and chopping enough wood for the stove to last me for a week. After that, just before sunset, I went round the island a couple of times in my canoe for precaution's sake. I had never dreamed of doing this before, but when a man is alone he does things that never occur to him when he is one of a large party.

How lonely the island seemed when I landed again! The sun was down, and twilight is unknown in these northern regions. The darkness comes up at once. The canoe safely pulled up and turned over on her face, I groped my way up the little narrow pathway to the verandah. The six lamps were soon burning merrily in the front room; but in the kitchen, where I 'dined', the shadows were so gloomy, and the lamplight so inadequate, that the stars could be seen peeping through the cracks between the rafters.

I turned in early that night. Though it was calm and there was no wind, the creaking of my bedstead and the musical gurgle of the water over the rocks below were not the only sounds that reached my ears. As I lay awake, the appalling emptiness of the house grew upon me. The corridors and vacant rooms seemed to echo innumerable footsteps, shufflings, the rustle of skirts, and a constant undertone of whispering. When sleep at length overtook me, the breathings and noises, however, passed gently to mingle with the voices of my dreams.

A week passed by, and the 'reading' progressed favourably. On the tenth day of my solitude, a strange thing happened. I awoke after a good night's sleep to find myself possessed with a marked repugnance for my room. The air seemed to stifle me. The more I tried to define the cause of this dislike, the more unreasonable it appeared. There was something about the room that made me afraid. Absurd as it seems, this feeling clung to me obstinately while dressing, and more than once I caught myself shivering, and conscious of an inclination to get out of the room as quickly as possible. The more I tried to laugh it away, the more real it became; and when at last I was dressed, and went out into the passage, and downstairs into the kitchen, it was with feelings of relief, such as I might imagine would accompany one's escape from the presence of a dangerous contagious disease.

While cooking my breakfast, I carefully recalled every night spent in the room, in the hope that I might in some way connect the dislike I now felt with some disagreeable incident that had occurred in it. But the only thing I could recall was one stormy night when I suddenly awoke and heard the boards creaking so loudly in the corridor that I was convinced there were people in the house. So certain was I of this, that I had descended the stairs, gun in hand, only to find the doors and windows securely fastened, and the mice and black-beetles in sole possession of the floor. This was certainly not sufficient to account for the strength of my feelings.

The morning hours I spent in steady reading; and when I broke off in the middle of the day for a swim and luncheon, I was very much surprised, if not a little alarmed, to find that my dislike for the room had, if anything, grown stronger. Going upstairs to get a book, I experienced the most marked aversion to entering the room, and while within I was conscious all the time of an uncomfortable feeling that was half uneasiness and half apprehension. The result of it was that, instead of reading, I spent the afternoon on the water paddling and fishing, and when I got home about sundown, brought with me half a dozen delicious black bass for the supper-table and the larder.

As sleep was an important matter to me at this time, I had decided that if my aversion to the room was so strongly marked on my return as it had been before, I would move my bed down into the sitting-room, and sleep there. This was, I argued, in no sense a concession to an absurd and fanciful fear, but simply a precaution to ensure a good night's sleep. A bad night involved the loss of the next day's reading,—a loss I was not prepared to incur.

I accordingly moved my bed downstairs into a corner of the sitting-room facing the door, and was moreover uncommonly glad when the operation was completed, and the door of the bedroom closed finally upon the shadows, the silence, and the strange *fear* that shared the room with them.

The croaking stroke of the kitchen clock sounded the hour of eight as I finished washing up my few dishes, and closing the kitchen door behind me, passed into the front room. All the lamps were lit, and their reflectors, which I had polished up during the day, threw a blaze of light into the room.

Outside the night was still and warm. Not a breath of air was stirring; the waves were silent, the trees motionless, and heavy clouds hung like an oppressive curtain over the heavens. The darkness seemed to have rolled up with unusual swiftness, and not the faintest glow of colour remained to show where the sun had set. There was present in the atmosphere that ominous and overwhelming silence which so often precedes the most violent storms.

I sat down to my books with my brain unusually clear, and in my heart the pleasant satisfaction of knowing that five black bass were lying in the ice-house, and that tomorrow morning the old farmer would arrive with fresh bread and eggs. I was soon absorbed in my books.

As the night wore on the silence deepened. Even the chipmunks were still; and the boards of the floors and walls ceased creaking. I read on steadily till, from the gloomy shadows of the kitchen, came the hoarse sound of the clock striking nine. How loud the strokes sounded! They were like blows of a big hammer. I closed one book and opened another, feeling that I was just warming up to my work.

This, however, did not last long. I presently found that I was reading the same paragraphs over twice, simple paragraphs that did not require such effort. Then I noticed that my mind began to wander to other things, and the effort to recall my thoughts became harder with each digression. Concentration was growing momentarily more difficult. Presently I discovered that I had turned over two pages instead of one, and had not noticed my mistake until I was well down the page. This was becoming serious. What was the disturbing influence? It could not be physical fatigue. On the contrary, my mind was unusually alert, and in a more receptive condition than usual. I made a new and determined effort to read, and for a short time succeeded in giving my whole attention to my subject. But in a very few moments again I found myself leaning back in my chair, staring vacantly into space.

Something was evidently at work in my subconsciousness. There was something I had neglected to do. Perhaps the kitchen door and windows were not fastened. I accordingly went to see, and found that they were! The fire perhaps needed attention. I went to see, and found that it was all right! I looked at the lamps, went upstairs into every bedroom in turn, and then went round the house, and even into the ice-house. Nothing was wrong; everything was in its place. Yet something *was* wrong! The conviction grew stronger and stronger within me.

When I at length settled down to my books again and tried to read, I became aware, for the first time, that the room seemed growing cold. Yet the day had been oppressively warm, and evening had brought no relief. The six big lamps, moreover, gave out heat enough to warm the room pleasantly. But a chilliness, that perhaps crept up from the lake, made itself felt in the room, and caused me to get up to close the glass door opening on to the verandah.

For a brief moment I stood looking out at the shaft of light that fell from the windows and shone some little distance down the pathway, and out for a few feet into the lake.

As I looked, I saw a canoe glide into the pathway of light, and immediately crossing it, pass out of sight again into the darkness. It was perhaps a hundred feet from the shore, and it moved swiftly.

I was surprised that a canoe should pass the island at that time of night, for all the summer visitors from the other side of the lake had gone home weeks before, and the island was a long way out of any line of water traffic.

My reading from this moment did not make very good progress, for somehow the picture of that canoe, gliding so dimly and swiftly across the narrow track of light on the black waters, silhouetted itself against the background of my mind with singular vividness. It kept coming between my eyes and the printed page. The more I thought about it the more surprised I became. It was of larger build than any I had seen during the past summer months, and was more like the old Indian war canoes with the high curving bows and stern and wide beam. The more I tried to read, the less success attended my efforts; and finally I closed my books and went out on the verandah to walk up and down a bit, and shake the chilliness out of my bones.

The night was perfectly still, and as dark as imaginable. I stumbled down the path to the little landing wharf, where the water made the very faintest of gurgling under the timbers. The sound of a big tree falling in the mainland forest, far across the lake, stirred echoes in the heavy air, like the first guns of a distant night attack. No other sound disturbed the stillness that reigned supreme.

As I stood upon the wharf in the broad splash of light that followed me from the sitting-room windows, I saw another canoe cross the pathway of uncertain light upon the water, and disappear at once into the impenetrable gloom that lay beyond. This time I saw more distinctly than before. It was like the former canoe, a big birch-bark, with high-crested bows and stern and broad beam. It was paddled by two Indians, of whom the one in the stern—the steerer—appeared to be a very large man. I could see this very plainly; and though the second canoe was much nearer the island than the first, I judged that they were both on their way home to the Government Reservation, which was situated some fifteen miles away upon the mainland.

I was wondering in my mind what could possibly bring any Indians down to this part of the lake at such an hour of the night, when a third canoe, of precisely similar build, and also occupied by two Indians, passed silently round the end of the wharf. This time the canoe was very much nearer shore, and it suddenly flashed into my mind that the three canoes were in reality one and the same, and that only one canoe was circling the island!

This was by no means a pleasant reflection, because, if it were the correct solution of the unusual appearance of the three canoes in this lonely part of the lake at so late an hour, the purpose of the two men could only reasonably be considered to be in some way connected with myself. I had never known of the Indians attempting any violence upon the settlers who shared the wild, inhospitable country with them; at the same time, it was not beyond the region of possibility to suppose . . . But then I did not care even to think of such hideous possibilities, and my imagination immediately sought relief in all manner of other solutions to the problem, which indeed came readily enough to my mind, but did not succeed in recommending themselves to my reason.

Meanwhile, by a sort of instinct, I stepped back out of the bright light in which I had hitherto been standing, and waited in the deep shadow of a rock to see if the canoe would again make its appearance. Here I could see, without being seen, and the precaution seemed a wise one.

After less than five minutes the canoe, as I had anticipated, made its fourth appearance. This time it was not twenty yards from the wharf, and I saw that the Indians meant to land. I recognized the two men as those who had passed before, and the steerer was certainly an immense fellow. It was unquestionably the same canoe. There could be no longer any doubt that for some purpose of their own the men had been going round and round the island for some time, waiting for an opportunity to land. I strained my eyes to follow them in the darkness, but the night had completely swallowed them up, and not even the faintest swish of the paddles reached my ears as the Indians plied their long and powerful strokes. The canoe would be round again in a few moments, and this time it was possible that the men might land. It was well to be prepared. I knew nothing of their intentions, and two to one (when the two are big Indians!) late at night on a lonely island was not exactly my idea of pleasant intercourse.

In a corner of the sitting-room, leaning up against the back wall, stood my Marlin rifle, with ten cartridges in the magazine and one lying snugly in the greased breech. There was just time to get up to the house and take up a position of defence in that corner. Without an instant's hesitation I ran up to the verandah, carefully picking my way among the trees, so as to avoid being seen in the light. Entering the room, I shut the door leading to the verandah, and as quickly as possible turned out every one of the six lamps. To be in a room so brilliantly lighted, where my every movement could be observed from outside, while I could see nothing but impenetrable darkness at every window, was by all laws of warfare an unnecessary concession to the enemy. And this enemy, if enemy it was to be, was far too wily and dangerous to be granted any such advantages.

I stood in the corner of the room with my back against the wall, and my hand on the cold rifle-barrel. The table, covered with my books, lay between me and the door, but for the first few minutes after the lights were out the darkness was so intense that nothing could be discerned at all. Then, very gradually, the outline of the room became visible, and the framework of the windows began to shape itself dimly before my eyes.

After a few minutes the door (its upper half of glass), and the two windows that looked out upon the front verandah, became specially distinct; and I was glad that this was so, because if the Indians came up to the house I should be able to see their approach, and gather something of their plans. Nor was I mistaken, for there presently came to my ears the peculiar hollow sound of a canoe landing and being carefully dragged up over the rocks. The paddles I distinctly heard being placed underneath, and the silence that ensued thereupon I rightly interpreted to mean that the Indians were stealthily approaching the house. . . .

While it would be absurd to claim that I was not alarmed—even frightened—at the gravity of the situation and its possible outcome, I speak the whole truth when I say that I was not overwhelmingly afraid for myself. I was conscious that even at this stage of the night I was passing into a psychical condition in which my sensations seemed no longer normal. Physical fear at no time entered into the nature of my feelings; and though I kept my hand upon my rifle the greater part of the night, I was all the time conscious that its assistance could be of little avail against the terrors that I had to face. More than once I seemed to feel most curiously that I was in no real sense a part of the proceedings, nor actually involved in them, but that I was playing the part of a spectator—a spectator, moreover, on a psychic rather than on a material plane. Many of my sensations that night were too vague for definite description and analysis, but the main feeling that will stay with me to the end of my days is the awful horror of it all, and the miserable sensation that if the strain had lasted a little longer than was actually the case my mind must inevitably have given way.

Meanwhile I stood still in my corner, and waited patiently for what was to come. The house was as still as the grave, but the inarticulate voices of the night sang in my ears, and I seemed to hear the blood running in my veins and dancing in my pulses.

If the Indians came to the back of the house, they would find the kitchen door and window securely fastened. They could not get in there without making considerable noise, which I was bound to hear. The only mode of getting in was by means, of the door that faced me, and I kept my eyes glued on that door without taking them off for the smallest fraction of a second.

My sight adapted itself every minute better to the darkness. I saw the table that nearly filled the room, and left only a narrow passage on each side. I could also make out the straight backs of the wooden chairs pressed up against it, and could even distinguish my papers and inkstand lying on the white oilcloth covering. I thought of the gay faces that had gathered round that table during the summer, and I longed for the sunlight as I had never longed for it before.

Less than three feet to my left the passage-way led to the kitchen, and the stairs leading to the bedrooms above commenced in this passage-way, but almost in the sitting-room itself. Through the windows I could see the dim motionless outlines of the trees: not a leaf stirred, not a branch moved.

A few moments of this awful silence, and then I was aware of a soft tread on the boards of the verandah, so stealthy that it seemed an impression directly on my brain rather than upon the nerves of hearing. Immediately afterwards a black figure darkened the glass door, and I perceived that a face was pressed against the upper panes. A shiver ran down my back, and my hair was conscious of a tendency to rise and stand at right angles to my head.

It was the figure of an Indian, broad-shouldered and immense; indeed, the largest figure of a man I have ever seen outside of a circus hall, By some power of light that seemed to generate itself in the brain, I saw the strong dark face with the aquiline nose and high cheek-bones flattened against the glass. The direction of the gaze I could not determine; but faint gleams of light as the big eyes rolled round and showed their whites, told me plainly that no corner of the room escaped their searching.

For what seemed fully five minutes the dark figure stood there, with the huge shoulders bent forward so as to bring the head down to the level of the glass; while behind him, though not nearly so large, the shadowy form of the other Indian swayed to and fro like a bent tree. While I waited in an agony of suspense and agitation for their next movement little currents of icy sensation ran up and down my spine and my heart seemed alternately to stop beating and then start off again with terrifying rapidity. They must have heard its thumping and the singing of the blood in my head! Moreover, I was conscious, as I felt a cold stream of perspiration trickle down my face, of a desire to scream, to shout, to bang the walls like a child, to make a noise, or do anything that would relieve the suspense and bring things to a speedy climax.

It was probably this inclination that led me to another discovery, for when I tried to bring my rifle from behind my back to raise it and have it pointed at the door ready to fire, I found that I was powerless to move.

The muscles, paralysed by this strange fear, refused to obey the will. Here indeed was a terrifying complication!

* * * * *

There was a faint sound of rattling at the brass knob, and the door was pushed open a couple of inches. A pause of a few seconds, and it was pushed open still further. Without a sound of footsteps that was appreciable to my ears, the two figures glided into the room, and the man behind gently closed the door after him.

They were alone with me between the four walls. Could they see me standing there, so still and straight in my corner? Had they, perhaps, already seen me? My blood surged and sang like the roll of drums in an orchestra; and though I did my best to suppress my breathing, it sounded like the rushing of wind through a pneumatic tube.

My suspense as to the next move was soon at an end—only, however, to give place to a new and keener alarm. The men had hitherto exchanged no words and no signs, but there were general indications of a movement across the room, and whichever way they went they would have to pass round the table. If they came my way they would have to pass within six inches of my person. While I was considering this very disagreeable possibility, I perceived that the smaller Indian (smaller by comparison) suddenly raised his arm and pointed to the ceiling. The other fellow raised his head and followed the direction of his companion's arm. I began to understand at last. They were going upstairs, and the room directly overhead to which they pointed had been until this night my bedroom. It was the room in which I had experienced that very morning so strange a sensation of fear, and but for which I should then have been lying asleep in the narrow bed against the window.

The Indians then began to move silently around the room; they were going upstairs, and they were coming round my side of the table. So stealthy were their movements that, but for the abnormally sensitive state of the nerves, I should never have heard them. As it was, their catlike tread was distinctly audible. Like two monstrous black cats they came round the table toward me, and for the first time I perceived that the smaller of the two dragged something along the floor behind him. As it trailed along over the floor with a soft, sweeping sound, I somehow got the impression that it was a large dead thing with outstretched wings, or a large, spreading cedar branch. Whatever it was, I was unable to see it even in outline, and I was too terrified, even had I possessed the power over my muscles, to move my neck forward in the effort to determine its nature.

Nearer and nearer they came. The leader rested a giant hand upon the table as he moved. My lips were glued together, and the air seemed to burn in my nostrils. I tried to close my eyes, so that I might not see as they passed me; but my eyelids had stiffened, and refused to obey. Would they never get by me? Sensation seemed also to have left my legs, and it was as if I were standing on mere supports of wood or stone. Worse still, I was conscious that I was losing the power of balance, the power to stand upright, or even to lean backwards against the wall. Some force was drawing me forward, and a dizzy terror seized me that I should lose my balance, and topple forward against the Indians just as they were in the act of passing me.

Even moments drawn out into hours must come to an end some time, and almost before I knew it the figures had passed me and had their feet upon the lower step of the stairs leading to the upper bedrooms. There could not have been six inches between us, and yet I was conscious only of a current of cold air that followed them. They had not touched me, and I was convinced that they had not seen me. Even the trailing thing on the floor behind them had not touched my feet, as I had dreaded it would, and on such an occasion as this I was grateful even for the smallest mercies.

The absence of the Indians from my immediate neighbourhood brought little sense of relief. I stood shivering and shuddering in my corner, and, beyond being able to breathe more freely, I felt no whit less uncomfortable. Also, I was aware that a certain light, which, without apparent source or rays, had enabled me to follow their every gesture and movement, had gone out of the room with their departure. An unnatural darkness now filled the room, and pervaded its every corner so that I could barely make out the positions of the windows and the glass doors.

As I said before, my condition was evidently an abnormal one. The capacity for feeling surprise seemed, as in dreams, to be wholly absent. My senses recorded with unusual accuracy every smallest occurrence, but I was able to draw only the simplest deductions.

The Indians soon reached the top of the stairs, and there they halted for a moment. I had not the faintest clue as to their next movement. They appeared to hesitate. They were listening attentively. Then I heard one of them, who by the weight of his soft tread must have been the giant, cross the narrow corridor and enter the room directly overhead—my own little bedroom. But for the insistence of that unaccountable dread I had experienced there in the morning, I should at that very moment have been lying in the bed with the big Indian in the room standing beside me.

For the space of a hundred seconds there was silence, such as might have existed before the birth of sound. It was followed by a long quivering shriek of terror, which rang out into the night, and ended in a short gulp before it had run its full course. At the same moment the other Indian left his place at the head of the stairs, and joined his companion in the bedroom. I heard the 'thing' trailing behind him along the floor. A thud followed, as of something heavy falling, and then all became as still and silent as before.

It was at this point that the atmosphere, surcharged all day with the electricity of a fierce storm, found relief in a dancing flash of brilliant lightning simultaneously with a crash of loudest thunder. For five seconds every article in the room was visible to me with amazing distinctness, and through the windows I saw the tree trunks standing in solemn rows. The thunder pealed and echoed across the lake and among the distant islands, and the flood-gates of heaven then opened and let out their rain in streaming torrents.

The drops fell with a swift rushing sound upon the still waters of the lake, which leaped up to meet them, and pattered with the rattle of shot on the leaves of the maples and the roof of the cottage. A moment later, and another flash, even more brilliant and of longer duration than the first, lit up the sky from zenith to horizon, and bathed the room momentarily in dazzling whiteness. I could see the rain glistening on the leaves and branches outside. The wind rose suddenly, and in less than a minute the storm that had been gathering all day burst forth in its full fury.

Above all the noisy voices of the elements, the slightest sounds in the room overhead made themselves heard, and in the few seconds of deep silence that followed the shriek of terror and pain, I was aware that the movements had commenced again. The men were leaving the room and approaching the top of the stairs. A short pause, and they began to descend. Behind them, tumbling from step to step, I could hear that trailing 'thing' being dragged along. It had become ponderous!

I awaited their approach with a degree of calmness, almost of apathy, which was only explicable on the ground that after a certain point Nature applies her own anaesthetic, and a merciful condition of numbness super venes. On they came, step by step, nearer and nearer, with the shuffling sound of the burden behind growing louder as they approached.

They were already half-way down the stairs when I was galvanized afresh into a condition of terror by the consideration of a new and horrible possibility. It was the reflection that if another vivid flash of lightning were to come when the shadowy procession was in the room, perhaps when it was actually passing in front of me, I should see everything in detail, and worse, be seen myself! I could only hold my breath and wait—wait while the minutes lengthened into hours, and the procession made its slow progress round the room.

The Indians had reached the foot of the staircase. The form of the huge leader loomed in the doorway of the passage, and the burden with an ominous thud had dropped from the last step to the floor. There was a moment's pause while I saw the Indian turn and stoop to assist his companion. Then the procession moved forward again, entered the room close on my left, and began to move slowly round my side of the table. The leader was already beyond me, and his companion, dragging on the floor behind him the burden, whose confused outline I could dimly make out, was exactly in front of me, when the cavalcade came to a dead halt. At the same moment, with the strange suddenness of thunderstorms, the splash of the rain ceased altogether, and the wind died away into utter silence.

For the space of five seconds my heart seemed to stop beating, and then the worst came. A double flash of lightning lit up the room and its contents with merciless vividness.

The huge Indian leader stood a few feet past me on my right. One leg was stretched forward in the act of taking a step. His immense shoulders were turned towards his companion, and in all their magnificent fierceness I saw the outline of his features. His gaze was directed upon the burden his companion was dragging along the floor; but his profile, with the big aquiline nose, high cheek-bone, straight black hair, and bold chin, burnt itself in that brief instant into my brain, never again to fade.

Dwarfish, compared with this gigantic figure, appeared the proportions of the other Indian, who, within twelve inches of my face, was stooping over the thing he was dragging in a position that lent to his person the additional horror of deformity. And the burden, lying upon a sweeping cedar branch which he held and dragged by a long stem, was the body of a white man. The scalp had been neatly lifted, and blood lay in a broad smear upon the cheeks and forehead.

Then, for the first time that night, the terror that had paralysed my muscles and my will lifted its unholy spell from my soul. With a loud cry I stretched out my arms to seize the big Indian by the throat, and, grasping only air, tumbled forward unconscious upon the ground.

I had recognized the body, and *the face was my own!* . . .

It was bright daylight when a man's voice recalled me to consciousness. I was lying where I had fallen, and the farmer was standing in the room with the loaves of bread in his hands. The horror of the night was still in my heart, and as the bluff settler helped me to my feet and picked up the rifle which had fallen with me, with many questions and expressions of condolence, I imagined my brief replies were neither self-explanatory nor even intelligible.

That day, after a thorough and fruitless search of the house, I left the island, and went over to spend my last ten days with the farmer; and when time came for me to leave, the necessary reading had been accomplished, and my nerves had completely recovered their balance.

On the day of my departure the farmer started early in his big boat with my belongings to row to the point, twelve miles distant, where a little steamer ran twice a week for the accommodation of hunters. Late in the afternoon I went off in another direction in my canoe, wishing to see the island once again, where I had been the victim of so strange an experience.

In due course I arrived there, and made a tour of the island. I also made a search of the little house, and it was not without a curious sensation in my heart that I entered the little upstairs bedroom. There seemed nothing unusual.

Just after I re-embarked, I saw a canoe gliding ahead of me around the curve of the island. A canoe was an unusual sight at this time of the year, and this one seemed to have sprung from nowhere. Altering my course a little, I watched it disappear around the next projecting point of rock. It had high curving bows, and there were two Indians in it. I lingered with some excitement, to see if it would appear again round the other side of the island; and in less than five minutes it came into view. There were less than two hundred yards between us, and the Indians, sitting on their haunches, were paddling swiftly in my direction.

I never paddled faster in my life than I did in those next few minutes. When I turned to look again, the Indians had altered their course, and were again circling the island.

The sun was sinking behind the forests on the mainland, and the crimson-coloured clouds of sunset were reflected in the waters of the lake, when I looked round for the last time, and saw the big bark canoe and its two dusky occupants still going round the island. Then the shadows deepened rapidly; the lake grew black, and the night wind blew its first breath in my face as I turned a corner, and a projecting bluff of rock hid from my view both island and canoe.

# THE SECRET OF MACARGER'S GULCH

## AMBROSE BIERCE

North westwardly from Indian Hill, about nine miles as the crow flies, is Macarger's Gulch. It is not much of a gulch—a mere depression between two wooded ridges of inconsiderable height. From its mouth up to its head-for gulches, like rivers, have an anatomy of their own—the distance does not exceed two miles, and the width at bottom is at only one place more than a dozen yards; for most of the distance on either side of the little brook which drains it in winter, and goes dry in the early spring, there is no level ground at all; the steep slopes of the hills, covered with an almost impenetrable growth of manzanita and chemisal, are parted by nothing but the width of the water course. No one but an occasional enterprising hunter of the vicinity ever goes into Macarger's Gulch, and five miles away it is unknown, even by name. Within that distance in any direction are far more conspicuous topographical features without names, and one might try in vain to ascertain by local inquiry the origin of the name of this one.

About midway between the head and the mouth of Macarger's Gulch, the hill on the right as you ascend is cloven by another gulch, a short dry one, and at the junction of the two is a level space of two or three acres, and there a few years ago stood an old board house containing one small room. How the component parts of the house, few and simple as they were, had been assembled at that almost inaccessible point is a problem in the solution of which there would be greater satisfaction than advantage. Possibly the creek bed is a reformed road. It is certain that the gulch was at one time pretty thoroughly prospected by miners, who must have had some means of getting in with at least pack animals carrying tools and supplies; their profits, apparendy, were not such as would have justified any considerable outlay to connect Macarger's Gulch with any center of civilization enjoying the distinction of a sawmill. The house, however, was there, most of it. It lacked a door and a window frame, and the chimney of mud and stones had fallen into an unlovely heap, overgrown with rank weeds. Such humble furniture as there may once have been and much of the lower weatherboarding, had served as fuel in the camp fires of hunters; as had also, probably, the curbing of an old well, which at the time I write of existed in the form of a rather wide but not very deep depression near by.

One afternoon in the summer of 1874, I passed up Macarger's Gulch from the narrow valley into which it opens, by following the dry bed of the brook. I was quail-shooting and had made a bag of about a dozen birds by the time I had reached the house described, of whose existence I was until then unaware. After rather carelessly inspecting the ruin I resumed my sport, and having fairly good success prolonged it until near sunset, when it occurred to me that I was a long way from any human habitation—too far to reach one by nightfall. But in my game bag was food, and the old house would afford shelter, if shelter were needed on a warm and dewless night in the foothills of the Sierra Nevada, where one may sleep in comfort on the pine needles, without covering. I am fond of solitude and love the night, so my resolution to "camp out" was soon taken, and by the time that it was dark I had made my bed of boughs and grasses in a corner of the room and was roasting a quail at a fire that I had kindled on the hearth. The smoke escaped out of the ruined chimney, the light illuminated the room with a kindly glow, and as I ate my simple meal of plain bird and drank the remains of a bottle of red wine which had served me all the afternoon in place of the water, which the region did not supply, I experienced a sense of comfort which better fare and accommodations do not always give.

Nevertheless, there was something lacking. I had a sense of comfort, but not of security. I detected myself staring more frequently at the open doorway and blank window than I could find warrant for doing. Outside these apertures all was black, and I was unable to repress a certain feeling of apprehension as my fancy pictured the outer world and filled it with unfriendly entities, natural and supernatural—chief among which, in their respective classes, were the grizzly bear, which I knew was occasionally still seen in that region, and the ghost, which I had reason to think was not. Unfortunately, our feelings do not always respect the law of probabilities, and to me that evening, the possible and the impossible were equally disquieting.

Everyone who has had experience in the matter must have observed that one confronts the actual and imaginary perils of the night with far less apprehension in the open air than in a house with an open doorway. I felt this now as I lay on my leafy couch in a corner of the room next to the chimney and permitted my fire to die out. So strong became my sense of the presence of something malign and menacing in the place, that I found myself almost unable to withdraw my eyes from the opening, as in the deepening darkness it became more and more indistinct. And when the last little flame flickered and went out I grasped the shotgun which I had laid at my side and actually turned the muzzle in the direction of the now invisible entrance, my thumb on one of the hammers, ready to cock the piece, my breath suspended, my muscles rigid and tense. But later I laid down the weapon with a sense of shame and mortification. What did I fear, and why? —I, to whom the night had been a more familiar face than that of man—I, in whom that element of hereditary superstition from which none of us is altogether free had given to solitude and darkness and silence only a more alluring interest and charm! I was unable to comprehend my folly, and losing in the conjecture the thing conjectured of, I fell asleep. And then I dreamed.

I was in a great city in a foreign land—a city whose people were of my own race, with minor differences of speech and costume; yet precisely what these were I could not say; my sense of them was indistinct. The city was dominated by a great castle upon an overlooking height whose name I knew, but could not speak. I walked through many streets, some broad and straight with high, modern buildings, some narrow, gloomy, and tortuous, between the gables of quaint old houses whose overhanging stories, elaborately ornamented with carvings in wood and stone, almost met above my head.

I sought someone whom I had never seen, yet knew that I should recognize when found. My quest was not aimless and fortuitous; it had a definite method.

I turned from one street into another without hesitation and threaded a maze of intricate passages, devoid of the fear of losing my way.

Presently I stopped before a low door in a plain stone house which might have been the dwelling of an artisan of the better sort, and without announcing myself, entered. The room, rather sparely furnished, and lighted by a single window with small diamond-shaped panes, had but two occupants; a man and a woman. They took no notice of my intrusion, a circumstance which, in the manner of dreams, appeared entirely natural. They were not conversing; they sat apart, unoccupied and sullen.

The woman was young and rather stout, with fine large eyes and a certain grave beauty; my memory of her expression is exceedingly vivid, but in dreams one does not observe the details of faces. About her shoulders was a plaid shawl. The man was older, dark, with an evil face made more forbidding by a long scar extending from near the left temple diagonally downward into the black mustache; though in my dreams it seemed rather to haunt the face as a thing apart—I can express it no otherwise—than to belong to it. The moment that I found the man and woman I knew them to be husband and wife.

What followed, I remember indistinctly; all was confused and inconsistent—made so, I think, by gleams of consciousness. It was as if two pictures, the scene of my dream, and my actual surroundings, had been blended, one overlying the other, until the former, gradually fading, disappeared, and I was broad awake in the deserted cabin, entirely and tranquilly conscious of my situation.

My foolish fear was gone, and opening my eyes I saw that my fire, not altogether burned out, had revived by the falling of a stick and was again lighting the room. I had probably slept only a few minutes, but my commonplace dream had somehow so strongly impressed me that I was no longer drowsy; and after a little while I rose, pushed the embers of my fire together, and lighting my pipe proceeded in a rather ludicrously methodical way to meditate upon my vision.

It would have puzzled me then to say in what respect it was worth attention. In the first moment of serious thought that I gave to the matter I recognized the city of my dream as Edinburgh, where I had never been; so if the dream was a memory it was a memory of pictures and description. The recognition somehow deeply impressed me; it was as if something in my mind insisted rebelliously against will and reason on the importance of all this. And that faculty, whatever it was, asserted also a control of my speech. "Surely," I said aloud, quite involuntarily, "the MacGregors must have come here from Edinburgh."

At the moment, neither the substance of this remark nor the fact of my making it, surprised me in the least; it seemed entirely natural that I should know the name of my dreamfolk and something of their history. But the absurdity of it all soon dawned upon me: I laughed aloud, knocked the ashes from my pipe and again stretched myself upon my bed of boughs and grass, where I lay staring absently into my failing fire, with no further thought of either my dream or my surroundings. Suddenly the single remaining flame crouched for a moment, then, springing upward, lifted itself clear of its embers and expired in air. The darkness was absolute.

At that instant—almost, it seemed, before the gleam of the blaze had faded from my eyes—there was a dull, dead sound, as of some heavy body falling upon the floor, which shook beneath me as I lay. I sprang to a sitting posture and groped at my side for my gun; my notion was that some wild beast had leaped in through the open window. While the flimsy structure was still shaking from the impact I heard the sound of blows, the scuffling of feet upon the floor, and then—it seemed to come from almost within reach of my hand, the sharp shrieking of a woman in mortal agony. So horrible a cry I had never heard nor conceived; it utterly unnerved me; I was conscious for a moment of nothing but my own terror! Fortunately my hand now found the weapon of which it was in search, and the familiar touch somewhat restored me. I leaped to my feet, straining my eyes to pierce the darkness. The violent sounds had ceased, but more terrible than these, I heard, at what seemed long intervals, the faint intermittent gasping of some living, dying thing!

As my eyes grew accustomed to the dim light of the coals in the fireplace, I saw first the shapes of the door and window, looking blacker than the black of the walls. Next, the distinction between wall and floor became discernible, and at last I was sensible to the form and full expanse of the floor from end to end and side to side. Nothing was visible and the silence was unbroken.

With a hand that shook a little, the other still grasping my gun, I restored my fire and made a critical examination of the place. There was nowhere any sign that the cabin had been entered. My own tracks were visible in the dust covering the floor, but there were no others. I relit my pipe, provided fresh fuel by ripping a thin board or two from the inside of the house-I did not care to go into the darkness out of doors—and passed the rest of the night smoking and thinking, and feeding my fire; not for added years of life would I have permitted that little flame to expire again.

Some years afterward I met in Sacramento a man named Morgan, to whom I had a note of introduction from a friend in San Francisco. Dining with him one evening at his home I observed various "trophies" upon the wall, indicating that he was fond of shooting. It turned out that he was, and in relating some of his feats he mentioned having been in the region of my adventure.

"Mr. Morgan," I asked abruptly, "do you know a place up there called Macarger's Gulch?"

"I have good reason to," he replied; "it was I who gave to the newspapers, last year, the accounts of the finding of the skeleton there."

I had not heard of it; the accounts had been published, it appeared, while I was absent in the East.

"By the way," said Morgan, "the name of the gulch is a corruption; it should have been called 'MacGregor's.' My dear," he added, speaking to his wife, "Mr. Elderson has upset his wine."

That was hardly accurate—I had simply dropped it, glass and all.

"There was an old shanty once in the gulch," Morgan resumed when the ruin wrought by my awkwardness had been repaired, "but just previously to my visit it had been blown down, or rather blown away, for its débris was scattered all about, the very floor being parted, plank from plank. Between two of the sleepers still in position I and my companion observed the remnant of a plaid shawl, and examining it found that it was wrapped about the shoulders of the body of a woman, of which but little remained besides the bones, partly covered with fragments of clothing, and brown dry skin. But we will spare Mrs. Morgan," he added with a smile. The lady had indeed exhibited signs of disgust rather than sympathy.

"It is necessary to say, however," he went on, "that the skull was fractured in several places, as by blows of some blunt instrument; and that instrument itself—a pick-handle, still stained with blood—lay under the boards near by."

Mr. Morgan turned to his wife. "Pardon me, my dear," he said with affected solemnity, "for mentioning these disagreeable particulars, the natural though regrettable incidents of a conjugal quarrel—resulting, doubtless, from the luckless wife's insubordination."

"I ought to be able to overlook it," the lady replied with composure; "you have so many times asked me to in those very words."

I thought he seemed rather glad to go on with his story. "From these and other circumstances," he said, "the coroner's jury found that the deceased, Janet MacGregor, came to her death from blows inflicted by some person to the jury unknown; but it was added that the evidence pointed strongly to her husband, Thomas MacGregor, as the guilty person. But Thomas MacGregor has never been found nor heard of. It was learned that the couple came from Edinburgh, but not—my dear, do you not observe that Mr. Elderson's boneplate has water in it?" I had deposited a chicken bone in my finger bowl.

"In a little cupboard I found a photograph of MacGregor, but it did not lead to his capture."

"Will you let me see it?" I said.

The picture showed a dark man with an evil face made more forbidding by a long scar extending from near the temple diagonally downward into the black mustache.

"By the way, Mr. Elderson," said my affable host, "may I know why you asked about 'Macarger's Gulch'?"

"I lost a mule near there once," I replied, "and the mischance has—has quite upset me."

"My dear," said Mr. Morgan, with the mechanical intonation of an interpreter translating, "the loss of Mr. Elderson's mule has peppered his coffee."

# THE ROMANCE OF CERTAIN OLD CLOTHES

## HENRY JAMES

### 1

Towards the middle of the eighteenth century there lived in the Province of Massachusetts a widowed gentlewoman, the mother of three children, by name Mrs. Veronica Wingrave. She had lost her husband early in life, and had devoted herself to the care of her progeny. These young persons grew up in a manner to reward her tenderness and to gratify her highest hopes. The first-born was a son, whom she had called Bernard, in remembrance of his father. The others were daughters - born at an interval of three years apart. Good looks were traditional in the family, and this youthful trio were not likely to allow the tradition to perish. The boy was of that fair and ruddy complexion and that athletic structure which in those days (as in these) were the sign of good English descent - a frank, affectionate young fellow, a deferential son, a patronising brother, a steadfast friend. Clever, however, he was not; the wit of the family had been apportioned chiefly to his sisters. The late Mr. William Wingrave had been a great reader of Shakespeare, at a time when this pursuit implied more freedom of thought than at the present day, and in a community where it required much courage to patronise the drama even in the closet; and he had wished to call attention to his admiration of the great poet by calling his daughters out of his favourite plays. Upon the elder he had bestowed the romantic name of Rosalind, and the younger he had called Perdita, in memory of a little girl born between them, who had lived but a few weeks.

When Bernard Wingrave came to his sixteenth year his mother put a brave face upon it and prepared to execute her husband's last injunction. This had been a formal command that, at the proper age, his son should be sent out to England, to complete his education at the university of Oxford, where he himself had acquired his taste for elegant literature. It was Mrs. Wingrave's belief that the lad's equal was not to be found in the two hemispheres, but she had the old traditions of literal obedience. She swallowed her sobs, and made up her boy's trunk and his simple provincial outfit, and sent him on his way across the seas. Bernard presented himself at his father's college, and spent five years in England, without great honour, indeed, but with a vast deal of pleasure and no discredit. On leaving the university he made the journey to France. In his twenty-fourth year he took ship for home, prepared to find poor little New England (New England was very small in those days) a very dull, unfashionable residence. But there had been changes at home, as well as in Mr. Bernard's opinions. He found his mother's house quite habitable, and his sisters grown into two very charming young ladies, with all the accomplishments and graces of the young women of Britain, and a certain native-grown originality and wildness, which, if it was not an accomplishment, was certainly a grace the more. Bernard privately assured his mother that his sisters were fully a match for the most genteel young women in the old country; whereupon poor Mrs. Wingrave, you may be sure, bade them hold up their heads. Such was Bernard's opinion, and such, in a tenfold higher degree, was the opinion of Mr. Arthur Lloyd. This gentleman was a college-mate of Mr. Bernard, a young man of reputable family, of a good person and a handsome inheritance; which latter appurtenance he proposed to invest in trade in the flourishing colony. He and Bernard were sworn friends; they had crossed the ocean together, and the young American had lost no time in presenting him at his mother's house, where he had made quite as good an impression as that which he had received and of which I have just given a hint.

The two sisters were at this time in all the freshness of their youthful bloom; each wearing, of course, this natural brilliancy in the manner that became her best. They were equally dissimilar in appearance and character. Rosalind, the elder - now in her twenty-second year - was tall and white, with calm gray eyes and auburn tresses; a very faint likeness to the Rosalind of Shakespeare's comedy, whom I imagine a brunette (if you will), but a slender, airy creature, full of the softest, quickest impulses. Miss Wingrave, with her slightly lymphatic fairness, her fine arms, her majestic height, her slow utterance, was not cut out for adventures. She would never have put on a man's jacket and hose; and, indeed, being a very plump beauty, she may have had reasons apart from her natural dignity. Perdita, too, might very well have exchanged the sweet melancholy of her name against something more in consonance with her aspect and disposition. She had the cheek of a gipsy and the eye of an eager child, as well as the smallest waist and lightest foot in all the country of the Puritans. When you spoke to her she never made you wait, as her handsome sister was wont to do (while she looked at you with a cold fine eye), but gave you your choice of a dozen answers before you had uttered half your thought. The young girls were very glad to see their brother once more; but they found themselves quite able to spare part of their attention for their brother's friend. Among the young men their friends and neighbours, the *belle jeunesse* of the Colony, there were many excellent fellows, several devoted swains, and some two or three who enjoyed the reputation of universal charmers and conquerors. But the homebred arts and somewhat boisterous gallantry of these honest colonists were completely eclipsed by the good looks, the fine clothes, the punctilious courtesy, the perfect elegance, the immense information, of Mr. Arthur Lloyd. He was in reality no paragon; he was a capable, honourable, civil youth, rich in pounds sterling, in his health and complacency and his little capital of uninvested affections. But he was a gentleman; he had a handsome person; he had studied and travelled; he spoke French, he played on the flute, and he read verses aloud with very great taste. There were a dozen reasons why Miss Wingrave and her sister should have thought their other male acquaintance made but a poor figure before such a perfect man of the world. Mr. Lloyd's anecdotes told our little New England maidens a great deal more of the ways and means of people of fashion in European capitals than he had any idea of doing. It was delightful to sit by and hear him and Bernard talk about the fine people and fine things they had seen. They would all gather round the fire after tea, in the little wainscoted parlour, and the two young men would remind each other, across the rug, of this, that and the other adventure. Rosalind and Perdita would often have given their ears to know exactly what adventure it was, and where it happened, and who was there, and what the ladies had on; but in those days a well bred young woman was not expected to break into the conversation of her elders, or to ask too many questions; and the poor girls used therefore to sit fluttering behind the more languid - or more discreet - curiosity of their mother.

## 2

That they were both very fine girls Arthur Lloyd was not slow to discover; but it took him some time to make up his mind whether he liked the big sister or the little sister best. He had a strong presentiment - an emotion of a nature entirely too cheerful to be called a foreboding - that he was destined to stand up before the parson with one of them; yet he was unable to arrive at a preference, and for such a consummation a preference was certainly necessary, for Lloyd had too much young blood in his veins to make a choice by lot and be cheated of the satisfaction of falling in love. He resolved to take things as they came - to let his heart speak. Meanwhile he was on a very pleasant footing. Mrs. Wingrave showed a dignified indifference to his 'intentions', equally remote from a carelessness of her daughter's honour and from that sharp alacrity to make him come to the point, which, in his quality of a young man of property, he had too often encountered in the worldly matrons of his native islands. As for Bernard, all that he asked was that his friend should treat his sisters as his own; and as for the poor girls themselves, however each may have secretly longed that their visitor should do or say something 'marked', they kept a very modest and contented demeanour.

Towards each other, however, they were somewhat more on the offensive. They were good friends enough, and accommodating bedfellows (they shared the same four-poster), betwixt whom it would take more than a day for the seeds of jealousy to sprout and bear fruit; but they felt that the seeds had been sown on the day that Mr. Lloyd came into the house. Each made up her mind that, if she should be slighted, she would bear her grief in silence, and that no one should be any the wiser; for if they had a great deal of ambition, they had also a large share of pride. But each prayed in secret, nevertheless, that upon *her* the selection, the distinction, might fall. They had need of a vast deal of patience, of self-control, of dissimulation. In those days a young girl of decent breeding could make no advances whatever, and barely respond, indeed, to those that were made. She was expected to sit still in her chair, with her eyes on the carpet, watching the spot where the mystic handkerchief should fall. Poor Arthur Lloyd was obliged to carry on his wooing in the little wainscoted parlour, before the eyes of Mrs. Wingrave, her son, and his prospective sister-in-law. But youth and love are so cunning that a hundred signs and tokens might travel to and fro, and not one of these three pairs of eyes detect them in their passage. The two maidens were almost always together, and had plenty of chances to betray themselves. That each knew she was being watched, however, made not a grain of difference in the little offices they mutually rendered, or in the various household tasks they performed in common. Neither flinched nor fluttered beneath the silent battery of her sister's eyes. The only apparent change in their habits was that they had less to say to each other. It was impossible to talk about Mr. Lloyd, and it was ridiculous to talk about anything else. By tacit agreement they began to wear all their choice finery, and to devise such little implements of conquest, in the way of ribbons and top-knots and kerchiefs, as were sanctioned by indubitable modesty. They executed in the same inarticulate fashion a contract of fair play in this exciting game. "Is it better so?" Rosalind would ask, tying a bunch of ribbons on her bosom, and turning about from her glass to her sister. Perdita would look up gravely from her work and examine the decoration. "I think you had better give it another loop," she would say, with great solemnity, looking hard at her sister with eyes that added, 'upon my honour!'

So they were for ever stitching and trimming their petticoats, and pressing out their muslins, and contriving washes and ointments and cosmetics, like the ladies in the household of the vicar of Wakefield. Some three or four months went by; it grew to be midwinter, and as yet Rosalind knew that if Perdita had nothing more to boast of than she, there was not much to be feared from her rivalry. But Perdita by this time - the charming Perdita - felt that her secret had grown to be tenfold more precious than her sister's.

One afternoon Miss Wingrave sat alone - that was a rare accident - before her toilet-glass, combing out her long hair. It was getting too dark to see; she lit the two candles in their sockets, on the frame of her mirror, and then went to the window to draw her curtains. It was a gray December evening; the landscape was bare and bleak, and the sky heavy with snow-clouds. At the end of the large garden into which her window looked was a wall with a little postern door, opening into a lane. The door stood ajar, as she could vaguely see in the gathering darkness, and moved slowly to and fro, as if some one were swaying it from the lane without. It was doubtless a servant-maid who had been having a tryst with her sweetheart. But as she was about to drop her curtain Rosalind saw her sister step into the garden and hurry along the path which led to the house. She dropped the curtain, all save a little crevice for her eyes. As Perdita came up the path she seemed to be examining something in her hand, holding it close to her eyes. When she reached the house she stopped a moment, looked intently at the object, and pressed it to her lips.

Poor Rosalind slowly came back to her chair and sat down before her glass, where, if she had looked at it less abstractedly, she would have seen her handsome features sadly disfigured by jealousy. A moment afterwards the door opened behind her and her sister came into the room, out of breath, and her cheeks aglow with the chilly air.

Perdita started. "Ah," said she, "I thought you were with our mother." The ladies were to go to a tea-party, and on such occasions it was the habit of one of the young girls to help their mother to dress. Instead of coming in, Perdita lingered at the door.

"Come in, come in," said Rosalind. "We have more than an hour yet. I should like you very much to give a few strokes to my hair." She knew that her sister wished to retreat, and that she could see in the glass all her movements in the room. "Nay, just help me with my hair," she said, "and I will go to Mamma."

Perdita came reluctantly, and took the brush. She saw her sister's eyes, in the glass, fastened hard upon her hands. She had not made three passes when Rosalind clapped her own right hand upon her sister's left, and started out of her chair. "Whose ring is that?" she cried, passionately, drawing her towards the light.

On the young girl's third finger glistened a little gold ring, adorned with a very small sapphire. Perdita felt that she need no longer keep her secret, yet that she must put a bold face on her avowal. "It's mine," she said proudly.

"Who gave it to you?" cried the other.

Perdita hesitated a moment. "Mr. Lloyd."

"Mr. Lloyd is generous, all of a sudden."

"Ah no," cried Perdita, with spirit, "not all of a sudden! He offered it to me a month ago."

"And you needed a month's begging to take it?" said Rosalind, looking at the little trinket, which indeed was not especially elegant, although it was the best that the jeweller of the Province could furnish. "I wouldn't have taken it in less than two."

"It isn't the ring," Perdita answered, "it's what it means!"

"It means that you are not a modest girl!" cried Rosalind.

"Pray, does your mother know of your intrigue? Does Bernard?"

"My mother has approved my 'intrigue', as you call it. Mr. Lloyd has asked for my hand, and Mamma has given it. Would you have had him apply to you, dearest sister?"

Rosalind gave her companion a long look, full of passionate envy and sorrow. Then she dropped her lashes on her pale cheeks and turned away. Perdita felt that it had not been a pretty scene; but it was her sister's fault. However, the elder girl rapidly called back her pride, and turned herself about again. "You have my very best wishes," she said, with a low curtsey. "I wish you every happiness, and a very long life."

Perdita gave a bitter laugh. "Don't speak in that tone!" she cried. "I would rather you should curse me outright. Come, Rosy," she added, "he couldn't marry both of us."

"I wish you very great joy," Rosalind repeated, mechanically, sitting down to her glass again, "and a very long life, and plenty of children."

There was something in the sound of these words not at all to Perdita's taste. "Will you give me a year to live at least?" she said.

"In a year I can have one little boy - or one little girl at least. If you will give me your brush again I will do your hair."

"Thank you," said Rosalind. "You had better go to Mamma. It isn't becoming that a young lady with a promised husband should wait on a girl with none."

"Nay," said Perdita, good-humouredly, "I have Arthur to wait upon me. You need my service more than I need yours." But her sister motioned her away, and she left the room. When she had gone poor Rosalind fell on her knees before her dressing-table, buried her head in her arms, and poured out a flood of tears and sobs. She felt very much the better for this effusion of sorrow. When her sister came back she insisted upon helping her to dress - on her wearing her prettiest things. She forced upon her acceptance a bit of lace of her own, and declared that now that she was to be married she should do her best to appear worthy of her lover's choice. She discharged these offices in stern silence; but, such as they were, they had to do duty as an apology and an atonement; she never made any other.

Now that Lloyd was received by the family as an accepted suitor nothing remained but to fix the wedding-day. It was appointed for the following April, and in the interval preparations were diligently made for the marriage. Lloyd, on his side, was busy with his commercial arrangements, and with establishing a correspondence with the great mercantile house to which he had attached himself in England. He was therefore not so frequent a visitor at Mrs. Wingrave's as during the months of his diffidence and irresolution, and poor Rosalind had less to suffer than she had feared from the sight of the mutual endearments of the young lovers. Touching his future sister-in-law Lloyd had a perfectly clear conscience. There had not been a particle of love-making between them, and he had not the slightest suspicion that he had dealt her a terrible blow. He was quite at his ease; life promised so well, both domestically and financially. The great revolt of the Colonies was not yet in the air, and that his connubial felicity should taxe a tragic turn it was absurd, it was blasphemous, to apprehend. Meanwhile, at Mrs. Wingrave's, there was a greater rustling of silks, a more rapid clicking of scissors and flying of needles, than ever. The good lady had determined that her daughter should carry from home the genteelest outfit that her money could buy or that the country could furnish. All the sage women in the Province were convened, and their united taste was brought to bear on Perdita's wardrobe.

Rosalind's situation, at this moment, was assuredly not to be envied. The poor girl had an inordinate love of dress, and the very best taste in the world, as her sister perfectly well knew. Rosalind was tall, she was stately and sweeping, she was made to carry stiff brocade and masses of heavy lace, such as belong to the toilet of a rich man's wife. But Rosalind sat aloof, with her beautiful arms folded and her head averted, while her mother and sister and the venerable women aforesaid worried and wondered over their materials, oppressed by the multitude of their resources. One day there came in a beautiful piece of white silk, brocaded with heavenly blue and silver, sent by the bridegroom himself - it not being thought amiss in those days that the husband-elect should contribute to the bride's trousseau. Perdita could think of no form or fashion which would do sufficient honour to the splendour of the material.

"Blue's your colour, sister, more than mine," she said, with appealing eyes. "It's a pity it's not for you. You would know what to do with it."

Rosalind got up from her place and looked at the great shining fabric, as it lay spread over the back of a chair. Then she took it up in her hands and felt it - lovingly, as Perdita could see - and turned about toward the mirror with it.

She let it roll down to her feet, and flung the other end over her shoulder, gathering it in about her waist with her white arm, which was bare to the elbow. She threw back her head, and looked at her image, and a hanging tress of her auburn hair fell upon the gorgeous surface of the silk. It made a dazzling picture. The women standing about uttered a little "Look, look!" of admiration. "Yes, indeed," said Rosalind, quietly, "blue is my colour." But Perdita could see that her fancy had been stirred, and that she would now fall to work and solve all their silken riddles. And indeed she behaved very well, as Perdita, knowing her insatiable love of millinery, was quite ready to declare. Innumerable yards of lustrous silk and satin, of muslin, velvet and lace, passed through her cunning hands, without a jealous word coming from her lips. Thanks to her industry, when the wedding-day came Perdita was prepared to espouse more of the vanities of life than any fluttering young bride who had yet received the sacramental blessing of a New England divine.

It had been arranged that the young couple should go out and spend the first days of their wedded life at the country-house of an English gentleman - a man of rank and a very kind friend to Arthur Lloyd. He was a bachelor; he declared he should be delighted to give up the place to the influence of Hymen. After the ceremony at church - it had been performed by an English clergyman - young Mrs. Lloyd hastened back to her mother's house to change her nuptial robes for a riding-dress. Rosalind helped her to effect the change, in the little homely room in which they had spent their undivided younger years. Perdita then hurried off to bid farewell to her mother, leaving Rosalind to follow. The parting was short; the horses were at the door, and Arthur was impatient to start. But Rosalind had not followed, and Perdita hastened back to her room, opening the door abruptly. Rosalind, as usual, was before the glass, but in a position which caused the other to stand still, amazed. She had dressed herself in Perdita's cast-off wedding veil and wreath, and on her neck she had hung the full string of pearls which the young girl had received from her husband as a wedding-gift. These things had been hastily laid aside, to await their possessor's disposal on her return from the country. Bedizened in this unnatural garb Rosalind stood before the mirror, plunging a long look into its depths and reading heaven knows what audacious visions. Perdita was horrified. It was a hideous image of their old rivalry come to life again. She made a step toward her sister, as if to pull off the veil and the flowers. But catching her eyes in the glass, she stopped.

"Farewell, sweetheart," she said. "You might at least have waited till I had got out of the house!" And she hurried away from the room.

Mr. Lloyd had purchased in Boston a house which to the taste of those days appeared as elegant as it was commodious; and here he very soon established himself with his young wife. He was thus separated by a distance of twenty miles from the residence of his mother-in-law. Twenty miles, in that primitive era of roads and conveyances, were as serious a matter as a hundred at the present day, and Mrs. Wingrave saw but little of her daughter during the first twelvemonth of her marriage. She suffered in no small degree from Perdita's absence; and her affliction was not diminished by the fact that Rosalind had fallen into terribly low spirits and was not to be roused or cheered but by change of air and company. The real cause of the young lady's dejection the reader will not be slow to suspect. Mrs. Wingrave and her gossips, however, deemed her complaint a mere bodily ill, and doubted not that she would obtain relief from the remedy just mentioned. Her mother accordingly proposed, on her behalf, a visit to certain relatives on the paternal side, established in New York, who had long complained that they were able to see so little of their New England cousins. Rosalind was despatched to these good people, under a suitable escort, and remained with them for several months. In the interval her brother Bernard, who had begun the practice of the law, made up his mind to take a wife. Rosalind came home to the wedding, apparently cured of her heartache, with bright roses and lilies in her face and a proud smile on her lips. Arthur Lloyd came over from Boston to see his brother-in-law married, but without his wife, who was expecting very soon to present him with an heir. It was nearly a year since Rosalind had seen him. She was glad—she hardly knew why—that Perdita had stayed at home. Arthur looked happy, but he was more grave and important than before his marriage. She thought he looked 'interesting'—for although the word, in its modern sense, was not then invented, we may be sure that the idea was. The truth is, he was simply anxious about his wife and her coming ordeal.

Nevertheless, he by no means failed to observe Rosalind's beauty and splendour, and to note how she effaced the poor little bride. The allowance that Perdita had enjoyed for her dress had now been transferred to her sister, who turned it to wonderful account. On the morning after the wedding he had a lady's saddle put on the horse of the servant who had come with him from town, and went out with the young girl for a ride. It was a keen, clear morning in January; the ground was bare and hard, and the horses in good condition - to say nothing of Rosalind, who was charming in her hat and plume, and her dark blue riding coat, trimmed with fur. They rode all the morning, they lost their way, and were obliged to stop for dinner at a farm-house. The early winter dusk had fallen when they got home. Mrs. Wingrave met them with a long face. A messenger had arrived at noon from Mrs. Lloyd; she was beginning to be ill, she desired her husband's immediate return. The young man, at the thought that he had lost several hours, and that by hard riding he might already have been with his wife, uttered a passionate oath. He barely consented to stop for a mouthful of supper, but mounted the messenger's horse and started off at a gallop. He reached home at midnight. His wife had been delivered of a little girl. "Ah, why weren't you with me?" she said, as he came to her bedside.

"I was out of the house when the man came. I was with Rosalind," said Lloyd, innocently.

Mrs. Lloyd made a little moan, and turned away. But she continued to do very well, and for a week her improvement was uninterrupted. Finally, however, through some indiscretion in the way of diet or exposure, it was checked, and the poor lady grew rapidly worse. Lloyd was in despair. It very soon became evident that she was breathing her last. Mrs. Lloyd came to a sense of her approaching end, and declared that she was reconciled with death. On the third evening after the change took place she told her husband that she felt she should not get through the night. She dismissed her servants, and also requested her mother to withdraw, Mrs. Wingrave having arrived on the preceding day. She had had her infant placed on the bed beside her, and she lay on her side, with the child against her breast, holding her husband's hands. The night-lamp was hidden behind the heavy curtains of the bed, but the room was illumined with a red glow from the immense fire of logs on the hearth.

"It seems strange not to be warmed into life by such a fire as that," the young woman said, feebly trying to smile, "if I had but a little of it in my veins! But I have given all *my* fire to this little spark of mortality." And she dropped her eyes on her child. Then raising them she looked at her husband with a long, penetrating gaze. The last feeling which lingered in her heart was one of suspicion. She had not recovered from the shock which Arthur had given her by telling her that in the hour of her agony he had been with Rosalind. She trusted her husband very nearly as well as she loved him; but now that she was called away for ever she felt a cold horror of her sister.

She felt in her soul that Rosalind had never ceased to be jealous of her good fortune; and a year of happy security had not effaced the young girl's image, dressed in her wedding-garments, and smiling with simulated triumph.

Now that Arthur was to be alone, what might not Rosalind attempt? She was beautiful, she was engaging; what arts might she not use, what impression might she not make upon the young man's saddened heart? Mrs. Lloyd looked at her husband in silence. It seemed hard, after all, to doubt of his constancy. His fine eyes were filled with tears; his face was convulsed with weeping; the clasp of his hands was warm and passionate. How noble he looked, how tender, how faithful and devoted! 'Nay,' thought Perdita, 'he's not for such a one as Rosalind. He'll never forget me. Nor does Rosalind truly care for him; she cares only for vanities and finery and jewels.' And she lowered her eyes on her white hands, which her husband's liberality had covered with rings, and on the lace ruffles which trimmed the edge of her night-dress. 'She covets my rings and my laces more than she covets my husband.'

At this moment the thought of her sister's rapacity seemed to cast a dark shadow between her and the helpless figure of her little girl. "Arthur," she said, "you must take off my rings. I shall not be buried in them. One of these days my daughter shall wear them - my rings and my laces and silks. I had them all brought out and shown me to-day. It's a great wardrobe - there's not such another in the Province; I can say it without vanity, now that I have done with it. It will be a great inheritance for my daughter when she grows into a young woman. There are things there that a man never buys twice, and if they are lost you will never again see the like. So you will watch them well. Some dozen things I have left to Rosalind; I have named them to my mother. I have given her that blue and silver; it was meant for her; I wore it only once, I looked ill in it. But the rest are to be sacredly kept for this little innocent. It's such a providence that she should be my colour; she can wear my gowns; she has her mother's eyes. You know the same fashions come back every twenty years. She can wear my gowns as they are. They will lie there quietly waiting till she grows into them - wrapped in camphor and rose-leaves, and keeping their colours in the sweet-scented darkness. She shall have black hair, she shall wear my carnation satin. Do you promise me, Arthur?"

"Promise you what, dearest?"

"Promise me to keep your poor little wife's old gowns."

"Are you afraid I shall sell them?"

"No, but that they may get scattered. My mother will have them properly wrapped up, and you shall lay them away under a double-lock. Do you know the great chest in the attic, with the iron bands? There is no end to what it will hold. You can put them all there. My mother and the housekeeper will do it, and give you the key. And you will keep the key in your secretary, and never give it to any one but your child. Do you promise me?"

"Ah, yes, I promise you," said Lloyd, puzzled at the intensity with which his wife appeared to cling to this idea.

"Will you swear?" repeated Perdita.

"Yes, I swear."

"Well - I trust you - I trust you," said the poor lady, looking into his eyes with eyes in which, if he had suspected her vague apprehensions, he might have read an appeal quite as much as an assurance.

Lloyd bore his bereavement rationally and manfully. A month after his wife's death, in the course of business, circumstances arose which offered him an opportunity of going to England. He took advantage of it, to change the current of his thoughts. He was absent nearly a year, during which his little girl was tenderly nursed and guarded by her grandmother. On his return he had his house again thrown open, and announced his intention of keeping the same state as during his wife's lifetime. It very soon came to be predicted that he would marry again, and there were at least a dozen young women of whom one may say that it was by no fault of theirs that, for six months after his return, the prediction did not come true.

During this interval he still left his little daughter in Mrs. Wingrave's hands, the latter assuring him that a change of residence at so tender an age would be full of danger for her health. Finally, however, he declared that his heart longed for his daughter's presence and that she must be brought up to town. He sent his coach and his housekeeper to fetch her home. Mrs. Wingrave was in terror lest something should befall her on the road; and, in accordance with this feeling, Rosalind offered to accompany her. She could return the next day. So she went up to town with her little niece, and Mr. Lloyd met her on the threshold of his house, overcome with her kindness and with paternal joy. Instead of returning the next day Rosalind stayed out the week; and when at last she reappeared, she had only come for her clothes. Arthur would not hear of her coming home, nor would the baby. That little person cried and choked if Rosalind left her; and at the sight of her grief Arthur lost his wits, and swore that she was going to die. In fine, nothing would suit them but that the aunt should remain until the little niece had grown used to strange faces.

It took two months to bring this consummation about; for it was not until this period had elapsed that Rosalind took leave of her brother-in-law. Mrs. Wingrave had shaken her head over her daughter's absence; she had declared

that it was not becoming, that it was the talk of the whole country. She had reconciled herself to it only because, during the girl's visit, the household enjoyed an
unwonted term of peace. Bernard Wingrave had brought his wife home to live,
between whom and her sister-in-law there was as little love as you please. Rosalind was perhaps no angel; but in the daily practice of life she was a sufficiently
good-natured girl, and if she quarrelled with Mrs. Bernard, it was not without
provocation. Quarrel, however, she did, to the great annoyance not only of her
antagonist, but of the two spectators of these constant altercations. Her stay in
the household of her brother-in-law, therefore, would have been delightful, if
only because it removed her from contact with the object of her antipathy at
home. It was doubly - it was ten times - delightful, in that it kept her near the
object of her early passion. Mrs. Lloyd's sharp suspicions had fallen very far
short of the truth. Rosalind's sentiment had been a passion at first, and a passion
it remained - a passion of whose radiant heat, tempered to the delicate state of
his feelings, Mr. Lloyd very soon felt the influence. Lloyd, as I have hinted, was
not a modern Petrarch; it was not in his nature to practise an ideal constancy. He
had not been many days in the house with his sister-in-law before he began to
assure himself that she was, in the language of that day, a devilish fine woman.

Whether Rosalind really practised those insidious arts that her sister had
been tempted to impute to her it is needless to inquire. It is enough to say that
she found means to appear to the very best advantage. She used to seat herself
every morning before the big fireplace in the dining-room, at work upon a piece
of tapestry, with her little niece disporting herself on the carpet at her feet, or
on the train of her dress, and playing with her woollen balls. Lloyd would have
been a very stupid fellow if he had remained insensible to the rich suggestions of
this charming picture. He was exceedingly fond of his little girl, and was never
weary of taking her in his arms and tossing her up and down, and making her
crow with delight. Very often, however, he would venture upon greater liberties
than the young lady was yet prepared to allow, and then she would suddenly
vociferate her displeasure. Rosalind, at this, would drop her tapestry, and put out
her handsome hands with the serious smile of the young girl whose virgin fancy
has revealed to her all a mother's healing arts. Lloyd would give up the child,
their eyes would meet, their hands would touch, and Rosalind would extinguish
the little girl's sobs upon the snowy folds of the kerchief that crossed her bosom.
Her dignity was perfect, and nothing could be more discreet than the manner
in which she accepted her brother-in-law's hospitality. It may almost be said,
perhaps, that there was something harsh in her reserve. Lloyd had a provoking

feeling that she was in the house and yet was unapproachable. Half-an-hour after supper, at the very outset of the long winter evenings, she would light her candle, make the young man a most respectful curtsey, and march off to bed. If these were arts, Rosalind was a great artist. But their effect was so gentle, so gradual, they were calculated to work upon the young widower's fancy with a *crescendo* so finely shaded, that, as the reader has seen, several weeks elapsed before Rosalind began to feel sure that her returns would cover her outlay. When this became morally certain she packed up her trunk and returned to her mother's house. For three days she waited; on the fourth Mr. Lloyd made his appearance - a respectful but pressing suitor. Rosalind heard him to the end, with great humility, and accepted him with infinite modesty. It is hard to imagine that Mrs. Lloyd would have forgiven her husband; but if anything might have disarmed her resentment it would have been the ceremonious continence of this interview. Rosalind imposed upon her lover but a short probation. They were married, as was becoming, with great privacy - almost with secrecy - in the hope perhaps, as was waggishly remarked at the time, that the late Mrs. Lloyd wouldn't hear of it.

The marriage was to all appearance a happy one, and each party obtained what each had desired - Lloyd 'a devilish fine woman', and Rosalind - but Rosalind's desires, as the reader will have observed, had remained a good deal of a mystery. There were, indeed, two blots upon their felicity, but time would perhaps efface them. During the first three years of her marriage Mrs Lloyd failed to become a mother, and her husband on his side suffered heavy losses of money. This latter circumstance compelled a material retrenchment in his expenditure, and Rosalind was perforce less of a fine lady than her sister had been. She contrived, however, to carry it like a woman of considerable fashion. She had long since ascertained that her sister's copious wardrobe had been sequestrated for the benefit of her daughter, and that it lay languishing in thankless gloom in the dusty attic. It was a revolting thought that these exquisite fabrics should await the good pleasure of a little girl who sat in a high chair and ate bread-and-milk with a wooden spoon. Rosalind had the good taste, however, to say nothing about the matter until several months had expired. Then, at last, she timidly broached it to her husband. Was it not a pity that so much finery should be lost? For lost it would be, what with colours fading, and moths eating it up, and the change of fashions. But Lloyd gave her so abrupt and peremptory a refusal, that she saw, for the present, her attempt was vain. Six months went by, however, and brought with them new needs and new visions. Rosalind's thoughts hovered lovingly about her sister's relics. She went up and looked at the chest in which they lay imprisoned. There was a sullen defiance in its three great padlocks and its iron bands which only quickened her cupidity. There was something exasperating in its incorruptible immobility. It was like a grim and grizzled old household servant, who locks his jaws over a family secret. And then there was a look of capacity in its vast extent, and a sound as of dense fulness, when Rosalind knocked its side with the toe of her little shoe, which caused her to flush with baffled longing. "It's absurd," she cried; "it's improper, it's wicked"; and she forthwith resolved upon another attack upon her husband. On the following day, after dinner, when he had had his wine, she boldly began it. But he cut her short with great sternness.

"Once for all, Rosalind," said he, "it's out of the question. I shall be gravely displeased if you return to the matter."

"Very good," said Rosalind. "I am glad to learn the esteem in which I am held. Gracious heaven," she cried, "I am a very happy woman! It's an agreeable thing to feel one's self sacrificed to a caprice!" And her eyes filled with tears of anger and disappointment. Lloyd had a good-natured man's horror of a woman's sobs, and he attempted - I may say he condescended - to explain. "It's not a caprice, dear, it's a promise," he said - "an oath."

"An oath? It's a pretty matter for oaths! And to whom, pray?"

"To Perdita," said the young man, raising his eyes for an instant, but immediately dropping them.

"Perdita - ah, Perdita!" and Rosalind's tears broke forth. Her bosom heaved with stormy sobs - sobs which were the long-deferred sequel of the violent fit of weeping in which she had indulged herself on the night when she discovered her sister's betrothal. She had hoped, in her better moments, that she had done with her jealousy; but her temper, on that occasion, had taken an ineffaceable fold.

"And pray, what right had Perdita to dispose of my future?" she cried. "What right had she to bind you to meanness and cruelty? Ah, I occupy a dignified place, and I make a very fine figure! I am welcome to what Perdita has left! And what has she left? I never knew till now how little! Nothing, nothing, nothing." This was very poor logic, but it was very good as a 'scene'. Lloyd put his arm around his wife's waist and tried to kiss her, but she shook him off with magnificent scorn. Poor fellow! He had coveted a 'devilish fine woman', and he had got one. Her scorn was intolerable. He walked away with his ears tingling - irresolute, distracted. Before him was his secretary, and in it the sacred key which with his own hand he had turned in the triple lock. He marched up and opened it, and took the key from a secret drawer, wrapped in a little packet which he had sealed with his own honest bit of blazonry. *Je garde,* said the motto - 'I keep'. But he was ashamed to put it back. He flung it upon the table beside his wife.

"Put it back!" she cried. "I want it not. I hate it!"

"I wash my hands of it," cried her husband. "God forgive me!"

Mrs. Lloyd gave an indignant shrug of her shoulders, and swept out of the room, while the young man retreated by another door. Ten minutes later Mrs. Lloyd returned, and found the room occupied by her little step-daughter and the nursery-maid. The key was not on the table. She glanced at the child. Her little niece was perched on a chair, with the packet in her hands. She had broken the seal with her own small fingers. Mrs. Lloyd hastily took possession of the key. At the habitual supper-hour Arthur Lloyd came back from his counting-room. It was the month of June, and supper was served by daylight. The meal was placed on the table, but Mrs. Lloyd failed to make her appearance. The servant whom his master sent to call her came back with the assurance that her room was empty, and that the women informed him that she had not been seen since dinner. They had, in truth, observed her to have been in tears, and, supposing her to be shut up in her chamber, had not disturbed her. Her husband called her name in various parts of the house, but without response. At last it occurred to him that he might find her by taking the way to the attic. The thought gave him a strange feeling of discomfort, and he bade his servants remain behind, wishing no witness in his quest. He reached the foot of the staircase leading to the topmost flat, and stood with his hand on the banisters, pronouncing his wife's name. His voice trembled. He called again louder and more firmly. The only sound which disturbed the absolute silence was a faint echo of his own tones, repeating his question under the great eaves. He nevertheless felt irresistibly moved to ascend the staircase. It opened upon a wide hall, lined with wooden closets, and terminating in a window which looked westward, and admitted the last rays of the sun. Before the window stood the great chest. Before the chest, on her knees, the young man saw with amazement and horror the figure of his wife. In an instant he crossed the interval between them, bereft of utterance. The lid of the chest stood open, exposing, amid their perfumed napkins, its treasure of stuffs and jewels. Rosalind had fallen backward from a kneeling posture, with one hand supporting her on the floor and the other pressed to her heart. On her limbs was the stiffness of death, and on her face, in the fading light of the sun, the terror of something more than death. Her lips were parted in entreaty, in dismay, in agony; and on her blanched brow and cheeks there glowed the marks of ten hideous wounds from two vengeful ghostly hands.

# THE LOST GHOST
## MARY E. WILKINS FREEMAN

**M**rs. John Emerson, sitting with her needlework beside the window, looked out and saw Mrs. Rhoda Meserve coming down the street, and knew at once by the trend of her steps and the cant of her head that she meditated turning in at her gate. She also knew by a certain something about her general carriage—a thrusting forward of the neck, a bustling hitch of the shoulders— that she had important news. Rhoda Meserve always had the news as soon as the news was in being, and generally Mrs. John Emerson was the first to whom she imparted it. The two women had been friends ever since Mrs. Meserve had married Simon Meserve and come to the village to live.

Mrs. Meserve was a pretty woman, moving with graceful flirts of ruffling skirts; her clear-cut, nervous face, as delicately tinted as a shell, looked brightly from the plumy brim of a black hat at Mrs. Emerson in the window. Mrs. Emerson was glad to see her coming. She returned the greeting with enthusiasm, then rose hurriedly, ran into the cold parlour and brought out one of the best rocking-chairs. She was just in time, after drawing it up beside the opposite window, to greet her friend at the door.

"Good-afternoon," said she. "I declare, I'm real glad to see you. I've been alone all day. John went to the city this morning. I thought of coming over to your house this afternoon, but I couldn't bring my sewing very well. I am putting the ruffles on my new black dress skirt."

"Well, I didn't have a thing on hand except my crochet work," responded Mrs. Meserve, "and I thought I'd just run over a few minutes."

"I'm real glad you did," repeated Mrs. Emerson. "Take your things right off. Here, I'll put them on my bed in the bedroom. Take the rocking-chair."

Mrs. Meserve settled herself in the parlour rocking-chair, while Mrs. Emerson carried her shawl and hat into the little adjoining bedroom. When she returned Mrs. Meserve was rocking peacefully and was already at work hooking blue wool in and out.

"That's real pretty," said Mrs. Emerson.

"Yes, I think it's pretty," replied Mrs. Meserve.

"I suppose it's for the church fair?"

"Yes. I don't suppose it'll bring enough to pay for the worsted, let alone the work, but I suppose I've got to make something."

"How much did that one you made for the fair last year bring?"

"Twenty-five cents."

"It's wicked, ain't it?"

"I rather guess it is. It takes me a week every minute I can get to make one. I wish those that bought such things for twenty-five cents had to make them. Guess they'd sing another song. Well, I suppose I oughtn't to complain as long as it is for the Lord, but sometimes it does seem as if the Lord didn't get much out of it."

"Well, it's pretty work," said Mrs. Emerson, sitting down at the opposite window and taking up her dress skirt.

"Yes, it is real pretty work. I just *love* to crochet."

The two women rocked and sewed and crocheted in silence for two or three minutes. They were both waiting. Mrs. Meserve waited for the other's curiosity to develop in order that her news might have, as it were, a befitting stage entrance. Mrs. Emerson waited for the news. Finally she could wait no longer.

"Well, what's the news?" said she.

"Well, I don't know as there's anything very particular," hedged the other woman, prolonging the situation.

"Yes, there is; you can't cheat me," replied Mrs. Emerson.

"Now, how do you know?"

"By the way you look."

Mrs. Meserve laughed consciously and rather vainly.

"Well, Simon says my face is so expressive I can't hide anything more than five minutes no matter how hard I try," said she. "Well, there is some news. Simon came home with it this noon. He heard it in South Dayton. He had some business over there this morning. The old Sargent place is let."

Mrs. Emerson dropped her sewing and stared.

"You don't say so!"

"Yes, it is."

"Who to?"

"Why, some folks from Boston that moved to South Dayton last year. They haven't been satisfied with the house they had there—it wasn't large enough. The man has got considerable property and can afford to live pretty well. He's got a wife and his unmarried sister in the family. The sister's got money, too. He does business in Boston and it's just as easy to get to Boston from here as from South Dayton, and so they're coming here. You know the old Sargent house is a splendid place."

"Yes, it's the handsomest house in town, but-"

"Oh, Simon said they told him about that and he just laughed. Said he wasn't afraid and neither was his wife and sister. Said he'd risk ghosts rather than little tucked-up sleeping-rooms without any sun, like they've had in the Dayton house. Said he'd rather risk *seeing* ghosts, than risk being ghosts themselves. Simon said they said he was a great hand to joke."

"Oh, well," said Mrs. Emerson, "it is a beautiful house, and maybe there isn't anything in those stories. It never seemed to me they came very straight anyway. I never took much stock in them. All I thought was—if his wife was nervous."

"Nothing in creation would hire me to go into a house that I'd ever heard a word against of that kind," declared Mrs. Meserve with emphasis. "I wouldn't go into that house if they would give me the rent. I've seen enough of haunted houses to last me as long as I live."

Mrs. Emerson's face acquired the expression of a hunting hound.

"Have you?" she asked in an intense whisper.

"Yes, I have. I don't want any more of it."

"Before you came here?" "Yes; before I was married—when I was quite a girl."

Mrs. Meserve had not married young. Mrs. Emerson had mental calculations when she heard that.

"Did you really live in a house that was-" she whispered fearfully.

Mrs. Meserve nodded solemnly.

"Did you really ever—see—anything-"

Mrs. Meserve nodded.

"You didn't see anything that did you any harm?"

"No, I didn't see anything that did me harm looking at it in one way, but it don't do anybody in this world any good to see things that haven't any business to be seen in it. You never get over it."

There was a moment's silence. Mrs. Emerson's features seemed to sharpen.

"Well, of course I don't want to urge you," said she, "if you don't feel like talking about it; but maybe it might do you good to tell it out, if it's on your mind, worrying you."

"I try to put it out of my mind," said Mrs. Meserve.

"Well, it's just as you feel."

"I never told anybody but Simon," said Mrs. Meserve. "I never felt as if it was wise perhaps. I didn't know what folks might think. So many don't believe in anything they can't understand, that they might think my mind wasn't right. Simon advised me not to talk about it. He said he didn't believe it was anything supernatural, but he had to own up that he couldn't give any explanation for it to save his life. He had to own up that he didn't believe anybody could. Then he said he wouldn't talk about it. He said lots of folks would sooner tell folks my head wasn't right than to own up they couldn't see through it."

"I'm sure I wouldn't say so," returned Mrs. Emerson reproachfully. "You know better than that, I hope."

"Yes, I do," replied Mrs. Meserve. "I know you wouldn't say so."

"And I wouldn't tell it to a soul if you didn't want me to."

"Well, I'd rather you wouldn't."

"I won't speak of it even to Mr. Emerson."

"I'd rather you wouldn't even to him."

"I won't."

Mrs. Emerson took up her dress skirt again; Mrs. Meserve hooked up another loop of blue wool. Then she began:

"Of course," said she, "I ain't going to say positively that I believe or disbelieve in ghosts, but all I can tell you is what I saw. I can't explain it. I don't pretend I can, for I can't. If you can, well and good; I shall be glad, for it will stop tormenting me as it has done and always will otherwise. There hasn't been a day nor a night since it happened that I haven't thought of it, and always I have felt the shivers go down my back when I did."

"That's an awful feeling," Mrs. Emerson said.

"Ain't it? Well, it happened before I was married, when I was a girl and lived in East Wilmington. It was the first year I lived there. You know my family all died five years before that. I told you."

Mrs. Emerson nodded.

"Well, I went there to teach school, and I went to board with a Mrs. Amelia Dennison and her sister, Mrs. Bird. Abby, her name was—Abby Bird. She was a widow; she had never had any children. She had a little money—Mrs. Dennison didn't have any—and she had come to East Wilmington and bought the house they lived in. It was a real pretty house, though it was very old and run down. It had cost Mrs. Bird a good deal to put it in order. I guess that was the reason they took me to board. I guess they thought it would help along a little. I guess what I paid for my board about kept us all in victuals. Mrs. Bird had enough to live on if they were careful, but she had spent so much fixing up the old house that they must have been a little pinched for awhile.

"Anyhow, they took me to board, and I thought I was pretty lucky to get in there. I had a nice room, big and sunny and furnished pretty, the paper and paint all new, and everything as neat as wax. Mrs. Dennison was one of the best cooks I ever saw, and I had a little stove in my room, and there was always a nice fire there when I got home from school. I thought I hadn't been in such a nice place since I lost my own home, until I had been there about three weeks.

"I had been there about three weeks before I found it out, though I guess it had been going on ever since they had been in the house, and that was most four months. They hadn't said anything about it, and I didn't wonder, for there they had just bought the house and been to so much expense and trouble fixing it up.

"Well, I went there in September. I begun my school the first Monday. I remember it was a real cold fall, there was a frost the middle of September, and I had to put on my winter coat. I remember when I came home that night (let me see, I began school on a Monday, and that was two weeks from the next Thursday), I took off my coat downstairs and laid it on the table in the front entry. It was a real nice coat—heavy black broadcloth trimmed with fur; I had had it the winter before. Mrs. Bird called after me as I went upstairs that I ought not to leave it in the front entry for fear somebody might come in and take it, but I only laughed and called back to her that I wasn't afraid. I never was much afraid of burglars.

"Well, though it was hardly the middle of September, it was a real cold night. I remember my room faced west, and the sun was getting low, and the sky was a pale yellow and purple, just as you see it sometimes in the winter when there is going to be a cold snap. I rather think that was the night the frost came the first time. I know Mrs. Dennison covered up some flowers she had in the front yard, anyhow. I remember looking out and seeing an old green plaid shawl of hers over the verbena bed. There was a fire in my little wood-stove. Mrs. Bird made it, I know. She was a real motherly sort of woman; she always seemed to be the happiest when she was doing something to make other folks happy and comfortable. Mrs. Dennison told me she had always been so. She said she had coddled her husband within an inch of his life. 'It's lucky Abby never had any children,' she said, 'for she would have spoilt them.'

"Well, that night I sat down beside my nice little fire and ate an apple. There was a plate of nice apples on my table. Mrs. Bird put them there. I was always very fond of apples. Well, I sat down and ate an apple, and was having a beautiful time, and thinking how lucky I was to have got board in such a place with such nice folks, when I heard a queer little sound at my door. It was such a little hesitating sort of sound that it sounded more like a fumble than a knock, as if some one very timid, with very little hands, was feeling along the door, not quite daring to knock. For a minute I thought it was a mouse. But I waited and it came again, and then I made up my mind it was a knock, but a very little scared one, so I said, 'Come in.'

"But nobody came in, and then presently I heard the knock again. Then I got up and opened the door, thinking it was very queer, and I had a frightened feeling without knowing why.

"Well, I opened the door, and the first thing I noticed was a draught of cold air, as if the front door downstairs was open, but there was a strange close smell about the cold draught. It smelled more like a cellar that had been shut up for years, than out-of-doors. Then I saw something. I saw my coat first. The thing that held it was so small that I couldn't see much of anything else. Then I saw a little white face with eyes so scared and wishful that they seemed as if they might eat a hole in anybody's heart. It was a dreadful little face, with something about it which made it different from any other face on earth, but it was so pitiful that somehow it did away a good deal with the dreadful-ness. And there were two little hands spotted purple with the cold, holding up my winter coat, and a strange little far-away voice said: 'I can't find my mother.'

"'For Heaven's sake,' I said, 'who are you?'

"Then the little voice said again: 'I can't find my mother.'

"All the time I could smell the cold and I saw that it was about the child; that cold was clinging to her as if she had come out of some deadly cold place. Well, I took my coat, I did not know what else to do, and the cold was clinging to that. It was as cold as if it had come off ice. When I had the coat I could see the child more plainly. She was dressed in one little white garment made very simply. It was a nightgown, only very long, quite covering her feet, and I could see dimly through it her little thin body mottled purple with the cold. Her face did not look so cold; that was a clear waxen white. Her hair was dark, but it looked as if it might be dark only because it was so damp, almost wet, and might really be light hair. It clung very close to her forehead, which was round and white. She would have been very beautiful if she had not been so dreadful.

"'Who are you?' says I again, looking at her.

"She looked at me with her terrible pleading eyes and did not say anything.

"'What are you?' says I. Then she went away. She did not seem to run or walk like other children. She flitted, like one of those little filmy white butter-flies, that don't seem like real ones they are so light, and move as if they had no weight. But she looked back from the head of the stairs. 'I can't find my mother,' said she, and I never heard such a voice.

"'Who is your mother?' says I, but she was gone.

"Well, I thought for a moment I should faint away. The room got dark and I heard a singing in my ears. Then I flung my coat onto the bed. My hands were as cold as ice from holding it, and I stood in my door, and called first Mrs. Bird and then Mrs. Dennison. I didn't dare go down over the stairs where that had gone. It seemed to me I should go mad if I didn't see somebody or something like other folks on the face of the earth. I thought I should never make anybody hear, but I could hear them stepping about downstairs, and I could smell biscuits baking for supper. Somehow the smell of those biscuits seemed the only natural thing left to keep me in my right mind. I didn't dare go over those stairs. I just stood there and called, and finally I heard the entry door open and Mrs. Bird called back:

"'What is it? Did you call, Miss Arms?'

"'Come up here; come up here as quick as you can, both of you,' I screamed out; 'quick, quick, quick!'

"I heard Mrs. Bird tell Mrs. Dennison: 'Come quick, Amelia, something is the matter in Miss Arms' room.' It struck me even then that she expressed herself rather queerly, and it struck me as very queer, indeed, when they both got upstairs and I saw that they knew what had happened, or that they knew of what nature the happening was.

"'What is it, dear?' asked Mrs. Bird, and her pretty, loving voice had a strained sound. I saw her look at Mrs. Dennison and I saw Mrs. Dennison look back at her.

"'For God's sake,' says I, and I never spoke so before—'for God's sake, what was it brought my coat upstairs?'

"'What was it like?' asked Mrs. Dennison in a sort of failing voice, and she looked at her sister again and her sister looked back at her.

"'It was a child I have never seen here before. It looked like a child,' says I, 'but I never saw a child so dreadful, and it had on a nightgown, and said she couldn't find her mother. Who was it? What was it?'

"I thought for a minute Mrs. Dennison was going to faint, but Mrs. Bird hung onto her and rubbed her hands, and whispered in her ear (she had the cooingest kind of voice), and I ran and got her a glass of cold water. I tell you it took considerable courage to go downstairs alone, but they had set a lamp on the entry table so I could see. I don't believe I could have spunked up enough to have gone downstairs in the dark, thinking every second that child might be close to me. The lamp and the smell of the biscuits baking seemed to sort of keep my courage up, but I tell you I didn't waste much time going down those stairs and out into the kitchen for a glass of water. I pumped as if the house was afire, and I grabbed the first thing I came across in the shape of a tumbler: it was a painted one that Mrs. Dennison's Sunday school class gave her, and it was meant for a flower vase.

"Well, I filled it and then ran upstairs. I felt every minute as if something would catch my feet, and I held the glass to Mrs. Dennison's lips, while Mrs. Bird held her head up, and she took a good long swallow, then she looked hard at the tumbler.

"' Yes,' says I, 'I know I got this one, but I took the first I came across, and it isn't hurt a mite.'

"'Don't get the painted flowers wet,' says Mrs. Dennison very feebly, 'they'll wash off if you do.'

"'I'll be real careful,' says I. I knew she set a sight by that painted tumbler.

"The water seemed to do Mrs. Dennison good, for presently she pushed Mrs. Bird away and sat up. She had been laying down on my bed.

"'I'm all over it now,' says she, but she was terribly white, and her eyes looked as if they saw something outside things. Mrs. Bird wasn't much better, but she always had a sort of settled sweet, good look that nothing could disturb to any great extent. I knew I looked dreadful, for I caught a glimpse of myself in the glass, and I would hardly have known who it was.

"Mrs. Dennison, she slid off the bed and walked sort of tottery to a chair. 'I was silly to give way so,' says she.

"'No, you wasn't silly, sister,' says Mrs. Bird. 'I don't know what this means any more than you do, but whatever it is, no one ought to be called silly for being overcome by anything so different from other things which we have known all our lives.'

"Mrs. Dennison looked, at her sister, then she looked at me, then back at her sister again, and Mrs. Bird spoke as if she had been asked a question.

"'Yes,' says she, 'I do think Miss Arms ought to be told—that is, I think she ought to be told all we know ourselves.'

"'That isn't much,' said Mrs. Dennison with a dying-away sort of sigh. She looked as if she might faint away again any minute. She was a real delicate-looking woman, but it turned out she was a good deal stronger than poor Mrs. Bird.

"'No, there isn't much we do know,' says Mrs. Bird, 'but what little there is she ought to know. I felt as if she ought to when she first came here.'

"'Well, I didn't feel quite right about it,' said Mrs. Dennison, 'but I kept hoping it might stop, and any way, that it might never trouble her, and you had put so much in the house, and we needed the money, and I didn't know but she might be nervous and think she couldn't come, and I didn't want to take a man boarder.'

"'And aside from the money, we were very anxious to have you come, my dear,' says Mrs. Bird.

"'Yes,' says Mrs. Dennison, 'we wanted the young company in the house; we were lonesome, and we both of us took a great liking to you the minute we set eyes on you.'

"And I guess they meant what they said, both of them. They were beautiful women, and nobody could be any kinder to me than they were, and I never blamed them for not telling me before, and, as they said, there wasn't really much to tell."

"They hadn't any sooner fairly bought the house, and moved into it, than they began to see and hear things. Mrs. Bird said they were sitting together in the sitting-room one evening when they heard it the first time. She said her sister was knitting lace (Mrs. Dennison made beautiful knitted lace) and she was reading the *Missionary Herald* (Mrs. Bird was very much interested in mission work), when all of a sudden they heard something. She heard it first and she laid down her *Missionary Herald* and listened, and then Mrs. Dennison she saw her listening and she drops her lace. 'What is it you are listening to, Abby?' says she. Then it came again and they both heard, and the cold shivers went down their backs to hear it, though they didn't know why. 'It's the cat, isn't it?' says Mrs. Bird.

"'It isn't any cat,' says Mrs. Dennison.

"'Oh, I guess it *must* be the cat; maybe she's got a mouse,' says Mrs. Bird, real cheerful, to calm down Mrs. Dennison, for she saw she was 'most scared to death, and she was always afraid of her fainting away. Then she opens the door and calls, 'Kitty, kitty, kitty !' They had brought their cat with them in a basket when they came to East Wilmington to live. It was a real handsome tiger cat, a tommy, and he knew a lot.

"Well, she called 'Kitty, kitty, kitty!' and sure enough the kitty came, and when he came in the door he gave a big yawl that didn't sound unlike what they had heard.

"'There, sister, here he is; you see it was the cat,' says Mrs. Bird. 'Poor kitty!'

"But Mrs. Dennison she eyed the cat, and she give a great screech.

"'What's that? What's that?' says she.

"'What's what?' says Mrs. Bird, pretending to herself that she didn't see what her sister meant.

"'Somethin's got hold of that cat's tail,' says Mrs. Dennison. 'Somethin's got hold of his tail. It's pulled straight out, an' he can't get away. Just hear him yawl!'

"'It isn't anything,' says Mrs. Bird, but even as she said that she could see a little hand holding fast to that cat's tail, and then the child seemed to sort of clear out of the dimness behind the hand, and the child was sort of laughing then, instead of looking sad, and she said that was a great deal worse. She said that laugh was the most awful and the saddest thing she ever heard.

"Well, she was so dumfounded that she didn't know what to do, and she couldn't sense at first that it was anything supernatural. She thought it must be one of the neighbour's children who had run away and was making free of their house, and was teasing their cat, and that they must be just nervous to feel so upset by it. So she speaks up sort of sharp.

"'Don't you know that you mustn't pull the kitty's tail?' says she. 'Don't you know you hurt the poor kitty, and she'll scratch you if you don't take care. Poor kitty, you mustn't hurt her.'

"And with that she said the child stopped pulling that cat's tail and went to stroking her just as soft and pitiful, and the cat put his hack up and rubbed and purred as if he liked it. The cat never seemed a mite afraid, and that seemed queer, for I had always heard that animals were dreadfully afraid of ghosts; but then, that was a pretty harmless little sort of ghost.

"Well, Mrs. Bird said the child stroked that cat, while she and Mrs. Dennison stood watching it, and holding onto each other, for, no matter how hard they tried to think it was all right, it didn't look right. Finally Mrs. Dennison she spoke.

"'What's your name, little girl?' says she.

"Then the child looks up and stops stroking the cat, and says she can't find her mother, just the way she said it to me. Then Mrs. Dennison she gave such a gasp that Mrs. Bird thought she was going to faint away, but she didn't. 'Well, who is your mother?' says she. But the child just says again 'I can't find my mother—I can't find my mother.'

"'Where do you live, dear?' says Mrs. Bird.

"'I can't find my mother,' says the child.

"Well, that was the way it was. Nothing happened. Those two women stood there hanging onto each other, and the child stood in front of them, and they asked her questions, and everything she would say was: I can't find my mother.'

"Then Mrs. Bird tried to catch hold of the child, for she thought in spite of what she saw that perhaps she was nervous and it was a real child, only perhaps not quite right in its head, that had run away in her little nightgown after she had been put to bed.

"She tried to catch the child. She had an idea of putting a shawl around it and going out—she was such a little thing she could have carried her easy enough—and trying to find out to which of the neighbours she belonged. But the minute she moved toward the child there wasn't any child there; there was only that little voice seeming to come from nothing, saying 'I can't find my mother,' and presently that died away.

"Well, that same thing kept happening, or something very much the same. Once in awhile Mrs. Bird would be washing dishes, and all at once the child would be standing beside her with the dish-towel, wiping them. Of course, that was terrible. Mrs. Bird would wash the dishes all over. Sometimes she didn't tell Mrs. Dennison, it made her so nervous. Sometimes when they were making cake they would find the raisins all picked over, and sometimes little sticks of kindling-wood would be found laying beside the kitchen stove. They never knew when they would come across that child, and always she kept saying over and over that she couldn't find her mother. They never tried talking to her, except once in awhile Mrs. Bird would get desperate and ask her something, but the child never seemed to hear it; she always kept right on saying that she couldn't find her mother.

"After they had told me all they had to tell about their experience with the child, they told me about the house and the people that had lived there before they did. It seemed something dreadful had happened in that house. And the land agent had never let on to them. I don't think they would have bought it if he had, no matter how cheap it was, for even if folks aren't really afraid of anything, they don't want to live in houses where such dreadful things have happened that you keep thinking about them. I know after they told me I should never have stayed there another night, if I hadn't thought so much of them, no matter how comfortable I was made; and I never was nervous, either. But I stayed. Of course, it didn't happen in my room. If it had I could not have stayed."

"What was it?" asked Mrs. Emerson in an awed voice.

"It was an awful thing. That child had lived in the house with her father and mother two years before. They had come—or the father had—from a real good family. He had a good situation: he was a drummer for a big leather house in the city, and they lived real pretty, with plenty to do with. But the mother was a real wicked woman. She was as handsome as a picture, and they said she came from good sort of people enough in Boston, but she was bad clean through, though she was real pretty spoken and most everybody liked her. She used to dress out and make a great show, and she never seemed to take much interest in the child, and folks began to say she wasn't treated right.

"The woman had a hard time keeping a girl. For some reason one wouldn't stay. They would leave and then talk about her awfully, telling all kinds of things.

People didn't believe it at first; then they began to. They said that the woman made that little thing, though she wasn't. much over five years old, and small and babyish for her age, do most of the work, what there was done; they said the house used to look like a pigsty when she didn't have help. They said the little thing used to stand on a chair and wash dishes, and they'd seen her carrying in sticks of wood most as big as she was many a time, and they'd heard her mother scolding her. The woman was a fine singer, and had a voice like a screech-owl when she scolded.

"The father was away most of the time, and when that happened he had been away out West for some weeks. There had been a married man hanging about the mother for some time, and folks had talked some; but they weren't sure there was anything wrong, and he was a man very high up, with money, so they kept pretty still for fear he would hear of it and make trouble for them, and of course nobody was sure, though folks did say afterward that the father of the child had ought to have been told.

"But that was very easy to say; it wouldn't have been so easy to find anybody who would have been willing to tell him such a thing as that, especially when they weren't any too sure. He set his eyes by his wife, too. They said all he seemed to think of was to earn money to buy things to deck her out in. And he about worshiped the child, too. They said he was a real nice man. The men that are treated so bad mostly are real nice men. I've always noticed that.

"Well, one morning that man that there had been whispers about was missing. He had been gone quite a while, though, before they really knew that he was missing, because he had gone away and told his wife that he had to go to New York on business and might be gone a week, and not to worry if he didn't get home, and not to worry if he didn't write, because he should be thinking from day to day that he might take the next train home and there would be no use in writing. So the wife waited, and she tried not to worry until it was two days over the week, then she run into a neighbour's and fainted dead away on the floor; and then they made inquiries and found out that he had skipped— with some money that didn't belong to him, too.

"Then folks began to ask where was that woman, and they found out by comparing notes that nobody had seen her since the man went away; but three or four women remembered that she had told them that she thought of taking the child and going to Boston to visit her folks, so when they hadn't seen her around, and the house shut, they jumped to the conclusion that was where she was. They were the neighbours that lived right around her, but they didn't have much to do with her, and she'd gone out of her way to tell them about her Boston plan, and they didn't make much reply when she did.

"Well, there was this house shut up, and the man and woman missing and the child. Then all of a sudden one of the women that lived the nearest remembered something. She remembered that she had waked up three nights running, thinking she heard a child crying somewhere, and once she waked up her husband, but he said it must be the Bisbees' little girl, and she thought it must be. The child wasn't well and was always crying. It used to have colic spells, especially at night. So she didn't think any more about it until this came up, then all of a sudden she did think of it. She told what she had heard, and finally folks began to think they had better enter that house and see if there was anything wrong.

"Well, they did enter it, and they found that child dead, locked in one of the rooms. (Mrs. Dennison and Mrs. Bird never used that room; it was a back bedroom on the second floor.)

"Yes, they found that poor child there, starved to death, and frozen, though they weren't sure she had frozen to death, for she was in bed with clothes enough to keep her pretty warm when she was alive. But she had been there a week, and she was nothing but skin and bone. It looked as if the mother had locked her into the house when she went away, and told her not to make any noise for fear the neighbours would hear her and find out that she herself had gone.

"Mrs. Dennison said she couldn't really believe that the woman had meant to have her own child starved to death. Probably she thought the little thing would raise somebody, or folks would try to get in the house and find her. Well, whatever she thought, there the child was, dead.

"But that wasn't all. The father came home, right in the midst of it; the child was just buried, and he was beside himself. And he went on the track of his wife, and he found her, and he shot her dead; it was in all the papers at the time; then he disappeared. Nothing had been seen of him since. Mrs. Dennison said that she thought he had either made way with himself or got out of the country, nobody knew, but they did know there was something wrong with the house.

"I knew folks acted queer when they asked me how I liked it when we first came here,' says Mrs. Dennison, 'but I never dreamed why till we saw the child that night.'"

"I never heard anything like it in my life," said Mrs. Emerson, staring at the other woman with awestruck eyes.

"I thought you'd say so," said Mrs. Meserve. "You don't wonder that I ain't disposed to speak light when I hear there is anything queer about a house, do you?"

"No, I don't, after that," Mrs. Emerson said.

"But that ain't all," said Mrs. Meserve. "Did you see it again?" Mrs. Emerson asked.

"Yes, I saw it a number of times before the last time. It was lucky I wasn't nervous, or I never could have stayed there, much as I liked the place and much as I thought of those two women; they were beautiful women, and no mistake. I loved those women. I hope Mrs. Dennison will come and see me sometime.

"Well, I stayed, and I never knew when I'd see that child. I got so I was very careful to bring everything of mine upstairs, and not leave any little thing in my room that needed doing, for fear she would come lugging up my coat or hat or gloves or I'd find things done when there'd been no live being in the room to do them. I can't tell you how I dreaded seeing her; and worse than the seeing her was the hearing her say, 'I can't find my mother.' It was enough to make your blood run cold. I never heard a living child cry for its mother that was anything so pitiful as that dead one. It was enough to break your heart.

"She used to come and say that to Mrs. Bird oftener than to any one else. Once I heard Mrs. Bird say she wondered if it was possible that the poor little thing couldn't really find her mother in the other world, she had been such a wicked woman.

"But Mrs. Dennison told her she didn't think she ought to speak so nor even think so, and Mrs. Bird said she shouldn't wonder if she was right. Mrs. Bird was always very easy to put in the wrong. She was a good woman, and one that couldn't do things enough for other folks. It seemed as if that was what she lived on. I don't think she was ever so scared by that poor little ghost, as much as she pitied it, and she was 'most heartbroken because she couldn't do anything for it, as she could have done for a live child.

"'It seems to me sometimes as if I should die if I can't get that awful little white robe off that child and get her in some clothes and feed her and stop her looking for her mother,' I heard her say once, and she was in earnest. She cried when she said it. That wasn't long before she died.

"Now I am coming to the strangest part of it all. Mrs. Bird died very sudden. One morning—it was Saturday, and there wasn't any school—I went downstairs to breakfast, and Mrs. Bird wasn't there; there was nobody but Mrs. Dennison. She was pouring out the coffee when I came in. 'Why, where's Mrs. Bird?' says I.

"'Abby ain't feeling very well this morning,' says she; 'there isn't much the matter, I guess, but she didn't sleep very well, and her head aches, and she's sort of chilly, and I told her I thought she'd better stay in bed till the house gets warm.' It was a very cold morning.

"'Maybe she's got cold,' says I.

"'Yes, I guess she has,' says Mrs. Dennison. 'I guess she's got cold. She'll be up before long. Abby ain't one to stay in bed a minute longer than she can help.'

"Well, we went on eating our breakfast, and all at once a shadow flickered across one wall of the room and over the ceiling the way a shadow will sometimes when somebody passes the window outside. Mrs. Dennison and I both looked up, then out of the window; then Mrs. Dennison she gives a scream.

"'Why, Abby's crazy!' says she. 'There she is out this bitter cold morning, and—and-' She didn't finish, but she meant the child. For we were both looking out, and we saw, as plain as we ever saw anything in our lives, Mrs. Abby Bird walking off over the white snow-path with that child holding fast to her hand, nestling close to her as if she had found her own mother.

"'She's dead,' says Mrs. Dennison, clutching hold of me hard. 'She's dead; my sister is dead!'

"She was. We hurried upstairs as fast as we could go, and she was dead in her bed, and smiling as if she was dreaming, and one arm and hand was stretched out as if something had hold of it; and it couldn't be straightened even at the last—it lay out over her casket at the funeral."

"Was the child ever seen again?" asked Mrs. Emerson in a shaking voice.

"No," replied Mrs. Meserve; "that child was never seen again after she went out of the yard with Mrs. Bird."

# MAN-SIZE IN MARBLE
## E. NESBIT

Although every word of this story is as true as despair, I do not expect people to believe it. Nowadays a "rational explanation" is required before belief is possible. Let me then, at once, offer the "rational explanation" which finds most favour among those who have heard the tale of my life's tragedy. It is held that we were "under a delusion," Laura and I, on that October 31st; and that this supposition places the whole matter on a satisfactory and believable basis. The reader can judge, when he, too, has heard my story, how far this is an "explanation," and in what sense it is "rational." There were three who took part in this: Laura and I and another man. The other man still lives, and can speak to the truth of the least credible part of my story.

\* \* \* \* \*

I never in my life knew what it was to have as much money as I required to supply the most ordinary needs—good colours, books, and cab-fares—and when we were married we knew quite well that we should only be able to live at all by "strict punctuality and attention to business." I used to paint in those days, and Laura used to write, and we felt sure we could keep the pot at least simmering. Living in town was out of the question, so we went to look for a cottage in the country, which should be at once sanitary and picturesque. So rarely do these two qualities meet in one cottage that our search was for some time quiet fruitless. We tried advertisements, but most of the desirable rural residences which we did look at proved to be lacking in both essentials, and when a cottage chanced to have drains it always had stucco as well and was shaped like a tea-caddy. And if we found a vine or rose-covered porch, corruption invariably lurked within. Our minds got so befogged by the eloquence of house-agents and the rival disadvantages of the fever-traps and outrages to beauty which we had seen and scorned, that I very much doubt whether either of us, on our wedding morning, knew the difference between a house and a haystack. But when we got away from friends and house-agents, on our honeymoon, our wits grew clear again, and we knew a pretty cottage when at last we saw one. It was at Brenzett—a little village set on a hill over against the southern marshes. We had gone there, from the seaside village where we were staying, to see the church, and two fields from the church we found this cottage. It stood quite by itself, about two miles from the village. It was a long, low building, with rooms sticking out in unexpected places. There was a bit of stone-work—ivy-covered and moss-grown, just two old rooms, all that was left of a big house that had once stood there—and round this stonework the house had grown up. Stripped of its roses and jasmine it would have been hideous. As it stood it was charming, and after a brief examination we took it. It was absurdly cheap. The rest of our honeymoon we spent in grubbing about in second-hand shops in the county town, picking up bits of old oak and Chippendale chairs for our furnishing. We wound up with a run up to town and a visit to Liberty's, and soon the low oak-beamed lattice-windowed rooms began to be home. There was a jolly old-fashioned garden, with grass paths, and no end of holly-hocks and sunflowers, and big lilies. From the window you could see the marsh-pastures, and beyond them the blue, thin line of the sea. We were as happy as the summer was glorious, and settled down into work sooner than we ourselves expected. I was never tired of sketching the view and the wonderful cloud effects from the open lattice, and Laura would sit at the table and write verses about them, in which I mostly played the part of foreground.

We got a tall old peasant woman to do for us. Her face and figure were good, though her cooking was of the homeliest; but she understood all about gardening, and told us all the old names of the coppices and cornfields, and the stories of the smugglers and highwaymen, and, better still, of the "things that walked," and of the "sights" which met one in lonely glens of a starlight night. She was a great comfort to us, because Laura hated housekeeping as much as I loved folklore, and we soon came to leave all the domestic business to Mrs. Dorman, and to use her legends in little magazine stories which brought in the jingling guinea.

We had three months of married happiness, and did not have a single quarrel. One October evening I had been down to smoke a pipe with the doctor—our only neighbour—a pleasant young Irishman. Laura had stayed at home to finish a comic sketch of a village episode for the *Monthly Marplot*. I left her laughing over her own jokes, and came in to find her a crumpled heap of pale muslin weeping on the window seat.

"Good heavens, my darling, what's the matter?" I cried, taking her in my arms. She leaned her little dark head against my shoulder and went on crying. I had never seen her cry before—we had always been so happy, you see—and I felt sure some frightful misfortune had happened.

"What *is* the matter? Do speak."

"It's Mrs. Dorman," she sobbed.

"What has she done?" I inquired, immensely relieved.

"She says she must go before the end of the month, and she says her niece is ill; she's gone down to see her now, but I don't believe that's the reason, because her niece is always ill. I believe someone has been setting her against us. Her manner was so queer—"

"Never mind, Pussy," I said; "whatever you do, don't cry, or I shall have to cry too, to keep you in countenance, and then you'll never respect your man again!"

She dried her eyes obediently on my handkerchief, and even smiled faintly.

"But you see," she went on, "it is really serious, because these village people are so sheepy, and if one won't do a thing you may be quite sure none of the others will. And I shall have to cook the dinners, and wash up the hateful greasy plates; and you'll have to carry cans of water about, and clean the boots and knives—and we shall never have any time for work, or earn any money, or anything. We shall have to work all day, and only be able to rest when we are waiting for the kettle to boil!"

I represented to her that even if we had to perform these duties, the day would still present some margin for other toils and recreations. But she refused to see the matter in any but the greyest light. She was very unreasonable, my Laura, but I could not have loved her any more if she had been as reasonable as Whately.

"I'll speak to Mrs. Dorman when she comes back, and see if I can't come to terms with her," I said. "Perhaps she wants a rise in her screw. It will be all right. Let's walk up to the church."

The church was a large and lonely one, and we loved to go there, especially upon bright nights. The path skirted a wood, cut through it once, and ran along the crest of the hill through two meadows, and round the churchyard wall, over which the old yews loomed in black masses of shadow. This path, which was partly paved, was called "the bier balk," for it had long been the way by which the corpses had been carried to burial. The churchyard was richly treed, and was shaded by great elms which stood just outside and stretched their majestic arms in benediction over the happy dead. A large, low porch let one into the building by a Norman doorway and a heavy oak door studded with iron. Inside, the arches rose into darkness, and between them the reticulated windows, which stood out white in the moonlight. In the chancel, the windows were of rich glass, which showed in faint light their noble colouring, and made the black oak of the choir pews hardly more solid than the shadows. But on each side of the altar lay a grey marble figure of a knight in full plate armour lying upon a low slab, with hands held up in everlasting prayer, and these figures, oddly enough, were always to be seen if there was any glimmer of light in the church. Their names were lost, but the peasants told of them that they had been fierce and wicked men, marauders by land and sea, who had been the scourge of their time, and had been guilty of deeds so foul that the house they had lived in—the big house, by the way, that had stood on the site of our cottage—had been stricken by lightning and the vengeance of Heaven. But for all that, the gold of their heirs had bought them a place in the church. Looking at the bad hard faces reproduced in the marble, this story was easily believed.

The church looked at its best and weirdest on that night, for the shadows of the yew trees fell through the windows upon the floor of the nave and touched the pillars with tattered shade. We sat down together without speaking, and watched the solemn beauty of the old church, with some of that awe which inspired its early builders. We walked to the chancel and looked at the sleeping warriors. Then we rested some time on the stone seat in the porch, looking out over the stretch of quiet moonlit meadows, feeling in every fibre of our being the peace of the night and of our happy love; and came away at last with a sense that even scrubbing and blackleading were but small troubles at their worst.

Mrs. Dorman had come back from the village, and I at once invited her to a *tête-à-tête*.

"Now, Mrs. Dorman," I said, when I had got her into my painting room, "what's all this about your not staying with us?"

"I should be glad to get away, sir, before the end of the month," she answered, with her usual placid dignity.

"Have you any fault to find, Mrs. Dorman?"

"None at all, sir; you and your lady have always been most kind, I'm sure—"

"Well, what is it? Are your wages not high enough?"

"No, sir, I gets quite enough."

"Then why not stay?"

"I'd rather not"—with some hesitation—"my niece is ill."

"But your niece has been ill ever since we came." No answer. There was a long and awkward silence. I broke it.

"Can't you stay for another month?" I asked. "No, sir. I'm bound to go by Thursday." And this was Monday!

"Well, I must say, I think you might have let us know before. There's no time now to get any one else, and your mistress is not fit to do heavy housework. Can't you stay till next week?"

"I might be able to come back next week."

I was now convinced that all she wanted was a brief holiday, which we should have been willing enough to let her have, as soon as we could get a substitute.

"But why must you go this week?" I persisted. "Come, out with it."

Mrs. Dorman drew the little shawl, which she always wore, tightly across her bosom, as though she were cold. Then she said, with a sort of effort—

"They say, sir, as this was a big house in Catholic times, and there was a many deeds done here."

The nature of the "deeds" might be vaguely inferred from the inflection of Mrs. Dorman's voice—which was enough to make one's blood run cold. I was glad that Laura was not in the room. She was always nervous, as highly-strung natures are, and I felt that these tales about our house, told by this old peasant woman, with her impressive manner and contagious credulity, might have made our home less dear to my wife.

"Tell me all about it, Mrs. Dorman," I said; "you needn't mind about telling me. I'm not like the young people who make fun of such things."

Which was partly true.

"Well, sir"—she sank her voice—"you may have seen in the church, beside the altar, two shapes."

"You mean the effigies of the knights in armour," I said cheerfully.

"I mean them two bodies, drawed out man-size in marble," she returned, and I had to admit that her description was a thousand times more graphic than mine, to say nothing of a certain weird force and uncanniness about the phrase "drawed out man-size in marble."

"They do say, as on All Saints' Eve them two bodies sits up on their slabs, and gets off of them, and then walks down the aisle, *in their marble*"—(another good phrase, Mrs. Dorman)—"and as the church clock strikes eleven they walks out of the church door, and over the graves, and along the bier-balk and if it's a wet night there's the marks of their feet in the morning."

"And where do they go?" I asked, rather fascinated.

"They comes back here to their home, sir, and if anyone meets them—"

"Well, what then?" I asked.

But no—not another word could I get from her save that her niece was ill and she must go. After what I had heard I scorned to discuss the niece, and tried to get from Mrs. Dorman more details of the legend. I could get nothing but warnings.

"Whatever you do, sir, lock the door early on All Saints' Eve, and make the cross-sign over the doorstep and on the windows."

"But has anyone ever seen these things?" I persisted.

"That's not for me to say. I know what I know, sir."

"Well, who was here last year?"

"No one, sir; the lady as owned the house only stayed here in summer, and she always went to London a full month afore *the* night. And I'm sorry to inconvenience you and your lady, but my niece is ill and I must go on Thursday."

I could have shaken her for her absurd reiteration of that obvious fiction, after she had told me her real reasons.

She was determined to go, nor could our united entreaties move her in the least.

I did not tell Laura the legend of the shapes that "walked in their marble," partly because a legend concerning our house might perhaps trouble my wife, and partly, I think, from some more occult reason. This was not quite the same to me as any other story, and I did not want to talk about it till the day was over. I had very soon ceased to think of the legend, however. I was painting a portrait of Laura, against the lattice window, and I could not think of much else. I had got a splendid background of yellow and grey sunset, and was working away with enthusiasm at her face. On Thursday Mrs. Dorman went. She relented, at parting, so far as to say—

"Don't you put yourself about too much, ma'am, and if there's any little thing I can do next week, I'm sure I shan't mind."

From which I inferred that she wished to come back to us after Hallowe'en. Up to the last she adhered to the fiction of the niece with touching fidelity.

Thursday passed off pretty well. Laura showed marked ability in the matter of steak and potatoes, and I confess that my knives, and the plates, which I insisted upon washing, were better done than I had dared to expect.

Friday came. It is about what happened on that Friday that this is written. I wonder if I should have believed it, if anyone had told it to me. I will write the story of it as quickly and plainly as I can. Everything that happened on that day is burnt into my brain. I shall not forget anything, nor leave anything out.

I got up early, I remember, and lighted the kitchen fire, and had just achieved a smoky success, when my little wife came running down, as sunny and sweet as the clear October morning itself. We prepared breakfast together, and found it very good fun. The housework was soon done, and when brushes and brooms and pails were quiet again, the house was still indeed. It is wonderful what a difference one makes in a house. We really missed Mrs. Dorman, quite apart from considerations concerning pots and pans. We spent the day in dusting our books and putting them straight, and dined gaily on cold steak and coffee. Laura was, if possible, brighter and gayer and sweeter than usual, and I began to think that a little domestic toil was really good for her. We had never been so merry since we were married, and the walk we had that afternoon was, I think, the happiest time of all my life. When we had watched the deep scarlet clouds slowly pale into leaden grey against a pale-green sky, and saw the white mists curl up along the hedgerows in the distant marsh, we came back to the house, silently, hand in hand.

"You are sad, my darling," I said, half-jestingly, as we sat down together in our little parlour. I expected a disclaimer, for my own silence had been the silence of complete happiness. To my surprise she said—

"Yes. I think I am sad, or rather I am uneasy. I don't think I'm very well. I have shivered three or four times since we came in, and it is not cold, is it?"

"No," I said, and hoped it was not a chill caught from the treacherous mists that roll up from the marshes in the dying light. No—she said, she did not think so. Then, after a silence, she spoke suddenly—

"Do you ever have presentiments of evil?"

"No," I said, smiling, "and I shouldn't believe in them if I had."

"I do," she went on; "the night my father died I knew it, though he was right away in the north of Scotland," I did not answer in words.

She sat looking at the fire for some time in silence, gently stroking my hand. At last she sprang up, came behind me, and, drawing my head back, kissed me.

"There, it's over now," she said. "What a baby I am! Come, light the candles, and we'll have some of these new Rubinstein duets."

And we spent a happy hour or two at the piano.

At about half-past ten I began to long for the good-night pipe, but Laura looked so white that I felt it would be brutal of me to fill our sitting-room with the fumes of strong cavendish.

"I'll take my pipe outside," I said.

"Let me come, too."

"No, sweetheart, not tonight; you're much too tired. I shan't be long. Get to bed, or I shall have an invalid to nurse tomorrow as well as the boots to clean."

I kissed her and was turning to go, when she flung her arms round my neck, and held me as if she would never let me go again. I stroked her hair.

"Come, Pussy, you're over-tired. The housework has been too much for you."

She loosened her clasp a little and drew a deep breath.

"No. We've been very happy today, Jack, haven't we? Don't stay out too long." "I won't, my dearie."

I strolled out of the front door, leaving it unlatched. What a night it was! The jagged masses of heavy dark cloud were rolling at intervals from horizon to horizon, and thin white wreaths covered the stars. Through all the rush of the cloud river, the moon swam, breasting the waves and disappearing again in the darkness. When now and again her light reached the woodlands they seemed to be slowly and noiselessly waving in time to the swing of the clouds above them. There was a strange grey light over all the earth; the fields had that shadowy bloom over them which only comes from the marriage of dew and moonshine, or frost and starlight.

I walked up and down, drinking in the beauty of the quiet earth and the changing sky. The night was absolutely silent. Nothing seemed to be abroad. There was no scurrying of rabbits, or twitter of the half-asleep birds. And though the clouds went sailing across the sky, the wind that drove them never came low enough to rustle the dead leaves in the woodland paths. Across the meadows I could see the church tower standing out black and grey against the sky. I walked there thinking over our three months of happiness—and of my wife, her dear eyes, her loving ways. Oh, my little girl! My own little girl; what a vision came then of a long, glad life for you and me together!

I heard a bell-bleat from the church. Eleven already! I turned to go in, but the night held me. I could not go back into our little warm rooms yet. I would go up to the church. I felt vaguely that it would be good to carry my love and thankfulness to the sanctuary whither so many loads of sorrow and gladness had been borne by the men and women of the dead years.

I looked in at the low window as I went by. Laura was half lying on her chair in front of the fire. I could not see her face, only her little head showed dark against the pale blue wall. She was quite still. Asleep, no doubt, my heart reached out to her, as I went on. There must be a God, I thought, and a God who was good. How otherwise could anything so sweet and dear as she have ever been imagined?

I walked slowly along the edge of the wood. A sound broke the stillness of the night, it was a rustling in the wood. I stopped and listened. The sound stopped too. I went on, and now distinctly heard another step than mine answer mine like an echo. It was a poacher or a wood-stealer, most likely, for these were not unknown in our Arcadian neighbourhood. But whoever it was, he was a fool not to step more lightly. I turned into the wood, and now the footstep seemed to come from the path I had just left. It must be an echo, I thought. The wood looked perfect in the moonlight. The large dying ferns and the brush-wood showed where through thinning foliage the pale light came down. The tree trunks stood up like Gothic columns all around me. They reminded me of the church, and I turned into the bier-balk, and passed through the corpse-gate between the graves to the low porch. I paused for a moment on the stone seat where Laura and I had watched the fading landscape. Then I noticed that the door of the church was open, and I blamed myself for having left it unlatched the other night. We were the only people who ever cared to come to the church except on Sundays, and I was vexed to think that through our carelessness the damp autumn airs had had a chance of getting in and injuring the old fabric. I went in. It will seem strange, perhaps, that I should have gone half-way up the aisle before I remembered—with a sudden chill, followed by as sudden a rush of self-contempt—that this was the very day and hour when, according to tradition, the "shapes drawn out man-size in marble" began to walk.

Having thus remembered the legend, and remembered it with a shiver, of which I was ashamed, I could not do otherwise than walk up towards the altar, just to look at the figures—as I said to myself; really what I wanted was to assure myself, first, that I did not believe the legend, and, secondly, that it was not true. I was rather glad that I had come. I thought now I could tell Mrs. Dorman how vain her fancies were, and how peacefully the marble figures slept on through the ghastly hour. With my hands in my pockets I passed up the aisle. In the grey dim light the eastern end of the church looked larger than usual, and the arches above the two tombs looked larger too. The moon came out and showed me the reason. I stopped short, my heart gave a leap that nearly choked me, and then sank sickeningly.

The "bodies drawn out man-size" *were gone,* and their marble slabs lay wide and bare in the vague moonlight that slanted through the east window.

Were they really gone? or was I mad? Clenching my nerves, I stooped and passed my hand over the smooth slabs, and felt their flat unbroken surface. Had someone taken the things away? Was it some vile practical joke? I would make sure, anyway. In an instant I had made a torch of a newspaper, which happened to be in my pocket, and lighting it held it high above my head. Its yellow glare illumined the dark arches and those slabs. The figures *were* gone. And I was alone in the church; or was I alone?

And then a horror seized me, a horror indefinable and indescribable—an overwhelming certainty of supreme and accomplished calamity. I flung down the torch and tore along the aisle and out through the porch, biting my lips as I ran to keep myself from shrieking aloud. Oh, was I mad—or what was this that possessed me? I leaped the churchyard wall and took the straight cut across the fields, led by the light from our windows. Just as I got over the first stile, a dark figure seemed to spring out of the ground. Mad still with that certainty of misfortune, I made for the thing that stood in my path, shouting, "Get out of the way, can't you!"

But my push met with a more vigorous resistance than I had expected. My arms were caught just above the elbow and held as in a vice, and the raw-boned Irish doctor actually shook me.

"Would ye?" he cried, in his own unmistakable accents—"would ye, then?"

"Let me go, you fool," I gasped. "The marble figures have gone from the church; I tell you they've gone."

He broke into a ringing laugh. "I'll have to give ye a draught tomorrow, I see. Ye've bin smoking too much and listening to old wives' tales."

"I tell you, I've seen the bare slabs."

"Well, come back with me. I'm going up to old Palmer's—his daughter's ill; we'll look in at the church and let me see the bare slabs."

"You go, if you like," I said, a little less frantic for his laughter; "I'm going home to my wife."

"Rubbish, man," said he; "d'ye think I'll permit of that? Are ye to go saying all yer life that ye've seen solid marble endowed with vitality, and me to go all me life saying ye were a coward? No, sir—ye shan't do ut."

The night air—a human voice—and I think also the physical contact with this six feet of solid common sense, brought me back a little to my ordinary self, and the word "coward" was a mental shower-bath.

"Come on, then," I said sullenly; "perhaps you're right."

He still held my arm tightly. We got over the stile and back to the church. All was still as death. The place smelt very damp and earthy. We walked up the aisle. I am not ashamed to confess that I shut my eyes: I knew the figures would not be there. I heard Kelly strike a match.

"Here they are, ye see, right enough; ye've been dreaming or drinking, asking yer pardon for the imputation."

I opened my eyes. By Kelly's expiring vesta I saw two shapes lying "in their marble" on their slabs. I drew a deep breath, and caught his hand.

"I'm awfully indebted to you," I said. "It must have been some trick of light, or I have been working rather hard, perhaps that's it. Do you know, I was quite convinced they were gone."

"I'm aware of that," he answered rather grimly; "ye'll have to be careful of that brain of yours, my friend, I assure ye."

He was leaning over and looking at the right-hand figure, whose stony face was the most villainous and deadly in expression.

"By Jove," he said, "something has been afoot here—this hand is broken."

And so it was. I was certain that it had been perfect the last time Laura and I had been there.

"Perhaps someone has *tried* to remove them," said the young doctor.

"That won't account for my impression," I objected.

"Too much painting and tobacco will account for that, well enough."

"Come along," I said, "or my wife will be getting anxious. You'll come in and have a drop of whisky and drink confusion to ghosts and better sense to me."

"I ought to go up to Palmer's, but it's so late now I'd best leave it till the morning," he replied. "I was kept late at the Union, and I've had to see a lot of people since. All right, I'll come back with ye."

I think he fancied I needed him more than did Palmer's girl, so, discussing how such an illusion could have been possible, and deducing from this experience large generalities concerning ghostly apparitions, we walked up to our cottage. We saw, as we walked up the garden-path, that bright light streamed out of the front door, and presently saw that the parlour door was open too. Had she gone out?

"Come in," I said, and Dr. Kelly followed me into the parlour. It was all ablaze with candles, not only the wax ones, but at least a dozen guttering, glaring tallow dips, stuck in vases and ornaments in unlikely places. Light, I knew, was Laura's remedy for nervousness. Poor child! Why had I left her? Brute that I was.

We glanced round the room, and at first we did not see her. The window was open, and the draught set all the candles flaring one way. Her chair was empty and her handkerchief and book lay on the floor. I turned to the window. There, in the recess of the window, I saw her. Oh, my child, my love, had she gone to that window to watch for me? And what had come into the room behind her? To what had she turned with that look of frantic fear and horror? Oh, my little one, had she thought that it was I whose step she heard, and turned to meet—what?

She had fallen back across a table in the window, and her body lay half on it and half on the window-seat, and her head hung down over the table, the brown hair loosened and fallen to the carpet. Her lips were drawn back, and her eyes wide, wide open. They saw nothing now. What had they seen last?

The doctor moved towards her, but I pushed him aside and sprang to her; caught her in my arms and cried—

"It's all right, Laura! I've got you safe, wifie."

She fell into my arms in a heap. I clasped her and kissed her, and called her by all her pet names, but I think I knew all the time that she was dead. Her hands were tightly clenched. In one of them she held something fast. When I was quite sure that she was dead, and that nothing mattered at all any more, I let him open her hand to see what she held.

It was a grey marble finger.

# THE QUEEN OF SPADES
## ALEXANDER SERGEYEVICH PUSHKIN

At the house of Naroumov, a cavalry officer, the long winter night had been passed in gambling. At five in the morning breakfast was served to the weary players. The winners ate with relish; the losers, on the contrary, pushed back their plates and sat brooding gloomily. Under the influence of the good wine, however, the conversation then became general.

"Well, Sourine?" said the host inquiringly.

"Oh, I lost as usual. My luck is abominable. No matter how cool I keep, I never win."

"How is it, Herman, that you never touch a card?" remarked one of the men, addressing a young officer of the Engineering Corps. "Here you are with the rest of us at five o'clock in the morning, and you have neither played nor bet all night."

"Play interests me greatly," replied the person addressed, "but I hardly care to sacrifice the necessaries of life for uncertain superfluities."

"Herman is a German, therefore economical; that explains it," said Tomsky, "But the person I can't quite understand, is my grandmother, the Countess Anna Fedorovna."

"Why?" inquired a chorus of voices.

"I can't understand why my grandmother never gambles." "I don't see anything very striking in the fact that a woman of eighty refuses to gamble," objected Naroumov. "Have you never heard her story?" "No—"

"Well, then, listen to it. To begin with, sixty years ago my grandmother went to Paris, where she was all the fashion. People crowded each other in the streets to get a chance to see the 'Muscovite Venus,' as she was called. All the great ladies played faro, then. On one occasion, while playing with the Duke of Orleans, she lost an enormous sum. She told her husband of the debt, but he refused outright to pay it. Nothing could induce him to change his mind on the subject, and grandmother was at her wits' ends. Finally, she remembered a friend of hers, Count Saint-Germain. You must have heard of him, as many wonderful stories have been told about him. He is said to have discovered the elixir of life, the philosopher's stone, and many other equally marvelous things. He had money at his disposal, and my grandmother knew it. She sent him a note asking him to come to see her. He obeyed her summons and found her in great distress. She painted the cruelty of her husband in the darkest colors, and ended by telling the Count that she depended upon his friendship and generosity.

"'I could lend you the money,' replied the Count, after a moment of thoughtfulness, 'but I know that you would not enjoy a moment's rest until you had returned it; it would only add to your embarrassment. There is another way of freeing yourself.'

"'But I have no money at all," insisted my grandmother.

"'There is no need of money. Listen to me.'

"The Count then told her a secret which any of us would give a good deal to know."

The young gamesters were all attention. Tomsky lit his pipe, took a few whiffs, then continued:

"The next evening, grandmother appeared at Versailles at the Queen's gaming-table. The Duke of Orleans was the dealer. Grandmother made some excuse for not having brought any money, and began to punt. She chose three cards in succession, again and again, winning every time, and was soon out of debt."

"A fable," remarked Herman; "perhaps the cards were marked."

"I hardly think so," replied Tomsky, with an air of importance.

"So you have a grandmother who knows three winning cards, and you haven't found out the magic secret."

"I must say I have not. She had four sons, one of them, being my father, all of whom are devoted to play; she never told the secret to one of them. But my uncle told me this much, on his word of honor. Tchaplitzky, who died in poverty after having squandered millions, lost at one time, at play, nearly three hundred thousand rubles. He was desperate and grandmother took pity on him. She told him the three cards, making him swear never to use them again. He returned to the game, staked fifty thousand rubles on each card, and came out ahead, after paying his debts."

As day was dawning the party now broke up, each one draining his glass and taking his leave.

The Countess Anna Fedorovna was seated before her mirror in her dressing-room. Three women were assisting at her toilet. The old Countess no longer made the slightest pretensions to beauty, but she still clung to all the habits of her youth, and spent as much time at her toilet as she had done sixty years before. At the window a young girl, her ward, sat at her needlework.

"Good afternoon, grandmother," cried a young officer, who had just entered the room. "I have come to ask a favor of you."

"What, Pavel?"

"I want to be allowed to present one of my friends to you, and to take you to the ball on Tuesday night."

"Take me to the ball and present him to me there." After a few more remarks the officer walked up to the window where Lisaveta Ivanovna sat.

"Whom do you wish to present?" asked the girl.

"Naroumov; do you know him?"

"No; is he a soldier?"

"Yes."

"An engineer?"

"No; why do you ask?"

The girl smiled and made no reply.

Pavel Tomsky took his leave, and, left to herself, Lisaveta glanced out of the window. Soon, a young officer appeared at the corner of the street; the girl blushed and bent her head low over her canvas.

This appearance of the officer had become a daily occurrence. The man was totally unknown to her, and as she was not accustomed to coquetting with the soldiers she saw on the street, she hardly knew how to explain his presence.

His persistence finally roused an interest entirely strange to her. One day, she even ventured to smile upon, her admirer, for such he seemed to be.

The reader need hardly be told that the officer was no other than Herman, the would-be gambler, whose imagination had been strongly excited by the story told by Tomsky of the three magic cards.

"Ah," he thought, "if the old Countess would only reveal the secret to me. Why not try to win her good-will and appeal to her sympathy?" With this idea in mind, he took up his daily station before the house, watching the pretty face at the window, and trusting to fate to bring about the desired acquaintance.

One day, as Lisaveta was standing on the pavement about to enter the carriage after the Countess, she felt herself jostled and a note was thrust into her hand. Turning, she saw the young officer at her elbow. As quick as thought, she put the note in her glove and entered the carriage. On her return from the drive, she hastened to her chamber to read the missive, in a state of excitement mingled with fear. It was a tender and respectful declaration of affection, copied word for word from a German novel. Of this fact, Lisa was, of course, ignorant.

The young girl was much impressed by the missive, but she felt that the writer must not be encouraged. She therefore wrote a few lines of explanation and, at the first opportunity, dropped it, with the letter, out of the window. The officer hastily crossed the street, picked up the papers and entered a shop to read them.

In no wise daunted by this rebuff, he found the opportunity to send her another note in a few days. He received no reply, but, evidently understanding the female heart, he persevered, begging for an interview.

He was rewarded at last by the following:

"To-night we go to the ambassador's ball. We shall remain, until two o'clock. I can arrange for a meeting in this way. After our departure, the servants will probably all go out, or go to sleep. At half-past eleven enter the vestibule boldly, and if you see any one, inquire for the Countess; if not, ascend the stairs, turn to the left and go on until you come to a door, which opens into her bedchamber. Enter this room and behind a screen you will find another door leading to a corridor; from this a spiral staircase leads to my sitting-room. I shall expect to find you there on my return."

Herman trembled like a leaf as the appointed hour drew near. He obeyed instructions fully, and, as he met no one, he reached the old lady's bedchamber without difficulty. Instead of going out of the small door behind the screen, however, he concealed himself in a closet to await the return of the old Countess.

The hours dragged slowly by; at last he heard the sound of wheels. Immediately lamps were lighted and servants began moving about. Finally the old woman tottered into the room, completely exhausted. Her women removed her wraps and proceeded to get her in readiness for the night, Herman watched the proceedings with a curiosity not unmingled with superstitious fear. When at last she was attired in cap and gown, the old woman looked less uncanny than when she wore her ball-dress of blue brocade.

She sat down in an easy chair beside a table, as she was in the habit of doing before retiring, and her women withdrew. As the old lady sat swaying to and fro, seemingly oblivious to her surroundings, Herman crept out of his hiding-place.

At the slight noise the old woman opened her eyes, and gazed at the intruder with a half-dazed expression.

"Have no fear, I beg of you," said Herman, in a calm voice. "I have not come to harm you, but to ask a favor of you instead." The Countess looked at him in silence, seemingly without comprehending him. Herman thought she might be deaf, so he put his lips close to her ear and repeated his remark. The listener remained perfectly mute.

"You could make my fortune without its costing you anything," pleaded, the young man; "only tell me the three cards which are sure to win, and—"

Herman, paused as the old woman opened her lips as if about to speak.

"It was only a jest; I swear to you, it was only a jest," came from the withered lips.

"There was no jesting about it. Remember Tchaplitzky, who, thanks to you, was able to pay his debts."

An expression of interior agitation passed over the face of the old woman; then she relapsed into her former apathy.

"Will you tell me the names of the magic cards, or not?" asked Herman after a pause.

There was no reply.

The young man then drew a pistol from, his pocket, exclaiming: "You old witch, I'll force you to tell me!"

At the sight of the weapon the Countess gave a second sign of life. She threw back her head and put out her hands as if to protect herself; then they dropped and she sat motionless.

Herman grasped her arm roughly, and was about to renew his threats, when he saw that she was dead!

\* \* \* \* \*

Seated in her room, still in her ball-dress, Lisaveta gave herself up to her reflections. She had expected to find the young officer there, but she felt relieved to see that he was not.

Strangely enough, that very night at the ball, Tomsky had rallied her about her preference for the young officer, assuring her that he knew more than she supposed he did.

"Of whom are you speaking?" she had asked in alarm, fearing her adventure had been discovered.

"Of the remarkable man," was the reply. "His name is Herman."

Lisa made no reply.

"This Herman," continued Tomsky, "is a romantic character; he has the profile of a Napoleon and the heart of a Mephistopheles. It is said he has at least three crimes on his conscience. But how pale you are."

"It is only a slight headache. But why do you talk to me of this Herman?"

"Because I believe he has serious intentions concerning you."

"Where has he seen, me?"

"At church, perhaps, or on the street."

The conversation was interrupted at this point, to the great regret of the young girl. The words of Tomsky made a deep impression upon her, and she realized how imprudently she had acted. She was thinking of all this and a great deal more when the door of her apartment suddenly opened, and Herman stood before her. She drew back at sight of him, trembling violently.

"Where have you been?" she asked in a frightened whisper.

"In the bedchamber of the Countess. She is dead," was the calm reply.

"My God! What are you saying?" cried the girl.

"Furthermore, I believe that I was the cause of her death."

The words of Tomsky flashed through Lisa's mind.

Herman sat down and told her all. She listened with a feeling of terror and disgust. So those passionate letters, that audacious pursuit were not the result of tenderness and love. It was money that he desired. The poor girl felt that she had in a sense been an accomplice in the death of her benefactress. She began to weep bitterly. Herman regarded her in silence.

"You are a monster!" exclaimed Lisa, drying her eyes.

"I didn't intend to kill her; the pistol was not even loaded.

"How are you going to get out of the house?" inquired Lisa. "It is nearly daylight. I intended to show you the way to a secret staircase, while the Countess was asleep, as we would have to cross her chamber. Now I am afraid to do so."

"Direct me, and I will find the way alone," replied Herman. She gave him minute instructions and a key with which to open the street door. The young man pressed the cold, inert hand, then, went out. The death of the Countess had surprised no one, as it had long been expected. Her funeral was attended by every one of note in the vicinity. Herman mingled with the throng without attracting any especial attention. After all the friends had taken their last look at the dead face, the young man approached the bier. He prostrated himself on the cold floor, and remained motionless for a long time. He rose at last with a face almost as pale as that of the corpse itself, and went up the steps to look into the casket. As he looked clown it seemed to him that the rigid face returned his glance mockingly, closing one eye. He turned abruptly away, made a false step, and fell to the floor. He was picked up, and, at the same moment, Lisaveta was carried out in a faint.

Herman did not recover his usual composure during the entire day. He dined alone at an out-of-the-way restaurant, and drank a great deal, in the hope of stifling his emotion. The wine only served to stimulate his imagination. He returned home and threw himself down on his bed without undressing.

During the night he awoke with a start; the moon shone into his chamber, making everything plainly visible. Some one looked in at the window, then quickly disappeared. He paid no attention to this, but soon he heard the vestibule door open. He thought it was his orderly, returning late, drunk as usual. The step was an unfamiliar one, and he heard the shuffling sound of loose slippers.

The door of his room opened, and a woman, in white entered. She came close to the bed, and the terrified man recognized the Countess.

"I have come to you against my will," she said abruptly; "but I was commanded to grant your request. The tray, seven, and ace in succession are the magic cards. Twenty-four hours must elapse between the use of each card, and after the three have been used, you must never play again." The phantom then turned and walked away. Herman heard the outside door close, and again saw the form pass the window. He rose and went out into the hall, 'where his orderly lay asleep on the floor. The door was closed. Finding no trace of a visitor, he returned, to his room, lit his candle, and wrote down what he had just heard.

Two fixed ideas cannot exist in the brain at the same time any more than two bodies can occupy the same point in space. The tray, seven, and ace soon chased away the thoughts of the dead woman, and all other thoughts from the brain of the young officer. All his ideas merged, into a single one: how to turn to advantage the secret paid for so dearly. He even thought of resigning his commission and going to Paris to force a fortune from conquered fate. Chance rescued him from his embarrassment.

Tchekalinsky, a man who had passed his whole life at cards, opened a club at St. Petersburg. His long experience secured for him the confidence of his companions, and his hospitality and genial humor conciliated society.

The gilded youth flocked around him, neglecting society, preferring the charms of faro to those of their sweethearts. Naroumov invited Herman to accompany him to the club, and the young man accepted the invitation only too willingly.

The two officers found the apartments full. Generals and statesmen played whist; young men lounged on sofas, eating ices or smoking. In the principal salon stood a long table, at which about twenty men sat playing faro, the host of the establishment being the banker.

He was a man of about sixty, gray-haired and respectable. His ruddy face shone with genial humor; his eyes sparkled and a constant smile hovered, around his lips.

Naroumov presented Herman. The host gave him. a cordial handshake, begged him not to stand upon ceremony, and returned, to his dealing. More than thirty cards were already on the table. Tchekalinsky paused after each coup, to allow the punters time to recognize their gains or losses, politely answering all questions and constantly smiling.

After the deal was over, the cards were shuffled and the game began again. "Permit me to choose a card," said Herman, stretching out his hand over the head of a portly gentleman, to reach a livret. The banker bowed without replying.

Herman chose a card, and wrote the amount of his stake upon it with a piece of chalk.

"How much is that?" asked the banker; "excuse me, sir, but I do not see well."

"Forty thousand rubles," said Herman coolly.

All eyes were instantly turned upon the speaker.

"He has lost his wits," thought Naroumov.

"Allow me to observe," said Tchekalinsky, with his eternal smile, "that your stake is excessive."

"What of it?" replied Herman, nettled. "Do you accept it or not?" The banker nodded in assent. "I have only to remind you that the cash will be necessary; of course your word, is good, but in order to keep the confidence of my patrons, I prefer the ready money."

Herman, took a bank-check from his pocket and handed it to his host. The latter examined it attentively, then laid it on the card chosen. He began dealing: to the right, a nine; to the left, a tray, "The tray wins," said Herman, showing the card he held—a tray. A murmur ran through the crowd. Tchekalinsky frowned for a second only, then his smile returned. He took a roll of bank-bills from his pocket and counted out the required sum. Herman received it and at once left the table.

The next evening saw him at the place again. Every one eyed him curiously, and Tchekalinsky greeted him cordially.

He selected his card and placed upon it his fresh stake. The banker began dealing: to the right, a nine; to the left, a seven.

Herman then showed his card—a seven spot. The onlookers exclaimed, and the host was visibly disturbed. He counted out ninety-four-thousand rubles and passed them to Herman, who accepted them without showing the least surprise, and at once withdrew.

The following evening he went again. His appearance was the signal for the cessation, of all occupation, every one being eager to watch the developments of events. He selected his card—an ace.

The dealing began: to the right, a queen; to the left, an ace.

"The ace wins," remarked Herman, turning up his card without glancing at it.

"Your queen is killed," remarked Tchekalinsky quietly.

Herman trembled; looking down, he saw, not the ace he had selected, but the queen of spades. He could scarcely believe his eyes. It seemed impossible that he could have made such a mistake. As he stared, at the card it seemed to him that the queen winked one eye at him mockingly.

"The old woman!" he exclaimed involuntarily.

The croupier raked in the money while he looked on in stupid terror. When, he left the table, all made way for him to pass; the cards were shuffled, and the gambling went on.

Herman became a lunatic. He was confined at the hospital at Oboukov, where he spoke to no one, but kept constantly murmuring in a monotonous tone: "The tray, seven, ace! The tray, seven, queen!"

# THE STORY OF THE SPANIARDS, HAMMERSMITH

## E. AND H. HERON

Lieutenant Roderick Houston, of H.M.S. *Sphinx,* had practically nothing beyond his pay, and he was beginning to be very tired of the West African station, when he received the pleasant intelligence that a relative had left him a legacy. This consisted of a satisfactory sum in ready money and a house in Hammersmith, which was rated at over £200 a year, and was said in addition to be comfortably furnished. Houston, therefore, counted on its rental to bring his income up to a fairly desirable figure. Further information from home, however, showed him that he had been rather premature in his expectations, whereupon, being a man of action, he applied for two months' leave, and came home to look after his affairs himself.

When he had been a week in London he arrived at the conclusion that he could not possibly hope single-handed to tackle the difficulties which presented themselves. He accordingly wrote the following letter to his friend, Flaxman Low:

The Spaniards, Hammersmith, 23-3-1892. Dear Low,—Since we parted some three years ago, I have heard very little of you. It was only yesterday that I met our mutual friend, Sammy Smith ("Silkworm" of our schooldays), who told me that your studies have developed in a new direction, and that you are now a good deal interested in psychical subjects. If this be so, I hope to induce you to come and stay with me here for a few days by promising to introduce you to a problem in your own line. I am just now living at "The Spaniards," a house that has lately been left to me, and which in the first instance was built by an old fellow named Van Nuysen, who married a great-aunt of mine. It is a good house, but there is said to be "something wrong" with it. It lets easily, but unluckily the tenants cannot be persuaded to remain above a week or two. They complain that the place is haunted by something—presumably a ghost—because its vagaries bear just that brand of inconsequence which stamps the common run of manifestations.

It occurs to me that you may care to investigate the matter with me. If so, send me a wire when to expect you.

Yours ever,
Roderick Houston.

Houston waited in some anxiety for an answer. Low was the sort of man one could rely on in almost any emergency. Sammy Smith had told him a characteristic anecdote of Low's career at Oxford, where, although his intellectual triumphs may be forgotten, he will always be remembered by the story that when Sands, of Queen's, fell ill on the day before the Varsity sports, a telegram was sent to Low's rooms: "Sands ill. You must do the hammer for us." Low's reply was pithy: "I'll be there." Thereupon he finished the treatise upon which he was engaged, and next day his strong, lean figure was to be seen swinging the hammer amidst vociferous cheering, for that was the occasion on which he not only won the event, but beat the record.

On the fifth day Low's answer came from Vienna. As he read it, Houston recalled the high forehead, long neck—with its accompanying low collar—and thin moustache of his scholarly, athletic friend, and smiled. There was so much more in Flaxman Low than anyone gave him credit for.

My dear Houston,—Very glad to hear of you again. In response to your kind invitation, I thank you for the opportunity of meeting the ghost, and still more for the pleasure of your companionship. I came here to inquire into a somewhat similar affair. I hope, however, to be able to leave tomorrow, and will be with you some time on Friday evening.

Very sincerely yours,

Flaxman Low.

P.S.—By the way, will it be convenient to give your servants a holiday during the term of my visit, as, if my investigations are to be of any value, not a grain of dust must be disturbed in your house, excepting by ourselves?—F.L.

"The Spaniards" was within some fifteen minutes' walk of Hammersmith Bridge. Set in the midst of a fairly respectable neighbourhood, it presented an odd contrast to the commonplace dullness of the narrow streets crowded about it. As Flaxman Low drove up in the evening light, he reflected that the house might have come from the back of beyond—it gave an impression of something old-world and something exotic.

It was surrounded by a ten-foot wall, above which the upper storey was visible, and Low decided that this intensely English house still gave some curious suggestion of the tropics. The interior of the house carried out the same idea, with its sense of space and air, cool tints and wide, matted passages.

"So you have seen something yourself since you came?" Low said, as they sat at dinner, for Houston had arranged that meals should be sent in for them from an hotel.

"I've heard tapping up and down the passage upstairs. It is an uncarpeted landing which runs the whole length of the house. One night, when I was quicker than usual, I saw what looked like a bladder disappear into one of the bedrooms—your room it is to be, by the way—and the door closed behind it," replied Houston discontentedly. "The usual meaningless antics of a ghost."

"What had the tenants who lived here to say about it?" went on Low.

"Most of the people saw and heard just what I have told you, and promptly went away. The only one who stood out for a little while was old Filderg—you know the man? Twenty years ago he made an effort to cross the Australian deserts—he stopped for eight weeks. When he left he saw the house-agent, and said he was afraid he had done a little shooting practice in the upper passage, and he hoped it wouldn't count against him in the bill, as it was done in defence of his life. He said something had jumped on to the bed and tried to strangle him. He described it as cold and glutinous, and he pursued it down the passage, firing at it. He advised the owner to have the house pulled down; but, of course, my cousin did nothing of the kind. It's a very good house, and he did not see the sense of spoiling his property."

"That's very true," replied Flaxman Low, looking round. "Mr. Van Nuysen had been in the West Indies, and kept his liking for spacious rooms."

"Where did you hear anything about him?" asked Houston in surprise.

"I have heard nothing beyond what you told me in your letter; but I see a couple of bottles of Gulf weed and a lace-plant ornament, such as people used to bring from the West Indies in former days."

"Perhaps I should tell you the history of the old man," said Houston doubtfully; "but we aren't proud of it!"

Flaxman Low considered a moment.

"When was the ghost seen for the first time?"

"When the first tenant took the house. It was let after old Van Nuysen's time."

"Then it may clear the way if you will tell me something of him."

"He owned sugar plantations in Trinidad, where he passed the greater part of his life, while his wife mostly remained in England—incompatibility of temper it was said. When he came home for good and built this house they still lived apart, my aunt declaring that nothing on earth would persuade her to return to him. In course of time he became a confirmed invalid, and he then insisted on my aunt joining him. She lived here for perhaps a year, when she was found dead in bed one morning—in your room."

"What caused her death?"

"She had been in the habit of taking narcotics, and it was supposed that she smothered herself while under their influence."

"That doesn't sound very satisfactory," remarked Flaxman Low.

"Her husband was satisfied with it anyhow, and it was no one else's business. The family were only too glad to have the affair hushed up."

"And what became of Mr. Van Nuysen?"

"That I can't tell you. He disappeared a short time after. Search was made for him in the usual way, but nobody knows to this day what became of him."

"Ah, that was strange, as he was such an invalid," said Low, and straightway fell into a long fit of abstraction,

from which he was roused by hearing Houston curse the incurable foolishness and imbecility of ghostly behaviour. Flaxman woke up at this. He broke a walnut thoughtfully and began in a gentle voice:

"My dear fellow, we are apt to be hasty in our condemnation of the general behaviour of ghosts. It may appear incalculably foolish in our eyes, and I admit there often seems to be a total absence of any apparent object or intelligent action. But remember that what appears to us to be foolishness may be wisdom in the spirit world, since our unready senses can only catch broken glimpses of what is, I have not the slightest doubt, a coherent whole, if we could trace the connection."

"There may be something in that," replied Houston indifferently. "People naturally say that this ghost is the ghost of old Van Nuysen. But what connection can possibly exist between what I have told you of him and the manifestations—a tapping up and down the passage and the drawing about of a bladder like a child at play? It sounds idiotic!"

"Certainly. Yet it need not necessarily be so. There are isolated facts, we must look for the links which lie between. Suppose a saddle and a horse-shoe were to be shown to a man who had never seen a horse, I doubt whether he, however intelligent, could evolve the connecting idea! The ways of spirits are strange to us simply because we need further data to help us to interpret them."

"It's a new point of view," returned Houston, "but upon my word, you know, Low, I think you're wasting your time!"

Flaxman Low smiled slowly; his grave, melancholy face brightened.

"I have," said he, "gone somewhat deeply into the subject. In other sciences one reasons by analogy. Psychology is unfortunately a science with a future but without a past, or more probably it is a lost science of the ancients. However that may be, we stand today on the frontier of an unknown world, and progress is the result of individual effort; each solution of difficult phenomena forms a step towards the solution of the next problem. In this case, for example, the bladder-like object may be the key to the mystery."

Houston yawned.

"It all seems pretty senseless, but perhaps you may be able to read reason into it. If it were anything tangible, anything a man could meet with his fists, it would be easier."

"I entirely agree with you. But suppose we deal with this affair as it stands, on similar lines, I mean on prosaic, rational lines, as we should deal with a purely human mystery."

"My dear fellow," returned Houston, pushing his chair back from the table wearily, "you shall do just as you like, only get rid of the ghost!"

For some time after Low's arrival nothing very special happened. The tappings continued, and more than once Low had been in time to see the bladder disappear into the closing door of his bedroom, though, unluckily, he never chanced to be inside the room on these occasions, and however quickly he followed the bladder, he never succeeded in seeing anything further. He made a thorough examination of the house, and left no space unaccounted for in his careful measurement. There were no cellars, and the foundation of the house consisted of a thick layer of concrete.

At length, on the sixth night, an event took place, which, as Flaxman Low remarked, came very near to putting an end to the investigations as far as he was concerned. For the preceding two nights he and Houston had kept watch in the hope of getting a glimpse of the person or thing which tapped so persistently up and down the passage. But they were disappointed, for there were no manifestations. On the third evening, therefore, Low went off to his room a little earlier than usual, and fell asleep almost immediately.

He says he was awakened by feeling a heavy weight upon his feet, something that seemed inert and motionless. He recollected that he had left the gas burning, but the room was now in darkness.

Next he was aware that the thing on the bed had slowly shifted, and was gradually travelling up towards his chest. How it came on the bed he had no idea. Had it leaped or climbed? The sensation he experienced as it moved was of some ponderous, pulpy body, not crawling or creeping, but spreading! It was horrible! He tried to move his lower limbs, but could not because of the deadening weight. A feeling of drowsiness began to overpower him, and a deadly cold, such as he said he had before felt at sea when in the neighbourhood of icebergs, chilled upon the air.

With a violent struggle he managed to free his arms, but the thing grew more irresistible as it spread upwards. Then he became conscious of a pair of glassy eyes, with livid, everted lids, looking into his own. Whether they were human eyes or beast eyes, he could not tell, but they were watery, like the eyes of a dead fish, and gleamed with a pale, internal lustre.

Then he owns he grew afraid. But he was still cool enough to notice one peculiarity about this ghastly visitant—although the head was within a few inches of his own, he could detect no breathing. It dawned upon him that he was about to be suffocated, for, by the same method of extension, the thing was now coming over his face! It felt cold and clammy, like a mass of mucilage or a monstrous snail. And every instant the weight became greater. He is a powerful man, and he struck with his fists again and again at the head. Some substance yielded under the blows with a sickening sensation of bruised flesh.

With a lucky twist he raised himself in the bed and battered away with all the force he was capable of in his cramped position. The only effect was an occasional shudder or quake that ran through the mass as his half-arm blows rained upon it. At last, by chance, his hand knocked against the candle beside him. In a moment he recollected the matches. He seized the box, and struck a light.

As he did so, the lump slid to the floor. He sprang out of bed, and lit the candle. He felt a cold touch upon his leg, but when he looked down there was nothing to be seen. The door, which he had locked overnight, was now open, and he rushed out into the passage. All was still and silent with the throbbing vacancy of night time.

After searching round, he returned to his room. The bed still gave ample proof of the struggle that had taken place, and by his watch he saw the hour to be between two and three.

As there seemed nothing more to be done, he put on his dressing-gown, lit his pipe, and sat down to write an account of the experience he had just passed through for the Psychical Research Society—from which paper the above is an abstract.

He is a man of strong nerves, but he could not disguise from himself that he had been at handgrips with some grotesque form of death. What might be the nature of his assailant he could not determine, but his experience was supported by the attack which had been made on Filderg, and also—it was impossible to avoid the conclusion—by the manner of Mrs. Van Nuysen's death.

He thought the whole situation over carefully in connection with the tapping and the disappearing bladder, but, turn these events how he would, he could make nothing of them. They were entirely incongruous. A little later he went and made a shakedown in Houston's room.

"What was the thing?" asked Houston, when Low had ended his story of the encounter.

Low shrugged his shoulders.

"At least it proves that Filderg did not dream," he said.

"But this is monstrous! We are more in the dark than ever. There's nothing for it but to have the house pulled down. Let us leave today."

"Don't be in a hurry, my dear fellow. You would rob me of a very great pleasure; besides, we may be on the verge of some valuable discovery. This series of manifestations is even more interesting than the Vienna mystery I was telling you of."

"Discovery or not," replied the other, "I don't like it."

The first thing next morning Low went out for a quarter of an hour. Before breakfast a man with a barrowful of sand came into the garden. Low looked up from his paper, leant out of the window, and gave some order.

When Houston came down a few minutes later he saw the yellowish heap on the lawn with some surprise.

"Hullo! What's this?" he asked.

"I ordered it," replied Low.

"All right. What's it for?"

"To help us in our investigations. Our visitor is capable of being felt, and he or it left a very distinct impression on the bed. Hence I gather it can also leave an impression on sand. It would be an immense advance if we could arrive at any correct notion of what sort of feet the ghost walks on. I propose to spread a layer of this sand in the upper passage, and the result should be footmarks if the tapping comes tonight."

That evening the two men made a fire in Houston's bedroom, and sat there smoking and talking, to leave the ghost "a free run for once," as Houston phrased it. The tapping was heard at the usual hour, and presently the accustomed pause at the other end of the passage and the quiet closing of the door.

Low heaved a long sigh of satisfaction as he listened.

"That's my bedroom door," he said; "I know the sound of it perfectly. In the morning, and with the help of daylight, we shall see what we shall see."

As soon as there was light enough for the purpose of examining the footprints, Low roused Houston.

Houston was as full of excitement as a boy, but his spirits fell by the time he had passed from end to end of the passage.

"There are marks," he said, "but they are as perplexing as everything else about this haunting brute, whatever it is. I suppose you think this is the print left by the thing which attacked you the night before last?"

"I fancy it is," said Low, who was still bending over the floor eagerly. "What do you make of it, Houston?"

"The brute has only one leg, to start with," replied Houston, "and that leaves the mark of a large, clawless pad! It's some animal—some ghoulish monster!"

"On the contrary," said Low, "I think we have now every reason to conclude that it is a man?"

"A man? What man ever left footmarks like these?"

"Look at these hollows and streaks at the sides; they are the traces of the sticks we have heard tapping."

"You don't convince me," returned Houston doggedly.

"Let us wait another twenty-four hours, and tomorrow night, if nothing further occurs, I will give you my conclusions. Think it over. The tapping, the bladder, and the fact that Mr. Van Nuysen had lived in Trinidad. Add to these things this single padlike print. Does nothing strike you by way of a solution?"

Houston shook his head.

"Nothing. And I fail to connect any of these things with what happened both to you and Filderg."

"Ah! now," said Flaxman Low, his face clouding a little, "I confess you lead me into a somewhat different region, though to me the connection is perfect."

Houston raised his eyebrows and laughed.

"If you can unravel this tangle of hints and events and diagnose the ghost, I shall be extremely astonished," he said. "What can you make of the footless impression?"

"Something, I hope. In fact, that mark may be a clue—an outrageous one, perhaps, but still a clue."

That evening the weather broke, and by night the storm had risen to a gale, accompanied by sharp bursts of rain.

"It's a noisy night," remarked Houston; "I don't suppose we'll hear the ghost, supposing it does turn up."

This was after dinner, as they were about to go into the smoking-room. Houston, finding the gas low in the hall, stopped to turn it higher; at the same time asking Low to see if the jet on the upper landing was also alight.

Flaxman Low glanced up and uttered a slight exclamation, which brought Houston to his side.

Looking down at them from over the banisters was a face—a blotched, yellowish face, flanked by two swollen, protruding ears, the whole aspect being strangely leonine. It was but a glimpse, a clash of meeting glances, as it were, a glare of defiance, and the face was quickly withdrawn as the two men literally leapt up the stairs.

"There's nothing here," exclaimed Houston, after a search had been carried out through every room above.

"I didn't suppose we'd find anything," returned Low.

"This fairly knots up the thread," said Houston. "You can't pretend to unravel it now."

"Come down," said Low briefly; "I'm ready to give you my opinion, such as it is."

Once in the smoking-room, Houston busied himself in turning on all the light he could procure, then he saw to securing the windows, and piled up an immense fire, while Flaxman Low, who, as usual, had a cigarette in his mouth, sat on the edge of the table and watched him with some amusement.

"You saw that abominable face?" cried Houston, as he threw himself into a chair. "It was as material as yours or mine. But where did he go to? He must be somewhere about."

"We saw him clearly. That is sufficient for our purpose."

"You are very good at enumerating points, Low. Now just listen to my list. The difficulties grow with every fresh discovery. We're at a deadlock now, I take it? The sticks and the tapping point to an old man, the playing with a bladder to a child; the footmark might be the pad of a tiger minus claws, yet the thing that attacked you at night was cold and pulpy. And, lastly, by way of a wind-up, we see a lion-like, human face! If you can make all these items square with each other, I'll be happy to hear what you have got to say."

"You must first allow me to ask you a question. I understood you to say that no blood relationship existed between you and old Mr. Van Nuysen?"

"Certainly not. He was quite an outsider," answered Houston brusquely.

"In that case you are welcome to my conclusions. All the things you have mentioned point to one explanation. This house is haunted by the ghost of Mr. Van Nuysen, and he was a leper."

Houston stood up and stared at his companion.

"What a horrible notion! I must say I fail to see how you have arrived at such a conclusion."

"Take the chain of evidence in rather different order," said Low. "Why should a man tap with a stick?"

"Generally because he's blind."

"In cases of blindness, one stick is used for guidance. Here we have two for support."

"A man who has lost the use of his feet."

"Exactly; a man who has from some cause partially lost the use of his feet."

"But the bladder and the lion-like face?" went on Houston.

"The bladder, or what seemed to us to resemble a bladder, was one of his feet, contorted by the disease and probably swathed in linen, which foot he dragged rather than used; consequently, in passing through a door, for example, he would be in the habit of drawing it in after him. Now, as regards the single footmark we saw. In one form of leprosy, the smaller bones of the extremities frequently fall away. The pad-like impression was, as I believe, the mark of the foot—a toeless foot which he used, because in a more advanced stage of the disease the maimed hand or foot heals and becomes callous."

"Go on," said Houston; "it sounds as if it might be true. And the lion-like face I can account for myself. I have been in China, and have seen it before in lepers."

"Mr. Van Nuysen had been in Trinidad for many years, as we know, and while there he probably contracted the disease."

"I suppose so. After his return," added Houston, "he shut himself up almost entirely, and gave out that he was a martyr to rheumatic gout, this awful thing being the true explanation."

"It also accounts for Mrs. Van Nuysen's determination not to return to her husband."

Houston appeared much disturbed.

"We can't drop it here, Low," he said, in a constrained voice. "There is a good deal more to be cleared up yet. Can you tell me more?"

"From this point I find myself on less certain ground," replied Low unwillingly. "I merely offer a suggestion, remember—I don't ask you to accept it. I believe Mrs. Van Nuysen was murdered!"

"What?" exclaimed Houston. "By her husband?"

"Indications tend that way."

"But, my good fellow—"

"He suffocated her and then made away with himself. It is a pity that his body was not recovered. The condition of the remains would be the only really satisfactory test of my theory. If the skeleton could even now be found, the fact that he was a leper would be finally settled."

There was a prolonged pause until Houston put another question.

"Wait a minute, Low," he said. "Ghosts are admittedly immaterial. In this instance our spook has an extremely palpable body. Surely this is rather unusual? You have made everything else more or less plain. Can you tell me why this dead leper should have tried to murder you and old Filderg? And also how he came to have the actual physical power to do so?"

Low removed his cigarette to look thoughtfully at the end of it. "Now I lapse into the purely theoretical," he answered. "Cases have been known where the assumption of diabolical agency is apparently justifiable."

"Diabolical agency?—I don't follow you."

"I will try to make myself clear, though the subject is still in a stage of vagueness and immaturity. Van Nuysen committed a murder of exceptional atrocity, and afterwards killed himself. Now, bodies of suicides are known to be peculiarly susceptible to spiritual influences, even to the point of arrested corruption. Add to this our knowledge that the highest aim of an evil spirit is to gain possession of a material body. If I carried out my theory to its logical conclusion, I should say that Van Nuysen's body is hidden somewhere on these premises—that this body is intermittently animated by some spirit, which at certain periods is forced to re-enact the gruesome tragedy of the Van Nuysens. Should any living person chance to occupy the position of the first victim, so much the worse for him!"

For some minutes Houston made no remark on this singular expression of opinion.

"But have you ever met with anything of the sort before?" he said at last.

"I can recall," replied Flaxman Low thoughtfully, "quite a number of cases which would seem to bear out this hypothesis. Among them a curious problem of haunting exhaustively examined by Busner in the early part of 1888, at which I was myself lucky enough to assist. Indeed, I may add that the affair which I have recently been engaged upon in Vienna offers some rather similar features. There, however, we had to stop short of excavation, by which alone any specific results might have been attained."

"Then you are of opinion," said Houston, "that pulling the house to pieces might cast some further light upon this affair?"

"I cannot see any better course," said Mr. Low.

Then Houston closed the discussion by a very definite declaration.

"This house shall come down!"

So "The Spaniards" was pulled down.

Such is the story of "The Spaniards," Hammersmith, and it has been given the first place in this series* because, although it may not be of so strange a nature as some that will follow it, yet it seems to us to embody in a high degree the peculiar methods by which Mr. Flaxman Low is wont to approach these cases.

The work of demolition, begun at the earliest possible moment, did not occupy very long, and during its early stages, under the boarding at an angle of the landing was found a skeleton. Several of the phalanges were missing, and other indications also established beyond a doubt the fact that the remains were the remains of a leper.

The skeleton is now in the museum of one of our city hospitals. It bears a scientific ticket, and is the only evidence extant of the correctness of Mr. Flaxman Low's methods and the possible truth of his extraordinary theories.

*"Real Ghost Stories," *Pearson's Magazine* (1898); J.E.

# NUMBER 13

## M. R. JAMES

Among the towns of Jutland, Viborg justly holds a high place. It is the seat of a bishopric; it has a handsome but almost entirely new cathedral, a charming garden, a lake of great beauty, and many storks. Near it is Hald, accounted one of the prettiest things in Denmark; and hard by is Finderup, where Marsk Stig murdered King Erik dipping on St. Cecilia's Day, in the year 1286. Fifty-six blows of square-headed iron maces were traced on Erik's skull when his tomb was opened in the seventeenth century. But I am not writing a guide-book.

There are good hotels in Viborg—Preisler's and the Phoenix are all that can be desired. But my cousin, whose experiences I have to tell you now, went to the Golden Lion the first time that he visited Viborg. He has not been there since, and the following pages will, perhaps, explain the reason of his abstention.

The Golden Lion is one of the very few houses in the town that were not destroyed in the great fire of 1726, which practically demolished the cathedral, the Sognekirke, the Raadhuus, and so much else that was old and interesting. It is a great red-brick house—that is, the front is of brick, with corbie steps on the gables and a text over the door; but the courtyard into which the omnibus drives is of black and white wood and plaster.

The sun was declining in the heavens when my cousin walked up to the door, and the light smote full upon the imposing facade of the house. He was delighted with the old-fashioned aspect of the place, and promised himself a thoroughly satisfactory and amusing stay in an inn so typical of old Jutland.

It was not business in the ordinary sense of the word that had brought Mr Anderson to Viborg. He was engaged upon some researches into the Church history of Denmark, and it had come to his knowledge that in the Rigsarkiv of Viborg there were papers, saved from the fire, relating to the last days of Roman Catholicism in the country. He proposed, therefore, to spend a considerable time—perhaps as much as a fortnight or three weeks—in examining and copying these, and he hoped that the Golden Lion would be able to give him a room of sufficient size to serve alike as a bedroom and a study. His wishes were explained to the landlord, and, after a certain amount of thought, the latter suggested that perhaps it might be the best way for the gentleman to look at one or two of the larger rooms and pick one for himself. It seemed a good idea.

The top floor was soon rejected as entailing too much getting upstairs after the day's work; the second floor contained no room of exactly the dimensions required; but on the first floor there was a choice of two or three rooms which would, so far as size went, suit admirably.

The landlord was strongly in favour of Number 17, but Mr Anderson pointed out that its windows commanded only the blank wall of the next house, and that it would be very dark in the afternoon. Either Number 12 or Number 14 would be better, for both of them looked on the street, and the bright evening light and the pretty view would more than compensate him for the additional amount of noise.

Eventually Number 12 was selected. Like its neighbours, it had three windows, all on one side of the room; it was fairly high and unusually long. There was, of course, no fireplace, but the stove was handsome and rather old—a cast-iron erection, on the side of which was a representation of Abraham sacrificing Isaac, and the inscription, 'I Bog Mose, Cap. 22,' above. Nothing else in the room was remarkable; the only interesting picture was an old coloured print of the town, date about 1820.

Supper-time was approaching, but when Anderson, refreshed by the ordinary ablutions, descended the staircase, there were still a few minutes before the bell rang. He devoted them to examining the list of his fellow-lodgers. As is usual in Denmark, their names were displayed on a large blackboard, divided into columns and lines, the numbers of the rooms being painted in at the beginning of each line. The list was not exciting. There was an advocate, or Sagfoerer, a German, and some bagmen from Copenhagen. The one and only point which suggested any food for thought was the absence of any Number 13 from the tale of the rooms, and even this was a thing which Anderson had already noticed half a dozen times in his experience of Danish hotels. He could not help wondering whether the objection to that particular number, common as it is, was so widespread and so strong as to make it difficult to let a room so ticketed, and he resolved to ask the landlord if he and his colleagues in the profession had actually met with many clients who refused to be accommodated in the thirteenth room.

He had nothing to tell me (I am giving the story as I heard it from him) about what passed at supper, and the evening, which was spent in unpacking and arranging his clothes, books, and papers, was not more eventful. Towards eleven o'clock he resolved to go to bed, but with him, as with a good many other people nowadays, an almost necessary preliminary to bed, if he meant to sleep, was the reading of a few pages of print, and he now remembered that the particular book which he had been reading in the train, and which alone would satisfy him at that present moment, was in the pocket of his great-coat, then hanging on a peg outside the dining-room.

To run down and secure it was the work of a moment, and, as the passages were by no means dark, it was not difficult for him to find his way back to his own door. So, at least, he thought; but when he arrived there, and turned the handle, the door entirely refused to open, and he caught the sound of a hasty movement towards it from within. He had tried the wrong door, of course. Was his own room to the right or to the left? He glanced at the number: it was 13. His room would be on the left; and so it was. And not before he had been in bed for some minutes, had read his wonted three or four pages of his book, blown out his light, and turned over to go to sleep, did it occur to him that, whereas on the blackboard of the hotel there had been no Number 13, there was undoubtedly a room numbered 13 in the hotel. He felt rather sorry he had not chosen it for his own. Perhaps he might have done the landlord a little service by occupying it, and given him the chance of saying that a well-born English gentleman had lived in it for three weeks and liked it very much. But probably it was used as a servant's room or something of the kind. After all, it was most likely not so large or good a room as his own. And he looked drowsily about the room, which was fairly perceptible in the half-light from the street-lamp. It was a curious effect, he thought. Rooms usually look larger in a dim light than a full one, but this seemed to have contracted in length and grown proportionately higher. Well, well! sleep was more important than these vague ruminations—and to sleep he went.

On the day after his arrival Anderson attacked the Rigsarkiv of Viborg. He was, as one might expect in Denmark, kindly received, and access to all that he wished to see was made as easy for him as possible. The documents laid before him were far more numerous and interesting than he had at all anticipated. Besides official papers, there was a large bundle of correspondence relating to Bishop Joergen Friis, the last Roman Catholic who held the see, and in these there cropped up many amusing and what are called 'intimate' details of private life and individual character. There was much talk of a house owned by the Bishop, but not inhabited by him, in the town. Its tenant was apparently somewhat of a scandal and a stumbling-block to the reforming party. He was a disgrace, they wrote, to the city; he practised secret and wicked arts, and had sold his soul to the enemy. It was of a piece with the gross corruption and superstition of the Babylonish Church that such a viper and blood-sucking *Troldmand* should be patronized and harboured by the Bishop. The Bishop met these reproaches boldly; he protested his own abhorrence of all such things as secret arts, and required his antagonists to bring the matter before the proper court—of course, the spiritual court—and sift it to the bottom. No one could be more ready and willing than himself to condemn Mag Nicolas Francken if the evidence showed him to have been guilty of any of the crimes informally alleged against him.

Anderson had not time to do more than glance at the next letter of the Protestant leader, Rasmus Nielsen, before the record office was closed for the day, but he gathered its general tenor, which was to the effect that Christian men were now no longer bound by the decisions of Bishops of Rome, and that the Bishop's Court was not, and could not be, a fit or competent tribunal to judge so grave and weighty a cause.

On leaving the office, Mr Anderson was accompanied by the old gentleman who presided over it, and, as they walked, the conversation very naturally turned to the papers of which I have just been speaking.

Herr Scavenius, the Archivist of Viborg, though very well informed as to the general run of the documents under his charge, was not a specialist in those of the Reformation period. He was much interested in what Anderson had to tell him about them. He looked forward with great pleasure, he said, to seeing the publication in which Mr Anderson spoke of embodying their contents. 'This house of the Bishop Friis,' he added, 'it is a great puzzle to me where it can have stood. I have studied carefully the topography of old Viborg, but it is most unlucky—of the old terrier of the Bishop's property which was made in 1560, and of which we have the greater part in the Arkiv—just the piece which had the list of the town property is missing. Never mind. Perhaps I shall some day succeed to find him.'

After taking some exercise—I forget exactly how or where—Anderson went back to the Golden Lion, his supper, his game of patience, and his bed. On the way to his room it occurred to him that he had forgotten to talk to the landlord about the omission of Number 13 from the hotel board, and also that he might as well make sure that Number 13 did actually exist before he made any reference to the matter.

The decision was not difficult to arrive at. There was the door with its number as plain as could be, and work of some kind was evidently going on inside it, for as he neared the door he could hear footsteps and voices, or a voice, within. During the few seconds in which he halted to make sure of the number, the footsteps ceased, seemingly very near the door, and he was a little startled at hearing a quick hissing breathing as of a person in strong excitement. He went on to his own room, and again he was surprised to find how much smaller it seemed now than it had when he selected it. It was a slight disappointment, but only slight. If he found it really not large enough, he could very easily shift to another. In the meantime he wanted something—as far as I remember it was a pocket-handkerchief—out of his portmanteau, which had been placed by the porter on a very inadequate trestle or stool against the wall at the farthest end of the room from his bed. Here was a very curious thing: the portmanteau was not to be seen. It had been moved by officious servants; doubtless the contents had been put in the wardrobe. No, none of them were there. This was vexatious. The idea of a theft he dismissed at once. Such things rarely happen in Denmark, but some piece of stupidity had certainly been performed (which is not so uncommon), and the *stuepige* must be severely spoken to. Whatever it was that he wanted, it was not so necessary to his comfort that he could not wait till the morning for it, and he therefore settled not to ring the bell and disturb the servants. He went to the window—the right-hand window it was—and looked out on the quiet street. There was a tall building opposite, with large spaces of dead wall; no passers-by; a dark night; and very little to be seen of any kind.

The light was behind him, and he could see his own shadow clearly cast on the wall opposite. Also the shadow of the bearded man in the room on the left, who passed to and fro in shirtsleeves once or twice, and was seen first brushing his hair, and later on in a nightgown. Also the shadow of the occupant of Number 13 on the right. This might be more interesting. Number 13 was, like himself, leaning on his elbows on the window-sill looking out into the street. He seemed to be a tall thin man—or was it by any chance a woman?—at least, it was someone who covered his or her head with some kind of drapery before going to bed, and, he thought, must be possessed of a red lamp-shade—and the lamp must be flickering very much. There was a distinct playing up and down of a dull red light on the opposite wall. He craned out a little to see if he could make any more of the figure, but beyond a fold of some light, perhaps white, material on the window-sill he could see nothing.

Now came a distant step in the street, and its approach seemed to recall Number 13 to a sense of his exposed position, for very swiftly and suddenly he swept aside from the window, and his red light went out. Anderson, who had been smoking a cigarette, laid the end of it on the window-sill and went to bed.

Next morning he was woken by the *stuepige* with hot water, etc. He roused himself, and after thinking out the correct Danish words, said as distinctly as he could:

'You must not move my portmanteau. Where is it?'

As is not uncommon, the maid laughed, and went away without making any distinct answer.

Anderson, rather irritated, sat up in bed, intending to call her back, but he remained sitting up, staring straight in front of him. There was his portmanteau on its trestle, exactly where he had seen the porter put it when he first arrived. This was a rude shock for a man who prided himself on his accuracy of observation. How it could possibly have escaped him the night before he did not pretend to understand; at any rate, there it was now.

The daylight showed more than the portmanteau; it let the true proportions of the room with its three windows appear, and satisfied its tenant that his choice after all had not been a bad one. When he was almost dressed he walked to the middle one of the three windows to look out at the weather. Another shock awaited him. Strangely unobservant he must have been last night. He could have sworn ten times over that he had been smoking at the right-hand window the last thing before he went to bed, and here was his cigarette-end on the sill of the middle window.

He started to go down to breakfast. Rather late, but Number 13 was later: here were his boots still outside his door—a gentleman's boots. So then Number 13 was a man, not a woman. Just then he caught sight of the number on the door. It was 14. He thought he must have passed Number 13 without noticing it. Three stupid mistakes in twelve hours were too much for a methodical, accurate-minded man, so he turned back to make sure. The next number to 14 was number 12, his own room. There was no Number 13 at all.

After some minutes devoted to a careful consideration of everything he had had to eat and drink during the last twenty-four hours, Anderson decided to give the question up. If his eyes or his brain were giving way he would have plenty of opportunities for ascertaining that fact; if not, then he was evidently being treated to a very interesting experience. In either case the development of events would certainly be worth watching.

During the day he continued his examination of the episcopal correspondence which I have already summarized. To his disappointment, it was incomplete. Only one other letter could be found which referred to the affair of Mag Nicolas Francken. It was from the Bishop Joergen Friis to Rasmus Nielsen. He said:

> Although we are not in the least degree inclined to assent to your judgement concerning our court, and shall be prepared if need be to withstand you to the uttermost in that behalf, yet forasmuch as our trusty and well-beloved Mag Nicolas Francken, against whom you have dared to allege certain false and malicious charges, hath been suddenly removed from among us, it is apparent that the question for this time falls. But forasmuch as you further allege that the Apostle and Evangelist St John in his heavenly Apocalypse describes the Holy Roman Church under the guise and symbol of the Scarlet Woman, be it known to you,' etc.

Search as he might, Anderson could find no sequel to this letter nor any clue to the cause or manner of the 'removal' of the *casus belli*. He could only suppose that Francken had died suddenly; and as there were only two days between the date of Nielsen's last letter—when Francken was evidently still in being— and that of the Bishop's letter, the death must have been completely unexpected.

In the afternoon he paid a short visit to Hald, and took his tea at Baekkelund; nor could he notice, though he was in a somewhat nervous frame of mind, that there was any indication of such a failure of eye or brain as his experiences of the morning had led him to fear.

At supper he found himself next to the landlord.

'What,' he asked him, after some indifferent conversation, 'is the reason why in most of the hotels one visits in this country the number thirteen is left out of the list of rooms? I see you have none here.'

The landlord seemed amused.

'To think that you should have noticed a thing like that! I've thought about it once or twice myself, to tell the truth. An educated man, I've said, has no business with these superstitious notions. I was brought up myself here in the high school of Viborg, and our old master was always a man to set his face against anything of that kind. He's been dead now this many years—a fine upstanding man he was, and ready with his hands as well as his head. I recollect us boys, one snowy day—'

Here he plunged into reminiscence.

'Then you don't think there is any particular objection to having a Number 13?' said Anderson.

'Ah! to be sure. Well, you understand, I was brought up to the business by my poor old father. He kept an hotel in Aarhuus first, and then, when we were born, he moved to Viborg here, which was his native place, and had the Phoenix here until he died. That was in 1876. Then I started business in Silkeborg, and only the year before last I moved into this house.'

Then followed more details as to the state of the house and business when first taken over.

'And when you came here, was there a Number 13?'

'No, no. I was going to tell you about that. You see, in a place like this, the commercial class—the travellers—are what we have to provide for in general. And put them in Number 13? Why, they'd as soon sleep in the street, or sooner. As far as I'm concerned myself, it wouldn't make a penny difference to me what the number of my room was, and so I've often said to them; but they stick to it that it brings them bad luck. Quantities of stories they have among them of men that have slept in a Number 13 and never been the same again, or lost their best customers, or—one thing and another,' said the landlord, after searching for a more graphic phrase.

'Then what do you use your Number 13 for?' said Anderson, conscious as he said the words of a curious anxiety quite disproportionate to the importance of the question.

'My Number 13? Why, don't I tell you that there isn't such a thing in the house? I thought you might have noticed that. If there was it would be next door to your own room.'

'Well, yes; only I happened to think—that is, I fancied last night that I had seen a door numbered thirteen in that passage; and, really, I am almost certain I must have been right, for I saw it the night before as well.'

Of course, Herr Kristensen laughed this notion to scorn, as Anderson had expected, and emphasized with much iteration the fact that no Number 13 existed or had existed before him in that hotel.

Anderson was in some ways relieved by his certainty, but still puzzled, and he began to think that the best way to make sure whether he had indeed been subject to an illusion or not was to invite the landlord to his room to smoke a cigar later on in the evening. Some photographs of English towns which he had with him formed a sufficiently good excuse.

Herr Kristensen was flattered by the invitation, and most willingly accepted it. At about ten o'clock he was to make his appearance, but before that Anderson had some letters to write, and retired for the purpose of writing them. He almost blushed to himself at confessing it, but he could not deny that it was the fact that he was becoming quite nervous about the question of the existence of Number 13; so much so that he approached his room by way of Number 11, in order that he might not be obliged to pass the door, or the place where the door ought to be. He looked quickly and suspiciously about the room when he entered it, but there was nothing, beyond that indefinable air of being smaller than usual, to warrant any misgivings. There was no question of the presence or absence of his portmanteau tonight. He had himself emptied it of its contents and lodged it under his bed. With a certain effort he dismissed the thought of Number 13 from his mind, and sat down to his writing.

His neighbours were quiet enough. Occasionally a door opened in the passage and a pair of boots was thrown out, or a bagman walked past humming to himself, and outside, from time to time, a cart thundered over the atrocious cobble-stones, or a quick step hurried along the flags.

Anderson finished his letters, ordered in whisky and soda, and then went to the window and studied the dead wall opposite and the shadows upon it.

As far as he could remember, Number 14 had been occupied by the lawyer, a staid man, who said little at meals, being generally engaged in studying a small bundle of papers beside his plate. Apparently, however, he was in the habit of giving vent to his animal spirits when alone. Why else should he be dancing? The shadow from the next room evidently showed that he was. Again and again his thin form crossed the window, his arms waved, and a gaunt leg was kicked up with surprising agility. He seemed to be barefooted, and the floor must be well laid, for no sound betrayed his movements. Sagfoerer Herr Anders Jensen, dancing at ten o'clock at night in a hotel bedroom, seemed a fitting subject for a historical painting in the grand style; and Anderson's thoughts, like those of Emily in the 'Mysteries of Udolpho', began to 'arrange themselves in the following lines':

When I return to my hotel, at ten o'clock p.m., the waiters think I am unwell; I do not care for them. But when I've locked my chamber door, and put my boots outside, I dance all night upon the floor.

And even if my neighbours swore, I'd go on dancing all the more, for I'm acquainted with the law, and in despite of all their jaw, their protests I deride.

Had not the landlord at this moment knocked at the door, it is probable that quite a long poem might have been laid before the reader. To judge from his look of surprise when he found himself in the room, Herr Kristensen was struck, as Anderson had been, by something unusual in its aspect. But he made no remark. Andersons photographs interested him mightily, and formed the text of many autobiographical discourses. Nor is it quite clear how the conversation could have been diverted into the desired channel of Number 13, had not the lawyer at this moment begun to sing, and to sing in a manner which could leave no doubt in anyone's mind that he was either exceedingly drunk or raving mad. It was a high, thin voice that they heard, and it seemed dry, as if from long disuse. Of words or tune there was no question. It went sailing up to a surprising height, and was carried down with a despairing moan as of a winter wind in a hollow chimney, or an organ whose wind fails suddenly. It was a really horrible sound, and Anderson felt that if he had been alone he must have fled for refuge and society to some neighbour bagman's room. The landlord sat open-mouthed.

'I don't understand it,' he said at last, wiping his forehead. 'It is dreadful. I have heard it once before, but I made sure it was a cat.' 'Is he mad?' said Anderson.

'He must be; and what a sad thing! Such a good customer, too, and so successful in his business, by what I hear, and a young family to bring up.'

Just then came an impatient knock at the door, and the knocker entered, without waiting to be asked. It was the lawyer, in *deshabille* and very rough-haired; and very angry he looked.

'I beg pardon, sir,' he said, 'but I should be much obliged if you would kindly desist—'

Here he stopped, for it was evident that neither of the persons before him was responsible for the disturbance; and after a moment's lull it swelled forth again more wildly than before.

'But what in the name of Heaven does it mean?' broke out the lawyer. 'Where is it? Who is it? Am I going out of my mind?'

'Surely, Herr Jensen, it comes from your room next door? Isn't there a cat or something stuck in the chimney?'

This was the best that occurred to Anderson to say and he realized its futility as he spoke; but anything was better than to stand and listen to that horrible voice, and look at the broad, white face of the landlord, all perspiring and quivering as he clutched the arms of his chair.

'Impossible,' said the lawyer, 'impossible. There is no chimney. I came here because I was convinced the noise was going on here. It was certainly in the next room to mine.'

'Was there no door between yours and mine?' said Anderson eagerly.

'No, sir,' said Herr Jensen, rather sharply. At least, not this morning.'

Ah!' said Anderson. 'Nor tonight?'

'I am not sure,' said the lawyer with some hesitation.

Suddenly the crying or singing voice in the next room died away, and the singer was heard seemingly to laugh to himself in a crooning manner. The three men actually shivered at the sound. Then there was a silence.

'Come,' said the lawyer, 'what have you to say, Herr Kristensen? What does this mean?'

'Good Heaven!' said Kristensen. 'How should I tell! I know no more than you, gentlemen. I pray I may never hear such a noise again.'

'So do I,' said Herr Jensen, and he added something under his breath. Anderson thought it sounded like the last words of the Psalter, 'omnis spiritus laudet Dominum, but he could not be sure.

'But we must do something,' said Anderson—'the three of us. Shall we go and investigate in the next room?'

'But that is Herr Jensen's room,' wailed the landlord. 'It is no use; he has come from there himself.'

'I am not so sure,' said Jensen. 'I think this gentleman is right: we must go and see.'

The only weapons of defence that could be mustered on the spot were a stick and umbrella. The expedition went out into the passage, not without quakings. There was a deadly quiet outside, but a light shone from under the next door. Anderson and Jensen approached it. The latter turned the handle, and gave a sudden vigorous push. No use. The door stood fast.

'Herr Kristensen,' said Jensen, 'will you go and fetch the strongest servant you have in the place? We must see this through.'

The landlord nodded, and hurried off, glad to be away from the scene of action. Jensen and Anderson remained outside looking at the door.

'It *is* Number 13, you see,' said the latter. 'Yes; there is your door, and there is mine,' said Jensen. 'My room has three windows in the daytime,' said Anderson with difficulty, suppressing a nervous laugh.

'By George, so has mine!' said the lawyer, turning and looking at Anderson. His back was now to the door. In that moment the door opened, and an arm came out and clawed at his shoulder. It was clad in ragged, yellowish linen, and the bare skin, where it could be seen, had long grey hair upon it.

Anderson was just in time to pull Jensen out of its reach with a cry of disgust and fright, when the door shut again, and a low laugh was heard.

Jensen had seen nothing, but when Anderson hurriedly told him what a risk he had run, he fell into a great state of agitation, and suggested that they should retire from the enterprise and lock themselves up in one or other of their rooms.

However, while he was developing this plan, the landlord and two able-bodied men arrived on the scene, all looking rather serious and alarmed. Jensen met them with a torrent of description and explanation, which did not at all tend to encourage them for the fray.

The men dropped the crowbars they had brought, and said flatly that they were not going to risk their throats in that devil's den. The landlord was miserably nervous and undecided, conscious that if the danger were not faced his hotel was ruined, and very loth to face it himself. Luckily Anderson hit upon a way of rallying the demoralized force.

'Is this,' he said, 'the Danish courage I have heard so much of? It isn't a German in there, and if it was, we are five to one.'

The two servants and Jensen were stung into action by this, and made a dash at the door.

'Stop!' said Anderson. 'Don't lose your heads. You stay out here with the light, landlord, and one of you two men break in the door, and don't go in when it gives way.'

The men nodded, and the younger stepped forward, raised his crowbar, and dealt a tremendous blow on the upper panel. The result was not in the least what any of them anticipated. There was no cracking or rending of wood—only a dull sound, as if the solid wall had been struck. The man dropped his tool with a shout, and began rubbing his elbow. His cry drew their eyes upon him for a moment; then Anderson looked at the door again. It was gone; the plaster wall of the passage stared him in the face, with a considerable gash in it where the crowbar had struck it. Number 13 had passed out of existence.

For a brief space they stood perfectly still, gazing at the blank wall. An early cock in the yard beneath was heard to crow; and as Anderson glanced in the direction of the sound, he saw through the window at the end of the long passage that the eastern sky was paling to the dawn.

'Perhaps,' said the landlord, with hesitation, 'you gentlemen would like another room for tonight—a double-bedded one?'

Neither Jensen nor Anderson was averse to the suggestion. They felt inclined to hunt in couples after their late experience. It was found convenient, when each of them went to his room to collect the articles he wanted for the night, that the other should go with him and hold the candle. They noticed that both Number 12 and Number 14 had *three* windows.

* * * * *

Next morning the same party reassembled in Number 12. The landlord was naturally anxious to avoid engaging outside help, and yet it was imperative that the mystery attaching to that part of the house should be cleared up. Accordingly the two servants had been induced to take upon them the function of carpenters. The furniture was cleared away, and, at the cost of a good many irretrievably damaged planks, that portion of the floor was taken up which lay nearest to Number 14.

You will naturally suppose that a skeleton—say that of Mag Nicolas Francken—was discovered. That was not so. What they did find lying between the beams which supported the flooring was a small copper box. In it was a neatly-folded vellum document, with about twenty lines of writing. Both Anderson and Jensen (who proved to be something of a palaeographer) were much excited by this discovery, which promised to afford the key to these extraordinary phenomena.

* * * * *

I possess a copy of an astrological work which I have never read. It has, by way of frontispiece, a woodcut by Hans Sebald Beham, representing a number of sages seated round a table. This detail may enable connoisseurs to identify the book. I cannot myself recollect its title, and it is not at this moment within reach; but the fly-leaves of it are covered with writing, and, during the ten years in which I have owned the volume, I have not been able to determine which way up this writing ought to be read, much less in what language it is. Not dissimilar was the position of Anderson and Jensen after the protracted examination to which they submitted the document in the copper box.

After two days' contemplation of it, Jensen, who was the bolder spirit of the two, hazarded the conjecture that the language was either Latin or Old Danish.

Anderson ventured upon no surmises, and was very willing to surrender the box and the parchment to the Historical Society of Viborg to be placed in their museum.

I had the whole story from him a few months later, as we sat in a wood near Upsala, after a visit to the library there, where we—or, rather, I—had laughed over the contract by which Daniel Salthenius (in later life Professor of Hebrew at Koenigsberg) sold himself to Satan. Anderson was not really amused.

'Young idiot!' he said, meaning Salthenius, who was only an undergraduate when he committed that indiscretion, 'how did he know what company he was courting?'

And when I suggested the usual considerations he only grunted. That same afternoon he told me what you have read; but he refused to draw any inferences from it, and to assent to any that I drew for him.

# THE APPARITION OF MRS. VEAL

## DANIEL DEFOE

This thing is so rare in all its circumstances, and on so good authority, that my reading and conversation have not given me anything like it. It is fit to gratify the most ingenious and serious inquirer. Mrs. Bargrave is the person to whom Mrs. Veal appeared after her death; she is my intimate friend, and I can avouch for her reputation for these fifteen or sixteen years, on my own knowledge; and I can confirm the good character she had from her youth to the time of my acquaintance. Though, since this relation, she is calumniated by some people that are friends to the brother of Mrs. Veal who appeared, who think the relation of this appearance to be a reflection, and endeavor what they can to blast Mrs. Bargrave s reputation and to laugh the story out of countenance. But by the circumstances thereof, and the cheerful disposition of Mrs. Bargrave, notwithstanding the ill usage of a very wicked husband, there is not yet the least sign of dejection in her face; nor did I ever hear her let fall a desponding or murmuring expression; nay, not when actually under her husband's barbarity, which I have been a witness to, and several other persons of undoubted reputation.

Now you must know Mrs. Veal was a maiden gentlewoman of about thirty years of age, and for some years past had been troubled with fits, which were perceived coming on her by her going off from her discourse very abruptly to some impertinence. She was maintained by an only brother, and kept his house in Dover. She was a very pious woman, and her brother a very sober man to all appearance; but now he does all he can to null and quash the story. Mrs. Veal was intimately acquainted with Mrs. Bargrave from her childhood. Mrs. Veal's circumstances were then mean; her father did not take care of his children as he ought, so that they were exposed to hardships. And Mrs. Bargrave in those days had as unkind a father, though she wanted neither for food nor clothing; while Mrs. Veal wanted for both, insomuch that she would often say, "Mrs. Bargrave, you are not only the best, but the only friend I have in the world; and no circumstance of life shall ever dissolve my friendship." They would often condole each other's adverse fortunes, and read together *Drelincourt upon Death,* and other good books; and so, like two Christian friends, they comforted each other under their sorrow.

Some time after, Mr. Veal's friends got him a place in the custom-house at Dover, which occasioned Mrs. Veal, by little and little, to fall off from her intimacy with Mrs. Bargrave, though there was never any such thing as a quarrel; but an indifferency came on by degrees, till at last Mrs. Bargrave had not seen her in two years and a half, though above a twelvemonth of the time Mrs. Bargrave hath been absent from Dover, and this last half-year has been in Canterbury about two months of the time, dwelling in a house of her own.

In this house, on the eighth of September, one thousand seven hundred and five, she was sitting alone in the forenoon, thinking over her unfortunate life, and arguing herself into a due resignation to Providence, though her condition seemed hard: "And," said she, "I have been provided for hitherto, and doubt not but I shall be still, and am well satisfied that my afflictions shall end when it is most fit for me." And then took up her sewing work, which she had no sooner done but she hears a knocking at the door; she went to see who was there, and this proved to be Mrs. Veal, her old friend, who was in a riding-habit. At that moment of time the clock struck twelve at noon.

"Madam," says Mrs. Bargrave, "I am surprised to see you, you have been so long a stranger"; but told her she was glad to see her, and offered to salute her, which Mrs. Veal complied with, till their lips almost touched, and then Mrs. Veal drew her hand across her own eyes, and said, "I am not very well," and so waived it. She told Mrs. Bargrave she was going a journey, and had a great mind to see her first. "But," says Mrs. Bargrave, "how can you take a journey alone? I am amazed at it, because I know you have a fond brother." "Oh," says Mrs. Veal, "I gave my brother the slip, and came away, because I had so great a desire to see you before I took my journey." So Mrs. Bargrave went in with her into another room within the first, and Mrs. Veal sat her down in an elbow-chair, in which Mrs. Bargrave was sitting when she heard Mrs. Veal knock. "Then," says Mrs. Veal, "my dear friend, I am come to renew our old friendship again, and beg your pardon for my breach of it; and if you can forgive me, you are the best of women." "Oh," says Mrs. Bargrave, "do not mention such a thing; I have not had an uneasy thought about it." "What did you think of me?" says Mrs. Veal. Says Mrs. Bargrave, "I thought you were like the rest of the world, and that prosperity had made you forget yourself and me." Then Mrs. Veal reminded Mrs. Bargrave of the many friendly offices she did her in former days, and much of the conversation they had with each other in the times of their adversity; what books they read, and what comfort in particular they received from Drelincourt's *Book of Death,* which was the best, she said, on the subject ever wrote. She also mentioned Doctor Sherlock, and two Dutch books, which were translated, wrote upon death, and several others. But Drelincourt, she said, had the clearest notions of death and of the future state of any who had handled that subject. Then she asked Mrs. Bargrave whether she had Drelincourt. She said, "Yes." Says Mrs. Veal, "Fetch it." And so Mrs. Bargrave goes up-stairs and brings it down. Says Mrs. Veal, "Dear Mrs. Bargrave, if the eyes of our faith were as open as the eyes of our body, we should see numbers of angels about us for our guard. The notions we have of Heaven now are nothing like what it is, as Drelincourt says; therefore be comforted under your afflictions, and believe that the Almighty has a particular regard to you, and that your afflictions are marks of Gods favor; and when they have done the business they are sent for, they shall be removed from you. And believe me, my dear friend, believe what I say to you, one minute of future happiness will infinitely reward you for all your sufferings. For I can never believe" (and claps her hand upon her knee with great earnestness, which, indeed, ran through most of her discourse) "that ever God will suffer you to spend all your days in this afflicted state. But be assured that your afflictions shall leave you, or you them, in a short time." She spake in that pathetical and heavenly manner that Mrs. Bargrave wept several times, she was so deeply affected with it.

Then Mrs. Veal mentioned Doctor Kendrick's *Ascetic,* at the end of which he gives an account of the lives of the primitive Christians. Their pattern she recommended to our imitation, and said, "Their conversation was not like this of our age. For now," says she, "there is nothing but vain, frothy discourse, which is far different from theirs. Theirs was to edification, and to build one another up in faith, so that they were not as we are, nor are we as they were. But," said she, "we ought to do as they did; there was a hearty friendship among them; but where is it now to be found?" Says Mrs. Bargrave, "It is hard indeed to find a true friend in these days." Says Mrs. Veal, "Mr. Norris has a fine copy of verses, called *Friendship in Perfection,* which I wonderfully admire. Have you seen the book?" says Mrs. Veal. "No," says Mrs. Bargrave, "but I have the verses of my own writing out." "Have you?" says Mrs. Veal; "then fetch them"; which she did from above stairs, and offered them to Mrs. Veal to read, who refused, and waived the thing, saying, "holding down her head would make it ache"; and then desiring Mrs. Bargrave to read them to her, which she did. As they were admiring *Friendship,* Mrs. Veal said, "Dear Mrs. Bargrave, I shall love you forever." In these verses there is twice used the word "Elysian." "Ah!" says Mrs. Veal, "these poets have such names for Heaven." She would often draw her hand across her own eyes, and say, "Mrs. Bargrave, do not you think I am mightily impaired by my fits?" "No," says Mrs. Bargrave; "I think you look as well as ever I knew you."

After this discourse, which the apparition put in much finer words than Mrs. Bargrave said she could pretend to, and as much more than she can remember—for it cannot be thought that an hour and three quarters' conversation could all be retained, though the main of it she thinks she does—she said to Mrs. Bargrave she would have her write a letter to her brother, and tell him she would have him give rings to such and such; and that there was a purse of gold in her cabinet, and that she would have two broad pieces given to her cousin Watson.

Talking at this rate, Mrs. Bargrave thought that a fit was coming upon her, and so placed herself on a chair just before her knees, to keep her from falling to the ground, if her fits should occasion it; for the elbow-chair, she thought, would keep her from falling on either side. And to divert Mrs. Veal, as she thought, took hold of her gown-sleeve several times, and commended it. Mrs. Veal told her it was a scoured silk, and newly made up. But, for all this, Mrs. Veal persisted in her request, and told Mrs. Bargrave she must not deny her. And she would have her tell her brother all their conversation when she had the opportunity. "Dear Mrs. Veal," says Mrs. Bargrave, "this seems so impertinent that I cannot tell how to comply with it; and what a mortifying story will our conversation be to a young gentleman. Why," says Mrs. Bargrave, "it is much better, methinks, to do it yourself." "No," says Mrs. Veal; "though it seems impertinent to you now, you will see more reasons for it hereafter." Mrs. Bargrave, then, to satisfy her importunity, was going to fetch a pen and ink, but Mrs. Veal said, "Let it alone now, but do it when I am gone; but you must be sure to do it"; which was one of the last things she enjoined her at parting, and so she promised her.

Then Mrs. Veal asked for Mrs. Bargrave's daughter. She said she was not at home. "But if you have a mind to see her," says Mrs. Bargrave, "I'll send for her." "Do," says Mrs. Veal; on which she left her, and went to a neighbor's to see her; and by the time Mrs. Bargrave was returning, Mrs. Veal was got without the door in the street, in the face of the beast-market, on a Saturday (which is market-day), and stood ready to part as soon as Mrs. Bargrave came to her. She asked her why she was in such haste. She said she must be going, though perhaps she might not go her journey till Monday; and told Mrs. Bargrave she hoped she should see her again at her cousin Watson's before she went whither she was going. Then she said she would take her leave of her, and walked from Mrs. Bargrave, in her view, till a turning interrupted the sight of her, which was three-quarters after one in the afternoon.

Mrs. Veal died the seventh of September, at twelve o'clock at noon, of her fits, and had not above four hours' senses before her death, in which time she received the sacrament. The next day after Mrs. Veal's appearance, being Sunday, Mrs. Bargrave was mightily indisposed with a cold and sore throat, that she could not go out that day; but on Monday morning she sends a person to Captain Watson's to know if Mrs. Veal was there. They wondered at Mrs. Bargrave's inquiry, and sent her word she was not there, nor was expected. At this answer, Mrs. Bargrave told the maid she had certainly mistook the name or made some blunder. And though she was ill, she put on her hood and went herself to Captain Watson's, though she knew none of the family, to see if Mrs. Veal was there or not. They said they wondered at her asking, for that she had not been in town; they were sure, if she had, she would have been there. Says Mrs. Bargrave, "I am sure she was with me on Saturday almost two hours." They said it was impossible, for they must have seen her if she had. In comes Captain Watson, while they were in dispute, and said that Mrs. Veal was certainly dead, and the escutcheons were making. This strangely surprised Mrs. Bargrave, when she sent to the person immediately who had the care of them, and found it true. Then she related the whole story to Captain Watson's family; and what gown she had on, and how striped; and that Mrs. Veal told her that it was scoured. Then Mrs. Watson cried out, "You have seen her indeed, for none knew but Mrs.

Veal and myself that the gown was scoured." And Mrs. Watson owned that she described the gown exactly; "for," said she, "I helped her to make it up." This Mrs. Watson blazed all about the town, and avouched the demonstration of truth of Mrs. Bargrave's seeing Mrs. Veal's apparition. And Captain Watson carried two gentlemen immediately to Mrs. Bargrave's house to hear the relation from her own mouth. And when it spread so fast that gentlemen and persons of quality, the judicious and sceptical part of the world, flocked in upon her, it at last became such a task that she was forced to go out of the way; for they were in general extremely satisfied of the truth of the thing, and plainly saw that Mrs. Bargrave was no hypochondriac, for she always appears with such a cheerful air and pleasing mien that she has gained the favor and esteem of all the gentry, and it is thought a great favor if they can but get the relation from her own mouth. I should have told you before that Mrs. Veal told Mrs. Bargrave that her sister and brother-in-law were just come down from London to see her. Says Mrs. Bargrave, "How came you to order matters so strangely?" "It could not be helped," said Mrs. Veal. And her brother and sister did come to see her, and entered the town of Dover just as Mrs. Veal was expiring. Mrs. Bargrave asked her whether she would drink some tea. Says Mrs. Veal, "I do not care if I do; but I'll warrant you this mad fellow"—meaning Mrs. Bargrave's husband—"has broke all your trinkets." "But," says Mrs. Bargrave, "I'll get something to drink in for all that"; but Mrs. Veal waived it, and said, "It is no matter; let it alone"; and so it passed.

All the time I sat with Mrs. Bargrave, which was some hours, she recollected fresh sayings of Mrs. Veal. And one material thing more she told Mrs. Bargrave, that old Mr. Bretton allowed Mrs. Veal ten pounds a year, which was a secret, and unknown to Mrs. Bargrave till Mrs. Veal told her.

Mrs. Bargrave never varies in her story, which puzzles those who doubt of the truth, or are unwilling to believe it. A servant in the neighbor's yard adjoining to Mrs. Bargrave's house heard her talking to somebody an hour of the time Mrs. Veal was with her. Mrs. Bargrave went out to her next neighbor's the very moment she parted with Mrs. Veal, and told her what ravishing conversation she had had with an old friend, and told the whole of it. Drelincourt's *Book of Death* is, since this happened, bought up strangely. And it is to be observed that, notwithstanding all the trouble and fatigue Mrs. Bargrave has undergone upon this account, she never took the value of a farthing, nor suffered her daughter to take anything of anybody, and therefore can have no interest in telling the story.

But Mr. Veal does what he can to stifle the matter, and said he would see Mrs. Bargrave; but yet it is certain matter of fact that he has been at Captain

Watson's since the death of his sister, and yet never went near Mrs. Bargrave; and some of his friends report her to be a liar, and that she knew of Mr. Bretton's ten pounds a year. But the person who pretends to say so has the reputation to be a notorious liar among persons whom I know to be of undoubted credit. Now, Mr. Veal is more of a gentleman than to say she lies, but says a bad husband has crazed her; but she needs only present herself, and it will effectually confute that pretence. Mr. Veal says he asked his sister on her death-bed whether she had a mind to dispose of anything. And she said no. Now the things which Mrs. Veal's apparition would have disposed of were so trifling, and nothing of justice aimed at in the disposal, that the design of it appears to me to be only in order to make Mrs. Bargrave satisfy the world of the reality thereof as to what she had seen and heard, and to secure her reputation among the reasonable and understanding part of mankind. And then, again, Mr. Veal owns that there was a purse of gold; but it was not found in her cabinet, but in a comb-box. This looks improbable; for that Mrs. Watson owned that Mrs. Veal was so very careful of the key of her cabinet that she would trust nobody with it; and if so, no doubt she would not trust her gold out of it. And Mrs. Veal's often drawing her hands over her eyes, and asking Mrs. Bargrave whether her fits had not impaired her, looks to me as if she did it on purpose to remind Mrs. Bargrave of her fits, to prepare her not to think it strange that she should put her upon writing to her brother, to dispose of rings and gold, which look so much like a dying person's request; and it took accordingly with Mrs. Bargrave as the effect of her fits coming upon her, and was one of the many instances of her wonderful love to her and care of her, that she should not be affrighted, which, indeed, appears in her whole management, particularly in her coming to her in the daytime, waiving the salutation, and when she was alone; and then the manner of her parting, to prevent a second attempt to salute her.

Now, why Mr. Veal should think this relation a reflection—as it is plain he does, by his endeavoring to stifle it—I cannot imagine; because the generality believe her to be a good spirit, her discourse was so heavenly. Her two great errands were, to comfort Mrs. Bargrave in her affliction, and to ask her forgiveness for her breach of friendship, and with a pious discourse to encourage her. So that, after all, to suppose that Mrs. Bargrave could hatch such an invention as this, from Friday noon to Saturday noon—supposing that she knew of Mrs. Veal's death the very first moment—without jumbling circumstances, and without any interest, too, she must be more witty, fortunate, and wicked, too, than any indifferent person, I dare say, will allow. I asked Mrs. Bargrave several times if she was sure she felt the gown. She answered, modestly, "If my senses be to be relied on, I am sure of it." I asked her if she heard a sound when she clapped her hand upon her knee. She said she did not remember she did, but said she appeared to be as much a substance as I did who talked with her. "And I may," said she, "be as soon persuaded that your apparition is talking to me now as that I did not really see her; for I was under no manner of fear, and received her as a friend, and parted with her as such. I would not," says she, "give one farthing to make any one believe it; I have no interest in it; nothing but trouble is entailed upon me for a long time, for aught I know; and, had it not come to light by accident, it would never have been made public." But now she says she will make her own private use of it, and keep herself out of the way as much as she can; and so she has done since. She says she had a gentleman who came thirty miles to her to hear the relation; and that she had told it to a roomful of people at the time. Several particular gentlemen have had the story from Mrs. Bargrave's own mouth.

This thing has very much affected me, and I am as well satisfied as I am of the best-grounded matter of fact. And why we should dispute matter of fact, because we cannot solve things of which we can have no certain or demonstrative notions, seems strange to me; Mrs. Bargrave's authority and sincerity alone would have been undoubted in any other case.

# ROUND THE FIRE
## CATHERINE CROWE

'My story will be a very short one,' said Mrs M.; 'for I must tell you that though, like everybody else, I have heard a great many ghost stories, and have met people who assured me they had seen such things, I cannot, for my own part, bring myself to believe in them; but a circumstance occurred when I was abroad that you may perhaps consider of a ghostly nature, though I cannot.

'I was travelling through Germany, with no one but my maid - it was before the time of railways, and on my road from Leipsic to Dresden I stopped at an inn that appeared to have been long ago part of an aristocratic residence - a castle, in short; for there was a stone wall and battlements, and a tower at one side; while the other was a prosaic-looking square building that had evidently been added in modern times. The inn *stood* at one end of a small village, in which some of the houses looked so antique that they might, I thought, be coeval with the castle itself. There were a good many travellers, but the host said he could accommodate me; and when I asked to see my room, he led me up to the towers, and showed me a tolerably comfortable one. There were only two apartments on each floor; so I asked him if I could have the other for my maid, and he said yes, if no other traveller arrived. None came, and she slept there.

'I supped at the *table d'hote,* and retired to bed early, as I had an excursion to make on the following day; and I was sufficiently tired with my journey to fall asleep directly.

'I don't know how long I had slept - but I think some hours, when I awoke quite suddenly, almost with a start, and beheld near the foot of the bed the *most* hideous, dreadful-looking old woman, in an antique dress, that imagination can conceive. She seemed to be approaching me - not as if walking, but gliding, with her left arm and hand extended towards me.

'"Merciful God, deliver me!" I exclaimed under my first impulse of amazement; and as I said the words she disappeared.'

'Then, though you don't believe in ghosts, you thought it was one when you saw it,'said I.

'I don't know what I thought - I admit I was a good deal frightened, and it was a long time before I fell asleep again.

'In the morning,' continued Mrs M., 'my maid knocked, and I told her to come in; but the door was locked, and I had to get out of bed to admit her - I thought I might have forgotten to fasten it. As soon as I was up I examined every part of the room, but I could find nothing to account for this intrusion. There was neither trap nor moving panel, nor door that I could see, except the one I had locked. However, I made up my mind not to speak of the circumstance, for I fancied I must have been deceived in supposing myself awake, and that it was only a dream; more particularly as there was no light in my room, and I could not comprehend how I could have seen this woman.

'I went out early, and was away the greater part of the day. When I returned I found more travellers had arrived, and that they had given the room next mine to a German lady and her daughter, who were at the *table d'hote.* I therefore had a bed made up in my room for my maid; and before I lay down, I searched thoroughly, that I might be sure nobody was concealed there.

'In the middle of the night - I suppose about the same time I had been disturbed on the preceding one - I and my maid were awakened by a piercing scream; and I heard the voice of the German girl in the adjoining room, exclaiming, *"Ach! meine mutter! meine mutter!"*

'For some time afterwards I heard them talking, and then I fell asleep -wondering, I confess, whether they had had a visit from the frightful old woman. They left me in no doubt the next morning. They came down to breakfast greatly excited - told everybody the cause - described the old woman exactly as I had seen her, and departed from the house incontently, declaring they would not stay there another hour.'

'What did the host say to it?' we asked.

'Nothing; he said we must have dreamed it - and I suppose we did.'

'Your story,' said I, 'reminds me of a very interesting letter which I received soon after the publication of *The Night Side of Nature*. It was from a clergyman who gave his name, and said he was chaplain to a nobleman. He related that in a house he inhabited, or had inhabited, a lady had one evening gone upstairs and seen, to her amazement, in a room, the door of which was open, a lady in an antique dress standing before a chest of drawers and apparently examining their contents. She stood still, wondering who this stranger could be, when the figure turned her face towards her and, to her horror, she saw there were no eyes. Other members of the family saw the same apparition also. I believe there were further particulars; but I unfortunately lost this letter, with some others, in the confusion of changing my residence.

The absence of eyes I take to be emblematical of moral blindness; for in the world of spirits there is no deceiving each other by false seemings; as we are, so we appear.'

'Then,' said Mrs W.C., 'the apparition - if it was an apparition - that two of my servants saw lately, must be in a very degraded state.

'There is a road, and on one side of it a path, just beyond my garden wall. Not long ago two of my servants were in the dusk of the evening walking up this path, when they saw a large, dark object coming towards them. At first they thought it was an animal; and when it got close one of them stretched out her hand to touch it; but she could feel nothing, and it passed on between her and the garden wall, although there was *no space*, the path being only wide enough for two; and on looking back, they saw it walking down the hill behind them. Three men were coming up on the path, and as the thing approached they jumped off into the road.

'"Good heavens, what is that!" cried the women.

'"I don't know," replied the men; "I never saw such a thing as that before."

The women came home greatly agitated; and we have since heard there is a tradition that the spot is haunted by the ghost of a man who was killed in a quarry close by.'

'I have travelled a great deal,' said our next speaker, the Chevalier de La C.G. 'and, certainly, I have never been in any country where instances of these spiritual appearances were not adduced on apparently credible authority. I have heard numerous stories of the sort, but the one that most readily occurs to me at present was told to me not long ago, in Paris, by Count P. - the nephew of the celebrated Count P. whose name occurs in the history of the remarkable incidents connected with the death of the Emperor Paul.

'Count P., my authority for the following story, was attached to the Russian embassy; and he told me, one evening, when the conversation turned on the inconveniences of travelling in the East of Europe, that on one occasion, when in Poland, he found himself about seven o'clock in an autumn evening on a forest road, where there was no possibility of finding a house of public entertainment within many miles. There was a frightful storm; the road, not good at the best, was almost impracticable from the weather, and his horses were completely knocked up. On consulting his people what was best to be done, they said that to go back was as impossible as to go forward; but that by turning a little out of the main road, they should soon reach a castle where possibly shelter might be procured for the night. The count gladly consented, and it was not long before they found themselves at the gate of what appeared a building on a very splendid scale. The courier quickly alighted and rang at the bell, and while waiting for admission he inquired who the castle belonged to, and was told that it was Count X's.

It was some time before the bell was answered, but at length an elderly man appeared at a wicket, with a lantern, and peeped out. On perceiving the equipage, he came forward and stepped up to the carriage, holding the light aloft to discover who was inside. Count P. handed him his card, and explained his distress.

"There is no one here, my lord," replied the man, "but myself and my family; the castle is not inhabited."

"That's bad news," said the count; "but nevertheless, you can give me what I am most in need of, and that is shelter for the night."

"'Willingly," said the man, "if your lordship will put up with such accommodation as we can hastily prepare."

"'So," said the count, "I alighted and walked in; and the old man unbarred the great gates to admit my carriages and people. We found ourselves in an immense *com*, with the castle *en face*, and stables and offices on each side. As we had *afourgon* with us, with provender for the cattle and provisions for ourselves, we wanted nothing but beds and a good fire; and as the only one lighted was in the old man's apartments, he first took us there. They consisted of a suite of small rooms in the left wing, that had probably been formerly occupied by the upper servants. They were comfortably furnished, and he and his large family appeared to be very well lodged. Besides the wife, there were three sons, with their wives and children, and two nieces; and in a part of the offices, where I saw a light, I was told there were labourers and women servants, for it was a valuable estate, with a fine forest, and the sons acted as *gardes chasse.*

"'Is there much game in the forest?" I asked.

"'A great deal of all sorts," they answered.

"'Then I suppose during the season the family live here?"

"'Never," they replied. "None of the family ever reside here."

"'Indeed!" I said; "how is that? It seems a very fine place."

"'Superb," answered the wife of the custodian; "but the castle is haunted."

'She said this with a simple gravity that made me laugh; upon which they all stared at me with the most edifying amazement.

"'I beg your pardon," I said; "but you know, perhaps, in great cities, such as I usually inhabit, there are no ghosts."

"'Indeed!" said they. "No ghosts!"

"'At least," I said, "I never heard of any; and we don't believe in such things."

'They looked at each other with surprise, but said nothing; not appearing to have any desire to convince me. "But do you mean to say," said I, "that that is the reason the family don't live here, and that the castle is abandoned on that account?"

"'Yes," they replied, "that is the reason nobody has resided here for many years."

"'But how can you live here then?"

"'We are never troubled in this part of the building," said she. "We hear noises, but we are used to that."

"'Well, if there is a ghost, I hope I shall see it," said I.

"'God forbid!" said the woman, crossing herself. "But we shall guard against that; your seigneurie will sleep not far from this, where you will be quite safe."

"'Oh! but," said I, "I am quite serious: if there is a ghost I should particularly like to see him, and I should be much obliged to you to put me in the apartments he most frequents."

They opposed this proposition earnestly, and begged me not to think of it; besides, they said if anything was to happen to my lord, how should they answer for it; but as I insisted, the women went to call the members of the family who were lighting fires and preparing beds in some rooms on the same floor as they occupied themselves. When they came they were as earnest against the indulgence of my wishes as the women had been. Still I insisted.

"'Are you afraid,' I said, "to go yourselves in the haunted chambers?"

"'No,' they answered. "We are the custodians of the castle and have to keep the rooms clean and well aired lest the furniture be spoiled - my lord talks always of removing it, but it has never been removed yet - but we would not sleep up there for all the world."

"Then it is the upper floors that are haunted?"

"'Yes, especially the long room, no one could pass a night there; the last that did is in a lunatic asylum now at Warsaw," said the custodian. "'What happened to him?"

"I don't know," said the man; "he was never able to tell." "'Who was he?' I asked.

"He was a lawyer. My lord did business with him; and one day he was speaking of this place, and saying that it was a pity he was not at liberty to pull it down and sell the materials; but he cannot, because it is family property and goes with the title; and the lawyer said he wished it was his, and that no ghost should keep him out of it. My lord said that it was easy for any one to say that who knew nothing about it, and that he must suppose the family had not abandoned such a fine place without good reasons. But the lawyer said it was some trick, and that it was coiners, or robbers, who had got a footing in the castle, and contrived to frighten people away that they might keep it to themselves; so my lord said if he could prove that he should be very much obliged to him, and more than that, he would give him a great sum — I don't know how much. So the lawyer said he would; and my lord wrote to me that he was coming to inspect the property, and I was to let him do anything he liked.

"'Well, he came, and with him his son, a fine young man and a soldier. They asked me all sorts of questions, and went over the castle and examined every part of it. From what they said I could see that they thought the ghost was all nonsense, and that I and my family were in collusion with the robbers or coiners. However, I did not care for that; my lord knew that the castle had been haunted before I was born.

"'I had prepared rooms on this floor for them — the same I am preparing for your lordship, and they slept there, keeping the keys of the upper rooms to themselves, so I did not interfere with them. But one morning, very early, we were awakened by someone knocking at our bedroom door, and when we opened it we saw Mr Thaddeus - that was the lawyer's son - standing there half-dressed and as pale as a ghost; and he said his father was very ill and he begged us to go to him; to our surprise he led us upstairs to the haunted chamber, and there we found the poor gentleman speechless, and we thought they had gone up there early and that he had had a stroke. But it was not so; Mr Thaddeus said that after we were all in bed they had gone up there to pass the night. I know they thought that there was no ghost but us, and that's why they would not let us know their intention. They laid down upon some sofas, wrapt up in their fur cloaks, and resolved to keep awake, and they did so for some time, but at last the young man was overcome by drowsiness; he struggled against it, but could not conquer it, and the last thing he recollects was his father shaking him and saying, 'Thaddeus, Thaddeus, for God's sake keep awake!' But he could not, and he knew no more till he woke and saw that day was breaking, and found his father sitting in a corner of the room speechless, and looking like a corpse; and there he was when we went up. The young man thought he'd been taken ill or had a stroke, as we supposed at first; but when we found they had passed the night in the haunted chambers, we had no doubt what had happened-he had seen some terrible sight and so lost his senses."

"'He lost his senses, I should say, from terror when his son fell asleep," said I, "and he felt himself alone. He could have been a man of no nerve. At all events, what you tell me raises my curiosity. Will you take me upstairs and shew me these rooms?"

"'Willingly," said the man, and fetching a bunch of keys and a light, and calling one of his sons to follow him with another, he led the way up the great staircase to a suite of apartments on the first floor. The rooms were lofty and large, and the man said the furniture was very handsome, but old. Being all covered with canvas cases, I could not judge of it. "Which is the long room?" I said.

'Upon which he led me into a long narrow room that might rather have been called a gallery. There were sofas along each side, something like a dais at the upper end; and several large pictures hanging on the walls.

'I had with me a bull dog, of a very fine breed, that had been given me in England by Lord F. She had followed me upstairs - indeed, she followed me everywhere - and I watched her narrowly as she went smelling about, but there were no indications of her perceiving anything extraordinary. Beyond this gallery there was only a small octagon room, with a door that led out upon another staircase. When I had examined it all thoroughly, I returned to the long room and told the man as that was the place especially frequented by the ghost, I should feel much obliged if he would allow me to pass the night there. I could take upon myself to say that Count X. would have no objection.

"'It is not that,' replied the man; "but the danger to your lordship," and he conjured me not to insist on such a perilous experiment.

'When he found I was resolved, he gave way, but on condition that I signed a paper, stating that in spite of his representations I had determined to sleep in the long room.

'I confess the more anxious these people seemed to prevent my sleeping there, the more curious I was; not that I believed in the ghost the least in the world. I thought that the lawyer had been right in his conjecture, but that he hadn't nerve enough to investigate whatever he saw or heard; and that they had succeeded in frightening him out of his senses. I saw what an excellent place these people had got, and how much it was their interest to maintain the idea that the castle was uninhabitable. Now, I have pretty good nerves — I have been in situations that have tried them severely - and I did not believe that any ghost, if there was such a thing, or any jugglery by which a semblance of one might be contrived, would shake them. As for any real danger, I did not apprehend it; the people knew who I was, and any mischief happening to me would have led to consequences they well understood. So they lighted fires in both the grates of the gallery and as they had abundance of dry wood they soon blazed up. I was determined not to leave the room after I was once in it, lest, if my suspicions were correct, they might have time to make their arrangements; so I desired my people to bring up my supper, and I ate it there.

'My courier said he had always heard the castle was haunted, but he dare say there was no ghost but the people below, who had a very comfortable berth of it; and he offered to pass the night with me, but I declined any companion and preferred trusting to myself and my dog. My valet, on the contrary, strongly advised me against the enterprise, assuring me that he had lived with a family in France whose chateau was haunted, and had left his place in consequence.

'By the time I had finished my supper it was ten o'clock, and everything was prepared for the night. My bed, though an impromptu, was very comfortable, made of amply stuffed cushions and thick coverlets, placed in front of the fire. I was provided with light and plenty of wood; and I had my regimental cutlass, and a case of excellent pistols, which I carefully primed and loaded in presence of the custodian, saying, "You see I am determined to fire at the ghost, so if he cannot stand a bullet he had better not pay me a visit."

The old man shook his head calmly, but made no answer. Having desired the courier, who said he should not go to bed, to come upstairs immediately if he heard the report of firearms, I dismissed my people and locked the doors, barricading each with a heavy ottoman besides. There was no arras or hangings of any sort behind which a door could be concealed; and I went round the room, the walls of which were panelled with white and gold, knocking every part, but neither the sound, nor Dido, the dog, gave any indications of there being anything unusual. Then I undressed and lay down with my sword and my pistols beside me; and Dido at the foot of my bed, where she always slept.

'I confess I was in a state of pleasing excitement; my curiosity and my love of adventure were roused; and whether it was ghost, or robber, or coiner, I was to have a visit from, the interview was likely to be equally interesting. It was half-past ten when I lay down; my expectations were too vivid to admit of sleep; and after an attempt at a French novel, I was obliged to give it up; I could not fix my attention to it. Besides, my chief care was not to be surprised. I could not help thinking the custodian and his family had some secret way of getting into the room, and I hoped to detect them in the act; so I lay with my eyes and ears open in a position that gave me a view of every part of it, till my travelling clock struck twelve, which being pre-eminently the ghostly hour, I thought the critical moment was arrived. But no, no sound, no interruption of any sort to the silence and solitude of the night occurred. When half-past twelve and one struck, I pretty well made up my mind that I should be disappointed in my expectations, and that the ghost, whoever he was, knew better than to encounter Dido and a brace of well charged pistols; but just as I arrived at this conclusion an unaccountable *frisson* came over me, and I saw Dido, who tired with her day's journey had lain till now quietly curled up asleep, begin to move, and slowly get upon her feet. I thought she was only going to turn, but, instead of lying down, she stood still with her ears erect and her head towards the dais, uttering a low growl.

'The dais, I should mention, was but the skeleton of a dais, for the draperies were taken off. There was only remaining a canopy covered with crimson velvet, and an arm-chair covered with velvet too, but cased in canvas like the rest of the furniture. I had examined this part of the room thoroughly, and had moved the chair aside to ascertain that there was nothing under it.

'Well, I sat up in bed and looked steadily in the same direction as the dog, but I could see nothing at first, though it appeared that she did; but as I looked I began to perceive something like a cloud in the chair, while at the same time a chill which seemed to pervade the very marrow in my bones crept through me, yet the fire was good; and it was not the chill of fear, for I cocked my pistols with perfect self-possession and abstained from giving Dido the signal to advance, because I wished eagerly to see the denouement of the adventure.

'Gradually this cloud took a form, and assumed the shape of a tall white figure that reached from the ceiling to the floor of the dais, which was raised by two steps. "At him, Dido! At him!" I said, and away she dashed to the steps, but instantly turned and crept back completely cowed. As her courage was undoubted, I own this astonished me, and I should have fired, but that I was perfectly satisfied that what I saw was not a substantial human form, for I had seen it grow into its present shape and height from the undefined cloud that first appeared in the chair. I laid my hand on the dog, who had crept up to my side, and I felt her shaking in her skin. I was about to rise myself and approach the figure, though I confess I was a good deal awestruck, when it stepped majestically from the dais, and seemed to be advancing. "At him!" I said, "At him, Dido!" and I gave the dog every encouragement to go forward; she made a sorry attempt, but returned when she had got half-way and crouched beside me whining with terror. The figure advanced upon me; the cold became icy; the dog crouched and trembled; and I, as it approached, honestly confess,' said Count P., 'that I hid my head under the bedclothes and did not venture to look up till morning. I know not what it was - as it passed over me I felt a sensation of undefinable horror, that no words can describe - and I can only say that nothing on earth would tempt me to pass another night in that room, and I am sure if Dido could speak you'd find her of the same opinion.

'I had desired to be called at seven o'clock, and when the custodian, who accompanied my valet, found me safe and in my perfect senses, I must say the poor man appeared greatly relieved; and when I descended the whole family seemed to look upon me as a hero. I thought it only just to them to admit that something had happened in the night that I felt impossible to account for, and that I should not recommend anybody who was not very sure of their nerves to repeat the experiment.'

When the Chevalier had concluded this extraordinary story, I suggested that the apparition of the castle very much resembled that mentioned by the late Professor Gregory, in his letters oh mesmerism, as having appeared in the Tower of London some years ago, and, from the alarm it created, having occasioned the death of a lady, the wife of an officer quartered there, and one of the sentries. Every one who had read that very interesting publication was struck by the resemblance.

# THE ISLE OF VOICES

## R. L. STEVENSON

Keola was married with Lehua, daughter of Kalamake, the wise man of Molokai, and he kept his dwelling with the father of his wife. There was no man more cunning than that prophet; he read the stars, he could divine by the bodies of the dead, and by the means of evil creatures: he could go alone into the highest parts of the mountain, into the region of the hobgoblins, and there he would lay snares to entrap the spirits of the ancient.

For this reason no man was more consulted in all the Kingdom of Hawaii. Prudent people bought, and sold, and married, and laid out their lives by his counsels; and the King had him twice to Kona to seek the treasures of Kamehameha. Neither was any man more feared: of his enemies, some had dwindled in sickness by the virtue of his incantations, and some had been spirited away, the life and the clay both, so that folk looked in vain for so much as a bone of their bodies. It was rumoured that he had the art or the gift of the old heroes. Men had seen him at night upon the mountains, stepping from one cliff to the next; they had seen him walking in the high forest, and his head and shoulders were above the trees.

This Kalamake was a strange man to see. He was come of the best blood in Molokai and Maui, of a pure descent; and yet he was more white to look upon than any foreigner: his hair the colour of dry grass, and his eyes red and very blind, so that "Blind as Kalamake, that can see across to-morrow," was a byword in the islands.

Of all these doings of his father-in-law, Keola knew a little by the common repute, a little more he suspected, and the rest he ignored. But there was one thing troubled him. Kalamake was a man that spared for nothing, whether to eat or to drink, or to wear; and for all he paid in bright new dollars. "Bright as Kalamake's dollars," was another saying in the Eight Isles. Yet he neither sold, nor planted, nor took hire — only now and then from his sorceries — and there was no source conceivable for so much silver coin.

It chanced one day Keola's wife was gone upon a visit to Kaunakakai, on the lee side of the island, and the men were forth at the sea-fishing. But Keola was an idle dog, and he lay in the verandah and watched the surf beat on the shore and the birds fly about the cliff. It was a chief thought with him always—the thought of the bright dollars. When he lay down to bed he would be wondering why they were so many, and when he woke at morn he would be wondering why they were all new; and the thing was never absent from his mind. But this day of all days he made sure in his heart of some discovery. For it seems he had observed the place where Kalamake kept his treasure, which was a lock-fast desk against the parlour wall, under the print of Kamehameha the Fifth, and a photograph of Queen Victoria with her crown; and it seems again that, no later than the night before, he found occasion to look in, and behold! the bag lay there empty. And this was the day of the steamer; he could see her smoke off Kalaupapa; and she must soon arrive with a month's goods, tinned salmon and gin, and all manner of rare luxuries for Kalamake.

"Now if he can pay for his goods to-day," Keola thought, "I shall know for certain that the man is a warlock, and the dollars come out of the Devil's pocket."

While he was so thinking, there was his father-in-law behind him, looking vexed.

"Is that the steamer?" he asked.

"Yes," said Keola. "She has but to call at Pelekunu, and then she will be here."

"There is no help for it then," returned Kalamake, "and I must take you in my confidence, Keola, for the lack of anyone better. Come here within the house."

So they stepped together into the parlour, which was a very fine room, papered and hung with prints, and furnished with a rocking- chair, and a table and a sofa in the European style. There was a shelf of books besides, and a family Bible in the midst of the table, and the lock-fast writing desk against the wall; so that anyone could see it was the house of a man of substance.

Kalamake made Keola close the shutters of the windows, while he himself locked all the doors and set open the lid of the desk. From this he brought forth a pair of necklaces hung with charms and shells, a bundle of dried herbs, and the dried leaves of trees, and a green branch of palm.

"What I am about," said he, "is a thing beyond wonder. The men of old were wise; they wrought marvels, and this among the rest; but that was at night, in the dark, under the fit stars and in the desert. The same will I do here in my own house and under the plain eye of day."

So saying, he put the bible under the cushion of the sofa so that it was all covered, brought out from the same place a mat of a wonderfully fine texture, and heaped the herbs and leaves on sand in a tin pan. And then he and Keola put on the necklaces and took their stand upon the opposite corners of the mat.

"The time comes," said the warlock; "be not afraid."

With that he set flame to the herbs, and began to mutter and wave the branch of palm. At first the light was dim because of the closed shutters; but the herbs caught strongly afire, and the flames beat upon Keola, and the room glowed with the burning; and next the smoke rose and made his head swim and his eyes darken, and the sound of Kalamake muttering ran in his ears. And suddenly, to the mat on which they were standing came a snatch or twitch, that seemed to be more swift than lightning. In the same wink the room was gone and the house, the breath all beaten from Keola's body. Volumes of light rolled upon his eyes and head, and he found himself transported to a beach of the sea under a strong sun, with a great surf roaring: he and the warlock standing there on the same mat, speechless, gasping and grasping at one another, and passing their hands before their eyes.

"What was this?" cried Keola, who came to himself the first, because he was the younger. "The pang of it was like death."

"It matters not," panted Kalamake. "It is now done."

"And, in the name of God, where are we?" cried Keola.

"That is not the question," replied the sorcerer. "Being here, we have matter in our hands, and that we must attend to. Go, while I recover my breath, into the borders of the wood, and bring me the leaves of such and such a herb, and such and such a tree, which you will find to grow there plentifully — three handfuls of each. And be speedy. We must be home again before the steamer comes; it would seem strange if we had disappeared." And he sat on the sand and panted.

Keola went up the beach, which was of shining sand and coral, strewn with singular shells; and he thought in his heart —

"How do I not know this beach? I will come here again and gather shells."

In front of him was a line of palms against the sky; not like the palms of the Eight Islands, but tall and fresh and beautiful, and hanging out withered fans like gold among the green, and he thought in his heart —

"It is strange I should not have found this grove. I will come here again, when it is warm, to sleep." And he thought, "How warm it has grown suddenly!" For it was winter in Hawaii, and the day had been chill. And he thought also, "Where are the grey mountains? And where is the high cliff with the hanging forest and the wheeling birds?" And the more he considered, the less he might conceive in what quarter of the islands he was fallen.

In the border of the grove, where it met the beach, the herb was growing, but the tree further back. Now, as Keola went toward the tree, he was aware of a young woman who had nothing on her body but a belt of leaves.

"Well!" thought Keola, "they are not very particular about their dress in this part of the country." And he paused, supposing she would observe him and escape; and seeing that she still looked before her, stood and hummed aloud. Up she leaped at the sound. Her face was ashen; she looked this way and that, and her mouth gaped with the terror of her soul. But it was a strange thing that her eyes did not rest upon Keola.

"Good day," said he. "You need not be so frightened; I will not eat you." And he had scarce opened his mouth before the young woman fled into the bush.

"These are strange manners," thought Keola. And, not thinking what he did, ran after her.

As she ran, the girl kept crying in some speech that was not practised in Hawaii, yet some of the words were the same, and he knew she kept calling and warning others. And presently he saw more people running — men, women and children, one with another, all running and crying like people at a fire. And with that he began to grow afraid himself, and returned to Kalamake bringing the leaves. Him he told what he had seen.

"You must pay no heed," said Kalamake. "All this is like a dream and shadows. All will disappear and be forgotten."

"It seemed none saw me," said Keola.

"And none did," replied the sorcerer. "We walk here in the broad sun invisible by reason of these charms. Yet they hear us; and therefore it is well to speak softly, as I do."

With that he made a circle round the mat with stones, and in the midst he set the leaves.

"It will be your part," said he, "to keep the leaves alight, and feed the fire slowly. While they blaze (which is but for a little moment) I must do my errand; and before the ashes blacken, the same power that brought us carries us away. Be ready now with the match; and do you call me in good time lest the flames burn out and I be left."

As soon as the leaves caught, the sorcerer leaped like a deer out of the circle, and began to race along the beach like a hound that has been bathing. As he ran, he kept stooping to snatch shells; and it seemed to Keola that they glittered as he took them. The leaves blazed with a clear flame that consumed them swiftly; and presently Keola had but a handful left, and the sorcerer was far off, running and stopping.

"Back!" cried Keola. "Back! The leaves are near done."

At that Kalamake turned, and if he had run before, now he flew. But fast as he ran, the leaves burned faster. The flame was ready to expire when, with a great leap, he bounded on the mat. The wind of his leaping blew it out; and with that the beach was gone, and the sun and the sea, and they stood once more in the dimness of the shuttered parlour, and were once more shaken and blinded; and on the mat betwixt them lay a pile of shining dollars. Keola ran to the shutters; and there was the steamer tossing in the swell close in.

The same night Kalamake took his son-in-law apart, and gave him five dollars in his hand.

"Keola," said he, "if you are a wise man (which I am doubtful of) you will think you slept this afternoon on the verandah, and dreamed as you were sleeping. I am a man of few words, and I have for my helpers people of short memories."

Never a word more said Kalamake, nor referred again to that affair. But it ran all the while in Keola's head — if he were lazy before, he would now do nothing.

"Why should I work," thought he, "when I have a father-in-law who makes dollars of sea-shells?"

Presently his share was spent. He spent it all upon fine clothes. And then he was sorry:

"For," thought he, "I had done better to have bought a concertina, with which I might have entertained myself all day long." And then he began to grow vexed with Kalamake.

"This man has the soul of a dog," thought he. "He can gather dollars when he pleases on the beach, and he leaves me to pine for a concertina! Let him beware: I am no child, I am as cunning as he, and hold his secret." With that he spoke to his wife Lehua, and complained of her father's manners.

"I would let my father be," said Lehua. "He is a dangerous man to cross."

"I care that for him!" cried Keola; and snapped his fingers. "I have him by the nose. I can make him do what I please." And he told Lehua the story.

But she shook her head.

"You may do what you like," said she; "but as sure as you thwart my father, you will be no more heard of. Think of this person, and that person; think of Hua, who was a noble of the House of Representatives, and went to Honolulu every year; and not a bone or a hair of him was found. Remember Kamau, and how he wasted to a thread, so that his wife lifted him with one hand. Keola, you are a baby in my father's hands; he will take you with his thumb and finger and eat you like a shrimp."

Now Keola was truly afraid of Kalamake, but he was vain too; and these words of his wife's incensed him.

"Very well," said he, "if that is what you think of me, I will show how much you are deceived." And he went straight to where his father-in-law was sitting in the parlour.

"Kalamake," said he, "I want a concertina."

"Do you, indeed?" said Kalamake.

"Yes," said he, "and I may as well tell you plainly, I mean to have it. A man who picks up dollars on the beach can certainly afford a concertina."

"I had no idea you had so much spirit," replied the sorcerer. "I thought you were a timid, useless lad, and I cannot describe how much pleased I am to find I was mistaken. Now I begin to think I may have found an assistant and successor in my difficult business. A concertina? You shall have the best in Honolulu. And to-night, as soon as it is dark, you and I will go and find the money."

"Shall we return to the beach?" asked Keola.

"No, no!" replied Kalamake; "you must begin to learn more of my secrets. Last time I taught you to pick shells; this time I shall teach you to catch fish. Are you strong enough to launch Pili's boat?"

"I think I am," returned Keola. "But why should we not take your own, which is afloat already?"

"I have a reason which you will understand thoroughly before to- morrow," said Kalamake. "Pili's boat is the better suited for my purpose. So, if you please, let us meet there as soon as it is dark; and in the meanwhile, let us keep our own counsel, for there is no cause to let the family into our business."

Honey is not more sweet than was the voice of Kalamake, and Keola could scarce contain his satisfaction.

"I might have had my concertina weeks ago," thought he, "and there is nothing needed in this world but a little courage."

Presently after he spied Lehua weeping, and was half in a mind to tell her all was well.

"But no," thinks he; "I shall wait till I can show her the concertina; we shall see what the chit will do then. Perhaps she will understand in the future that her husband is a man of some intelligence."

As soon as it was dark father and son-in-law launched Pili's boat and set the sail. There was a great sea, and it blew strong from the leeward; but the boat was swift and light and dry, and skimmed the waves. The wizard had a lantern, which he lit and held with his finger through the ring; and the two sat in the stern and smoked cigars, of which Kalamake had always a provision, and spoke like friends of magic and the great sums of money which they could make by its exercise, and what they should buy first, and what second; and Kalamake talked like a father.

Presently he looked all about, and above him at the stars, and back at the island, which was already three parts sunk under the sea, and he seemed to con- sider ripely his position.

"Look!" says he, "there is Molokai already far behind us, and Maui like a cloud; and by the bearing of these three stars I know I am come where I desire. This part of the sea is called the Sea of the Dead. It is in this place extraordi- narily deep, and the floor is all covered with the bones of men, and in the holes of this part gods and goblins keep their habitation. The flow of the sea is to the north, stronger than a shark can swim, and any man who shall here be thrown out of a ship it bears away like a wild horse into the uttermost ocean. Presently he is spent and goes down, and his bones are scattered with the rest, and the gods devour his spirit."

Fear came on Keola at the words, and he looked, and by the light of the stars and the lantern, the warlock seemed to change.

"What ails you?" cried Keola, quick and sharp.

"It is not I who am ailing," said the wizard; "but there is one here very sick."

With that he changed his grasp upon the lantern, and, behold I as he drew his finger from the ring, the finger stuck and the ring was burst, and his hand was grown to be of the bigness of three.

At that sight Keola screamed and covered his face.

But Kalamake held up the lantern. "Look rather at my face!" said he — and his head was huge as a barrel; and still he grew and grew as a cloud grows on a mountain, and Keola sat before him screaming, and the boat raced on the great seas.

"And now," said the wizard, "what do you think about that concertina? and are you sure you would not rather have a flute? No?" says he; "that is well, for I do not like my family to be changeable of purpose. But I begin to think I had better get out of this paltry boat, for my bulk swells to a very unusual degree, and if we are not the more careful, she will presently be swamped."

With that he threw his legs over the side. Even as he did so, the greatness of the man grew thirty-fold and forty-fold as swift as sight or thinking, so that he stood in the deep seas to the armpits, and his head and shoulders rose like a high isle, and the swell beat and burst upon his bosom, as it beats and breaks against a cliff. The boat ran still to the north, but he reached out his hand, and took the gunwale by the finger and thumb, and broke the side like a biscuit, and Keola was spilled into the sea. And the pieces of the boat the sorcerer crushed in the hollow of his hand and flung miles away into the night.

"Excuse me taking the lantern," said he; "for I have a long wade before me, and the land is far, and the bottom of the sea uneven, and I feel the bones under my toes."

And he turned and went off walking with great strides; and as often as Keola sank in the trough he could see him no longer; but as often as he was heaved upon the crest, there he was striding and dwindling, and he held the lamp high over his head, and the waves broke white about him as he went.

Since first the islands were fished out of the sea, there was never a man so terrified as this Keola. He swam indeed, but he swam as puppies swim when they are cast in to drown, and knew not wherefore. He could but think of the hugeness of the swelling of the warlock, of that face which was great as a mountain, of those shoulders that were broad as an isle, and of the seas that beat on them in vain. He thought, too, of the concertina, and shame took hold upon him; and of the dead men's bones, and fear shook him.

Of a sudden he was aware of something dark against the stars that tossed, and a light below, and a brightness of the cloven sea; and he heard speech of men. He cried out aloud and a voice answered; and in a twinkling the bows of a ship hung above him on a wave like a thing balanced, and swooped down. He caught with his two hands in the chains of her, and the next moment was buried in the rushing seas, and the next hauled on board by seamen.

They gave him gin and biscuit and dry clothes, and asked him how he came where they found him, and whether the light which they had seen was the lighthouse, Lae o Ka Laau. But Keola knew white men are like children and only believe their own stories; so about himself he told them what he pleased, and as for the light (which was Kalamake's lantern) he vowed he had seen none.

This ship was a schooner bound for Honolulu, and then to trade in the low islands; and by a very good chance for Keola she had lost a man off the bowsprit in a squall. It was no use talking. Keola durst not stay in the Eight Islands. Word goes so quickly, and all men are so fond to talk and carry news, that if he hid in the north end of Kauai or in the south end of Kau, the wizard would have wind of it before a month, and he must perish. So he did what seemed the most prudent, and shipped sailor in the place of the man who had been drowned.

In some ways the ship was a good place. The food was extraordinarily rich and plenty, with biscuits and salt beef every day, and pea-soup and puddings made of flour and suet twice a week, so that Keola grew fat. The captain also was a good man, and the crew no worse than other whites. The trouble was the mate, who was the most difficult man to please Keola had ever met with, and beat and cursed him daily, both for what he did and what he did not. The blows that he dealt were very sore, for he was strong; and the words he used were very unpalatable, for Keola was come of a good family and accustomed to respect. And what was the worst of all, whenever Keola found a chance to sleep, there was the mate awake and stirring him up with a rope's end. Keola saw it would never do; and he made up his mind to run away.

They were about a month out from Honolulu when they made the land. It was a fine starry night, the sea was smooth as well as the sky fair; it blew a steady trade; and there was the island on their weather bow, a ribbon of palm trees lying flat along the sea. The captain and the mate looked at it with the night glass, and named the name of it, and talked of it, beside the wheel where Keola was steering. It seemed it was an isle where no traders came. By the captain's way, it was an isle besides where no man dwelt; but the mate thought otherwise.

"I don't give a cent for the directory," said he, "I've been past here one night in the schooner EUGENIE; it was just such a night as this; they were fishing with torches, and the beach was thick with lights like a town."

"Well, well," says the captain, "it's steep-to, that's the great point; and there ain't any outlying dangers by the chart, so we'll just hug the lee side of it. Keep her romping full, don't I tell you!" he cried to Keola, who was listening so hard that he forgot to steer.

And the mate cursed him, and swore that Kanaka was for no use in the world, and if he got started after him with a belaying pin, it would be a cold day for Keola.

And so the captain and mate lay down on the house together, and Keola was left to himself.

"This island will do very well for me," he thought; "if no traders deal there, the mate will never come. And as for Kalamake, it is not possible he can ever get as far as this."

With that he kept edging the schooner nearer in. He had to do this quietly, for it was the trouble with these white men, and above all with the mate, that you could never be sure of them; they would all be sleeping sound, or else pretending, and if a sail shook, they would jump to their feet and fall on you with a rope's end. So Keola edged her up little by little, and kept all drawing. And presently the land was close on board, and the sound of the sea on the sides of it grew loud.

With that, the mate sat up suddenly upon the house.

"What are you doing?" he roars. "You'll have the ship ashore!"

And he made one bound for Keola, and Keola made another clean over the rail and plump into the starry sea. When he came up again, the schooner had payed off on her true course, and the mate stood by the wheel himself, and Keola heard him cursing. The sea was smooth under the lee of the island; it was warm besides, and Keola had his sailor's knife, so he had no fear of sharks. A little way before him the trees stopped; there was a break in the line of the land like the mouth of a harbour; and the tide, which was then flowing, took him up and carried him through. One minute he was without, and the next within: had floated there in a wide shallow water, bright with ten thousand stars, and all about him was the ring of the land, with its string of palm trees. And he was amazed, because this was a kind of island he had never heard of.

The time of Keola in that place was in two periods — the period when he was alone, and the period when he was there with the tribe. At first he sought everywhere and found no man; only some houses standing in a hamlet, and the marks of fires. But the ashes of the fires were cold and the rains had washed them away; and the winds had blown, and some of the huts were overthrown. It was here he took his dwelling, and he made a fire drill, and a shell hook, and fished and cooked his fish, and climbed after green cocoanuts, the juice of which he drank, for in all the isle there was no water. The days were long to him, and the nights terrifying. He made a lamp of cocoa-shell, and drew the oil of the ripe nuts, and made a wick of fibre; and when evening came he closed up his hut, and lit his lamp, and lay and trembled till morning. Many a time he thought in his heart he would have been better in the bottom of the sea, his bones rolling there with the others.

All this while he kept by the inside of the island, for the huts were on the shore of the lagoon, and it was there the palms grew best, and the lagoon itself abounded with good fish. And to the outer slide he went once only, and he looked but the once at the beach of the ocean, and came away shaking. For the look of it, with its bright sand, and strewn shells, and strong sun and surf, went sore against his inclination.

"It cannot be," he thought, "and yet it is very like. And how do I know? These white men, although they pretend to know where they are sailing, must take their chance like other people. So that after all we may have sailed in a circle, and I may be quite near to Molokai, and this may be the very beach where my father-in-law gathers his dollars."

So after that he was prudent, and kept to the land side.

It was perhaps a month later, when the people of the place arrived - the fill of six great boats. They were a fine race of men, and spoke a tongue that sounded very different from the tongue of Hawaii, but so many of the words were the same that it was not difficult to understand. The men besides were very courteous, and the women very towardly; and they made Keola welcome, and built him a house, and gave him a wife; and what surprised him the most, he was never sent to work with the young men.

And now Keola had three periods. First he had a period of being very sad, and then he had a period when he was pretty merry. Last of all came the third, when he was the most terrified man in the four oceans.

The cause of the first period was the girl he had to wife. He was in doubt about the island, and he might have been in doubt about the speech, of which he had heard so little when he came there with the wizard on the mat. But about his wife there was no mistake conceivable, for she was the same girl that ran from him crying in the wood. So he had sailed all this way, and might as well have stayed in Molokai; and had left home and wife and all his friends for no other cause but to escape his enemy, and the place he had come to was that wizard's hunting ground, and the shore where he walked invisible. It was at this period when he kept the most close to the lagoon side, and as far as he dared, abode in the cover of his hut.

The cause of the second period was talk he heard from his wife and the chief islanders. Keola himself said little. He was never so sure of his new friends, for he judged they were too civil to be wholesome, and since he had grown better acquainted with his father-in-law the man had grown more cautious. So he told them nothing of himself, but only his name and descent, and that he came from the Eight Islands, and what fine islands they were; and about the king's palace in Honolulu, and how he was a chief friend of the king and the missionaries. But he put many questions and learned much. The island where he was was called the Isle of Voices; it belonged to the tribe, but they made their home upon another, three hours' sail to the southward. There they lived and had their permanent houses, and it was a rich island, where were eggs and chickens and pigs, and ships came trading with rum and tobacco. It was there the schooner had gone after Keola deserted; there, too, the mate had died, like the fool of a white man as he was. It seems, when the ship came, it was the beginning of the sickly season in that isle, when the fish of the lagoon are poisonous, and all who eat of them swell up and die. The mate was told of it; he saw the boats preparing, because in that season the people leave that island and sail to the Isle of Voices; but he was a fool of a white man, who would believe no stories but his own, and he caught one of these fish, cooked it and ate it, and swelled up and died, which was good news to Keola. As for the Isle of Voices, it lay solitary the most part of the year; only now and then a boat's crew came for copra, and in the bad season, when the fish at the main isle were poisonous, the tribe dwelt there in a body. It had its name from a marvel, for it seemed the seaside of it was all beset with invisible devils; day and night you heard them talking one with another in strange tongues; day and night little fires blazed up and were extinguished on the beach; and what was the cause of these doings no man might conceive. Keola asked them if it were the same in their own island where they stayed, and they told him no, not there; nor yet in any other of some hundred isles that lay all about them in that sea; but it was a thing peculiar to the Isle of Voices. They told him also that these fires and voices were ever on the seaside and in the seaward fringes of the wood, and a man might dwell by the lagoon two thousand years (if he could live so long) and never be any way troubled; and even on the seaside the devils did no harm if let alone. Only once a chief had cast a spear at one of the voices, and the same night he fell out of a cocoanut palm and was killed.

Keola thought a good bit with himself. He saw he would be all right when the tribe returned to the main island, and right enough where he was, if he kept by the lagoon, yet he had a mind to make things righter if he could. So he told the high chief he had once been in an isle that was pestered the same way, and the folk had found a means to cure that trouble.

"There was a tree growing in the bush there," says he, "and it seems these devils came to get the leaves of it. So the people of the isle cut down the tree wherever it was found, and the devils came no more."

They asked what kind of tree this was, and he showed them the tree of which Kalamake burned the leaves. They found it hard to believe, yet the idea tickled them. Night after night the old men debated it in their councils, but the high chief (though he was a brave man) was afraid of the matter, and reminded them daily of the chief who cast a spear against the voices and was killed, and the thought of that brought all to a stand again.

Though he could not yet bring about the destruction of the trees, Keola was well enough pleased, and began to look about him and take pleasure in his days; and, among other things, he was the kinder to his wife, so that the girl began to love him greatly. One day he came to the hut, and she lay on the ground lamenting.

"Why," said Keola, "what is wrong with you now?"

She declared it was nothing.

The same night she woke him. The lamp burned very low, but he saw by her face she was in sorrow.

"Keola," she said, "put your ear to my mouth that I may whisper, for no one must hear us. Two days before the boats begin to be got ready, go you to the sea-side of the isle and lie in a thicket. We shall choose that place before-hand, you and I; and hide food; and every night I shall come near by there singing. So when a night comes and you do not hear me, you shall know we are clean gone out of the island, and you may come forth again in safety."

The soul of Keola died within him.

"What is this?" he cried. "I cannot live among devils. I will not be left behind upon this isle. I am dying to leave it."

"You will never leave it alive, my poor Keola," said the girl; "for to tell you the truth, my people are eaters of men; but this they keep secret. And the reason they will kill you before we leave is because in our island ships come, and Donat-Kimaran comes and talks for the French, and there is a white trader there in a house with a verandah, and a catechist. Oh, that is a fine place indeed! The trader has barrels filled with flour, and a French warship once came in the lagoon and gave everybody wine and biscuit. Ah, my poor Keola, I wish I could take you there, for great is my love to you, and it is the finest place in the seas except Papeete."

So now Keola was the most terrified man in the four oceans. He had heard tell of eaters of men in the south islands, and the thing had always been a fear to him; and here it was knocking at his door. He had heard besides, by travellers, of their practices, and how when they are in a mind to eat a man, they cherish and fondle him like a mother with a favourite baby. And he saw this must be his own case; and that was why he had been housed, and fed, and wived, and liberated from all work; and why the old men and the chiefs discoursed with him like a person of weight. So he lay on his bed and railed upon his destiny; and the flesh curdled on his bones.

The next day the people of the tribe were very civil, as their way was. They were elegant speakers, and they made beautiful poetry, and jested at meals, so that a missionary must have died laughing. It was little enough Keola cared for their fine ways; all he saw was the white teeth shining in their mouths, and his gorge rose at the sight; and when they were done eating, he went and lay in the bush like a dead man.

The next day it was the same, and then his wife followed him.

"Keola," she said, "if you do not eat, I tell you plainly you will be killed and cooked to-morrow. Some of the old chiefs are murmuring already. They think you are fallen sick and must lose flesh."

With that Keola got to his feet, and anger burned in him.

"It is little I care one way or the other," said he. "I am between the devil and the deep sea. Since die I must, let me die the quickest way; and since I must be eaten at the best of it, let me rather be eaten by hobgoblins than by men. Farewell," said he, and he left her standing, and walked to the sea-side of that island.

It was all bare in the strong sun; there was no sign of man, only the beach was trodden, and all about him as he went, the voices talked and whispered, and the little fires sprang up and burned down. All tongues of the earth were spoken there; the French, the Dutch, the Russian, the Tamil, the Chinese. Whatever land knew sorcery, there were some of its people whispering in Keola's ear. That beach was thick as a cried fair, yet no man seen; and as he walked he saw the shells vanish before him, and no man to pick them up. I think the devil would have been afraid to be alone in such a company; but Keola was past fear and courted death. When the fires sprang up, he charged for them like a bull. Bodiless voices called to and fro; unseen hands poured sand upon the flames; and they were gone from the beach before he reached them.

"It is plain Kalamake is not here," he thought, "or I must have been killed long since."

With that he sat him down in the margin of the wood, for he was tired, and put his chin upon his hands. The business before his eyes continued: the beach babbled with voices, and the fires sprang up and sank, and the shells vanished and were renewed again even while he looked.

"It was a by-day when I was here before," he thought, "for it was nothing to this."

And his head was dizzy with the thought of these millions and millions of dollars, and all these hundreds and hundreds of persons culling them upon the beach and flying in the air higher and swifter than eagles.

"And to think how they have fooled me with their talk of mints," says he, "and that money was made there, when it is clear that all the new coin in all the world is gathered on these sands! But I will know better the next time!" said he.

And at last, he knew not very well how or when, sleep feel on Keola, and he forgot the island and all his sorrows.

Early the next day, before the sun was yet up, a bustle woke him. He awoke in fear, for he thought the tribe had caught him napping: but it was no such matter. Only, on the beach in front of him, the bodiless voices called and shouted one upon another, and it seemed they all passed and swept beside him up the coast of the island.

"What is afoot now?" thinks Keola. And it was plain to him it was something beyond ordinary, for the fires were not lighted nor the shells taken, but the bodiless voices kept posting up the beach, and hailing and dying away; and others following, and by the sound of them these wizards should be angry.

"It is not me they are angry at," thought Keola, "for they pass me close."

As when hounds go by, or horses in a race, or city folk coursing to a fire, and all men join and follow after, so it was now with Keola; and he knew not what he did, nor why he did it, but there, lo and behold! he was running with the voices.

So he turned one point of the island, and this brought him in view of a second; and there he remembered the wizard trees to have been growing by the score together in a wood. From this point there went up a hubbub of men crying not to be described; and by the sound of them, those that he ran with shaped their course for the same quarter. A little nearer, and there began to mingle with the outcry the crash of many axes. And at this a thought came at last into his mind that the high chief had consented; that the men of the tribe had set to cutting down these trees; that word had gone about the isle from sorcerer to sorcerer, and these were all now assembling to defend their trees. Desire of strange things swept him on. He posted with the voices, crossed the beach, and came into the borders of the wood, and stood astonished. One tree had fallen, others were part hewed away. There was the tribe clustered. They were back to back, and bodies lay, and blood flowed among their feet. The hue of fear was on all their faces; their voices went up to heaven shrill as a weasel's cry.

Have you seen a child when he is all alone and has a wooden sword, and fights, leaping and hewing with the empty air? Even so the man-eaters huddled back to back, and heaved up their axes, and laid on, and screamed as they laid on, and behold! no man to contend with them! only here and there Keola saw an axe swinging over against them without hands; and time and again a man of the tribe would fall before it, clove in twain or burst asunder, and his soul sped howling.

For awhile Keola looked upon this prodigy like one that dreams, and then fear took him by the midst as sharp as death, that he should behold such doings. Even in that same flash the high chief of the clan espied him standing, and pointed and called out his name. Thereat the whole tribe saw him also, and their eyes flashed, and their teeth clashed.

"I am too long here," thought Keola, and ran further out of the wood and down the beach, not caring whither.

"Keola!" said, a voice close by upon the empty sand.

"Lehua! is that you?" he cried, and gasped, and looked in vain for her; but by the eyesight he was stark alone.

"I saw you pass before," the voice answered: "but you would not hear me. Quick! get the leaves and the herbs, and let us free."

"You are there with the mat?" he asked.

"Here, at your side;" said she. And he felt her arms about him. "Quick! the leaves and the herbs, before my father can get back!"

So Keola ran for his life, and fetched the wizard fuel; and Lehua guided him back, and set his feet upon the mat, and made the fire. All the time of its burning, the sound of the battle towered out of the wood; the wizards and the man-eaters hard at fight; the wizards, the viewless ones, roaring out aloud like bulls upon a mountain, and the men of the tribe replying shrill and savage out of the terror of their souls. And all the time of the burning, Keola stood there and listened, and shook, and watched how the unseen hands of Lehua poured the leaves. She poured them fast, and the flame burned high, and scorched Keola's hands; and she speeded and blew the burning with her breath. The last leaf was eaten, the flame fell, and the shock followed, and there were Keola and Lehua in the room at home.

Now, when Keola could see his wife at last he was mighty pleased, and he was mighty pleased to be home again in Molokai and sit down beside a bowl of poi — for they make no poi on board ships, and there was none in the Isle of Voices — and he was out of the body with pleasure to be clean escaped out of the hands of the eaters of men. But there was another matter not so clear, and Lehua and Keola talked of it all night and were troubled. There was Kalamake left upon the isle. If, by the blessing of God, he could but stick there, all were well; but should he escape and return to Molokai, it would be an ill day for his daughter and her husband. They spoke of his gift of swelling, and whether he could wade that distance in the seas. But Keola knew by this time where that island was — and that is to say, in the Low or Dangerous Archipelago. So they fetched the atlas and looked upon the distance in the map, and by what they could make of it, it seemed a far way for an old gentleman to walk. Still, it would not do to make too sure of a warlock like Kalamake, and they determined at last to take counsel of a white missionary.

So the first one that came by, Keola told him everything. And the missionary was very sharp on him for taking the second wife in the low island; but for all the rest, he vowed he could make neither head nor tail of it.

"However," says he, "if you think this money of your father's ill gotten, my advice to you would be, give some of it to the lepers and some to the missionary fund. And as for this extraordinary rigmarole, you cannot do better than keep it to yourselves."

But he warned the police at Honolulu that, by all he could make out, Kalamake and Keola had been coining false money, and it would not be amiss to watch them.

Keola and Lehua took his advice, and gave many dollars to the lepers and the fund. And no doubt the advice must have been good, for from that day to this, Kalamake has never more been heard of. But whether he was slain in the battle by the trees, or whether he is still kicking his heels upon the Isle of Voices, who shall say?

# THE PLATTNER STORY

## H. G. WELLS

Whether the story of Gottfried Plattner is to be credited or not, is a pretty question in the value of evidence. On the one hand, we have seven witnesses—to be perfectly exact, we have six and a half pairs of eyes, and one undeniable fact; and on the other we have—what is it?—prejudice, common sense, the inertia of opinion. Never were there seven more honest-seeming witnesses; never was there a more undeniable fact that the inversion of Gottfried Plattner's anatomical structure, and—never was there a more preposterous story than the one they have to tell! The most preposterous part of the story is the worthy Gottfried's contribution (for I count him as one of the seven). Heaven forbid that I should be led into giving countenance to superstition by a passion for impartiality, and so come to share the fate of Eusapia's patrons! Frankly, I believe there is something crooked about this business of Gottfried Plattner; but what that crooked factor is, I will admit as frankly, I do not know. I have been surprised at the credit accorded to the story in the most unexpected and authoritative quarters. The fairest way to the reader, however, will be for me to tell it without further comment.

Gottfried Plattner is, in spite of his name, a free-born Englishman. His father was an Alsatian who came to England in the Sixties, married a respectable English girl of unexceptionable antecedents, and died, after a wholesome and uneventful life (devoted, I understand, chiefly to the laying of parquet flooring), in 1887. Gottfried's age is seven-and-twenty. He is, by virtue of his heritage of three languages, Modern Languages Master in a small private school in the South of England. To the casual observer he is singularly like any other Modern Languages Master in any other small private school. His costume is neither very costly nor very fashionable, but, on the other hand, it is not markedly cheap or shabby; his complexion, like his height and his bearing, is inconspicuous. You would notice perhaps that, like the majority of people, his face was not absolutely symmetrical, his right eye a little larger than the left, and his jaw a trifle heavier on the right side. If you, as an ordinary careless person, were to bare his chest and feel his heart beating, you would probably find it quite like the heart of anyone else. But here you and the trained observer would part company. If you found his heart quite ordinary, the trained observer would find it quite otherwise. And once the thing was pointed out to you, you too would perceive the peculiarity easily enough. It is that Gottfried's heart beats on the right side of his body.

Now that is not the only singularity of Gottfried's structure, although it is the only one that would appeal to the untrained mind. Careful sounding of Gottfried's internal arrangements, by a well-known surgeon, seems to point to the fact that all the other unsymmetrical parts of his body are similarly misplaced. The right lobe of his liver is on the left side, the left on his right; while his lungs, too, are similarly contraposed. What is still more singular, unless Gottfried is a consummate actor we must believe that his right hand has recently become his left. Since the occurrences we are about to consider (as impartially as possible), he has found the utmost difficulty in writing except from right to left across the paper with his left hand. He cannot throw with his right hand, he is perplexed at meal times between knife and fork, and his ideas of the rule of the road—he is a cyclist—are still a dangerous confusion. And there is not a scrap of evidence to show that before these occurrences Gottfried was at all left-handed.

There is yet another wonderful fact in this preposterous business. Gottfried produces three photographs of himself. You have him at the age of five or six, thrusting fat legs at you from under a plaid frock, and scowling. In that photograph his left eye is a little larger than his right, and his jaw is a trifle heavier on the left side. This is the reverse of his present living conditions. The photograph of Gottfried at fourteen seems to contradict these facts, but that is because it is one of those cheap "Gem" photographs that were then in vogue, taken direct upon metal, and therefore reversing things just as a looking-glass would. The third photograph represents him at one-and-twenty, and confirms the record of the others. There seems here evidence of the strongest confirmatory character that Gottfried has exchanged his left side for his right. Yet how a human being can be so changed, short of a fantastic and pointless miracle, it is exceedingly hard to suggest.

In one way, of course, these facts might be explicable on the supposition that Plattner has undertaken an elaborate mystification on the strength of his heart's displacement. Photographs may be fudged, and left-handedness imitated. But the character of the man does not lend itself to any such theory. He is quiet, practical, unobtrusive, and thoroughly sane from the Nordau standpoint. He likes beer and smokes moderately, takes walking exercise daily, and has a healthily high estimate of the value of his teaching. He has a good but untrained tenor voice, and takes a pleasure in singing airs of a popular and cheerful character. He is fond, but not morbidly fond, of reading—chiefly fiction pervaded with a vaguely pious optimism,—sleeps well, and rarely dreams. He is, in fact, the very last person to evolve a fantastic fable. Indeed, so far from forcing this story upon the world, he has been singularly reticent on the matter. He meets inquirers with a certain engaging—bashfulness is almost the word, that disarms the most suspicious. He seems genuinely ashamed that anything so unusual has occurred to him.

It has to be regretted that Plattner's aversion to the idea of postmortem dissection may postpone, perhaps for ever, the positive proof that his entire body has had its left and right sides transposed. Upon that fact mainly the credibility of his story hangs. There is no way of taking a man and moving him about *in space*, as ordinary people understand space, that will result in our changing his sides. Whatever you do, his right is still his right, his left his left. You can do that with a perfectly thin and flat thing, of course. If you were to cut a figure of paper, any figure with a right and left side, you could change its sides simply by lifting it up and turning it over. But with a solid it is different. Mathematical theorists tell us that the only way in which the right and left sides of a solid body can be changed is by taking that body clean out of space as we know it,— taking it out of ordinary existence, that is, and turning it somewhere outside space. This is a little abstruse, no doubt, but anyone with a slight knowledge of mathematical theory will assure the reader of its truth. To put the thing in technical language, the curious inversion of Plattner's right and left sides is proof that he has moved out of our space into what is called the Fourth Dimension, and that he has returned again to our world. Unless we choose to consider ourselves the victims of an elaborate and motiveless fabrication, we are almost bound to believe that this has occurred.

So much for the tangible facts. We come now to the account of the phenomena that attended his temporary disappearance from the world. It appears that in the Sussexville Proprietary School, Plattner not only discharged the duties of Modern Language Master, but also taught chemistry, commercial geography, bookkeeping, shorthand, drawing, and any other additional subject to which the changing fancies of the boys' parents might direct attention. He knew little or nothing of these various subjects, but in secondary as distinguished from Board or elementary schools, knowledge in the teacher is, very properly, by no means so necessary as high moral character and gentlemanly tone. In chemistry he was particularly deficient, knowing, he says, nothing beyond the Three Gases (whatever the three gases may be). As, however, his pupils began by knowing nothing, and derived all their information from him, this caused him (or anyone) but little inconvenience for several terms. Then a little boy named Whibble joined the school, who had been educated, it seems, by some mischievous relative into an inquiring habit of mind. This little boy followed Plattner's lessons with marked and sustained interest, and in order to exhibit his zeal on the subject, brought at various times substances for Plattner to analyse. Plattner, flattered by this evidence of his power to awaken interest and trusting to the boy's ignorance, analysed these and even made general statements as to their composition. Indeed he was so far stimulated by his pupil as to obtain a work upon analytical chemistry, and study it during his supervision of the evening's preparation. He was surprised to find chemistry quite an interesting subject.

So far the story is absolutely commonplace. But now the greenish powder comes upon the scene. The source of that greenish powder seems, unfortunately, lost. Master Whibble tells a tortuous story of finding it done up in a packet in a disused limekiln near the Downs. It would have been an excellent thing for Plattner, and possibly for Master Whibble's family, if a match could have been applied to that powder there and then. The young gentleman certainly did not bring it to school in a packet, but in a common eight-ounce graduated medicine bottle, plugged with masticated newspaper. He gave it to Plattner at the end of the afternoon school. Four boys had been detained after school prayers in order to complete some neglected tasks, and Plattner was supervising these in the small classroom in which the chemical teaching was conducted. The appliances for the practical teaching of chemistry in the Sussexville Proprietary School, as in most private schools in this country, are characterised by a severe simplicity. They are kept in a cupboard standing in a recess and having about the same capacity as a common travelling trunk. Plattner, being bored with his passive superintendence, seems to have welcomed the intervention of Whibble with his green powder as an agreeable diversion, and, unlocking this cupboard, proceeded at once with his analytical experiments. Whibble sat, luckily for himself, at a safe distance, regarding him. The four malefactors, feigning a profound absorption in their work, watched him furtively with the keenest interest. For even within the limits of the Three Gases, Plattner's practical chemistry was, I understand, temerarious.

They are practically unanimous in their account of Plattner's proceedings. He poured a little of the green powder into a test-tube, and tried the substance with water, hydrochloric acid, nitric acid, and sulphuric acid in succession. Getting no result, he emptied out a little heap—nearly half the bottleful, in fact—upon a slate and tried a match. He held the medicine bottle in his left hand. The stuff began to smoke and melt, and then—exploded with deafening violence and a blinding flash.

The five boys, seeing the flash and being prepared for catastrophes, ducked below their desks, and were none of them seriously hurt. The window was blown out into the playground, and the blackboard on its easel was upset. The slate was smashed to atoms. Some plaster fell from the ceiling. No other damage was done to the school edifice or appliances, and the boys at first, seeing nothing of Plattner, fancied he was knocked down and lying out of their sight below the desks. They jumped out of their places to go to his assistance, and were amazed to find the space empty. Being still confused by the sudden violence of the report, they hurried to the open door, under the impression that he must have been hurt, and have rushed out of the room. But Carson, the foremost, nearly collided in the doorway with the principal, Mr. Lidgett.

Mr. Lidgett is a corpulent, excitable man with one eye. The boys describe him as stumbling into the room mouthing some of those tempered expletives irritable schoolmasters accustom themselves to use—lest worse befall. "Wretched mumchancer!" he said. "Where's Mr. Plattner?" The boys are agreed on the very words. ("Wobbler," "snivelling puppy," and "mumchancer" are, it seems, among the ordinary small change of Mr. Lidgett's scholastic commerce.)

Where's Mr. Plattner? That was a question that was to be repeated many times in the next few days. It really seemed as though that frantic hyperbole, "blown to atoms," had for once realised itself. There was not a visible particle of Plattner to be seen; not a drop of blood nor a stitch of clothing to be found. Apparently he had been blown clean out of existence and left not a wrack behind. Not so much as would cover a sixpenny piece, to quote a proverbial expression! The evidence of his absolute disappearance, as a consequence of that explosion, is indubitable.

It is not necessary to enlarge here upon the commotion excited in the Sussexville Proprietary School, and in Sussexville and elsewhere, by this event. It is quite possible, indeed, that some of the readers of these pages may recall the hearing of some remote and dying version of that excitement during the last summer holidays. Lidgett, it would seem, did everything in his power to suppress and minimise the story. He instituted a penalty of twenty-five lines for any mention of Plattner's name among the boys, and stated in the school-room that he was clearly aware of his assistant's whereabouts. He was afraid, he explains, that the possibility of an explosion happening, in spite of the elaborate precautions taken to minimise the practical teaching of chemistry, might injure the reputation of the school; and so might any mysterious quality in Plattner's departure. Indeed, he did everything in his power to make the occurrence seem as ordinary as possible. In particular, he cross-examined the five eye-witnesses of the occurrence so searchingly that they began to doubt the plain evidence of their senses. But, in spite of these efforts, the tale, in a magnified and distorted state, made a nine days' wonder in the district, and several parents withdrew their sons on colourable pretexts. Not the least remarkable point in the matter is the fact that a large number of people in the neighbourhood dreamed singularly vivid dreams of Plattner during the period of excitement before his return, and that these dreams had a curious uniformity. In almost all of them Plattner was seen, sometimes singly, sometimes in company wandering about through a coruscating iridescence. In all cases his face was pale and distressed, and in some he gesticulated towards the dreamer. One or two of the boys, evidently under the influence of nightmare, fancied that Plattner approached them with remarkable swiftness, and seemed to look closely into their very eyes. Others fled with Plattner from the pursuit of vague and extraordinary creatures of a globular shape. But all these fancies were forgotten in inquiries and speculations when, on the Wednesday next but one after the Monday of the explosion, Plattner returned.

The circumstances of his return were as singular as those of his departure. So far as Mr. Lidgett's somewhat choleric outline can be filled in from Plattner's hesitating statements, it would appear that on Wednesday evening, towards the hour of sunset, the former gentleman, having dismissed evening preparation, was engaged in his garden, picking and eating strawberries, a fruit of which he is inordinately fond. It is a large old-fashioned garden, secured from observation, fortunately, by a high and ivy-covered red-brick wall. Just as he was stooping over a particularly prolific plant, there was a flash in the air and a heavy thud, and before he could look round, some heavy body struck him violently from behind. He was pitched forward, crushing the strawberries he held in his hand, and with such force that his silk hat—Mr. Lidgett adheres to the older ideas of scholastic costume—was driven violently down upon his forehead, and almost over one eye. This heavy missile, which slid over him sideways and collapsed into a sitting posture among the strawberry plants, proved to be our long-lost Mr. Gottfried Plattner, in an extremely dishevelled condition. He was collarless and hatless, his linen was dirty, and there was blood upon his hands. Mr. Lidgett was so indignant and surprised that he remained on all-fours, and with his hat jammed down on his eye, while he expostulated vehemently with Plattner for his disrespectful and unaccountable conduct.

This scarcely idyllic scene completes what I may call the exterior version of the Plattner story—its exoteric aspect. It is quite unnecessary to enter here into all the details of his dismissal by Mr. Lidgett. Such details, with the full names and dates and references, will be found in the larger report of these occurrences that was laid before the Society for the Investigation of Abnormal Phenomena. The singular transposition of Plattner's right and left sides was scarcely observed for the first day or so, and then first in connection with his disposition to write from right to left across the blackboard. He concealed rather than ostended this curious confirmatory circumstance, as he considered it would unfavourably affect his prospects in a new situation. The displacement of his heart was discovered some months after, when he was having a tooth extracted under anaesthetics. He then, very unwillingly, allowed a cursory surgical examination to be made of himself, with a view to a brief account in the *Journal of Anatomy*. That exhausts the statement of the material facts; and we may now go on to consider Plattner's account of the matter.

But first let us clearly differentiate between the preceding portion of this story and what is to follow. All I have told thus far is established by such evidence as even a criminal lawyer would approve. Every one of the witnesses is still alive; the reader, if he have the leisure, may hunt the lads out to-morrow, or even brave the terrors of the redoubtable Lidgett, and cross-examine and trap and test to his heart's content; Gottfried Plattner, himself, and his twisted heart and his three photographs are producible. It may be taken as proved that he did disappear for nine days as the consequence of an explosion; that he returned almost as violently, under circumstances in their nature annoying to Mr. Lidgett, whatever the details of those circumstances may be; and that he returned inverted, just as a reflection returns from a mirror. From the last fact, as I have already stated, it follows almost inevitably that Plattner, during those nine days, must have been in some state of existence altogether out of space. The evidence of these statements is, indeed, far stronger than that upon which most murderers are hanged. But for his own particular account of where he had been, with its confused explanations and well-nigh self-contradictory details, we have only Mr. Gottfried Plattner's word. I do not wish to discredit that, but I must point out—what so many writers upon obscure psychic phenomena fail to do— that we are passing here from the practically undeniable to that kind of matter which any reasonable man is entitled to believe or reject as he thinks proper. The previous statements render it plausible; its discordance with common experience tilts it towards the incredible. I would prefer not to sway the beam of the reader's judgment either way, but simply to tell the story as Plattner told it me.

He gave me his narrative, I may state, at my house at Chislehurst; and so soon as he had left me that evening, I went into my study and wrote down everything as I remembered it. Subsequently he was good enough to read over a type-written copy, so that its substantial correctness is undeniable.

He states that at the moment of the explosion he distinctly thought he was killed. He felt lifted off his feet and driven forcibly backward. It is a curious fact for psychologists that he thought clearly during his backward flight, and wondered whether he should hit the chemistry cupboard or the blackboard easel. His heels struck ground, and he staggered and fell heavily into a sitting position on something soft and firm. For a moment the concussion stunned him. He became aware at once of a vivid scent of singed hair, and he seemed to hear the voice of Lidgett asking for him. You will understand that for a time his mind was greatly confused.

At first he was distinctly under the impression that he was still in the classroom. He perceived quite distinctly the surprise of the boys and the entry of Mr. Lidgett. He is quite positive upon that score. He did not hear their remarks, but that he ascribed to the deafening effect of the experiment. Things about him seemed curiously dark and faint, but his mind explained that on the obvious but mistaken idea that the explosion had engendered a huge volume of dark smoke. Through the dimness the figures of Lidgett and the boys moved, as faint and silent as ghosts. Plattner's face still tingled with the stinging heat of the flash. He was, he says, "all muddled." His first definite thoughts seem to have been of his personal safety. He thought he was perhaps blinded and deafened. He felt his limbs and face in a gingerly manner. Then his perceptions grew clearer, and he was astonished to miss the old familiar desks and other schoolroom furniture about him. Only dim, uncertain, grey shapes stood in the place of these. Then came a thing that made him shout aloud, and awoke his stunned faculties to instant activity. *Two of the boys, gesticulating, walked one after the other clean through him!* Neither manifested the slightest consciousness of his presence. It is difficult to imagine the sensation he felt. They came against him, he says, with no more force than a wisp of mist.

Plattner's first thought after that was that he was dead. Having been brought up with thoroughly sound views in these matters, however, he was a little surprised to find his body still about him. His second conclusion was that he was not dead, but that the others were: that the explosion had destroyed Sussexville Proprietary School and every soul in it except himself. But that, too, was scarcely satisfactory. He was thrown back upon astonished observation.

Everything about him was extraordinarily dark: at first it seemed to have an altogether ebony blackness. Overhead was a black firmament. The only touch of light in the scene was a faint greenish glow at the edge of the sky in one direction, which threw into prominence a horizon of undulating black hills. This, I say, was his impression at first. As his eye grew accustomed to the darkness, he began to distinguish a faint quality of differentiating greenish colour in the circumambient night. Against this background the furniture and occupants of the classroom, it seems, stood out like phosphorescent spectres, faint and impalpable. He extended his hand, and thrust it without an effort through the wall of the room by the fireplace.

He describes himself as making a strenuous effort to attract attention. He shouted to Lidgett, and tried to seize the boys as they went to and fro. He only desisted from these attempts when Mrs. Lidgett, whom he as an Assistant Master naturally disliked, entered the room. He says the sensation of being in the world, and yet not a part of it, was an extraordinarily disagreeable one. He compared his feelings not inaptly to those of a cat watching a mouse through a window. Whenever he made a motion to communicate with the dim, familiar world about him, he found an invisible, incomprehensible barrier preventing intercourse.

He then turned his attention to his solid environment. He found the medicine bottle still unbroken in his hand, with the remainder of the green powder therein. He put this in his pocket, and began to feel about him. Apparently, he was sitting on a boulder of rock covered with a velvety moss. The dark country about him he was unable to see, the faint, misty picture of the schoolroom blotting it out, but he had a feeling (due perhaps to a cold wind) that he was near the crest of a hill, and that a steep valley fell away beneath his feet. The green glow along the edge of the sky seemed to be growing in extent and intensity. He stood up, rubbing his eyes.

It would seem that he made a few steps, going steeply downhill, and then stumbled, nearly fell, and sat down again upon a jagged mass of rock to watch the dawn. He became aware that the world about him was absolutely silent. It was as still as it was dark, and though there was a cold wind blowing up the hill-face, the rustle of grass, the sighing of the boughs that should have accompanied it, were absent. He could hear, therefore, if he could not see, that the hillside upon which he stood was rocky and desolate. The green grew brighter every moment, and as it did so a faint, transparent blood-red mingled with, but did not mitigate, the blackness of the sky overhead and the rocky desolations about him. Having regard to what follows, I am inclined to think that that redness may have been an optical effect due to contrast. Something black fluttered momentarily against the livid yellow-green of the lower sky, and then the thin and penetrating voice of a bell rose out of the black gulf below him. An oppressive expectation grew with the growing light.

It is probable that an hour or more elapsed while he sat there, the strange green light growing brighter every moment, and spreading slowly, in flamboyant fingers, upwards towards the zenith. As it grew, the spectral vision of *our* world became relatively or absolutely fainter. Probably both, for the time must have been about that of our earthly sunset. So far as his vision of our world went, Plattner by his few steps downhill, had passed through the floor of the classroom, and was now, it seemed, sitting in mid-air in the larger schoolroom downstairs. He saw the boarders distinctly, but much more faintly than he had seen Lidgett. They were preparing their evening tasks, and he noticed with interest that several were cheating with their Euclid riders by means of a crib, a compilation whose existence he had hitherto never suspected. As the time passed they faded steadily, as steadily as the light of the green dawn increased.

Looking down into the valley, he saw that the light had crept far down its rocky sides, and that the profound blackness of the abyss was now broken by a minute green glow, like the light of a glow-worm. And almost immediately the limb of a huge heavenly body of blazing green rose over the basaltic undulations of the distant hills, and the monstrous hill-masses about him came out gaunt and desolate, in green light and deep, ruddy black shadows. He became aware of a vast number of ball-shaped objects drifting as thistledown drifts over the high ground. There were none of these nearer to him than the opposite side of the gorge. The bell below twanged quicker and quicker, with something like impatient insistence, and several lights moved hither and thither. The boys at work at their desks were now almost imperceptibly faint.

This extinction of our world, when the green sun of this other universe rose, is a curious point upon which Plattner insists. During the Other-World night it is difficult to move about, on account of the vividness with which the things of this world are visible. It becomes a riddle to explain why, if this is the case, we in this world catch no glimpse of the Other-World. It is due, perhaps, to the comparatively vivid illumination of this world of ours. Plattner describes the midday of the Other-World, at its brightest, as not being nearly so bright as this world at full moon, while its night is profoundly black. Consequently, the amount of light, even in an ordinary dark room, is sufficient to render the things of the Other-World invisible, on the same principle that faint phosphorescence is only visible in the profoundest darkness. I have tried, since he told me his story, to see something of the Other-World by sitting for a long space in a photographer's dark room at night. I have certainly seen indistinctly the form of greenish slopes and rocks, but only, I must admit, very indistinctly indeed. The reader may possibly be more successful. Plattner tells me that since his return he has seen and recognised places in the Other-World in his dreams, but this is probably due to his memory of these scenes. It seems quite possible that people with unusually keen eyesight may occasionally catch a glimpse of this strange Other-World about us.

However, this is a digression. As the green sun rose, a long street of black buildings became perceptible, though only darkly and indistinctly, in the gorge, and, after some hesitation, Plattner began to clamber down the precipitous descent towards them. The descent was long and exceedingly tedious, being so not only by the extraordinary steepness, but also by reason of the looseness of the boulders with which the whole face of the hill was strewn. The noise of his descent—now and then his heels struck fire from the rocks—seemed now the only sound in the universe, for the beating of the bell had ceased. As he drew nearer he perceived that the various edifices had a singular resemblance to tombs and mausoleums and monuments, saving only that they were all uniformly black instead of being white as most sepulchres are. And then he saw, crowding out of the largest building very much as people disperse from church, a number of pallid, rounded, pale-green figures. These scattered in several directions about the broad street of the place, some going through side alleys and reappearing upon the steepness of the hill, others entering some of the small black buildings which lined the way.

At the sight of these things drifting up towards him, Plattner stopped, staring. They were not walking, they were indeed limbless; and they had the appearance of human heads beneath which a tadpole-like body swung. He was too astonished at their strangeness, too full indeed of strangeness, to be seriously alarmed by them. They drove towards him, in front of the chill wind that was blowing uphill, much as soap-bubbles drive before a draught. And as he looked at the nearest of those approaching, he saw it was indeed a human head, albeit with singularly large eyes, and wearing such an expression of distress and anguish as he had never seen before upon mortal countenance. He was surprised to find that it did not turn to regard him, but seemed to be watching and following some unseen moving thing. For a moment he was puzzled, and then it occurred to him that this creature was watching with its enormous eyes something that was happening in the world he had just left. Nearer it came, and nearer, and he was too astonished to cry out. It made a very faint fretting sound as it came close to him. Then it struck his face with a gentle pat—its touch was very cold—and drove past him, and upward towards the crest of the hill.

An extraordinary conviction flashed across Plattner's mind that this head had a strong likeness to Lidgett. Then he turned his attention to the other heads that were now swarming thickly up the hillside. None made the slightest sign of recognition. One or two, indeed, came close to his head and almost followed the example of the first, but he dodged convulsively out of the way. Upon most of them he saw the same expression of unavailing regret he had seen upon the first and heard the same faint sounds of wretchedness from them. One or two wept, and one rolling swiftly uphill wore an expression of diabolical rage. But others were cold, and several had a look of gratified interest in their eyes. One, at least, was almost in an ecstasy of happiness. Plattner does not remember that he recognized any more likenesses in those he saw at this time.

For several hours, perhaps, Plattner watched these strange things dispersing themselves over the hills, and not till long after they had ceased to issue from the clustering black buildings in the gorge did he resume his downward climb. The darkness about him increased so much that he had a difficulty in stepping true. Overhead the sky was now a bright pale green. He felt neither hunger nor thirst. Later, when he did, he found a chilly stream running down the centre of the gorge, and the rare moss upon the boulders, when he tried it at last in desperation, was good to eat.

He groped about among the tombs that ran down the gorge, seeking vaguely for some clue to these inexplicable things. After a long time he came to the entrance of the big mausoleum-like building from which the heads had issued. In this he found a group of green lights burning upon a kind of basaltic altar, and a bell-rope from a belfry overhead hanging down into the centre of the place. Round the wall ran a lettering of fire in a character unknown to him. While he was still wondering at the purport of these things, he heard the receding tramp of heavy feet echoing far down the street. He ran out into the darkness again, but he could see nothing. He had a mind to pull the bell-rope, and finally decided to follow the footsteps. But although he ran far, he never overtook them; and his shouting was of no avail. The gorge seemed to extend an interminable distance. It was as dark as earthly starlight throughout its length, while the ghastly green day lay along the upper edges of its precipices. There were none of the heads, now, below. They were all, it seemed, busily occupied along the upper slopes. Looking up, he saw them drifting hither and thither, some hovering stationary, some flying swiftly through the air. It reminded him, he said, of "big snowflakes"; only these were black and pale green.

In pursuing the firm, undeviating footsteps that he never overtook, in groping into new regions of this endless devil's dyke, in clambering up and down the pitiless heights, in wandering about the summits, and in watching the drifting faces, Plattner states that he spent the better part of seven or eight days. He did not keep count, he says. Though once or twice he found eyes watching him, he had word with no living soul. He slept among the rocks on the hillside. In the gorge things earthly were invisible, because, from the earthly standpoint, it was far underground. On the altitudes, so soon as the earthly day began, the world became visible to him. He found himself sometimes stumbling over the dark green rocks, or arresting himself on a precipitous brink, while all about him the green branches of the Sussexville lanes were swaying; or, again, he seemed to be walking through the Sussexville streets, or watching unseen the private business of some household. And then it was he discovered, that to almost every human being in our world there pertained some of these drifting heads; that everyone in the world is watched intermittently by these helpless disembodiments. What are they—these Watchers of the Living? Plattner never learned. But two that presently found and followed him, were like his childhood's memory of his father and mother. Now and then other faces turned their eyes upon him: eyes like those of dead people who had swayed him, or injured him, or helped him in his youth and manhood. Whenever they looked at him, Plattner was overcome with a strange sense of responsibility. To his mother he ventured to speak; but she made no answer. She looked sadly, steadfastly, and tenderly—a little reproachfully, too, it seemed—into his eyes.

He simply tells this story: he does not endeavour to explain. We are left to surmise who these Watchers of the Living may be, or if they are indeed the Dead, why they should so closely and passionately watch a world they have left for ever. It may be—indeed to my mind it seems just—that, when our life has closed, when evil or good is no longer a choice for us, we may still have to witness the working out of the train of consequences we have laid. If human souls continue after death, then surely human interests continue after death. But that is merely my own guess at the meaning of the things seen. Plattner offers no interpretation, for none was given him. It is well the reader should understand this clearly. Day after day, with his head reeling, he wandered about this green-lit world outside the world, weary and, towards the end, weak and hungry. By day—by our earthly day, that is—the ghostly vision of the old familiar scenery of Sussexville, all about him, irked and worried him. He could not see where to put his feet, and ever and again with a chilly touch one of these Watching Souls would come against his face. And after dark the multitude of these Watchers about him, and their intent distress, confused his mind beyond describing. A great longing to return to the earthly life that was so near and yet so remote consumed him. The unearthliness of things about him produced a positively painful mental distress. He was worried beyond describing by his own particular followers. He would shout at them to desist from staring at him, scold at them, hurry away from them. They were always mute and intent. Run as he might over the uneven ground they followed his destinies.

On the ninth day, towards evening, Plattner heard the invisible footsteps approaching, far away down the gorge. He was then wandering over the broad crest of the same hill upon which he had fallen in his entry into this strange Other-World of his. He turned to hurry down into the gorge, feeling his way hastily, and was arrested by the sight of the thing that was happening in a room in a back street near the school. Both of the people in the room he knew by sight. The windows were open, the blinds up, and the setting sun shone clearly into it, so that it came out quite brightly at first, a vivid oblong of room, lying like a magic-lantern picture upon the black landscape and the livid green dawn. In addition to the sunlight, a candle had just been lit in the room.

On the bed lay a lank man, his ghastly white face terrible upon the tumbled pillow. His clenched hands were raised above his head. A little table beside the bed carried a few medicine bottles, some toast and water, and an empty glass. Every now and then the lank man's lips fell apart, to indicate a word he could not articulate. But the woman did not notice that he wanted anything, because she was busy turning out papers from an old-fashioned bureau in the opposite corner of the room. At first the picture was very vivid indeed, but as the green dawn behind it grew brighter and brighter, so it became fainter and more and more transparent.

As the echoing footsteps paced nearer and nearer, those footsteps that sound so loud in that Other-World and come so silently in this, Plattner perceived about him a great multitude of dim faces gathering together out of the darkness and watching the two people in the room. Never before had he seen so many of the Watchers of the Living. A multitude had eyes only for the sufferer in the room, another multitude, in infinite anguish, watched the woman as she hunted with greedy eyes for something she could not find. They crowded about Plattner, they came across his sight and buffeted his face, the noise of their unavailing regrets was all about him. He saw clearly only now and then. At other times the pictures quivered dimly, through the veil of green reflections upon their movements. In the room it must have been very still, and Plattner says the candle flame streamed up into a perfectly vertical line of smoke, but in his ears each footfall and its echoes beat like a clap of thunder. And the faces! Two more particularly, near the woman's: one a woman's also, white and clear-featured, a face which might have once been cold and hard but which was now softened by the touch of a wisdom strange to earth. The other might have been the woman's father. Both were evidently absorbed in the contemplation of some act of hateful meanness, so it seemed, which they could no longer guard against and prevent. Behind were others, teachers it may be who had taught ill, friends whose influence had failed. And over the man, too—a multitude, but none that seemed to be parents or teachers! Faces that might once have been coarse, now purged to strength by sorrow! And in the forefront one face, a girlish one, neither angry nor remorseful but merely patient and weary, and, as it seemed to Plattner, waiting for relief. His powers of description fail him at the memory of this multitude of ghastly countenances. They gathered on the stroke of the bell. He saw them all in the space of a second. It would seem that he was so worked upon by his excitement that quite involuntarily his restless fingers took the bottle of green powder out of his pocket and held it before him. But he does not remember that.

Abruptly the footsteps ceased. He waited for the next and there was silence, and then suddenly, cutting through the unexpected stillness like a keen, thin blade, came the first stroke of the bell. At that the multitudinous faces swayed to and fro, and a louder crying began all about him. The woman did not hear; she was burning something now in the candle flame. At the second stroke everything grew dim, and a breath of wind, icy cold, blew through the host of watchers. They swirled about him like an eddy of dead leaves in the spring, and at the third stroke something was extended through them to the bed. You have heard of a beam of light. This was like a beam of darkness, and looking again at it, Plattner saw that it was a shadowy arm and hand.

The green sun was now topping the black desolations of the horizon, and the vision of the room was very faint. Plattner could see that the white of the bed struggled, and was convulsed; and that the woman looked round over her shoulder at it, startled.

The cloud of watchers lifted high like a puff of green dust before the wind, and swept swiftly downward towards the temple in the gorge. Then suddenly Plattner understood the meaning of the shadowy black arm that stretched across his shoulder and clutched its prey. He did not dare turn his head to see the Shadow behind the arm. With a violent effort, and covering his eyes, he set himself to run, made perhaps twenty strides, then slipped on a boulder and fell. He fell forward on his hands; and the bottle smashed and exploded as he touched the ground.

In another moment he found himself, stunned and bleeding, sitting face to face with Lidgett in the old walled garden behind the school.

There the story of Plattner's experiences ends. I have resisted, I believe successfully, the natural disposition of a writer of fiction to dress up incidents of this sort. I have told the thing as far as possible in the order in which Plattner told it to me. I have carefully avoided any attempt at style, effect, or construction. It would have been easy, for instance, to have worked the scene of the death-bed into a kind of plot in which Plattner might have been involved. But quite apart from the objection-ableness of falsifying a most extraordinary true story, any such trite devices would spoil, to my mind, the peculiar effect of this dark world, with its livid green illumination and its drifting Watchers of the Living, which, unseen and unapproachable to us, is yet lying all about us.

It remains to add, that a death did actually occur in Vincent Terrace, just beyond the school garden, and, so far as can be proved, at the moment of Plattner's return. Deceased was a rate-collector and insurance agent. His widow, who was much younger than himself, married last month a Mr. Whymper, a veterinary surgeon of Allbeeding. As the portion of this story given here has in various forms circulated orally in Sussexville, she has consented to my use of her name, on condition that I make it distinctly known that she emphatically contradicts every detail of Plattner's account of her husband's last moments. She burnt no will, she says, although Plattner never accused her of doing so: her husband made but one will, and that just after their marriage. Certainly, from a man who had never seen it, Plattner's account of the furniture of the room was curiously accurate.

One other thing, even at the risk of an irksome repetition, I must insist upon lest I seem to favour the credulous superstitious view. Plattner's absence from the world for nine days is, I think, proved. But that does not prove his story. It is quite conceivable that even outside space hallucinations may be possible. That, at least, the reader must bear distinctly in mind.

# ON THE BRIGHTON ROAD
## RICHARD MIDDLETON

S lowly the sun had climbed up the hard white downs, till it broke with little of the mysterious ritual of dawn upon a sparkling world of snow. There had been a hard frost during the night, and the birds, who hopped about here and there with scant tolerance of life, left no trace of their passage on the silver pavements. In places the sheltered caverns of the hedges broke the monotony of the whiteness that had fallen upon the coloured earth, and overhead the sky melted from orange to deep blue, from deep blue to a blue so pale that it suggested a thin paper screen rather than illimitable space. Across the level fields there came a cold, silent wind which blew fine dust of snow from the trees, but hardly stirred the crested hedges. Once above the sky-line, the sun seemed to climb more quickly, and as it rose higher it began to give out a heat that blended with the keenness of the wind.

It may have been this strange alternation of heat and cold that disturbed the tramp in his dreams, for he struggled for a moment with the snow that covered him, like a man who finds himself twisted uncomfortably in the bed-clothes, and then sat up with staring, questioning eyes. "Lord! I thought I was in bed," he said to himself as he took in the vacant landscape, "and all the while I was out here." He stretched his limbs, and, rising carefully to his feet, shook the snow off his body. As he did so the wind set him shivering, and he knew that his bed had been warm.

"Come, I feel pretty fit," he thought. "I suppose I am lucky to wake at all in this. Or unlucky—it isn't much of a business to come back to." He looked up and saw the downs shining against the blue like the Alps on a picture-postcard. "That means another forty miles or so, I suppose," he continued grimly. "Lord knows what I did yesterday. Walked till I was done, and now I'm only about twelve miles from Brighton. Damn the snow, damn Brighton, damn everything!" The sun crept up higher and higher, and he started walking patiently along the road with his back turned to the hills.

"Am I glad or sorry that it was only sleep that took me, glad or sorry, glad or sorry?" His thoughts seemed to arrange themselves in a metrical accompaniment to the steady thud of his footsteps, and he hardly sought an answer to his question. It was good enough to walk to.

Presently, when three milestones had loitered past, he overtook a boy who was stooping to light a cigarette. He wore no overcoat, and looked unspeakably fragile against the snow. "Are you on the road, guv'nor?" asked the boy huskily as he passed.

"I think I am," the tramp said.

"Oh! then I'll come a bit of the way with you if you don't walk too fast. It's a bit lonesome walking this time of day." The tramp nodded his head, and the boy started limping along by his side.

"I'm eighteen," he said casually. "I bet you thought I was younger."

"Fifteen, I'd have said."

"You'd have backed a loser. Eighteen last August, and I've been on the road six years. I ran away from home five times when I was a little 'un, and the police took me back each time. Very good to me, the police was. Now I haven't got a home to run away from."

"Nor have I," the tramp said calmly.

"Oh, I can see what you are," the boy panted; "you're a gentleman come down. It's harder for you than for me." The tramp glanced at the limping, feeble figure and lessened his pace.

"I haven't been at it as long as you have," he admitted.

"No, I could tell that by the way you walk. You haven't got tired yet. Perhaps you expect something the other end?"

The tramp reflected for a moment. "I don't know," he said bitterly, "I'm always expecting things."

"You'll grow out of that," the boy commented. "It's warmer in London, but it's harder to come by grub. There isn't much in it really."

"Still, there's the chance of meeting somebody there who will understand—"

"Country people are better," the boy interrupted. "Last night I took a lease of a barn for nothing and slept with the cows, and this morning the farmer routed me out and gave me tea and toke because I was little. Of course, I score there; but in London, soup on the Embankment at night, and all the rest of the time coppers moving you on."

"I dropped by the roadside last night and slept where I fell. It's a wonder I didn't die," the tramp said. The boy looked at him sharply.

"How do you know you didn't?" he said.

"I don't see it," the tramp said, after a pause.

"I tell you," the boy said hoarsely, "people like us can't get away from this sort of thing if we want to. Always hungry and thirsty and dog-tired and walking all the time. And yet if anyone offers me a nice home and work my stomach feels sick. Do I look strong? I know I'm little for my age, but I've been knocking about like this for six years, and do you think I'm not dead? I was drowned bathing at Margate, and I was killed by a gipsy with a spike; he knocked my head right in, and twice I was froze like you last night, and a motor cut me down on this very road, and yet I'm walking along here now, walking to London to walk away from it again, because I can't help it. Dead! I tell you we can't get away if we want to."

The boy broke off in a fit of coughing, and the tramp paused while he recovered.

"You'd better borrow my coat for a bit, Tommy," he said, "your cough's pretty bad."

"You go to hell!" the boy said fiercely, puffing at his cigarette; "I'm all right. I was telling you about the road. You haven't got down to it yet, but you'll find out presently. We're all dead, all of us who're on it, and we're all tired, yet somehow we can't leave it. There's nice smells in the summer, dust and hay and the wind smack in your face on a hot day; and it's nice waking up in the wet grass on a fine morning. I don't know, I don't know—" he lurched forward suddenly, and the tramp caught him in his arms.

"I'm sick," the boy whispered—"sick."

The tramp looked up and down the road, but he could see no houses or any sign of help. Yet even as he supported the boy doubtfully in the middle of the road a motor-car suddenly flashed in the middle distance, and came smoothly through the snow.

"What's the trouble?" said the driver quietly as he pulled up. "I'm a doctor." He looked at the boy keenly and listened to his strained breathing.

"Pneumonia," he commented. "I'll give him a lift to the infirmary, and you, too, if you like."

The tramp thought of the workhouse and shook his head. "I'd rather walk," he said.

The boy winked faintly as they lifted him into the car.

"I'll meet you beyond Reigate," he murmured to the tramp. "You'll see." And the car vanished along the white road.

All the morning the tramp splashed through the thawing snow, but at midday he begged some bread at a cottage door and crept into a lonely barn to eat it. It was warm in there, and after his meal he fell asleep among the hay. It was dark when he woke, and started trudging once more through the slushy roads.

Two miles beyond Reigate a figure, a fragile figure, slipped out of the darkness to meet him.

"On the road, guv'nor?" said a husky voice. "Then I'll come a bit of the way with you if you don't walk too fast. It's a bit lonesome walking this time of day."

"But the pneumonia!" cried the tramp aghast.

"I died at Crawley this morning," said the boy.

# THE LAST HOUSE IN C— STREET
## DINAH M. MULOCK

I am not a believer in ghosts in general; I see no good in them. They come—
that is, are reported to come—so irrelevantly, purposelessly—so ridiculously, in
short—that one's common sense as regards this world, one's supernatural sense
of the other, are alike revolted. Then nine out of ten 'capital ghost stories' are
so easily accounted for; and in the tenth, when all natural explanation fails, one
who has discovered the extraordinary difficulty there is in all society in getting
hold of that very slippery article called a fact, is strongly inclined to shake a
dubious head, ejaculating, 'Evidence! it is all a question of evidence!'

But my unbelief springs from no dogged or contemptuous scepticism as
to the possibility—however great the improbability—of that strange impression
upon, or communication to, spirit in matter, from spirit wholly immaterialised,
which is vulgarly called 'a ghost.' There is no credulity more blind, no ignorance
more childish, that that of the sage who tries to measure 'heaven and earth and
the things under the earth,' with the small two-foot rule of his own brains. The

presumption of mere folly alone would argue concerning any mystery of the universe, 'It is inexplicable, and therefore impossible.'

Premising these opinions, though simply as opinions, I am about to relate what I must confess seems to me a thorough ghost story; its external and circumstantial evidence being indisputable, while its psychological causes and results, though not easy of explanation, are still more difficult to be explained away. The ghost, like Hamlet's, was an honest ghost. From her daughter—an old lady, who, bless her good and gentle memory! has since learned the secrets of all things - I heard this veritable tale.

'My dear,' said Mrs MacArthur to me—it was in the early days of table-moving, when young folk ridiculed and elder folk were shocked at the notion of calling up one's departed ancestors into one's dinner-table, and learning the wonders of the angelic world by the bobbings of a hat or the twirlings of a plate;—'My dear,' continued the old lady, 'I do not like trifling with spirits.'

'Why not? Do you believe in them?'

'A little.'

'Did you ever see one?' 'Never. But once, I heard one.'

She looked serious, as if she hardly liked to speak about it, either from a sense of awe or from fear of ridicule. But it was impossible to laugh at any illusions of the gentle old lady, who never uttered a harsh or satirical word to a living soul. Likewise the evident awe with which she mentioned the circumstance was rather remarkable in one who had a large stock of common sense, little wonder, and no ideality.

I was very curious to hear Mrs MacArthur's ghost story.

'My dear, it was a long time ago, so long that you may fancy I forget and confuse the circumstances. But I do not. Sometimes I think one recollects more clearly things that happened in one's teens—I was eighteen that year—than a great many nearer events. And besides, I had other reasons for remembering vividly everything belonging to this time,—for I was in love, you must know.'

She looked at me with a mild deprecating smile, as if hoping my youthfulness would not consider the thing so very impossible or ridiculous. No; I was all interest at once.

'In love with Mr MacArthur,' I said, scarcely as a question, being at that Arcadian time of life when one takes as a natural necessity, and believes in as an undoubted truth, that all people, that is, good people, marry their first love.

'No, my dear; not with Mr MacArthur.'

I was so astonished, so completely dumbfounded–for I had woven a sort of ideal round my good old friend–that I suffered Mrs MacArthur to knit in silence for full five minutes. My surprise was not lessened when she said, with a gratified little smile -

'He was a young gentleman of good parts; and he was very fond of me. Proud, too, rather. For though you might not think it, my dear, I was actually a beauty in those days.'

I had very little doubt of it. The slight lithe figure, the tiny hands and feet,–if you had walked behind Mrs MacArthur down the street you might have taken her for a young woman still. Certainly, people lived slower and easier in the last generation than in ours.

'Yes, I was the beauty of Bath. Mr Everest fell in love with me there. I was much gratified; for I had just been reading Miss Burney's Cecilia, and I thought him exactly like Mortimer Delvil. A very pretty story, Cecilia; did you ever read it?'

'No.' And, to arrive quicker at her tale, I leaped to the only conclusion which could reconcile the two facts of my good old friend having had a lover named Everest, and being now Mrs MacArthur. 'Was it *his* ghost you saw?'

'No, my dear, no; thank goodness, he is alive still. He calls here sometimes; he has been a faithful friend to our family. Ah!' with a slow shake of the head, half pleased, half pensive, 'you would hardly believe, my dear, what a very pretty fellow he was.'

One could scarcely smile at the odd phrase, pertaining to last-century novels and to the loves of our great-grandmothers. I listened patiently to the wandering reminiscences which still further delayed the ghost story.

'But, Mrs MacArthur, was it in Bath that you saw or heard what I think you were going to tell me? The ghost, you know?'

'Don't call it *that*; it sounds as if you were laughing at it. And you must not, for it is really true; as true as that I sit here, an old lady of seventy-five, and that then I was a young gentlewoman of eighteen. Nay, my dear, I will tell you all about it.

'We had been staying in London, my father and mother, Mr Everest, and I. He had persuaded them to take me; he wanted to show me a little of the world, though even his world was but a narrow one, my dear, - for he was a law student, living poorly and working hard.

'He took lodgings for us near the Temple; in C— street, the last house there, looking on to the river. He was very fond of the river; and often of evenings, when his work was too heavy to let him take us to Ranelagh or to the play, he used to walk with my father and mother and me up and down the Temple Gardens. Were you ever in the Temple Gardens? It is a pretty place now - a quiet, grey nook in the midst of noise and bustle; the stars look wonderful through those great trees; but still it is not like what it was then, when I was a girl.'

Ah! no; impossible.

'It was in the Temple Gardens, my dear, that I remember we took our last walk - my mother, Mr Everest, and I - before she went home to Bath. She was very anxious and restless to go, being too delicate for London gaieties. Besides, she had a large family at home, of which I was the eldest; and we were anxiously expecting another baby in a month or two. Nevertheless, my dear mother had gone about with me, taken me to all the shows and sights that I, a hearty and happy girl, longed to see, and entered into them with almost as great enjoyment as my own.

'But tonight she was pale, rather grave, and steadfastly bent on returning home.

'We did all we could to persuade her to the contrary, for on the next night but one was to have been the crowning treat of all our London pleasures: we were to see *Hamlet* at Drury-lane, with John Kemble and Sarah Siddons! Think of that, my dear. Ah! you have no such sights now. Even my grave father longed to go, and urged in his mild way that we should put off our departure. But my mother was determined.

'At last Mr Everest said - I could show you the very spot where he stood, with the river–it was high water–lapping against the wall, and the evening sun shining on the Southwark houses opposite. He said–it was very wrong, of course, my dear; but then he was in love, and might be excused -

'"Madam," said he, "it is the first time I ever knew you think of yourself alone."

'"Myself, Edmond?"

'"Pardon me, but would it not be possible for you to return home, leaving behind, for two days only, Dr. Thwaite and Mistress Dorothy?"

'"Leave them behind–leave them behind!" She mused over the words. "What say you, Dorothy?"

'I was silent. In very truth, I had never been parted from her in all my life. It had never crossed my mind to wish to part from her, or to enjoy any pleasure without her, till–till within the last three months. "Mother, don't suppose I—"

'But here I caught sight of Mr Everest and stopped.

'"Pray continue, Mistress Dorothy."

'No, I could not. He looked so vexed, so hurt; and we had been so happy together. Also, we might not meet again for years, for the journey between London and Bath was then a serious one, even to lovers; and he worked very hard–had few pleasures in his life. It did indeed seem almost selfish of my mother.

Though my lips said nothing, perhaps my sad eyes said only too much, and my mother felt it.

'She walked with us a few yards, slowly and thoughtfully. I could see her now, with her pale, tired face, under the cherry-coloured ribbons of her hood. She had been very handsome as a young woman, and was most sweet-looking still–my dear, good mother!

'"Dorothy, we will discuss this no more. I am very sorry, but I must go home. However, I will persuade your father to remain with you till the week's end. Are you satisfied!'

'"No," was the first filial impulse of my heart; but Edmund pressed my arm with such an entreating look, that almost against my will I answered "Yes."

'Mr Everest overwhelmed my mother with his delight and gratitude. She walked up and down for some time longer, leaning on his arm–she was very fond of him; then stood looking on the river, upwards and downwards.

'"I suppose this is my last walk in London. Thank you for all the care you have taken of me. And when I am gone home–mind, oh, mind, Edmond, that you take special care of Dorothy."

'These words, and the tone in which they were spoken, fixed themselves on my mind– first, from gratitude, not unmingled with regret, as if I had not been so considerate to her as she to me; *afterwards*—But we often err, my dear, in dwelling too much on that word. We finite creatures have only to deal with "now"–nothing whatever to do with "afterwards." In this case, I have ceased to blame myself or others. Whatever was, being past, was right to be, and could not have been otherwise.

'My mother went home next morning, alone. We were to follow in a few days, though she would not allow us to fix any time. Her departure was so hurried that I remember nothing about it, save her answer to my father's urgent desire–almost command–that if anything went amiss she would immediately let him know.

'"Under all circumstances, wife," he reiterated, "this you promise?"

'"I promise."

'Though when she was gone he declared she need not have said it so earnestly, since we should be at home almost as soon as the slow Bath coach could take her there and bring us back a letter. And besides, there was nothing likely to happen. But he fidgeted a good deal, being unused to her absence in their happy wedded life. He was, like most men, glad to blame anybody but himself, and the whole day, and the next, was cross at intervals with both Edmond and me; but we bore it–and patiently.

'"It will be all right when we get him to the theatre. He has no real cause for anxiety about her. What a dear woman she is, and a precious - your mother, Dorothy!"

'I rejoiced to hear my lover speak thus, and thought there hardly ever was young gentlewoman so blessed as I.

'We went to the play. Ah, you know nothing of what a play is, nowadays. You never saw John Kemble and Mrs Siddons. Though in dresses and shows it was far inferior to the *Hamlet* you took me to see last week, my dear–and though I perfectly well remember being on the point of laughing when in the most solemn scene, it became clearly evident that the Ghost had been drinking. Strangely enough, no after events connected therewith ever were able to drive from my mind the vivid impression of this my first play. Strange, also, that the play should have been *Hamlet*. Do you think that Shakespeare believed in—in what people call "ghosts?"'

I could not say; but I thought Mrs MacArthur's ghost very long in coming.

'Don't, my dear–don't; do anything but laugh at it.'

She was visibly affected, and it was not without an effort that she proceeded in her story.

'I wish you to understand exactly my position that night–a young girl, her head full of the enchantment of the stage–her heart of something not less engrossing. Mr Everest had supped with us, leaving us both in the best of spirits; indeed my father had gone to bed, laughing heartily at the remembrance of the antics of Mr Grimaldi, which had almost obliterated the Queen and Hamlet from his memory, on which the ridiculous always took a far stronger hold than the awful or sublime.

'I was sitting–let me see–at the window, chatting with my maid Patty, who was brushing the powder out of my hair. The window was open half-way, and looking out on the Thames; and the summer night being very warm and starry, made it almost like sitting out of doors. There was none of the awe given by the solitude of a closed room, when every sound is magnified, and every shadow seems alive.

'As I said, we had been chatting and laughing; for Patty and I were both very young, and she had a sweetheart, too. She, like every one of our household, was a warm admirer of Mr Everest. I had just been half scolding, half smiling at her praises of him, when St Paul's great clock came booming over the silent river.

"'Eleven," counted Patty. "Terrible late we be, Mistress Dorothy: not like Bath hours, I reckon."

"'Mother will have been in bed an hour ago," said I, with a little self-reproach at not having thought of her till now.

The next minute my maid and I both started up with a simultaneous exclamation.

"'Did you hear that?"

"'Yes, a bat flying against the window."

"'But the lattices are open, Mistress Dorothy."

'So they were; and there was no bird or bat or living thing about—only the quiet summer night, the river, and the stars.

"'I be certain sure I heard it. And I think it was like—just a bit like-somebody tapping."

"'Nonsense, Patty!" But it had struck me thus—though I said it was a bat. It was exactly like the sound of fingers against a pane—very soft, gentle fingers; such as, in passing into her flower-garden, my mother used often to tap outside the school-room casement at home.

"'I wonder, did father hear anything. It—the bird, you know, Patty-might have flown at his window, too?"

"'Oh, Mistress Dorothy!" Patty would not be deceived. I gave her the brush to finish my hair, but her hand shook too much. I shut the window, and we both sat down facing it.

'At that minute, distinct, clear, and unmistakeable, like a person giving a summons in passing by, we heard once more the tapping on the pane. But nothing was seed; not a single shadow came between us and the open air; the bright starlight.

'Startled I was, and awed, but I was not frightened. The sound gave me even an inexplicable delight. But I had hardly time to recognise my feelings, still less to analyse them, when a loud cry came from my father's room.

"'Dolly,-Dolly!"

'Now my mother and I had both one name, but he always gave her the old-fashioned pet name, - I was invariably Dorothy. Still I did not pause to think, but ran to his locked door and answered.

'It was a long time before he took any notice, though I heard him talking to himself, and moaning. He was subject to bad dreams, especially before his attacks of gout. So my first alarm lightened. I stood listening, knocking at intervals, until at last he replied.

'"What do 'ee want, child?"

'"Is anything the matter, father?"

'"Nothing. Go to thy bed, Dorothy."

'"Did you not call? Do you want any one?"

'"Not thee. O Dolly, my poor Dolly,"–and he seemed to be almost sobbing, "why did I let thee leave me?

'"Father, you are not going to be ill? It is not the gout, is it? (for that was the time when he wanted my mother most, and, indeed, when he was wholly unmanageable by any one but her.)

'"Go away. Get to thy bed, girl; I don't want 'ee."

'I thought he was angry with me for having been in some sort the cause of our delay, and retired very miserable. Patty and I sat up a good while longer, discussing the dreary prospect of my father's having a fit of the gout here in London lodgings, with only us to nurse him, and my mother away. Our alarm was so great that we quite forgot the curious circumstance which had first attracted us, till Patty spoke up from her bed on the floor.

'"I hope master aren't going to be very ill, and that noise – you know - came for a warning. Do 'ee think it *was* a bird, Mistress Dorothy?" '"Very likely. Now, Patty, let us go to sleep."

'But I did not, for all night I heard my father groaning at intervals. I was certain it was the gout, and wished from the bottom of my heart that we had gone home with mother.

'What was my surprise when, quite early, I heard him rise and go down, just as if nothing was ailing him! I found him sitting at the breakfast-table in his travelling coat, looking very haggard and miserable, but evidently bent on a journey.

'"Father, you are not going to Bath?"

'"Yes, I be."

'"Not till the evening coach starts," I cried, alarmed. "We can't, you know?"

"Ill take a post-chaise, then. We must be off in an hour."

'An hour! The cruel pain of parting–(my dear, I believe I used to feel things keenly when I was young)–shot through me–through and through. A single hour, and I should have said good-bye to Edmond -one of those heart-breaking farewells when we seem to leave half of our poor young life behind us, forgetting that the only real parting is when there is no love left to part from. A few years, and I wondered how I could have crept away and wept in such intolerable agony at the mere bidding good-bye to Edmond–Edmond, who loved me!

'Every minute seemed a day till he came in, as usual, to breakfast. My red eyes and my father's corded trunk explained all.

"'Dr Thwaite, you are not going?"

"'Yes, I am," repeated my father. He sat moodily leaning on the table - would not taste his breakfast.

"'Not till the night coach, surely? I was to take you and Mistress Dorothy to see Mr Benjamin West, the king's painter."

"'Let king and painters alone, lad; I am going home to my Dolly."

'Mr Everest used many arguments, gay and grave, upon which I hung with earnest conviction and hope. He made things so clear always; he was a man of much brighter parts than my father, and had great influence over him.

"'Dorothy," he whispered, "help me to persuade the Doctor. It is so little time I beg for, only a few hours; and before so long a parting."–Ay, longer than he thought, or I.

"'Children," cried my father at last, "you are a couple of fools. Wait till you have been married twenty years. I must go to my Dolly. I know there is something amiss at home."

'I should have felt alarmed, but I saw Mr Everest smile; and besides, I was yet glowing under his fond look, as my father spoke of our being "married twenty years."

"'Father, you have surely no reason for thinking this? If you have, tell us."

'My father just lifted his head, and looked at me woefully in the face.

"'Dorothy, last night, as sure as I see you now, I saw your mother." "'Is that all?" cried Mr Everest, laughing: "why, my good sir, very likely you did; you were dreaming about her." "I had not gone to sleep." "How did you see her?"

"'Coming into my room, just as she used to do in our bedroom at home, with the candle in her hand and the baby asleep on her arm."

"'Did she speak?" asked Mr Everest, with another and rather satirical smile; "remember, you saw *Hamlet* last night. Indeed, sir–indeed, Dorothy–it was a mere dream. I do not believe in ghosts; it would be an insult to common sense, to human wisdom—nay, even to Divinity itself."

'Edmond spoke so earnestly, justly, and withal so affectionately, that perforce I agreed; and even my father began to feel rather ashamed of his own weakness. He, a sensible man and the head of a family, to yield to a mere superstitious fancy, springing probably from a hot supper and an over-excited brain! To the same cause Mr Everest attributed the other incident, which somewhat hesitatingly I told him.

'"Dear, it was a bird; nothing but a bird. One flew in at my window last spring; it had hurt itself, and I kept it, and nursed it, and petted it. It was such a pretty gentle little thing, it put me in mind of Dorothy."

'"Did it?" said I.

'"And at last it got well and flew away." "Ah! that was not like Dorothy."

'Thus, my father being persuaded, it was not hard to persuade me. We settled to remain till evening. Edmond and I, with my maid Patty went about together chiefly in Mr West's Gallery, and in the quiet shade of our favourite Temple Gardens. And if for those four stolen hours, and the sweetness in them, I afterwards suffered untold remorse and bitterness, I have entirely forgiven myself, as I know my dear mother would have forgiven me, long ago.'

Mrs MacArthur stopped, wiped her eyes, and then continued -speaking more in the matter-of-fact way that old people speak in, than she had been lately doing.

'Well, my dear, where was I?'

'In the Temple Gardens.'

'Yes, yes. Then we came home to dinner. My father always enjoyed his dinner, and his nap afterwards; he had nearly recovered himself now: only looked tired from loss of rest. Edmond and I sat in the window, watching the barges and wherries down the Thames; there were no steam-boats then, you know.

'Some one knocked at the door with a message for my father, but he slept so heavily he did not hear. Mr Everest went to see what it was; I stood at the window. I remember mechanically watching the red sail of a Margate hoy that was going down the river, and thinking with a sharp pang how dark the room seemed to grow, in a moment, with Edmond not there.

'Re-entering, after a somewhat long absence, he never looked at me, but went straight to my father.

'"Sir, it is almost time for you to start; (oh! Edmond). "There is a coach at the door; and, pardon me, but I think you should travel quickly."

'My father sprang to his feet.

'"Dear sir, wait one moment; I have received news from Bath. You have another little daughter, sir, and—"

'"Dolly, my Dolly!" Without another word my father rushed away, leaped into the post-chaise that was waiting and drove off.

'"Edmond!" I gasped.

'"My poor little girl—my own Dorothy!"

'By the tenderness of his embrace, less lover-like than brother-like—by his tears, for I could feel them on my neck–I knew, as well as if he had told me, that I should never see my dear mother any more.

'She had died in childbirth,' continued the old lady after a long pause -'died at night, at the same hour and minute that I had heard the tapping on the window-pane, and my father had thought he saw her coming into his room with a baby on her arm.

'Was the baby dead, too?'

'They thought so then, but it afterwards revived.'

'What a strange story!'

'I do not ask you to believe in it. How and why and what it was I cannot tell; I only know that it assuredly was as I have told it.'

'And Mr Everest?' I inquired, after some hesitation.

The old lady shook her head. 'Ah, my dear, you may perhaps learn-though I hope you will not–how very, very seldom things turn out as one expects when one is young. After that day I did not see Mr Everest for twenty years.'

'How wrong of him–how—'

'Don't blame him; it was not his fault. You see, after that time my father took a prejudice against him–not unnatural, perhaps; and *she* was not there to make things straight. Besides, my own conscience was very sore, and there were the six children at home, and the little baby had no mother: so at last I made up my mind. I should have loved him just the same if we had waited twenty years. I told him so: but he could not see things in that light. Don't blame him, my dear, don't blame him. It was as well, perhaps, as it happened.'

'Did he marry?'

'Yes, after a few years; and loved his wife dearly. When I was about one-and-thirty, I married Mr MacArthur. So neither of us was unhappy, you see–at least, not more so than most people; and we became sincere friends afterwards. Mr and Mrs Everest come to see me still, almost every Sunday. Why, you foolish child, you are not crying?'

Ay, I was–but scarcely at the ghost story.

# THE FURNISHED ROOM

## O. HENRY

Restless, shifting, fugacious as time itself is a certain vast bulk of the population of the red brick district of the lower West Side. Homeless, they have a hundred homes. They flit from furnished room to furnished room, transients forever—transients in abode, transients in heart and mind. They sing "Home, Sweet Home" in ragtime; they carry their *lares et penates* in a bandbox; their vine is entwined about a picture hat; a rubber plant is their fig tree.

Hence the houses of this district, having had a thousand dwellers, should have a thousand tales to tell, mostly dull ones, no doubt; but it would be strange if there could not be found a ghost or two in the wake of all these vagrant guests.

One evening after dark a young man prowled among these crumbling red mansions, ringing their bells. At the twelfth he rested his lean hand baggage upon the step and wiped the dust from his hatband and forehead. The bell sounded faint and far away in some remote, hollow depths. To the door of this, the twelfth house whose bell he had rung, came a housekeeper who made him think of an unwholesome, surfeited worm that had eaten its nut to a hollow shell and now sought to fill the vacancy with edible lodgers.

He asked if there was a room to let.

"Come in," said the housekeeper. Her voice came from her throat; her throat seemed lined with fur. "I have the third-floor-back, vacant since a week back. Should you wish to look at it?"

The young man followed her up the stairs. A faint light from no particular source mitigated the shadows of the halls. They trod noiselessly upon a stair carpet that its own loom would have forsworn. It seemed to have become vegetable; to have degenerated in that rank, sunless air to lush lichen or spreading moss that grew in patches to the staircase and was viscid under the foot like organic matter. At each turn of the stairs were vacant niches in the wall. Perhaps plants had once been set within them. If so they had died in that foul and tainted air. It may be that statues of the saints had stood there, but it was not difficult to conceive that imps and devils had dragged them forth in the darkness and down to the unholy depths of some furnished pit below.

"This is the room," said the housekeeper, from her furry throat. "It's a nice room. It ain't often vacant. I had some most elegant people in it last summer—no trouble at all, and paid in advance to the minute. The water's at the end of the hall. Sprowls and Mooney kept it three months. They done a vaudeville sketch. Miss B'retta Sprowls—you may have heard of her—oh, that was just the stage names— right there over the dresser is where the marriage certificate hung, framed. The gas is here, and you see there is plenty of closet room. It's a room everybody likes. It never stays idle long."

"Do you have many theatrical people rooming here?" asked the young man.

"They comes and goes. A good proportion of my lodgers is connected with the theaters. Yes, sir, this is the theatrical district. Actor people never stays long anywhere. I get my share. Yes, they comes and they goes."

He engaged the room, paying for a week in advance. He was tired, he said, and would take possession at once. He counted out the money. The room had been made ready, she said, even to towels and water. As the housekeeper moved away he put, for the thousandth time, the question that he carried at the end of his tongue.

"A young girl—Miss Vashner—Miss Eloise Vashner—do you remember such a one among your lodgers? She would be singing on the stage, most likely. A fair girl, of medium height and slender, with reddish, gold hair and a dark mole near her left eyebrow."

"No, I don't remember the name. Them stage people has names they change as often as their rooms. They comes and they goes. No, I don't call that one to mind."

No. Always no. Five months of ceaseless interrogation and the inevitable negative. So much time spent by days in questioning managers, agents, schools and choruses; by night among the audiences of theaters from all-star casts down to music halls so low that he dreaded to find what he most hoped for. He who had loved her best had tried to find her. He was sure that since her disappearance from home this great, water-girt city held her somewhere, but it was like a monstrous quicksand, shifting its particles constantly, with no foundation, its upper granules of today buried tomorrow in ooze and slime.

The furnished room received its latest guest with a first glow of pseudo hospitality, a hectic, haggard, perfunctory welcome like the specious smile of a demirep. The sophistical comfort came in reflected gleams from the decayed furniture, the ragged brocade upholstery of a couch and two chairs, a foot-wide cheap pier glass between the two windows, from one or two gilt picture frames and a brass bedstead in a corner.

The guest reclined, inert, upon a chair, while the room, confused in speech as though it were an apartment in Babel, tried to discourse to him of its divers tenantry.

A polychromatic rug like some brilliant-flowered rectangular, tropical islet lay surrounded by a billowy sea of soiled matting. Upon the gay-papered wall were those pictures that pursue the homeless one from house to house—The Huguenot Lovers, The First Quarrel, The Wedding Breakfast, Psyche at the Fountain. The mantel's chastely severe outline was ingloriously veiled behind some pert drapery drawn rakishly askew like the sashes of the Amazonian ballet. Upon it was some desolate flotsam cast aside by the room's marooned when a lucky sail had borne them to a fresh port—a trifling vase or two, pictures of actresses, a medicine bottle, some stray cards out of a deck.

One by one, as the characters of a cryptograph become explicit, the little signs left by the furnished room's procession of guests developed a significance. The threadbare space in the rug in front of the dresser told that lovely women had marched in the throng. The tiny fingerprints on the wall spoke of little prisoners trying to feel their way to sun and air. A splattered stain, raying like the shadow of a bursting bomb, witnessed where a hurled glass or bottle had splintered with its contents against the wall. Across the pier glass had been scrawled with a diamond in staggering letters the name "Marie." It seemed that the succession of dwellers in the furnished room had turned in fury—perhaps tempted beyond forebearance by its garish coldness—and wreaked upon it their passions.

The furniture was chipped and bruised; the couch, distorted by bursting springs, seemed a horrible monster that had been slain during the stress of some grotesque convulsion. Some more potent upheaval had cloven a great slice from the marble mantel. Each plank in the floor owned its particular cant and shriek as from a separate and individual agony. It seemed incredible that all this malice and injury had been wrought upon the room by those who had called it for a time their home; and yet it may have been the cheated home instinct surviving blindly, the resentful rage at false household gods that had kindled their wrath. A hut that is our own we can sweep and adorn and cherish.

The young tenant in the chair allowed these thoughts to file, soft shod, through his mind, while there drifted into the room furnished sounds and furnished scents. He heard in one room a tittering and incontinent, slack laughter; in others the monologue of a scold, the rattling of dice, a lullaby, and one crying dully; above him a banjo tinkled with spirit. Doors banged somewhere; the elevated trains roared intermittently; a cat yowled miserably upon a back fence. And he breathed the breath of the house—a dank savor rather than a smell—a cold, musty effluvium as from underground vaults mingled with the reeking exhalations of linoleum and mildewed and rotten woodwork.

Then suddenly, as he rested there, the room was filled with the strong, sweet odor of mignonette. It came as upon a single buffet of wind with such sureness and fragrance and emphasis that it almost seemed a living visitant. And the man cried aloud: "What, 'dear?" as if he had been called, and sprang up and faced about. The rich odor clung to him and wrapped him around. He reached out his arms for it, all his senses for the time confused and commingled. How could one be peremptorily called by an odor? Surely it must have been a sound. But, was it not the sound that had touched, that had caressed him?

"She has been in this room," he cried, and he sprang to wrest from it a token, for he knew he would recognize the smallest thing that had belonged to her or that she had touched. This enveloping scent of mignonette, the odor that she had loved and made her own—whence came it?

The room had been but carelessly set in order. Scattered upon the flimsy dresser scarf were half a dozen hairpins—those discreet, indistinguishable friends of womankind, feminine of gender, infinite of mood and uncommunicative of tense. These he ignored, conscious of their triumphant lack of identity. Ransacking the drawers of the dresser he came upon a discarded, tiny, ragged handkerchief. He pressed it to his face. It was racy and insolent with heliotrope; he hurled it to the floor. In another drawer he found odd buttons, a theater program, a pawnbroker's card, two lost marshmallows, a book on the divination of dreams. In the last was a woman's black satin hair bow, which halted him, poised between ice and fire. But the black satin hair bow also is femininity's demure, impersonal common ornament and tells no tales.

And then he traversed the room like a hound on the scent, skimming the walls, considering the corners of the bulging matting on his hands and knees, rummaging mantel and tables, the curtains and hangings, the drunken cabinet in the corner, for a visible sign, unable to perceive that she was there beside, around, against, within, above him, clinging to him, wooing him, calling him so poignantly through the finer senses that even his grosser ones became cognizant of the call. Once again he answered loudly: "Yes, dear!" and turned, wild-eyed, to gaze on vacancy, for he could not yet discern form and color and love and outstretched arms in the odor of mignonette. Oh, God! whence that odor, and since when have odors had a voice to call? Thus he groped.

He burrowed in crevices and corners, and found corks and cigarettes. These he passed in passive contempt. But once he found in a fold of the matting a half-smoked cigar, and this he ground beneath his heel with a green and trenchant oath. He sifted the room from end to end. He found dreary and ignoble small records of many a peripatetic tenant; but of her whom he sought, and who may have lodged there, and whose spirit seemed to hover there, he found no trace.

And then he thought of the housekeeper.

He ran from the haunted room downstairs and to a door that showed a crack of light. She came out to his knock. He smothered his excitement as best he could.

"Will you tell me, madam," he besought her, "who occupied the room I have before I came?"

"Yes, sir. I can tell you again. 'Twas Sprowls and Mooney, as I said. Miss B'retta Sprowls it was in the theaters, but Missis Mooney she was. My house is well known for respectability. The marriage certificate hung, framed, on a nail over—"

"What kind of a lady was Miss Sprowls—in looks, I mean?"

"Why, black-haired, sir, short, and stout, with a comical face. They left a week ago Tuesday."

"And before they occupied it?"

"Why, there was a single gentleman connected with the draying business. He left owing me a week. Before him was Missis Crowder and her two children, that stayed four months; and back of them was old Mr. Doyle, whose sons paid for him. He kept the room six months. That goes back a year, sir, and further I do not remember."

He thanked her and crept back to his room. The room was dead. The essence that had vivified it was gone. The perfume of mignonette had departed. In its place was the old, stale odor of moldy house furniture, of atmosphere in storage.

The ebbing of his hope drained his faith. He sat staring at the yellow, singing gaslight. Soon he walked to the bed and began to tear the sheets into strips. With the blade of his knife he drove them tightly into every crevice around windows and door. When all was snug and taut he turned out the light, turned the gas full on again, and laid himself gratefully upon the bed.

It was Mrs. McCool's night to go with the can for beer. So she fetched it and sat with Mrs. Purdy in one of those subterranean retreats where housekeepers foregather and the worm dieth seldom.

"I rented out my third-floor-back this evening," said Mrs. Purdy, across a fine circle of foam. "A young man took it. He went up to bed two hours ago."

"Now, did ye, Mrs. Purdy, ma'am?" said Mrs. McCool, with intense admiration. "You do be a wonder for rentin' rooms of that kind. And did ye tell him, then?" she concluded in a husky whisper laden with mystery.

"Rooms," said Mrs. Purdy, in her furriest tones, "are furnished for to rent. I did not tell him, Mrs. McCool."

"'Tis right ye are, ma'am; 'tis by renting rooms we kape alive. Ye have the rale sense for business, ma'am. There be many people will rayjict the rentin' of a room if they be tould a suicide has been after dyin' in the bed of it."

"As you say, we has our living to be making," remarked Mrs. Purdy.

"Yis, ma'am; 'tis true. 'Tis just one wake ago this day I helped ye lay out the third-floor-back. A pretty slip of a colleen she was to be killin' herself wid the gas—a swate little face she had, Mrs. Purdy, ma'am."

"She'd a-been called handsome, as you say," said Mrs. Purdy, assenting but critical, "but for that mole she had a-growin' by her left eyebrow. Do fill up your glass again, Mrs. McCool."

# HAMLET'S GHOST
## WILLIAM SHAKESPEARE

### ACT 1. SCENE IV

SCENE IV. The platform.

Enter HAMLET, HORATIO, and MARCELLUS HAMLET. The air bites shrewdly; it is very cold.

 HORATIO It is a nipping and an eager air.

 HAMLET What hour now?

 HORATIO I think it lacks of twelve.

 HAMLET No, it is struck.

 HORATIO Indeed? I heard it not: then it draws near the season Wherein the spirit held his wont to walk.

 A flourish of trumpets, and ordnance shot off, within.

 What does this mean, my lord?

HAMLET The king doth wake to-night and takes his rouse, Keeps wassail, and the swaggering up-spring reels; And, as he drains his draughts of Rhenish down, The kettle-drum and trumpet thus bray out The triumph of his pledge.

HORATIO Is it a custom?

HAMLET Ay, marry, is't: But to my mind, though I am native here And to the manner born, it is a custom More honour'd in the breach than the observance. This heavy-headed revel east and west Makes us traduced and tax'd of other nations: They clepe us drunkards, and with swinish phrase Soil our addition; and indeed it takes From our achievements, though perform'd at height, The pith and marrow of our attribute. So, oft it chances in particular men, That for some vicious mole of nature in them, As, in their birth—wherein they are not guilty, Since nature cannot choose his origin— By the o'ergrowth of some complexion, Oft breaking down the pales and forts of reason, Or by some habit that too much o'er-leavens The form of plausive manners, that these men, Carrying, I say, the stamp of one defect, Being nature's livery, or fortune's star,— Their virtues else—be they as pure as grace, As infinite as man may undergo— Shall in the general censure take corruption From that particular fault: the dram of eale Doth all the noble substance of a doubt To his own scandal.

HORATIO Look, my lord, it comes!

Enter Ghost

HAMLET Angels and ministers of grace defend us! Be thou a spirit of health or goblin damn'd, Bring with thee airs from heaven or blasts from hell, Be thy intents wicked or charitable, Thou comest in such a questionable shape That I will speak to thee: I'll call thee Hamlet, King, father, royal Dane: O, answer me! Let me not burst in ignorance; but tell Why thy canonized bones, hearsed in death, Have burst their cerements; why the sepulchre, Wherein we saw thee quietly inurn'd, Hath oped his ponderous and marble jaws, To cast thee up again. What may this mean, That thou, dead corse, again in complete steel Revisit'st thus the glimpses of the moon, Making night hideous; and we fools of nature So horridly to shake our disposition With thoughts beyond the reaches of our souls? Say, why is this? wherefore? what should we do?

Ghost beckons HAMLET

HORATIO It beckons you to go away with it, As if it some impartment did desire To you alone.

MARCELLUS Look, with what courteous action It waves you to a more removed ground: But do not go with it.

HORATIO No, by no means.

HAMLET It will not speak; then I will follow it.

HORATIO Do not, my lord.

HAMLET Why, what should be the fear? I do not set my life in a pin's fee; And for my soul, what can it do to that, Being a thing immortal as itself? It waves me forth again: I'll follow it.

HORATIO What if it tempt you toward the flood, my lord, Or to the dreadful summit of the cliff That beetles o'er his base into the sea, And there assume some other horrible form, Which might deprive your sovereignty of reason And draw you into madness? think of it: The very place puts toys of desperation, Without more motive, into every brain That looks so many fathoms to the sea And hears it roar beneath.

HAMLET It waves me still. Go on; I'll follow thee.

MARCELLUS You shall not go, my lord.

HAMLET Hold off your hands.

HORATIO Be ruled; you shall not go.

HAMLET My fate cries out, And makes each petty artery in this body As hardy as the Nemean lion's nerve. Still am I call'd. Unhand me, gentlemen. By heaven, I'll make a ghost of him that lets me! I say, away! Go on; I'll follow thee.

Exeunt Ghost and HAMLET

HORATIO He waxes desperate with imagination.

MARCELLUS Let's follow; 'tis not fit thus to obey him.

HORATIO Have after. To what issue will this come?

MARCELLUS Something is rotten in the state of Denmark.

HORATIO Heaven will direct it.

MARCELLUS Nay, let's follow him.

Exeunt

Act 1. Scene V

SCENE V. Another part of the platform.

Enter GHOST and HAMLET HAMLET Where wilt thou lead me? speak; I'll go no further.

Ghost Mark me.

HAMLET I will.

Ghost My hour is almost come, When I to sulphurous and tormenting flames Must render up myself.

HAMLET Alas, poor ghost!

Ghost Pity me not, but lend thy serious hearing To what I shall unfold.

HAMLET Speak; I am bound to hear.

Ghost So art thou to revenge, when thou shalt hear.

HAMLET What?

Ghost I am thy father's spirit, Doom'd for a certain term to walk the night, And for the day confined to fast in fires, Till the foul crimes done in my days of nature Are burnt and purged away. But that I am forbid To tell the secrets of my prison-house, I could a tale unfold whose lightest word Would harrow up thy soul, freeze thy young blood, Make thy two eyes, like stars, start from their spheres, Thy knotted and combined locks to part And each particular hair to stand on end, Like quills upon the fretful porpentine: But this eternal blazon must not be To ears of flesh and blood. List, list, O, list! If thou didst ever thy dear father love—

HAMLET O God!

Ghost Revenge his foul and most unnatural murder.

HAMLET Murder!

Ghost Murder most foul, as in the best it is; But this most foul, strange and unnatural.

HAMLET Haste me to know't, that I, with wings as swift As meditation or the thoughts of love, May sweep to my revenge.

Ghost I find thee apt; And duller shouldst thou be than the fat weed That roots itself in ease on Lethe wharf, Wouldst thou not stir in this. Now, Hamlet, hear: 'Tis given out that, sleeping in my orchard, A serpent stung me; so the whole ear of Denmark Is by a forged process of my death Rankly abused: but know, thou noble youth, The serpent that did sting thy father's life Now wears his crown.

HAMLET O my prophetic soul! My uncle!

Ghost Ay, that incestuous, that adulterate beast, With witchcraft of his wit, with traitorous gifts,— O wicked wit and gifts, that have the power So to seduce!—won to his shameful lust The will of my most seeming-virtuous queen: O Hamlet, what a falling-off was there! From me, whose love was of that dignity That it went hand in hand even with the vow I made to her in marriage, and to decline Upon a wretch whose natural gifts were poor To those of mine! But virtue, as it never will be moved, Though lewdness court it in a shape of heaven, So lust, though to a radiant angel link'd, Will sate itself in a celestial bed, And prey on garbage. But, soft! methinks I scent the morning air; Brief let me be. Sleeping within my orchard, My custom always of the afternoon, Upon my secure hour thy uncle stole, With juice of cursed hebenon in a vial, And in the porches of my ears did pour The leperous distilment; whose effect Holds such an enmity with blood of man That swift as quicksilver it courses through The natural gates and alleys of the body, And with a sudden vigour doth posset And curd, like eager droppings into milk, The thin and wholesome blood: so did it mine; And a most instant tetter bark'd about, Most lazar-like, with vile and loathsome crust, All my smooth body. Thus was I, sleeping, by a brother's hand Of life, of crown, of queen, at once dispatch'd: Cut off even in the blossoms of my sin, Unhousel'd, disappointed, unanel'd, No reckoning made, but sent to my account With all my imperfections on my head: O, horrible! O, horrible! most horrible! If thou hast nature in thee, bear it not; Let not the royal bed of Denmark be A couch for luxury and damned incest. But, howsoever thou pursuest this act, Taint not thy mind, nor let thy soul contrive Against thy mother aught: leave her to heaven And to those thorns that in her bosom lodge, To prick and sting her. Fare thee well at once! The glow-worm shows the matin to be near, And 'gins to pale his uneffectual fire: Adieu, adieu! Hamlet, remember me.

Exit

HAMLET O all you host of heaven! O earth! what else? And shall I couple hell? O, fie! Hold, hold, my heart; And you, my sinews, grow not instant old, But bear me stiffly up. Remember thee! Ay, thou poor ghost, while memory holds a seat In this distracted globe. Remember thee! Yea, from the table of my memory I'll wipe away all trivial fond records, All saws of books, all forms, all pressures past, That youth and observation copied there; And thy commandment all alone shall live Within the book and volume of my brain, Unmix'd with baser matter: yes, by heaven! O most pernicious woman! O villain, villain, smiling, damned villain! My tables,—meet it is I set it down, That one may smile, and smile, and be a villain; At least I'm sure it may be so in Denmark:

Writing

So, uncle, there you are. Now to my word; It is 'Adieu, adieu! remember me.' I have sworn 't.

MARCELLUS HORATIO [Within] My lord, my lord,—

MARCELLUS [Within] Lord Hamlet,—

HORATIO [Within] Heaven secure him!

HAMLET So be it!

HORATIO [Within] Hillo, ho, ho, my lord!

HAMLET Hillo, ho, ho, boy! come, bird, come.

Enter HORATIO and MARCELLUS

MARCELLUS How is't, my noble lord?

HORATIO What news, my lord?

HAMLET O, wonderful!

HORATIO Good my lord, tell it.

HAMLET No; you'll reveal it.

HORATIO Not I, my lord, by heaven.

MARCELLUS Nor I, my lord.

HAMLET How say you, then; would heart of man once think it? But you'll be secret?

HORATIO MARCELLUS Ay, by heaven, my lord.

HAMLET There's ne'er a villain dwelling in all Denmark But he's an arrant knave.

HORATIO There needs no ghost, my lord, come from the grave To tell us this.

HAMLET Why, right; you are i' the right; And so, without more circumstance at all, I hold it fit that we shake hands and part: You, as your business and desire shall point you; For every man has business and desire, Such as it is; and for mine own poor part, Look you, I'll go pray.

HORATIO These are but wild and whirling words, my lord.

HAMLET I'm sorry they offend you, heartily; Yes, 'faith heartily.

HORATIO There's no offence, my lord.

HAMLET Yes, by Saint Patrick, but there is, Horatio, And much offence too. Touching this vision here, It is an honest ghost, that let me tell you: For your desire to know what is between us, O'ermaster 't as you may. And now, good friends, As you are friends, scholars and soldiers, Give me one poor request.

HORATIO What is't, my lord? we will.

HAMLET Never make known what you have seen to-night.

HORATIO MARCELLUS My lord, we will not.

HAMLET Nay, but swear't.

HORATIO In faith, My lord, not I.

MARCELLUS Nor I, my lord, in faith.

HAMLET Upon my sword.

MARCELLUS We have sworn, my lord, already.

HAMLET Indeed, upon my sword, indeed.

Ghost [Beneath] Swear.

HAMLET Ah, ha, boy! say'st thou so? art thou there, truepenny? Come on—you hear this fellow in the cellarage— Consent to swear.

HORATIO Propose the oath, my lord.

HAMLET Never to speak of this that you have seen, Swear by my sword.

Ghost [Beneath] Swear.

HAMLET Hic et ubique? then we'll shift our ground. Come hither, gentlemen, And lay your hands again upon my sword: Never to speak of this that you have heard, Swear by my sword.

Ghost [Beneath] Swear.

HAMLET Well said, old mole! canst work i' the earth so fast? A worthy pioner! Once more remove, good friends.

HORATIO O day and night, but this is wondrous strange!

HAMLET And therefore as a stranger give it welcome. There are more things in heaven and earth, Horatio, Than are dreamt of in your philosophy. But come; Here, as before, never, so help you mercy, How strange or odd soe'er I bear myself, As I perchance hereafter shall think meet To put an antic disposition on, That you, at such times seeing me, never shall, With arms encumber'd thus, or this headshake, Or by pronouncing of some doubtful phrase, As 'Well, well, we know,' or 'We could, an if we would,' Or 'If we list to speak,' or 'There be, an if they might,' Or such ambiguous giving out, to note That you know aught of me: this not to do, So grace and mercy at your most need help you, Swear.

Ghost [Beneath] Swear.

HAMLET Rest, rest, perturbed spirit!

They swear

So, gentlemen, With all my love I do commend me to you: And what so poor a man as Hamlet is May do, to express his love and friending to you, God willing, shall not lack. Let us go in together; And still your fingers on your lips, I pray. The time is out of joint: O cursed spite, That ever I was born to set it right! Nay, come, let's go together.

Exeunt

# CATERPILLARS

## E. F. BENSON

I saw a month or two ago in an Italian paper that the Villa Cascana, in which I once stayed, had been pulled down, and that a manufactory of some sort was in process of erection on its site. There is therefore no longer any reason for refraining from writing of those things which I myself saw (or imagined I saw) in a certain room and on a certain landing of the villa in question, nor from mentioning the circumstances which followed, which may or may not (according to the opinion of the reader) throw some light on, or be somehow connected with this experience.

The Villa Cascana was in all ways but one a perfectly delightful house, yet, if it were standing now, nothing in the world—I use the phrase in its literal sense—would induce me to set foot in it again, for I believe it to have been haunted in a very terrible and practical manner. Most ghosts, when all is said and done, do not do much harm; they may perhaps terrify, but the person whom they visit usually gets over their visitation. They may on the other hand be entirely friendly and beneficent. But the appearances in the Villa Cascana were not beneficent, and had they made their "visit" in a very slightly different manner, I do not suppose I should have got over it any more than Arthur Inglis did.

The house stood on an ilex-clad hill not far from Sestri di Levante on the Italian Rivera, looking out over the iridescent blues of that enchanted sea, while behind it rose the pale green chestnut woods that climb up the hillsides till they give place to the pines that, black in contrast with them, crown the slopes. All round it the garden in the luxuriance of mid-spring bloomed and was fragrant, and the scent of magnolia and rose, borne on the salt freshness of the winds from the sea, flowed like a stream through the cool, vaulted rooms.

On the ground floor a broad pillared *loggia* ran round three sides of the house, the top of which formed a balcony for certain rooms on the first floor. The main staircase, broad and of grey marble steps, led up from the hall to the landing outside these rooms, which were three in number, namely, two big sitting-rooms and a bedroom arranged *en suite*. The latter was unoccupied, the sitting-rooms were in use. From here the main staircase continued up to the second floor, where were situated certain bedrooms, one of which I occupied, while on the other side of the first-floor landing some half-dozen steps led to another suite of rooms, where, at the time I am speaking of, Arthur Inglis, the artist, had his bedroom and studio. Thus the landing outside my bedroom, at the top of the house, commanded both the landing of the first floor, and also the steps that led to Inglis' rooms. Jim Stanley and his wife, finally (whose guest I was), occupied rooms in another wing of the house, where also were the servants' quarters.

I arrived just in time for lunch on a brilliant noon of mid-May. The garden was shouting with colour and fragrance, and not less delightful after my broiling walk up from the *marina*, should have been the coming from the reverberating heat and blaze of the day into the marble coolness of the villa. Only (the reader has my bare word for this, and nothing more), the moment I set foot in the house I felt that something was wrong. This feeling, I may say, was quite vague, though very strong, and I remember that when I saw letters waiting for me on the table in the hall I felt certain that the explanation was here: I was convinced that there was bad news of some sort for me. Yet when I opened them I found no such explanation of my premonition: my correspondents all reeked of prosperity. Yet this clear miscarriage of a presentiment did not dissipate my uneasiness. In that cool fragrant house there was something wrong.

I am at pains to mention this because it may explain why it was that, though I am as a rule so excellent a sleeper that the extinction of a light on getting into bed is apparently contemporaneous with being called on the following morning, I slept very badly on my first night in the Villa Cascana. It may also explain that fact that when I did sleep (if it was indeed in sleep that I saw what I thought I saw) I dreamed in a very vivid and original manner, original, that is to say, in the sense that something which, as far as I knew, had never previously entered into my consciousness, usurped it then. But since, in addition to this evil premonition, certain words and events occurring during the rest of the day, might have suggested something of what I thought happened that night, it will be well to relate them.

After lunch, then, I went round the house with Mrs. Stanley, and during our tour she referred, it is true, to the unoccupied bedroom on the first floor, which opened out of the room where we had lunched.

"We left that unoccupied," she said, "because Jim and I have a charming bedroom and dressing-room, as you saw, in the wing, and if we used it ourselves we should have to turn the dining-room into a dressing-room and have our meals downstairs. As it is, however, we have our little flat there, Arthur Inglis has his little flat in the other passage; and I remembered (aren't I extraordinary?) that you once said that the higher up you were in a house the better you were pleased. So I put you at the top of the house, instead of giving you that room."

It is true, that a doubt, vague as my uneasy premonition, crossed my mind at this. I did not see why Mrs. Stanley should have explained all this, if there had not been more to explain. I allow, therefore, that the thought that there was something to explain about the unoccupied bedroom was momentarily present to my mind.

The second thing that may have borne on my dream was this.

At dinner the conversation turned for a moment on ghosts. Inglis, with the certainty of conviction, expressed his belief that anybody who could possibly believe in the existence of supernatural phenomena was unworthy of the name of an ass. The subject instantly dropped. As far as I can recollect, nothing else occurred or was said that could bear on what follows.

We all went to bed rather early, and personally I yawned my way upstairs, feeling hideously sleepy. My room was rather hot, and I threw all the windows wide, and from without poured in the white light of the moon, and the love-song of many nightingales. I undressed quickly, and got into bed, but though I had felt so sleepy before, I now felt extremely wide-awake. But I was quite content to be awake: I did not toss or turn, I felt perfectly happy listening to the song and seeing the light. Then, it is possible, I may have gone to sleep, and what follows may have been a dream. I thought anyhow that after a time the nightingales ceased singing and the moon sank. I thought also that if, for some unexplained reason I was going to lie awake all night, I might as well read, and I remembered that I had left a book in which I was interested in the dining-room on the first floor. So I got out of bed, lit a candle, and went downstairs. I entered the room, saw on a side-table the book I had come to look for, and then, simultaneously, saw that the door into the unoccupied bedroom was open. A curious grey light, not of dawn nor of moonshine, came out of it, and I looked in. The bed stood just opposite the door, a big four-poster, hung with tapestry at the head. Then I saw that the greyish light of the bedroom came from the bed, or rather from what was on the bed. For it was covered with great caterpillars, a foot or more in length, which crawled over it. They were faintly luminous, and it was the light from them that showed me the room. Instead of the sucker-feet of ordinary caterpillars they had rows of pincers like crabs, and they moved by grasping what they lay on with their pincers, and then sliding their bodies forward. In colour these dreadful insects were yellowish grey, and they were covered with irregular lumps and swellings. There must have been hundreds of them, for they formed a sort of writhing, crawling pyramid on the bed. Occasionally one fell off on to the floor, with a soft fleshy thud, and though the floor was of hard concrete, it yielded to the pincer-feet as if it had been putty, and crawling back, the caterpillar would mount on to the bed again, to rejoin its fearful companions. They appeared to have no faces, so to speak, but at one end of them there was a mouth that opened sideways in respiration.

Then, as I looked, it seemed to me as if they all suddenly became conscious of my presence. All the mouths at any rate were turned in my direction, and next moment they began dropping off the bed with those soft fleshy thuds on to the floor, and wriggling towards me. For one second the paralysis of nightmare was on me, but the next I was running upstairs again to my room, and I remember feeling the cold of the marble steps on my bare feet. I rushed into my bedroom, and slammed the door behind me, and then—I was certainly wide awake now—I found myself standing by my bed with the sweat of terror pouring from me. The noise of the banged door still rang in my ears. But, as would have been more usual, if this had been mere nightmare, the terror that had been mine when I saw those foul beasts crawling about the bed or dropping softly on to the floor did not cease then. Awake now, if dreaming before, I did not at all recover from the horror of dream: it did not seem to me that I had dreamed. And until dawn, I sat or stood, not daring to lie down, thinking that every rustle or movement that I heard was the approach of the caterpillars. To them and the claws that bit into the cement the wood of the door was child's play: steel would not keep them out.

But with the sweet and noble return of day the horror vanished: the whisper of wind became benignant again: the nameless fear, whatever it was, was smoothed out and terrified me no longer. Dawn broke, hueless at first; then it grew dove-coloured, then the flaming pageant of light spread over the sky.

\* \* \* \* \*

The admirable rule of the house was that everybody had breakfast where and when he pleased, and in consequence it was not till lunch-time that I met any of the other members of our party, since I had breakfast on my balcony, and wrote letters and other things till lunch. In fact, I got down to that meal rather late, after the other three had begun. Between my knife and fork there was a small pill-box of cardboard, and as I sat down Inglis spoke.

"Do look at that," he said, "since you are interested in natural history. I found it crawling on my counterpane last night, and I don't know what it is."

I think that before I opened the pill-box I expected something of the sort which I found in it. Inside it, anyhow, was a small caterpillar, greyish-yellow in colour, with curious bumps and excrescences on its rings. It was extremely active, and hurried round the box, this way and that. Its feet were unlike the feet of any caterpillar I ever saw: they were like the pincers of a crab. I looked, and shut the lid down again.

"No, I don't know it," I said, "but it looks rather unwholesome. What are you going to do with it?"

"Oh, I shall keep it," said Inglis. "It has begun to spin: I want to see what sort of a moth it turns into."

I opened the box again, and saw that these hurrying movements were indeed the beginning of the spinning of the web of its cocoon. Then Inglis spoke again.

"It has got funny feet, too," he said. "They are like crabs' pincers. What's the Latin for crab? Oh, yes, Cancer. So in case it is unique, let's christen it: 'Cancer Inglisensis'."

Then something happened in my brain, some momentary piecing together of all that I had seen or dreamed. Something in his words seemed to me to throw light on it all, and my own intense horror at the experience of the night before linked itself on to what he had just said. In effect, I took the box and threw it, caterpillar and all, out of the window. There was a gravel path just outside, and beyond it a fountain playing into a basin. The box fell on to the middle of this.

Inglis laughed.

"So the students of the occult don't like solid facts," he said. "My poor caterpillar!"

The talk went off again at once on to other subjects, and I have only given in detail, as they happened, these trivialities in order to be sure myself that I have recorded everything that could have borne on occult subjects or on the subject of caterpillars. But at the moment when I threw the pill-box into the fountain, I lost my head: my only excuse is that, as is probably plain, the tenant of it was, in miniature, exactly what I had seen crowded on to the bed in the unoccupied room. And though this translation of those phantoms into flesh and blood—or whatever it is that caterpillars are made of—ought perhaps to have relieved the horror of the night, as a matter of fact it did nothing of the kind. It only made the crawling pyramid that covered the bed in the unoccupied room more hideously real.

\* \* \* \* \*

After lunch we spent a lazy hour or two strolling about the garden or sitting in the *loggia,* and it must have been about four o'clock when Stanley and I started off to bathe, down the path that led by the fountain into which I had thrown the pill-box. The water was shallow and clear, and at the bottom of it I saw its white remains. The soaking had disintegrated the cardboard, and it had become no more than a few strips and shreds of sodden paper. The centre of the fountain was a marble Italian Cupid which squirted the water out of a wine-skin held under its arm. And crawling up its leg was the caterpillar. Strange and scarcely credible as it seemed, it must have survived the falling-to-bits of its prison, and made its way to shore, and there it was, out of arm's reach, weaving and waving this way and that as it evolved its cocoon.

Then, as I looked at it, it seemed to me again that, like the caterpillar I had seen last night, it saw me, and breaking out of the threads that surrounded it, it crawled down the marble leg of the Cupid and began swimming like a snake across the water of the fountain towards me. It came with extraordinary speed (the fact of a caterpillar being able to swim was new to me), and in another moment was crawling up the marble lip of the basin. Just then Inglis joined us.

"Why if it isn't old 'Cancer Inglisensis' again," he said, catching sight of the beast. "What a tearing hurry it is in."

We were standing side by side on the path, and when the caterpillar had advanced to within about a yard of us, it stopped, and began waving again, as if in doubt as to the direction in which it should go. Then it appeared to make up its mind, and crawled on to Inglis' shoe.

"It likes me best," he said, "but I don't really know that I like it. And as it won't drown I think perhaps—"

He shook it off his shoe on to the gravel path and trod on it.

* * * * *

All the afternoon the air got heavier and heavier with the Sirocco that was without doubt coming up from the south, and that night again I went up to bed feeling very sleepy, but below my drowsiness, so to speak, there was the consciousness, stronger than before, that there was something wrong in the house, that something dangerous was close at hand. But I fell asleep at once, and—how long after I do not know—either woke or dreamed I awoke, feeling that I must get up at once *or I should be too late.* Then (dreaming or awake) I lay and fought this fear, telling myself that I was but the prey of my own nerves disordered by Sirocco or what not, and at the same time quite clearly knowing in another part of my mind, so to speak, that every moment's delay added to the danger. At last this second feeling became irresistible, and I put on coat and trousers and went out of my room on to the landing. And then I saw that I had already delayed too long, and that I was now too late.

The whole of the landing of the first floor below was invisible under the swarm of caterpillars that crawled there. The folding doors into the sitting-room from which opened the bedroom where I had seen them last night, were shut, but they were squeezing through the cracks of it, and dropping one by one through the keyhole, elongating themselves into mere string as they passed, and growing fat and lumpy again on emerging. Some, as if exploring, were nosing about the steps into the passage at the end of which were Inglis' rooms, others were crawling on the lowest steps of the staircase that led up to where I stood. The landing, however, was completely covered with them: I was cut off. And of the frozen horror that seized me when I saw that, I can give no idea in words.

* * * * *

Then at last a general movement began to take place, and they grew thicker on the steps that led to Inglis' room. Gradually, like some hideous tide of flesh, they advanced along the passage, and I saw the foremost, visible by the pale grey luminousness that came from them, reach his door. Again and again I tried to shout and warn him, in terror all the time that they should turn at the sound of my voice and mount my stair instead, but for all my efforts I felt that no sound came from my throat. They crawled along the hinge-crack of his door, passing through as they had done before, and still I stood there making impotent efforts to shout to him, to bid him escape while there was time.

\* \* \* \* \*

At last the passage was completely empty: they had all gone, and at that moment I was conscious for the first time of the cold of the marble landing on which I stood barefooted. The dawn was just beginning to break in the Eastern sky.

\* \* \* \* \*

Six months later I met Mrs. Stanley in a country house in England. We talked on many subjects and at last she said:

"I don't think I have seen you since I got that dreadful news about Arthur Inglis a month ago." "I haven't heard," said I. "No? He has got cancer. They don't even advise an operation, for there is no hope of a cure: he is riddled with it, the doctors say."

Now during all these six months I do not think a day had passed on which I had not had in my mind the dreams (or whatever you like to call them) which I had seen in the Villa Cascana.

"It is awful, is it not?" she continued, "and I feel, I can't help feeling, that he may have—"

"Caught it at the villa?" I asked.

She looked at me in blank surprise.

"Why did you say that?" she asked. "How did you know?"

Then she told me. In the unoccupied bedroom a year before there had been a fatal case of cancer. She had, of course, taken the best advice and had been told that the utmost dictates of prudence would be obeyed so long as she did not put anybody to sleep in the room, which had also been thoroughly disinfected and newly white-washed and painted. But—

# THE BLACK MATE
## JOSEPH CONRAD

A good many years ago there were several ships loading at the Jetty, London Dock. I am speaking here of the 'eighties of the last century, of the time when London had plenty of fine ships in the docks, though not so many fine buildings in its streets.

The ships at the Jetty were fine enough; they lay one behind the other; and the *Sapphire*, third from the end, was as good as the rest of them, and nothing more. Each ship at the Jetty had, of course, her chief officer on board. So had every other ship in dock.

The policeman at the gates knew them all by sight, without being able to say at once, without thinking, to what ship any particular man belonged. As a matter of fact, the mates of the ships then lying in the London Dock were like the majority of officers in the Merchant Service—a steady, hard-working, staunch, un-romantic-looking set of men, belonging to various classes of society, but with the professional stamp obliterating the personal characteristics, which were not very marked anyhow.

This last was true of them all, with the exception of the mate of the *Sapphire*. Of him the policemen could not be in doubt. This one had a presence.

He was noticeable to them in the street from a great distance; and when in the morning he strode down the Jetty to his ship, the lumpers and the dock labourers rolling the bales and trundling the cases of cargo on their hand-trucks would remark to each other:

"Here's the black mate coming along."

That was the name they gave him, being a gross lot, who could have no appreciation of the man's dignified bearing. And to call him black was the superficial impressionism of the ignorant.

Of course, Mr. Bunter, the mate of the *Sapphire*, was not black. He was no more black than you or I, and certainly as white as any chief mate of a ship in the whole of the Port of London. His complexion was of the sort that did not take the tan easily; and I happen to know that the poor fellow had had a month's illness just before he joined the *Sapphire*.

From this you will perceive that I knew Bunter. Of course I knew him. And, what's more, I knew his secret at the time, this secret which—never mind just now. Returning to Bunter's personal appearance, it was nothing but ignorant prejudice on the part of the foreman stevedore to say, as he did in my hearing: "I bet he's a furriner of some sort." A man may have black hair without being set down for a Dago. I have known a West-country sailor, boatswain of a fine ship, who looked more Spanish than any Spaniard afloat I've ever met. He looked like a Spaniard in a picture.

Competent authorities tell us that this earth is to be finally the inheritance of men with dark hair and brown eyes. It seems that already the great majority of mankind is dark-haired in various shades. But it is only when you meet one that you notice how men with really black hair, black as ebony, are rare. Bunter's hair was absolutely black, black as a raven's wing. He wore, too, all his beard (clipped, but a good length all the same), and his eyebrows were thick and bushy. Add to this steely blue eyes, which in a fair-haired man would have been nothing so extraordinary, but in that sombre framing made a startling contrast, and you will easily understand that Bunter was noticeable enough.

If it had not been for the quietness of his movements, for the general soberness of his demeanour, one would have given him credit for a fiercely passionate nature.

Of course, he was not in his first youth; but if the expression "in the force of his age" has any meaning, he realized it completely. He was a tall man, too, though rather spare. Seeing him from his poop indefatigably busy with his duties, Captain Ashton, of the clipper ship *Elsinore*, lying just ahead of the *Sapphire*, remarked once to a friend that "Johns has got somebody there to hustle his ship along for him."

Captain Johns, master of the *Sapphire*, having commanded ships for many years, was well known without being much respected or liked. In the company of his fellows he was either neglected or chaffed. The chaffing was generally undertaken by Captain Ashton, a cynical and teasing sort of man. It was Captain Ashton who permitted himself the unpleasant joke of proclaiming once in company that "Johns is of the opinion that every sailor above forty years of age ought to be poisoned—shipmasters in actual command excepted."

It was in a City restaurant, where several well-known shipmasters were having lunch together. There was Captain Ashton, florid and jovial, in a large white waistcoat and with a yellow rose in his buttonhole; Captain Sellers in a sack-coat, thin and pale-faced, with his iron-gray hair tucked behind his ears, and, but for the absence of spectacles, looking like an ascetical mild man of books; Captain Hell, a bluff sea-dog with hairy fingers, in blue serge and a black felt hat pushed far back off his crimson forehead. There was also a very young shipmaster, with a little fair moustache and serious eyes, who said nothing, and only smiled faintly from time to time.

Captain Johns, very much startled, raised his perplexed and credulous glance, which, together with a low and horizontally wrinkled brow, did not make a very intellectual *ensemble*. This impression was by no means mended by the slightly pointed form of his bald head.

Everybody laughed outright, and, thus guided, Captain Johns ended by smiling rather sourly, and attempted to defend himself. It was all very well to joke, but nowadays, when ships, to pay anything at all, had to be driven hard on the passage and in harbour, the sea was no place for elderly men. Only young men and men in their prime were equal to modern conditions of push and hurry. Look at the great firms: almost every single one of them was getting rid of men showing any signs of age. He, for one, didn't want any oldsters on board his ship.

And, indeed, in this opinion Captain Johns was not singular. There was at that time a lot of seamen, with nothing against them but that they were grizzled, wearing out the soles of their last pair of boots on the pavements of the City in the heart-breaking search for a berth.

Captain Johns added with a sort of ill-humoured innocence that from holding that opinion to thinking of poisoning people was a very long step.

This seemed final but Captain Ashton would not let go his joke.

"Oh, yes. I am sure you would. You said distinctly 'of no use.' What's to be done with men who are 'of no use?' You are a kind-hearted fellow, Johns. I am sure that if only you thought it over carefully you would consent to have them poisoned in some painless manner."

Captain Sellers twitched his thin, sinuous lips.

"Make ghosts of them," he suggested, pointedly.

At the mention of ghosts Captain Johns became shy, in his perplexed, sly, and unlovely manner.

Captain Ashton winked.

"Yes. And then perhaps you would get a chance to have a communication with the world of spirits. Surely the ghosts of seamen should haunt ships. Some of them would be sure to call on an old shipmate."

Captain Sellers remarked drily:

"Don't raise his hopes like this. It's cruel. He won't see anything. You know, Johns, that nobody has ever seen a ghost."

At this intolerable provocation Captain Johns came out of his reserve. With no perplexity whatever, but with a positive passion of credulity giving momentary lustre to his dull little eyes, he brought up a lot of authenticated instances. There were books and books full of instances. It was merest ignorance to deny supernatural apparitions. Cases were published every month in a special newspaper. Professor Cranks saw ghosts daily. And Professor Cranks was no small potatoes either. One of the biggest scientific men living. And there was that newspaper fellow—what's his name?—who had a girl-ghost visitor. He printed in his paper things she said to him. And to say there were no ghosts after that!

"Why, they have been photographed! What more proof do you want?"

Captain Johns was indignant. Captain Bell's lips twitched, but Captain Ashton protested now.

"For goodness' sake don't keep him going with that. And by the by, Johns, who's that hairy pirate you've got for your new mate? Nobody in the Dock seems to have seen him before."

Captain Johns, pacified by the change of subjects, answered simply that Willy, the tobacconist at the corner of Fenchurch Street, had sent him along.

Willy, his shop, and the very house in Fenchurch Street, I believe, are gone now. In his time, wearing a careworn, absent-minded look on his pasty face, Willy served with tobacco many southern-going ships out of the Port of

London. At certain times of the day the shop would be full of shipmasters. They sat on casks, they lounged against the counter.

Many a youngster found his first lift in life there; many a man got a sorely needed berth by simply dropping in for four pennyworth of birds'-eye at an auspicious moment. Even Willy's assistant, a redheaded, uninterested, delicate-looking young fellow, would hand you across the counter sometimes a bit of valuable intelligence with your box of cigarettes, in a whisper, lips hardly moving, thus: "The *Bellona*, South Dock. Second officer wanted. You may be in time for it if you hurry up."

And didn't one just fly!

"Oh, Willy sent him," said Captain Ashton. "He's a very striking man. If you were to put a red sash round his waist and a red handkerchief round his head he would look exactly like one of them buccaneering chaps that made men walk the plank and carried women off into captivity. Look out, Johns, he don't cut your throat for you and run off with the *Sapphire*. What ship has he come out of last?"

Captain Johns, after looking up credulously as usual, wrinkled his brow, and said placidly that the man had seen better days. His name was Bunter.

"He's had command of a Liverpool ship, the *Samaria*, some years ago. He lost her in the Indian Ocean, and had his certificate suspended for a year. Ever since then he has not been able to get another command. He's been knocking about in the Western Ocean trade lately."

"That accounts for him being a stranger to everybody about the Docks," Captain Ashton concluded as they rose from table.

Captain Johns walked down to the Dock after lunch. He was short of stature and slightly bandy. His appearance did not inspire the generality of mankind with esteem; but it must have been otherwise with his employers. He had the reputation of being an uncomfortable commander, meticulous in trifles, always nursing a grievance of some sort and incessantly nagging. He was not a man to kick up a row with you and be done with it, but to say nasty things in a whining voice; a man capable of making one's life a perfect misery if he took a dislike to an officer.

That very evening I went to see Bunter on board, and sympathized with him on his prospects for the voyage. He was subdued. I suppose a man with a secret locked up in his breast loses his buoyancy. And there was another reason why I could not expect Bunter to show a great elasticity of spirits. For one thing he had been very seedy lately, and besides—but of that later.

Captain Johns had been on board that afternoon and had loitered and dodged about his chief mate in a manner which had annoyed Bunter exceedingly.

"What could he mean?" he asked with calm exasperation. "One would think he suspected I had stolen something and tried to see in what pocket I had stowed it away; or that somebody told him I had a tail and he wanted to find out how I managed to conceal it. I don't like to be approached from behind several times in one afternoon in that creepy way and then to be looked up at suddenly in front from under my elbow. Is it a new sort of peep-bo game? It doesn't amuse me. I am no longer a baby."

I assured him that if anyone were to tell Captain Johns that he—Bunter—had a tail, Johns would manage to get himself to believe the story in some mysterious manner. He would. He was suspicious and credulous to an inconceivable degree. He would believe any silly tale, suspect any man of anything, and crawl about with it and ruminate the stuff, and turn it over and over in his mind in the most miserable, inwardly whining perplexity. He would take the meanest possible view in the end, and discover the meanest possible course of action by a sort of natural genius for that sort of thing.

Bunter also told me that the mean creature had crept all over the ship on his little, bandy legs, taking him along to grumble and whine to about a lot of trifles. Crept about the decks like a wretched insect—like a cockroach, only not so lively.

Thus did the self-possessed Bunter express himself with great disgust. Then, going on with his usual stately deliberation, made sinister by the frown of his jet-black eyebrows:

"And the fellow is mad, too. He tried to be sociable for a bit, and could find nothing else but to make big eyes at me, and ask me if I believed 'in communication beyond the grave.' Communication beyond—I didn't know what he meant at first. I didn't know what to say. 'A very solemn subject, Mr. Bunter,' says he. I've given a great deal of study to it."

Had Johns lived on shore he would have been the predestined prey of fraudulent mediums; or even if he had had any decent opportunities between the voyages. Luckily for him, when in England, he lived somewhere far away in Leytonstone, with a maiden sister ten years older than himself, a fearsome virago twice his size, before whom he trembled. It was said she bullied him terribly in general; and in the particular instance of his spiritualistic leanings she had her own views.

These leanings were to her simply satanic. She was reported as having declared that, "With God's help, she would prevent that fool from giving himself up to the Devils." It was beyond doubt that Johns' secret ambition was to get into personal communication with the spirits of the dead—if only his sister would let him. But she was adamant. I was told that while in London he had to account to her for every penny of the money he took with him in the morning, and for every hour of his time. And she kept the bankbook, too.

Bunter (he had been a wild youngster, but he was well connected; had ancestors; there was a family tomb somewhere in the home counties)—Bunter was indignant, perhaps on account of his own dead. Those steely-blue eyes of his flashed with positive ferocity out of that black-bearded face. He impressed me—there was so much dark passion in his leisurely contempt.

"The cheek of the fellow! Enter into relations with . . . A mean little cad like this! It would be an impudent intrusion. He wants to enter! . . . What is it? A new sort of snobbishness or what?"

I laughed outright at this original view of spiritism—or whatever the ghost craze is called. Even Bunter himself condescended to smile. But it was an austere, quickly vanished smile. A man in his almost, I may say, tragic position couldn't be expected—you understand. He was really worried. He was ready eventually to put up with any dirty trick in the course of the voyage. A man could not expect much consideration should he find himself at the mercy of a fellow like Johns. A misfortune is a misfortune, and there's an end of it. But to be bored by mean, low-spirited, inane ghost stories in the Johns style, all the way out to Calcutta and back again, was an intolerable apprehension to be under. Spiritism was indeed a solemn subject to think about in that light. Dreadful, even!

Poor fellow! Little we both thought that before very long he himself . . . However, I could give him no comfort. I was rather appalled myself.

Bunter had also another annoyance that day. A confounded berthing master came on board on some pretence or other, but in reality, Bunter thought, simply impelled by an inconvenient curiosity—inconvenient to Bunter, that is. After some beating about the bush, that man suddenly said:

"I can't help thinking. I've seen you before somewhere, Mr. Mate. If I heard your name, perhaps Bunter—"

That's the worst of a life with a mystery in it—he was much alarmed. It was very likely that the man had seen him before—worse luck to his excellent memory. Bunter himself could not be expected to remember every casual dock walloper he might have had to do with. Bunter brazened it out by turning upon the man, making use of that impressive, black-as-night sternness of expression his unusual hair furnished him with:

"My name's Bunter, sir. Does that enlighten your inquisitive intellect? And I don't ask what your name may be. I don't want to know. I've no use for it, sir. An individual who calmly tells me to my face that he is _not sure_ if he has seen me before, either means to be impudent or is no better than a worm, sir. Yes, I said a worm—a blind worm!"

Brave Bunter. That was the line to take. He fairly drove the beggar out of the ship, as if every word had been a blow. But the pertinacity of that brass-bound Paul Pry was astonishing. He cleared out of the ship, of course, before Bunter's ire, not saying anything, and only trying to cover up his retreat by a sickly smile. But once on the Jetty he turned deliberately round, and set himself to stare in dead earnest at the ship. He remained planted there like a mooring-post, absolutely motionless, and with his stupid eyes winking no more than a pair of cabin portholes.

What could Bunter do? It was awkward for him, you know. He could not go and put his head into the bread-locker. What he did was to take up a position abaft the mizzen-rigging, and stare back as unwinking as the other. So they remained, and I don't know which of them grew giddy first; but the man on the Jetty, not having the advantage of something to hold on to, got tired the soonest, flung his arm, giving the contest up, as it were, and went away at last.

Bunter told me he was glad the *Sapphire*, "that gem amongst ships" as he alluded to her sarcastically, was going to sea next day. He had had enough of the Dock. I understood his impatience. He had steeled himself against any possible worry the voyage might bring, though it is clear enough now that he was not prepared for the extraordinary experience that was awaiting him already, and in no other part of the world than the Indian Ocean itself; the very part of the world where the poor fellow had lost his ship and had broken his luck, as it seemed for good and all, at the same time.

As to his remorse in regard to a certain secret action of his life, well, I understand that a man of Bunter's fine character would suffer not a little. Still, between ourselves, and without the slightest wish to be cynical, it cannot be denied that with the noblest of us the fear of being found out enters for some considerable part into the composition of remorse. I didn't say this in so many words to Bunter, but, as the poor fellow harped a bit on it, I told him that there were skeletons in a good many honest cupboards, and that, as to his own particular guilt, it wasn't writ large on his face for everybody to see—so he needn't worry as to that. And besides, he would be gone to sea in about twelve hours from now.

He said there was some comfort in that thought, and went off then to spend his last evening for many months with his wife. For all his wildness, Bunter had made no mistake in his marrying. He had married a lady. A perfect lady. She was a dear little woman, too. As to her pluck, I, who know what times they had to go through, I cannot admire her enough for it. Real, hard-wearing every day and day after day pluck that only a woman is capable of when she is of the right sort—the undismayed sort I would call it.

The black mate felt this parting with his wife more than any of the previous ones in all the years of bad luck. But she was of the undismayed kind, and showed less trouble in her gentle face than the black-haired, buccaneer-like, but dignified mate of the *Sapphire*. It may be that her conscience was less disturbed than her husband's. Of course, his life had no secret places for her; but a woman's conscience is somewhat more resourceful in finding good and valid excuses. It depends greatly on the person that needs them, too.

They had agreed that she should not come down to the Dock to see him off. "I wonder you care to look at me at all," said the sensitive man. And she did not laugh.

Bunter was very sensitive; he left her rather brusquely at the last. He got on board in good time, and produced the usual impression on the mud-pilot in the broken-down straw hat who took the *Sapphire* out of dock. The river-man was very polite to the dignified, striking-looking chief mate. "The five-inch manilla for the check-rope, Mr.—Bunter, thank you—Mr. Bunter, please." The sea-pilot who left the "gem of ships" heading comfortably down Channel off Dover told some of his friends that, this voyage, the *Sapphire* had for chief mate a man who seemed a jolly sight too good for old Johns. "Bunter's his name. I wonder where he's sprung from? Never seen him before in any ship I piloted in or out all these years. He's the sort of man you don't forget. You couldn't. A thorough good sailor, too. And won't old Johns just worry his head off! Unless the old fool should take fright at him—for he does not seem the sort of man that would let himself be put upon without letting you know what he thinks of you. And that's exactly what old Johns would be more afraid of than of anything else."

As this is really meant to be the record of a spiritualistic experience which came, if not precisely to Captain Johns himself, at any rate to his ship, there is no use in recording the other events of the passage out. It was an ordinary passage, the crew was an ordinary crew, the weather was of the usual kind. The black mate's quiet, sedate method of going to work had given a sober tone to the life of the ship. Even in gales of wind everything went on quietly somehow.

There was only one severe blow which made things fairly lively for all hands for full four-and-twenty hours. That was off the coast of Africa, after passing the Cape of Good Hope. At the very height of it several heavy seas were shipped with no serious results, but there was a considerable smashing of breakable objects in the pantry and in the staterooms. Mr. Bunter, who was so greatly respected on board, found himself treated scurvily by the Southern Ocean, which, bursting open the door of his room like a ruffianly burglar, carried off several useful things, and made all the others extremely wet.

Later, on the same day, the Southern Ocean caused the *Sapphire* to lurch over in such an unrestrained fashion that the two drawers fitted under Mr. Bunter's sleeping-berth flew out altogether, spilling all their contents. They ought, of course, to have been locked, and Mr. Bunter had only to thank himself for what had happened. He ought to have turned the key on each before going out on deck.

His consternation was very great. The steward, who was paddling about all the time with swabs, trying to dry out the flooded cuddy, heard him exclaim "Hallo!" in a startled and dismayed tone. In the midst of his work the steward felt a sympathetic concern for the mate's distress.

Captain Johns was secretly glad when he heard of the damage. He was indeed afraid of his chief mate, as the sea-pilot had ventured to foretell, and afraid of him for the very reason the sea-pilot had put forward as likely.

Captain Johns, therefore, would have liked very much to hold that black mate of his at his mercy in some way or other. But the man was irreproachable, as near absolute perfection as could be. And Captain Johns was much annoyed, and at the same time congratulated himself on his chief officer's efficiency.

He made a great show of living sociably with him, on the principle that the more friendly you are with a man the more easily you may catch him tripping; and also for the reason that he wanted to have somebody who would listen to his stories of manifestations, apparitions, ghosts, and all the rest of the imbecile spook-lore. He had it all at his fingers' ends; and he spun those ghostly yarns in a persistent, colourless voice, giving them a futile turn peculiarly his own.

"I like to converse with my officers," he used to say. "There are masters that hardly ever open their mouths from beginning to end of a passage for fear of losing their dignity. What's that, after all—this bit of position a man holds!"

His sociability was most to be dreaded in the second dog-watch, because he was one of those men who grow lively towards the evening, and the officer on duty was unable then to find excuses for leaving the poop. Captain Johns would pop up the companion suddenly, and, sidling up in his creeping way to poor Bunter, as he walked up and down, would fire into him some spiritualistic proposition, such as:

"Spirits, male and female, show a good deal of refinement in a general way, don't they?"

To which Bunter, holding his black-whiskered head high, would mutter:

"I don't know."

"Ah! that's because you don't want to. You are the most obstinate, prejudiced man I've ever met, Mr. Bunter. I told you you may have any book out of my bookcase. You may just go into my stateroom and help yourself to any volume."

And if Bunter protested that he was too tired in his watches below to spare any time for reading, Captain Johns would smile nastily behind his back, and remark that of course some people needed more sleep than others to keep themselves fit for their work. If Mr. Bunter was afraid of not keeping properly awake when on duty at night, that was another matter.

"But I think you borrowed a novel to read from the second mate the other day—a trashy pack of lies," Captain Johns sighed. "I am afraid you are not a spiritually minded man, Mr. Bunter. That's what's the matter."

Sometimes he would appear on deck in the middle of the night, looking very grotesque and bandy-legged in his sleeping suit. At that sight the persecuted Bunter would wring his hands stealthily, and break out into moisture all over his forehead. After standing sleepily by the binnacle, scratching himself in an unpleasant manner, Captain Johns was sure to start on some aspect or other of his only topic.

He would, for instance, discourse on the improvement of morality to be expected from the establishment of general and close intercourse with the spirits of the departed. The spirits, Captain Johns thought, would consent to associate familiarly with the living if it were not for the unbelief of the great mass of mankind. He himself would not care to have anything to do with a crowd that would not believe in his—Captain Johns'—existence. Then why should a spirit? This was asking too much.

He went on breathing hard by the binnacle and trying to reach round his shoulder-blades; then, with a thick, drowsy severity, declared:

"Incredulity, sir, is the evil of the age!"

It rejected the evidence of Professor Cranks and of the journalist chap. It resisted the production of photographs.

For Captain Johns believed firmly that certain spirits had been photographed. He had read something of it in the papers. And the idea of it having been done had got a tremendous hold on him, because his mind was not critical. Bunter said afterwards that nothing could be more weird than this little man, swathed in a sleeping suit three sizes too large for him, shuffling with excitement in the moonlight near the wheel, and shaking his fist at the serene sea.

"Photographs! photographs!" he would repeat, in a voice as creaky as a rusty hinge.

The very helmsman just behind him got uneasy at that performance, not being capable of understanding exactly what the "old man was kicking up a row with the mate about."

Then Johns, after calming down a bit, would begin again.

"The sensitised plate can't lie. No, sir."

Nothing could be more funny than this ridiculous little man's conviction—his dogmatic tone. Bunter would go on swinging up and down the poop like a deliberate, dignified pendulum. He said not a word. But the poor fellow had not a trifle on his conscience, as you know; and to have imbecile ghosts rammed down his throat like this on top of his own worry nearly drove him crazy. He knew that on many occasions he was on the verge of lunacy, because he could not help indulging in half-delirious visions of Captain Johns being picked up by the scruff of the neck and dropped over the taffrail into the ship's wake—the sort of thing no sane sailorman would think of doing to a cat or any other animal, anyhow. He imagined him bobbing up—a tiny black speck left far astern on the moonlit ocean.

I don't think that even at the worst moments Bunter really desired to drown Captain Johns. I fancy that all his disordered imagination longed for was merely to stop the ghostly inanity of the skipper's talk.

But, all the same, it was a dangerous form of self-indulgence. Just picture to yourself that ship in the Indian Ocean, on a clear, tropical night, with her sails full and still, the watch on deck stowed away out of sight; and on her poop, flooded with moonlight, the stately black mate walking up and down with measured, dignified steps, preserving an awful silence, and that grotesquely mean little figure in striped flannelette alternately creaking and droning of "personal intercourse beyond the grave."

It makes me creepy all over to think of. And sometimes the folly of Captain Johns would appear clothed in a sort of weird utilitarianism. How useful it would be if the spirits of the departed could be induced to take a practical interest in the affairs of the living! What a help, say, to the police, for instance, in the detection of crime! The number of murders, at any rate, would be considerably reduced, he guessed with an air of great sagacity. Then he would give way to grotesque discouragement.

Where was the use of trying to communicate with people that had no faith, and more likely than not would scorn the offered information? Spirits had their feelings. They were *all* feelings in a way. But he was surprised at the forbearance shown towards murderers by their victims. That was the sort of apparition that no guilty man would dare to pooh-pooh. And perhaps the undiscovered murderers—whether believing or not—were haunted. They wouldn't be likely to boast about it, would they?

"For myself," he pursued, in a sort of vindictive, malevolent whine, "if anybody murdered me I would not let him forget it. I would wither him up—I would terrify him to death."

The idea of his skipper's ghost terrifying anyone was so ludicrous that the black mate, little disposed to mirth as he was, could not help giving vent to a weary laugh.

And this laugh, the only acknowledgment of a long and earnest discourse, offended Captain Johns.

"What's there to laugh at in this conceited manner, Mr. Bunter?" he snarled. "Supernatural visitations have terrified better men than you. Don't you allow me enough soul to make a ghost of?"

I think it was the nasty tone that caused Bunter to stop short and turn about.

"I shouldn't wonder," went on the angry fanatic of spiritism, "if you weren't one of them people that take no more account of a man than if he were a beast. You would be capable, I don't doubt, to deny the possession of an immortal soul to your own father."

And then Bunter, being bored beyond endurance, and also exasperated by the private worry, lost his self-possession.

He walked up suddenly to Captain Johns, and, stooping a little to look close into his face, said, in a low, even tone:

"You don't know what a man like me is capable of."

Captain Johns threw his head back, but was too astonished to budge. Bunter resumed his walk; and for a long time his measured footsteps and the low wash of the water alongside were the only sounds which troubled the silence brooding over the great waters. Then Captain Johns cleared his throat uneasily, and, after sidling away towards the companion for greater safety, plucked up enough courage to retreat under an act of authority:

"Raise the starboard clew of the mainsail, and lay the yards dead square, Mr. Bunter. Don't you see the wind is nearly right aft?"

Bunter at once answered "Ay, ay, sir," though there was not the slightest necessity to touch the yards, and the wind was well out on the quarter. While he was executing the order Captain Johns hung on the companion-steps, growling to himself: "Walk this poop like an admiral and don't even notice when the yards want trimming!"—loud enough for the helmsman to overhear. Then he sank slowly backwards out of the man's sight; and when he reached the bottom of the stairs he stood still and thought.

"He's an awful ruffian, with all his gentlemanly airs. No more gentleman mates for me."

Two nights afterwards he was slumbering peacefully in his berth, when a heavy thumping just above his head (a well-understood signal that he was wanted on deck) made him leap out of bed, broad awake in a moment.

"What's up?" he muttered, running out barefooted. On passing through the cabin he glanced at the clock. It was the middle watch. "What on earth can the mate want me for?" he thought.

Bolting out of the companion, he found a clear, dewy moonlit night and a strong, steady breeze. He looked around wildly. There was no one on the poop except the helmsman, who addressed him at once.

"It was me, sir. I let go the wheel for a second to stamp over your head. I am afraid there's something wrong with the mate."

"Where's he got to?" asked the captain sharply.

The man, who was obviously nervous, said:

"The last I saw of him was as he-fell down the port poop-ladder."

"Fell down the poop-ladder! What did he do that for? What made him?"

"I don't know, sir. He was walking the port side. Then just as he turned towards me to come aft . . . "

"You saw him?" interrupted the captain.

"I did. I was looking at him. And I heard the crash, too—something awful. Like the mainmast going overboard. It was as if something had struck him."

Captain Johns became very uneasy and alarmed. "Come," he said sharply. "Did anybody strike him? What did you see?"

"Nothing, sir, so help me! There was nothing to see. He just gave a little sort of hallo! threw his hands before him, and over he went—crash. I couldn't hear anything more, so I just let go the wheel for a second to call you up."

"You're scared!" said Captain Johns. "I am, sir, straight!"

Captain Johns stared at him. The silence of his ship driving on her way seemed to contain a danger—a mystery. He was reluctant to go and look for his mate himself, in the shadows of the main-deck, so quiet, so still.

All he did was to advance to the break of the poop, and call for the watch. As the sleepy men came trooping aft, he shouted to them fiercely:

"Look at the foot of the port poop-ladder, some of you! See the mate lying there?"

Their startled exclamations told him immediately that they did see him. Somebody even screeched out emotionally: "He's dead!"

Mr. Bunter was laid in his bunk and when the lamp in his room was lit he looked indeed as if he were dead, but it was obvious also that he was breathing yet. The steward had been roused out, the second mate called and sent on deck to look after the ship, and for an hour or so Captain Johns devoted himself silently to the restoring of consciousness. Mr. Bunter at last opened his eyes, but he could not speak. He was dazed and inert. The steward bandaged a nasty scalp-wound while Captain Johns held an additional light. They had to cut away a lot of Mr. Bunter's jet-black hair to make a good dressing. This done, and after gazing for a while at their patient, the two left the cabin.

"A rum go, this, steward," said Captain Johns in the passage.

"Yessir."

"A sober man that's right in his head does not fall down a poop-ladder like a sack of potatoes. The ship's as steady as a church."

"Yessir. Fit of some kind, I shouldn't wonder."

"Well, I should. He doesn't look as if he were subject to fits and giddiness. Why, the man's in the prime of life. I wouldn't have another kind of mate—not if I knew it. You don't think he has a private store of liquor, do you, eh? He seemed to me a bit strange in his manner several times lately. Off his feed, too, a bit, I noticed."

"Well, sir, if he ever had a bottle or two of grog in his cabin, that must have gone a long time ago. I saw him throw some broken glass overboard after the last gale we had; but that didn't amount to anything. Anyway, sir, you couldn't call Mr. Bunter a drinking man."

"No," conceded the captain, reflectively. And the steward, locking the pantry door, tried to escape out of the passage, thinking he could manage to snatch another hour of sleep before it was time for him to turn out for the day.

Captain Johns shook his head.

"There's some mystery there."

"There's special Providence that he didn't crack his head like an eggshell on the quarter-deck mooring-bits, sir. The men tell me he couldn't have missed them by more than an inch."

And the steward vanished skilfully.

Captain Johns spent the rest of the night and the whole of the ensuing day between his own room and that of the mate.

In his own room he sat with his open hands reposing on his knees, his lips pursed up, and the horizontal furrows on his forehead marked very heavily. Now and then raising his arm by a slow, as if cautious movement, he scratched lightly the top of his bald head. In the mate's room he stood for long periods of time with his hand to his lips, gazing at the half-conscious man.

For three days Mr. Bunter did not say a single word. He looked at people sensibly enough but did not seem to be able to hear any questions put to him. They cut off some more of his hair and swathed his head in wet cloths. He took some nourishment, and was made as comfortable as possible. At dinner on the third day the second mate remarked to the captain, in connection with the affair:

"These half-round brass plates on the steps of the poop-ladders are beastly dangerous things!"

"Are they?" retorted Captain Johns, sourly. "It takes more than a brass plate to account for an able-bodied man crashing down in this fashion like a felled ox."

The second mate was impressed by that view. There was something in that, he thought.

"And the weather fine, everything dry, and the ship going along as steady as a church!" pursued Captain Johns, gruffly.

As Captain Johns continued to look extremely sour, the second mate did not open his lips any more during the dinner. Captain Johns was annoyed and hurt by an innocent remark, because the fitting of the aforesaid brass plates had been done at his suggestion only the voyage before, in order to smarten up the appearance of the poop-ladders.

On the fourth day Mr. Bunter looked decidedly better; very languid yet, of course, but he heard and understood what was said to him, and even could say a few words in a feeble voice.

Captain Johns, coming in, contemplated him attentively, without much visible sympathy.

"Well, can you give us your account of this accident, Mr. Bunter?"

Bunter moved slightly his bandaged head, and fixed his cold blue stare on Captain Johns' face, as if taking stock and appraising the value of every feature;

the perplexed forehead, the credulous eyes, the inane droop of the mouth. And he gazed so long that Captain Johns grew restive, and looked over his shoulder at the door.

"No accident," breathed out Bunter, in a peculiar tone.

"You don't mean to say you've got the falling sickness," said Captain Johns. "How would you call it signing as chief mate of a clipper ship with a thing like that on you?"

Bunter answered him only by a sinister look. The skipper shuffled his feet a little.

"Well, what made you have that tumble, then?"

Bunter raised himself a little, and, looking straight into Captain Johns' eyes said, in a very distinct whisper:

"You—were—right!"

He fell back and closed his eyes. Not a word more could Captain Johns get out of him; and, the steward coming into the cabin, the skipper withdrew.

But that very night, unobserved, Captain Johns, opening the door cautiously, entered again the mate's cabin. He could wait no longer. The suppressed eagerness, the excitement expressed in all his mean, creeping little person, did not escape the chief mate, who was lying awake, looking frightfully pulled down and perfectly impassive.

"You are coming to gloat over me, I suppose," said Bunter without moving, and yet making a palpable hit.

"Bless my soul!" exclaimed Captain Johns with a start, and assuming a sobered demeanour. "There's a thing to say!"

"Well, gloat, then! You and your ghosts, you've managed to get over a live man."

This was said by Bunter without stirring, in a low voice, and with not much expression.

"Do you mean to say," inquired Captain Johns, in an awe-struck whisper, "that you had a supernatural experience that night? You saw an apparition, then, on board my ship?"

Reluctance, shame, disgust, would have been visible on poor Bunter's countenance if the great part of it had not been swathed up in cotton-wool and bandages. His ebony eyebrows, more sinister than ever amongst all that lot of white linen, came together in a frown as he made a mighty effort to say:

"Yes, I have seen."

The wretchedness in his eyes would have awakened the compassion of any other man than Captain Johns. But Captain Johns was all agog with triumphant

excitement. He was just a little bit frightened, too. He looked at that unbeliev-
ing scoffer laid low, and did not even dimly guess at his profound, humiliating
distress. He was not generally capable of taking much part in the anguish of
his fellow-creatures. This time, moreover, he was excessively anxious to know
what had happened. Fixing his credulous eyes on the bandaged head, he asked,
trembling slightly:

"And did it—did it knock you down?"

"Come! am I the sort of man to be knocked down by a ghost?" protested
Bunter in a little stronger tone. "Don't you remember what you said yourself the
other night? Better men than me—Ha! you'll have to look a long time before
you find a better man for a mate of your ship."

Captain Johns pointed a solemn finger at Bunter's bedplace.

"You've been terrified," he said. "That's what's the matter. You've been
terrified. Why, even the man at the wheel was scared, though he couldn't see
anything. He *felt* the supernatural. You are punished for your incredulity, Mr.
Bunter. You were terrified."

"And suppose I was," said Bunter. "Do you know what I had seen? Can
you conceive the sort of ghost that would haunt a man like me? Do you think
it was a ladyish, afternoon call, another-cup-of-tea-please apparition that visits
your Professor Cranks and that journalist chap you are always talking about?
No; I can't tell you what it was like. Every man has his own ghosts. You couldn't
conceive . . . "

Bunter stopped, out of breath; and Captain Johns remarked, with the glow
of inward satisfaction reflected in his tone:

"I've always thought you were the sort of man that was ready for anything;
from pitch-and-toss to wilful murder, as the saying goes. Well, well! So you were
terrified."

"I stepped back," said Bunter, curtly. "I don't remember anything else."

"The man at the wheel told me you went backwards as if something had
hit you."

"It was a sort of inward blow," explained Bunter. "Something too deep for
you, Captain Johns, to understand. Your life and mine haven't been the same.
Aren't you satisfied to see me converted?"

"And you can't tell me any more?" asked Captain Johns, anxiously.

"No, I can't. I wouldn't. It would be no use if I did. That sort of experience
must be gone through. Say I am being punished. Well, I take my punishment,
but talk of it I won't."

"Very well," said Captain Johns; "you won't. But, mind, I can draw my own conclusions from that."

"Draw what you like; but be careful what you say, sir. You don't terrify me. You aren't a ghost."

"One word. Has it any connection with what you said to me on that last night, when we had a talk together on spiritualism?"

Bunter looked weary and puzzled.

"What did I say?"

"You told me that I couldn't know what a man like you was capable of."

"Yes, yes. Enough!"

"Very good. I am fixed, then," remarked Captain Johns. "All I say is that I am jolly glad not to be you, though I would have given almost anything for the privilege of personal communication with the world of spirits. Yes, sir, but not in that way."

Poor Bunter moaned pitifully.

"It has made me feel twenty years older."

Captain Johns retired quietly. He was delighted to observe this overbearing ruffian humbled to the dust by the moralizing agency of the spirits. The whole occurrence was a source of pride and gratification; and he began to feel a sort of regard for his chief mate.

It is true that in further interviews Bunter showed himself very mild and deferential. He seemed to cling to his captain for spiritual protection. He used to send for him, and say, "I feel so nervous," and Captain Johns would stay patiently for hours in the hot little cabin, and feel proud of the call.

For Mr. Bunter was ill, and could not leave his berth for a good many days. He became a convinced spiritualist, not enthusiastically—that could hardly have been expected from him—but in a grim, unshakable way. He could not be called exactly friendly to the disembodied inhabitants of our globe, as Captain Johns was. But he was now a firm, if gloomy, recruit of spiritualism.

One afternoon, as the ship was already well to the north in the Gulf of Bengal, the steward knocked at the door of the captain's cabin, and said, without opening it:

"The mate asks if you could spare him a moment, sir. He seems to be in a state in there."

Captain Johns jumped up from the couch at once.

"Yes. Tell him I am coming."

He thought: Could it be possible there had been another spiritual manifestation—in the daytime, too!

He revelled in the hope. It was not exactly that, however. Still, Bunter, whom he saw sitting collapsed in a chair—he had been up for several days, but not on deck as yet—poor Bunter had something startling enough to communicate. His hands covered his face. His legs were stretched straight out, dismally.

"What's the news now?" croaked Captain Johns, not unkindly, because in truth it always pleased him to see Bunter—as he expressed it—tamed.

"News!" exclaimed the crushed sceptic through his iands. "Ay, news enough, Captain Johns. Who will be able to deny the awfulness, the genuineness? Another man would have dropped dead. You want to know what I had seen. All I can tell you is that since I've seen it my hair is turning white."

Bunter detached his hands from his face, and they hung on each side of his chair as if dead. He looked broken in the dusky cabin.

"You don't say!" stammered out Captain Johns. "Turned white! Hold on a bit! I'll light the lamp!"

When the lamp was lit, the startling phenomenon could be seen plainly enough. As if the dread, the horror, the anguish of the supernatural were being exhaled through the pores of his skin, a sort of silvery mist seemed to cling to the cheeks and the head of the mate. His short beard, his cropped hair, were growing, not black, but gray—almost white.

When Mr. Bunter, thin-faced and shaky, came on deck for duty, he was clean-shaven, and his head was white. The hands were awe-struck. "Another man," they whispered to each other. It was generally and mysteriously agreed that the mate had "seen something," with the exception of the man at the wheel at the time, who maintained that the mate was "struck by something."

This distinction hardly amounted to a difference. On the other hand, everybody admitted that, after he picked up his strength a bit, he seemed even smarter in his movements than before.

One day in Calcutta, Captain Johns, pointing out to a visitor his white-headed chief mate standing by the main-hatch, was heard to say oracularly:

"That man's in the prime of life."

Of course, while Bunter was away, I called regularly on Mrs. Bunter every Saturday, just to see whether she had any use for my services. It was understood I would do that. She had just his half-pay to live on—it amounted to about a pound a week. She had taken one room in a quiet little square in the East End.

And this was affluence to what I had heard that the couple were reduced to for a time after Bunter had to give up the Western Ocean trade—he used to go as mate of all sorts of hard packets after he lost his ship and his luck together—it was affluence to that time when Bunter would start at seven o'clock in the morning with but a glass of hot water and a crust of dry bread. It won't stand thinking about, especially for those who know Mrs. Bunter. I had seen something of them, too, at that time; and it just makes me shudder to remember what that born lady had to put up with. Enough!

Dear Mrs. Bunter used to worry a good deal after the _Sapphire_ left for Calcutta. She would say to me: "It must be so awful for poor Winston"—Winston is Bunter's name—and I tried to comfort her the best I could. Afterwards, she got some small children to teach in a family, and was half the day with them, and the occupation was good for her.

In the very first letter she had from Calcutta, Bunter told her he had had a fall down the poop-ladder, and cut his head, but no bones broken, thank God. That was all. Of course, she had other letters from him, but that vagabond Bunter never gave me a scratch of the pen the solid eleven months. I supposed, naturally, that everything was going on all right. Who could imagine what was happening?

Then one day dear Mrs. Bunter got a letter from a legal firm in the City, advising her that her uncle was dead—her old curmudgeon of an uncle—a retired stockbroker, a heartless, petrified antiquity that had lasted on and on. He was nearly ninety, I believe; and if I were to meet his venerable ghost this minute, I would try to take him by the throat and strangle him.

The old beast would never forgive his niece for marrying Bunter; and years afterwards, when people made a point of letting him know that she was in London, pretty nearly starving at forty years of age, he only said: "Serve the little fool right!" I believe he meant her to starve. And, lo and behold, the old cannibal died intestate, with no other relatives but that very identical little fool. The Bunters were wealthy people now.

Of course, Mrs. Bunter wept as if her heart would break. In any other woman it would have been mere hypocrisy. Naturally, too, she wanted to cable the news to her Winston in Calcutta, but I showed her, *Gazette* in hand, that the ship was on the homeward-bound list for more than a week already. So we sat down to wait, and talked meantime of dear old Winston every day. There were just one hundred such days before the *Sapphire* got reported "All well" in the chops of the Channel by an incoming mailboat.

"I am going to Dunkirk to meet him," says she. The *Sapphire* had a cargo of jute for Dunkirk. Of course, I had to escort the dear lady in the quality of her "ingenious friend." She calls me "our ingenious friend" to this day; and I've observed some people—strangers—looking hard at me, for the signs of the ingenuity, I suppose.

After settling Mrs. Bunter in a good hotel in Dunkirk, I walked down to the docks—late afternoon it was—and what was my surprise to see the ship actually fast alongside. Either Johns or Bunter, or both, must have been driving her hard up Channel. Anyway, she had been in since the day before last, and her crew was already paid off. I met two of her apprenticed boys going off home on leave with their dunnage on a Frenchman's barrow, as happy as larks, and I asked them if the mate was on board.

"There he is, on the quay, looking at the moorings," says one of the youngsters as he skipped past me.

You may imagine the shock to my feelings when I beheld his white head. I could only manage to tell him that his wife was at an hotel in town. He left me at once, to go and get his hat on board. I was mightily surprised by the smartness of his movements as he hurried up the gangway.

Whereas the black mate struck people as deliberate, and strangely stately in his gait for a man in the prime of life, this white-headed chap seemed the most wonderfully alert of old men. I don't suppose Bunter was any quicker on his pins than before. It was the colour of the hair that made all the difference in one's judgment.

The same with his eyes. Those eyes, that looked at you so steely, so fierce, and so fascinating out of a bush of a buccaneer's black hair, now had an innocent almost boyish expression in their good-humoured brightness under those white eyebrows.

I led him without any delay into Mrs. Bunter's private sitting-room. After she had dropped a tear over the late cannibal, given a hug to her Winston, and told him that he must grow his moustache again, the dear lady tucked her feet upon the sofa, and I got out of Bunter's way.

He started at once to pace the room, waving his long arms. He worked himself into a regular frenzy, and tore Johns limb from limb many times over that evening.

"Fell down? Of course I fell down, by slipping backwards on that fool's patent brass plates. 'Pon my word, I had been walking that poop in charge of the ship, and I didn't know whether I was in the Indian Ocean or in the moon.

I was crazy. My head spun round and round with sheer worry. I had made my last application of your chemist's wonderful stuff." (This to me.) "All the store of bottles you gave me got smashed when those drawers fell out in the last gale. I had been getting some dry things to change, when I heard the cry: 'All hands on deck!' and made one jump of it, without even pushing them in properly. Ass! When I came back and saw the broken glass and the mess, I felt ready to faint.

"No; look here—deception is bad; but not to be able to keep it up after one has been forced into it. You know that since I've been squeezed out of the Western Ocean packets by younger men, just on account of my grizzled muzzle—you know how much chance I had to ever get a ship. And not a soul to turn to. We have been a lonely couple, we two—she threw away everything for me—and to see her want a piece of dry bread—"

He banged with his fist fit to split the Frenchman's table in two.

"I would have turned a sanguinary pirate for her, let alone cheating my way into a berth by dyeing my hair. So when you came to me with your chemist's wonderful stuff—"

He checked himself.

"By the way, that fellow's got a fortune when he likes to pick it up. It is a wonderful stuff—you tell him salt water can do nothing to it. It stays on as long as your hair will."

"All right," I said. "Go on."

Thereupon he went for Johns again with a fury that frightened his wife, and made me laugh till I cried.

"Just you try to think what it would have meant to be at the mercy of the meanest creature that ever commanded a ship! Just fancy what a life that crawling Johns would have led me! And I knew that in a week or so the white hair would begin to show. And the crew. Did you ever think of that? To be shown up as a low fraud before all hands. What a life for me till we got to Calcutta! And once there—kicked out, of course. Half-pay stopped. Annie here alone without a penny—starving; and I on the other side of the earth, ditto. You see?

"I thought of shaving twice a day. But could I shave my head, too? No way—no way at all. Unless I dropped Johns overboard; and even then—

"Do you wonder now that with all these things boiling in my head I didn't know where I was putting down my foot that night? I just felt myself falling—then crash, and all dark.

"When I came to myself that bang on the head seemed to have steadied my wits somehow. I was so sick of everything that for two days I wouldn't speak to anyone. They thought it was a slight concussion of the brain. Then the idea dawned upon me as I was looking at that ghost-ridden, wretched fool. 'Ah, you love ghosts,' I thought. 'Well, you shall have something from beyond the grave.'

"I didn't even trouble to invent a story. I couldn't imagine a ghost if I wanted to. I wasn't fit to lie connectedly if I had tried. I just bulled him on to it. Do you know, he got, quite by himself, a notion that at some time or other I had done somebody to death in some way, and that—"

"Oh, the horrible man!" cried Mrs. Bunter from the sofa. There was a silence.

"And didn't he bore my head off on the home passage!" began Bunter again in a weary voice. "He loved me. He was proud of me. I was converted. I had had a manifestation. Do you know what he was after? He wanted me and him 'to make a *seance*,' in his own words, and to try to call up that ghost (the one that had turned my hair white—the ghost of my supposed victim), and, as he said, talk it over with him—the ghost—in a friendly way.

"'Or else, Bunter,' he says, 'you may get another manifestation when you least expect it, and tumble overboard perhaps, or something. You ain't really safe till we pacify the spirit-world in some way.'

"Can you conceive a lunatic like that? No—say?"

I said nothing. But Mrs. Bunter did, in a very decided tone.

"Winston, I don't want you to go on board that ship again any more."

"My dear," says he, "I have all my things on board yet."

"You don't want the things. Don't go near that ship at all."

He stood still; then, dropping his eyes with a faint smile, said slowly, in a dreamy voice:

"The haunted ship."

"And your last," I added.

We carried him off, as he stood, by the night train. He was very quiet; but crossing the Channel, as we two had a smoke on deck, he turned to me suddenly, and, grinding his teeth, whispered:

"He'll never know how near he was being dropped overboard!"

He meant Captain Johns. I said nothing.

But Captain Johns, I understand, made a great to-do about the disappearance of his chief mate. He set the French police scouring the country for the body. In the end, I fancy he got word from his owners' office to drop all this fuss—that it was all right. I don't suppose he ever understood anything of that mysterious occurrence.

To this day he tries at times (he's retired now, and his conversation is not very coherent)—he tries to tell the story of a black mate he once had, "a murderous, gentlemanly ruffian, with raven-black hair which turned white all at once in consequence of a manifestation from beyond the grave." An avenging apparition. What with reference to black and white hair, to poop-ladders, and to his own feelings and views, it is difficult to make head or tail of it. If his sister (she's very vigorous still) should be present she cuts all this short—peremptorily:

"Don't you mind what he says. He's got devils on the brain."

# A TOUGH TUSSLE

## AMBROSE BIERCE

One night in the autumn of 1861 a man sat alone in the heart of a forest in western Virginia. The region was one of the wildest on the continent—the Cheat Mountain country. There was no lack of people close at hand, however; within a mile of where the man sat was the now silent camp of a whole Federal brigade. Somewhere about—it might be still nearer—was a force of the enemy, the numbers unknown.

It was this uncertainty as to its numbers and position that accounted for the man's presence in that lonely spot; he was a young officer of a Federal infantry regiment and his business there was to guard his sleeping comrades in the camp against a surprise. He was in command of a detachment of men constituting a picket-guard. These men he had stationed just at nightfall in an irregular line, determined by the nature of the ground, several hundred yards in front of where he now sat. The line ran through the forest, among the rocks and laurel thickets, the men fifteen or twenty paces apart, all in concealment and under injunction of strict silence and unremitting vigilance. In four hours, if nothing occurred, they would be relieved by a fresh detachment from the reserve now resting in care of its captain some distance away to the left and rear. Before stationing his men the young officer of whom we are writing had pointed out to his two sergeants the spot at which he would be found if it should be necessary to consult him, or if his presence at the front line should be required.

It was a quiet enough spot—the fork of an old wood-road, on the two branches of which, prolonging themselves deviously forward in the dim moonlight, the sergeants were themselves stationed, a few paces at the rear of the line. If driven sharply back by a sudden onset of the enemy and pickets are not expected to make a stand after firing the men would come into the converging roads and naturally following them to their point of intersection could be rallied and "formed." In his small way the author of these dispositions was something of a strategist; if Napoleon had planned as intelligently at Waterloo he would have won that memorable battle and been overthrown later.

Second-Lieutenant Brainerd Byring was a brave and efficient officer, young and comparatively inexperienced as he was in the business of killing his fellow-men. He had enlisted in the very first days of the war as a private, with no military knowledge whatever, had been made first-sergeant of his company on account of his education and engaging manner, and had been lucky enough to lose his captain by a Confederate bullet; in the resulting promotions he had gained a commission. He had been in several engagements, such as they were— at Philippi, Rich Mountain, Carrick's Ford and Greenbrier—and had borne himself with such gallantry as not to attract the attention of his superior officers.

The exhilaration of battle was agreeable to him, but the sight of the dead, with their clay faces, blank eyes and stiff bodies, which when not unnaturally shrunken were unnaturally swollen, had always intolerably affected him. He felt towards them a kind of reasonless antipathy that was something more than the physical and spiritual repugnance common to us all. Doubtless this feeling was due to his unusually acute sensibilities—his keen sense of the beautiful, which these hideous things outraged. Whatever may have been the cause, he could not look upon a dead body without a loathing which had in it an element of resentment. What others have respected as the dignity of death had to him no existence—was altogether unthinkable. Death was a thing to be hated. It was not picturesque, it had no tender and solemn side—a dismal thing, hideous in all its manifestations and suggestions. Lieutenant Byring was a braver man than anybody knew, for nobody knew his horror of that which he was ever ready to incur.

Having posted his men, instructed his sergeants and retired to his station, he seated himself on a log, and with senses all alert began his vigil. For greater ease he loosened his sword-belt and taking his heavy revolver from his holster laid it on the log beside him. He felt very comfortable, though he hardly gave the fact a thought, so intently did he listen for any sound from the front which might have a menacing significance—a shout, a shot, or the footfall of one of his sergeants coming to apprise him of something worth knowing. From the vast, invisible ocean of moonlight overhead fell, here and there, a slender, broken stream that seemed to plash against the intercepting branches and trickle to earth, forming small white pools among the clumps of laurel. But these leaks were few and served only to accentuate the blackness of his environment, which his imagination found it easy to people with all manner of unfamiliar shapes, menacing, uncanny, or merely grotesque.

He to whom the portentous conspiracy of night and solitude and silence in the heart of a great forest is not an unknown experience needs not to be told what another world it all is—how even the most commonplace and familiar objects take on another character. The trees group themselves differently; they draw closer together, as if in fear. The very silence has another quality than the silence of the day. And it is full of half-heard whispers—whispers that startle—ghosts of sounds long dead. There are living sounds, too, such as are never heard under other conditions: notes of strange night-birds, the cries of small animals in sudden encounters with stealthy foes or in their dreams, a rustling in the dead leaves—it may be the leap of a wood-rat, it may be the footfall of a panther. What caused the breaking of that twig?—what the low, alarmed twittering in that bushful of birds? There are sounds without a name, forms without substance, translations in space of objects which have not been seen to move, movements wherein nothing is observed to change its place. Ah, children of the sunlight and the gaslight, how little you know of the world in which you live!

Surrounded at a little distance by armed and watchful friends, Byring felt utterly alone. Yielding himself to the solemn and mysterious spirit of the time and place, he had forgotten the nature of his connection with the visible and audible aspects and phases of the night. The forest was boundless; men and the habitations of men did not exist. The universe was one primeval mystery of darkness, without form and void, himself the sole, dumb questioner of its eternal secret. Absorbed in thoughts born of this mood, he suffered the time to slip away unnoted.

Meantime the infrequent patches of white light lying amongst the tree-trunks had undergone changes of size, form and place. In one of them near by, just at the roadside, his eye fell upon an object that he had not previously observed. It was almost before his face as he sat; he could have sworn that it had not before been there. It was partly covered in shadow, but he could see that it was a human figure. Instinctively he adjusted the clasp of his sword-belt and laid hold of his pistol—again he was in a world of war, by occupation an assassin.

The figure did not move. Rising, pistol in hand, he approached. The figure lay upon its back, its upper part in shadow, but standing above it and looking down upon the face, he saw that it was a dead body. He shrugged and turned from it with a feeling of sickness and disgust, resumed his seat upon the log, and forgetting military prudence struck a match and lit a cigar. In the sudden blackness that followed the extinction of the flame he felt a sense of relief; he could no longer see the object of his aversion. Nevertheless, he kept his eyes set in that direction until it appeared again with growing distinctness. It seemed to have moved a trifle nearer.

"Damn the thing!" he muttered. "What does it want?"

It did not appear to be in need of anything but a soul.

Byring turned away his eyes and began humming a tune, but he broke off in the middle of a bar and looked at the dead body. Its presence annoyed him, though he could hardly have had a quieter neighbour. He was conscious, too, of a vague, indefinable feeling that was new to him. It was not fear, but rather a sense of the supernatural—in which he did not at all believe.

"I have inherited it," he said to himself. "I suppose it will require a thousand ages—perhaps ten thousand—for humanity to outgrow this feeling. Where and when did it originate? Away back, probably, in what is called the cradle of the human race—the plains of Central Asia. What we inherit as a superstition our barbarous ancestors must have held as a reasonable conviction. Doubtless they believed themselves justified by facts whose nature we cannot even conjecture in thinking a dead body a malign thing endowed with some strange power of mischief, with perhaps a will and a purpose to exert it. Possibly they had some awful form of religion of which that was one of the chief doctrines, sedulously taught by their priesthood, as ours teach the immortality of the soul. As the Aryans moved slowly on, to and through the Caucasus passes, and spread over Europe, new conditions of life must have resulted in the formulation of new religions. The old belief in the malevolence of the dead body was lost from the creeds and even perished from tradition, but it left its heritage of terror, which is transmitted from generation to generation—is as much a part of us as are our blood and bones."

In following out his thought he had forgotten that which suggested it; but now his eye fell again upon the corpse. The shadow had now altogether uncovered it. He saw the sharp profile, the chin in the air, the whole face, ghastly white in the moonlight. The clothing was grey, the uniform of a Confederate soldier. The coat and waistcoat, unbuttoned, had fallen away on each side, exposing the white shirt. The chest seemed unnaturally prominent, but the abdomen had sunk in, leaving a sharp projection at the line of the lower ribs. The arms were extended, the left knee was thrust upward. The whole posture impressed Byring as having been studied with a view to the horrible.

"Bah!" he exclaimed; "he was an actor—he knows how to be dead."

He drew away his eyes, directing them resolutely along one of the roads leading to the front, and resumed his philosophising where he had left off.

"It may be that our Central Asian ancestors had not the custom of burial. In that case it is easy to understand their fear of the dead, who really were a menace and an evil. They bred pestilences. Children were taught to avoid the places where they lay and to run away if by inadvertence they came near a corpse. I think, indeed, I'd better go away from this chap."

He half rose to do so, then remembered that he had told his men in front and the officer in the rear who was to relieve him that he could at any time be found at that spot. It was a matter of pride, too. If he abandoned his post he feared they would think he feared the corpse. He was no coward and he was unwilling to incur anybody's ridicule. So he again seated himself, and to prove his courage looked boldly at the body. The right arm—the one farthest from him—was now in shadow. He could barely see the hand which, he had before observed, lay at the root of a clump of laurel. There had been no change, a fact which gave him a certain comfort, he could not have said why. He did not at once remove his eyes; that which we do not wish to see has a strange fascination, sometimes irresistible. Of the woman who covers her eyes with her hands and looks between the fingers let it be said that the wits have dealt with her not altogether justly.

Byring suddenly became conscious of a pain in his right hand. He withdrew his eyes from his enemy and looked at it. He was grasping the hilt of his drawn sword so tightly that it hurt him. He observed, too, that he was leaning forward in a strained attitude—crouching like a gladiator ready to spring at the throat of an antagonist. His teeth were clenched and he was breathing hard. This matter was soon set right, and as his muscles relaxed and he drew a long breath he felt keenly enough the ludicrousness of the incident. It affected him to laughter. Heavens! what sound was that? what mindless devil was uttering an unholy glee in mockery of human merriment? He sprang to his feet and looked about him, not recognising his own laugh.

He could no longer conceal from himself the horrible fact of his cowardice; he was thoroughly frightened! He would have run from the spot, but his legs refused their office; they gave way beneath him and he sat again upon the log, violently trembling. His face was wet, his whole body bathed in a chill perspiration. He could not even cry out. Distinctly he heard behind him a stealthy tread, as of some wild animal, and dared not look over his shoulder. Had the soulless living joined forces with the soulless dead?—was it an animal? Ah, if he could but be assured of that! But by no effort of will could he now unfix his gaze from the face of the dead man.

I repeat that Lieutenant Byring was a brave and intelligent man. But what would you have? Shall a man cope, single-handed, with so monstrous an alliance as that of night and solitude and silence and the dead—while an incalculable host of his own ancestors shriek into the ear of his spirit their coward counsel, sing their doleful death-songs in his heart, and disarm his very blood of all its iron? The odds are too great—courage was not made for so rough use as that.

One sole conviction now had the man in possession: that the body had moved. It lay nearer to the edge of its plot of light—there could be no doubt of it. It had also moved its arms, for, look, they are both in the shadow! A breath of cold air struck Byring full in the face; the boughs of trees above him stirred and moaned. A strongly defined shadow passed across the face of the dead, left it luminous, passed back upon it and left it half obscured. The horrible thing was visibly moving! At that moment a single shot rang out upon the picket-line— a lonelier and louder, though more distant, shot than ever had been heard by mortal ear! It broke the spell of that enchanted man; it slew the silence and the solitude, dispersed the hindering host from Central Asia and released his modern manhood. With a cry like that of some great bird pouncing upon its prey he sprang forward, hot-hearted for action!

Shot after shot now came from the front. There were shoutings and confusion, hoof-beats and desultory cheers. Away to the rear, in the sleeping camp, were a singing of bugles and grumble of drums. Pushing through the thickets on either side the roads came the Federal pickets, in full retreat, firing backward at random as they ran. A straggling group that had followed back one of the roads, as instructed, suddenly sprang away into the bushes as half a hundred horsemen thundered by them, striking wildly with their sabres as they passed. At headlong speed these mounted madmen shot past the spot where Byring had sat, and vanished round an angle of the road, shouting and firing their pistols. A moment later there was a roar of musketry, followed by dropping shots—they had encountered the reserve guard in line; and back they came in dire confusion, with here and there an empty saddle and many a maddened horse, bullet-stung, snorting and plunging with pain. It was all over—"an affair of outposts."

The line was re-established with fresh men, the roll called, the stragglers were re-formed. The Federal commander with a part of his staff, imperfectly clad, appeared upon the scene, asked a few questions, looked exceedingly wise and retired. After standing at arms for an hour the brigade in camp "swore a prayer or two" and went to bed.

Early the next morning a fatigue-party, commanded by a captain and accompanied by a surgeon, searched the ground for dead and wounded. At the fork of the road, a little to one side, they found two bodies lying close together— that of a Federal officer and that of a Confederate private. The officer had died of a sword-thrust through the heart, but not, apparently, until he had inflicted upon his enemy no fewer than five dreadful wounds. The dead officer lay on his face in a pool of blood, the weapon still in his breast. They turned him on his back and the surgeon removed it.

"Gad!" said the captain—"it is Byring!" adding, with a glance at the other, "they had a tough tussle."

The surgeon was examining the sword. It was that of a line officer of Federal infantry—exactly like the one worn by the captain. It was, in fact, Byring's own. The only other weapon discovered was an undischarged revolver in the dead officer's belt.

The surgeon laid down the sword and approached the other body. It was frightfully gashed and stabbed, but there was no blood. He took hold of the left foot and tried to straighten the leg. In the effort the body was displaced. The dead do not wish to be moved—it protested with a faint, sickening odour. Where it had lain were a few maggots, manifesting an imbecile activity.

The surgeon looked at the captain. The captain looked at the surgeon.

# NAPOLEON AND THE SPECTRE
## CHARLOTTE BRONTË

Well, as I was saying, the Emperor got into bed.

'Chevalier,' says he to his valet, 'let down those window-curtains, and shut the casement before you leave the room.'

Chevalier did as he was told, and then, taking up his candlestick, departed.

In a few minutes the Emperor felt his pillow becoming rather hard, and he got up to shake it. As he did so a slight rustling noise was heard near the bed-head. His Majesty listened, but all was silent as he lay down again.

Scarcely had he settled into a peaceful attitude of repose, when he was disturbed by a sensation of thirst. Lifting himself on his elbow, he took a glass of lemonade from the small stand which was placed beside him. He refreshed himself by a deep draught. As he returned the goblet to its station a deep groan burst from a kind of closet in one corner of the apartment.

'Who's there?' cried the Emperor, seizing his pistols. 'Speak, or I'll blow your brains out.'

This threat produced no other effect than a short, sharp laugh, and a dead silence followed.

The Emperor started from his couch, and, hastily throwing on a *robe-de-chambre* which hung over the back of a chair, stepped courageously to the haunted closet. As he opened the door something rustled. He sprang forward sword in hand. No soul or even substance appeared, and the rustling, it was evident, proceeded from the falling of a cloak, which had been suspended by a peg from the door.

Half ashamed of himself he returned to bed.

Just as he was about once more to close his eyes, the light of the three wax tapers, which burned in a silver branch over the mantelpiece, was suddenly darkened. He looked up. A black, opaque shadow obscured it. Sweating with terror, the Emperor put out his hand to seize the bell-rope, but some invisible being snatched it rudely from his grasp, and at the same instant the ominous shade vanished.

'Pooh!' exclaimed Napoleon, 'it was but an ocular delusion.'

'Was it?' whispered a hollow voice, in deep mysterious tones, close to his ear. 'Was it a delusion, Emperor of France? No! all thou hast heard and seen is sad forewarning reality. Rise, lifter of the Eagle Standard! Awake, swayer of the Lily Sceptre! Follow me, Napoleon, and thou shalt see more.'

As the voice ceased, a form dawned on his astonished sight. It was that of a tall, thin man, dressed in a blue surtout edged with gold lace. It wore a black cravat very tightly round its neck, and confined by two little sticks placed behind each ear. The countenance was livid; the tongue protruded from between the teeth, and the eyes all glazed and bloodshot started with frightful prominence from their sockets.

'Mon *Dieu!*' exclaimed the Emperor, 'what do I see? Spectre, whence cometh thou?'

The apparition spoke not, but gliding forward beckoned Napoleon with uplifted finger to follow.

Controlled by a mysterious influence, which deprived him of the capability of either thinking or acting for himself, he obeyed in silence.

The solid wall of the apartment fell open as they approached, and, when both had passed through, it closed behind them with a noise like thunder.

They would now have been in total darkness had it not been for a dim light which shone round the ghost and revealed the damp walls of a long, vaulted passage. Down this they proceeded with mute rapidity. Ere long a cool, refreshing breeze, which rushed wailing up the vault and caused the Emperor to wrap his loose nightdress closer round, announced their approach to the open air.

This they soon reached, and Nap found himself in one of the principal streets of Paris.

'Worthy Spirit,' said he, shivering in the chill night air, 'permit me to return and put on some additional clothing. I will be with you again presently.'

'Forward,' replied his companion sternly.

He felt compelled, in spite of the rising indignation which almost choked him, to obey.

On they went through the deserted streets till they arrived at a lofty house built on the banks of the Seine. Here the Spectre stopped, the gates rolled back to receive them, and they entered a large marble hall which was partly concealed by a curtain drawn across, through the half transparent folds of which a bright light might be seen burning with dazzling lustre. A row of fine female figures, richly attired, stood before this screen. They wore on their heads garlands of the most beautiful flowers, but their faces were concealed by ghastly masks representing death's-heads.

'What is all this mummery?' cried the Emperor, making an effort to shake off the mental shackles by which he was so unwillingly restrained, 'Where am I, and why have I been brought here?'

'Silence,' said the guide, lolling out still further his black and bloody tongue. 'Silence, if thou wouldst escape instant death.'

The Emperor would have replied, his natural courage overcoming the temporary awe to which he had at first been subjected, but just then a strain of wild, supernatural music swelled behind the huge curtain, which waved to and fro, and bellied slowly out as if agitated by some internal commotion or battle of waving winds. At the same moment an overpowering mixture of the scents of mortal corruption, blent with the richest Eastern odours, stole through the haunted hall.

A murmur of many voices was now heard at a distance, and something grasped his arm eagerly from behind.

He turned hastily round. His eyes met the well-known countenance of Marie Louise.

'What! are you in this infernal place, too?' said he. 'What has brought you here?'

'Will your Majesty permit me to ask the same question of yourself?' said the Empress, smiling.

He made no reply; astonishment prevented him.

No curtain now intervened between him and the light. It had been removed as if by magic, and a splendid chandelier appeared suspended over his head. Throngs of ladies, richly dressed, but without death's-head masks, stood round, and a due proportion of gay cavaliers was mingled with them. Music was still sounding, but it was seen to proceed from a band of mortal musicians stationed in an orchestra near at hand. The air was yet redolent of incense, but it was incense unblended with stench.

'Mon *Dieu!*' cried the Emperor, 'how is all this come about? Where in the world is Piche?'

'Piche?' replied the Empress. 'What does your Majesty mean? Had you not better leave the apartment and retire to rest?'

'Leave the apartment? Why, where am I?'

'In my private drawing-room, surrounded by a few particular persons of the Court whom I had invited this evening to a ball. You entered a few minutes since in your nightdress with your eyes fixed and wide open. I suppose from the astonishment you now testify that you were walking in your sleep.'

The Emperor immediately fell into a fit of catalepsy, in which he continued during the whole of that night and the greater part of the next day.

# JOHN JAGO'S GHOST
## WILKIE COLLINS

### I THE SICK MAN

'Heart all right,' said the doctor. 'Lungs all right. No organic disease that I can discover. Philip Lefrank, don't alarm yourself. You are not going to die yet. The disease you are suffering from is—overwork. The remedy in your case is—rest.'

So the doctor spoke, in my chambers in the Temple (London); having been sent for to see me about half an hour after I had alarmed my clerk by fainting at my desk. I have no wish to intrude myself needlessly on the reader's attention but it may be necessary to add, in the way of explanation, that I am a 'junior' barrister in good practice. I come from the Channel Island of Jersey. The French spelling of my name (Lefranc) was Anglicised generations since, in the days when the letter 'k' was still used in England at the end of words which now terminate in 'c'. We hold our heads high, nevertheless, as a Jersey family. It is to this day a trial to my father to hear his son described as a member of the English bar.

'Rest!' I repeated, when my medical adviser had done. 'My good friend, are you aware that it is term time? The courts are sitting. Look at the briefs waiting for me on that table! Rest means ruin in my case.'

'And work,' added the doctor, quietly, 'means death.'

I started. He was not trying to frighten me: he was plainly in earnest.

'It is merely a question of time,' he went on. 'You have a fine constitution; you are a young man; but you cannot deliberately overwork your brain, and derange your nervous system, much longer. Go away at once. If you are a good sailor, take a sea-voyage. The ocean-air is the best of all air to build you up again. No: I don't want to write a prescription. I decline to physic you. I have no more to say.

With those words my medical friend left the room. I was obstinate: I went into court the same day.

The senior counsel in the case on which I was engaged applied to me for some information which it was my duty to give him. To my horror and amazement, I was perfectly unable to collect my ideas: facts and dates all mingled together confusedly in my mind. I was led out of court thoroughly terrified about myself. The next day my briefs went back to the attorneys; and I followed my doctor's advice by taking my passage for America in the first steamer that sailed for New York.

I had chosen the voyage to America in preference to any other trip by sea, with a special object in view. A relative of my mother's had emigrated to the United States many years since, and had thriven there as a farmer. He had given me a general invitation to visit him if I ever crossed the Atlantic. The long period of inaction, under the name of rest, to which the doctor's decision had condemned me, could hardly be more pleasantly occupied, as I thought, than by paying a visit to my relation, and seeing what I could of America in that way. After a brief sojourn at New York, I started by railway for the residence of my host—Mr Isaac Meadowcroft, of Morwick Farm.

There are some of the grandest natural prospects on the face of creation in America. There is also to be found in certain States of the Union, by way of wholesome contrast, scenery as flat, as monotonous, and as uninteresting to the traveller, as any that the earth can show. The part of the country in which Mr Meadowcroft's farm was situated fell within this latter category. I looked round me when I stepped out of the railway-carriage on the platform at Morwick Station; and I said to myself, 'If to be cured means, in my case, to be dull, I have accurately picked out the very place for the purpose.'

I look back at those words by the light of later events; and I pronounce them, as you will soon pronounce them, to be the words of an essentially rash man, whose hasty judgment never stopped to consider what surprises time and chance together might have in store for him.

Mr Meadowcroft's eldest son, Ambrose, was waiting at the station to drive me to the farm.

There was no forewarning, in the appearance of Ambrose Meadowcroft, of the strange and terrible events that were to follow my arrival at Morwick. A healthy, handsome young fellow, one of thousands of other healthy, handsome young fellows, said, 'How d'ye do, Mr Lefrank? Glad to see you, sir. Jump into the buggy: the man will look after your portmanteau.' With equally conventional politeness I answered, 'Thank you. How are you all at home?' So we started on the way to the farm.

Our conversation on the drive began with the subjects of agriculture and breeding. I displayed my total ignorance of crops and cattle before we had travelled ten yards on our journey. Ambrose Meadowcroft cast about for another topic, and failed to find it. Upon this I cast about on my side, and asked, at a venture, if I had chosen a convenient time for my visit. The young farmer's stolid brown face instantly brightened. I had evidently hit, haphazard, on an interesting subject.

'You couldn't have chosen a better time,' he said. 'Our house has never been so cheerful as it is now.

'Have you any visitors staying with you?'

'It's not exactly a visitor. It's a new member of the family who has come to live with us.'

'A new member of the family? May I ask who it is?'

Ambrose Meadowcroft considered before he replied; touched his horse with the whip; looked at me with a certain sheepish hesitation; and suddenly burst out with the truth, in the plainest possible words:

'It's just the nicest girl, sir, you ever saw in your life.'

'Ay, ay! A friend of your sister's, I suppose?'

'A friend? Bless your heart! it's our little American cousin—Naomi Colebrook.'

I vaguely remembered that a younger sister of Mr Meadowcroft's had married an American merchant in the remote past, and had died many years since, leaving an only child. I was now further informed that the father also was dead.

In his last moments he had committed his helpless daughter to the compassionate care of his wife's relations at Morwick.

'He was always a speculating man,' Ambrose went on. 'Tried one thing after another, and failed in all. Died, sir, leaving barely enough to bury him. My father was a little doubtful, before she came here, how his American niece would turn out. We are English, you know; and, though we do live in the United States, we stick fast to our English ways and habits. We don't much like American women in general, I can tell you; but, when Naomi made her appearance, she conquered us all. Such a girl! Took her place as one of the family directly. Learnt to make herself useful in the dairy in a week's time. I tell you this—she hasn't been with us quite two months yet; and we wonder already how we ever got on without her!'

Once started on the subject of Naomi Colebrook, Ambrose held to that one topic, and talked on it without intermission. It required no great gift of penetration to discover the impression which the American cousin had produced in this case. The young fellow's enthusiasm communicated itself, in a certain tepid degree, to me. I really felt a mild flutter of anticipation at the prospect of seeing Naomi, when we drew up, towards the close of evening, at the gates of Morwick Farm.

## II THE NEW FACES

Immediately on my arrival, I was presented to Mr Meadowcroft, the father. The old man had become a confirmed invalid, confined by chronic rheumatism to his chair. He received me kindly, and a little wearily as well. His only unmarried daughter (he had long since been left a widower) was in the room, in attendance on her father. She was a melancholy, middle-aged woman, without visible attractions of any sort—one of those persons who appear to accept the obligation of living, under protest, as a burden which they would never have consented to bear if they had only been consulted first. We three had a dreary little interview in a parlour of bare walls; and then I was permitted to go upstairs, and unpack my portmanteau in my own room.

'Supper will be at nine o'clock, sir,' said Miss Meadowcroft.

She pronounced those words as if 'supper' was a form of domestic offence, habitually committed by the men, and endured by the women. I followed the groom up to my room, not over well pleased with my first experience of the farm.

No Naomi, and no romance, thus far!

My room was clean—oppressively clean. I quite longed to see a little dust somewhere. My library was limited to the Bible and the Prayer-book. My view from the window showed me a dead flat in a partial state of cultivation, fading sadly from view in the waning light. Above the head of my spruce white bed hung a scroll, bearing a damnatory quotation from Scripture in emblazoned letters of red and black. The dismal presence of Miss Meadowcroft had passed over my bedroom, and had blighted it. My spirits sank as I looked round me. Supper-time was still an event in the future. I lit the candles, and took from my portmanteau what I firmly believe to have been the first French novel ever produced at Morwick Farm. It was one of the masterly and charming stories of Dumas the elder. In five minutes I was in a new world, and my melancholy room was full of the liveliest French company. The sound of an imperative and uncompromising bell recalled me in due time to the regions of reality. I looked at my watch. Nine o'clock.

Ambrose met me at the bottom of the stairs, and showed me the way to the supper-room.

Mr Meadowcroft's invalid-chair had been wheeled to the head of the table. On his right-hand side sat his sad and silent daughter. She signed to me, with a ghostly solemnity, to take the vacant place on the left of her father. Silas Meadowcroft came in at the same moment, and was presented to me by his brother. There was a strong family likeness between them, Ambrose being the taller and the handsomer man of the two. But there was no marked character in either face. I set them down as men with undeveloped qualities, waiting (the good and evil qualities alike) for time and circumstances to bring them to their full growth.

The door opened again while I was still studying the two brothers, without, I honestly confess, being very favourably impressed by either of them. A new member of the family-circle, who instantly attracted my attention, entered the room.

He was short, spare, and wiry; singularly pale for a person whose life was passed in the country. The face was in other respects, besides this, a striking face to see. As to the lower part, it was covered with a thick black beard and moustache, at a time when shaving was the rule, and beards the rare exception, in America. As to the upper part of the face, it was irradiated by a pair of wild, glittering brown eyes, the expression of which suggested to me that there was something not quite right with the man's mental balance. A perfectly sane person in all his sayings and doings, so far as I could see, there was still something in those wild brown eyes which suggested to me, that, under exceptionally trying circumstances, he might surprise his oldest friends by acting in some exceptionally violent or foolish way. 'A little cracked'—that, in the popular phrase, was my impression of the stranger who now made his appearance in the supper-room.

Mr Meadowcroft the elder, having not spoken one word thus far, himself introduced the new-coiner to me, with a side-glance at his sons, which had something like defiance in it—a glance which, as I was sorry to notice, was returned with a similar appearance of defiance by the two young men.

'Philip Lefrank, this is my overlooker, Mr Jago,' said the old man, formally presenting us. 'John Jago, this is my young relative by marriage, Mr Lefrank. He is not well: he has come over the ocean for rest, and change of scene. Mr Jago is an American, Philip. I hope you have no prejudice against Americans. Make acquaintance with Mr Jago. Sit together.' He cast another dark look at his sons; and the sons again returned it. They pointedly drew back from John Jago as he approached the empty chair next to me, and moved round to the opposite side of the table. It was plain that the man with the beard stood high in the father's favour, and that he was cordially disliked for that or for some other reason by the sons.

The door opened once more. A young lady quietly joined the party at the supper-table.

Was the young lady Naomi Colebrook? I looked at Ambrose, and saw the answer in his face. Naomi at last!

A pretty girl, and, so far as I could judge by appearances, a good girl too. Describing her generally, I may say that she had a small head, well carried, and well set on her shoulders; bright, grey eyes, that looked at you honestly, and meant what they looked; a trim, slight little figure—too slight for our English notions of beauty; a strong American accent; and (a rare thing in America) a pleasantly-toned voice, which made the accent agreeable to English ears. Our first impressions of people are, in nine cases out often, the right impressions. I liked Naomi Colebrook at first sight; liked her pleasant smile; liked her hearty shake of the hand when we were presented to each other. 'If I get on well with nobody else in this house,' I thought to myself, 'I shall certainly get on well with *you.*'

For once in a way, I proved a true prophet. In the atmosphere of smouldering enmities at Morwick Farm, the pretty American girl and I remained firm and true friends from first to last.

Ambrose made room for Naomi to sit between his brother and himself. She changed colour for a moment, and looked at him, with a pretty, reluctant tenderness, as she took her chair. I strongly suspected the young farmer of squeezing her hand privately, under cover of the tablecloth.

The supper was not a merry one. The only cheerful conversation was the conversation across the table between Naomi and me.

For some incomprehensible reason, John Jago seemed to be ill at ease in the presence of his young countrywoman. He looked up at Naomi doubtingly from his plate, and looked down again slowly with a frown. When I addressed him, he answered constrainedly. Even when he spoke to Mr Meadowcroft, he was still on his guard—on his guard against the two young men, as I fancied by the direction which his eyes took on these occasions. When we began our meal, I had noticed for the first time that Silas Meadowcroft's left hand was strapped up with surgical plaster; and I now further observed that John Jago's wandering brown eyes, furtively looking at everybody round the table in turn, looked with a curious cynical scrutiny at the young man's injured hand.

By way of making my first evening at the farm all the more embarrassing to me as a stranger, I discovered before long that the father and sons were talking indirectly at each other, through Mr Jago and through me. When old Mr Meadowcroft spoke disparagingly to his overlooker of some past mistake made in the cultivation of the arable land of the farm, old Mr Meadowcroft's eyes pointed the application of his hostile criticism straight in the direction of his two sons. When the two sons seized a stray remark of mine about animals in general, and applied it satirically to the mismanagement of sheep and oxen in particular, they looked at John Jago, while they talked to me. On occasions of this sort—and they happened frequently—Naomi struck in resolutely at the right moment, and turned the talk to some harmless topic. Every time she took a prominent part in this way in keeping the peace, melancholy Miss Meadowcroft looked slowly round at her in stern and silent disparagement of her interference. A more dreary and more disunited family-party I never sat at the table with. Envy, hatred, malice, and uncharitableness are never so essentially detestable to my mind as when they are animated by a sense of propriety, and work under the surface. But for my interest in Naomi, and my other interest in the little love-looks which I now and then surprised passing between her and Ambrose, I should never have sat through that supper. I should certainly have taken refuge in my French novel and my own room.

At last the unendurably long meal, served with ostentatious profusion, was at an end. Miss Meadowcroft rose with her ghostly solemnity, and granted me my dismissal in these words:

'We are early people at the farm, Mr Lefrank. I wish you good-night.'

She laid her bony hands on the back of Mr Meadowcroft's invalid-chair, cut him short in his farewell salutation to me, and wheeled him out to his bed as if she were wheeling him out to his grave.

'Do you go to your room immediately, sir? If not, may I offer you a cigar?—provided the young gentlemen will permit it.'

So, picking his words with painful deliberation, and pointing his reference to 'the young gentlemen' with one sardonic sidelook at them, Mr John Jago performed the duties of hospitality on his side. I excused myself from accepting the cigar. With studied politeness, the man of the glittering brown eyes wished me a good night's rest, and left the room.

Ambrose and Silas both approached me hospitably, with their open cigar-cases in their hands.

'You were quite right to say "No,"' Ambrose began. 'Never smoke with John Jago. His cigars will poison you.'

'And never believe a word John Jago says to you,' added Silas. 'He is the greatest liar in America, let the other be whom he may.'

Naomi shook her forefinger reproachfully at them, as if the two sturdy young farmers had been two children.

'What will Mr Lefrank think?' she said, 'if you talk in that way of a person whom your father respects and trusts? Go and smoke. I am ashamed of both of you.'

Silas slunk away without a word of protest. Ambrose stood his ground, evidently bent on making his peace with Naomi before he left her.

Seeing that I was in the way, I walked aside towards a glass door at the lower end of the room. The door opened on the trim little farm-garden, bathed at that moment in lovely moonlight. I stepped out to enjoy the scene, and found my way to a seat under an elm-tree. The grand repose of Nature had never looked so unutterably solemn and beautiful as it now appeared, after what I had seen and heard inside the house. I understood, or thought I understood, the sad despair of humanity which led men into monasteries in the old time. The misanthropical side of my nature (where is the sick man who is not conscious of that side of him?) was fast getting the upper hand of me—when I felt a light touch laid on my shoulder, and found myself reconciled to my species once more by Naomi Colebrook.

## III THE MOONLIGHT-MEETING

'I want to speak to you,' Naomi began. 'You don't think ill of me for following you out here? We are not accustomed to stand much on ceremony in
America.'

'You are quite right in America. Pray sit down.'

She seated herself by my side, looking at me frankly and fearlessly by the
light of the moon.

'You are related to the family here,' she resumed, 'and I am related too. I
guess I may say to you what I couldn't say to a stranger. I am right glad you have
come here, Mr Lefrank; and for a reason, sir, which you don't suspect.'

'Thank you for the compliment you pay me, Miss Colebrook, whatever the
reason may be.'

She took no notice of my reply: she steadily pursued her own train of
thought.

'I guess you may do some good, sir, in this wretched house,' the girl went
on, with her eyes still earnestly fixed on my face. 'There is no love, no trust, no
peace at Morwick Farm. They want somebody here—except Ambrose: don't
think ill of Ambrose; he is only thoughtless—I say, the rest of them want somebody here to make them ashamed of their hard hearts, and their horrid, false,
envious ways. You are a gentleman; you know more than they know: they can't
help themselves, they must look up to you. Try, Mr Lefrank, when you have the
opportunity—pray try, sir, to make peace among them. You heard what went
on at supper-time; and you were disgusted with it. Oh, yes, you were! I saw you
frown to yourself; and I know what that means in you Englishmen.'

There was no choice but to speak one's mind plainly to Naomi. I acknowledged the impression which had been produced on me at supper-time just as
plainly as I have acknowledged it in these pages. Naomi nodded her head in
undisguised approval of my candour.

'That will do; that's speaking out,' she said. 'But—oh, my! you put it a
deal too mildly, sir, when you say the men don't seem to be on friendly terms
together here. They hate each other. That's the word, Mr Lefrank—hate; bitter,
bitter, bitter hate!' She clenched her little fists; she shook them vehemently, by
way of adding emphasis to her last words; and then she suddenly remembered
Ambrose. 'Except Ambrose,' she added, opening her hand again, and laying it
very earnestly on my arm. 'Don't go and misjudge Ambrose, sir. There is no
harm in poor Ambrose.'

The girl's innocent frankness was really irresistible.

'Should I be altogether wrong,' I asked, 'If I guessed that you were a little partial to Ambrose?'

An Englishwoman would have felt, or would at least have assumed, some little hesitation at replying to my question. Naomi did not hesitate for an instant.

'You are quite right, sir,' she said, with the most perfect composure. 'If things go well, I mean to marry Ambrose.'

'If things go well,' I repeated. 'What does that mean? Money?'

She shook her head.

'It means a fear that I have in my own mind,' she answered—'a fear, Mr Lefrank, of matters taking a bad turn among the men here—the wicked, hard-hearted, unfeeling men. I don't mean Ambrose, sir: I mean his brother Silas, and John Jago. Did you notice Silas's hand? John Jago did that, sir, with a knife.'

'By accident?' I asked.

'On purpose,' she answered. 'In return for a blow.'

This plain revelation of the state of things at Morwick Farm rather staggered me. Blows and knives under the rich and respectable roof-tree of old Mr Meadowcroft!—blows and knives, not among the labourers, but among the masters! My first impression was like your first impression, no doubt. I could hardly believe it.

'Are you sure of what you say?' I enquired.

'I have it from Ambrose. Ambrose would never deceive me. Ambrose knows all about it.'

My curiosity was powerfully excited. To what sort of household had I rashly voyaged across the ocean in search of rest and quiet?

'May I know all about it too?' I said.

'Well, I will try and tell you what Ambrose told me. But you must promise me one thing first, sir. Promise you won't go away and leave us when you know the whole truth. Shake hands on it, Mr Lefrank; come, shake hands on it.'

There was no resisting her fearless frankness. I shook hands on it. Naomi entered on her narrative the moment I had given her my pledge, without wasting a word by way of preface.

'When you are shown over the farm here,' she began, 'you will see that it is really two farms in one. On this side of it, as we look from under this tree, they raise crops: on the other side—on much the larger half of the land, mind—they raise cattle. When Mr Meadowcroft got too old and too sick to look after his farm himself, the boys (I mean Ambrose and Silas) divided the work between them. Ambrose looked after the crops, and Silas after the cattle. Things didn't go well, somehow, under their management. I can't tell you why. I am only sure Ambrose was not in fault. The old man got more and more dissatisfied, especially about his beasts. His pride is in his beasts. Without saying a word to the boys, he looked about privately (I think he was wrong in that, sir; don't you?)— he looked about privately for help; and, in an evil hour, he heard of John Jago. Do you like John Jago, Mr Lefrank?'

'So far, no. I don't like him.'

'Just my sentiments, sir. But I don't know: it's likely we may be wrong. There's nothing against John Jago, except that he is so odd in his ways. They do say he wears all that nasty hair on his face (I hate hair on a man's face) on account of a vow he made when he lost his wife. Don't you think, Mr Lefrank, a man must be a little mad who shows his grief at losing his wife by vowing that he will never shave himself again? Well, that's what they do say John Jago vowed. Perhaps it's a lie. People are such liars here! Anyway, it's truth (the boys themselves confess that), when John came to the farm, he came with a first-rate character. The old father here isn't easy to please; and he pleased the old father. Yes, that's so. Mr Meadowcroft don't like my countrymen in general. He's like his sons—English, bitter English, to the marrow of his bones. Somehow, in spite of that, John Jago got round him; maybe because John does certainly know his business. Oh, yes! Cattle and crops, John knows his business. Since he's been overlooker, things have prospered as they didn't prosper in the time of the boys. Ambrose owned as much to me himself. Still, sir, it's hard to be set aside for a stranger; isn't it? John gives the orders now. The boys do the work; but they have no voice in it when John and the old man put their heads together over the business of the farm. I have been long in telling you of it, sir; but now you know how the envy and the hatred grew among the men, before my time. Since I have been here, things seem to get worse and worse. There's hardly a day goes by that hard words don't pass between the boys and John, or the boys and their father. The old man has an aggravating way, Mr Lefrank—a nasty way, as we do call it—of taking John Jago's part. Do speak to him about it when you get the chance. The main blame of the quarrel between Silas and John the other day lies at his door, I think. I don't want to excuse Silas, either. It was brutal of him—though he is Ambrose's brother—to strike John, who is the smaller and weaker man of the two. But it was worse than brutal in John, to out with his knife, and try to stab Silas. Oh, he did it! If Silas had not caught the knife in his hand (his hand's awfully cut, I can tell you; I dressed it myself), it might have ended, for anything I know, in murder—'

She stopped as the word passed her lips, looked back over her shoulder, and started violently.

I looked where my companion was looking. The dark figure of a man was standing, watching us, in the shadow of the elm-tree. I rose directly to approach him. Naomi recovered her self-possession, and checked me before I could interfere.

'Who are you?' she asked, turning sharply towards the stranger. 'What do you want there?'

The man stepped out from the shadow into the moonlight, and stood revealed to us as John Jago. 'I hope I am not intruding?' he said, looking hard at me.

'What do you want?' Naomi repeated.

'I don't wish to disturb you, or to disturb this gentleman,' he proceeded. 'When you are quite at leisure, Miss Naomi, you would be doing me a favour if you would permit me to say a few words to you in private.'

He spoke with the most scrupulous politeness; trying, and trying vainly, to conceal some strong agitation which was in possession of him. His wild brown eyes—wilder than ever in the moonlight—rested entreatingly, with a strange underlying expression of despair, on Naomi's face. His hands, clasped tightly in front of him, trembled incessantly. Little as I liked the man, he did really impress me as a pitiable object at that moment.

'Do you mean that you want to speak to me to-night?' Naomi asked, in undisguised surprise.

'Yes, miss, if you please, at your leisure and at Mr Lefrank's.' Naomi hesitated.

'Won't it keep till to-morrow?' she said.

'I shall be away on farm-business to-morrow, miss, for the whole day. Please to give me a few minutes this evening.' He advanced a step towards her: his voice faltered, and dropped timidly to a whisper. 'I really have something to say to you, Miss Naomi. It would be a kindness on your part—a very, very great kindness—if you will let me say it before I rest to-night.'

I rose again to resign my place to him. Once more Naomi checked me. 'No,' she said. 'Don't stir.' She addressed John Jago very reluctantly: 'If you are so much in earnest about it, Mr John, I suppose it must be. I can't guess what you can possibly have to say to me which cannot be said before a third person. However, it wouldn't be civil, I suppose, to say "No" in my place. You know it's my business to wind up the hall-clock at ten every night. If you choose to come and help me, the chances are that we shall have the hall to ourselves. Will that do?'

'Not in the hall, miss, if you will excuse me.'

'Not in the hall!'

'And not in the house either, if I may make so bold.'

'What do you mean?' She turned impatiently, and appealed to me. 'Do you understand him?'

John Jago signed to me imploringly to let him answer for himself. 'Bear with me, Miss Naomi,' he said. 'I think I can make you understand me. There are eyes on the watch, and ears on the watch, in the house; and there are some footsteps—I won't say whose—so soft, that no person can hear them.'

The last allusion evidently made itself understood. Naomi stopped him before he could say more.

'Well, where is it to be?' she asked, resignedly. 'Will the garden do, Mr John?'

'Thank you kindly, miss: the garden will do.' He pointed to a gravel-walk beyond us, bathed in the full flood of the moonlight. 'There,' he said, 'where we can see all round us, and be sure that nobody is listening. At ten o'clock.' He paused, and addressed himself to me. 'I beg to apologise, sir, for intruding myself on your conversation. Please to excuse me.' His eyes rested with a last, anxious, pleading look on Naomi's face. He bowed to us, and melted away into the shadow of the tree. The distant sound of a door, closed softly, came to us through the stillness of the night. John Jago had re-entered the house.

Now that he was out of hearing, Naomi spoke to me very earnestly:

'Don't suppose, sir, I have any secrets with him,' she said. 'I know no more than you do what he wants with me. I have half a mind not to keep the appointment. It's close on ten now. What would you do in my place?'

'Having made the appointment,' I answered, 'it seems to be due to yourself to keep it. If you feel the slightest alarm, I will wait in another part of the garden, so that I can hear if you call me.'

She received my proposal with a saucy toss of the head, and a smile of pity for my ignorance.

'You are a stranger, Mr Lefrank, or you would never talk to me in that way. In America, we don't do the men the honour of letting them alarm us. In America, the women take care of themselves. He has got my promise to meet him, as you say; and I must keep my promise. Only think,' she added, speaking more to herself than to me, 'of John Jago finding out Miss Meadowcroft's nasty, sly, underhand ways in the house! Most men would never have noticed her!'

I was completely taken by surprise. Sad and severe Miss Meadowcroft a listener and a spy! What next at Morwick Farm?

'Was that hint at the watchful eyes and ears, and the soft footsteps, really an allusion to Mr Meadowcroft's daughter?' I asked.

'Of course it was. Ah! she has imposed on you as she imposes on everybody else. The false wretch! She is secretly at the bottom of half the bad feeling among the men. I am certain of it—she keeps Mr Meadowcroft's mind bitter towards the boys. Old as she is, Mr Lefrank, and ugly as she is, she wouldn't object (if she could only make him ask her) to be John Jago's second wife. No, sir; and she wouldn't break her heart if the boys were not left a stick or a stone on the farm when the father dies. I have watched her, and I know it. Ah! I could tell you such things. But there's no time now—there's ten o'clock striking! we must say goodnight. I am right glad I have spoken to you, sir. I say again, at parting, what I have said already: Use your influence, pray use your influence, to soften them, and to make them ashamed of themselves, in this wicked house. We will have more talk about what you can do, to-morrow, when you are shown over the farm. Say goodbye now; I must keep my appointment. Look! here is John Jago stealing out again in the shadow of the tree! Good-night, friend Lefrank; and pleasant dreams.'

With one hand she took mine, and pressed it cordially: with the other she pushed me away without ceremony in the direction of the house. A charming girl!—an irresistible girl! I was nearly as bad as the boys. I declare, I almost hated John Jago, too, as we crossed each other in the shadow of the tree.

Arrived at the glass door, I stopped, and looked back at the gravel-walk.

They had met. I saw the two shadowy figures slowly pacing backwards and forwards in the moonlight, the woman a little in advance of the man. What was he saying to her? Why was he so anxious that not a word of it should be heard? Our presentiments are sometimes, in certain rare cases, the faithful prophecy of the future. A vague distrust of that moonlight-meeting stealthily took a hold on my mind. 'Will mischief come of it?' I asked myself, as I closed the door and entered the house.

Mischief did come of it. You shall hear how.

## IV THE BEECHEN STICK

Persons of sensitive nervous temperament, sleeping for the first time in a strange house, and in a bed that is new to them, must make up their minds to pass a wakeful night. My first night at Morwick Farm was no exception to this rule. The little sleep I had was broken and disturbed by dreams. Towards six o'clock in the morning my bed became unendurable to me. The sun was shining in brightly at the window. I determined to try the reviving influence of a stroll in the fresh morning air.

Just as I got out of bed, I heard footsteps and voices under my window.

The footsteps stopped, and the voices became recognisable. I had passed the night with my window open: I was able, without exciting notice from below, to look out.

The persons beneath me were Silas Meadowcroft, John Jago, and three strangers, whose dress and appearance indicated plainly enough that they were labourers on the farm. Silas was swinging a stout beechen stick in his hand, and was speaking to Jago, coarsely and insolently enough, of his moonlight-meeting with Naomi on the previous night.

'Next time you go courting a young lady in secret,' said Silas, 'make sure that the moon goes down first, or wait for a cloudy sky. You were seen in the garden, Master Jago; and you may as well tell us the truth for once in a way. Did you find her open to persuasion, sir? Did she say "Yes?"'

John Jago kept his temper.

'If you must have your joke, Mr Silas,' he said, quietly and firmly, 'be pleased to joke on some other subject. You are quite wrong, sir, in what you suppose to have passed between the young lady and me.'

Silas turned about, and addressed himself ironically to the three labourers.

'You hear him, boys? He can't tell the truth, try him as you may. He wasn't making love to Naomi in the garden last night—oh, dear, no! He has had one wife already; and he knows better than to take the yoke on his shoulders for the second time!'

Greatly to my surprise, John Jago met this clumsy jesting with a formal and serious reply.

'You are quite right, sir,' he said. 'I have no intention of marrying for the second time. What I was saying to Miss Naomi doesn't matter to you. It was not at all what you choose to suppose; it was something of quite another kind, with which you have no concern. Be pleased to understand once for all, Mr Silas, that not so much as the thought of making love to the young lady has ever entered my head. I respect her; I admire her good qualities: but if she was the only woman left in the world, and if I was a much younger man than I am, I should never think of asking her to be my wife.' He burst out suddenly into a harsh, uneasy laugh. 'No, no! not my style, Mr Silas—not my style!'

Something in those words, or in his manner of speaking them, appeared to exasperate Silas. He dropped his clumsy irony, and addressed himself directly to John Jago in a tone of savage contempt.

'Not your style?' he repeated. 'Upon my soul, that's a cool way of putting it, for a man in your place! What do you mean by calling her "not your style?" You impudent beggar! Naomi Colebrook is meat for your master!'

John Jago's temper began to give way at last. He approached defiantly a step or two nearer to Silas Meadowcroft.

'Who is my master?' he asked.

'Ambrose will show you, if you go to him,' answered the other. 'Naomi is his sweetheart, not mine. Keep out of his way, if you want to keep a whole skin on your bones.'

John Jago cast one of his sardonic side-looks at the farmer's wounded left hand. 'Don't forget your own skin, Mr Silas, when you threaten mine! I have set my mark on you once, sir. Let me by on my business, or I may mark you for a second time.'

Silas lifted his beechen stick. The labourers, roused to some rude sense of the serious turn which the quarrel was taking, got between the two men, and parted them. I had been hurriedly dressing myself while the altercation was proceeding; and I now ran downstairs to try what my influence could do towards keeping the peace at Morwick Farm.

The war of angry words was still going on when I joined the men outside.

'Be off with you on your business, you cowardly hound!' I heard Silas say. 'Be off with you to the town! and take care you don't meet Ambrose on the way!'

'Take you care you don't feel my knife again before I go!' cried the other man.

Silas made a desperate effort to break away from the labourers who were holding him.

'Last time you only felt my fist!' he shouted. 'Next time you shall feel this!' He lifted the stick as he spoke. I stepped up, and snatched it out of his hand.

'Mr Silas,' I said, 'I am an invalid, and I am going out for a walk. Your stick will be useful to me. I beg leave to borrow it.'

The labourers burst out laughing. Silas fixed his eyes on me with a stare of angry surprise. John Jago, immediately recovering his self-possession, took off his hat, and made me a deferential bow.

'I had no idea, Mr Lefrank, that we were disturbing you,' he said. 'I am very much ashamed of myself, sir. I beg to apologise.'

'I accept your apology, Mr Jago,' I answered, 'on the understanding that you, as the older man, will set the example of forbearance, if your temper is tried on any future occasion as it has been tried to-day. And I have further to request,' I added, addressing myself to Silas, 'that you will do me a favour, as your father's guest. The next time your good spirits lead you into making jokes at Mr Jago's expense, don't carry them quite so far. I am sure you meant no harm, Mr Silas. Will you gratify me by saying so yourself? I want to see you and Mr Jago shake hands.'

John Jago instantly held out his hand, with an assumption of good feeling which was a little over-acted, to my thinking. Silas Meadowcroft made no advance of the same friendly sort on his side.

'Let him go about his business,' said Silas. 'I won't waste any more words on him, Mr Lefrank, to please you. But (saving your presence) I'm damned if I take his hand!'

Further persuasion was plainly useless, addressed to such a man as this. Silas gave me no further opportunity of remonstrating with him, even if I had been inclined to do so. He turned about in sulky silence, and, retracing his steps along the path, disappeared round the corner of the house. The labourers withdrew next, in different directions, to begin the day's work. John Jago and I were alone.

I left it to the man of the wild brown eyes to speak first.

'In half an hour's time, sir,' he said, 'I shall be going on business to Narrabee, our market-town here. Can I take any letters to the post for you? or is there anything else that I can do in the town?'

I thanked him, and declined both proposals. He made me another deferential bow, and withdrew into the house. I mechanically followed the path, in the direction which Silas had taken before me.

Turning the corner of the house, and walking on for a little way, I found myself at the entrance to the stables, and face to face with Silas Meadowcroft once more. He had his elbows on the gate of the yard, swinging it slowly backwards and forwards, and turning and twisting a straw between his teeth. When he saw me approaching him, he advanced a step from the gate, and made an effort to excuse himself, with a very ill grace.

'No offence, mister. Ask me what you will besides, and I'll do it for you. But don't ask me to shake hands with John Jago; I hate him too badly for that. If I touched him with one hand, sir, I tell you this, I should throttle him with the other!'

'That's your feeling towards the man, Mr Silas, is it?'

'That's my feeling, Mr Lefrank; and I'm not ashamed of it, either.'

'Is there any such place as a church in your neighbourhood, Mr Silas?'

'Of course there is.

'And do you ever go to it?'

'Of course I do.'

'At long intervals, Mr Silas?'

'Every Sunday, sir, without fail.'

Some third person behind me burst out laughing; some third person had been listening to our talk. I turned round, and discovered Ambrose Meadowcroft.

'I understand the drift of your catechism, though my brother doesn't,' he said. 'Don't be hard on Silas, sir. He isn't the only Christian who leaves his Christianity in the pew when he goes out of church. You will never make us friends with John Jago, try as you may. Why, what have you got there, Mr Lefrank? May I die if it isn't my stick! I have been looking for it everywhere!'

The thick beechen stick had been feeling uncomfortably heavy in my invalid hand for some time past. There was no sort of need for my keeping it any longer. John Jago was going away to Narrabee, and Silas Meadowcroft's savage temper was subdued to a sulky repose. I handed the stick back to Ambrose. He laughed as he took it from me.

You can't think how strange it feels, Mr Lefrank, to be out without one's stick,' he said. 'A man gets used to his stick, sir; doesn't he? Are you ready for your breakfast?'

'Not just yet. I thought of taking a little walk first.'

'All right, sir. I wish I could go with you; but I have got my work to do this morning, and Silas has his work too. If you go back by the way you came, you will find yourself in the garden. If you want to go further, the wicket-gate at the end will lead you into the lane.'

Through sheer thoughtlessness, I did a very foolish thing. I turned back as I was told, and left the brothers together at the gate of the stable-yard.

## V THE NEWS FROM NARRABEE

Arrived at the garden, a thought struck me. The cheerful speech and easy manner of Ambrose plainly indicated that he was ignorant thus far of the quarrel which had taken place under my window. Silas might confess to having taken his brother's stick, and might mention whose head he had threatened with it. It was not only useless, but undesirable, that Ambrose should know of the quarrel. I retraced my steps to the stable-yard. Nobody was at the gate. I called alternately to Silas and to Ambrose. Nobody answered. The brothers had gone away to their work.

Returning to the garden, I heard a pleasant voice wishing me 'Good morning.' I looked round. Naomi Colebrook was standing at one of the lower windows of the farm. She had her working-apron on, and she was industriously brightening the knives for the breakfast-table, on an old-fashioned board. A sleek black cat balanced himself on her shoulder, watching the flashing motion of the knife as she passed it rapidly to and fro on the leather-covered surface of the board.

'Come here,' she said, 'I want to speak to you.'

I noticed, as I approached, that her pretty face was clouded and anxious. She pushed the cat irritably off her shoulder: she welcomed me with only the faint reflection of her bright, customary smile.

'I have seen John Jago,' she said. 'He has been hinting at something which he says happened under your bedroom-window this morning. When I begged him to explain himself he only answered, "Ask Mr Lefrank: I must be off to Narrabee." What does it mean? Tell me right away, sir! I'm out of temper, and I can't wait!'

Except that I made the best instead of the worst of it, I told her what had happened under my window as plainly as I have told it here. She put down the knife that she was cleaning, and folded her hands before her, thinking.

'I wish I had never given John Jago that meeting,' she said. 'When a man asks anything of a woman, the woman, I find, mostly repents it if she says yes.'

She made that quaint reflection with a very troubled brow. The moonlight-meeting had left some unwelcome remembrances in her mind. I saw that as plainly as I saw Naomi herself.

What had John Jago said to her? I put the question with all needful delicacy, making my apologies beforehand.

'I should like to tell *you*,' she began, with a strong emphasis on the last word.

There she stopped. She turned pale; then suddenly flushed again to the deepest red. She took up the knife once more, and went on cleaning it as industriously as ever.

'I mustn't tell you,' she resumed, with her head down over the knife. 'I have promised not to tell anybody. That's the truth. Forget all about it, sir, as soon as you can. Hush! here's the spy who saw us last night on the walk, and who told Silas!'

Dreary Miss Meadowcroft opened the kitchen-door. She carried an ostentatiously large Prayer Book; and she looked at Naomi as only a jealous woman of middle age can look at a younger and prettier woman than herself.

'Prayers, Miss Colebrook,' she said, in her sourest manner. She paused, and noticed me standing under the window. 'Prayers, Mr Lefrank,' she added, with a look of devout pity, directed exclusively to my address.

'We will follow you directly, Miss Meadowcroft,' said Naomi.

'I have no desire to intrude on your secrets, Miss Colebrook.'

With that acrid answer, our priestess took herself and her Prayer Book out of the kitchen. I joined Naomi, entering the room by the garden-door. She met me eagerly.

'I am not quite easy about something,' she said. 'Did you tell me that you left Ambrose and Silas together?'

'Yes.'

'Suppose Silas tells Ambrose of what happened this morning?'

The same idea, as I have already mentioned, had occurred to my mind. I did my best to reassure Naomi.

'Mr Jago is out of the way,' I replied. 'You and I can easily put things right in his absence.'

She took my arm.

'Come in to prayers,' she said. 'Ambrose will be there, and I shall find an opportunity of speaking to him.'

Neither Ambrose nor Silas was in the breakfast-room when we entered it. After waiting vainly for ten minutes, Mr Meadowcroft told his daughter to read the prayers. Miss Meadowcroft read, thereupon, in the tone of an injured woman taking the throne of mercy by storm, and insisting on her rights. Breakfast followed; and still the brothers were absent. Miss Meadowcroft looked at her father, and said, 'From bad to worse, sir. What did I tell you?' Naomi instantly applied the antidote: 'The boys are no doubt detained over their work, uncle.' She turned to me. 'You want to see the farm, Mr Lefrank. Come and help me to find the boys.'

For more than an hour we visited one part of the farm after another, without discovering the missing men. We found them at last near the outskirts of a small wood, sitting, talking together, on the trunk of a felled tree.

Silas rose as we approached, and walked away, without a word of greeting or apology, into the wood. As he got on his feet I noticed that his brother whispered something in his ear; and I heard him answer, 'All right!'

'Ambrose, does that mean you have something to keep a secret from us?' asked Naomi, approaching her lover with a smile. 'Is Silas ordered to hold his tongue?'

Ambrose kicked sulkily at the loose stones lying about him. I noticed, with a certain surprise, that his favourite stick was not in his hand, and was not lying near him.

'Business,' he said, in answer to Naomi, not very graciously—'business between Silas and me. That's what it means, if you must know.'

Naomi went on, woman-like, with her questions, heedless of the reception which they might meet with from an irritated man.

'Why were you both away at prayers and breakfast-time?' she asked next. 'We had too much to do,' Ambrose gruffly replied, 'and we were too far from the house.'

'Very odd,' said Naomi. 'This has never happened before, since I have been at the farm.'

'Well, live and learn. It has happened now.'

The tone in which he spoke would have warned any man to let him alone. But warnings which speak by implication only are thrown away on women. The woman, having still something in her mind to say, said it.

'Have you seen anything of John Jago this morning?'

The smouldering ill temper of Ambrose burst suddenly—why, it was impossible to guess—into a flame.

'How many more questions am I to answer?' he broke out, violently. 'Are you the parson, putting me through my catechism? I have seen nothing of John Jago and I have got my work to go on with. Will that do for you?'

He turned with an oath, and followed his brother into the wood. Naomi's bright eyes looked up at me, flashing with indignation.

'What does he mean, Mr Lefrank, by speaking to me in that way? Rude brute! How dare he do it?' She paused: her voice, look, and manner suddenly changed. 'This has never happened before, sir. Has anything gone wrong? I declare, I shouldn't know Ambrose again, he is so changed. Say, how does it strike you?'

I still made the best of a bad case.

'Something has upset his temper,' I said. 'The merest trifle, Miss Colebrook, upsets a man's temper sometimes. I speak as a man, and I know it. Give him time, and he will make his excuses, and all will be well again.'

My presentation of the case entirely failed to reassure my pretty companion. We went back to the house. Dinner-time came, and the brothers appeared. Their father spoke to them of their absence from morning prayers—with needless severity, as I thought. They resented the reproof with needless indignation on their side, and left the room. A sour smile of satisfaction showed itself on Miss Meadowcroft's thin lips. She looked at her father; then raised her eyes sadly to the ceiling, and said, 'We can only pray for them, sir.'

Naomi disappeared after dinner. When I saw her again, she had some news for me.

'I have been with Ambrose,' she said, 'and he has begged my pardon. We have made it up, Mr Lefrank. Still—still—'

'Still—*what*, Miss Naomi?'

'He is not like himself, sir. He denies it; but I can't help thinking he is hiding something from me.'

The day wore on: the evening came. I returned to my French novel. But not even Dumas himself could keep my attention to the story. What else I was thinking of I cannot say. Why I was out of spirits I am unable to explain. I wished myself back in England: I took a blind, unreasoning hatred to Morwick Farm.

Nine o'clock struck; and we all assembled again at supper, with the exception of John Jago. He was expected back to supper; and we waited for him a quarter of an hour, by Mr Meadowcroft's own directions. John Jago never appeared.

The night wore on, and still the absent man failed to return. Miss Meadowcroft volunteered to sit up for him. Naomi eyed her, a little maliciously I must own, as the two women parted for the night. I withdrew to my room, and again I was unable to sleep. When sunrise came, I went out, as before, to breathe the morning air.

On the staircase I met Miss Meadowcroft ascending to her own room. Not a curl of her stiff grey hair was disarranged: nothing about the impenetrable woman betrayed that she had been watching through the night.

'Has Mr Jago not returned?' I asked.

Miss Meadowcroft slowly shook her head, and frowned at me.

'We are in the hands of Providence, Mr Lefrank. Mr Jago must have been detained for the night at Narrabee.'

The daily routine of the meals resumed its unalterable course. Breakfast-time came and dinner-time came, and no John Jago darkened the doors of Morwick Farm. Mr Meadowcroft and his daughter consulted together, and determined to send in search of the missing man. One of the more intelligent of the labourers was despatched to Narrabee to make enquiries.

The man returned late in the evening, bringing startling news to the farm. He had visited all the inns and all the places of business resort in Narrabee; he had made endless enquiries in every direction, with this result—no one had set eyes on John Jago. Everybody declared that John Jago had not entered the town.

We all looked at each other, excepting the two brothers, who were seated together in a dark corner of the room. The conclusion appeared to be inevitable. John Jago was a lost man.

## VI THE LIME-KILN

Mr Meadowcroft was the first to speak.

'Somebody must find John,' he said.

'Without losing a moment,' added his daughter.

Ambrose suddenly stepped out of the dark corner of the room.

'I will enquire,' he said.

Silas followed him.

'I will go with you,' he added.

Mr Meadowcroft interposed his authority.

'One of you will be enough; for the present, at least. Go you, Ambrose. Your brother may be wanted later. If any accident has happened (which God forbid), we may have to enquire in more than one direction. Silas, you will stay at the farm.'

The brothers withdrew together—Ambrose to prepare for his journey, Silas to saddle one of the horses for him. Naomi slipped out after them. Left in company with Mr Meadowcroft and his daughter (both devoured by anxiety about the missing man, and both trying to conceal it under an assumption of devout resignation to circumstances, I need hardly add that I, too, retired, as soon as it was politely possible for me to leave the room. Ascending the stairs on my way to my own quarters, I discovered Naomi half hidden in a recess formed by an old-fashioned window-seat on the first landing. My bright little friend was in sore trouble. Her apron was over her face, and she was crying bitterly. Ambrose had not taken his leave as tenderly as usual. She was more firmly persuaded than ever that 'Ambrose was hiding something from her.' We all waited anxiously for the next day. The next day made the mystery deeper than ever.

The horse which had taken Ambrose to Narrabee was ridden back to the farm by a groom from the hotel. He delivered a written message from Ambrose which startled us. Further enquiries had positively proved that the missing man had never been near Narrabee. The only attainable tidings of his whereabouts were tidings derived from vague report. It was said that a man like John Jago had been seen the previous day in a railway car, travelling on the line to New York. Acting on this imperfect information, Ambrose had decided on verifying the truth of the report by extending his enquiries to New York.

This extraordinary proceeding forced the suspicion on me that something had really gone wrong. I kept my doubts to myself; but I was prepared, from that moment, to see the disappearance of John Jago followed by very grave results.

The same day the results declared themselves.

Time enough had now elapsed for report to spread through the district the news of what had happened at the farm. Already aware of the bad feeling existing between, the men, the neighbours had been now informed (no doubt by the labourers present) of the deplorable scene that had taken place under my bedroom-window. Public opinion declares itself in America without the slightest reserve, or the slightest care for consequences. Public opinion declared on this occasion that the lost man was the victim of foul play, and held one or both of the brothers Meadowcroft responsible for his disappearance. Later in the day, the reasonableness of this serious view of the case was confirmed in the popular mind by a startling discovery. It was announced that a Methodist preacher lately settled at Morwick, and greatly respected throughout the district, had dreamed of John Jago in the character of a murdered man, whose bones were hidden at Morwick Farm. Before night the cry was general for a verification of the preacher's dream. Not only in the immediate district, but in the town of Narrabee itself, the public voice insisted on the necessity of a search for the mortal remains of John Jago at Morwick Farm.

In the terrible turn which matters had now taken, Mr Meadowcroft the elder displayed a spirit and an energy for which I was not prepared.

'My sons have their faults,' he said—'serious faults, and nobody knows it better than I do. My sons have behaved badly and ungratefully towards John Jago; I don't deny that either. But Ambrose and Silas are not murderers. Make your search. I ask for it; no, I insist on it, after what has been said, injustice to my family and my name!'

The neighbours took him at his word. The Morwick section of the American nation organised itself on the spot. The sovereign people met in committee, made speeches, elected competent persons to represent the public interests, and began the search the next day. The whole proceeding, ridiculously informal from a legal point of view, was carried on by these extraordinary people with as stern and strict a sense of duty as if it had been sanctioned by the highest tribunal in the land.

Naomi met the calamity that had fallen on the household as resolutely as her uncle himself. The girl's courage rose with the call which was made on it. Her one anxiety was for Ambrose.

'He ought to be here,' she said to me. 'The wretches in this neighbourhood are wicked enough to say that his absence is a confession of his guilt.'

She was right. In the present temper of the popular mind the absence of Ambrose was a suspicious circumstance in itself.

'We might telegraph to New York,' I suggested, 'if you only knew where a message would be likely to find him.'

'I know the hotel which the Meadowcrofts use at New York,' she replied. 'I was sent there, after my father's death, to wait till Miss Meadowcroft could take me to Morwick.'

We decided on telegraphing to the hotel. I was writing the message, and Naomi was looking over my shoulder, when we were startled by a strange voice speaking close behind us.

'Oh! that's his address, is it?' said the voice. 'We wanted his address rather badly.' The speaker was a stranger to me. Naomi recognised him as one of the neighbours. 'What do you want his address for?' she asked, sharply.

'I guess we've found the mortal remains of John Jago, miss,' the man replied. 'We have got Silas already, and we want Ambrose, too, on suspicion of murder.'

'It's a lie!' cried Naomi, furiously—'a wicked lie!'

The man turned to me.

'Take her into the next room, mister,' he said, 'and let her see for herself.'

We went together into the next room.

In one corner, sitting by her father, and holding his hand, we saw stern and stony Miss Meadowcroft, weeping silently. Opposite to them, crouched on the window-seat,—his eyes wandering, his hands hanging helpless,—we next discovered Silas Meadowcroft, plainly self-betrayed as a panic-stricken man. A few of the persons who had been engaged in the search were seated near, watching him. The mass of the strangers present stood congregated round a table in the middle of the room. They drew aside as I approached with Naomi, and allowed us to have a clear view of certain objects placed on the table.

The centre object of the collection was a little heap of charred bones. Round this were ranged a knife, two metal buttons, and a stick partially burnt. The knife was recognised by the labourers as the weapon John Jago habitually carried about with him—the weapon with which he had wounded Silas Meadowcroft's hand. The buttons Naomi herself declared to have a peculiar pattern on them, which had formerly attracted her attention to John Jago's coat. As for the stick, burnt as it was, I had no difficulty in identifying the quaintly-carved knob at the top. It was the heavy beechen stick which I had snatched out of Silas's hand, and which I had restored to Ambrose on his claiming it as his own. In reply to my enquiries, I was informed that the bones, the knife, the buttons, and the stick had all been found together in a lime-kiln then in use on the farm.

'Is it serious?' Naomi whispered to me, as we drew back from the table.

It would have been sheer cruelty to deceive her now.

'Yes,' I whispered back; 'it is serious.'

The search committee conducted its proceedings with the strictest regularity. The proper applications were made forthwith to a justice of the peace, and the justice issued his warrant. That night Silas was committed to prison; and an officer was despatched to arrest Ambrose in New York.

For my part, I did the little I could to make myself useful. With the silent sanction of Mr Meadowcroft and his daughter, I went to Narrabee, and secured the best legal assistance for the defence which the town could place at my disposal. This done, there was no choice but to wait for news of Ambrose, and for the examination before the magistrate which was to follow. I shall pass over the misery in the house during the interval of expectation: no useful purpose could be served by describing it now. Let me only say that Naomi's conduct strengthened me in the conviction that she possessed a noble nature. I was unconscious of the state of my own feelings at the time; but I am now disposed to think that this was the epoch at which I began to envy Ambrose the wife whom he had won.

The telegraph brought us our first news of Ambrose. He had been arrested at the hotel, and he was on his way to Morwick. The next day he arrived, and followed his brother to prison. The two were confined in separate cells, and were forbidden all communication with each other.

Two days later, the preliminary examination took place. Ambrose and Silas Meadowcroft were charged before the magistrate with the wilful murder of John Jago. I was cited to appear as one of the witnesses; and, at Naomi's own request, I took the poor girl into court, and sat by her during the proceedings.

My host also was present in his invalid-chair, with his daughter by his side. Such was the result of my voyage across the ocean in search of rest and quiet; and thus did time and chance fulfil my first hasty forebodings of the dull life I was to lead at Morwick Farm!

## VII THE MATERIALS FOR THE DEFENCE

On our way to the chairs allotted to us in the magistrate's court, we passed the platform on which the prisoners were standing together.

Silas took no notice of us. Ambrose made a friendly sign of recognition, and then rested his hand on the 'bar' in front of him. As she passed beneath him, Naomi was just tall enough to reach his hand on tiptoe. She took it. 'I know you are innocent,' she whispered, and gave him one look of loving encouragement as she followed me to her place. Ambrose never lost his self-control. I may have been wrong; but I thought this a bad sign.

The case, as stated for the prosecution, told strongly against the suspected men.

Ambrose and Silas Meadowcroft were charged with the murder of John Jago (by means of the stick or by use of some other weapon), and with the deliberate destruction of the body by throwing it into the quick-lime. In proof of this latter assertion, the knife which the deceased habitually carried about him, and the metal buttons which were known to belong to his coat, were produced. It was argued that these indestructible substances, and some fragments of the larger bones, had alone escaped the action of the burning lime. Having produced medical witnesses to support this theory by declaring the bones to be human, and having thus circumstantially asserted the discovery of the remains in the kiln, the prosecution next proceeded to prove that the missing man had been murdered by the two brothers, and had been by them thrown into the quick-lime as a means of concealing their guilt.

Witness after witness deposed to the inveterate enmity against the deceased displayed by Ambrose and Silas. The threatening language they habitually used towards him; their violent quarrels with him, which had become a public scandal throughout the neighbourhood, and which had ended (on one occasion at least) in a blow; the disgraceful scene which had taken place under my window; and the restoration to Ambrose, on the morning of the fatal quarrel, of the very stick which had been found among the remains of the dead man—these facts and events, and a host of minor circumstances besides, sworn to by witnesses whose credit was unimpeachable, pointed with terrible directness to the conclusion at which the prosecution had arrived.

I looked at the brothers as the weight of the evidence pressed more and more heavily against them. To outward view at least, Ambrose still maintained his self-possession. It was far otherwise with Silas. Abject terror showed itself in his ghastly face; in his great knotty hands, clinging convulsively to the bar at which he stood; in his staring eyes, fixed in vacant horror on each witness who appeared. Public feeling judged him on the spot. There he stood, self-betrayed already, in the popular opinion, as a guilty man!

The one point gained in cross-examination by the defence related to the charred bones.

Pressed on this point, a majority of the medical witnesses admitted that their examination had been a hurried one, and that it was just possible that the bones might yet prove to be the remains of an animal, and not of a man. The presiding magistrate decided, upon this, that a second examination should be made, and that the number of the medical experts should be increased.

Here the preliminary proceedings ended. The prisoners were remanded for three days.

The prostration of Silas at the close of the enquiry was so complete, that it was found necessary to have two men to support him on his leaving the court. Ambrose leaned over the bar to speak to Naomi before he followed the gaoler out. 'Wait,' he whispered confidently, 'till they hear what I have to say!' Naomi kissed her hand to him affectionately, and turned to me with the bright tears in her eyes.

'Why don't they hear what he has to say at once?' she asked. 'Anybody can see that Ambrose is innocent. It's a crying shame, sir, to send him back to prison. Don't you think so yourself?'

If I had confessed what I really thought, I should have said that Ambrose had proved nothing to my mind, except that he possessed rare powers of self-control. It was impossible to acknowledge this to my little friend. I diverted her mind from the question of her lover's innocence, by proposing that we should get the necessary order and visit him in his prison on the next day. Naomi dried her tears, and gave me a little grateful squeeze of the hand.

'Oh, my! what a good fellow you are!' cried the outspoken American girl. 'When your time comes to be married, sir, I guess the woman won't repent saying "Yes" to you.'

Mr Meadowcroft preserved unbroken silence as we walked back to the farm on either side of his invalid-chair. His last reserves of resolution seemed to have given way under the overwhelming strain laid on them by the proceedings in court. His daughter, in stern indulgence to Naomi, mercifully permitted her opinion to glimmer on us only, through the medium of quotation from Scripture-texts. If the texts meant anything, they meant that she had foreseen all that had happened, and that the one sad aspect of the case, to her mind, was the death of John Jago, unprepared to meet his end.

I obtained the order of admission to the prison the next morning.

We found Ambrose still confident of the favourable result, for his brother and for himself, of the enquiry before the magistrate. He seemed to be almost as eager to tell, as Naomi was to hear, the true story of what had happened at the lime-kiln. The authorities of the prison—present, of course, at the interview—warned him to remember that what he said might be taken down in writing and produced against him in court.

'Take it down, gentlemen, and welcome,' Ambrose replied. 'I have nothing to fear; I am only telling the truth.'

With that he turned to Naomi, and began his narrative, as nearly as I can remember, in these words:

'I may as well make a clean breast of it at starting, my girl. After Mr Lefrank left us that morning, I asked Silas how he came by my stick. In telling me how, Silas also told me of the words that had passed between him and John Jago under Mr Lefrank's window. I was angry and jealous; and I own it freely, Naomi, I thought the worst that could be thought about you and John.'

Here Naomi stopped him without ceremony.

'Was that what made you speak to me as you spoke when we found you at the wood?' she asked.

'Yes.'

'And was that what made you leave me, when you went away to Narrabee, without giving me a kiss at parting?'

'It was.'

'Beg my pardon for it before you say a word more.'

'I beg your pardon.'

'Say you are ashamed of yourself.'

'I am ashamed of myself,' Ambrose answered, penitently.

'Now you may go on,' said Naomi. 'Now I'm satisfied.'

Ambrose went on.

'We were on our way to the clearing at the other side of the wood while Silas was talking to me; and, as ill luck would have it, we took the path that led by the lime-kiln. Turning the corner, we met John Jago on his way to Narrabee. I was too angry, I tell you, to let him pass quietly. I gave him a bit of my mind. His blood was up too, I suppose; and he spoke out, on his side, as freely as I did. I own I threatened him with the stick; but I'll swear to it I meant him no harm. You know—after dressing Silas's hand—that John Jago is ready with his knife. He comes from out West, where they are always ready with one weapon or another handy in their pockets. It's likely enough *he* didn't mean to harm me, either; but how could I be sure of that? When he stepped up to me, and showed his weapon, I dropped the stick, and closed with him. With one hand I wrenched the knife away from him; and with the other I caught him by the collar of his rotten old coat, and gave him a shaking that made his bones rattle in his skin. A big piece of the cloth came away in my hand. I shied it into the quick-lime close by us, and I pitched the knife after the cloth; and, if Silas hadn't stopped me, I think it's likely I might have shied John Jago himself into the lime next. As it was, Silas kept hold of me. Silas shouted out to him, "Be off with you! and don't come back again, if you don't want to be burnt in the kiln!" He stood looking at us for a minute, fetching his breath, and holding his torn coat round him. Then he spoke with a deadly-quiet voice and a deadly-quiet look: "Many a true word, Mr Silas," he says, "is spoken in jest. I shall not come back again." He turned about, and left us. We stood staring at each other like a couple of fools. "You don't think he means it?" I says. "Bosh!" says Silas. "He's too sweet on Naomi not to come back." What's the matter now, Naomi?'

I had noticed it too. She started and turned pale, when Ambrose repeated to her what Silas had said to him.

'Nothing is the matter,' Naomi answered. 'Your brother has no right to take liberties with my name. Go on. Did Silas say any more while he was about it?'

'Yes: he looked into the kiln; and he says, "What made you throw away the knife, Ambrose?"—"How does a man know why he does anything," I says, "when he does it in a passion?"—"It's a ripping-good knife," says Silas: "in your place, I should have kept it." I picked up the stick off the ground. "Who says I've lost it yet?" I answered him; and with that I got up on the side of the kiln, and began sounding for the knife, to bring it, you know, by means of the stick, within easy reach of a shovel, or some such thing. "Give us your hand," I says to Silas. "Let me stretch out a bit, and I'll have it in no time." Instead of finding the knife, I came nigh to falling myself into the burning lime. The vapour overpowered me, I suppose. All I know is, I turned giddy, and dropped the stick in the kiln. I should have followed the stick, to a dead certainty, but for Silas pulling me back by the hand. "Let it be," says Silas. "If I hadn't had hold of you, John Jago's knife might have been the death of you, after all!" He led me away by the arm, and we went on together on the road to the wood. We stopped where you found us, and sat down on the felled tree. We had a little more talk about John Jago. It ended in our agreeing to wait and see what happened, and to keep our own counsel in the mean time. You and Mr Lefrank came upon us, Naomi, while we were still talking; and you guessed right when you guessed that we had a secret from you. You know the secret now.

There he stopped. I put a question to him—the first that I had asked yet. 'Had you or your brother any fear at that time of the charge which has since been brought against you?' I said.

'No such thought entered our heads, sir,' Ambrose answered. 'How could we foresee that the neighbours would search the kiln, and say what they have said of us? All we feared was, that the old man might hear of the quarrel, and be bitterer against us than ever. I was the more anxious of the two to keep things secret, because I had Naomi to consider as well as the old man. Put yourself in my place, and you will own, sir, that the prospect at home was not a pleasant one for me, if John Jago really kept away from the farm, and if it came out that it was all my doing.'

(This was certainly an explanation of his conduct; but it was not quite satisfactory to my mind.)

'As you believe, then,' I went on, 'John Jago has carried out his threat of not returning to the farm? According to you, he is now alive and in hiding somewhere?'

'Certainly!' said Ambrose.

'Certainly!' repeated Naomi.

'Do you believe the report that he was seen travelling on the railway to New York?'

'I believe it firmly, sir; and, what is more, I believe I was on his track. I was only too anxious to find him; and I say I could have found him, if they would have let me stay in New York.'

I looked at Naomi.

'I believe it too,' she said. 'John Jago is keeping away.'

'Do you suppose he is afraid of Ambrose and Silas?'

She hesitated.

'He may be afraid of them,' she replied, with a strong emphasis on the word *may*.

'But you don't think it likely?' She hesitated again. I pressed her again.

'Do you think there is any other motive for his absence?'

Her eyes dropped to the floor. She answered obstinately, almost doggedly,— 'I can't say.'

I addressed myself to Ambrose.

'Have you anything more to tell us?' I asked.

'No,' he said. 'I have told you all I know about it.'

I rose to speak to the lawyer whose services I had retained. He had helped us to get the order of admission, and he had accompanied us to the prison. Seated apart, he had kept silence throughout, attentively watching the effect of Ambrose Meadowcroft's narrative on the officers of the prison and on me.

'Is this the defence?' I enquired, in a whisper.

'This is the defence, Mr Lefrank. What do you think, between ourselves?' 'Between ourselves, I think the magistrate will commit them for trial.' 'On the charge of murder?' 'Yes; on the charge of murder.'

## VIII THE CONFESSION

My replies to the lawyer accurately expressed the conviction in my mind. The narrative related by Ambrose had all the appearance, in my eyes, of a fabricated story, got up, and clumsily got up, to pervert the plain meaning of the circumstantial evidence produced by the prosecution. I reached this conclusion reluctantly and regretfully, for Naomi's sake. I said all I could say to shake the absolute confidence which she felt in the discharge of the prisoners at the next examination.

The day of the adjourned enquiry arrived.

Naomi and I again attended the court together. Mr Meadowcroft was unable, on this occasion, to leave the house. His daughter was present, walking to the court by herself, and occupying a seat by herself.

On his second appearance at the 'bar,' Silas was more composed, and more like his brother. No new witnesses were called by the prosecution. We began the battle over the medical evidence relating to the charred bones; and, to some extent, we won the victory. In other words, we forced the doctors to acknowledge that they differed widely in their opinions. They confessed that they were not certain. Two went still further, and declared that the bones were the bones of an animal, not of a man. We made the most of this; and then we entered upon the defence, founded on Ambrose Meadowcroft's story.

Necessarily, no witnesses could be called on our side. Whether this circumstance discouraged him, or whether he privately shared my opinion of his client's statement, I cannot say—it is only certain that the lawyer spoke mechanically, doing his best, no doubt, but doing it without genuine conviction or earnestness on his own part. Naomi cast an anxious glance at me as he sat down. The girl's hand, when I took it, turned cold in mine. She saw plain signs of the failure of the defence in the look and manner of the counsel for the prosecution; but she waited resolutely until the presiding magistrate announced his decision. I had only too clearly foreseen what he would feel it to be his duty to do. Naomi's head dropped on my shoulder as he said the terrible words which committed Ambrose and Silas Meadowcroft to take their trial on the charge of murder.

I led her out of the court into the air. As I passed the 'bar,' I saw Ambrose, deadly pale, looking after us as we left him; the magistrate's decision had evidently daunted him. His brother Silas had dropped in abject terror on the gaoler's chair; the miserable wretch shook and shuddered dumbly like a cowed dog.

Miss Meadowcroft returned with us to the farm, preserving unbroken silence on the way back. I could detect nothing in her bearing which suggested any compassionate feeling for the prisoners in her stern and secret nature. On Naomi's withdrawal to her own room, we were left together for a few minutes; and then, to my astonishment, the outwardly merciless woman showed me that she, too, was one of Eve's daughters, and could feel and suffer, in her own hard way, like the rest of us. She suddenly stepped close up to me, and laid her hand on my arm.

'You are a lawyer, ain't you?' she asked.

'Yes.'

'Have you had any experience in your profession?'

'Ten years' experience.'

'Do you think—' She stopped abruptly; her hard face softened; her eyes dropped to the ground. 'Never mind,' she said, confusedly. 'I'm upset by all this misery, though I may not look like it. Don't notice me.'

She turned away. I waited, in the firm persuasion that the unspoken question in her mind would sooner or later force its way to utterance by her lips. I was right. She came back to me unwillingly, like a woman acting under some influence which the utmost exertion of her will was powerless to resist.

'Do you believe John Jago is still a living man?'

She put the question vehemently, desperately, as if the words rushed out of her mouth in spite of her.

'I do not believe it,' I answered.

'Remember what John Jago has suffered at the hands of my brothers,' she persisted. 'Is it not in your experience that he should take a sudden resolution to leave the farm?'

I replied, as plainly as before—

'It is not in my experience.'

She stood looking at me for a moment with a face of blank despair; then bowed her grey head in silence, and left me. As she crossed the room to the door, I saw her look upward; and I heard her say to herself softly, between her teeth, 'Vengeance is mine, I will repay, saith the Lord.'

It was the requiem of John Jago, pronounced by the woman who loved him.

When I next saw her, her mask was on once more. Miss Meadowcroft was herself again. Miss Meadowcroft could sit by, impenetrably calm, while the lawyers discussed the terrible position of her brothers, with the scaffold in view as one of the possibilities of the 'case'.

Left by myself, I began to feel uneasy about Naomi. I went upstairs, and, knocking softly at her door, made my enquiries from outside. The clear young voice answered me sadly, 'I am trying to bear it: I won't distress you when we meet again.' I descended the stairs, feeling my first suspicion of the true nature of my interest in the American girl. Why had her answer brought the tears into my eyes? I went out walking, alone, to think undisturbedly. Why did the tones of her voice dwell on my ear all the way? Why did my hand still feel the last cold, faint pressure of her fingers when I led her out of court?

I took a sudden resolution to go back to England.

When I returned to the farm, it was evening. The lamp was not yet lit in the hall. Pausing to accustom my eyes to the obscurity in-doors, I heard the voice of the lawyer whom we had employed for the defence, speaking to some one very earnestly.

'I'm not to blame,' said the voice. 'She snatched the paper out of my hand before I was aware of her.'

'Do you want it back?' asked the voice of Miss Meadowcroft.

'No: it's only a copy. If keeping it will help to quiet her, let her keep it by all means. Good evening.'

Saying those last words, the lawyer approached me on his way out of the house. I stopped him without ceremony: I felt an ungovernable curiosity to know more.

'Who snatched the paper out of your hand?' I asked, bluntly.

The lawyer started. I had taken him by surprise. The instinct of professional reticence made him pause before he answered me.

In the brief interval of silence, Miss Meadowcroft replied to my question from the other end of the hall.

'Naomi Colebrook snatched the paper out of his hand.'

'What paper?'

A door opened softly behind me. Naomi herself appeared on the threshold; Naomi herself answered my question.

'I will tell you,' she whispered. 'Come in here.'

One candle only was burning in the room. I looked at her by the dim light. My resolution to return to England instantly became one of the lost ideas of my life.

'Good God!' I exclaimed, 'what has happened now?'

She gave me the paper which she had taken from the lawyer's hand.

The 'copy' to which he had referred, was a copy of the written confession of Silas Meadowcroft on his return to prison. He accused his brother Ambrose of the murder of John Jago. He declared on his oath that he had seen his brother Ambrose commit the crime.

In the popular phrase, I could 'hardly believe my own eyes.' I read the last sentences of the confession for the second time: . . . I heard their voices at the lime-kiln. They were having words about Cousin Naomi. I ran to the place to part them. I was not in time. I saw Ambrose strike the deceased a terrible blow on the head with his (Ambrose's) heavy stick. The deceased dropped without a cry. I put my hand on his heart. He was dead. I was horribly frightened. Ambrose threatened to kill me next if I said a word to any living soul. He took up the body and cast it into the quick-lime, and threw the stick in after it. We went on together to the wood. We sat down on a felled tree outside the wood. Ambrose made up the story that we were to tell if what he had done was found out. He made me repeat it after him like a lesson. We were still at it when Cousin Naomi and Mr Lefrank came up to us. They know the rest. This, on my oath, is a true confession. I make it of my own free will, repenting me sincerely that I did not make it before.

(Signed) SILAS MEADOWCROFT

I laid down the paper, and looked at Naomi once more. She spoke to me with a strange composure. Immovable determination was in her eye; immovable determination was in her voice.

'Silas has lied away his brother's life to save himself,' she said. 'I see cowardly falsehood and cowardly cruelty in every line on that paper. Ambrose is innocent, and the time has come to prove it.'

'You forget,' I said, 'that we have just failed to prove it.'

She took no notice of my objection.

'John Jago is alive, in hiding from us,' she went on. 'Help me, friend Lefrank, to advertise for him in the newspapers.'

I drew back from her in speechless distress. I own I believed that the new misery which had fallen on her had affected her brain.

'You don't believe it?' she said. 'Shut the door.'

I obeyed her. She seated herself, and pointed to a chair near her.

'Sit down,' she proceeded. 'I am going to do a wrong thing, but there is no help for it. I am going to break a sacred promise. You remember that moonlight night when I met him on the garden-walk?'

'John Jago?'

'Yes. Now listen. I am going to tell you what passed between John Jago and me.'

## IX THE ADVERTISEMENT

I waited in silence for the disclosure that was now to come. Naomi began by asking me a question.

'You remember when we went to see Ambrose in prison?' she said.

'Perfectly.'

'Ambrose told us of something which his villain of a brother said of John Jago and me. Do you remember what it was?'

I remembered perfectly. Silas had said, 'John Jago is too sweet On Naomi not to come back.'

'That's so,' Naomi remarked, when I had repeated the words. 'I couldn't help starting when I heard what Silas had said; and I thought you noticed me.'

'I did notice you.'

'Did you wonder what it meant?'

'Yes.'

'I'll tell you. It meant this: What Silas Meadowcroft said to his brother of John Jago, was what I myself was thinking of John Jago at that very moment. It startled me to find my own thought in a man's mind, spoken for me by a man. I am the person, sir, who has driven John Jago away from Morwick Farm; and I am the person who can and will bring him back again.'

There was something in her manner, more than in her words, which let the light in suddenly on my mind.

'You have told me the secret,' I said. 'John Jago is in love with you.'

'Mad about me!' she rejoined, dropping her voice to a whisper. 'Stark, staring mad!—that's the only word for him. After we had taken a few turns on the gravel-walk, he suddenly broke out like a man beside himself. He fell down on his knees; he kissed my gown, he kissed my feet; he sobbed and cried for love of me. I'm not badly off for courage, sir, considering I'm a woman. No man, that I can call to mind, ever really scared me before. But, I own, John Jago frightened me: oh, my! he did frighten me! My heart was in my mouth, and my knees shook under me. I begged and prayed of him to get up and go away. No; there he knelt, and held by the skirt of my gown. The words poured out from him like—well, like nothing I can think of but water from a pump. His happiness and his life, and his hopes in earth and heaven, and Lord only knows what besides, all depended, he said, on a word from me. I plucked up spirit enough at that to remind him that I was promised to Ambrose. "I think you ought to be ashamed of yourself," I said, "to own that you are wicked enough to love me when you know I am promised to another man!" When I spoke to him, he took a new turn: he began abusing Ambrose. That straightened me up. I snatched my gown out of his hand, and I gave him my whole mind. "I hate you!" I said. "Even if I wasn't promised to Ambrose, I wouldn't marry you; no! not if there wasn't another man left in the world to ask me. I hate you, Mr Jago! I hate you!" He saw I was in earnest at last. He got up from my feet, and he settled down quiet again, all on a sudden. "You have said enough" (that was how he answered me). "You have broken my life. I have no hopes and no prospects now. I had a pride in the farm, miss, and a pride in my work; I bore with your brutish cousins' hatred of me; I was faithful to Mr Meadowcroft's interests; all for your sake, Naomi Colebrook—all for your sake! I have done with it now; I have done with my life at the farm. You will never be troubled with me again. I am going away, as the dumb creatures go when they are sick, to hide myself in a corner, and die. Do me one last favour. Don't make me the laughing-stock of the whole neighbourhood.

I can't bear that: it maddens me, only to think of it. Give me your promise never to tell any living soul what I have said to you to-night—your sacred promise to the man whose life you have broken!" I did as he bade me: I gave him my sacred promise with the tears in my eyes. Yes; that is so. After telling him I hated him (and I did hate him), I cried over his misery; I did. Mercy, what fools women are! What is the horrid perversity, sir, which makes us always ready to pity the men? He held out his hand to me; and he said, "Good bye for ever!' and I pitied him. I said, "I'll shake hands with you if you will give me your promise in exchange for mine. I beg of you not to leave the farm. What will my uncle do if you go away? Stay here, and be friends with me; and forget and forgive, Mr John." He gave me his promise (he can refuse me nothing); and he gave it again when I saw him again the next morning. Yes, I'll do him justice, though I do hate him! I believe he honestly meant to keep his word as long as my eye was on him. It was only when he was left to himself that the Devil tempted him to break his promise, and leave the farm. I was brought up to believe in the Devil, Mr Lefrank; and I find it explains many things. It explains John Jago. Only let me find out where he has gone, and I'll engage he shall come back and clear Ambrose of the suspicion which his vile brother has cast on him. Here is the pen all ready for you. Advertise for him, friend Lefrank; and do it right away, for my sake!'

I let her run on, without attempting to dispute her conclusions, until she could say no more. When she put the pen into my hand, I began the composition of the advertisement, as obediently as if I, too, believed that John Jago was a living man.

In the case of anyone else, I should have openly acknowledged that my own convictions remained unshaken. If no quarrel had taken place at the lime-kiln, I should have been quite ready, as I viewed the case, to believe that John Jago's disappearance was referable to the terrible disappointment which Naomi had inflicted on him. The same morbid dread of ridicule which had led him to assert that he cared nothing for Naomi, when he and Silas had quarrelled under my bedroom-window, might also have impelled him to withdraw himself secretly and suddenly from the scene of his discomfiture. But to ask me to believe, after what had happened at the lime-kiln, that he was still living, was to ask me to take Ambrose Meadowcroft's statement for granted as a true statement of facts.

I had refused to do this from the first; and I still persisted in taking that course. If I had been called upon to decide the balance of probability between the narrative related by Ambrose in his defence and the narrative related by

Silas in his confession. I must have owned, no matter how unwillingly, that the confession was, to my mind, the least incredible story of the two.

Could I say this to Naomi? I would have written fifty advertisements enquiring for John Jago rather than say it; and you would have done the same, if you had been as fond of her as I was.

I drew out the advertisement, for insertion in 'The Morwick Mercury,' in these terms:

MURDER.—Printers of newspapers throughout the United States are desired to publish that Ambrose Meadowcroft and Silas Meadowcroft, of Morwick Farm, Morwick County, are committed for trial on the charge of murdering John Jago, now missing from the farm and from the neighbourhood. Any person who can give information of the existence of said Jago may save the lives of two wrongly accused men by making immediate communication. Jago is about five feet four inches high. He is spare and wiry; his complexion is extremely pale; his eyes are dark, and very bright and restless. The lower part of his face is concealed by a thick black beard and mustache. The whole appearance of the man is wild and flighty.

I added the date and address. That evening a servant was sent on horseback to Narrabee to procure the insertion of the advertisement in the next issue of the newspaper.

When we parted that night, Naomi looked almost like her brighter and happier self. Now that the advertisement was on its way to the printing-office, she was more than sanguine: she was certain of the result.

'You don't know how you have comforted me,' she said, in her frank, warm-hearted way, when we parted for the night. 'All the newspapers will copy it, and we shall hear of John Jago before the week is out.' She turned to go, and came back again to me. 'I will never forgive Silas for writing that confession!' she whispered in my ear. 'If he ever lives under the same roof with Ambrose again, I—well, I believe I wouldn't marry Ambrose if he did. There!'

She left me. Through the wakeful hours of the night my mind dwelt on her last words. That she should contemplate, under any circumstances, even the bare possibility of not marrying Ambrose, was, I am ashamed to say, a direct encouragement to certain hopes which I had already begun to form in secret. The next day's mail brought me a letter on business. My clerk wrote to enquire if there was any chance of my returning to England in time to appear in court at the opening of next law term. I answered, without hesitation, 'It is still impossible for me to fix the date of my return.' Naomi was in the room while I was writing.

How would she have answered, I wonder, if I had told her the truth, and said, 'You are responsible for this letter?'

## X THE SHERIFF AND THE GOVERNOR

The question of time was now a serious question at Morwick Farm. In six weeks, the court for the trial of criminal cases was to be opened at Narrabee.

During this interval, no new event of any importance occurred.

Many idle letters reached us relating to the advertisement for John Jago; but no positive information was received. Not the slightest trace of the lost man turned up; not the shadow of a doubt was cast on the assertion of the prosecution, that his body had been destroyed in the kiln. Silas Meadowcroft held firmly to the horrible confession that he had made. His brother Ambrose, with equal resolution, asserted his innocence, and reiterated the statement which he had already advanced. At regular periods I accompanied Naomi to visit him in the prison. As the day appointed for the opening of the court approached, he seemed to falter a little in his resolution; his manner became restless; and he grew irritably suspicious about the merest trifles. This change did not necessarily imply the consciousness of guilt: it might merely have indicated natural nervous agitation as the time for the trial drew near. Naomi noticed the alteration in her lover. It greatly increased her anxiety, though it never shook her confidence in Ambrose.

Except at meal-times, I was left, during the period of which I am now writing, almost constantly alone with the charming American girl. Miss Meadowcroft searched the newspapers for tidings of the living John Jago in the privacy of her own room. Mr Meadowcroft would see nobody but his daughter and his doctor, and occasionally one or two old friends. I have since had reason to believe that Naomi, in these days of our intimate association, discovered the true nature of the feeling with which she had inspired me. But she kept her secret. Her manner towards me steadily remained the manner of a sister: she never over-stepped by a hair's breadth the safe limits of the character she had assumed.

The sittings of the court began. After hearing the evidence, and examining the confession of Silas Meadowcroft, the grand jury found a true bill against both the prisoners. The day appointed for the trial was the first day in the new week.

I had carefully prepared Naomi's mind for the decision of the grand jury. She bore the new blow bravely.

'If you are not tired of it,' she said, 'come with me to the prison to-morrow. Ambrose will need a little comfort by that time.' She paused, and looked at the day's letters lying on the table. 'Still not a word about John Jago,' she said. 'And all the papers have copied the advertisement. I felt so sure we should hear of him long before this!'

'Do you still feel sure that he is living?' I ventured to ask.

'I am as certain of it as ever,' she replied firmly. 'He is somewhere in hiding: perhaps he is in disguise. Suppose we know no more of him than we know now, when the trial begins? Suppose the jury—' She stopped, shuddering. Death—shameful death on the scaffold—might be the terrible result of the consultation of the jury. 'We have waited for news to come to us long enough,' Naomi resumed. 'We must find the tracks of John Jago for ourselves. There is a week yet before the trial begins. Who will help me to make enquiries? Will you be the man, friend Lefrank?'

It is needless to add (though I knew nothing would come of it) that I consented to be the man.

We arranged to apply that day for the order of admission to the prison, and, having seen Ambrose, to devote ourselves immediately to the contemplated search. How that search was to be conducted was more than I could tell, and more than Naomi could tell. We were to begin by applying to the police to help us to find John Jago, and we were then to be guided by circumstances. Was there ever a more hopeless programme than this?

'Circumstances' declared themselves against us at starting. I applied, as usual, for the order of admission to the prison, and the order was for the first time refused; no reason being assigned by the persons in authority for taking this course. Enquire as I might, the only answer given was, 'Not to-day.'

At Naomi's suggestion, we went to the prison to seek the explanation which was refused to us at the office. The gaoler on duty at the outer gate was one of Naomi's many admirers. He solved the mystery cautiously in a whisper. The sheriff and the governor of the prison were then speaking privately with Ambrose Meadowcroft in his cell: they had expressly directed that no persons should be admitted to see the prisoner that day but themselves.

What did it mean? We returned, wondering, to the farm. There Naomi, speaking by chance to one of the female servants, made certain discoveries.

Early that morning the sheriff had been brought to Morwick by an old friend of the Meadowcrofts. A long interview had been held between Mr Meadowcroft and his daughter and the official personage introduced by the friend. Leaving the farm, the sheriff had gone straight to the prison, and had proceeded with the governor to visit Ambrose in his cell. Was some potent influence being brought privately to bear on Ambrose? Appearances certainly suggested that enquiry. Supposing the influence to have been really exerted, the next question followed, What was the object in view? We could only wait and see. Our patience was not severely tried. The event of the next day enlightened us in a very unexpected manner. Before noon, the neighbours brought startling news from the prison to the farm. Ambrose Meadowcroft had confessed himself to be the murderer of John Jago! He had signed the confession in the presence of the sheriff and the governor on that very day! I saw the document. It is needless to reproduce it here. In substance, Ambrose confessed what Silas had confessed; claiming, however, to have only struck Jago under intolerable provocation, so as to reduce the nature of his offence against the law from murder to manslaughter. Was the confession really the true statement of what had taken place? or had the sheriff and the governor, acting in the interests of the family name, persuaded Ambrose to try this desperate means of escaping the ignominy of death on the scaffold? The sheriff and the governor preserved impenetrable silence until the pressure put on them judicially at the trial obliged them to speak. Who was to tell Naomi of this last and saddest of all the calamities which had fallen on her? Knowing how I loved her in secret, I felt an invincible reluctance to be the person who revealed Ambrose Meadowcroft's degradation to his betrothed wife. Had any other member of the family told her what had happened? The lawyer was able to answer me: Miss Meadowcroft had told her.

I was shocked when I heard it. Miss Meadowcroft was the last person in the house to spare the poor girl: Miss Meadowcroft would make the hard tidings doubly terrible to bear in the telling. I tried to find Naomi, without success. She had been always accessible at other times. Was she hiding herself from me now? The idea occurred to me as I was descending the stairs after vainly knocking at the door of her room. I was determined to see her. I waited a few minutes, and then ascended the stairs again suddenly. On the landing I met her, just leaving her room.

She tried to run back. I caught her by the arm, and detained her. With her free hand she held her handkerchief over her face so as to hide it from me.

'You once told me I had comforted you,' I said to her, gently. 'Won't you let me comfort you now?'

She still struggled to get away, and still kept her head turned from me.

'Don't you see that I am ashamed to look you in the face?' she said, in low, broken tones. 'Let me go.'

I still persisted in trying to sooth her. I drew her to the window-seat. I said I would wait until she was able to speak to me.

She dropped on the seat, and wrung her hands on her lap. Her downcast eyes still obstinately avoided meeting mine.

'Oh!' she said to herself, 'what madness possessed me? Is it possible that I ever disgraced myself by loving Ambrose Meadowcroft?' She shuddered as the idea found its way to expression on her lips. The tears rolled slowly over her cheeks. 'Don't despise me, Mr Lefrank!' she said, faintly.

I tried, honestly tried, to put the confession before her in its least unfavourable light.

'His resolution has given way,' I said. 'He has done this, despairing of proving his innocence, in terror of the scaffold.'

She rose, with an angry stamp of her foot. She turned her face on me with the deep red flush of shame in it, and the big tears glistening in her eyes.

'No more of him!' she said, sternly. 'If he is not a murderer, what else is he? A liar and a coward! In which of his characters does he disgrace me most? I have done with him for ever! I will never speak to him again!' She pushed me furiously away from her; advanced a few steps towards her own door; stopped, and came back to me. The generous nature of the girl spoke in her next words. 'I am not ungrateful to you, friend Lefrank. A woman in my place is only a woman; and, when she is shamed as I am, she feels it very bitterly. Give me your hand! God bless you!'

She put my hand to her lips before I was aware of her, and kissed it, and ran back into her room.

I sat down on the place which she had occupied. She had looked at me for one moment when she kissed my hand. I forgot Ambrose and his confession; I forgot the coming trial; I forgot my professional duties and my English friends. There I sat, in a fool's elysium of my own making, with absolutely nothing in my mind but the picture of Naomi's face at the moment when she had last looked at me!

I have already mentioned that I was in love with her. I merely add this to satisfy you that I tell the truth.

## XI THE PEBBLE AND THE WINDOW

Miss Meadowcroft and I were the only representatives of the family at the farm who attended the trial. We went separately to Narrabee. Excepting the ordinary greetings at morning and night, Miss Meadowcroft had not said one word to me since the time when I told her that I did not believe John Jago to be a living man.

I have purposely abstained from encumbering my narrative with legal details. I now propose to state the nature of the defence in the briefest outline only.

We insisted on making both the prisoners plead 'Not guilty.' This done, we took an objection to the legality of the proceedings at starting. We appealed to the old English law, that there should be no conviction for murder until the body of the murdered person was found, or proof of its destruction obtained beyond a doubt. We denied that sufficient proof had been obtained in the case now before the court.

The judges consulted, and decided that the trial should go on.

We took our next objection when the Confessions were produced in evidence. We declared that they had been extorted by terror, or by undue influence; and we pointed out certain minor particulars in which the two confessions failed to corroborate each other. For the rest, our defence on this occasion was, as to essentials, what our defence had been at the enquiry before the magistrate. Once more the judges consulted, and once more they overruled our objection. The Confessions were admitted in evidence.

On their side, the prosecution produced one new witness in support of their case. It is needless to waste time in recapitulating his evidence. He contradicted himself gravely on cross-examination. We showed plainly, and after investigation proved, that he was not to be believed on his oath.

The Chief Justice summed up.

He charged, in relation to the Confessions, that no weight should be attached to a confession incited by hope or fear; and he left it to the jury to determine whether the Confessions in this case had been so influenced. In the course of the trial, it had been shown for the defence that the sheriff and the governor of the prison had told Ambrose, with his father's knowledge and sanction, that the case was clearly against him; that the only chance of sparing his family the disgrace of his death by public execution lay in making a confession; and that they would do their best, if he did confess, to have his sentence commuted to transportation for life. As for Silas, he was proved to have been beside himself with terror when he made his abominable charge against his brother. We had vainly trusted to the evidence on these two points to induce the court to reject the Confessions; and we were destined to be once more disappointed in anticipating that the same evidence would influence the verdict of the jury on the side of mercy. After an absence of an hour, they returned into court with a verdict of 'Guilty' against both the prisoners.

Being asked in due form if they had anything to say in mitigation of their sentence, Ambrose and Silas solemnly declared their innocence, and publicly acknowledged that their respective confessions had been wrung from them with the hope of escaping the hangman's hands. This statement was not noticed by the bench. The prisoners were both sentenced to death.

On my return to the farm, I did not see Naomi. Miss Meadowcroft informed her of the result of the trial. Half an hour later, one of the women-servants handed to me an envelope bearing, my name on it in Naomi's handwriting.

The envelope enclosed a letter, and with it a slip of paper on which Naomi had hurriedly written these words: 'For God's sake, read the letter I send to you, and do something about it immediately!'

I looked at the letter. It assumed to be written by a gentleman in New York. Only the day before, he had, by the merest accident, seen the advertisement for John Jago, cut out of a newspaper and pasted into a book of 'curiosities' kept by a friend. Upon this he wrote to Morwick Farm to say that he had seen a man exactly answering to the description of John Jago, but bearing another name, working as a clerk in a merchant's office in Jersey City. Having time to spare before the mail went out, he had returned to the office to take another look at the man before he posted his letter. To his surprise, he was informed that the clerk had not appeared at his desk that day. His employer had sent to his lodgings, and had been informed that he had suddenly packed up his hand-bag after reading the newspaper at breakfast; had paid his rent honestly, and had gone away, nobody knew where!

It was late in the evening when I read these lines. I had time for reflection before it would be necessary for me to act.

Assuming the letter to be genuine, and adopting Naomi's explanation of the motive which had led John Jago to absent himself secretly from the farm, I reached the conclusion that the search for him might be usefully limited to Narrabee and to the surrounding neighbourhood.

The newspaper at his breakfast had no doubt given him his first information of the 'finding' of the grand jury, and of the trial to follow. It was in my experience of human nature that he should venture back to Narrabee under these circumstances, and under the influence of his infatuation for Naomi. More than this, it was again in my experience, I am sorry to say, that he should attempt to make the critical position of Ambrose a means of extorting Naomi's consent to listen favourably to his suit. Cruel indifference to the injury and the suffering which his sudden absence might inflict on others, was plainly implied in his secret withdrawal from the farm. The same cruel indifference, pushed to a further extreme, might well lead him to press his proposals privately on Naomi, and to fix her acceptance of them as the price to be paid for saving her cousin's life.

To these conclusions I arrived after much thinking. I had determined, on Naomi's account, to clear the matter up; but it is only candid to add, that my doubts of John Jago's existence remained unshaken by the letter. I believed it to be nothing more nor less than a heartless and stupid 'hoax.'

The striking of the hall-clock roused me from my meditations. I counted the strokes—midnight!

I rose to go up to my room. Everybody else in the farm had retired to bed, as usual, more than an hour since. The stillness in the house was breathless. I walked softly, by instinct, as I crossed the room to look out at the night. A lovely moonlight met my view: it was like the moonlight on the fatal evening when Naomi had met John Jago on the garden-walk.

My bedroom-candle was on the side-table: I had just lit it. I was just leaving the room, when the door suddenly opened, and Naomi herself stood before me!

Recovering the first shock of her sudden appearance, I saw instantly, in her eager eyes, in her deadly pale cheeks, that something serious had happened. A large cloak was thrown over her; a white handkerchief was tied over her head. Her hair was in disorder: she had evidently just risen in fear and in haste from her bed.

'What is it?' I asked, advancing to meet her.

She clung trembling with agitation to my arm.

'John Jago!' she whispered.

You will think my obstinacy invincible. I could hardly believe it, even then!

'Do you mean John Jago's ghost?' I asked.

'I have seen John Jago himself,' she answered.

'Where?'

'In the back yard, under my bedroom-window!'

The emergency was far too serious to allow of any consideration for the small proprieties of every-day life.

'Let me see him!' I said.

'I am here to fetch you,' she replied, in her frank and fearless way. 'Come upstairs with me.'

Her room was on the first floor of the house, and was the only bedroom which looked out on the back yard. On our way up the stairs she told me what had happened.

'I was in bed,' she said, 'but not asleep, when I heard a pebble strike against the window-pane. I waited, wondering what it meant. Another pebble was thrown against the glass. So far, I was surprised, but not frightened. I got up, and ran to the window to look out. There was John Jago, looking up at me in the moonlight!'

'Did he see you?'

'Yes. He said, "Come down and speak to me! I have something serious to say to you!"'

'Did you answer him?'

'As soon as I could fetch my breath, I said, "Wait a little," and ran downstairs to you. What shall I do?'

'Let me see him, and I will tell you.'

We entered her room. Keeping cautiously behind the window-curtain, I looked out.

There he was! His beard and moustache were shaved off: his hair was cut close. But there was no disguising his wild brown eyes, or the peculiar movement of his spare wiry figure, as he walked slowly to and fro in the moonlight, waiting for Naomi. For the moment, my own agitation almost overpowered me: I had so firmly disbelieved that John Jago was a living man!

'What shall I do?' Naomi repeated.

'Is the door of the dairy open?' I asked.

'No; but the door of the tool-house, round the corner, is not locked.'

'Very good. Show yourself at the window, and say to him, "I am coming directly."'

The brave girl obeyed me without a moment's hesitation.

There had been no doubt about his eyes and his gait: there was no doubt now about his voice, as he answered softly from below—'All right!'

'Keep him talking to you where he is now,' I said to Naomi, 'until I have time to get round by the other way to the tool-house. Then pretend to be fearful of discovery at the dairy; and bring him round the corner, so that I can hear him behind the door.'

We left the house together, and separated silently. Naomi followed my instructions with a woman's quick intelligence where stratagems are concerned.

I had hardly been a minute in the tool-house before I heard him speaking to Naomi on the other side of the door.

The first words which I caught distinctly related to his motive for secretly leaving the farm. Mortified pride—doubly mortified by Naomi's contemptuous refusal, and by the personal indignity offered to him by Ambrose—was at the bottom of his conduct in absenting himself from Morwick. He owned that he had seen the advertisement, and that it had actually encouraged him to keep in hiding!

'After being laughed at and insulted and denied, I was glad,' said the miserable wretch, 'to see that some of you had serious reason to wish me back again. It rests with you, Miss Naomi, to keep me here, and to persuade me to save Ambrose by showing myself, and owning to my name.'

'What do you mean?' I heard Naomi ask, sternly.

He lowered his voice; but I could still hear him.

'Promise you will marry me,' he said, 'and I will go before the magistrate tomorrow, and show him that I am a living man.'

'Suppose I refuse?'

'In that case you will lose me again, and none of you will find me till Ambrose is hanged.'

'Are you villain enough, John Jago, to mean what you say?' asked the girl, raising her voice.

'If you attempt to give the alarm,' he answered, 'as true as God's above us, you will feel my hand on your throat! It's my turn now, miss; and I am not to be trifled with. Will you have me for your husband,—yes or no?'

'No!' she answered, loudly and firmly.

I threw open the door, and seized him as he lifted his hand on her. He had not suffered from the nervous derangement which had weakened me, and he was the stronger man of the two. Naomi saved my life. She struck up his pistol as he pulled it out of his pocket with his free hand, and presented it at my head. The bullet was fired into the air. I tripped up his heels at the same moment. The report of the pistol had alarmed the house. We two together kept him on the ground until help arrived.

## XII THE END OF IT

John Jago was brought before the magistrate, and John Jago was identified the next day.

The lives of Ambrose and Silas were, of course, no longer in peril, so far as human justice was concerned. But there were legal delays to be encountered, and legal formalities to be observed, before the brothers could be released from prison in the characters of innocent men.

During the interval which thus elapsed, certain events happened which may be briefly mentioned here before I close my narrative.

Mr Meadowcroft the elder, broken by the suffering which he had gone through, died suddenly of a rheumatic affection of the heart. A codicil attached to his will abundantly justified what Naomi had told me of Miss Meadowcroft's influence over her father, and of the end she had in view in exercising it. A life-income only was left to Mr Meadowcroft's sons. The freehold of the farm was bequeathed to his daughter, with the testator's recommendation added, that she should marry his 'best and dearest friend, Mr John Jago.'

Armed with the power of the will, the heiress of Morwick sent an insolent message to Naomi, requesting her no longer to consider herself one of the inmates at the farm. Miss Meadowcroft, it should be here added, positively refused to believe that John Jago had ever asked Naomi to be his wife, or had ever threatened her, as I had heard him threaten her, if she refused. She accused me, as she accused Naomi, of trying meanly to injure John Jago in her estimation, out of hatred towards 'that much-injured man;' and she sent to me, as she had sent to Naomi, a formal notice to leave the house.

We two banished ones met the same day in the hall, with our travelling bags in our hands.

'We are turned out together, friend Lefrank,' said Naomi, with her quaintly comical smile. 'You will go back to England, I guess; and I must make my own living in my own country. Women can get employment in the States if they have a friend to speak for them. Where shall I find somebody who can give me a place?'

I saw my way to saying the right word at the right moment.

'I have got a place to offer you,' I replied, 'if you see no objection to accepting it.' She suspected nothing, so far. 'That's lucky, sir,' was all she said. 'Is it in a telegraph-office or in a dry-goods store?' I astonished my little American friend by taking her then and there in my arms, and giving her my first kiss. 'The office is by my fireside,' I said. 'The salary is anything in reason you like to ask me for. And the place, Naomi, if you have no objection to it, is the place of my wife.' I have no more to say, except that years have passed since I spoke those words, and that I am as fond of Naomi as ever.

Some months after our marriage, Mrs Lefrank wrote to a friend at Narrabee for news of what was going on at the farm. The answer informed us that Ambrose and Silas had emigrated to New Zealand, and that Miss Meadowcroft was alone at Morwick Farm.

John Jago had refused to marry her. John Jago had disappeared again, nobody knew where.

# THE TERROR
## GUY DE MAUPASSANT

You say you cannot possibly understand it, and I believe you. You think I am losing my mind? Perhaps I am, but for other reasons than those you imagine, my dear friend.

Yes, I am going to be married, and will tell you what has led me to take that step.

I may add that I know very little of the girl who is going to become my wife tomorrow; I have only seen her four or five times. I know that there is nothing unpleasing about her, and that is enough for my purpose. She is small, fair, and stout; so, of course, the day after to-morrow J shall ardently wish for a tall, dark, thin woman.

She is not rich, and belongs to the middle classes. She is a girl such as you may find by the gross, well adapted for matrimony, without any apparent faults, and with no particularly striking qualities. People say of her:

"Mile. Lajolle is a very nice girl," and to-morrow they will say: "What a very nice woman Madame Raymon is." She belongs, in a word, to that immense number of girls whom one is glad to have for one's wife, till the moment comes when one discovers that one happens to prefer all other women to that particular woman whom one has married.

"Well," you will say to me, "what on earth did you get married for?"

I hardly like to tell you the strange and seemingly improbable reason that urged me on to this senseless act; the fact, however, is that I am afraid of being alone.

I don't know how to tell you or to make you understand me, but my state of mind is so wretched that you will pity me and despise me.

I do not want to be alone any longer at night. I want to feel that there is some one close to me, touching me, a being who can speak and say something, no matter what it be.

I wish to be able to awaken somebody by my side, so that I may be able to ask some sudden question, a stupid question even, if I feel inclined, so that I may hear a human voice, and feel that there is some waking soul close to me, some one whose reason is at work; so that when I hastily light the candle I may see some human face by my side because—because—I am ashamed to confess it—because I am afraid of being alone.

Oh, you don't understand me yet.

I am not afraid of any danger; if a man were to come into the room, I should kill him without trembling. I am not afraid of ghosts, nor do I believe in the supernatural. I am not afraid of dead people, for I believe in the total annihilation of every being that disappears from the face of this earth.

Well—yes, well, it must be told: I am afraid of myself, afraid of that horrible sensation of incomprehensible fear.

You may laugh, if you like. It is terrible, and I cannot get over it. I am afraid of the walls, of the furniture, of the familiar objects; which are animated, as far as I am concerned, by a kind of animal life. Above all, I am afraid of my own dreadful thoughts, of my reason, which seems as if it were about to leave me, driven away by a mysterious and invisible agony.

At first I feel a vague uneasiness in my mind, which causes a cold shiver to run all over me. I look round, and of course nothing is to be seen, and I wish that there were something there, no matter what, as long as it were something tangible. I am frightened merely because I cannot understand my own terror.

If I speak, I am afraid of my own voice. If I walk, I am afraid of I know not what, behind the door, behind the curtains, in the cupboard, or under my bed, and yet all the time I know there is nothing anywhere, and I turn round suddenly because I am afraid of what is behind me, although there is nothing there, and I know it.

I become agitated. I feel that my fear increases, and so I shut myself up in my own room, get into bed, and hide under the clothes; and there, cowering down, rolled into a ball, I close my eyes in despair, and remain thus for an indefinite time, remembering that my candle is alight on the table by my bedside, and that I ought to put it out, and yet—I dare not do it!

It is very terrible, is it not, to be like that?

Formerly I felt nothing of all that. I came home quite calm, and went up and down my apartment without anything disturbing my peace of mind. Had any one told me that I should be attacked by a malady—for I can call it nothing else—of most improbable fear, such a stupid and terrible malady as it is, I should have laughed outright. I was certainly never afraid of opening the door in the dark. I went to bed slowly, without locking it, and never got up in the middle of the night to make sure that everything was firmly closed.

It began last year in a very strange manner on a damp autumn evening. When my servant had left the room, after I had dined, I asked myself what I was going to do. I walked up and down my room for some time, feeling tired without any reason for it, unable to work, and even without energy to read. A fine rain was falling, and I felt unhappy, a prey to one of those fits of despondency, without any apparent cause, which make us feel inclined to cry, or to talk, no matter to whom, so as to shake off our depressing thoughts.

I felt that I was alone, and my rooms seemed to me to be more empty than they had ever been before. I was in the midst of infinite and overwhelming solitude. What was I to do? I sat down, but a kind of nervous impatience seemed to affect my legs, so I got up and began to walk about again. I was, perhaps, rather feverish, for my hands, which I had clasped behind me, as one often does when walking slowly, almost seemed to burn one another. Then suddenly a cold shiver ran down my back, and I thought the damp air might have penetrated into my rooms, so I lit the fire for the first time that year, and sat down again and looked at the flames. But soon I felt that I could not possibly remain quiet, and so I got up again and determined to go out, to pull myself together, and to find a friend to bear me company.

I could not find any one, so I walked to the boulevard to try and meet some acquaintance or other there.

It was wretched everywhere, and the wet pavement glistened in the gaslight, while the oppressive warmth of the almost impalpable rain lay heavily over the streets and seemed to obscure the light of the lamps.

I went on slowly, saying to myself: "I shall not find a soul to talk to."

I glanced into several cafes, from the Madeleine as far as the Faubourg Poissonière, and saw many unhappy-looking individuals sitting at the tables, who did not seem even to have enough energy left to finish the refreshments they had ordered.

For a long time I wandered aimlessly up and down, and about midnight I started for home. I was very calm and very tired. My janitor opened the door at once, which was quite unusual for him, and I thought that another lodger had probably just come in.

When I go out I always double-lock the door of my room, and I found it merely closed, which surprised me; but I supposed that some letters had been brought up for me in the course of the evening.

I went in, and found my fire still burning so that it lighted up the room a little, and, while in the act of taking up a candle, I noticed somebody sitting in my armchair by the fire, warming his feet, with his back toward me.

I was not in the slightest degree frightened. I thought, very naturally, that some friend or other had come to see me. No doubt the porter, to whom I had said I was going out, had lent him his own key. In a moment I remembered all the circumstances of my return, how the street door had been opened immediately, and that my own door was only latched and not locked.

I could see nothing of my friend but his head, and he had evidently gone to sleep while waiting for me, so I went up to him to rouse him. I saw him quite distinctly; his right arm was hanging down and his legs were crossed; the position of his head, which was somewhat inclined to the left of the armchair, seemed to indicate that he was asleep. "Who can it be?" I asked myself. I could not see clearly, as the room was rather dark, so I put out my hand to touch him on the shoulder, and it came in contact with the back of the chair. There was nobody there; the seat was empty.

I fairly jumped with fright. For a moment I drew back as if confronted by some terrible danger; then I turned round again, impelled by an imperious standing upright, panting with fear, so upset that I could not collect my thoughts, and ready to faint.

But I am a cool man, and soon recovered myself. I thought: "It is a mere hallucination, that is all," and I immediately began to reflect on this phenomenon. Thoughts fly quickly at such moments.

I had been suffering from an hallucination, that was an incontestable fact. My mind had been perfectly lucid and had acted regularly and logically, so there was nothing the matter with the brain. It was only my eyes that had been deceived; they had had a vision, one of those visions which lead simple folk to believe in miracles. It was a nervous seizure of the optical apparatus, nothing more; the eyes were rather congested, perhaps.

I lit my candle, and when I stooped down to the fire in doing so I noticed that I was trembling, and I raised myself up with a jump, as if somebody had touched me from behind.

I was certainly not by any means calm.

I walked up and down a little, and hummed a tune or two. Then I double-locked the door and felt rather reassured; now, at any rate, nobody could come in.

I sat down again and thought over my adventure for a long time; then I went to bed and blew out my light.

For some minutes all went well; I lay quietly on my back, but presently an irresistible desire seized me to look round the room, and I turned over on my side.

My fire was nearly out, and the few glowing embers threw a faint light on the floor by the chair, where I fancied I saw the man sitting again.

I quickly struck a match, but I had been mistaken; there was nothing there. I got up, however, and hid the chair behind my bed, and tried to get to sleep, as the room was now dark; but I had not forgotten myself for more than five minutes, when in my dream I saw all the scene which I had previously witnessed as clearly as if it were reality. I woke up with a start, and having lit the candle, sat up in bed, without venturing even to try to go to sleep again.

Twice, however, sleep overcame me for a few moments in spite of myself, and twice I saw the same thing again, till I fancied I was going mad. When day broke, however, I thought that I was cured, and slept peacefully till noon.

It was all past and over. I had been feverish, had had the nightmare. I know not what. I had been ill, in fact, but yet thought I was a great fool.

I enjoyed myself thoroughly that evening. I dined at a restaurant and afterward went to the theatre, and then started for home. But as I got near the house I was once more seized by a strange feeling of uneasiness. I was afraid of seeing him again. I was not afraid of him, not afraid of his presence, in which I did not believe; but I was afraid of being deceived again. I was afraid of some fresh hallucination, afraid lest fear should take possession of me.

For more than an hour I wandered up and down the pavement; then, feeling that I was really too foolish, I returned home. I breathed so hard that I could hardly get upstairs, and remained standing outside my door for more than ten minutes; then suddenly I had a courageous impulse and my will asserted itself. I inserted my key into the lock, and went into the apartment with a candle in my hand. I kicked open my bedroom door, which was partly open, and cast a frightened glance toward the fireplace. There was nothing there. A-h!

What a relief and what a delight! What a deliverance! I walked up and down briskly and boldly, but I was not altogether reassured, and kept turning round with a jump; the very shadows in the corners disquieted me.

I slept badly, and was constantly disturbed by imaginary noises, but did not see him; no, that was all over.

Since that time I have been afraid of being alone at night. I feel that the spectre is there, close to me, around me; but it has not appeared to me again. And supposing it did, what would it matter, since I do not believe in it, and know that it is nothing?

However, it still worries me, because I am constantly thinking of it. *His right arm hanging down and his head inclined to the left like a man who was asleep—* I don't want to think about it!

Why, however, am I so persistently possessed with this idea? His feet were close to the fire!

He haunts me; it is very stupid, but who and what is he? I know that he does not exist except in my cowardly imagination, in my fears, and in my agony. There—enough of that!

Yes, it is all very well for me to reason with myself, *to stiffen my backbone,* so to say; but I cannot remain at home because I know he is there. I know I shall not see him again; he will not show himself again; that is all over. But he is there, all the same, in my thoughts. He remains invisible, but that does not prevent his being there. He is behind the doors, in the closed cupboard, in the wardrobe, under the bed, in every dark corner. If I open the door or the cupboard, if I take the candle to look under the bed and throw a light on the dark places, he is there no longer, but I feel that be is behind me. I turn round, certain that I shall not see him, that I shall never see him again; but for all that, he is behind me.

It is very stupid, it is dreadful; but what am I to do? I cannot help it. But if there were two of us in the place I feel certain that he would not be there any longer, for he is there just because I am alone, simply and solely because I am alone!

# NOT TO BE TAKEN AT BED-TIME
## ROSA MULHOLLAND

This is the legend of a house called the Devil's Inn, standing in the heather on the top of the Connemara mountains, in a shallow valley hollowed between five peaks. Tourists sometimes come in sight of it on September evenings; a crazy and weather-stained apparition, with the sun glaring at it angrily between the hills, and striking its shattered window-panes. Guides are known to shun it, however.

The house was built by a stranger, who came no one knew whence, and whom the people nicknamed Coll Dhu (Black-Coll), because of his sullen bearing and solitary habits. His dwelling they called the Devil's Inn, because no tired traveller had ever been asked to rest under its roof, nor friend known to cross its threshold. No one bore him company in his retreat but a wizen-faced old man, who shunned the good-morrow of the trudging peasant when he made occasional excursions to the nearest village for provisions for himself and master, and who was as secret as a stone concerning all the antecedents of both.

For the first year of their residence in the country, there had been much speculation as to who they were, and what they did with themselves up there among the clouds and eagles. Some said that Coll Dhu was a scion of the old family from whose hands the surrounding lands had passed; and that, embittered by poverty and pride, he had come to bury himself in solitude, and brood over his misfortunes. Others hinted of crime, and flight from another country; others again whispered of those who were cursed from their birth, and could never smile, nor yet make friends with a fellow-creature till the day of their death. But when two years had passed, the wonder had somewhat died out, and Coll Dhu was little thought of, except when a herd looking for sheep crossed the track of a big dark man walking the mountains gun in hand, to whom he did not dare say 'Lord save you!' or when a housewife rocking the cradle of a winter's night, crossed herself as a gust of storm thundered over her cabin-roof, with the exclamation, 'Oh, then, its Coll Dhu that has enough o' the fresh air about his head up there this night, the crature!'

Coll Dhu had lived thus in his solitude for some years, when it became known that Colonel Blake, the new lord of the soil, was coming to visit the country. By climbing one of the peaks encircling his eyrie, Coll could look sheer down a mountain-side, and see in miniature beneath him, a grey old dwelling with ivied chimneys and weather-slated walls, standing amongst straggling trees and grim warlike rocks, that gave it the look of a fortress, gazing out to the Atlantic for ever with the eager eyes of all its windows, as if demanding perpetually, 'What tidings from the New World?'

He could see now masons and carpenters crawling about below, like ants in the sun, over-running the old house from base to chimney, daubing here and knocking there, tumbling down walls that looked to Coll, up among the clouds, like a handful of jack-stones, and building up others that looked like the toy fences in a child's farm. Throughout several months he must have watched the busy ants at their task of breaking and mending again, disfiguring and beautifying; but when all was done he had not the curiosity to stride down and admire the handsome panelling of the new billiard-room, nor yet the fine view which the enlarged bay-window in the drawing-room commanded of the watery highway to Newfoundland.

Deep summer was melting into autumn, and the amber streaks of decay were beginning to creep out and trail over the ripe purple of moor and mountain, when Colonel Blake, his only daughter, and a party of friends, arrived in the country. The grey house below was alive with gaiety, but Coll Dhu no longer found an interest in observing it from his eyrie. When he watched the sun rise or set, he chose to ascend some crag that looked on no human habitation. When he sailed forth on his excursions, gun in hand, he set his face towards the most isolated wastes, dipping into the loneliest valleys, and scaling the nakedest ridges. When he came by chance within call of other excursionists, gun in hand he plunged into the shade of some hollow, and avoided an encounter. Yet it was fated, for all that, that he and Colonel Blake should meet.

Towards the evening of one bright September day, the wind changed, and in half an hour the mountains were wrapped in a thick blinding mist. Coll Dhu was far from his den, but so well had he searched these mountains, and inured himself to their climate, that neither storm, rain, nor fog, had power to disturb him. But while he stalked on his way, a faint and agonised cry from a human voice reached him through the smothering mist. He quickly tracked the sound, and gained the side of a man who was stumbling along in danger of death at every step.

'Follow me!' said Coll Dhu to this man, and, in an hour's time, brought him safely to the lowlands, and up to the walls of the eager-eyed mansion.

'I am Colonel Blake,' said the frank soldier, when, having left the fog behind them, they stood in the starlight under the lighted windows. Pray tell me quickly to whom I owe my life.'

As he spoke, he glanced up at his benefactor, a large man with a sombre sun-burned face.

'Colonel Blake,' said Coll Dhu, after a strange pause, 'your father suggested to my father to stake his estates at the gaming-table. They were staked, and the tempter won. Both are dead; but you and I live, and I have sworn to injure you.'

The colonel laughed good humouredly at the uneasy face above him.

'And you began to keep your oath tonight by saving my life?' said he. 'Come! I am a soldier, and know how to meet an enemy; but I had far rather meet a friend. I shall not be happy till you have eaten my salt. We have merrymaking tonight in honour of my daughter's birthday. Come in and join us?'

Coll Dhu looked at the earth doggedly.

'I have told you,' he said, 'who and what I am, and I will not cross your threshold.'

But at this moment (so runs the story) a French window opened among the flower-beds by which they were standing, and a vision appeared which stayed the words on Coll's tongue. A stately girl, clad in white satin, stood framed in the ivied window, with the warm light from within streaming around her richly-moulded figure into the night. Her face was as pale as her gown, her eyes were swimming in tears, but a firm smile sat on her lips as she held out both hands to her father. The light behind her touched the glistening folds of her dress–the lustrous pearls round her throat–the coronet of blood-red roses which encircled the knotted braids at the back of her head. Satin, pearls, and roses–had Coll Dhu, of the Devil's Inn, never set eyes upon such things before?

Evleen Blake was no nervous tearful miss. A few quick words–'Thank God! you're safe; the rest have been home an hour'–and a tight pressure of her father's fingers between her own jewelled hands, were all that betrayed the uneasiness she had suffered.

'Faith, my love, I owe my life to this brave gentleman!' said the blithe colonel. 'Press him to come in and be our guest, Evleen. He wants to retreat to his mountains, and lose himself again in the fog where I found him; or, rather, where he found me! Come, sir' (to Coll), 'you must surrender to this fair besieger.'

An introduction followed. 'Coll Dhu!' murmured Evleen Blake, for she had heard the common tales of him; but with a frank welcome she invited her father's preserver to taste the hospitality of that father's house.

'I beg you to come in, sir,' she said; 'but for you our gaiety must have been turned into mourning. A shadow will be upon our mirth if our benefactor disdains to join in it.'

With a sweet grace, mingled with a certain hauteur from which she was never free, she extended her white hand to the tall looming figure outside the window; to have it grasped and wrung in a way that made the proud girl's eyes flash their amazement, and the same little hand clench itself in displeasure, when it had hid itself like an outraged thing among the shining folds of her gown. Was this Coll Dhu mad, or rude?

The guest no longer refused to enter, but followed the white figure into a little study where a lamp burned; and the gloomy stranger, the bluff colonel, and the young mistress of the house, were fully discovered to each other's eyes. Evleen glanced at the newcomer's dark face, and shuddered with a feeling of indescribable dread and dislike; then, to her father, accounted for the shudder after a popular fashion, saying lightly: 'There is someone walking over my grave.'

So Coll Dhu was present at Evleen Blake's birthday ball. Here he was, under a roof which ought to have been his own, a stranger, known only by a nickname, shunned and solitary. Here he was, who had lived among the eagles and foxes, lying in wait with a fell purpose, to be revenged on the son of his father's foe for poverty and disgrace, for the broken heart of a dead mother, for the loss of a self-slaughtered father, for the dreary scattering of brothers and sisters. Here he stood, a Samson shorn of his strength; and all because a haughty girl had melting eyes, a winning mouth, and looked radiant in satin and roses.

Peerless where many were lovely, she moved among her friends, trying to be unconscious of the gloomy fire of those strange eyes which followed her unweariedly wherever she went. And when her father begged her to be gracious to the unsocial guest whom he would fain conciliate, she courteously conducted him to see the new picture-gallery adjoining the drawing-rooms; explained under what odd circumstances the colonel had picked up this little painting or that; using every delicate art her pride would allow to achieve her father's purpose, whilst maintaining at the same time her own personal reserve; trying to divert the guest's oppressive attention from herself to the objects for which she claimed his notice. Coll Dhu followed his conductress and listened to her voice, but what she said mattered nothing; nor did she wring many words of comment or reply from his lips, until they paused in a retired corner where the light was dim, before a window from which the curtain was withdrawn. The sashes were open, and nothing was visible but water; the night Atlantic, with the full moon riding high above a bank of clouds, making silvery tracks outward towards the distance of infinite mystery dividing two worlds. Here the following little scene is said to have been enacted.

'This window of my father's own planning, is it not creditable to his taste?' said the young hostess, as she stood, herself glittering like a dream of beauty, looking on the moonlight.

Coll Dhu made no answer; but suddenly, it is said, asked her for a rose from a cluster of flowers that nestled in the lace on her bosom.

For the second time that night Evleen Blake's eyes flashed with no gentle light. But this man was the saviour of her father. She broke off a blossom, and with such good grace, and also with such queen-like dignity as she might assume, presented it to him. Whereupon, not only was the rose seized, but also the hand that gave it, which was hastily covered with kisses.

Then her anger burst upon him.

'Sir,' she cried, 'if you are a gentleman you must be mad! If you are not mad, then you are not a gentleman!'

'Be merciful,' said Coll Dhu; 'I love you. My God, I never loved a woman before! Ah!' he cried, as a look of disgust crept over her face, 'you hate me. You shuddered the first time your eyes met mine. I love you, and you hate me!'

'I do,' cried Evleen, vehemently, forgetting everything but her indignation. 'Your presence is like something evil to me. Love me?–your looks poison me. Pray, sir, talk no more to me in this strain.'–'I will trouble you no longer,' said Coll Dhu. And, stalking to the window, he placed one powerful hand upon the sash, and vaulted from it out of her sight.

Bare-headed as he was, Coll Dhu strode off to the mountains, but not towards his own home. All the remaining dark hours of that night he is believed to have walked the labyrinths of the hills, until dawn began to scatter the clouds with a high wind. Fasting, and on foot from sunrise the morning before, he was then glad enough to see a cabin right in his way. Walking in, he asked for water to drink, and a corner where he might throw himself to rest.

There was a wake in the house, and the kitchen was full of people, all wearied out with the night's watch; old men were dozing over their pipes in the chimney-corner, and here and there a woman was fast asleep with her head on a neighbour's knee. All who were awake crossed themselves when Coll Dhu's figure darkened the door, because of his evil name; but an old man of the house invited him in, and offering him milk, and promising him a roasted potato by-and-by, conducted him to a small room off the kitchen, one end of which was strewed with heather, and where there were only two women sitting gossiping over a fire.

'A traveller,' said the old man, nodding his head at the women, who nodded back, as if to say 'he has the traveller's right.' And Coll Dhu flung himself on the heather, in the furthest corner of the narrow room.

The women suspended their talk for a while; but presently, guessing the intruder to be asleep, resumed it in voices above a whisper. There was but a patch of window with the grey dawn behind it, but Coll could see the figures by the firelight over which they bent: an old woman sitting forward with her withered hands extended to the embers, and a girl reclining against the hearth wall, with her healthy face, bright eyes, and crimson draperies, glowing by turns in the flickering blaze.

'I do' know,' said the girl, 'but it's the quarest marriage iver I hard of. Sure, it's not three weeks since he tould right an' left that he hated her like poison!'

'Whist, asthoreen!' said the colliagh, bending forward confidentially; 'throth an' we all know that o' him. But what could he do, the crature! When she put the burragh-bos on him!'

'The *what*?' asked the girl.

'Then the burragh-bos machree-o? That's the spanchel o' death, avourneen; an' well she has him tethered to her now, bad luck to her!'

The old woman rocked herself and stifled the Irish cry breaking from her wrinkled lips by burying her face in her cloak.

'But what is it?' asked the girl, eagerly. 'What's the burragh-bos, anyways, an' where did she get it?'

'Och, och! it's not fit for comin' over to young ears, but cuggir (whisper), acushla! It's a sthrip o' the skin o' a corpse, peeled from the crown o' the head to the heel, without crack or split, or the charm's broke; an' that, rowled up, and put on a sthring roun' the neck o' the wan that's cowld by the wan that wants to be loved. An' sure enough it puts the fire in their hearts, hot an' sthrong, afore twinty-four hours is gone.'

The girl had started from her lazy attitude, and gazed at her companion with eyes dilated by horror.

'Marciful Saviour!' she cried. 'Not a sowl on airth would bring the curse out o' heaven by sich a black doin'!'

'Aisy, Biddeen alanna! an' there's wan that does it, an' isn't the divil. Arrah, asthoreen, did ye niver hear tell o' Pexie na Pishrogie, that lives betune two hills o' Maam Turk?'

'I h'ard o' her,' said the girl, breathlessly.

'Well, sorra bit lie, but it's hersel' that does it. She'll do it for money any day. Sure they hunted her from the graveyard o' Salruck, where she had the dead raised; an' glory be to God! they would ha' murthered her, only they missed her thracks, an' couldn't bring it home to her afther.'

'Whist, a-wauher' (my mother), said the girl; 'here's the thraveller gettin' up to set off on his road again! Och, then, it's the short rest he tuk, the sowl!'

It was enough for Coll, however. He had got up, and now went back to the kitchen, where the old man had caused a dish of potatoes to be roasted, and earnestly pressed his visitor to sit down and eat of them. This Coll did readily; having recruited his strength by a meal, he betook himself to the mountains again, just as the rising sun was flashing among the waterfalls, and sending the night mists drifting down the glens. By sundown the same evening he was striding over the hills of Maam Turk, asking of herds his way to the cabin of one Pexie na Pishrogie.

In a hovel on a brown desolate heath, with scared-looking hills flying off into the distance on every side, he found Pexie: a yellow-faced hag, dressed in a dark-red blanket, with elf-locks of coarse black hair protruding from under an orange kerchief swathed round her wrinkled jaws. She was bending over a pot upon her fire, where herbs were simmering, and she looked lip with an evil glance when Coll Dhu darkened her door.

'The burragh-bos is it her honour wants?' she asked, when he had made known his errand. 'Ay, ay; but the arighad, the arighad (money) for Pexie. The burragh-bos is ill to get.'

'I will pay,' said Coll Dhu, laying a sovereign on the bench before her.

The witch sprang upon it, and chuckling, bestowed on her visitor a glance which made even Coll Dhu shudder.

'Her honour is a fine king,' she said, 'an' her is fit to get the burragh-bos. Ha! ha! her sail get the burragh-bos from Pexie. But the arighad is not enough. More, more!'

She stretched out her claw-like hand, and Coll dropped another sovereign into it. Whereupon she fell into more horrible convulsions of delight.

'Hark ye!' cried Coll. 'I have paid you well, but if your infernal charm does not work, I will have you hunted for a witch!'

'Work!' cried Pexie, rolling up her eyes. 'If Pexie's charrm not work, then her honour come back here an' carry these bits o' mountain away on her back. Ay, her will work. If the colleen hate her honour like the old diaoul hersel', still an' withal her love will love her honour like her own white sowl afore the sun sets or rises. That, (with a furtive leer) or the colleen dhas go wild mad afore wan hour.'

'Hag!' returned Coll Dhu; 'the last part is a hellish invention of your own. I heard nothing of madness. If you want more money, speak out, but play none of your hideous tricks on me.'

The witch fixed her cunning eyes on him, and took her cue at once from his passion.

'Her honour guess thrue,' she simpered; 'it is only the little bit more arighad poor Pexie want.'

Again the skinny hand was extended. Coll Dhu shrank from touching it, and threw his gold coin upon the table.

'King, king!' chuckled Pexie. 'Her honour is a grand king. Her honour is fit to get the burragh-bos. The colleen dhas sail love her like her own white sowl. Ha, ha!'

'When shall I get it?' asked Coll Dhu, impatiently.

'Her honour sall come back to Pexie in so many days, do-deag (twelve), so many days, fur that the burragh-bos is hard to get. The lonely graveyard is far away, an' the dead man is hard to raise—'

'Silence!' cried Coll Dhu; 'not a word more. I will have your hideous charm, but what it is, or where you get it, I will not know.'

Then, promising to come back in twelve days, he took his departure. Turning to look back when a little way across the heath, he saw Pexie gazing after him, standing on her black hill in relief against the lurid flames of the dawn, seeming to his dark imagination like a fury with all hell at her back.

At the appointed time Coll Dhu got the promised charm. He sewed it with perfumes into a cover of cloth of gold, and slung it to a fine-wrought chain. Lying in a casket which had once held the jewels of Coil's broken-hearted mother, it looked a glittering bauble enough. Meantime the people of the mountains were cursing over their cabin fires, because there had been another unholy raid upon their graveyard, and were banding themselves to hunt the criminal down.

A fortnight passed. How or where could Coll Dhu find an opportunity to put the charm round the neck of the colonel's proud daughter? More gold was dropped into Pexie's greedy claw, and then she promised to assist him in his dilemma.

Next morning the witch dressed herself in decent garb, smoothed her elf-locks under a snowy cap, smoothed the wrinkles out of her face, and with a basket on her arm locked the door of the hovel, and took her way to the lowlands. Pexie seemed to have given up her disreputable calling for that of a simple mushroom-gatherer. The housekeeper at the grey house bought poor Muireade's mushrooms of her every morning. Every morti-ing she left unfailingly a nosegay of wild flowers for Miss Evleen Blake, 'God bless her! She had never seen the darling young lady with her own two longing eyes, but sure hadn't she heard tell of her sweet purty face, miles away!' And at last, one morning, whom should she meet but Miss Evleen herself returning alone from a ramble. Whereupon poor Muireade 'made bold' to present her flowers in person.

'Ah,' said Evleen, 'it is you who leave me the flowers every morning? They are very sweet.'

Muireade had sought her only for a look at her beautiful face. And now that she had seen it, as bright as the sun, and as fair as the lily, she would take up her basket and go away contented. Yet she lingered a little longer.

'My lady never walk up big mountain?' said Pexie.

'No,' said Evleen, laughing; she feared she could not walk up a mountain.

'Ah yes; my lady ought to go, with more gran' ladies an' gentlemen, ridin' on purty little donkeys, up the big mountains. Oh, gran' things up big mountains for my lady to see!'

Thus she set to work, and kept her listener enchained for an hour, while she related wonderful stories of those upper regions. And as Evleen looked up to the burly crowns of the hills, perhaps she thought there might be sense in this wild old woman's suggestion. It ought to be a grand world up yonder.

Be that as it may, it was not long after this when Coll Dhu got notice that a party from the grey house would explore the mountains next day; that Evleen Blake would be one of the number; and that he, Coll, must prepare to house and refresh a crowd of weary people, who in the evening should be brought, hungry and faint, to his door. The simple mushroom-gatherer should be discovered laying in her humble stock among the green places between the hills, should volunteer to act as guide to the party, should lead them far out of their way through the mountains and up and down the most toilsome ascents and across dangerous places; to escape safely from which, the servants should be told to throw away the baskets of provisions which they carried.

Coll Dhu was not idle. Such a feast was set forth, as had never been spread so near the clouds before. We are told of wonderful dishes furnished by unwholesome agency, and from a place believed much hotter than is necessary for purposes of cookery. We are told also how Coll Dhu's barren chambers were suddenly hung with curtains of velvet, and with fringes of gold; how the blank white walls glowed with delicate colours and gilding; how gems of pictures sprang into sight between the panels; how the tables blazed with plate and gold, and glittered with the rarest glass; how such wines flowed, as the guests had never tasted; how servants in the richest livery, amongst whom the wizen-faced old man was a mere nonentity, appeared, and stood ready to carry in the wonderful dishes, at whose extraordinary fragrance the eagles came pecking to the windows, and the foxes drew near the walls, snuffing. Sure enough, in all good time, the weary party came within sight of the Devil's Inn, and Coll Dhu sallied forth to invite them across his lonely threshold. Colonel Blake (to whom Evleen, in her delicacy, had said no word of the solitary's strange behaviour to herself) hailed his appearance with delight, and the whole party sat down to Coll's banquet in high good humour. Also, it is said, in much amazement at the magnificence of the mountain rescue.

All went in to Coll's feast, save Evleen Blake, who remained standing on the threshold of the outer door; weary, but unwilling to rest there; hungry, but unwilling to eat there. Her white cambric dress was gathered on her arms, crushed and sullied with the toils of the day; her bright cheek was a little sunburned; her small dark head with its braids a little tossed, was bared to the mountain air and the glory of the sinking sun; her hands were loosely tangled in the strings of her hat; and her foot sometimes tapped the threshold-stone. So she was seen.

The peasants tell that Coll Dhu and her father came praying her to enter, and that the magnificent servants brought viands to the threshold; but no step would she move inward, no morsel would she taste.

'Poison, poison!' she murmured, and threw the food in handfuls to the foxes, who were snuffing on the heath.

But it was different when Muireade, the kindly old woman, the simple mushroom-gatherer, with all the wicked wrinkles smoothed out of her face, came to the side of the hungry girl, and coaxingly presented a savoury mess of her own sweet mushrooms, served on a common earthen platter.

'An' darlin', my lady, poor Muireade her cook them hersel', an' no thing o' this house touch them or look at poor Muireade's mushrooms.'

Then Evleen took the platter and ate a delicious meal. Scarcely was it finished when a heavy drowsiness fell upon her, and, unable to sustain herself on her feet, she presently sat down upon the door-stone. Leaning her head against the framework of the door, she was soon in a deep sleep, or trance. So she was found.

'Whimsical, obstinate little girl!' said the colonel, putting his hand on the beautiful slumbering head. And taking her in his arms he carried her into a chamber which had been (say the story-tellers) nothing but a bare and sorry closet in the morning hut which was now fitted up with Oriental splendour. And here on a luxurious couch she was laid, with a crimson coverlet wrapping her feet. And here in the tempered light coming through jewelled glass, where yesterday had been a coarse rough-hung window, her father looked his last upon her lovely face.

The colonel returned to his host and friends, and by-and-by the whole party sallied forth to see the after-glare of a fierce sunset swathing the hills in flames. It was not until they had gone some distance that Coll Dhu remembered to go back and fetch his telescope. He was not long absent. But he was absent long enough to enter that glowing chamber with a stealthy step, to throw a light chain around the neck of the sleeping girl, and to slip among the folds of her dress the hideous glittering burragh-bos.

After he had gone away again, Pexie came stealing to the door, and, opening it a little, sat down on the mat outside, with her cloak wrapped round her. An hour passed, and Evleen Blake still slept, her breathing scarcely stirring the deadly bauble on her breast. After that, she began to murmur and moan, and Pexie pricked up her ears. Presently a sound in the room told her that the victim was awake and had risen. Then Pexie put her face to the aperture of the door and looked in, gave a howl of dismay, and fled from the house, to be seen in that country no more.

The light was fading among the hills, and the ramblers were returning towards the Devil's Inn, when a group of ladies who were considerably in advance of the rest, met Evleen Blake advancing towards them on the heath, with her hair disordered as by sleep, and no covering on her head. They noticed something bright, like gold, shifting and glancing with the motion of her figure. There had been some jesting among them about Evleen's fancy for falling asleep on the door-step instead of coming in to dinner, and they advanced laughing, to rally her on the subject. But she stared at them in a strange way, as if she did not know them, and passed on. Her friends were rather offended, and commented on her fantastic humour; only one looked after her, and got laughed at by her companions for expressing uneasiness on the wilful young lady's account.

So they kept their way, and the solitary figure went fluttering on, the white robe blushing, and the fatal burragh-bos glittering in the reflection from the sky. A hare crossed her path, and she laughed out loudly, and clapping her hands, sprang after it. Then she stopped and asked questions of the stones, striking them with her open palm because they would not answer. (An amazed little herd sitting behind a rock, witnessed these strange proceedings.) By-and-by she began to call after the birds, in a wild shrill way startling the echoes of the hills as she went along. A party of gentlemen returning by a dangerous path, heard the unusual sound and stopped to listen.

'What is that?' asked one.

'A young eagle,' said Coll Dhu, whose face had become livid; 'they often give such cries.' 'It was uncommonly like a woman's voice!' was the reply; and immediately another wild note rang towards them from the rocks above; a bare saw-like ridge, shelving away to some distance ahead, and projecting one hungry tooth over an abyss. A few more moments and they saw Evleen Blake's light figure fluttering out towards this dizzy point.

'My Evleen!' cried the colonel, recognising his daughter, 'she is mad to venture on such a spot!'

'Mad!' repeated Coll Dhu. And then dashed off to the rescue with all the might and swiftness of his powerful limbs.

When he drew near her, Evleen had almost reached the verge of the terrible rock. Very cautiously he approached her, his object being to seize her in his strong arms before she was aware of his presence, and carry her many yards away from the spot of danger. But in a fatal moment Evleen turned her head and saw him. One wild ringing cry of hate and horror, which startled the very eagles and scattered a flight of curlews above her head, broke from her lips. A step backward brought her within a foot of death.

One desperate though wary stride, and she was struggling in Coll's embrace. One glance in her eyes, and he saw that he was striving with a mad woman. Back, back, she dragged him, and he had nothing to grasp by. The rock was slippery and his shod feet would not cling to it. Back, back! A hoarse panting, a dire swinging to and fro; and then the rock was standing naked against the sky, no one was there, and Coll Dhu and Evleen Blake lay shattered far below.

# THE HAUNTED HOUSE
## CHARLES DICKENS

Under none of the accredited ghostly circumstances, and environed by none of the conventional ghostly surroundings, did I first make acquaintance with the house which is the subject of this Christmas piece. I saw it in the daylight, with the sun upon it. There was no wind, no rain, no lightning, no thunder, no awful or unwonted circumstance, of any kind, to heighten its effect. More than that: I had come to it direct from a railway station: it was not more than a mile distant from the railway station; and, as I stood outside the house, looking back upon the way I had come, I could see the goods train running smoothly along the embankment in the valley. I will not say that everything was utterly commonplace, because I doubt if anything can be that, except to utterly commonplace people—and there my vanity steps in; but, I will take it on myself to say that anybody might see the house as I saw it, any fine autumn morning. The manner of my lighting on it was this.

I was travelling towards London out of the North, intending to stop by the way, to look at the house. My health required a temporary residence in the country; and a friend of mine who knew that, and who had happened to drive past the house, had written to me to suggest it as a likely place. I had got into the train at midnight, and had fallen asleep, and had woke up and had sat looking out of window at the brilliant Northern Lights in the sky, and had fallen asleep again, and had woke up again to find the night gone, with the usual discontented conviction on me that I hadn't been to sleep at all;—upon which question, in the first imbecility of that condition, I am ashamed to believe that I would have done wager by battle with the man who sat opposite me. That opposite man had had, through the night—as that opposite man always has—several legs too many, and all of them too long. In addition to this unreasonable conduct (which was only to be expected of him), he had had a pencil and a pocket-book, and had been perpetually listening and taking notes. It had appeared to me that these aggravating notes related to the jolts and bumps of the carriage, and I should have resigned myself to his taking them, under a general supposition that he was in the civil-engineering way of life, if he had not sat staring straight over my head whenever he listened. He was a goggle-eyed gentleman of a perplexed aspect, and his demeanour became unbearable. It was a cold, dead morning (the sun not being up yet), and when I had out-watched the paling light of the fires of the iron country, and the curtain of heavy smoke that hung at once between me and the stars and between me and the day, I turned to my fellow-traveller and said:

"I BEG your pardon, sir, but do you observe anything particular in me?" For, really, he appeared to be taking down, either my travelling-cap or my hair, with a minuteness that was a liberty.

The goggle-eyed gentleman withdrew his eyes from behind me, as if the back of the carriage were a hundred miles off, and said, with a lofty look of compassion for my insignificance:

"In you, sir?—B."

"B, sir?" said I, growing warm.

"I have nothing to do with you, sir," returned the gentleman; "pray let me listen—O."

He enunciated this vowel after a pause, and noted it down. At first I was alarmed, for an Express lunatic and no communication with the guard, is a serious position. The thought came to my relief that the gentleman might be what is popularly called a Rapper: one of a sect for (some of) whom I have the highest respect, but whom I don't believe in. I was going to ask him the question, when he took the bread out of my mouth.

"You will excuse me," said the gentleman contemptuously, "if I am too much in advance of common humanity to trouble myself at all about it. I have passed the night—as indeed I pass the whole of my time now—in spiritual intercourse." "O!" said I, somewhat snappishly.

"The conferences of the night began," continued the gentleman, turning several leaves of his note-book, "with this message: 'Evil communications corrupt good manners.'"

"Sound," said I; "but, absolutely new?"

"New from spirits," returned the gentleman.

I could only repeat my rather snappish "O!" and ask if I might be favoured with the last communication.

"'A bird in the hand,'" said the gentleman, reading his last entry with great solemnity, "'is worth two in the Bosh.'"

"Truly I am of the same opinion," said I; "but shouldn't it be Bush?"

"It came to me, Bosh," returned the gentleman. The gentleman then informed me that the spirit of Socrates had delivered this special revelation in the course of the night. "My friend, I hope you are pretty well. There are two in this railway carriage. How do you do? There are seventeen thousand four hundred and seventy-nine spirits here, but you cannot see them. Pythagoras is here. He is not at liberty to mention it, but hopes you like travelling." Galileo likewise had dropped in, with this scientific intelligence. "I am glad to see you, AMICO. COME STA? Water will freeze when it is cold enough. ADDIO!" In the course of the night, also, the following phenomena had occurred. Bishop Butler had insisted on spelling his name, "Bubler," for which offence against orthography and good manners he had been dismissed as out of temper. John Milton (suspected of wilful mystification) had repudiated the author-ship of Paradise Lost, and had introduced, as joint authors of that poem, two Unknown gentlemen, respectively named Grungers and Scadgingtone. And Prince Arthur, nephew of King John of England, had described himself as tolerably comfortable in the seventh circle, where he was learning to paint on velvet, under the direction of Mrs. Trimmer and Mary Queen of Scots. If this should meet the eye of the gentleman who favoured me with these disclosures, I trust he will excuse my confessing that the sight of the rising sun, and the contemplation of the magnificent Order of the vast Universe, made me impa-tient of them. In a word, I was so impatient of them, that I was mightily glad to get out at the next station, and to exchange these clouds and vapours for the free air of Heaven.

By that time it was a beautiful morning. As I walked away among such leaves as had already fallen from the golden, brown, and russet trees; and as I looked around me on the wonders of Creation, and thought of the steady, unchanging, and harmonious laws by which they are sustained; the gentleman's spiritual intercourse seemed to me as poor a piece of journey-work as ever this world saw. In which heathen state of mind, I came within view of the house, and stopped to examine it attentively.

It was a solitary house, standing in a sadly neglected garden: a pretty even square of some two acres. It was a house of about the time of George the Second; as stiff, as cold, as formal, and in as bad taste, as could possibly be desired by the most loyal admirer of the whole quartet of Georges. It was uninhabited, but had, within a year or two, been cheaply repaired to render it habitable; I say cheaply, because the work had been done in a surface manner, and was already decaying as to the paint and plaster, though the colours were fresh. A lop-sided board drooped over the garden wall, announcing that it was "to let on very reasonable terms, well furnished." It was much too closely and heavily shadowed by trees, and, in particular, there were six tall poplars before the front windows, which were excessively melancholy, and the site of which had been extremely ill chosen.

It was easy to see that it was an avoided house—a house that was shunned by the village, to which my eye was guided by a church spire some half a mile off—a house that nobody would take. And the natural inference was, that it had the reputation of being a haunted house.

No period within the four-and-twenty hours of day and night is so solemn to me, as the early morning. In the summer-time, I often rise very early, and repair to my room to do a day's work before breakfast, and I am always on those occasions deeply impressed by the stillness and solitude around me. Besides that there is something awful in the being surrounded by familiar faces asleep—in the knowledge that those who are dearest to us and to whom we are dearest, are profoundly unconscious of us, in an impassive state, anticipative of that mysterious condition to which we are all tending—the stopped life, the broken threads of yesterday, the deserted seat, the closed book, the unfinished but abandoned occupation, all are images of Death. The tranquillity of the hour is the tranquillity of Death. The colour and the chill have the same association. Even a certain air that familiar household objects take upon them when they first emerge from the shadows of the night into the morning, of being newer, and as they used to be long ago, has its counterpart in the subsidence of the worn face of maturity or age, in death, into the old youthful look. Moreover, I once saw the apparition of my father, at this hour. He was alive and well, and nothing ever came of it, but I saw him in the daylight, sitting with his back towards me, on a seat that stood beside my bed. His head was resting on his hand, and whether he was slumbering or grieving, I could not discern. Amazed to see him there, I sat up, moved my position, leaned out of bed, and watched him. As he did not move, I spoke to him more than once. As he did not move then, I became alarmed and laid my hand upon his shoulder, as I thought—and there was no such thing.

For all these reasons, and for others less easily and briefly statable, I find the early morning to be my most ghostly time. Any house would be more or less haunted, to me, in the early morning; and a haunted house could scarcely address me to greater advantage than then. I walked on into the village, with the desertion of this house upon my mind, and I found the landlord of the little inn, sanding his doorstep. I bespoke breakfast, and broached the subject of the house. "Is it haunted?" I asked.

The landlord looked at me, shook his head, and answered, "I say nothing."

"Then it IS haunted?"

"Well!" cried the landlord, in an outburst of frankness that had the appearance of desperation—"I wouldn't sleep in it." "Why not?"

"If I wanted to have all the bells in a house ring, with nobody to ring 'em; and all the doors in a house bang, with nobody to bang 'em; and all sorts of feet treading about, with no feet there; why, then," said the landlord, "I'd sleep in that house." "Is anything seen there?"

The landlord looked at me again, and then, with his former appearance of desperation, called down his stable-yard for "Ikey!" The call produced a high-shouldered young fellow, with a round red face, a short crop of sandy hair, a very broad humorous mouth, a turned-up nose, and a great sleeved waistcoat of purple bars, with mother-of-pearl buttons, that seemed to be growing upon him, and to be in a fair way—if it were not pruned—of covering his head and overrunning his boots.

"This gentleman wants to know," said the landlord, "if anything's seen at the Poplars."

"'Ooded woman with a howl," said Ikey, in a state of great freshness. "Do you mean a cry?" "I mean a bird, sir."

"A hooded woman with an owl. Dear me! Did you ever see her?" "I seen the howl." "Never the woman?"

"Not so plain as the howl, but they always keeps together." "Has anybody ever seen the woman as plainly as the owl?" "Lord bless you, sir! Lots." "Who?"

"Lord bless you, sir! Lots."

"The general-dealer opposite, for instance, who is opening his shop?" "Perkins? Bless you, Perkins wouldn't go a-nigh the place. No!" observed the young man, with considerable feeling; "he an't overwise, an't Perkins, but he an't such a fool as THAT." (Here, the landlord murmured his confidence in Perkins's knowing better.)

"Who is—or who was—the hooded woman with the owl? Do you know?"

"Well!" said Ikey, holding up his cap with one hand while he scratched his head with the other, "they say, in general, that she was murdered, and the howl he 'ooted the while." This very concise summary of the facts was all I could learn, except that a young man, as hearty and likely a young man as ever I see, had been took with fits and held down in 'em, after seeing the hooded woman. Also, that a personage, dimly described as "a hold chap, a sort of one-eyed tramp, answering to the name of Joby, unless you challenged him as Greenwood, and then he said, 'Why not? and even if so, mind your own business,'" had encountered the hooded woman, a matter of five or six times. But, I was not materially assisted by these witnesses: inasmuch as the first was in California, and the last was, as Ikey said (and he was confirmed by the landlord), anywheres.

Now, although I regard with a hushed and solemn fear, the mysteries, between which and this state of existence is interposed the barrier of the great trial and change that fall on all the things that live; and although I have not the audacity to pretend that I know anything of them; I can no more reconcile the mere banging of doors, ringing of bells, creaking of boards, and such-like insignificances, with the majestic beauty and pervading analogy of all the Divine rules that I am permitted to understand, than I had been able, a little while before, to yoke the spiritual intercourse of my fellow-traveller to the chariot of the rising sun. Moreover, I had lived in two haunted houses—both abroad. In one of these, an old Italian palace, which bore the reputation of being very badly haunted indeed, and which had recently been twice abandoned on that account, I lived eight months, most tranquilly and pleasantly: notwithstanding that the house had a score of mysterious bedrooms, which were never used, and possessed, in one large room in which I sat reading, times out of number at all ·
hours, and next to which I slept, a haunted chamber of the first pretensions. I gently hinted these considerations to the landlord. And as to this particular house having a bad name, I reasoned with him, Why, how many things had bad

names undeservedly, and how easy it was to give bad names, and did he not think that if he and I were persistently to whisper in the village that any weird-looking old drunken tinker of the neighbourhood had sold himself to the Devil, he would come in time to be suspected of that commercial venture! All this wise talk was perfectly ineffective with the landlord, I am bound to confess, and was as dead a failure as ever I made in my life.

To cut this part of the story short, I was piqued about the haunted house, and was already half resolved to take it. So, after breakfast, I got the keys from Perkins's brother-in-law (a whip and harness maker, who keeps the Post Office, and is under submission to a most rigorous wife of the Doubly Seceding Little Emmanuel persuasion), and went up to the house, attended by my landlord and by Ikey.

Within, I found it, as I had expected, transcendently dismal. The slowly changing shadows waved on it from the heavy trees, were doleful in the last degree; the house was ill-placed, ill-built, ill-planned, and ill-fitted. It was damp, it was not free from dry rot, there was a flavour of rats in it, and it was the gloomy victim of that indescribable decay which settles on all the work of man's hands whenever it's not turned to man's account. The kitchens and offices were too large, and too remote from each other. Above stairs and below, waste tracts of passage intervened between patches of fertility represented by rooms; and there was a mouldy old well with a green growth upon it, hiding like a murderous trap, near the bottom of the back-stairs, under the double row of bells. One of these bells was labelled, on a black ground in faded white letters, MASTER B. This, they told me, was the bell that rang the most.

"Who was Master B.?" I asked. "Is it known what he did while the owl hooted?"

"Rang the bell," said Ikey.

I was rather struck by the prompt dexterity with which this young man pitched his fur cap at the bell, and rang it himself. It was a loud, unpleasant bell, and made a very disagreeable sound. The other bells were inscribed according to the names of the rooms to which their wires were conducted: as "Picture Room," "Double Room," "Clock Room," and the like. Following Master B.'s bell to its source I found that young gentleman to have had but indifferent third-class accommodation in a triangular cabin under the cock-loft, with a corner fireplace which Master B. must have been exceedingly small if he were ever able to warm himself at, and a corner chimney-piece like a pyramidal staircase to the ceiling for Tom Thumb. The papering of one side of the room had dropped down bodily, with fragments of plaster adhering to it, and almost blocked up the door. It appeared that Master B., in his spiritual condition, always made a point of pulling the paper down. Neither the landlord nor Ikey could suggest why he made such a fool of himself.

Except that the house had an immensely large rambling loft at top, I made no other discoveries. It was moderately well furnished, but sparely. Some of the furniture—say, a third—was as old as the house; the rest was of various periods within the last half-century. I was referred to a corn-chandler in the market-place of the county town to treat for the house. I went that day, and I took it for six months.

It was just the middle of October when I moved in with my maiden sister (I venture to call her eight-and-thirty, she is so very handsome, sensible, and engaging). We took with us, a deaf stableman, my bloodhound Turk, two women servants, and a young person called an Odd Girl. I have reason to record of the attendant last enumerated, who was one of the Saint Lawrence's Union Female Orphans, that she was a fatal mistake and a disastrous engagement. The year was dying early, the leaves were falling fast, it was a raw cold day when we took possession, and the gloom of the house was most depressing. The cook (an amiable woman, but of a weak turn of intellect) burst into tears on beholding the kitchen, and requested that her silver watch might be delivered over to her sister (2 Tuppintock's Gardens, Liggs's Walk, Clapham Rise), in the event of anything happening to her from the damp. Streaker, the housemaid, feigned cheerfulness, but was the greater martyr. The Odd Girl, who had never been in the country, alone was pleased, and made arrangements for sowing an acorn in the garden outside the scullery window, and rearing an oak.

We went, before dark, through all the natural—as opposed to supernatural-miseries incidental to our state. Dispiriting reports ascended (like the smoke) from the basement in volumes, and descended from the upper rooms. There was no rolling-pin, there was no salamander (which failed to surprise me, for I don't know what it is), there was nothing in the house, what there was, was broken, the last people must have lived like pigs, what could the meaning of the landlord be? Through these distresses, the Odd Girl was cheerful and exemplary. But within four hours after dark we had got into a supernatural groove, and the Odd Girl had seen "Eyes," and was in hysterics.

My sister and I had agreed to keep the haunting strictly to ourselves, and my impression was, and still is, that I had not left Ikey, when he helped to unload the cart, alone with the women, or any one of them, for one minute.

Nevertheless, as I say, the Odd Girl had "seen Eyes" (no other explanation could ever be drawn from her), before nine, and by ten o'clock had had as much vinegar applied to her as would pickle a handsome salmon.

I leave a discerning public to judge of my feelings, when, under these untoward circumstances, at about half-past ten o'clock Master B.'s bell began to ring in a most infuriated manner, and Turk howled until the house resounded with his lamentations! I hope I may never again be in a state of mind so unchristian as the mental frame in which I lived for some weeks, respecting the memory of Master B. Whether his bell was rung by rats, or mice, or bats, or wind, or what other accidental vibration, or sometimes by one cause, sometimes another, and sometimes by collusion, I don't know; but, certain it is, that it did ring two nights out of three, until I conceived the happy idea of twisting Master B.'s neck—in other words, breaking his bell short off—and silencing that young gentleman, as to my experience and belief, for ever.

But, by that time, the Odd Girl had developed such improving powers of catalepsy, that she had become a shining example of that very inconvenient disorder. She would stiffen, like a Guy Fawkes endowed with unreason, on the most irrelevant occasions. I would address the servants in a lucid manner, pointing out to them that I had painted Master B.'s room and balked the paper, and taken Master B.'s bell away and balked the ringing, and if they could suppose that that confounded boy had lived and died, to clothe himself with no better behaviour than would most unquestionably have brought him and the sharpest particles of a birch-broom into close acquaintance in the present imperfect state of existence, could they also suppose a mere poor human being, such as I was, capable by those contemptible means of counteracting and limiting the powers of the disembodied spirits of the dead, or of any spirits?—I say I would become emphatic and cogent, not to say rather complacent, in such an address, when it would all go for nothing by reason of the Odd Girl's suddenly stiffening from the toes upward, and glaring among us like a parochial petrifaction.

Streaker, the housemaid, too, had an attribute of a most discomfiting nature. I am unable to say whether she was of an usually lymphatic temperament, or what else was the matter with her, but this young woman became a mere Distillery for the production of the largest and most transparent tears I ever met with. Combined with these characteristics, was a peculiar tenacity of hold in those specimens, so that they didn't fall, but hung upon her face and nose. In this condition, and mildly and deplorably shaking her head, her silence would throw me more heavily than the Admirable Crichton could have done in a verbal disputation for a purse of money. Cook, likewise, always covered me with confusion as with a garment, by neatly winding up the session with the protest that the Ouse was wearing her out, and by meekly repeating her last wishes regarding her silver watch.

As to our nightly life, the contagion of suspicion and fear was among us, and there is no such contagion under the sky. Hooded woman? According to the accounts, we were in a perfect Convent of hooded women. Noises? With that contagion downstairs, I myself have sat in the dismal parlour, listening, until I have heard so many and such strange noises, that they would have chilled my blood if I had not warmed it by dashing out to make discoveries. Try this in bed, in the dead of the night: try this at your own comfortable fire-side, in the life of the night. You can fill any house with noises, if you will, until you have a noise for every nerve in your nervous system.

I repeat; the contagion of suspicion and fear was among us, and there is no such contagion under the sky. The women (their noses in a chronic state of excoriation from smelling-salts) were always primed and loaded for a swoon, and ready to go off with hair-triggers. The two elder detached the Odd Girl on all expeditions that were considered doubly hazardous, and she always established the reputation of such adventures by coming back cataleptic. If Cook or Streaker went overhead after dark, we knew we should presently hear a bump on the ceiling; and this took place so constantly, that it was as if a fighting man were engaged to go about the house, administering a touch of his art which I believe is called The Auctioneer, to every domestic he met with.

It was in vain to do anything. It was in vain to be frightened, for the moment in one's own person, by a real owl, and then to show the owl. It was in vain to discover, by striking an accidental discord on the piano, that Turk always howled at particular notes and combinations. It was in vain to be a Rhadamanthus with the bells, and if an unfortunate bell rang without leave, to have it down inexorably and silence it. It was in vain to fire up chimneys, let torches down the well, charge furiously into suspected rooms and recesses. We changed servants, and it was no better. The new set ran away, and a third set came, and it was no better. At last, our comfortable housekeeping got to be so disorganised and wretched, that I one night dejectedly said to my sister: "Patty, I begin to despair of our getting people to go on with us here, and I think we must give this up."

My sister, who is a woman of immense spirit, replied, "No, John, don't give it up. Don't be beaten, John. There is another way." "And what is that?" said I.

"John," returned my sister, "if we are not to be driven out of this house, and that for no reason whatever, that is apparent to you or me, we must help ourselves and take the house wholly and solely into our own hands."

"But, the servants," said I.

"Have no servants," said my sister, boldly.

Like most people in my grade of life, I had never thought of the possibility of going on without those faithful obstructions. The notion was so new to me when suggested, that I looked very doubtful. "We know they come here to be frightened and infect one another, and we know they are frightened and do infect one another," said my sister.

"With the exception of Bottles," I observed, in a meditative tone. (The deaf stable-man. I kept him in my service, and still keep him, as a phenomenon of moroseness not to be matched in England.) "To be sure, John," assented my sister; "except Bottles. And what does that go to prove? Bottles talks to nobody, and hears nobody unless he is absolutely roared at, and what alarm has Bottles ever given, or taken! None."

This was perfectly true; the individual in question having retired, every night at ten o'clock, to his bed over the coach-house, with no other company than a pitchfork and a pail of water. That the pail of water would have been over me, and the pitchfork through me, if I had put myself without announcement in Bottles's way after that minute, I had deposited in my own mind as a fact worth remembering. Neither had Bottles ever taken the least notice of any of our many uproars. An imperturbable and speechless man, he had sat at his supper, with Streaker present in a swoon, and the Odd Girl marble, and had only put another potato in his cheek, or profited by the general misery to help himself to beefsteak pie. "And so," continued my sister, "I exempt Bottles. And considering, John, that the house is too large, and perhaps too lonely, to be kept well in hand by Bottles, you, and me, I propose that we cast about among our friends for a certain selected number of the most reliable and willing—form a Society here for three months-wait upon ourselves and one another—live cheerfully and socially—and see what happens."

I was so charmed with my sister, that I embraced her on the spot, and went into her plan with the greatest ardour. We were then in the third week of November; but, we took our measures so vigorously, and were so well seconded by the friends in whom we confided, that there was still a week of the month unexpired, when our party all came down together merrily, and mustered in the haunted house.

I will mention, in this place, two small changes that I made while my sister and I were yet alone. It occurring to me as not improbable that Turk howled in the house at night, partly because he wanted to get out of it, I stationed him in his kennel outside, but unchained; and I seriously warned the village that any man who came in his way must not expect to leave him without a rip in his own throat. I then casually asked Ikey if he were a judge of a gun? On his saying, "Yes, sir, I knows a good gun when I sees her," I begged the favour of his stepping up to the house and looking at mine. SHE'S a true one, sir," said Ikey, after inspecting a double-barrelled rifle that I bought in New York a few years ago. "No mistake about HER, sir."

"Ikey," said I, "don't mention it; I have seen something in this house." "No, sir?" he whispered, greedily opening his eyes. "'Ooded lady, sir?" "Don't be frightened," said I. "It was a figure rather like you." "Lord, sir?"

"Ikey!" said I, shaking hands with him warmly: I may say affectionately; "if there is any truth in these ghost-stories, the greatest service I can do you, is, to fire at that figure. And I promise you, by Heaven and earth, I will do it with this gun if I see it again!" The young man thanked me, and took his leave with some little precipitation, after declining a glass of liquor. I imparted my secret to him, because I had never quite forgotten his throwing his cap at the bell; because I had, on another occasion, noticed something very like a fur cap, lying not far from the bell, one night when it had burst out ringing; and because I had remarked that we were at our ghostliest whenever he came up in the evening to comfort the servants. Let me do Ikey no injustice. He was afraid of the house, and believed in its being haunted; and yet he would play false on the haunting side, so surely as he got an opportunity. The Odd Girl's case was exactly similar. She went about the house in a state of real terror, and yet lied monstrously and wilfully, and invented many of the alarms she spread, and made many of the sounds we heard. I had had my eye on the two, and I know it. It is not necessary for me, here, to account for this preposterous state of mind; I content myself with remarking that it is familiarly known to every intelligent man who has had fair medical, legal, or other watchful experience; that it is as well established and as common a state of mind as any with which observers are acquainted; and that it is one of the first elements, above all others, rationally to be suspected in, and strictly looked for, and separated from, any question of this kind.

To return to our party. The first thing we did when we were all assembled, was, to draw lots for bedrooms. That done, and every bedroom, and, indeed, the whole house, having been minutely examined by the whole body, we allotted the various household duties, as if we had been on a gipsy party, or a yachting party, or a hunting party, or were shipwrecked. I then recounted the floating rumours concerning the hooded lady, the owl, and Master B.: with others, still more filmy, which had floated about during our occupation, relative to some ridiculous old ghost of the female gender who went up and down, carrying the ghost of a round table; and also to an impalpable Jackass, whom nobody was ever able to catch. Some of these ideas I really believe our people below had communicated to one another in some diseased way, without conveying them in words. We then gravely called one another to witness, that we were not there to be deceived, or to deceive—which we considered pretty much the same thing—and that, with a serious sense of responsibility, we would be strictly true to one another, and would strictly follow out the truth. The understanding was established, that any one who heard unusual noises in the night, and who wished to trace them, should knock at my door; lastly, that on Twelfth Night, the last night of holy Christmas, all our individual experiences since that then present hour of our coming together in the haunted house, should be brought to light for the good of all; and that we would hold our peace on the subject till then, unless on some remarkable provocation to break silence.

We were, in number and in character, as follows: First—to get my sister and myself out of the way-there were we two. In the drawing of lots, my sister drew her own room, and I drew Master B.'s. Next, there was our first cousin John Herschel, so called after the great astronomer: than whom I suppose a better man at a telescope does not breathe. With him, was his wife: a charming creature to whom he had been married in the previous spring. I thought it (under the circumstances) rather imprudent to bring her, because there is no knowing what even a false alarm may do at such a time; but I suppose he knew his own business best, and I must say that if she had been MY wife, I never could have left her endearing and bright face behind. They drew the Clock Room. Alfred Starling, an uncommonly agreeable young fellow of eight-and-twenty for whom I have the greatest liking, was in the Double Room; mine, usually, and designated by that name from having a dressing-room within it, with two large and cumbersome windows, which no wedges I was ever able to make, would keep from shaking, in any weather, wind or no wind. Alfred is a young fellow who pretends to be "fast" (another word for loose, as I understand the term), but who is much too good and sensible for that nonsense, and who would have distinguished himself before now, if his father had not unfortunately left him a small independence of two hundred a year, on the strength of which his only occupation in life has been to spend six. I am in hopes, however, that his Banker may break, or that he may enter into some speculation guaranteed to pay twenty per cent.; for, I am convinced that if he could only be ruined, his fortune is made. Belinda Bates, bosom friend of my sister, and a most intellectual, amiable, and delightful girl, got the Picture Room. She has a fine genius for poetry, combined with real business earnestness, and "goes in"—to use an expression of Alfred's—for Woman's mission, Woman's rights, Woman's wrongs, and everything that is woman's with a capital W, or is not and ought to be, or is and ought not to be. "Most praiseworthy, my dear, and Heaven prosper you!" I whispered to her on the first night of my taking leave of her at the Picture-Room door, "but don't overdo it. And in respect of the great necessity there is, my darling, for more employments being within the reach of Woman than our civilisation has as yet assigned to her, don't fly at the unfortunate men, even those men who are at first sight in your way, as if they were the natural oppressors of your sex; for, trust me, Belinda, they do sometimes spend their wages among wives and daughters, sisters, mothers, aunts, and grandmothers; and the play is, really, not ALL Wolf and Red Riding-Hood, but has other parts in it." However, I digress. Belinda, as I have mentioned, occupied the Picture Room. We had but three other chambers: the Corner Room, the Cupboard Room, and the Garden Room. My old friend, Jack Governor, "slung his hammock," as he called it, in the Corner Room. I have always regarded Jack as the finest-looking sailor that ever sailed. He is gray now, but as handsome as he was a quarter of a century ago—nay, handsomer. A portly, cheery, well-built figure of a broad-shouldered man, with a frank smile, a brilliant dark eye, and a rich dark eyebrow. I remember those under darker hair, and they look all the better for their silver setting. He has been wherever his Union namesake flies, has Jack, and I have met old shipmates of his, away in the Mediterranean and on the other side of the Atlantic, who have beamed and brightened at the casual mention of his name, and have cried, "You know Jack Governor? Then you know a prince of men!" That he is! And so unmistakably a naval officer, that if you were to meet him coming out of an Esquimaux snow-hut in seal's skin, you would be vaguely persuaded he was in full naval uniform.

Jack once had that bright clear eye of his on my sister; but, it fell out that he married another lady and took her to South America, where she died. This was a dozen years ago or more. He brought down with him to our haunted house a little cask of salt beef; for, he is always convinced that all salt beef not of his own pickling, is mere carrion, and invariably, when he goes to London, packs a piece in his portmanteau. He had also volunteered to bring with him one "Nat Beaver," an old comrade of his, captain of a merchantman. Mr. Beaver, with a thick-set wooden face and figure, and apparently as hard as a block all over, proved to be an intelligent man, with a world of watery experiences in him, and great practical knowledge. At times, there was a curious nervousness about him, apparently the lingering result of some old illness; but, it seldom lasted many minutes. He got the Cupboard Room, and lay there next to Mr. Undery, my friend and solicitor: who came down, in an amateur capacity, "to go through with it," as he said, and who plays whist better than the whole Law List, from the red cover at the beginning to the red cover at the end.

I never was happier in my life, and I believe it was the universal feeling among us. Jack Governor, always a man of wonderful resources, was Chief Cook, and made some of the best dishes I ever ate, including unapproachable curries. My sister was pastrycook and confectioner. Starling and I were Cook's Mate, turn and turn about, and on special occasions the chief cook "pressed" Mr. Beaver. We had a great deal of out-door sport and exercise, but nothing was neglected within, and there was no ill-humour or misunderstanding among us, and our evenings were so delightful that we had at least one good reason for being reluctant to go to bed. We had a few night alarms in the beginning. On the first night, I was knocked up by Jack with a most wonderful ship's lantern in his hand, like the gills of some monster of the deep, who informed me that he "was going aloft to the main truck," to have the weathercock down. It was a stormy night and I remonstrated; but Jack called my attention to its making a sound like a cry of despair, and said somebody would be "hailing a ghost" presently, if it wasn't done. So, up to the top of the house, where I could hardly stand for the wind, we went, accompanied by Mr. Beaver; and there Jack, lantern and all, with Mr. Beaver after him, swarmed up to the top of a cupola, some two dozen feet above the chimneys, and stood upon nothing particular, coolly knocking the weathercock off, until they both got into such good spirits with the wind and the height, that I thought they would never come down. Another night, they turned out again, and had a chimney-cowl off. Another night, they cut a sobbing and gulping water-pipe away. Another night, they found out something else. On several occasions, they both, in the coolest manner, simultaneously dropped out of their respective bedroom windows, hand over hand by their counterpanes, to "overhaul" something mysterious in the garden.

The engagement among us was faithfully kept, and nobody revealed anything. All we knew was, if any one's room were haunted, no one looked the worse for it.

When I established myself in the triangular garret which had gained so distinguished a reputation, my thoughts naturally turned to Master B. My speculations about him were uneasy and manifold. Whether his Christian name was Benjamin, Bissextile (from his having been born in Leap Year), Bartholomew, or Bill. Whether the initial letter belonged to his family name, and that was Baxter, Black, Brown, Barker, Buggins, Baker, or Bird. Whether he was a foundling, and had been baptized B. Whether he was a lion-hearted boy, and B. was short for Briton, or for Bull. Whether he could possibly have been kith and kin to an illustrious lady who brightened my own childhood, and had come of the blood of the brilliant Mother Bunch? With these profitless meditations I tormented myself much. I also carried the mysterious letter into the appearance and pursuits of the deceased; wondering whether he dressed in Blue, wore Boots (he couldn't have been Bald), was a boy of Brains, liked Books, was good at Bowling, had any skill as a Boxer, even in his Buoyant Boyhood Bathed from a Bathing-machine at Bognor, Bangor, Bournemouth, Brighton, or Broadstairs, like a Bounding Billiard Ball? So, from the first, I was haunted by the letter B. It was not long before I remarked that I never by any hazard had a dream of Master B., or of anything belonging to him. But, the instant I awoke from sleep, at whatever hour of the night, my thoughts took him up, and roamed away, trying to attach his initial letter to something that would fit it and keep it quiet. For six nights, I had been worried this in Master B.'s room, when I began to perceive that things were going wrong.

The first appearance that presented itself was early in the morning when it was but just daylight and no more. I was standing shaving at my glass, when I suddenly discovered, to my consternation and amazement, that I was shaving—not myself—I am fifty—but a boy. Apparently Master B.!

I trembled and looked over my shoulder; nothing there. I looked again in the glass, and distinctly saw the features and expression of a boy, who was shaving, not to get rid of a beard, but to get one. Extremely troubled in my mind, I took a few turns in the room, and went back to the looking-glass, resolved to steady my hand and complete the operation in which I had been disturbed. Opening my eyes, which I had shut while recovering my firmness, I now met in the glass, looking straight at me, the eyes of a young man of four or five and twenty. Terrified by this new ghost, I closed my eyes, and made a strong effort to recover myself. Opening them again, I saw, shaving his cheek in the glass, my father, who has long been dead. Nay, I even saw my grandfather too, whom I never did see in my life.

Although naturally much affected by these remarkable visitations, I determined to keep my secret, until the time agreed upon for the present general disclosure. Agitated by a multitude of curious thoughts, I retired to my room, that night, prepared to encounter some new experience of a spectral character. Nor was my preparation needless, for, waking from an uneasy sleep at exactly two o'clock in the morning, what were my feelings to find that I was sharing my bed with the skeleton of Master B.!

I sprang up, and the skeleton sprang up also. I then heard a plaintive voice saying, "Where am I? What is become of me?" and, looking hard in that direction, perceived the ghost of Master B. The young spectre was dressed in an obsolete fashion: or rather, was not so much dressed as put into a case of inferior pepper-and-salt cloth, made horrible by means of shining buttons. I observed that these buttons went, in a double row, over each shoulder of the young ghost, and appeared to descend his back. He wore a frill round his neck. His right hand (which I distinctly noticed to be inky) was laid upon his stomach; connecting this action with some feeble pimples on his countenance, and his general air of nausea, I concluded this ghost to be the ghost of a boy who had habitually taken a great deal too much medicine.

"Where am I?" said the little spectre, in a pathetic voice. "And why was I born in the Calomel days, and why did I have all that Calomel given me?"

I replied, with sincere earnestness, that upon my soul I couldn't tell him.

"Where is my little sister," said the ghost, "and where my angelic little wife, and where is the boy I went to school with?" I entreated the phantom to be comforted, and above all things to take heart respecting the loss of the boy he went to school with. I represented to him that probably that boy never did, within human experience, come out well, when discovered. I urged that I myself had, in later life, turned up several boys whom I went to school with, and none of them had at all answered. I expressed my humble belief that that boy never did answer. I represented that he was a mythic character, a delusion, and a snare. I recounted how, the last time I found him, I found him at a dinner party behind a wall of white cravat, with an inconclusive opinion on every possible subject, and a power of silent boredom absolutely Titanic. I related how, on the strength of our having been together at "Old Doylance's," he had asked himself to breakfast with me (a social offence of the largest magnitude); how, fanning my weak embers of belief in Doylance's boys, I had let him in; and how, he had proved to be a fearful wanderer about the earth, pursuing the race of Adam with inexplicable notions concerning the currency, and with a proposition that the Bank of England should, on pain of being abolished, instantly strike off and circulate, God knows how many thousand millions of ten-and-sixpenny notes.

The ghost heard me in silence, and with a fixed stare. "Barber!" it apostrophised me when I had finished. "Barber?" I repeated—for I am not of that profession. "Condemned," said the ghost, "to shave a constant change of customers—now, me—now, a young man—now, thyself as thou art—now, thy father-now, thy grandfather; condemned, too, to lie down with a skeleton every night, and to rise with it every morning—"

(I shuddered on hearing this dismal announcement.) "Barber! Pursue me!"

I had felt, even before the words were uttered, that I was under a spell to pursue the phantom. I immediately did so, and was in Master B.'s room no longer.

Most people know what long and fatiguing night journeys had been forced upon the witches who used to confess, and who, no doubt, told the exact truth—particularly as they were always assisted with leading questions, and the Torture was always ready. I asseverate that, during my occupation of Master B.'s room, I was taken by the ghost that haunted it, on expeditions fully as long and wild as any of those. Assuredly, I was presented to no shabby old man with a goat's horns and tail (something between Pan and an old clothesman), holding conventional receptions, as stupid as those of real life and less decent; but, I came upon other things which appeared to me to have more meaning.

Confident that I speak the truth and shall be believed, I declare without hesitation that I followed the ghost, in the first instance on a broom-stick, and afterwards on a rocking-horse. The very smell of the animal's paint—especially when I brought it out, by making him warm—I am ready to swear to. I followed the ghost, afterwards, in a hackney coach; an institution with the peculiar smell of which, the present generation is unacquainted, but to which I am again ready to swear as a combination of stable, dog with the mange, and very old bellows. (In this, I appeal to previous generations to confirm or refute me.) I pursued the phantom, on a headless donkey: at least, upon a donkey who was so interested in the state of his stomach that his head was always down there, investigating it; on ponies, expressly born to kick up behind; on roundabouts and swings, from fairs; in the first cab-another forgotten institution where the fare regularly got into bed, and was tucked up with the driver. Not to trouble you with a detailed account of all my travels in pursuit of the ghost of Master B., which were longer and more wonderful than those of Sinbad the Sailor, I will confine myself to one experience from which you may judge of many. I was marvellously changed. I was myself, yet not myself. I was conscious of something within me, which has been the same all through my life, and which I have always recognised under all its phases and varieties as never altering, and yet I was not the I who had gone to bed in Master B.'s room. I had the smoothest of faces and the shortest of legs, and I had taken another creature like myself, also with the smoothest of faces and the shortest of legs, behind a door, and was confiding to him a proposition of the most astounding nature.

This proposition was, that we should have a Seraglio.

The other creature assented warmly. He had no notion of respectability, neither had I. It was the custom of the East, it was the way of the good Caliph Haroun Alraschid (let me have the corrupted name again for once, it is so scented with sweet memories!), the usage was highly laudable, and most worthy of imitation. "O, yes! Let us," said the other creature with a jump, "have a Seraglio."

It was not because we entertained the faintest doubts of the meritorious character of the Oriental establishment we proposed to import, that we perceived it must be kept a secret from Miss Griffin. It was because we knew Miss Griffin to be bereft of human sympathies, and incapable of appreciating the greatness of the great Haroun. Mystery impenetrably shrouded from Miss Griffin then, let us entrust it to Miss Bule.

We were ten in Miss Griffin's establishment by Hampstead Ponds; eight ladies and two gentlemen. Miss Bule, whom I judge to have attained the ripe age of eight or nine, took the lead in society. I opened the subject to her in the course of the day, and proposed that she should become the Favourite.

Miss Bule, after struggling with the diffidence so natural to, and charming in, her adorable sex, expressed herself as flattered by the idea, but wished to know how it was proposed to provide for Miss Pipson? Miss Bule—who was understood to have vowed towards that young lady, a friendship, halves, and no secrets, until death, on the Church Service and Lessons complete in two volumes with case and lock—Miss Bule said she could not, as the friend of Pipson, disguise from herself, or me, that Pipson was not one of the common. Now, Miss Pipson, having curly hair and blue eyes (which was my idea of anything mortal and feminine that was called Fair), I promptly replied that I regarded Miss Pipson in the light of a Fair Circassian. "And what then?" Miss Bule pensively asked. I replied that she must be inveigled by a Merchant, brought to me veiled, and purchased as a slave.

[The other creature had already fallen into the second male place in the State, and was set apart for Grand Vizier. He afterwards resisted this disposal of events, but had his hair pulled until he yielded.]

"Shall I not be jealous?" Miss Bule inquired, casting down her eyes. "Zobeide, no," I replied; "you will ever be the favourite Sultana; the first place in my heart, and on my throne, will be ever yours." Miss Bule, upon that assurance, consented to propound the idea to her seven beautiful companions. It occurring to me, in the course of the same day, that we knew we could trust a grinning and good-natured soul called Tabby, who was the serving drudge of the house, and had no more figure than one of the beds, and upon whose face there was always more or less black-lead, I slipped into Miss Bule's hand after supper, a little note to that effect; dwelling on the black-lead as being in a manner deposited by the finger of Providence, pointing Tabby out for Mesrour, the celebrated chief of the Blacks of the Hareem.

There were difficulties in the formation of the desired institution, as there are in all combinations. The other creature showed himself of a low character, and, when defeated in aspiring to the throne, pretended to have conscientious scruples about prostrating himself before the Caliph; wouldn't call him Commander of the Faithful; spoke of him slightingly and inconsistently as a mere "chap;" said he, the other creature, "wouldn't play"—Play!—and was otherwise coarse and offensive. This meanness of disposition was, however, put down by the general indignation of an united Seraglio, and I became blessed in the smiles of eight of the fairest of the daughters of men.

The smiles could only be bestowed when Miss Griffin was looking another way, and only then in a very wary manner, for there was a legend among the followers of the Prophet that she saw with a little round ornament in the middle of the pattern on the back of her shawl. But every day after dinner, for an hour, we were all together, and then the Favourite and the rest of the Royal Hareem competed who should most beguile the leisure of the Serene Haroun reposing from the cares of State—which were generally, as in most affairs of State, of an arithmetical character, the Commander of the Faithful being a fearful boggier at a sum.

On these occasions, the devoted Mesrour, chief of the Blacks of the Hareem, was always in attendance (Miss Griffin usually ringing for that officer, at the same time, with great vehemence), but never acquitted himself in a manner worthy of his historical reputation. In the first place, his bringing a broom into the Divan of the Caliph, even when Haroun wore on his shoulders the red robe of anger (Miss Pipson's pelisse), though it might be got over for the moment, was never to be quite satisfactorily accounted for. In the second place, his breaking out into grinning exclamations of "Lork you pretties!" was neither Eastern nor respectful. In the third place, when specially instructed to say "Bismillah!" he always said "Hallelujah!" This officer, unlike his class, was too good-humoured altogether, kept his mouth open far too wide, expressed approbation to an incongruous extent, and even once—it was on the occasion of the purchase of the Fair Circassian for five hundred thousand purses of gold, and cheap, too—embraced the Slave, the Favourite, and the Caliph, all round. (Parenthetically let me say God bless Mesrour, and may there have been sons and daughters on that tender bosom, softening many a hard day since!)

Miss Griffin was a model of propriety, and I am at a loss to imagine what the feelings of the virtuous woman would have been, if she had known, when she paraded us down the Hampstead Road two and two, that she was walking with a stately step at the head of Polygamy and Mahomedanism. I believe that a mysterious and terrible joy with which the contemplation of Miss Griffin, in this unconscious state, inspired us, and a grim sense prevalent among us that there was a dreadful power in our knowledge of what Miss Griffin (who knew all things that could be learnt out of book) didn't know, were the main-spring of the preservation of our secret. It was wonderfully kept, but was once upon the verge of self-betrayal. The danger and escape occurred upon a Sunday. We were all ten ranged in a conspicuous part of the gallery at church, with Miss Griffin at our head—as we were every Sunday—advertising the establishment in an unsecular sort of way—when the description of Solomon in his domestic glory happened to be read. The moment that monarch was thus referred to, conscience whispered me, "Thou, too, Haroun!" The officiating minister had a cast in his eye, and it assisted conscience by giving him the appearance of reading personally at me. A crimson blush, attended by a fearful perspiration, suffused my features. The Grand Vizier became more dead than alive, and the whole Seraglio reddened as if the sunset of Bagdad shone direct upon their lovely faces. At this portentous time the awful Griffin rose, and balefully surveyed the children of Islam. My own impression was, that Church and State had entered into a conspiracy with Miss Griffin to expose us, and that we should all be put into white sheets, and exhibited in the centre aisle. But, so Westerly—if I may be allowed the expression as opposite to Eastern associations—was Miss Griffin's sense of rectitude, that she merely suspected Apples, and we were saved.

I have called the Seraglio, united. Upon the question, solely, whether the Commander of the Faithful durst exercise a right of kissing in that sanctuary of the palace, were its peerless inmates divided. Zobeide asserted a counter-right in the Favourite to scratch, and the fair Circassian put her face, for refuge, into a green baize bag, originally designed for books. On the other hand, a young antelope of transcendent beauty from the fruitful plains of Camden Town (whence she had been brought, by traders, in the half-yearly caravan that crossed the intermediate desert after the holidays), held more liberal opinions, but stipulated for limiting the benefit of them to that dog, and son of a dog, the Grand Vizier—who had no rights, and was not in question. At length, the difficulty was compromised by the installation of a very youthful slave as Deputy. She, raised upon a stool, officially received upon her cheeks the salutes intended by the gracious Haroun for other Sultanas, and was privately rewarded from the coffers of the Ladies of the Hareem. And now it was, at the full height of enjoyment of my bliss, that I became heavily troubled. I began to think of my mother, and what she would say to my taking home at Midsummer eight of the most beautiful of the daughters of men, but all unexpected. I thought of the number of beds we made up at our house, of my father's income, and of the baker, and my despondency redoubled. The Seraglio and malicious Vizier, divining the cause of their Lord's unhappiness, did their utmost to augment it. They professed unbounded fidelity, and declared that they would live and die with him. Reduced to the utmost wretchedness by these protestations of attachment, I lay awake, for hours at a time, ruminating on my frightful lot. In my despair, I think I might have taken an early opportunity of falling on my knees before Miss Griffin, avowing my resemblance to Solomon, and praying to be dealt with according to the outraged laws of my country, if an unthought-of means of escape had not opened before me.

One day, we were out walking, two and two—on which occasion the Vizier had his usual instructions to take note of the boy at the turnpike, and if he profanely gazed (which he always did) at the beauties of the Hareem, to have him bowstrung in the course of the night—and it happened that our hearts were veiled in gloom. An unaccountable action on the part of the antelope had plunged the State into disgrace. That charmer, on the representation that the previous day was her birthday, and that vast treasures had been sent in a hamper for its celebration (both baseless assertions), had secretly but most pressingly invited thirty-five neighbouring princes and princesses to a ball and supper: with a special stipulation that they were "not to be fetched till twelve." This wandering of the antelope's fancy led to the surprising arrival at Miss Griffin's door, in divers equipages and under various escorts, of a great company in full dress, who were deposited on the top step in a flush of high expectancy, and who were dismissed in tears. At the beginning of the double knocks attendant on these ceremonies, the antelope had retired to a back attic, and bolted herself in; and at every new arrival, Miss Griffin had gone so much more and more distracted, that at last she had been seen to tear her front. Ultimate capitulation on the part of the offender, had been followed by solitude in the linen-closet, bread and water and a lecture to all, of vindictive length, in which Miss Griffin had used expressions: Firstly, "I believe you all of you knew of it;" Secondly, "Every one of you is as wicked as another;" Thirdly, "A pack of little wretches."

Under these circumstances, we were walking drearily along; and I especially, with my. Moosulmaun responsibilities heavy on me, was in a very low state of mind; when a strange man accosted Miss Griffin, and, after walking on at her side for a little while and talking with her, looked at me. Supposing him to be a minion of the law, and that my hour was come, I instantly ran away, with the general purpose of making for Egypt.

The whole Seraglio cried out, when they saw me making off as fast as my legs would carry me (I had an impression that the first turning on the left, and round by the public-house, would be the shortest way to the Pyramids), Miss Griffin screamed after me, the faithless Vizier ran after me, and the boy at the turnpike dodged me into a corner, like a sheep, and cut me off. Nobody scolded me when I was taken and brought back; Miss Griffin only said, with a stunning gentleness, This was very curious! Why had I run away when the gentleman looked at me?

If I had had any breath to answer with, I dare say I should have made no answer; having no breath, I certainly made none. Miss Griffin and the strange man took me between them, and walked me back to the palace in a sort of state; but not at all (as I couldn't help feeling, with astonishment) in culprit state.

When we got there, we went into a room by ourselves, and Miss Griffin called in to her assistance, Mesrour, chief of the dusky guards of the Hareem. Mesrour, on being whispered to, began to shed tears. "Bless you, my precious!" said that officer, turning to me; "your Pa's took bitter bad!" I asked, with a fluttered heart, "Is he very ill?" "Lord temper the wind to you, my lamb!" said the good Mesrour, kneeling down, that I might have a comforting shoulder for my head to rest on, "your Pa's dead!"

Haroun Alraschid took to flight at the words; the Seraglio vanished; from that moment, I never again saw one of the eight of the fairest of the daughters of men.

I was taken home, and there was Debt at home as well as Death, and we had a sale there. My own little bed was so superciliously looked upon by a Power unknown to me, hazily called "The Trade," that a brass coal-scuttle, a roasting-jack, and a birdcage, were obliged to be put into it to make a Lot of it, and then it went for a song. So I heard mentioned, and I wondered what song, and thought what a dismal song it must have been to sing! Then, I was sent to a great, cold, bare, school of big boys; where everything to eat and wear was thick and clumpy, without being enough; where everybody, large and small, was cruel; where the boys knew all about the sale, before I got there, and asked me what I had fetched, and who had bought me, and hooted at me, "Going, going, gone!" I never whispered in that wretched place that I had been Haroun, or had had a Seraglio: for, I knew that if I mentioned my reverses, I should be so worried, that I should have to drown myself in the muddy pond near the playground, which looked like the beer.

Ah me, ah me! No other ghost has haunted the boy's room, my friends, since I have occupied it, than the ghost of my own childhood, the ghost of my own innocence, the ghost of my own airy belief. Many a time have I pursued the phantom: never with this man's stride of mine to come up with it, never with these man's hands of mine to touch it, never more to this man's heart of mine to hold it in its purity. And here you see me working out, as cheerfully and thankfully as I may, my doom of shaving in the glass a constant change of customers, and of lying down and rising up with the skeleton allotted to me for my mortal companion.

THE TAVERN AT BRUGES

# THE BOLD DRAGOON; OR, THE ADVENTURE OF MY GRANDFATHER
## WASHINGTON IRVING

My grandfather was a bold dragoon, for it's a profession, d'ye see, that has run in the family. All my forefathers have been dragoons and died upon the field of honor except myself, and I hope my posterity may be able to say the same; however, I don't mean to be vainglorious. Well, my grandfather, as I said, was a bold dragoon, and had served in the Low Countries. In fact, he was one of that very army, which, according to my uncle Toby, "swore so terribly in Flanders." He could swear a good stick himself; and, moreover, was the very man that introduced the doctrine Corporal Trim mentions, of radical heat and radical moisture; or, in other words, the mode of keeping out the damps of ditch water by burnt brandy. Be that as it may, it's nothing to the purport of my story. I only tell it to show you that my grandfather was a man not easily to be humbugged. He had seen service; or, according to his own phrase, "he had seen the devil"—and that's saying everything.

Well, gentlemen, my grandfather was on his way to England, for which he intended to embark at Ostend;—bad luck to the place for one where I was kept by storms and head winds for three long days, and the divil of a jolly companion or pretty face to comfort me. Well, as I was saying, my grandfather was on his way to England, or rather to Ostend—no matter which, it's all the same. So one evening, towards nightfall, he rode jollily into Bruges. Very like you all know Bruges, gentlemen, a queer, old-fashioned Flemish town, once they say a great place for trade and money-making, in old times, when the Mynheers were in their glory; but almost as large and as empty as an Irishman's pocket at the present day.

Well, gentlemen, it was the time of the annual fair. All Bruges was crowded; and the canals swarmed with Dutch boats, and the streets swarmed with Dutch merchants; and there was hardly any getting along for goods, wares, and merchandises, and peasants in big breeches, and women in half a score of petticoats.

My grandfather rode jollily along in his easy, slashing way, for he was a saucy, sunshiny fellow—staring about him at the motley crowd, and the old houses with gable ends to the street and storks' nests on the chimneys; winking at the yafrows who showed their faces at the windows, and joking the women right and left in the street; all of whom laughed and took it in amazing good part; for though he did not know a word of their language, yet he always had a knack of making himself understood among the women.

Well, gentlemen, it being the time of the annual fair, all the town was crowded; every inn and tavern full, and my grandfather applied in vain from one to the other for admittance. At length he rode up to an old rackety inn that looked ready to fall to pieces, and which all the rats would have run away from, if they could have found room in any other house to put their heads. It was just such a queer building as you see in Dutch pictures, with a tall roof that reached up into the clouds; and as many garrets, one over the other, as the seven heavens of Mahomet. Nothing had saved it from tumbling down but a stork's nest on the chimney, which always brings good luck to a house in the Low Countries; and at the very time of my grandfather's arrival, there were two of these long-legged birds of grace, standing like ghosts on the chimney top. Faith, but they've kept the house on its legs to this very day; for you may see it any time you pass through Bruges, as it stands there yet; only it is turned into a brewery—a brewery of strong Flemish beer; at least it was so when I came that way after the battle of Waterloo.

My grandfather eyed the house curiously as he approached. It might Not altogether have struck his fancy, had he not seen in large letters over the door, HEER VERKOOPT MAN GOEDEN DRANK.

My grandfather had learnt enough of the language to know that the sign promised good liquor. "This is the house for me," said he, stopping short before the door.

The sudden appearance of a dashing dragoon was an event in an old inn, frequented only by the peaceful sons of traffic. A rich burgher of Antwerp, a stately ample man, in a broad Flemish hat, and who was the great man and great patron of the establishment, sat smoking a clean long pipe on one side of the door; a fat little distiller of Geneva from Schiedam, sat smoking on the other, and the bottle-nosed host stood in the door, and the comely hostess, in crimped cap, beside him; and the hostess' daughter, a plump Flanders lass, with long gold pendants in her ears, was at a side window.

"Humph!" said the rich burgher of Antwerp, with a sulky glance at the stranger.

"Der duyvel!" said the fat little distiller of Schiedam.

The landlord saw with the quick glance of a publican that the new guest was not at all, at all, to the taste of the old ones; and to tell the truth, he did not himself like my grandfather's saucy eye.

He shook his head—"Not a garret in the house but was full."

"Not a garret!" echoed the landlady.

"Not a garret!" echoed the daughter.

The burgher of Antwerp and the little distiller of Schiedam continued to smoke their pipes sullenly, eyed the enemy askance from under their broad hats, but said nothing.

My grandfather was not a man to be browbeaten. He threw the reins on his horse's neck, cocked his hat on one side, stuck one arm akimbo, slapped his broad thigh with the other hand—

"Faith and troth!" said he, "but I'll sleep in this house this very night!"

My grandfather had on a tight pair of buckskins—the slap went to the landlady's heart.

He followed up the vow by jumping off his horse, and making his way past the staring Mynheers into the public room. May be you've been in the barroom of an old Flemish inn—faith, but a handsome chamber it was as you'd wish to see; with a brick floor, a great fireplace, with the whole Bible history in glazed tiles; and then the mantel-piece, pitching itself head foremost out of the wall, with a whole regiment of cracked tea-pots and earthen jugs paraded on it; not to mention half a dozen great Delft platters hung about the room by way of pictures; and the little bar in one corner, and the bouncing bar-maid inside of it with a red calico cap and yellow ear-drops.

My grandfather snapped his fingers over his head, as he cast an eye round the room: "Faith, this is the very house I've been looking after," said he.

There was some farther show of resistance on the part of the garrison, but my grandfather was an old soldier, and an Irishman to boot, and not easily repulsed, especially after he had got into the fortress. So he blarney'd the landlord, kissed the landlord's wife, tickled the landlord's daughter, chucked the bar-maid under the chin; and it was agreed on all hands that it would be a thousand pities, and a burning shame into the bargain, to turn such a bold dragoon into the streets. So they laid their heads together, that is to say, my grandfather and the landlady, and it was at length agreed to accommodate him with an old chamber that had for some time been shut up.

"Some say it's haunted!" whispered the landlord's daughter, "but you're a bold dragoon, and I dare say you don't fear ghosts."

"The divil a bit!" said my grandfather, pinching her plump cheek; "but if I should be troubled by ghosts, I've been to the Red Sea in my time, and have a pleasant way of laying them, my darling!"

And then he whispered something to the girl which made her laugh, and give him a good-humored box on the ear. In short, there was nobody knew better how to make his way among the petticoats than my grandfather.

In a little while, as was his usual way, he took complete possession of the house: swaggering all over it;—into the stable to look after his horse; into the kitchen to look after his supper. He had something to say or do with every one; smoked with the Dutchmen; drank with the Germans; slapped the men on the shoulders, tickled the women under the ribs—never since the days of Ally Croaker had such a rattling blade been seen. The landlord stared at him with astonishment; the landlord's daughter hung her head and giggled whenever he came near; and as he turned his back and swaggered along, his tight jacket setting off his broad shoulders and plump buckskins, and his long sword trailing by his side, the maids whispered to one another—"What a proper man!"

At supper my grandfather took command of the table d'hote as though he had been at home; helped everybody, not forgetting himself; talked with every one, whether he understood their language or not; and made his way into the intimacy of the rich burgher of Antwerp, who had never been known to be sociable with any one during his life. In fact, he revolutionized the whole establishment, and gave it such a rouse, that the very house reeled with it. He outsat every one at table excepting the little fat distiller of Schiedam, who had sat soaking for a long time before he broke forth; but when he did, he was a very devil incarnate. He took a violent affection for my grandfather; so they sat drinking, and smoking, and telling stories, and singing Dutch and Irish songs, without understanding a word each other said, until the little Hollander was fairly swampt with his own gin and water, and carried off to bed, whooping and hiccuping, and trolling the burthen of a Low Dutch love song.

Well, gentlemen, my grandfather was shown to his quarters, up a huge staircase composed of loads of hewn timber; and through long rigmarole passages, hung with blackened paintings of fruit, and fish, and game, and country trollies, and huge kitchens, and portly burgomasters, such as you see about old-fashioned Flemish inns, till at length he arrived at his room.

An old-times chamber it was, sure enough, and crowded with all kinds of trumpery. It looked like an infirmary for decayed and superannuated furniture; where everything diseased and disabled was sent to nurse, or to be forgotten. Or rather, it might have been taken for a general congress of old legitimate moveables, where every kind and country had a representative. No two chairs were alike: such high backs and low backs, and leather bottoms and worsted bottoms, and straw bottoms, and no bottoms; and cracked marble tables with curiously carved legs, holding balls in their claws, as though they were going to play at ninepins.

My grandfather made a bow to the motley assemblage as he entered, and having undressed himself, placed his light in the fire-place, asking pardon of the tongs, which seemed to be making love to the shovel in the chimney corner, and whispering soft nonsense in its ear.

The rest of the guests were by this time sound asleep; for your Mynheers are huge sleepers. The house maids, one by one, crept up yawning to their attics, and not a female head in the inn was laid on a pillow that night without dreaming of the Bold Dragoon.

My grandfather, for his part, got into bed, and drew over him one of those great bags of down, under which they smother a man in the Low Countries; and there he lay, melting between, two feather beds, like an anchovy sandwich between two slices of toast and butter. He was a warm-complexioned man, and this smothering played the very deuce with him. So, sure enough, in a little while it seemed as if a legion of imps were twitching at him and all the blood in his veins was in fever heat.

He lay still, however, until all the house was quiet, excepting the snoring of the Mynheers from the different chambers; who answered one another in all kinds of tones and cadences, like so many bull-frogs in a swamp. The quieter the house became, the more unquiet became my grandfather. He waxed warmer and warmer, until at length the bed became too hot to hold him.

"May be the maid had warmed it too much?" said the curious gentleman, inquiringly.

"I rather think the contrary," replied the Irishman. "But be that as it may, it grew too hot for my grandfather."

"Faith there's no standing this any longer," says he; so he jumped out of bed and went strolling about the house.

"What for?" said the inquisitive gentleman.

"Why, to cool himself to be sure," replied the other, "or perhaps to find a more comfortable bed—or perhaps—but no matter what he went for—he never mentioned; and there's no use in taking up our time in conjecturing."

Well, my grandfather had been for some time absent from his room, and was returning, perfectly cool, when just as he reached the door he heard a strange noise within. He paused and listened. It seemed as if some one was trying to hum a tune in defiance of the asthma. He recollected the report of the room's being haunted; but he was no believer in ghosts. So he pushed the door gently ajar, and peeped in.

Egad, gentlemen, there was a gambol carrying on within enough to have astonished St. Anthony.

By the light of the fire he saw a pale weazen-faced fellow in a long flannel gown and a tall white nightcap with a tassel to it, who sat by the fire, with a bellows under his arm by way of bagpipe, from which he forced the asthmatical music that had bothered my grandfather. As he played, too, he kept twitching about with a thousand queer contortions; nodding his head and bobbing about his tasselled night-cap.

My grandfather thought this very odd, and mighty presumptuous, and was about to demand what business he had to play his wind instruments in another gentleman's quarters, when a new cause of astonishment met his eye. From the opposite side of the room a long-backed, bandy-legged chair, covered with leather, and studded all over in a coxcomical fashion with little brass nails, got suddenly into motion; thrust out first a claw foot, then a crooked arm, and at length, making a leg, slided gracefully up to an easy chair, of tarnished brocade, with a hole in its bottom, and led it gallantly out in a ghostly minuet about the floor.

The musician now played fiercer and fiercer, and bobbed his head and his nightcap about like mad. By degrees the dancing mania seemed to seize upon all the other pieces of furniture. The antique, long-bodied chairs paired off in couples and led down a country dance; a three-legged stool danced a hornpipe, though horribly puzzled by its supernumerary leg; while the amorous tongs seized the shovel round the waist, and whirled it about the room in a German waltz. In short, all the moveables got in motion, capering about; pirouetting, hands across, right and left, like so many devils, all except a great clothes-press, which kept curtseying and curtseying, like a dowager, in one corner, in exquisite time to the music;—being either too corpulent to dance, or perhaps at a loss for a partner.

My grandfather concluded the latter to be the reason; so, being, like a true Irishman, devoted to the sex, and at all times ready for a frolic, he bounced into the room, calling to the musician to strike up "Paddy O'Rafferty," capered up to the clothes-press and seized upon two handles to lead her out:—When, whizz!—the whole revel was at an end. The chairs, tables, tongs, and shovel slunk in an instant as quietly into their places as if nothing had happened; and the musician vanished up the chimney, leaving the bellows behind him in his hurry. My grandfather found himself seated in the middle of the floor, with the clothes-press sprawling before him, and the two handles jerked off and in his hands.

"Then after all, this was a mere dream!" said the inquisitive gentleman.

"The divil a bit of a dream!" replied the Irishman: "there never was a truer fact in this world. Faith, I should have liked to see any man tell my grandfather it was a dream."

Well, gentlemen, as the clothes-press was a mighty heavy body, and my grandfather likewise, particularly in rear, you may easily suppose two such heavy bodies coming to the ground would make a bit of a noise. Faith, the old mansion shook as though it had mistaken it for an earthquake. The whole garrison was alarmed. The landlord, who slept just below, hurried up with a candle to inquire the cause, but with all his haste his daughter had hurried to the scene of uproar before him. The landlord was followed by the landlady, who was followed by the bouncing bar-maid, who was followed by the simpering chambermaids all holding together, as well as they could, such garments as they had first lain hands on; but all in a terrible hurry to see what the devil was to pay in the chamber of the bold dragoon.

My grandfather related the marvellous scene he had witnessed, and the prostrate clothes-press, and the broken handles, bore testimony to the fact. There was no contesting such evidence; particularly with a lad of my grandfather's complexion, who seemed able to make good every word either with sword or shillelah. So the landlord scratched his head and looked silly, as he was apt to do when puzzled. The landlady scratched—no, she did not scratch her head,—but she knit her brow, and did not seem half pleased with the explanation. But the landlady's daughter corroborated it by recollecting that the last person who had dwelt in that chamber was a famous juggler who had died of St. Vitus's dance, and no doubt had infected all the furniture.

This set all things to rights, particularly when the chambermaids declared that they had all witnessed strange carryings on in that room;—and as they declared this "upon their honors," there could not remain a doubt upon the subject.

"And did your grandfather go to bed again in that room?" said the inquisitive gentleman.

"That's more than I can tell. Where he passed the rest of the night was a secret he never disclosed. In fact, though he had seen much service, he was but indifferently acquainted with geography, and apt to make blunders in his travels about inns at night, that it would have puzzled him sadly to account for in the morning."

"Was he ever apt to walk in his sleep?" said the knowing old gentleman.

"Never that I heard of."

# A GHOST STORY
## MARK TWAIN

I took a large room, far up Broadway, in a huge old building whose upper stories had been wholly unoccupied for years until I came. The place had long been given up to dust and cobwebs, to solitude and silence. I seemed groping among the tombs and invading the privacy of the dead, that first night I climbed up to my quarters. For the first time in my life a superstitious dread came over me; and as I turned a dark angle of the stairway and an invisible cobweb swung its slazy woof in my face and clung there, I shuddered as one who had encountered a phantom.

I was glad enough when I reached my room and locked out the mold and the darkness. A cheery fire was burning in the grate, and I sat down before it with a comforting sense of relief. For two hours I sat there, thinking of bygone times; recalling old scenes, and summoning half-forgotten faces out of the mists of the past; listening, in fancy, to voices that long ago grew silent for all time, and to once familiar songs that nobody sings now. And as my reverie softened down to a sadder and sadder pathos, the shrieking of the winds outside softened to a wail, the angry beating of the rain against the panes diminished to a tranquil patter, and one by one the noises in the street subsided, until the hurrying footsteps of the last belated straggler died away in the distance and left no sound behind. The fire had burned low. A sense of loneliness crept over me. I arose and undressed, moving on tiptoe about the room, doing stealthily what I had to do, as if I were environed by sleeping enemies whose slumbers it would be fatal to break. I covered up in bed, and lay listening to the rain and wind and the faint creaking of distant shutters, till they lulled me to sleep.

I slept profoundly, but how long I do not know. All at once I found myself awake, and filled with a shuddering expectancy. All was still.

All but my own heart—I could hear it beat. Presently the bedclothes began to slip away slowly toward the foot of the bed, as if some one were pulling them! I could not stir; I could not speak. Still the blankets slipped deliberately away, till my breast was uncovered. Then with a great effort I seized them and drew them over my head. I waited, listened, waited. Once more that steady pull began, and once more I lay torpid a century of dragging seconds till my breast was naked again. At last I roused my energies and snatched the covers back to their place and held them with a strong grip. I waited. By and by I felt a faint tug, and took a fresh grip. The tug strengthened to a steady strain—it grew stronger and stronger. My hold parted, and for the third time the blankets slid away. I groaned. An answering groan came from the foot of the bed! Beaded drops of sweat stood upon my forehead. I was more dead than alive. Presently I heard a heavy footstep in my room—the step of an elephant, it seemed to me—it was not like anything human. But it was moving from me-there was relief in that. I heard it approach the door—pass out without moving bolt or lock—and wander away among the dismal corridors, straining the floors and joists till they creaked again as it passed-and then silence reigned once more. When my excitement had calmed, I said to myself, "This is a dream-simply a hideous dream." And so I lay thinking it over until I convinced myself that it was a dream, and then a comforting laugh relaxed my lips and I was happy again. I got up and struck a light; and when I found that the locks and bolts were just as I had left them, another soothing laugh welled in my heart and rippled from my lips. I took my pipe and lit it, and was just sitting down before the fire, when-down went the pipe out of my nerveless fingers, the blood forsook my cheeks, and my placid breathing was cut short with a gasp! In the ashes on the hearth, side by side with my own bare footprint, was another, so vast that in comparison mine was but an infant's! Then I had had a visitor, and the elephant tread was explained.

I put out the light and returned to bed, palsied with fear. I lay a long time, peering into the darkness, and listening. Then I heard a grating noise overhead, like the dragging of a heavy body across the floor; then the throwing down of the body, and the shaking of my windows in response to the concussion. In distant parts of the building I heard the muffled slamming of doors. I heard, at intervals, stealthy footsteps creeping in and out among the corridors, and up and down the stairs. Sometimes these noises approached my door, hesitated, and went away again. I heard the clanking of chains faintly, in remote passages, and listened while the clanking grew nearer—while it wearily climbed the stairways, marking each move by the loose surplus of chain that fell with an accented rattle upon each succeeding step as the goblin that bore it advanced. I heard muttered sentences; half-uttered screams that seemed smothered violently; and the swish of invisible garments, the rush of invisible wings. Then I became conscious that my chamber was invaded-that I was not alone. I heard sighs and breathings about my bed, and mysterious whisperings. Three little spheres of soft phosphorescent light appeared on the ceiling directly over my head, clung and glowed there a moment, and then dropped-two of them upon my face and one upon the pillow. They, spattered, liquidly, and felt warm. Intuition told me they had turned to gouts of blood as they fell—I needed no light to satisfy myself of that. Then I saw pallid faces, dimly luminous, and white uplifted hands, floating bodiless in the air-floating a moment and then disappearing. The whispering ceased, and the voices and the sounds, and a solemn stillness followed. I waited and listened. I felt that I must have light or die. I was weak with fear. I slowly raised myself toward a sitting posture, and my face came in contact with a clammy hand! All strength went from me apparently, and I fell back like a stricken invalid. Then I heard the rustle of a garment—it seemed to pass to the door and go out.

When everything was still once more, I crept out of bed, sick and feeble, and lit the gas with a hand that trembled as if it were aged with a hundred years. The light brought some little cheer to my spirits. I sat down and fell into a dreamy contemplation of that great footprint in the ashes. By and by its outlines began to waver and grow dim. I glanced up and the broad gas-flame was slowly wilting away. In the same moment I heard that elephantine tread again. I noted its approach, nearer and nearer, along the musty halls, and dimmer and dimmer the light waned. The tread reached my very door and paused-the light had dwindled to a sickly blue, and all things about me lay in a spectral twilight. The door did not open, and yet I felt a faint gust of air fan my cheek, and presently was conscious of a huge, cloudy presence before me. I watched it with fascinated eyes. A pale glow stole over the Thing; gradually its cloudy folds took shape—an arm appeared, then legs, then a body, and last a great sad face looked out of the vapor. Stripped of its filmy housings, naked, muscular and comely, the majestic Cardiff Giant loomed above me!

All my misery vanished—for a child might know that no harm could come with that benignant countenance. My cheerful spirits returned at once, and in sympathy with them the gas flamed up brightly again. Never a lonely outcast was so glad to welcome company as I was to greet the friendly giant. I said:

"Why, is it nobody but you? Do you know, I have been scared to death for the last two or three hours? I am most honestly glad to see you. I wish I had a chair-Here, here, don't try to sit down in that thing-"

But it was too late. He was in it before I could stop him and down he went-I never saw a chair shivered so in my life. "Stop, stop, you'll ruin ev—"

Too late again. There was another crash, and another chair was resolved into its original elements.

"Confound it, haven't you got any judgment at' all? Do you want to ruin all the furniture on the place? Here, here, you petrified fool-" But it was no use. Before I could arrest him he had sat down on the bed, and it was a melancholy ruin.

"Now what sort of a way is that to do? First you come lumbering about the place bringing a legion of vagabond goblins along with you to worry me to death, and then when I overlook an indelicacy of costume which would not be tolerated anywhere by cultivated people except in a respectable theater, and not even there if the nudity were of your sex, you repay me by wrecking all the furniture you can find to sit down on. And why will you? You damage yourself as much as you do me. You have broken off the end of your spinal column, and littered up the floor with chips of your hams till the place looks like a marble yard. You ought to be ashamed of yourself-you are big enough to know better."

"Well, I will not break any more furniture. But what am I to do? I have not had a chance to sit down for a century." And the tears came into his eyes.

"Poor devil," I said, "I should not have been so harsh with you. And you are an orphan, too, no doubt. But sit down on the floor here-nothing else can stand your weight-and besides, we cannot be sociable with you away up there above me; I want you down where I can perch on this high counting-house stool and gossip with you face to face."

So he sat down on the floor, and lit a pipe which I gave him, threw one of my red blankets over his shoulders, inverted my sitz-bath on his head, helmet fashion, and made himself picturesque and comfortable. Then he crossed his ankles, while I renewed the fire, and exposed the flat, honeycombed bottoms of his prodigious feet to the grateful warmth.

"What is the matter with the bottom of your feet and the back of your legs, that they are gouged up so?"

"Infernal chilblains—I caught them clear up to the back of my head, roosting out there under Newell's farm. But I love the place; I love it as one loves his old home. There is no peace for me like the peace I feel when I am there."

We talked along for half an hour, and then I noticed that he looked tired, and spoke of it.

"Tired?" he said. "Well, I should think so. And now I will tell you all about it, since you have treated me so well. I am the spirit of the Petrified Man that lies across the street there in the museum. I am the ghost of the Cardiff Giant. I can have no rest, no peace, till they have given that poor body burial again. Now what was the most natural thing for me to do, to make men satisfy this wish? Terrify them into it! haunt the place where the body lay! So I haunted the museum night after night. I even got other spirits to help me. But it did no good, for nobody ever came to the museum at midnight. Then it occurred to me to come over the way and haunt this place a little. I felt that if I ever got a hearing I must succeed, for I had the most efficient company that perdition could furnish. Night after night we have shivered around through these mildewed halls, dragging chains, groaning, whispering, tramping up and down stairs, till, to tell you the truth, I am almost worn out. But when I saw a light in your room to-night I roused my energies again and went at it with a deal of the old freshness. But I am tired out-entirely fagged out. Give me, I beseech you, give me some hope!" I lit off my perch in a burst of excitement, and exclaimed:

"This transcends everything! everything that ever did occur! Why you poor blundering old fossil, you have had all your trouble for nothing—you have been haunting a plaster cast of yourself—the real Cardiff Giant is in Albany!—[A fact. The original fraud was ingeniously and fraudfully duplicated, and exhibited in New York as the "only genuine" Cardiff Giant (to the unspeakable disgust of the owners of the real colossus) at the very same time that the latter was drawing crowds at a museum is Albany.]-Confound it, don't you know your own remains?"

I never saw such an eloquent look of shame, of pitiable humiliation, overspread a countenance before.

The Petrified Man rose slowly to his feet, and said:

"Honestly, is that true?"

"As true as I am sitting here."

He took the pipe from his mouth and laid it on the mantel, then stood irresolute a moment (unconsciously, from old habit, thrusting his hands where his pantaloons pockets should have been, and meditatively dropping his chin on his breast); and finally said: "Well I never felt so absurd before. The Petrified Man has sold everybody else, and now the mean fraud has ended by selling its own ghost! My son, if there is any charity left in your heart for a poor friendless phantom like me, don't let this get out. Think how you would feel if you had made such an ass of yourself." I heard his stately tramp die away, step by step down the stairs and out into the deserted street, and felt sorry that he was gone, poor fellow-and sorrier still that he had carried off my red blanket and my bath-tub.

# AFTERWARD

## EDITH WHARTON

## I

"Oh, there is one, of course, but you'll never know it."

The assertion, laughingly flung out six months earlier in a bright June garden, came back to Mary Boyne with a sharp perception of its latent significance as she stood, in the December dusk, waiting for the lamps to be brought into the library.

The words had been spoken by their friend Alida Stair, as they sat at tea on her lawn at Pangbourne, in reference to the very house of which the library in question was the central, the pivotal "feature." Mary Boyne and her husband, in quest of a country place in one of the southern or southwestern counties, had, on their arrival in England, carried their problem straight to Alida Stair, who had successfully solved it in her own case; but it was not until they had rejected, almost capriciously, several practical and judicious suggestions that she threw it out: "Well, there's Lyng, in Dorsetshire. It belongs to Hugo's cousins, and you can get it for a song."

The reasons she gave for its being obtainable on these terms—its remoteness from a station, its lack of electric light, hot-water pipes, and other vulgar necessities—were exactly those pleading in its favor with two romantic Americans perversely in search of the economic drawbacks which were associated, in their tradition, with unusual architectural felicities.

"I should never believe I was living in an old house unless I was thoroughly uncomfortable," Ned Boyne, the more extravagant of the two, had jocosely insisted; "the least hint of 'convenience' would make me think it had been bought out of an exhibition, with the pieces numbered, and set up again." And they had proceeded to enumerate, with humorous precision, their various suspicions and exactions, refusing to believe that the house their cousin recommended was REALLY Tudor till they learned it had no heating system, or that the village church was literally in the grounds till she assured them of the deplorable uncertainty of the water-supply.

"It's too uncomfortable to be true!" Edward Boyne had continued to exult as the avowal of each disadvantage was successively wrung from her; but he had cut short his rhapsody to ask, with a sudden relapse to distrust: "And the ghost? You've been concealing from us the fact that there is no ghost!"

Mary, at the moment, had laughed with him, yet almost with her laugh, being possessed of several sets of independent perceptions, had noted a sudden flatness of tone in Alida's answering hilarity.

"Oh, Dorsetshire's full of ghosts, you know."

"Yes, yes; but that won't do. I don't want to have to drive ten miles to see somebody else's ghost. I want one of my own on the premises. IS there a ghost at Lyng?"

His rejoinder had made Alida laugh again, and it was then that she had flung back tantalizingly: "Oh, there IS one, of course, but you'll never know it."

"Never know it?" Boyne pulled her up. "But what in the world constitutes a ghost except the fact of its being known for one?"

"I can't say. But that's the story."

"That there's a ghost, but that nobody knows it's a ghost?"

"Well—not till afterward, at any rate."

"Till afterward?"

"Not till long, long afterward."

"But if it's once been identified as an unearthly visitant, why hasn't its signalement been handed down in the family? How has it managed to preserve its incognito?"

Alida could only shake her head. "Don't ask me. But it has."

"And then suddenly-" Mary spoke up as if from some cavernous depth of divination—"suddenly, long afterward, one says to one's self, THAT WAS it?'"

She was oddly startled at the sepulchral sound with which her question fell on the banter of the other two, and she saw the shadow of the same surprise flit across Alida's clear pupils. "I suppose so. One just has to wait."

"Oh, hang waiting!" Ned broke in. "Life's too short for a ghost who can only be enjoyed in retrospect. Can't we do better than that, Mary?"

But it turned out that in the event they were not destined to, for within three months of their conversation with Mrs. Stair they were established at Lyng, and the life they had yearned for to the point of planning it out in all its daily details had actually begun for them.

It was to sit, in the thick December dusk, by just such a wide-hooded fireplace, under just such black oak rafters, with the sense that beyond the mullioned panes the downs were darkening to a deeper solitude: it was for the ultimate indulgence in such sensations that Mary Boyne had endured for nearly fourteen years the soul-deadening ugliness of the Middle West, and that Boyne had ground on doggedly at his engineering till, with a suddenness that still made her blink, the prodigious windfall of the Blue Star Mine had put them at a stroke in possession of life and the leisure to taste it. They had never for a moment meant their new state to be one of idleness; but they meant to give themselves only to harmonious activities. She had her vision of painting and gardening (against a background of gray walls), he dreamed of the production of his long-planned book on the "Economic Basis of Culture"; and with such absorbing work ahead no existence could be too sequestered; they could not get far enough from the world, or plunge deep enough into the past.

Dorsetshire had attracted them from the first by a semblance of remoteness out of all proportion to its geographical position. But to the Boynes it was one of the ever-recurring wonders of the whole incredibly compressed island—a nest of counties, as they put it—that for the production of its effects so little of a given quality went so far: that so few miles made a distance, and so short a distance a difference.

"It's that," Ned had once enthusiastically explained, "that gives such depth to their effects, such relief to their least contrasts. They've been able to lay the butter so thick on every exquisite mouthful."

The butter had certainly been laid on thick at Lyng: the old gray house, hidden under a shoulder of the downs, had almost all the finer marks of commerce with a protracted past. The mere fact that it was neither large nor exceptional made it, to the Boynes, abound the more richly in its special sense—the sense of having been for centuries a deep, dim reservoir of life. The life had probably not been of the most vivid order: for long periods, no doubt, it had fallen as noiselessly into the past as the quiet drizzle of autumn fell, hour after hour, into the green fish-pond between the yews; but these back-waters of existence sometimes breed, in their sluggish depths, strange acuities of emotion, and Mary Boyne had felt from the first the occasional brush of an intenser memory.

The feeling had never been stronger than on the December afternoon when, waiting in the library for the belated lamps, she rose from her seat and stood among the shadows of the hearth. Her husband had gone off, after luncheon, for one of his long tramps on the downs. She had noticed of late that he preferred to be unaccompanied on these occasions; and, in the tried security of their personal relations, had been driven to conclude that his book was bothering him, and that he needed the afternoons to turn over in solitude the problems left from the morning's work. Certainly the book was not going as smoothly as she had imagined it would, and the lines of perplexity between his eyes had never been there in his engineering days. Then he had often looked fagged to the verge of illness, but the native demon of "worry" had never branded his brow. Yet the few pages he had so far read to her—the introduction, and a synopsis of the opening chapter—gave evidences of a firm possession of his subject, and a deepening confidence in his powers.

The fact threw her into deeper perplexity, since, now that he had done with "business" and its disturbing contingencies, the one other possible element of anxiety was eliminated. Unless it were his health, then? But physically he had gained since they had come to Dorsetshire, grown robuster, ruddier, and fresher-eyed. It was only within a week that she had felt in him the undefinable change that made her restless in his absence, and as tongue-tied in his presence as though it were SHE who had a secret to keep from him!

The thought that there WAS a secret somewhere between them struck her with a sudden smart rap of wonder, and she looked about her down the dim, long room.

"Can it be the house?" she mused.

The room itself might have been full of secrets. They seemed to be piling themselves up, as evening fell, like the layers and layers of velvet shadow dropping from the low ceiling, the dusky walls of books, the smoke-blurred sculpture of the hooded hearth.

"Why, of course—the house is haunted!" she reflected.

The ghost—Alida's imperceptible ghost-after figuring largely in the banter of their first month or two at Lyng, had been gradually discarded as too ineffectual for imaginative use. Mary had, indeed, as became the tenant of a haunted house, made the customary inquiries among her few rural neighbors, but, beyond a vague, "They du say so, Ma'am," the villagers had nothing to impart. The elusive specter had apparently never had sufficient identity for a legend to crystallize about it, and after a time the Boynes had laughingly set the matter down to their profit-and-loss account, agreeing that Lyng was one of the few houses good enough in itself to dispense with supernatural enhancements.

"And I suppose, poor, ineffectual demon, that's why it beats its beautiful wings in vain in the void," Mary had laughingly concluded.

"Or, rather," Ned answered, in the same strain, "why, amid so much that's ghostly, it can never affirm its separate existence as THE ghost." And thereupon their invisible housemate had finally dropped out of their references, which were numerous enough to make them promptly unaware of the loss.

Now, as she stood on the hearth, the subject of their earlier curiosity revived in her with a new sense of its meaning—a sense gradually acquired through close daily contact with the scene of the lurking mystery. It was the house itself, of course, that possessed the ghost-seeing faculty, that communed visually but secretly with its own past; and if one could only get into close enough communion with the house, one might surprise its secret, and acquire the ghost-sight on one's own account. Perhaps, in his long solitary hours in this very room, where she never trespassed till the afternoon, her husband HAD acquired it already, and was silently carrying the dread weight of whatever it had revealed to him. Mary was too well-versed in the code of the spectral world not to know that one could not talk about the ghosts one saw: to do so was almost as great a breach of good-breeding as to name a lady in a club. But this explanation did not really satisfy her. "What, after all, except for the fun of the frisson," she reflected, "would he really care for any of their old ghosts?" And thence she was thrown back once more on the fundamental dilemma: the fact that one's greater or less susceptibility to spectral influences had no particular bearing on the case, since, when one DID see a ghost at Lyng, one did not know it.

"Not till long afterward," Alida Stair had said. Well, supposing Ned HAD seen one when they first came, and had known only within the last week what had happened to him? More and more under the spell of the hour, she threw back her searching thoughts to the early days of their tenancy, but at first only to recall a gay confusion of unpacking, settling, arranging of books, and calling to each other from remote corners of the house as treasure after treasure of their habitation revealed itself to them. It was in this particular connection that she presently recalled a certain soft afternoon of the previous October, when, passing from the first rapturous flurry of exploration to a detailed inspection of the old house, she had pressed (like a novel heroine) a panel that opened at her touch, on a narrow flight of stairs leading to an unsuspected flat ledge of the roof—the roof which, from below, seemed to slope away on all sides too abruptly for any but practised feet to scale.

The view from this hidden coign was enchanting, and she had flown down to snatch Ned from his papers and give him the freedom of her discovery. She remembered still how, standing on the narrow ledge, he had passed his arm about her while their gaze flew to the long, tossed horizon-line of the downs, and then dropped contentedly back to trace the arabesque of yew hedges about the fish-pond, and the shadow of the cedar on the lawn.

"And now the other way," he had said, gently turning her about within his arm; and closely pressed to him, she had absorbed, like some long, satisfying draft, the picture of the gray-walled court, the squat lions on the gates, and the lime-avenue reaching up to the highroad under the downs.

It was just then, while they gazed and held each other, that she had felt his arm relax, and heard a sharp "Hullo!" that made her turn to glance at him.

Distinctly, yes, she now recalled she had seen, as she glanced, a shadow of anxiety, of perplexity, rather, fall across his face; and, following his eyes, had beheld the figure of a man—a man in loose, grayish clothes, as it appeared to her—who was sauntering down the lime-avenue to the court with the tentative gait of a stranger seeking his way. Her short-sighted eyes had given her but a blurred impression of slightness and grayness, with something foreign, or at least unlocal, in the cut of the figure or its garb; but her husband had apparently seen more—seen enough to make him push past her with a sharp "Wait!" and dash down the twisting stairs without pausing to give her a hand for the descent.

A slight tendency to dizziness obliged her, after a provisional clutch at the chimney against which they had been leaning, to follow him down more cautiously; and when she had reached the attic landing she paused again for a less definite reason, leaning over the oak banister to strain her eyes through the silence of the brown, sun-flecked depths below. She lingered there till, somewhere in those depths, she heard the closing of a door; then, mechanically impelled, she went down the shallow flights of steps till she reached the lower hall.

The front door stood open on the mild sunlight of the court, and hall and court were empty. The library door was open, too, and after listening in vain for any sound of voices within, she quickly crossed the threshold, and found her husband alone, vaguely fingering the papers on his desk.

He looked up, as if surprised at her precipitate entrance, but the shadow of anxiety had passed from his face, leaving it even, as she fancied, a little brighter and clearer than usual.

"What was it? Who was it?" she asked.

"Who?" he repeated, with the surprise still all on his side.

"The man we saw coming toward the house."

He seemed honestly to reflect. "The man? Why, I thought I saw Peters; I dashed after him to say a word about the stable-drains, but he had disappeared before I could get down."

"Disappeared? Why, he seemed to be walking so slowly when we saw him."

Boyne shrugged his shoulders. "So I thought; but he must have got up steam in the interval. What do you say to our trying a scramble up Meldon Steep before sunset?"

That was all. At the time the occurrence had been less than nothing, had, indeed, been immediately obliterated by the magic of their first vision from Meldon Steep, a height which they had dreamed of climbing ever since they had first seen its bare spine heaving itself above the low roof of Lyng. Doubtless it was the mere fact of the other incident's having occurred on the very day of their ascent to Meldon that had kept it stored away in the unconscious fold of association from which it now emerged; for in itself it had no mark of the por-tentous. At the moment there could have been nothing more natural than that Ned should dash himself from the roof in the pursuit of dilatory tradesmen. It was the period when they were always on the watch for one or the other of the specialists employed about the place; always lying in wait for them, and dash-ing out at them with questions, reproaches, or reminders. And certainly in the distance the gray figure had looked like Peters.

Yet now, as she reviewed the rapid scene, she felt her husband's explana-tion of it to have been invalidated by the look of anxiety on his face. Why had the familiar appearance of Peters made him anxious? Why, above all, if it was of such prime necessity to confer with that authority on the subject of the stable-drains, had the failure to find him produced such a look of relief? Mary could not say that any one of these considerations had occurred to her at the time, yet, from the promptness with which they now marshaled themselves at her summons, she had a sudden sense that they must all along have been there, waiting their hour.

## II

Weary with her thoughts, she moved toward the window. The library was now completely dark, and she was surprised to see how much faint light the outer world still held.

As she peered out into it across the court, a figure shaped itself in the tapering perspective of bare lines: it looked a mere blot of deeper gray in the grayness, and for an instant, as it moved toward her, her heart thumped to the thought, "It's the ghost!"

She had time, in that long instant, to feel suddenly that the man of whom, two months earlier, she had a brief distant vision from the roof was now, at his predestined hour, about to reveal himself as NOT having been Peters; and her spirit sank under the impending fear of the disclosure. But almost with the next tick of the clock the ambiguous figure, gaining substance and character, showed itself even to her weak sight as her husband's; and she turned away to meet him, as he entered, with the confession of her folly.

"It's really too absurd," she laughed out from the threshold, "but I never CAN remember!"

"Remember what?" Boyne questioned as they drew together.

"That when one sees the Lyng ghost one never knows it."

Her hand was on his sleeve, and he kept it there, but with no response in his gesture or in the lines of his fagged, preoccupied face.

"Did you think you'd seen it?" he asked, after an appreciable interval.

"Why, I actually took YOU for it, my dear, in my mad determination to spot it!"

"Me—just now?" His arm dropped away, and he turned from her with a faint echo of her laugh. "Really, dearest, you'd better give it up, if that's the best you can do."

"Yes, I give it up—I give it up. Have YOU?" she asked, turning round on him abruptly.

The parlor-maid had entered with letters and a lamp, and the light struck up into Boyne's face as he bent above the tray she presented.

"Have YOU?" Mary perversely insisted, when the servant had disappeared on her errand of illumination.

"Have I what?" he rejoined absently, the light bringing out the sharp stamp of worry between his brows as he turned over the letters.

"Given up trying to see the ghost." Her heart beat a little at the experiment she was making.

Her husband, laying his letters aside, moved away into the shadow of the hearth.

"I never tried," he said, tearing open the wrapper of a newspaper.

"Well, of course," Mary persisted, "the exasperating thing is that there's no use trying, since one can't be sure till so long afterward."

He was unfolding the paper as if he had hardly heard her; but after a pause, during which the sheets rustled spasmodically between his hands, he lifted his head to say abruptly, "Have you any idea HOW LONG?"

Mary had sunk into a low chair beside the fireplace. From her seat she looked up, startled, at her husband's profile, which was darkly projected against the circle of lamplight.

"No; none. Have YOU?" she retorted, repeating her former phrase with an added keenness of intention.

Boyne crumpled the paper into a bunch, and then inconsequently turned back with it toward the lamp.

"Lord, no! I only meant," he explained, with a faint tinge of impatience, "is there any legend, any tradition, as to that?"

"Not that I know of," she answered; but the impulse to add, "What makes you ask?" was checked by the reappearance of the parlor-maid with tea and a second lamp.

With the dispersal of shadows, and the repetition of the daily domestic office, Mary Boyne felt herself less oppressed by that sense of something mutely imminent which had darkened her solitary afternoon. For a few moments she gave herself silently to the details of her task, and when she looked up from it she was struck to the point of bewilderment by the change in her husband's face. He had seated himself near the farther lamp, and was absorbed in the perusal of his letters; but was it something he had found in them, or merely the shifting of her own point of view, that had restored his features to their normal aspect? The longer she looked, the more definitely the change affirmed itself. The lines of painful tension had vanished, and such traces of fatigue as lingered were of the kind easily attributable to steady mental effort. He glanced up, as if drawn by her gaze, and met her eyes with a smile.

"I'm dying for my tea, you know; and here's a letter for you," he said.

She took the letter he held out in exchange for the cup she proffered him, and, returning to her seat, broke the seal with the languid gesture of the reader whose interests are all inclosed in the circle of one cherished presence.

Her next conscious motion was that of starting to her feet, the letter falling to them as she rose, while she held out to her husband a long newspaper clipping.

"Ned! What's this? What does it mean?"

He had risen at the same instant, almost as if hearing her cry before she uttered it; and for a perceptible space of time he and she studied each other, like adversaries watching for an advantage, across the space between her chair and his desk.

"What's what? You fairly made me jump!" Boyne said at length, moving toward her with a sudden, half-exasperated laugh. The shadow of apprehension was on his face again, not now a look of fixed foreboding, but a shifting vigilance of lips and eyes that gave her the sense of his feeling himself invisibly surrounded.

Her hand shook so that she could hardly give him the clipping.

"This article—from the 'Waukesha Sentinel'—that a man named Elwell has brought suit against you—that there was something wrong about the Blue Star Mine. I can't understand more than half."

They continued to face each other as she spoke, and to her astonishment, she saw that her words had the almost immediate effect of dissipating the strained watchfulness of his look.

"Oh, THAT!" He glanced down the printed slip, and then folded it with the gesture of one who handles something harmless and familiar. "What's the matter with you this afternoon, Mary? I thought you'd got bad news."

She stood before him with her undefinable terror subsiding slowly under the reassuring touch of his composure.

"You knew about this, then—it's all right?"

"Certainly I knew about it; and it's all right."

"But what IS it? I don't understand. What does this man accuse you of?"

"Oh, pretty nearly every crime in the calendar." Boyne had tossed the clipping down, and thrown himself comfortably into an arm-chair near the fire. "Do you want to hear the story? It's not particularly interesting—just a squabble over interests in the Blue Star."

"But who is this Elwell? I don't know the name."

"Oh, he's a fellow I put into it—gave him a hand up. I told you all about him at the time."

"I daresay. I must have forgotten." Vainly she strained back among her memories. "But if you helped him, why does he make this return?"

"Oh, probably some shyster lawyer got hold of him and talked him over. It's all rather technical and complicated. I thought that kind of thing bored you."

His wife felt a sting of compunction. Theoretically, she deprecated the American wife's detachment from her husband's professional interests, but in practice she had always found it difficult to fix her attention on Boyne's report of the transactions in which his varied interests involved him. Besides, she had felt from the first that, in a community where the amenities of living could be obtained only at the cost of efforts as arduous as her husband's professional labors, such brief leisure as they could command should be used as an escape from immediate preoccupations, a flight to the life they always dreamed of living. Once or twice, now that this new life had actually drawn its magic circle about them, she had asked herself if she had done right; but hitherto such conjectures had been no more than the retrospective excursions of an active fancy. Now, for the first time, it startled her a little to find how little she knew of the material foundation on which her happiness was built.

She glanced again at her husband, and was reassured by the composure of his face; yet she felt the need of more definite grounds for her reassurance.

"But doesn't this suit worry you? Why have you never spoken to me about it?"

He answered both questions at once: "I didn't speak of it at first because it DID worry me—annoyed me, rather. But it's all ancient history now. Your correspondent must have got hold of a back number of the 'Sentinel.'"

She felt a quick thrill of relief. "You mean it's over? He's lost his case?"

There was a just perceptible delay in Boyne's reply. "The suit's been withdrawn—that's all."

But she persisted, as if to exonerate herself from the inward charge of being too easily put off. "Withdrawn because he saw he had no chance?"

"Oh, he had no chance," Boyne answered.

She was still struggling with a dimly felt perplexity at the back of her thoughts.

"How long ago was it withdrawn?"

He paused, as if with a slight return of his former uncertainty. "I've just had the news now; but I've been expecting it."

"Just now—in one of your letters?" "Yes; in one of my letters."

She made no answer, and was aware only, after a short interval of waiting, that he had risen, and strolling across the room, had placed himself on the sofa at her side. She felt him, as he did so, pass an arm about her, she felt his hand seek hers and clasp it, and turning slowly, drawn by the warmth of his cheek, she met the smiling clearness of his eyes.

"It's all right—it's all right?" she questioned, through the flood of her dissolving doubts; and "I give you my word it never was righter!" he laughed back at her, holding her close.

## III

One of the strangest things she was afterward to recall out of all the next day's incredible strangeness was the sudden and complete recovery of her sense of security.

It was in the air when she woke in her low-ceilinged, dusky room; it accompanied her down-stairs to the breakfast-table, flashed out at her from the fire, and re-duplicated itself brightly from the flanks of the urn and the sturdy flutings of the Georgian teapot. It was as if, in some roundabout way, all her diffused apprehensions of the previous day, with their moment of sharp concentration about the newspaper article,—as if this dim questioning of the future, and startled return upon the past,—had between them liquidated the arrears of some haunting moral obligation. If she had indeed been careless of her husband's affairs, it was, her new state seemed to prove, because her faith in him instinctively justified such carelessness; and his right to her faith had overwhelmingly affirmed itself in the very face of menace and suspicion. She had never seen him more untroubled, more naturally and unconsciously in possession of himself, than after the cross-examination to which she had subjected him: it was almost as if he had been aware of her lurking doubts, and had wanted the air cleared as much as she did.

It was as clear, thank Heaven! as the bright outer light that surprised her almost with a touch of summer when she issued from the house for her daily round of the gardens. She had left Boyne at his desk, indulging herself, as she passed the library door, by a last peep at his quiet face, where he bent, pipe in his mouth, above his papers, and now she had her own morning's task to perform. The task involved on such charmed winter days almost as much delighted loitering about the different quarters of her demesne as if spring were already at work on shrubs and borders. There were such inexhaustible possibilities still before her, such opportunities to bring out the latent graces of the old place, without a single irreverent touch of alteration, that the winter months were all too short to plan what spring and autumn executed. And her recovered sense of safety gave, on this particular morning, a peculiar zest to her progress through the sweet, still place. She went first to the kitchen-garden, where the espaliered pear-trees drew complicated patterns on the walls, and pigeons were fluttering and preening about the silvery-slated roof of their cot. There was something wrong about the piping of the hothouse, and she was expecting an authority from Dorchester, who was to drive out between trains and make a diagnosis of the boiler. But when she dipped into the damp heat of the greenhouses, among the spiced scents and waxy pinks and reds of old-fashioned exotics,—even the flora of Lyng was in the note!—she learned that the great man had not arrived, and the day being too rare to waste in an artificial atmosphere, she came out again and paced slowly along the springy turf of the bowling-green to the gardens behind the house. At their farther end rose a grass terrace, commanding, over the fish-pond and the yew hedges, a view of the long house-front, with its twisted chimney-stacks and the blue shadows of its roof angles, all drenched in the pale gold moisture of the air.

Seen thus, across the level tracery of the yews, under the suffused, mild light, it sent her, from its open windows and hospitably smoking chimneys, the look of some warm human presence, of a mind slowly ripened on a sunny wall of experience. She had never before had so deep a sense of her intimacy with it, such a conviction that its secrets were all beneficent, kept, as they said to children, "for one's good," so complete a trust in its power to gather up her life and Ned's into the harmonious pattern of the long, long story it sat there weaving in the sun.

She heard steps behind her, and turned, expecting to see the gardener, accompanied by the engineer from Dorchester. But only one figure was in sight, that of a youngish, slightly built man, who, for reasons she could not on the spot have specified, did not remotely resemble her preconceived notion of an authority on hot-house boilers. The new-comer, on seeing her, lifted his hat, and paused with the air of a gentleman-perhaps a traveler-desirous of having it immediately known that his intrusion is involuntary. The local fame of Lyng occasionally attracted the more intelligent sight-seer, and Mary half-expected to see the stranger dissemble a camera, or justify his presence by producing it. But he made no gesture of any sort, and after a moment she asked, in a tone responding to the courteous deprecation of his attitude: "Is there any one you wish to see?"

"I came to see Mr. Boyne," he replied. His intonation, rather than his accent, was faintly American, and Mary, at the familiar note, looked at him more closely. The brim of his soft felt hat cast a shade on his face, which, thus obscured, wore to her short-sighted gaze a look of seriousness, as of a person arriving "on business," and civilly but firmly aware of his rights.

Past experience had made Mary equally sensible to such claims; but she was jealous of her husband's morning hours, and doubtful of his having given any one the right to intrude on them.

"Have you an appointment with Mr. Boyne?" she asked.

He hesitated, as if unprepared for the question.

"Not exactly an appointment," he replied.

"Then I'm afraid, this being his working-time, that he can't receive you now. Will you give me a message, or come back later?"

The visitor, again lifting his hat, briefly replied that he would come back later, and walked away, as if to regain the front of the house. As his figure receded down the walk between the yew hedges, Mary saw him pause and look up an instant at the peaceful house-front bathed in faint winter sunshine; and it struck her, with a tardy touch of compunction, that it would have been more humane to ask if he had come from a distance, and to offer, in that case, to inquire if her husband could receive him. But as the thought occurred to her he passed out of sight behind a pyramidal yew, and at the same moment her attention was distracted by the approach of the gardener, attended by the bearded pepper-and-salt figure of the boiler-maker from Dorchester.

The encounter with this authority led to such far-reaching issues that they resulted in his finding it expedient to ignore his train, and beguiled Mary into spending the remainder of the morning in absorbed confabulation among the greenhouses. She was startled to find, when the colloquy ended, that it was nearly luncheon-time, and she half expected, as she hurried back to the house, to see her husband coming out to meet her. But she found no one in the court but an under-gardener raking the gravel, and the hall, when she entered it, was so silent that she guessed Boyne to be still at work behind the closed door of the library.

Not wishing to disturb him, she turned into the drawing-room, and there, at her writing-table, lost herself in renewed calculations of the outlay to which the morning's conference had committed her. The knowledge that she could permit herself such follies had not yet lost its novelty; and somehow, in contrast to the vague apprehensions of the previous days, it now seemed an element of her recovered security, of the sense that, as Ned had said, things in general had never been "righter."

She was still luxuriating in a lavish play of figures when the parlor-maid, from the threshold, roused her with a dubiously worded inquiry as to the expediency of serving luncheon. It was one of their jokes that Trimmle announced luncheon as if she were divulging a state secret, and Mary, intent upon her papers, merely murmured an absent-minded assent.

She felt Trimmle wavering expressively on the threshold as if in rebuke of such offhand acquiescence; then her retreating steps sounded down the passage, and Mary, pushing away her papers, crossed the hall, and went to the library door. It was still closed, and she wavered in her turn, disliking to disturb her husband, yet anxious that he should not exceed his normal measure of work. As she stood there, balancing her impulses, the esoteric Trimmle returned with the announcement of luncheon, and Mary, thus impelled, opened the door and went into the library.

Boyne was not at his desk, and she peered about her, expecting to discover him at the book-shelves, somewhere down the length of the room; but her call brought no response, and gradually it became clear to her that he was not in the library.

She turned back to the parlor-maid.

"Mr. Boyne must be up-stairs. Please tell him that luncheon is ready."

The parlor-maid appeared to hesitate between the obvious duty of obeying orders and an equally obvious conviction of the foolishness of the injunction laid upon her. The struggle resulted in her saying doubtfully, "If you please, Madam, Mr. Boyne's not up-stairs."

"Not in his room? Are you sure?"

"I'm sure, Madam."

Mary consulted the clock. "Where is he, then?"

"He's gone out," Trimmle announced, with the superior air of one who has respectfully waited for the question that a well-ordered mind would have first propounded.

Mary's previous conjecture had been right, then. Boyne must have gone to the gardens to meet her, and since she had missed him, it was clear that he had taken the shorter way by the south door, instead of going round to the court. She crossed the hall to the glass portal opening directly on the yew garden, but the parlor-maid, after another moment of inner conflict, decided to bring out recklessly, "Please, Madam, Mr. Boyne didn't go that way."

Mary turned back. "Where DID he go? And when?"

"He went out of the front door, up the drive, Madam." It was a matter of principle with Trimmle never to answer more than one question at a time.

"Up the drive? At this hour?" Mary went to the door herself, and glanced across the court through the long tunnel of bare limes. But its perspective was as empty as when she had scanned it on entering the house.

"Did Mr. Boyne leave no message?" she asked.

Trimmle seemed to surrender herself to a last struggle with the forces of chaos.

"No, Madam. He just went out with the gentleman."

"The gentleman? What gentleman?" Mary wheeled about, as if to front this new factor.

"The gentleman who called, Madam," said Trimmle, resignedly.

"When did a gentleman call? Do explain yourself, Trimmle!"

Only the fact that Mary was very hungry, and that she wanted to consult her husband about the greenhouses, would have caused her to lay so unusual an injunction on her attendant; and even now she was detached enough to note in Trimmle's eye the dawning defiance of the respectful subordinate who has been pressed too hard.

"I couldn't exactly say the hour, Madam, because I didn't let the gentleman in," she replied, with the air of magnanimously ignoring the irregularity of her mistress's course.

"You didn't let him in?"

"No, Madam. When the bell rang I was dressing, and Agnes-"

"Go and ask Agnes, then," Mary interjected. Trimmle still wore her look of patient magnanimity. "Agnes would not know, Madam, for she had unfortunately burnt her hand in trying the wick of the new lamp from town—" Trimmle, as Mary was aware, had always been opposed to the new lamp—"and so Mrs. Dockett sent the kitchen-maid instead."

Mary looked again at the clock. "It's after two! Go and ask the kitchen-maid if Mr. Boyne left any word."

She went into luncheon without waiting, and Trimmle presently brought her there the kitchen-maid's statement that the gentleman had called about one o'clock, that Mr. Boyne had gone out with him without leaving any message. The kitchen-maid did not even know the caller's name, for he had written it on a slip of paper, which he had folded and handed to her, with the injunction to deliver it at once to Mr. Boyne.

Mary finished her luncheon, still wondering, and when it was over, and Trimmle had brought the coffee to the drawing-room, her wonder had deepened to a first faint tinge of disquietude. It was unlike Boyne to absent himself without explanation at so unwonted an hour, and the difficulty of identifying the visitor whose summons he had apparently obeyed made his disappearance the more unaccountable. Mary Boyne's experience as the wife of a busy engineer, subject to sudden calls and compelled to keep irregular hours, had trained her to the philosophic acceptance of surprises; but since Boyne's withdrawal from business he had adopted a Benedictine regularity of life. As if to make up for the dispersed and agitated years, with their "stand-up" lunches and dinners rattled down to the joltings of the dining-car, he cultivated the last refinements of punctuality and monotony, discouraging his wife's fancy for the unexpected; and declaring that to a delicate taste there were infinite gradations of pleasure in the fixed recurrences of habit.

Still, since no life can completely defend itself from the unforeseen, it was evident that all Boyne's precautions would sooner or later prove unavailable, and Mary concluded that he had cut short a tiresome visit by walking with his caller to the station, or at least accompanying him for part of the way.

This conclusion relieved her from farther preoccupation, and she went out herself to take up her conference with the gardener. Thence she walked to the village post-office, a mile or so away; and when she turned toward home, the early twilight was setting in.

She had taken a foot-path across the downs, and as Boyne, meanwhile, had probably returned from the station by the highroad, there was little likelihood of their meeting on the way. She felt sure, however, of his having reached the house before her; so sure that, when she entered it herself, without even pausing to inquire of Trimmle, she made directly for the library. But the library was still empty, and with an unwonted precision of visual memory she immediately observed that the papers on her husband's desk lay precisely as they had lain when she had gone in to call him to luncheon.

Then of a sudden she was seized by a vague dread of the unknown. She had closed the door behind her on entering, and as she stood alone in the long, silent, shadowy room, her dread seemed to take shape and sound, to be there audibly breathing and lurking among the shadows. Her short-sighted eyes strained through them, half-discerning an actual presence, something aloof, that watched and knew; and in the recoil from that intangible propinquity she threw herself suddenly on the bell-rope and gave it a desperate pull.

The long, quavering summons brought Trimmle in precipitately with a lamp, and Mary breathed again at this sobering reappearance of the usual.

"You may bring tea if Mr. Boyne is in," she said, to justify her ring.

"Very well, Madam. But Mr. Boyne is not in," said Trimmle, putting down the lamp.

"Not in? You mean he's come back and gone out again?"

"No, Madam. He's never been back."

The dread stirred again, and Mary knew that now it had her fast.

"Not since he went out with—the gentleman?"

"Not since he went out with the gentleman."

"But who WAS the gentleman?" Mary gasped out, with the sharp note of some one trying to be heard through a confusion of meaningless noises.

"That I couldn't say, Madam." Trimmle, standing there by the lamp, seemed suddenly to grow less round and rosy, as though eclipsed by the same creeping shade of apprehension.

"But the kitchen-maid knows—wasn't it the kitchen-maid who let him in?"

"She doesn't know either, Madam, for he wrote his name on a folded paper."

Mary, through her agitation, was aware that they were both designating the unknown visitor by a vague pronoun, instead of the conventional formula which, till then, had kept their allusions within the bounds of custom. And at the same moment her mind caught at the suggestion of the folded paper.

"But he must have a name! Where is the paper?"

She moved to the desk, and began to turn over the scattered documents that littered it. The first that caught her eye was an unfinished letter in her husband's hand, with his pen lying across it, as though dropped there at a sudden summons.

"My dear Parvis,"-who was Parvis?-"I have just received your letter announcing Elwell's death, and while I suppose there is now no farther risk of trouble, it might be safer—"

She tossed the sheet aside, and continued her search; but no folded paper was discoverable among the letters and pages of manuscript which had been swept together in a promiscuous heap, as if by a hurried or a startled gesture.

"But the kitchen-maid SAW him. Send her here," she commanded, wondering at her dullness in not thinking sooner of so simple a solution.

Trimmle, at the behest, vanished in a flash, as if thankful to be out of the room, and when she reappeared, conducting the agitated underling, Mary had regained her self-possession, and had her questions pat.

The gentleman was a stranger, yes—that she understood. But what had he said? And, above all, what had he looked like? The first question was easily enough answered, for the disconcerting reason that he had said so little-had merely asked for Mr. Boyne, and, scribbling something on a bit of paper, had requested that it should at once be carried in to him.

"Then you don't know what he wrote? You're not sure it WAS his name?"

The kitchen-maid was not sure, but supposed it was, since he had written it in answer to her inquiry as to whom she should announce.

"And when you carried the paper in to Mr. Boyne, what did he say?"

The kitchen-maid did not think that Mr. Boyne had said anything, but she could not be sure, for just as she had handed him the paper and he was opening it, she had become aware that the visitor had followed her into the library, and she had slipped out, leaving the two gentlemen together.

"But then, if you left them in the library, how do you know that they went out of the house?"

This question plunged the witness into momentary inarticulateness, from which she was rescued by Trimmle, who, by means of ingenious circumlocutions, elicited the statement that before she could cross the hall to the back passage she had heard the gentlemen behind her, and had seen them go out of the front door together.

"Then, if you saw the gentleman twice, you must be able to tell me what he looked like."

But with this final challenge to her powers of expression it became clear that the limit of the kitchen-maid's endurance had been reached. The obligation of going to the front door to "show in" a visitor was in itself so subversive of the fundamental order of things that it had thrown her faculties into hopeless disarray, and she could only stammer out, after various panting efforts at evocation, "His hat, mum, was different-like, as you might say—"

"Different? How different?" Mary flashed out at her, her own mind, in the same instant, leaping back to an image left on it that morning, but temporarily lost under layers of subsequent impressions.

"His hat had a wide brim, you mean? and his face was pale—a youngish face?" Mary pressed her, with a white-lipped intensity of interrogation. But if the kitchen-maid found any adequate answer to this challenge, it was swept away for her listener down the rushing current of her own convictions. The stranger—the stranger in the garden! Why had Mary not thought of him before? She needed no one now to tell her that it was he who had called for her husband and gone away with him. But who was he, and why had Boyne obeyed his call?

## IV

It leaped out at her suddenly, like a grin out of the dark, that they had often called England so little—"such a confoundedly hard place to get lost in."

A CONFOUNDEDLY HARD PLACE TO GET LOST IN! That had been her husband's phrase. And now, with the whole machinery of official investigation sweeping its flash-lights from shore to shore, and across the dividing straits; now, with Boyne's name blazing from the walls of every town and village, his portrait (how that wrung her!) hawked up and down the country like the image of a hunted criminal; now the little compact, populous island, so policed, surveyed, and administered, revealed itself as a Sphinxlike guardian of abysmal mysteries, staring back into his wife's anguished eyes as if with the malicious joy of knowing something they would never know!

In the fortnight since Boyne's disappearance there had been no word of him, no trace of his movements. Even the usual misleading reports that raise expectancy in tortured bosoms had been few and fleeting. No one but the bewildered kitchen-maid had seen him leave the house, and no one else had seen "the gentleman" who accompanied him. All inquiries in the neighborhood failed to elicit the memory of a stranger's presence that day in the neighborhood of Lyng. And no one had met Edward Boyne, either alone or in company, in any of the neighboring villages, or on the road across the downs, or at either of the local railway-stations. The sunny English noon had swallowed him as completely as if he had gone out into Cimmerian night.

Mary, while every external means of investigation was working at its highest pressure, had ransacked her husband's papers for any trace of antecedent complications, of entanglements or obligations unknown to her, that might throw a faint ray into the darkness. But if any such had existed in the background of Boyne's life, they had disappeared as completely as the slip of paper on which the visitor had written his name. There remained no possible thread of guidance except—if it were indeed an exception—the letter which Boyne had apparently been in the act of writing when he received his mysterious summons. That letter, read and reread by his wife, and submitted by her to the police, yielded little enough for conjecture to feed on.

"I have just heard of Elwell's death, and while I suppose there is now no farther risk of trouble, it might be safer-" That was all. The "risk of trouble" was easily explained by the newspaper clipping which had apprised Mary of the suit brought against her husband by one of his associates in the Blue Star enterprise. The only new information conveyed in the letter was the fact of its showing Boyne, when he wrote it, to be still apprehensive of the results of the suit, though he had assured his wife that it had been withdrawn, and though the letter itself declared that the plaintiff was dead. It took several weeks of exhaustive cabling to fix the identity of the "Parvis" to whom the fragmentary communication was addressed, but even after these inquiries had shown him to be a Waukesha lawyer, no new facts concerning the Elwell suit were elicited. He appeared to have had no direct concern in it, but to have been conversant with the facts merely as an acquaintance, and possible intermediary; and he declared himself unable to divine with what object Boyne intended to seek his assistance.

This negative information, sole fruit of the first fortnight's feverish search, was not increased by a jot during the slow weeks that followed. Mary knew that the investigations were still being carried on, but she had a vague sense of their gradually slackening, as the actual march of time seemed to slacken. It was as though the days, flying horror-struck from the shrouded image of the one inscrutable day, gained assurance as the distance lengthened, till at last they fell back into their normal gait. And so with the human imaginations at work on the dark event. No doubt it occupied them still, but week by week and hour by hour it grew less absorbing, took up less space, was slowly but inevitably crowded out of the foreground of consciousness by the new problems perpetually bubbling up from the vaporous caldron of human experience.

Even Mary Boyne's consciousness gradually felt the same lowering of velocity. It still swayed with the incessant oscillations of conjecture; but they were slower, more rhythmical in their beat. There were moments of overwhelming lassitude when, like the victim of some poison which leaves the brain clear, but holds the body motionless, she saw herself domesticated with the Horror, accepting its perpetual presence as one of the fixed conditions of life.

These moments lengthened into hours and days, till she passed into a phase of stolid acquiescence. She watched the familiar routine of life with the incurious eye of a savage on whom the meaningless processes of civilization make but the faintest impression. She had come to regard herself as part of the routine, a spoke of the wheel, revolving with its motion; she felt almost like the furniture of the room in which she sat, an insensate object to be dusted and pushed about with the chairs and tables. And this deepening apathy held her fast at Lyng, in spite of the urgent entreaties of friends and the usual medical recommendation of "change." Her friends supposed that her refusal to move was inspired by the belief that her husband would one day return to the spot from which he had vanished, and a beautiful legend grew up about this imaginary state of waiting. But in reality she had no such belief: the depths of anguish inclosing her were no longer lighted by flashes of hope. She was sure that Boyne would never come back, that he had gone out of her sight as completely as if Death itself had waited that day on the threshold. She had even renounced, one by one, the various theories as to his disappearance which had been advanced by the press, the police, and her own agonized imagination. In sheer lassitude her mind turned from these alternatives of horror, and sank back into the blank fact that he was gone.

No, she would never know what had become of him—no one would ever know. But the house KNEW; the library in which she spent her long, lonely evenings knew. For it was here that the last scene had been enacted, here that the stranger had come, and spoken the word which had caused Boyne to rise and follow him. The floor she trod had felt his tread; the books on the shelves had seen his face; and there were moments when the intense consciousness of the old, dusky walls seemed about to break out into some audible revelation of their secret. But the revelation never came, and she knew it would never come. Lyng was not one of the garrulous old houses that betray the secrets intrusted to them. Its very legend proved that it had always been the mute accomplice, the incorruptible custodian of the mysteries it had surprised. And Mary Boyne, sitting face to face with its portentous silence, felt the futility of seeking to break it by any human means.

# V

"I don't say it WASN'T straight, yet don't say it WAS straight. It was business."

Mary, at the words, lifted her head with a start, and looked intently at the speaker.

When, half an hour before, a card with "Mr. Parvis" on it had been brought up to her, she had been immediately aware that the name had been a part of her consciousness ever since she had read it at the head of Boyne's unfinished letter. In the library she had found awaiting her a small neutral-tinted man with a bald head and gold eye-glasses, and it sent a strange tremor through her to know that this was the person to whom her husband's last known thought had been directed.

Parvis, civilly, but without vain preamble,—in the manner of a man who has his watch in his hand,—had set forth the object of his visit. He had "run over" to England on business, and finding himself in the neighborhood of Dorchester, had not wished to leave it without paying his respects to Mrs. Boyne; without asking her, if the occasion offered, what she meant to do about Bob Elwell's family.

The words touched the spring of some obscure dread in Mary's bosom. Did her visitor, after all, know what Boyne had meant by his unfinished phrase? She asked for an elucidation of his question, and noticed at once that he seemed surprised at her continued ignorance of the subject. Was it possible that she really knew as little as she said?

"I know nothing—you must tell me," she faltered out; and her visitor thereupon proceeded to unfold his story. It threw, even to her confused perceptions, and imperfectly initiated vision, a lurid glare on the whole hazy episode of the Blue Star Mine. Her husband had made his money in that brilliant speculation at the cost of "getting ahead" of some one less alert to seize the chance; the victim of his ingenuity was young Robert Elwell, who had "put him on" to the Blue Star scheme.

Parvis, at Mary's first startled cry, had thrown her a sobering glance through his impartial glasses.

"Bob Elwell wasn't smart enough, that's all; if he had been, he might have turned round and served Boyne the same way. It's the kind of thing that happens every day in business. I guess it's what the scientists call the survival of the fittest," said Mr. Parvis, evidently pleased with the aptness of his analogy.

Mary felt a physical shrinking from the next question she tried to frame; it was as though the words on her lips had a taste that nauseated her.

"But then—you accuse my husband of doing something dishonorable?"

Mr. Parvis surveyed the question dispassionately. "Oh, no, I don't. I don't even say it wasn't straight." He glanced up and down the long lines of books, as if one of them might have supplied him with the definition he sought. "I don't say it WASN'T straight, and yet I don't say it WAS straight. It was business." After all, no definition in his category could be more comprehensive than that.

Mary sat staring at him with a look of terror. He seemed to her like the indifferent, implacable emissary of some dark, formless power.

"But Mr. Elwell's lawyers apparently did not take your view, since I suppose the suit was withdrawn by their advice."

"Oh, yes, they knew he hadn't a leg to stand on, technically. It was when they advised him to withdraw the suit that he got desperate. You see, he'd borrowed most of the money he lost in the Blue Star, and he was up a tree. That's why he shot himself when they told him he had no show."

The horror was sweeping over Mary in great, deafening waves.

"He shot himself? He killed himself because of THAT?"

"Well, he didn't kill himself, exactly. He dragged on two months before he died." Parvis emitted the statement as unemotionally as a gramophone grinding out its "record."

"You mean that he tried to kill himself, and failed? And tried again?"

"Oh, he didn't have to try again," said Parvis, grimly.

They sat opposite each other in silence, he swinging his eye-glass thoughtfully about his finger, she, motionless, her arms stretched along her knees in an attitude of rigid tension.

"But if you knew all this," she began at length, hardly able to force her voice above a whisper, "how is it that when I wrote you at the time of my husband's disappearance you said you didn't understand his letter?"

Parvis received this without perceptible discomfiture. "Why, I didn't understand it—strictly speaking. And it wasn't the time to talk about it, if I had. The Elwell business was settled when the suit was withdrawn. Nothing I could have told you would have helped you to find your husband."

Mary continued to scrutinize him. "Then why are you telling me now?"

Still Parvis did not hesitate. "Well, to begin with, I supposed you knew more than you appear to—I mean about the circumstances of Elwell's death. And then people are talking of it now; the whole matter's been raked up again. And I thought, if you didn't know, you ought to."

She remained silent, and he continued: "You see, it's only come out lately what a bad state Elwell's affairs were in. His wife's a proud woman, and she fought on as long as she could, going out to work, and taking sewing at home, when she got too sick—something with the heart, I believe. But she had his bedridden mother to look after, and the children, and she broke down under it, and finally had to ask for help. That attracted attention to the case, and the papers took it up, and a subscription was started. Everybody out there liked Bob Elwell, and most of the prominent names in the place are down on the list, and people began to wonder why—"

Parvis broke off to fumble in an inner pocket. "Here," he continued, "here's an account of the whole thing from the 'Sentinel'—a little sensational, of course. But I guess you'd better look it over."

He held out a newspaper to Mary, who unfolded it slowly, remembering, as she did so, the evening when, in that same room, the perusal of a clipping from the "Sentinel" had first shaken the depths of her security.

As she opened the paper, her eyes, shrinking from the glaring head-lines, "Widow of Boyne's Victim Forced to Appeal for Aid," ran down the column of text to two portraits inserted in it. The first was her husband's, taken from a photograph made the year they had come to England. It was the picture of him that she liked best, the one that stood on the writing-table up-stairs in her bedroom. As the eyes in the photograph met hers, she felt it would be impossible to read what was said of him, and closed her lids with the sharpness of the pain.

"I thought if you felt disposed to put your name down—" she heard Parvis continue.

She opened her eyes with an effort, and they fell on the other portrait. It was that of a youngish man, slightly built, in rough clothes, with features somewhat blurred by the shadow of a projecting hat-brim. Where had she seen that outline before? She stared at it confusedly, her heart hammering in her throat and ears. Then she gave a cry.

"This is the man—the man who came for my husband!"

She heard Parvis start to his feet, and was dimly aware that she had slipped backward into the corner of the sofa, and that he was bending above her in alarm. With an intense effort she straightened herself, and reached out for the paper, which she had dropped.

"It's the man! I should know him anywhere!" she cried in a voice that sounded in her own ears like a scream.

Parvis's voice seemed to come to her from far off, down endless, fog-muffled windings.

"Mrs. Boyne, you're not very well. Shall I call somebody? Shall I get a glass of water?"

"No, no, no!" She threw herself toward him, her hand frantically clenching the newspaper. "I tell you, it's the man! I KNOW him! He spoke to me in the garden!"

Parvis took the journal from her, directing his glasses to the portrait. "It can't be, Mrs. Boyne. It's Robert Elwell."

"Robert Elwell?" Her white stare seemed to travel into space. "Then it was Robert Elwell who came for him."

"Came for Boyne? The day he went away?" Parvis's voice dropped as hers rose. He bent over, laying a fraternal hand on her, as if to coax her gently back into her seat. "Why, Elwell was dead! Don't you remember?"

Mary sat with her eyes fixed on the picture, unconscious of what he was saying.

"Don't you remember Boyne's unfinished letter to me—the one you found on his desk that day? It was written just after he'd heard of Elwell's death." She noticed an odd shake in Parvis's unemotional voice. "Surely you remember that!" he urged her.

Yes, she remembered: that was the profoundest horror of it. Elwell had died the day before her husband's disappearance; and this was Elwell's portrait; and it was the portrait of the man who had spoken to her in the garden. She lifted her head and looked slowly about the library. The library could have borne witness that it was also the portrait of the man who had come in that day to call Boyne from his unfinished letter. Through the misty surgings of her brain she heard the faint boom of half-forgotten words—words spoken by Alida Stair on the lawn at Pangbourne before Boyne and his wife had ever seen the house at Lyng, or had imagined that they might one day live there.

"This was the man who spoke to me," she repeated.

She looked again at Parvis. He was trying to conceal his disturbance under what he imagined to be an expression of indulgent commiseration; but the edges of his lips were blue. "He thinks me mad; but I'm not mad," she reflected; and suddenly there flashed upon her a way of justifying her strange affirmation.

She sat quiet, controlling the quiver of her lips, and waiting till she could trust her voice to keep its habitual level; then she said, looking straight at Parvis: "Will you answer me one question, please? When was it that Robert Elwell tried to kill himself?"

"When—when?" Parvis stammered.

"Yes; the date. Please try to remember."

She saw that he was growing still more afraid of her. "I have a reason," she insisted gently.

"Yes, yes. Only I can't remember. About two months before, I should say."

"I want the date," she repeated.

Parvis picked up the newspaper. "We might see here," he said, still humoring her. He ran his eyes down the page. "Here it is. Last October—the—"

She caught the words from him. "The 20th, wasn't it?" With a sharp look at her, he verified. "Yes, the 20th. Then you DID know?"

"I know now." Her white stare continued to travel past him. "Sunday, the 20th—that was the day he came first."

Parvis's voice was almost inaudible. "Came HERE first?"

"Yes."

"You saw him twice, then?"

"Yes, twice." She breathed it at him with dilated eyes. "He came first on the 20th of October. I remember the date because it was the day we went up Meldon Steep for the first time." She felt a faint gasp of inward laughter at the thought that but for that she might have forgotten.

Parvis continued to scrutinize her, as if trying to intercept her gaze.

"We saw him from the roof," she went on. "He came down the lime-avenue toward the house. He was dressed just as he is in that picture. My husband saw him first. He was frightened, and ran down ahead of me; but there was no one there. He had vanished."

"Elwell had vanished?" Parvis faltered.

"Yes." Their two whispers seemed to grope for each other. "I couldn't think what had happened. I see now. He TRIED to come then; but he wasn't dead enough—he couldn't reach us. He had to wait for two months; and then he came back again—and Ned went with him."

She nodded at Parvis with the look of triumph of a child who has successfully worked out a difficult puzzle. But suddenly she lifted her hands with a desperate gesture, pressing them to her bursting temples.

"Oh, my God! I sent him to Ned—I told him where to go! I sent him to this room!" she screamed out.

She felt the walls of the room rush toward her, like inward falling ruins; and she heard Parvis, a long way off, as if through the ruins, crying to her, and struggling to get at her. But she was numb to his touch, she did not know what he was saying. Through the tumult she heard but one clear note, the voice of Alida Stair, speaking on the lawn at Pangbourne.

"You won't know till afterward," it said. "You won't know till long, long afterward."

# THE BROWN HAND
## ARTHUR CONAN DOYLE

Every one knows that Sir Dominick Holden, the famous Indian surgeon, made me his heir, and that his death changed me in an hour from a hardworking and impecunious medical man to a well-to-do landed proprietor. Many know also that there were at least five people between the inheritance and me, and that Sir Dominick's selection appeared to be altogether arbitrary and whimsical. I can assure them, however, that they are quite mistaken, and that, although I only knew Sir Dominick in the closing years of his life, there were none the less very real reasons why he should show his goodwill towards me. As a matter of fact, though I say it myself, no man ever did more for another than I did for my Indian uncle. I cannot expect the story to be believed, but it is so singular that I should feel that it was a breach of duty if I did not put it upon record—so here it is, and your belief or incredulity is your own affair.

Sir Dominick Holden, C.B., K.C.S.I., and I don't know what besides, was the most distinguished Indian surgeon of his day. In the Army originally, he afterwards settled down into civil practice in Bombay, and visited as a consultant every part of India. His name is best remembered in connection with the Oriental Hospital, which he founded and supported. The time came, however, when his iron constitution began to show signs of the long strain to which he had subjected it, and his brother practitioners (who were not, perhaps, entirely disinterested upon the point) were unanimous in recommending him to return to England. He held on so long as he could, but at last he developed nervous symptoms of a very pronounced character, and so came back, a broken man, to his native county of Wiltshire. He bought a considerable estate with an ancient manor-house upon the edge of Salisbury Plain, and devoted his old age to the study of Comparative Pathology, which had been his learned hobby all his life, and in which he was a foremost authority.

We of the family were, as may be imagined, much excited by the news of the return of this rich and childless uncle to England. On his part, although by no means exuberant in his hospitality, he showed some sense of his duty to his relations, and each of us in turn had an invitation to visit him. From the accounts of my cousins it appeared to be a melancholy business, and it was with mixed feelings that I at last received my own summons to appear at Rodenhurst. My wife was so carefully excluded in the invitation that my first impulse was to refuse it, but the interests of the children had to be considered, and so, with her consent, I set out one October afternoon upon my visit to Wiltshire, with little thought of what that visit was to entail.

My uncle's estate was situated where the arable land of the plains begins to swell upwards into the rounded chalk hills which are characteristic of the county. As I drove from Dinton Station in the waning light of that autumn day, I was impressed by the weird nature of the scenery. The few scattered cottages of the peasants were so dwarfed by the huge evidences of prehistoric life, that the present appeared to be a dream and the past to be the obtrusive and masterful reality. The road wound through the valleys, formed by a succession of grassy hills, and the summit of each was cut and carved into the most elaborate fortifications, some circular, and some square, but all on a scale which has defied the winds and the rains of many centuries. Some call them Roman and some British, but their true origin and the reasons for this particular tract of country being so interlaced with entrenchments have never been finally made clear. Here and there on the long, smooth, olive-coloured slopes there rose small rounded barrows or tumuli. Beneath them lie the cremated ashes of the race which cut so deeply into the hills, but their graves tell us nothing save that a jar full of dust represents the man who once laboured under the sun.

It was through this weird country that I approached my uncle's residence of Rodenhurst, and the house was, as I found, in due keeping with its surroundings. Two broken and weather-stained pillars, each surmounted by a mutilated heraldic emblem, flanked the entrance to a neglected drive. A cold wind whistled through the elms which lined it, and the air was full of the drifting leaves. At the far end, under the gloomy arch of trees, a single yellow lamp burned steadily. In the dim half-light of the coming night I saw a long, low building stretching out two irregular wings, with deep eaves, a sloping gambrel roof, and walls which were criss-crossed with timber balks in the fashion of the Tudors. The cheery light of a fire flickered in the broad, latticed window to the left of the low-porched door, and this, as it proved, marked the study of my uncle, for it was thither that I was led by his butler in order to make my host's acquaintance.

He was cowering over his fire, for the moist chill of an English autumn had set him shivering. His lamp was unlit, and I only saw the red glow of the embers beating upon a huge, craggy face, with a Red Indian nose and cheek, and deep furrows and seams from eye to chin, the sinister marks of hidden volcanic fires. He sprang up at my entrance with something of an old-world courtesy and welcomed me warmly to Rodenhurst. At the same time I was conscious, as the lamp was carried in, that it was a very critical pair of light-blue eyes which looked out at me from under shaggy eyebrows, like scouts beneath a bush, and that this outlandish uncle of mine was carefully reading off my character with all the ease of a practised observer and an experienced man of the world.

For my part I looked at him, and looked again, for I had never seen a man whose appearance was more fitted to hold one's attention. His figure was the framework of a giant, but he had fallen away until his coat dangled straight down in a shocking fashion from a pair of broad and bony shoulders. All his limbs were huge and yet emaciated, and I could not take my gaze from his knobby wrists, and long, gnarled hands. But his eyes—those peering light-blue eyes—they were the most arrestive of any of his peculiarities. It was not their colour alone, nor was it the ambush of hair in which they lurked; but it was the expression which I read in them. For the appearance and bearing of the man were masterful, and one expected a certain corresponding arrogance in his eyes, but instead of that I read the look which tells of a spirit cowed and crushed, the furtive, expectant look of the dog whose master has taken the whip from the rack. I formed my own medical diagnosis upon one glance at those critical and yet appealing eyes. I believed that he was stricken with some mortal ailment, that he knew himself to be exposed to sudden death, and that he lived in terror of it. Such was my judgment—a false one, as the event showed; but I mention it that it may help you to realise the look which I read in his eyes.

My uncle's welcome was, as I have said, a courteous one, and in an hour or so I found myself seated between him and his wife at a comfortable dinner, with curious pungent delicacies upon the table, and a stealthy, quick-eyed Oriental waiter behind his chair. The old couple had come round to that tragic imitation of the dawn of life when husband and wife, having lost or scattered all those who were their intimates, find themselves face to face and alone once more, their work done, and the end nearing fast. Those who have reached that stage in sweetness and love, who can change their winter into a gentle Indian summer, have come as victors through the ordeal of life. Lady Holden was a small, alert woman with a kindly eye, and her expression as she glanced at him was a certificate of character to her husband. And yet, though I read a mutual love in their glances, I read also mutual horror, and recognised in her face some reflection of that stealthy fear which I had detected in his. Their talk was sometimes merry and sometimes sad, but there was a forced note in their merriment and a naturalness in their sadness which told me that a heavy heart beat upon either side of me.

We were sitting over our first glass of wine, and the servants had left the room, when the conversation took a turn which produced a remarkable effect upon my host and hostess. I cannot recall what it was which started the topic of the supernatural, but it ended in my showing them that the abnormal in psychical experiences was a subject to which I had, like many neurologists, devoted a great deal of attention. I concluded by narrating my experiences when, as a member of the Psychical Research Society, I had formed one of a committee of three who spent the night in a haunted house. Our adventures were neither exciting nor convincing, but, such as it was, the story appeared to interest my auditors in a remarkable degree. They listened with an eager silence, and I caught a look of intelligence between them which I could not understand. Lady Holden immediately afterwards rose and left the room.

Sir Dominick pushed the cigar-box over to me, and we smoked for some little time in silence. That huge bony hand of his was twitching as he raised it with his cheroot to his lips, and I felt that the man's nerves were vibrating like fiddle-strings. My instincts told me that he was on the verge of some intimate confidence, and I feared to speak lest I should interrupt it. At last he turned towards me with a spasmodic gesture like a man who throws his last scruple to the winds.

"From the little that I have seen of you it appears to me, Dr. Hardacre," said he, "that you are the very man I have wanted to meet."

"I am delighted to hear it, sir."

"Your head seems to be cool and steady. You will acquit me of any desire to flatter you, for the circumstances are too serious to permit of insincerities. You have some special knowledge upon these subjects, and you evidently view them from that philosophical standpoint which robs them of all vulgar terror. I presume that the sight of an apparition would not seriously discompose you?"

"I think not, sir."

"Would even interest you, perhaps?"

"Most intensely."

"As a psychical observer, you would probably investigate it in as impersonal a fashion as an astronomer investigates a wandering comet?"

"Precisely."

He gave a heavy sigh.

"Believe me, Dr. Hardacre, there was a time when I could have spoken as you do now. My nerve was a by-word in India. Even the Mutiny never shook it for an instant. And yet you see what I am reduced to—the most timorous man, perhaps, in all this county of Wiltshire. Do not speak too bravely upon this subject, or you may find yourself subjected to as long-drawn a test as I am—a test which can only end in the madhouse or the grave."

I waited patiently until he should see fit to go farther in his confidence. His preamble had, I need not say, filled me with interest and expectation.

"For some years, Dr. Hardacre," he continued, "my life and that of my wife have been made miserable by a cause which is so grotesque that it borders upon the ludicrous. And yet familiarity has never made it more easy to bear—on the contrary, as time passes my nerves become more worn and shattered by the constant attrition. If you have no physical fears, Dr. Hardacre, I should very much value your opinion upon this phenomenon which troubles us so."

"For what it is worth my opinion is entirely at your service. May I ask the nature of the phenomenon?"

"I think that your experiences will have a higher evidential value if you are not told in advance what you may expect to encounter. You are yourself aware of the quibbles of unconscious cerebration and subjective impressions with which a scientific sceptic may throw a doubt upon your statement. It would be as well to guard against them in advance."

"What shall I do, then?"

"I will tell you. Would you mind following me this way?" He led me out of the dining-room and down a long passage until we came to a terminal door. Inside there was a large bare room fitted as a laboratory, with numerous scientific instruments and bottles. A shelf ran along one side, upon which there stood a long line of glass jars containing pathological and anatomical specimens.

"You see that I still dabble in some of my old studies," said Sir Dominick. "These jars are the remains of what was once a most excellent collection, but unfortunately I lost the greater part of them when my house was burned down in Bombay in '92. It was a most unfortunate affair for me—in more ways than one. I had examples of many rare conditions, and my splenic collection was probably unique. These are the survivors."

I glanced over them, and saw that they really were of a very great value and rarity from a pathological point of view: bloated organs, gaping cysts, distorted bones, odious parasites—a singular exhibition of the products of India.

"There is, as you see, a small settee here," said my host. "It was far from our intention to offer a guest so meagre an accommodation, but since affairs have taken this turn, it would be a great kindness upon your part if you would consent to spend the night in this apartment. I beg that you will not hesitate to let me know if the idea should be at all repugnant to you."

"On the contrary," I said, "it is most acceptable."

"My own room is the second on the left, so that if you should feel that you are in need of company a call would always bring me to your side."

"I trust that I shall not be compelled to disturb you."

"It is unlikely that I shall be asleep. I do not sleep much. Do not hesitate to summon me."

And so with this agreement we joined Lady Holden in the drawing-room and talked of lighter things.

It was no affectation upon my part to say that the prospect of my night's adventure was an agreeable one. I had no pretence to greater physical courage than my neighbours, but familiarity with a subject robs it of those vague and undefined terrors which are the most appalling to the imaginative mind. The human brain is capable of only one strong emotion at a time, and if it be filled with curiosity or scientific enthusiasm, there is no room for fear. It is true that I had my uncle's assurance that he had himself originally taken this point of view, but I reflected that the breakdown of his nervous system might be due to his forty years in India as much as to any psychical experiences which had befallen him. I at least was sound in nerve and brain, and it was with something of the pleasurable thrill of anticipation with which the sportsman takes his position beside the haunt of his game that I shut the laboratory door behind me, and partially undressing, lay down upon the rug-covered settee.

It was not an ideal atmosphere for a bedroom. The air was heavy with many chemical odours, that of methylated spirit predominating. Nor were the decorations of my chamber very sedative. The odious line of glass jars with their relics of disease and suffering stretched in front of my very eyes. There was no blind to the window, and a three-quarter moon streamed its white light into the room, tracing a silver square with filigree lattices upon the opposite wall. When I had extinguished my candle this one bright patch in the midst of the general gloom had certainly an eerie and discomposing aspect. A rigid and absolute silence reigned throughout the old house, so that the low swish of the branches in the garden came softly and smoothly to my ears. It may have been the hypnotic lullaby of this gentle susurrus, or it may have been the result of my tiring day, but after many dozings and many efforts to regain my clearness of perception, I fell at last into a deep and dreamless sleep.

I was awakened by some sound in the room, and I instantly raised myself upon my elbow on the couch. Some hours had passed, for the square patch upon the wall had slid downwards and sideways until it lay obliquely at the end of my bed. The rest of the room was in deep shadow. At first I could see nothing, presently, as my eyes became accustomed to the faint light, I was aware, with a thrill which all my scientific absorption could not entirely prevent, that something was moving slowly along the line of the wall. A gentle, shuffling sound, as of soft slippers, came to my ears, and I dimly discerned a human figure walking stealthily from the direction of the door. As it emerged into the patch of moonlight I saw very clearly what it was and how it was employed. It was a man, short and squat, dressed in some sort of dark-grey gown, which hung straight from his shoulders to his feet. The moon shone upon the side of his face, and I saw that it was chocolate-brown in colour, with a ball of black hair like a woman's at the back of his head. He walked slowly, and his eyes were cast upwards towards the line of bottles which contained those gruesome remnants of humanity. He seemed to examine each jar with attention, and then to pass on to the next. When he had come to the end of the line, immediately opposite my bed, he stopped, faced me, threw up his hands with a gesture of despair, and vanished from my sight.

I have said that he threw up his hands, but I should have said his arms, for as he assumed that attitude of despair I observed a singular peculiarity about his appearance. He had only one hand! As the sleeves drooped down from the upflung arms I saw the left plainly, but the right ended in a knobby and unsightly stump. In every other way his appearance was so natural, and I had both seen and heard him so clearly, that I could easily have believed that he was an Indian servant of Sir Dominick's who had come into my room in search of something. It was only his sudden disappearance which suggested anything more sinister to me. As it was I sprang from my couch, lit a candle, and examined the whole room carefully. There were no signs of my visitor, and I was forced to conclude that there had really been something outside the normal laws of Nature in his appearance. I lay awake for the remainder of the night, but nothing else occurred to disturb me.

I am an early riser, but my uncle was an even earlier one, for I found him pacing up and down the lawn at the side of the house. He ran towards me in his eagerness when he saw me come out from the door.

"Well, well!" he cried. "Did you see him?"

"An Indian with one hand?"

"Precisely."

"Yes, I saw him"—and I told him all that occurred. When I had finished, he led the way into his study. "We have a little time before breakfast," said he. "It will suffice to give you an explanation of this extraordinary affair—so far as I can explain that which is essentially inexplicable. In the first place, when I tell you that for four years I have never passed one single night, either in Bombay, aboard ship, or here in England without my sleep being broken by this fellow, you will understand why it is that I am a wreck of my former self. His programme is always the same. He appears by my bedside, shakes me roughly by the shoulder, passes from my room into the laboratory, walks slowly along the line of my bottles, and then vanishes. For more than a thousand times he has gone through the same routine."

"What does he want?"

"He wants his hand."

"His hand?"

"Yes, it came about in this way. I was summoned to Peshawur for a consultation some ten years ago, and while there I was asked to look at the hand of a native who was passing through with an Afghan caravan. The fellow came from some mountain tribe living away at the back of beyond somewhere on the other side of Kaffiristan. He talked a bastard Pushtoo, and it was all I could do to understand him. He was suffering from a soft sarcomatous swelling of one of the metacarpal joints, and I made him realise that it was only by losing his hand that he could hope to save his life. After much persuasion he consented to the operation, and he asked me, when it was over, what fee I demanded. The poor fellow was almost a beggar, so that the idea of a fee was absurd, but I answered in jest that my fee should be his hand, and that I proposed to add it to my pathological collection.

"To my surprise he demurred very much to the suggestion, and he explained that according to his religion it was an all-important matter that the body should be reunited after death, and so make a perfect dwelling for the spirit. The belief is, of course, an old one, and the mummies of the Egyptians arose from an analogous superstition. I answered him that his hand was already off, and asked him how he intended to preserve it. He replied that he would pickle it in salt and carry it about with him. I suggested that it might be safer in my keeping than his, and that I had better means than salt for preserving it. On realising that I really intended to carefully keep it, his opposition vanished instantly. 'But remember, sahib,' said he, 'I shall want it back when I am dead.' I laughed at the remark, and so the matter ended. I returned to my practice, and he no doubt in the course of time was able to continue his journey to Afghanistan.

"Well, as I told you last night, I had a bad fire in my house at Bombay. Half of it was burned down, and, among other things, my pathological collection was largely destroyed. What you see are the poor remains of it. The hand of the hill-man went with the rest, but I gave the matter no particular thought at the time. That was six years ago.

"Four years ago—two years after the fire—I was awakened one night by a furious tugging at my sleeve. I sat up under the impression that my favourite mastiff was trying to arouse me. Instead of this, I saw my Indian patient of long ago, dressed in the long grey gown which was the badge of his people. He was holding up his stump and looking reproachfully at me. He then went over to my bottles, which at that time I kept in my room, and he examined them carefully, after which he gave a gesture of anger and vanished. I realised that he had just died, and that he had come to claim my promise that I should keep his limb in safety for him.

"Well, there you have it all, Dr. Hardacre. Every night at the same hour for four years this performance has been repeated. It is a simple thing in itself, but it has worn me out like water dropping on a stone. It has brought a vile insomnia with it, for I cannot sleep now for the expectation of his coming. It has poisoned my old age and that of my wife, who has been the sharer in this great trouble. But there is the breakfast gong, and she will be waiting impatiently to know how it fared with you last night. We are both much indebted to you for your gallantry, for it takes something from the weight of our misfortune when we share it, even for a single night, with a friend, and it reassures us as to our sanity, which we are sometimes driven to question."

This was the curious narrative which Sir Dominick confided to me—a story which to many would have appeared to be a grotesque impossibility, but which, after my experience of the night before, and my previous knowledge of such things, I was prepared to accept as an absolute fact. I thought deeply over the matter, and brought the whole range of my reading and experience to bear upon it. After breakfast, I surprised my host and hostess by announcing that I was returning to London by the next train.

"My dear doctor," cried Sir Dominick in great distress, "you make me feel that I have been guilty of a gross breach of hospitality in intruding this unfortunate matter upon you. I should have borne my own burden."

"It is, indeed, that matter which is taking me to London," I answered; "but you are mistaken, I assure you, if you think that my experience of last night was an unpleasant one to me. On the contrary, I am about to ask your permission to return in the evening and spend one more night in your laboratory. I am very eager to see this visitor once again."

My uncle was exceedingly anxious to know what I was about to do, but my fears of raising false hopes prevented me from telling him. I was back in my own consulting-room a little after luncheon, and was confirming my memory of a passage in a recent book upon occultism which had arrested my attention when I had read it.

"In the case of earth-bound spirits," said my authority, "some one dominant idea obsessing them at the hour of death is sufficient to hold them in this material world. They are the amphibia of this life and of the next, capable of passing from one to the other as the turtle passes from land to water. The causes which may bind a soul so strongly to a life which its body has abandoned are any violent emotion. Avarice, revenge, anxiety, love, and pity have all been known to have this effect. As a rule it springs from some unfulfilled wish, and when the wish has been fulfilled the material bond relaxes. There are many cases upon record which show the singular persistence of these visitors, and also their disappearance when their wishes have been fulfilled, or in some cases when a reasonable compromise has been effected."

"*A reasonable compromise effected*"—those were the words which I had brooded over all the morning, and which I now verified in the original. No actual atonement could be made here—but a reasonable compromise! I made my way as fast as a train could take me to the Shadwell Seamen's Hospital, where my old friend Jack Hewett was house-surgeon. Without explaining the situation I made him understand what it was that I wanted.

"A brown man's hand!" said he, in amazement. "What in the world do you want that for?"

"Never mind. I'll tell you some day. I know that your wards are full of Indians."

"I should think so. But a hand—" He thought a little and then struck a bell.

"Travers," said he to a student-dresser, "what became of the hands of the Lascar which we took off yesterday? I mean the fellow from the East India Dock who got caught in the steam winch."

"They are in the *post-mortem* room, sir."

"Just pack one of them in antiseptics and give it to Dr. Hardacre."

And so I found myself back at Rodenhurst before dinner with this curious outcome of my day in town. I still said nothing to Sir Dominick, but I slept that night in the laboratory, and I placed the Lascar's hand in one of the glass jars at the end of my couch.

So interested was I in the result of my experiment that sleep was out of the question. I sat with a shaded lamp beside me and waited patiently for my visitor. This time I saw him clearly from the first. He appeared beside the door, nebulous for an instant, and then hardening into as distinct an outline as any living man. The slippers beneath his grey gown were red and heelless, which accounted for the low, shuffling sound which he made as he walked. As on the previous night he passed slowly along the line of bottles until he paused before that which contained the hand. He reached up to it, his whole figure quivering with expectation, took it down, examined it eagerly, and then, with a face which was convulsed with disappointment, he hurled it down on the floor. There was a crash which resounded through the house, and when I looked up the mutilated Indian had disappeared. A moment later my door flew open and Sir Dominick rushed in.

"You are not hurt?" he cried.

"No—but deeply disappointed."

He looked in astonishment at the splinters of glass, and the brown hand lying upon the floor.

"Good God!" he cried. "What is this?"

I told him my idea and its wretched sequel. He listened intently, but shook his head.

"It was well thought of," said he, "but I fear that there is no such easy end to my sufferings. But one thing I now insist upon. It is that you shall never again upon any pretext occupy this room. My fears that something might have happened to you—when I heard that crash—have been the most acute of all the agonies which I have undergone. I will not expose myself to a repetition of it."

He allowed me, however, to spend the remainder of the night where I was, and I lay there worrying over the problem and lamenting my own failure. With the first light of morning there was the Lascar's hand still lying upon the floor to remind me of my fiasco. I lay looking at it—and as I lay suddenly an idea flew like a bullet through my head and brought me quivering with excitement out of my couch. I raised the grim relic from where it had fallen. Yes, it was indeed so. The hand was the *left* hand of the Lascar.

By the first train I was on my way to town, and hurried at once to the Seamen's Hospital. I remembered that both hands of the Lascar had been amputated, but I was terrified lest the precious organ which I was in search of might have been already consumed in the crematory. My suspense was soon ended. It had still been preserved in the *post-mortem* room. And so I returned to Rodenhurst in the evening with my mission accomplished and the material for a fresh experiment.

But Sir Dominick Holden would not hear of my occupying the laboratory again. To all my entreaties he turned a deaf ear. It offended his sense of hospitality, and he could no longer permit it. I left the hand, therefore, as I had done its fellow the night before, and I occupied a comfortable bedroom in another portion of the house, some distance from the scene of my adventures.

But in spite of that my sleep was not destined to be uninterrupted. In the dead of night my host burst into my room, a lamp in his hand. His huge gaunt figure was enveloped in a loose dressing-gown, and his whole appearance might certainly have seemed more formidable to a weak-nerved man than that of the Indian of the night before. But it was not his entrance so much as his expression which amazed me. He had turned suddenly younger by twenty years at the least. His eyes were shining, his features radiant, and he waved one hand in triumph over his head. I sat up astounded, staring sleepily at this extraordinary visitor. But his words soon drove the sleep from my eyes.

"We have done it! We have succeeded!" he shouted. "My dear Hardacre, how can I ever in this world repay you?"

"You don't mean to say that it is all right?"

"Indeed I do. I was sure that you would not mind being awakened to hear such blessed news."

"Mind! I should think not indeed. But is it really certain?"

"I have no doubt whatever upon the point. I owe you such a debt, my dear nephew, as I have never owed a man before, and never expected to. What can I possibly do for you that is commensurate? Providence must have sent you to my rescue. You have saved both my reason and my life, for another six months of this must have seen me either in a cell or a coffin. And my wife—it was wearing her out before my eyes. Never could I have believed that any human being could have lifted this burden off me." He seized my hand and wrung it in his bony grip.

"It was only an experiment—a forlorn hope—but I am delighted from my heart that it has succeeded. But how do you know that it is all right? Have you seen something?"

He seated himself at the foot of my bed.

"I have seen enough," said he. "It satisfies me that I shall be troubled no more. What has passed is easily told. You know that at a certain hour this creature always comes to me. To-night he arrived at the usual time, and aroused me with even more violence than is his custom. I can only surmise that his disappointment of last night increased the bitterness of his anger against me. He looked angrily at me, and then went on his usual round. But in a few minutes I saw him, for the first time since this persecution began, return to my chamber. He was smiling. I saw the gleam of his white teeth through the dim light. He stood facing me at the end of my bed, and three times he made the low Eastern salaam which is their solemn leave-taking. And the third time that he bowed he raised his arms over his head, and I saw his *two* hands outstretched in the air. So he vanished, and, as I believe, for ever."

\* \* \* \* \*

So that is the curious experience which won me the affection and the gratitude of my celebrated uncle, the famous Indian surgeon. His anticipations were realised, and never again was he disturbed by the visits of the restless hillman in search of his lost member. Sir Dominick and Lady Holden spent a very happy old age, unclouded, so far as I know, by any trouble, and they finally died during the great influenza epidemic within a few weeks of each other. In his lifetime he always turned to me for advice in everything which concerned that English life of which he knew so little; and I aided him also in the purchase and development of his estates. It was no great surprise to me, therefore, that I found myself eventually promoted over the heads of five exasperated cousins, and changed in a single day from a hard-working country doctor into the head of an important Wiltshire family. I at least have reason to bless the memory of the man with the brown hand, and the day when I was fortunate enough to relieve Rodenhurst of his unwelcome presence.

# THE AFFAIR AT GROVER STATION

## WILLA CATHER

I heard this story sitting on the rear platform of an accommodation freight that crawled along through the brown, sun-dried wilderness between Grover Station and Cheyenne. The narrator was 'Terrapin' Rodgers, who had been a classmate of mine at Princeton, and who was then cashier in the B—railroad office at Cheyenne. Rodgers was an Albany boy, but after his father failed in business, his uncle got 'Terrapin' a position on a Western railroad, and he left college and disappeared completely from our little world, and it was not until I was sent West by the University with a party of geologists who were digging for fossils in the region about Sterling, Colorado, that I saw him again. On this particular occasion Rodgers had been down at Sterling to spend Sunday with me, and I accompanied him when he returned to Cheyenne.

When the train pulled out of Grover Station, we were sitting smoking on the rear platform, watching the pale yellow disc of the moon that was just rising and that drenched the naked, grey plains in a soft lemon-coloured light. The telegraph poles scored the sky like a musical staff as they flashed by, and the stars, seen between the wires, looked like the notes of some erratic symphony. The stillness of the night and the loneliness and barrenness of the plains were conducive to an uncanny train of thought. We had just left Grover Station behind us, and the murder of the station agent at Grover, which had occurred the previous winter, was still the subject of much conjecturing and theorising all along that line of railroad. Rodgers had been an intimate friend of the murdered agent, and it was said that he knew more about the affair than any other living man, but with that peculiar reticence which at college had won him the soubriquet 'Terrapin', he had kept what he knew to himself, and even the most accomplished reporter on the *New York Journal,* who had travelled half-way across the continent for the express purpose of pumping Rodgers, had given him up as impossible. But I had known Rodgers a long time, and since I had been grubbing in the chalk about Sterling, we had fallen into a habit of exchanging confidences, for it is good to see an old face in a strange land. So, as the little red station house at Grover faded into the distance, I asked him point blank what he knew about the murder of Lawrence O'Toole. Rodgers took a long pull at his black-briar pipe as he answered me.

'Well, yes. I could tell you something about it, but the question is how much you'd believe, and whether you could restrain yourself from reporting it to the Society for Psychical Research. I never told the story but once, and then it was to the Division Superintendent, and when I finished the old gentleman asked if I were a drinking man, and remarking that a fertile imagination was not a desirable quality in a railroad employee, said it would be just as well if the story went no further. You see it's a gruesome tale, and someway we don't like to be reminded that there are more things in heaven and earth than our systems of philosophy can grapple with. However, I should rather like to tell the story to a man who would look at it objectively and leave it in the domain of pure incident where it belongs. It would unburden my mind, and I'd like to get a scientific man's opinion on the yarn. But I suppose I'd better begin at the beginning, with the dance which preceded the tragedy, just as such things follow each other in a play. I notice that Destiny, who is a good deal of an artist in her way, frequently falls back upon that elementary principle of contrast to make things interesting for us.

'It was the thirty-first of December, the morning of the incoming Governor's inaugural ball, and I got down to the office early, for I had a heavy day's work ahead of me, and I was going to the dance and wanted to close up by six o'clock. I had scarcely unlocked the door when I heard someone calling Cheyenne on the wire, and hurried over to the instrument to see what was wanted. It was Lawrence O'Toole, at Grover, and he said he was coming up for the ball on the extra, due in Cheyenne at nine o'clock that night. He wanted me to go up to see Miss Masterson and ask her if she could go with him. He had had some trouble in getting leave of absence, as the last regular train for Cheyenne then left Grover at 5:45 in the afternoon, and as there was an east-bound going through Grover at 7:30, the dispatcher didn't want him array, in case there should be orders for the 7:30 train. So Larry had made no arrangement with Miss Masterson, as he was uncertain about getting up until he was notified about the extra.

'I telephoned Miss Masterson and delivered Larry's message. She replied that she had made an arrangement to go to the dance with Mr Freymark, but added laughingly that no other arrangement held when Larry could come.

'About noon Freymark dropped in at the office, and I suspected he'd got his time from Miss Masterson. While he was hanging around, Larry called me up to tell me that Helen's flowers would be up from Denver on the Union Pacific passenger at five, and he asked me to have them sent up to her promptly and to call for her that evening in case the extra should be late. Freymark, of course, listened to the message, and when the sounder stopped, he smiled in a slow, disagreeable way, and saying, "Thank you. That's all I wanted to know," left the office.

'Lawrence O'Toole had been my predecessor in the cashier's office at Cheyenne, and he needs a little explanation now that he is under ground, though when he was in the world of living men, he explained himself better than any man I have ever met, East or West. I've knocked about a good deal since I cut loose from Princeton, and I've found that there are a great many good fellows in the world, but I've not found many better than Larry. I think I can say, without stretching a point, that he was the most popular man on the Division. He had a faculty of making everyone like him that amounted to a sort of genius. When he first went to working on the road, he was the agent's assistant down at Sterling, a mere kid fresh from Ireland, without a dollar in his pocket, and no sort of backing in the world but his quick wit and handsome face. It was a face that served him as a sight draft, good in all banks.

'Freymark was cashier at the Cheyenne office then, but he had been up to some dirty work with the company, and when it fell in the line of Larry's duty to expose him, he did so without hesitating. Eventually Freymark was discharged, and Larry was made cashier in his place. There was, after that, naturally, little love lost between them, and to make matters worse, Helen Masterson took a fancy to Larry, and Freymark had begun to consider himself pretty solid in that direction. I doubt whether Miss Masterson ever really liked the blackguard, but he was a queer fish, and she was a queer girl and she found him interesting.

'Old John J. Masterson, her father, had been United States Senator from Wyoming, and Helen had been educated at Wellesley and had lived in Washington a good deal. She found Cheyenne dull and had got into the Washington way of tolerating anything but stupidity, and Freymark certainly was not stupid. He passed as an Alsatian Jew, but he had lived a good deal in Paris and had been pretty much all over the world, and spoke the more general European languages fluently. He was a wiry, sallow, unwholesome looking man, slight and meagrely built, and he looked as though he had been dried through and through by the blistering heat of the tropics. His movements were as lithe and agile as those of a cat, and invested with a certain unusual, stealthy grace. His eyes were small and black as bright jet beads; his hair very thick and coarse and straight, black with a sort of purple lustre to it, and he always wore it correctly parted in the middle and brushed smoothly about his ears. He had a pair of the most impudent red lips that closed over white, regular teeth. His hands, of which he took the greatest care, were the yellow, wrinkled hands of an old man, and shrivelled at the finger tips, though I don't think he could have been much over thirty. The long and short of it is that the fellow was uncanny. You somehow felt that there was that in his present, or in his past, or in his-destiny which isolated him from other men. He dressed in excellent taste, was always accommodating, with the most polished manners and an address extravagantly deferential. He went into cattle after he lost his job with the company and had an interest in a ranch ten miles out, though he spent most of his time in Cheyenne at the Capitol card rooms. He had an insatiable passion for gambling, and he was one of the few men who make it pay.

'About a week before the dance, Larry's cousin, Harry Bums, who was a reporter on the London *Times,* stopped in Cheyenne on his way to 'Frisco, and Larry came up to meet him. We took Bums up to the club, and I noticed that he acted rather queerly when Freymark came in. Bums went down to Grover to spend a day with Larry, and on Saturday Larry wired me to come down and spend Sunday with him, as he had important news for me.

'I went, and the gist of his information was that Freymark, then going by another name, had figured in a particularly ugly London scandal that happened to be in Bums' beat, and his record had been exposed. He was, indeed, from Paris, but there was not a drop of Jewish blood in his veins, and he dated from farther back than Israel. His father was a French soldier who, during his service in the East, had bought a Chinese slave girl, had become attached to her, and married her, and after her death had brought her child back to Europe with him. He had entered the civil service and held several subordinate offices in the capital, where his son was educated. The boy, socially ambitious and extremely sensitive about his Asiatic blood, after having been blackballed at a club, had left and lived by an exceedingly questionable traffic in London, assuming a Jewish patronymic to account for his Oriental complexion and traits of feature. That explained everything. That explained why Freymark's hands were those of a centenarian. In his veins crept the sluggish amphibious blood of a race that was already old when Jacob tended the flocks of Laban upon the hills of Padan-Aram, a race that was in its mort cloth before Europe's swaddling clothes were made.

'Of course, the question at once came up as to what ought to be done with Bums' information. Cheyenne clubs are not exclusive, but a Chinaman who had been engaged in Freymark's peculiarly unsavoury traffic would be disbarred in almost any region outside of Whitechapel. One thing was sure: Miss Masterson must be informed of the matter at once.

"'On second thought,' said Larry, "I guess I'd better tell her myself. It will have to be done easy like, not to hurt her self-respect too much. Like as not I'll go off my head the first time I see him and call him rat-eater to his face."

'Well to get back to the day of the dance, I was wondering whether Larry would stay over to tell Miss Masterson about it the next day, for of course he couldn't spring such a thing on a girl at a party.

"That evening I dressed early and went down to the station at nine to meet Larry. The extra came in, but no Larry. I saw Connelly, the conductor, and asked him if he had seen anything of O'Toole, but he said he hadn't, that the station at Grover was open when he came through, but that he found no train orders and couldn't raise anyone, so he supposed O'Toole had come up on 153. I went back to the office and called Grover, but got no answer. Then I sat down at the instrument and called for fifteen minutes straight. I wanted to go then and hunt up the conductor on 153, the passenger that went through Grover at 5:30 in the afternoon, and ask him what he knew about Larry, but it was then 9:45 and I knew Miss Masterson would be waiting, so I jumped into the carriage and told the driver to make up time. On my way to the Mastersons' I did some tall thinking. I could find no explanation for O'Toole's non-appearance, but the business of the moment was to invent one for Miss Masterson that would neither alarm nor offend her. I couldn't exactly tell her he wasn't coming, for he might show up yet, so I decided to say the extra was late, and I didn't know when it would be in.

'Miss Masterson had been an exceptionally beautiful girl to begin with, and life had done a great deal for her. Fond as I was of Larry, I used to wonder whether a girl who had led such a full and independent existence would ever find the courage to face life with a railroad man who was so near the bottom of a ladder that is so long and steep.

'She came down the stairs in one of her Paris gowns that are as meat and drink to Cheyenne society reporters, with her arms full of American Beauty roses and her eyes and cheeks glowing. I noticed the roses then, though I didn't know that they were the boy's last message to the woman he loved. She paused half-way down the stain and looked at me, and then over my head into the drawing-room, and then her eyes questioned mine. I bungled at my explanation and she thanked me for coming, but she couldn't hide her disappointment, and scarcely glanced at herself in the mirror as I put her wrap about her shoulders.

'It was not a cheerful ride down to the Capitol. Miss Masterson did her duty by me bravely, but I found it difficult to be even decently attentive to what she was saying. Once arrived at Representative Hall, where the dance was held, the strain was relieved, for the fellows all pounced on her for dances, and there were friends of hers there from Helena and Laramie, and my responsibility was practically at an end. Don't expect me to tell you what a Wyoming inaugural ball is like. I'm not good at that sort of thing, and this dance is merely incidental to my story. Dance followed dance, and still no Larry. The dances I had with Miss Masterson were torture. She began to question and cross-question me, and when I got tangled up in my lies, she became indignant. Freymark was late in arriving. It must have been after midnight when he appeared, correct and smiling, having driven up from his ranch. He was effusively gay and insisted upon shaking hands with me, though I never willingly touched those clammy hands of his. He was constantly dangling about Miss Masterson, who made rather a point of being gracious to him. I couldn't much blame her under the circumstances, but it irritated me, and I'm not ashamed to say that I rather spied on them. When they were on the balcony I heard him say:

'"You see I've forgiven this morning entirely."

'She answered him rather coolly:

"'Ah, but you are constitutionally forgiving. However, I'll be fair and forgive too. It's more comfortable."

'Then he said in a slow, insinuating tone, and I could fairly see him thrust out those impudent red lips of his as he said it: "If I can teach you to forgive, I wonder whether I could not also teach you to forget? I almost think I could. At any rate I shall make you remember this night.

> *Rappelles-toi lorsque les destinées*
> *M'auront de toi pour jamas séparé."*

'As they came in, I saw him slip one of Larry's red roses into his pocket.

'It was not until near the end of the dance that the clock of destiny sounded the first stroke of the tragedy. I remember how gay the scene was, so gay that I had almost forgotten my anxiety in the music, flowers and laughter. The orchestra was playing a waltz, drawing the strains out long and sweet like the notes of a flute, and Freymark was dancing with Helen. I was not dancing myself then, and suddenly noticed some confusion among the waiters who stood watching by one of the doors, and Larry's black dog, Duke, all foam at the mouth, shot in the side and bleeding, dashed in through the door and eluding the caterer's men, ran half the length of the hall and threw himself at Freymark's feet, uttering a howl piteous enough to herald any sort of calamity. Freymark, who had not seen him before, turned with an exclamation of rage and a face absolutely livid and kicked the wounded brute half-way across the slippery floor. There was something fiendishly brutal and horrible in the episode, it was the breaking out of the barbarian blood through his mask of European civilisation, a jet of black mud that spurted up from some nameless pest hole of filthy heathen cities. The music stopped, people began moving about in a confused mass, and I saw Helen's eyes seeking mine appealingly. I hurried to her, and by the time I reached her Freymark had disappeared.

"'Get the carriage and take care of Duke," she said, and her voice trembled like that of one shivering with cold.

'When we were in the carriage, she spread one of the robes on her knee, and I lifted the dog up to her, and she took him in her arms, comforting him.

"'Where is Larry, and what does all this mean?" she asked. "You can't put me off any longer, for I danced with a man who came up on the extra."

'Then I made a clean breast of it, and told her what I knew, which was little enough.

'"Do you think he is ill?" she asked.

'I replied, "I don't know what to think. I'm all at sea,"—For since the appearance of the dog I was genuinely alarmed.

'She was silent for a long time, but when the rays of the electric street lights flashed at intervals into the carriage, I could see that she was leaning back with her eyes closed and the dog's nose against her throat. At last she said with a note of entreaty in her voice, "Can't you think of anything?" I saw that she was thoroughly frightened and told her that it would probably all end in a joke, and that I would telephone her as soon as I heard from Larry, and would more than likely have something amusing to tell her.

'It was snowing hard when we reached the Senator's, and when we got out of the carriage she gave Duke tenderly over to me and I remember how she dragged on my arm and how played out and exhausted she seemed.

'"You really must not worry at all," I said. "You know how uncertain railroad men are. It's sure to be better at the next inaugural ball; we'll all be dancing together then."

'"The next inaugural ball," she said as we went up the steps, putting out her hand to catch the snow-flakes.–"That seems a long way off."

'I got down to the office late next morning, and before I had time to try Grover, the dispatcher at Holyoke called me up to ask whether Larry were still in Cheyenne. He couldn't raise Grover, he said, and he wanted to give Larry train orders for 151, the east-bound passenger. When he heard what I had to say, he told me I had better go down to Grover on 151 myself, as the storm threatened to tie up all the trains and we might look for trouble.

'I had the veterinary surgeon fix up Duke's side, and I put him in the express car, and boarded the 151 with a mighty cold, uncomfortable sensation in the region of my diaphragm.

'It had snowed all night long, and the storm had developed into a blizzard, and the passenger had difficulty in making any headway at all.

'When we got into Grover I thought it was the most desolate spot I had ever looked on, and as the train pulled out, leaving me there, I felt like sending a message of farewell to the world. You know what Grover is, a red box of a station, section house barricaded by coal sheds and a little group of dwellings at the end of everything, with the desert running out on every side to the sky line. The houses and the station were covered with a coating of snow that clung to them like a wet plaster, and the siding was one deep snow drift, banked against the station door. The plain was a wide, white ocean of swirling, drifting snow, that beat and broke like the thrash of the waves in the merciless wind that swept, with nothing to break it, from the Rockies to the Missouri.

'When I opened the station door, the snow fell in upon the floor, and Duke sat down by the empty, fireless stove and began to howl and whine in a heart-breaking fashion. Larry's sleeping room upstairs was empty. Downstairs, everything was in order, and all the station work had been done up. Apparently the last thing Larry had done was to bill out a car of wool from the Oasis sheep ranch for Dewey, Gould & Co., Boston. The car had gone out on 153, the east-bound that left Grover at seven o'clock the night before, so he must have been there at that time. I copied the bill in the copybook, and went over to the section house to make inquiries.

'The section boss was getting ready to go out to look after his track. He said he had seen O'Toole at 5:30, when the west-bound passenger went through, and, not having seen him-since, supposed he was still in Cheyenne. I went over to Larry's boarding house, and the woman said he must be in Cheyenne, as he had eaten his supper at five o'clock the night before, so that he would have time to get his station work done and dress. The little girl, she said, had gone over at five to tell him that supper was ready. I questioned the child carefully. She said there was another man, a stranger, in the station with Larry when she went in and that though she didn't hear anything they said, and Larry was sitting with his chair tilted back and his feet on the stove, she somehow had thought they were quarrelling. The stranger, she said, was standing; he had a fur coat on and his eyes snapped like he was mad, and she was afraid of him. I asked her if she could recall anything else about him, and she said, "Yes, he had very red lips." When I heard that, my heart grew cold as a snow lump, and when I went out the wind seemed to go clear through me. It was evident enough that Freymark had gone down there to make trouble, had quarrelled with Larry and had boarded either the 5:30 passenger or the extra, and got the conductor to let him off at his ranch, and accounted for his late appearance at the dance.

'It was five o'clock then, but the 5:30 train was two hours late, so there was nothing to do but sit down and wait for the conductor, who had gone out on the seven o'clock east-bound the night before, and who must have seen Larry when he picked up the car of wool. It was growing dark by that time. The sky was a dull lead colour, and the snow had drifted about the little town until it was almost buried, and was still coming down so fast that you could scarcely see your hand before you.

'I was never so glad to hear anything as that whistle, when old 153 came lumbering and groaning in through the snow. I ran out on the platform to meet her, and her headlight looked like the face of an old friend. I caught the conductor's arm the minute he stepped off the train, but he wouldn't talk until he got in by the fire. He said he hadn't seen O'Toole at all the night before, but he had found the bill for the wool car on the table, with a note from Larry asking him to take the car out on the Q.T., and he had concluded that Larry had gone up to Cheyenne on the 5:30. I wired the Cheyenne office and managed to catch the express clerk who had gone through on the extra the night before. He wired me saying that he had not seen Larry board the extra, but that his dog had crept into his usual place in the express car, and he had supposed Larry was in the coach. He had seen Freymark get on at Grover, and the train had slowed up a trifle at his ranch to let him off, for Freymark stood in with some of the boys and sent his cattle shipments our way.

'When the night fairly closed down on me, I began to wonder how a gay, expansive fellow like O'Toole had ever stood six months at Grover. The snow had let up by that time, and the stars were beginning to glitter cold and bright through the hurrying clouds. I put on my ulster and went outside. I began a minute tour of inspection, I went through empty freight cars run down by the siding, searched the coal houses and primitive cellar, examining them carefully, and calling O'Toole name. Duke at my heels dragged himself painfully about, but seemed as much at sea as I, and betrayed the nervous suspense and alertness of a bird dog that has lost his game.

'I went back to the office and took the big station lamp upstairs to make a more careful examination of Larry's sleeping room. The suit of clothes that he usually wore at his work was hanging on the wall. His shaving things were lying about, and I recognised the silver-backed military hair brushes that Miss Masterson had given him at Christmas time, lying on his chiffonier. The upper drawer was open and a pair of white kid gloves was lying on the corner. A white string tie hung across his pipe rack, it was crumpled and had evidently proved unsatisfactory when he tied it. On the chiffonier lay several clean handkerchiefs with holes in them, where he had unfolded them and thrown them by in a hasty search for a whole one. A black silk muffler hung on the chair back, and a top hat was set awry on the head of a plaster cast of Parnell, Larry's hero. His dress suit was missing, so there was no doubt that he had dressed for the party. His overcoat lay on his trunk and his dancing shoes were on the floor, at the foot of the bed beside his everyday ones. I knew that his pumps were a little tight, he had joked about them when I was down the Sunday before the dance, but he had only one pair, and he couldn't have got another in Grover if he had tried himself. That set me to thinking. He was a dainty fellow about his shoes and I knew his collection pretty well. I went to his closet and found them all there. Even granting him a prejudice against overcoats, I couldn't conceive of his going out in that stinging weather without shoes. I noticed that a surgeon's case, such as are carried on passenger trains, and which Larry had once appropriated in Cheyenne, was open, and that the roll of medicated cotton had been pulled out and recently used. Each discovery I made served only to add to my perplexity. Granted that Freymark had been there, and granted that he had played the boy an ugly trick, he could not have spirited him away without the knowledge of the train crew.

'"Duke, old doggy," I said to the poor spaniel who was sniffing and whining about the bed, "you haven't done your duty. You must have seen what went on between your master and that clam-blooded Asiatic, and you ought to be able to give me a tip of some sort."

'I decided to go to bed and make a fresh start on the ugly business in the morning. The bed looked as though someone had been lying on it, so I started to beat it up a little before I got in. I took off the pillow and as I pulled up the mattress, on the edge of the ticking at the head of the bed, I saw a dark red stain about the size of my hand. I felt the cold sweat come out on me, and my hands were dangerously unsteady, as I carried the lamp over and set it down on the chair by the bed. But Duke was too quick for me, he had seen that stain and leaping on the bed began sniffing it, and whining like a dog that is being whipped to death. I bent down and felt it with my fingers. It was dry but the colour and stiffness were unmistakeably those of coagulated blood. I caught up my coat and vest and ran down stairs with Duke yelping at my heels. My first impulse was to go and call someone, but from the platform not a single light was visible, and I knew the section men had been in bed for hours. I remembered then, that Larry was often annoyed by haemorrhages at the nose in that high altitude, but even that did not altogether quiet my nerves, and I realised that sleeping in that bed was quite out of the question.

'Larry always kept a supply of brandy and soda on hand, so I made myself a stiff drink and filled the stove and locked the door, turned down the lamp and lay down on the operator's table. I had often slept there when I was night operator. At first it was impossible to sleep, for Duke kept starting up and limping to the door and scratching at it, yelping nervously. He kept this up until I was thoroughly unstrung, and though I'm ordinarily cool enough, there wasn't money enough in Wyoming to have bribed me to open that door. I felt cold all over every time I went near it, and I even drew the big rusty bolt that was never used, and it seemed to me that it groaned heavily as I drew it, or perhaps it was the wind outside that groaned. As for Duke, I threatened to put him out, and boxed his ears until I hurt his feelings, and he lay down in front of the door with his muzzle between his paws and his eyes shining like live coals and riveted on the crack under the door. The situation was gruesome enough, but the liquor had made me drowsy and at last I fell asleep.

'It must have been about three o'clock in the morning that I was awakened by the crying of the dog, a whimper low, continuous and pitiful, and indescribably human. While I was blinking my eyes in an effort to get thoroughly awake, I heard another sound, the grating sound of chalk on a wooden black board, or of a soft pencil on a slate. I turned my head to the right, and saw a man standing with his back to me, chalking something on the bulletin board. At a glance I recognised the broad, high shoulders and the handsome head of my friend. Yet there was that about the figure which kept me from calling his name or from moving a muscle where I lay. He finished his writing and dropped the chalk, and I distinctly heard its click as it fell. He made a gesture as though he were dusting his fingers, and then turned facing me, holding his left hand in front of his mouth. I saw him clearly in the soft light of the station lamp. He wore his dress clothes, and began moving towards the door silently as a shadow in his black stocking feet. There was about his movements an indescribable stiffness, as though his limbs had been frozen. His face was chalky white, his hair seemed damp and was plastered down close about his temples. His eyes were colourless jellies, dull as lead, and staring straight before him. When he reached the door, he lowered the hand he held before his mouth to lift the latch. His face was turned squarely towards me, and the lower jaw had fallen and was set rigidly upon his collar, the mouth was wide open and was *stuffed full of white cotton!* Then I knew it was a dead man's face I looked upon.

'The door opened, and that stiff black figure in stockings walked as noiselessly as a cat out into the night. I think I went quite mad then. I dimly remember that I rushed out upon the siding and ran up and down screaming, "Larry, Larry!" until the wind seemed to echo my call. The stars were out in myriads, and the snow glistened in their light, but I could see nothing but the wide, white plain, not even a dark shadow anywhere. When at last I found myself back in the station, I saw Duke lying before the door and dropped on my knees beside him, calling him by name. But Duke was past calling back. Master and dog had gone together, and I dragged him into the comer and covered his face, for his eyes were colourless and soft, like the eyes of that horrible face, once so beloved.

'The black board? O, I didn't forget that. I had chalked the time of the accommodation on it the night before, from sheer force of habit, for it isn't customary to mark the time of trains in unimportant stations like Grover. My writing had been rubbed out by a moist hand, for I could see the finger marks clearly, and in place of it was written in, blue chalk simply,

C.B. & Q. 26387

'I sat there drinking brandy and muttering to myself before that black board until those blue letters danced up and down, like magic lantern pictures when you jiggle the slides. I drank until the sweat poured off me like rain and my teeth chattered, and I turned sick at the stomach. At last an idea flashed upon me. I snatched the way bill off the hook. The car of wool that had left Grover for Boston the night before was numbered 26387.

'I must have got through the rest of the night somehow, for when the sun came up red and angry over the white plains, the section boss found me sitting by the stove, the lamp burning full blaze, the brandy bottle empty beside me, and with but one idea in my head, that box car 26387 must be stopped and opened as soon as possible, and that somehow it would explain.

'I figured that we could easily catch it in Omaha, and wired the freight agent there to go through it carefully and report anything unusual. That night I got a wire from the agent stating that the body of a man had been found under a woolsack at one end of the car with a fan and an invitation to the inaugural ball at Cheyenne in the pocket of his dress coat. I wired him not to disturb the body until I arrived, and started for Omaha. Before I left Grover the Cheyenne office wired me that Freymark had left town, going west over the Union Pacific. The company detectives never found him.

"The matter was clear enough then. Being a railroad man, he had hidden the body and sealed up the car and billed it out, leaving a note for the conductor. Since he was of a race without conscience or sensibilities, and since his past was more infamous than his birth, he had boarded the extra and had gone to the ball and danced with Miss Masterson with blood undried upon his hands.

'When I saw Larry O'Toole again, he was lying stiff and stark in the undertakers' rooms in Omaha. He was clad in his dress clothes, with black stockings on his feet, as I had seen him forty-eight hours before. Helen Masterson's fan was in his pocket. His mouth was wide open and stuffed full of white cotton.

'He had been shot in the mouth, the bullet lodging between the third and fourth vertebrae. The haemorrhage had been very slight and had been checked by the cotton. The quarrel had taken place about five in the afternoon. After supper Larry had dressed, all but his shoes, and had lain down to snatch a wink of sleep, trusting to the whistle of the extra to waken him. Freymark had gone back and shot him while he was asleep, afterwards placing his body in the wool car, which, but for my telegram, would not have been opened for weeks.

"That's the whole story. There is nothing more to tell except one detail that I did not mention to the superintendent. When I said good-bye to the boy before the undertaker and coroner took charge of the body, I lifted his right hand to take off a ring that Miss Masterson had given him and the ends of the fingers were covered with blue chalk.'